PHU VUONG AND ISA ENRIQUEZ

BLACKBLOOD

ACOLYTE

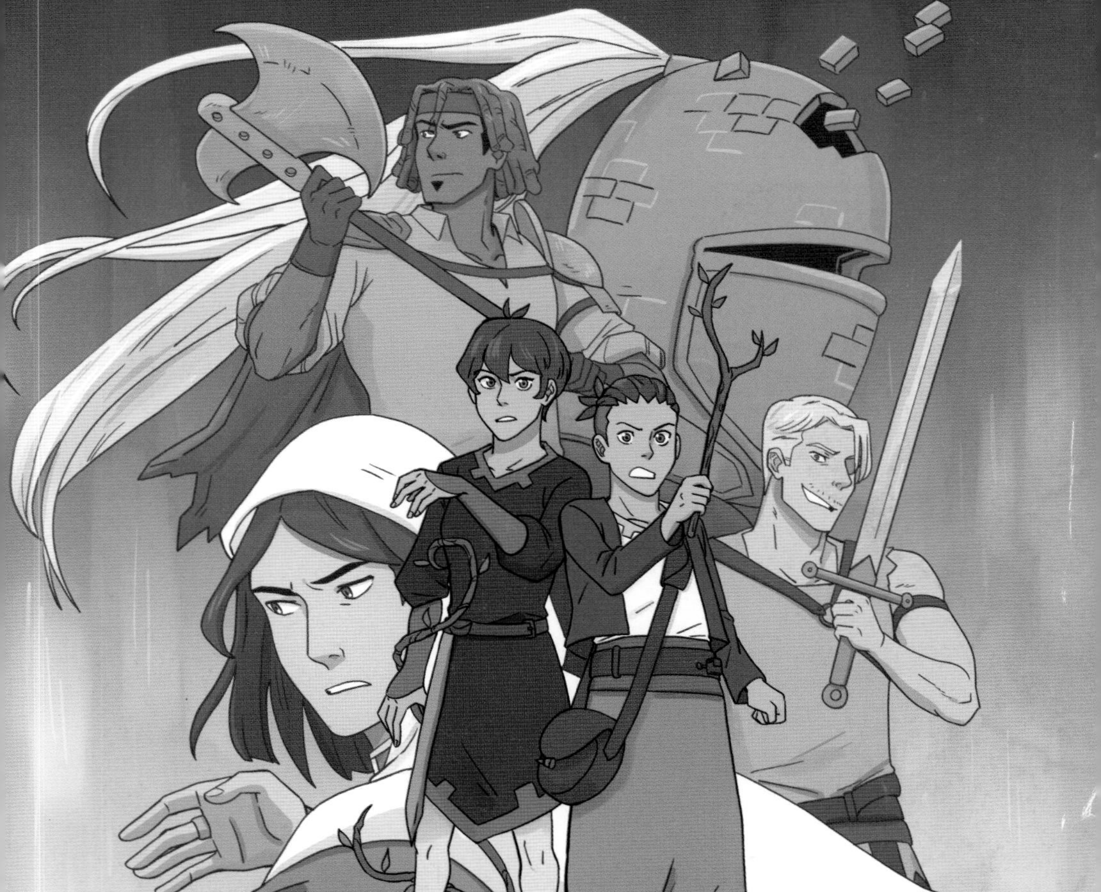

YELLOW JACKET

FOR OUR DAY 1 READERS,
HOPE YOU FIND THE REST OF THE
BOOK WAS WORTH THE WAIT
—PV

FOR MY MOM
—IE

YELLOW JACKET
an imprint of Little Bee Books

yellowjacketreads.com

ISBN 978-1-4998-1184-1 (pb) 10 9 8 7 6 5 4 3 2 1 | ISBN 978-1-4998-1185-8 (hc) 10 9 8 7 6 5 4 3 2 1 | ISBN 978-1-4998-1186-5 (eb)

New York, NY | Text copyright © 2021 by Phu Vuong | Illustrations copyright © 2021 by Isa Enriquez | Title design by Whitefox Designs
All rights reserved, including the right of reproduction in whole or in part in any form. | Yellow Jacket and associated colophon
are trademarks of Little Bee Books. | Library of Congress Cataloging-in-Publication Data is available upon request.
First Edition | Manufactured in China RRD 0621

For information about special discounts on bulk purchases, please contact Little Bee Books at sales@littlebeebooks.com.

CHAPTER 1:
A TIME WE NEVER KNEW

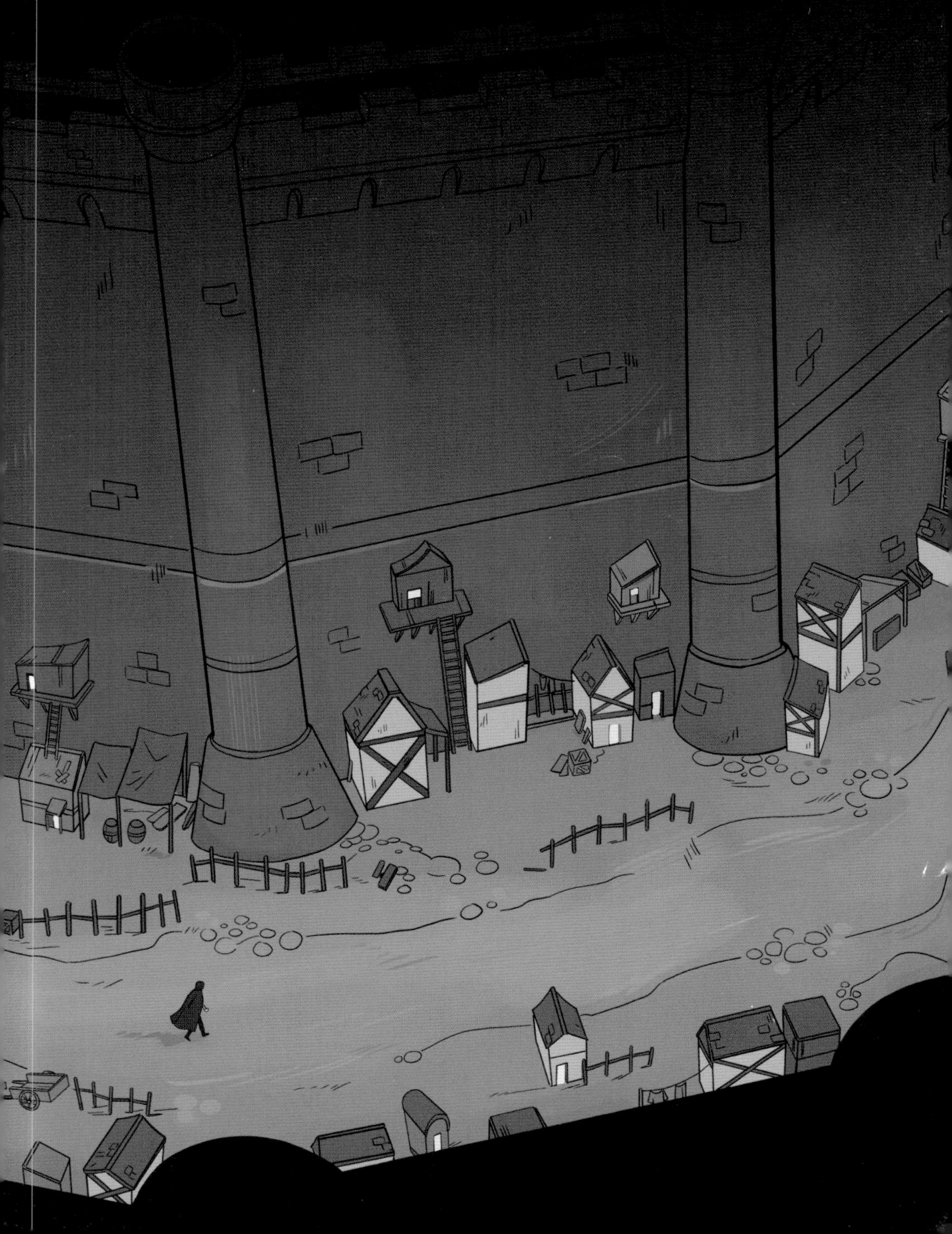

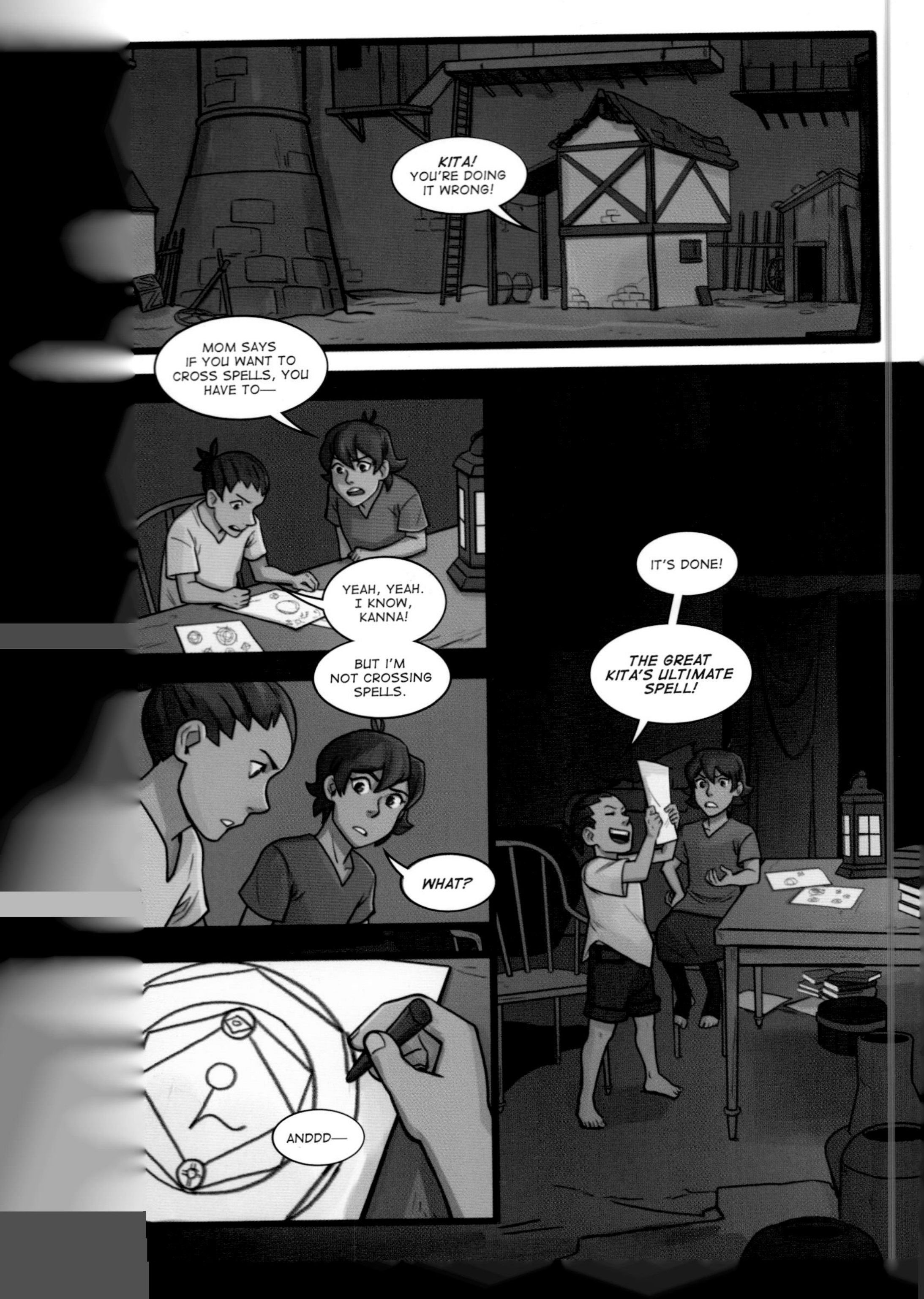
KITA! YOU'RE DOING IT WRONG!
MOM SAYS IF YOU WANT TO CROSS SPELLS, YOU HAVE TO—
YEAH, YEAH. I KNOW, KANNA!
BUT I'M NOT CROSSING SPELLS.
WHAT?
ANDDD—
IT'S DONE!
THE GREAT KITA'S ULTIMATE SPELL!

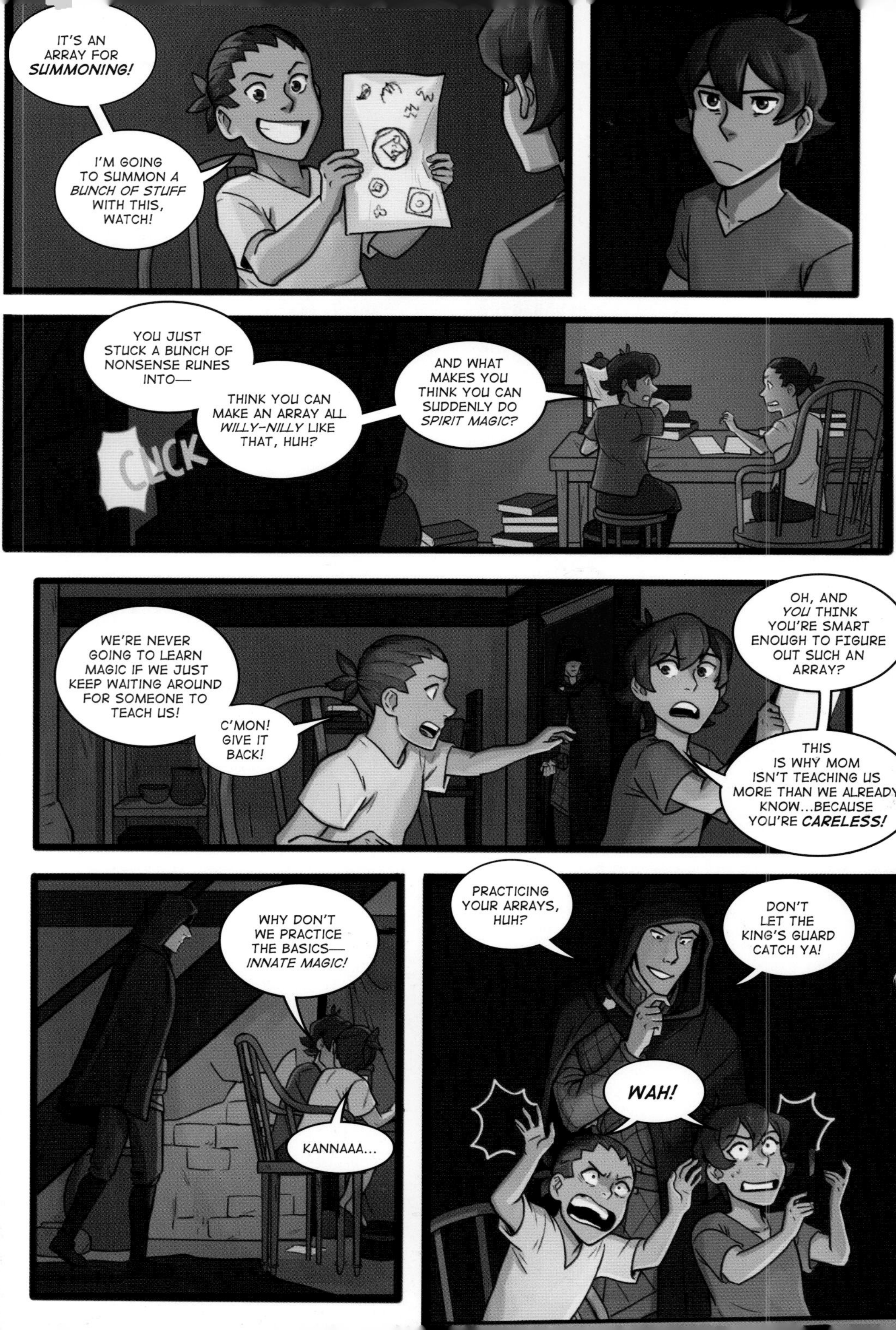
IT'S AN ARRAY FOR SUMMONING!
I'M GOING TO SUMMON A BUNCH OF STUFF WITH THIS, WATCH!
YOU JUST STUCK A BUNCH OF NONSENSE RUNES INTO—
THINK YOU CAN MAKE AN ARRAY ALL WILLY-NILLY LIKE THAT, HUH?
AND WHAT MAKES YOU THINK YOU CAN SUDDENLY DO SPIRIT MAGIC?
CLICK
WE'RE NEVER GOING TO LEARN MAGIC IF WE JUST KEEP WAITING AROUND FOR SOMEONE TO TEACH US!
C'MON! GIVE IT BACK!
OH, AND YOU THINK YOU'RE SMART ENOUGH TO FIGURE OUT SUCH AN ARRAY?
THIS IS WHY MOM ISN'T TEACHING US MORE THAN WE ALREADY KNOW...BECAUSE YOU'RE CARELESS!
WHY DON'T WE PRACTICE THE BASICS— INNATE MAGIC!
KANNAAA...
PRACTICING YOUR ARRAYS, HUH?
DON'T LET THE KING'S GUARD CATCH YA!
WAH!

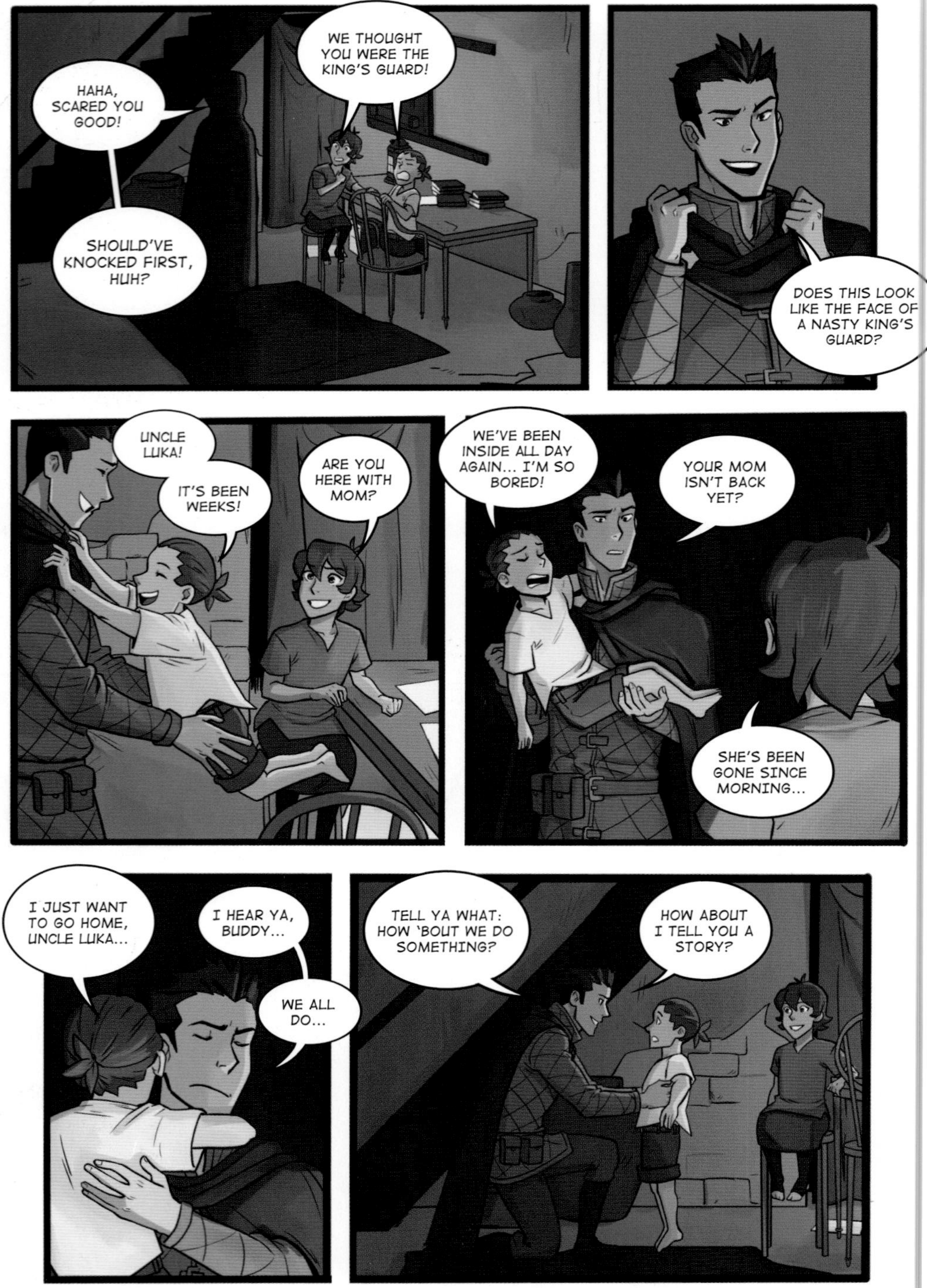
HAHA, SCARED YOU GOOD!
WE THOUGHT YOU WERE THE KING'S GUARD!
SHOULD'VE KNOCKED FIRST, HUH?
DOES THIS LOOK LIKE THE FACE OF A NASTY KING'S GUARD?
UNCLE LUKA!
IT'S BEEN WEEKS!
ARE YOU HERE WITH MOM?
WE'VE BEEN INSIDE ALL DAY AGAIN... I'M SO BORED!
YOUR MOM ISN'T BACK YET?
SHE'S BEEN GONE SINCE MORNING...
I JUST WANT TO GO HOME, UNCLE LUKA...
I HEAR YA, BUDDY...
WE ALL DO...
TELL YA WHAT: HOW 'BOUT WE DO SOMETHING?
HOW ABOUT I TELL YOU A STORY?

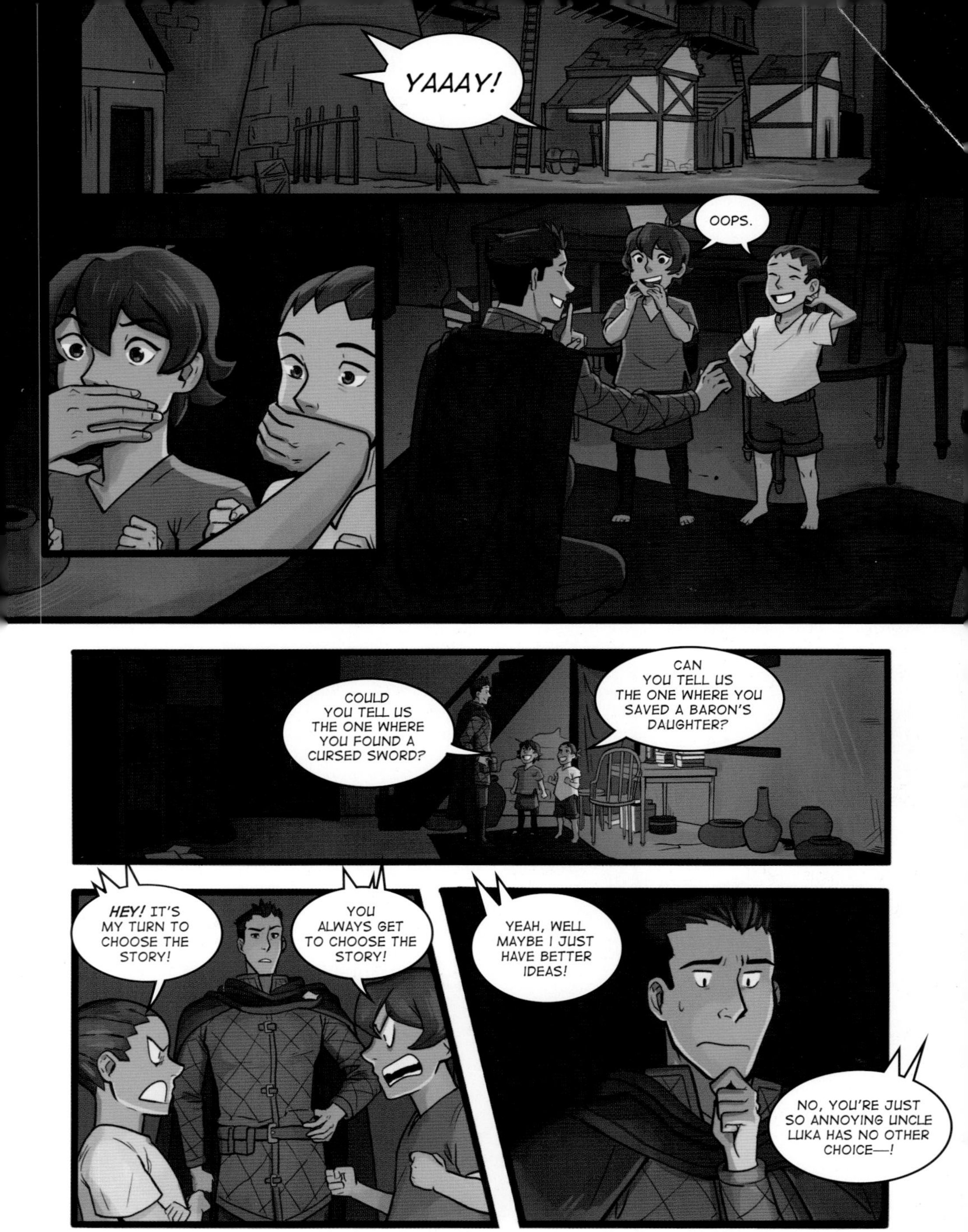
YAAAY!
OOPS.
COULD YOU TELL US THE ONE WHERE YOU FOUND A CURSED SWORD?
CAN YOU TELL US THE ONE WHERE YOU SAVED A BARON'S DAUGHTER?
HEY! IT'S MY TURN TO CHOOSE THE STORY!
YOU ALWAYS GET TO CHOOSE THE STORY!
YEAH, WELL MAYBE I JUST HAVE BETTER IDEAS!
NO, YOU'RE JUST SO ANNOYING UNCLE LUKA HAS NO OTHER CHOICE—!

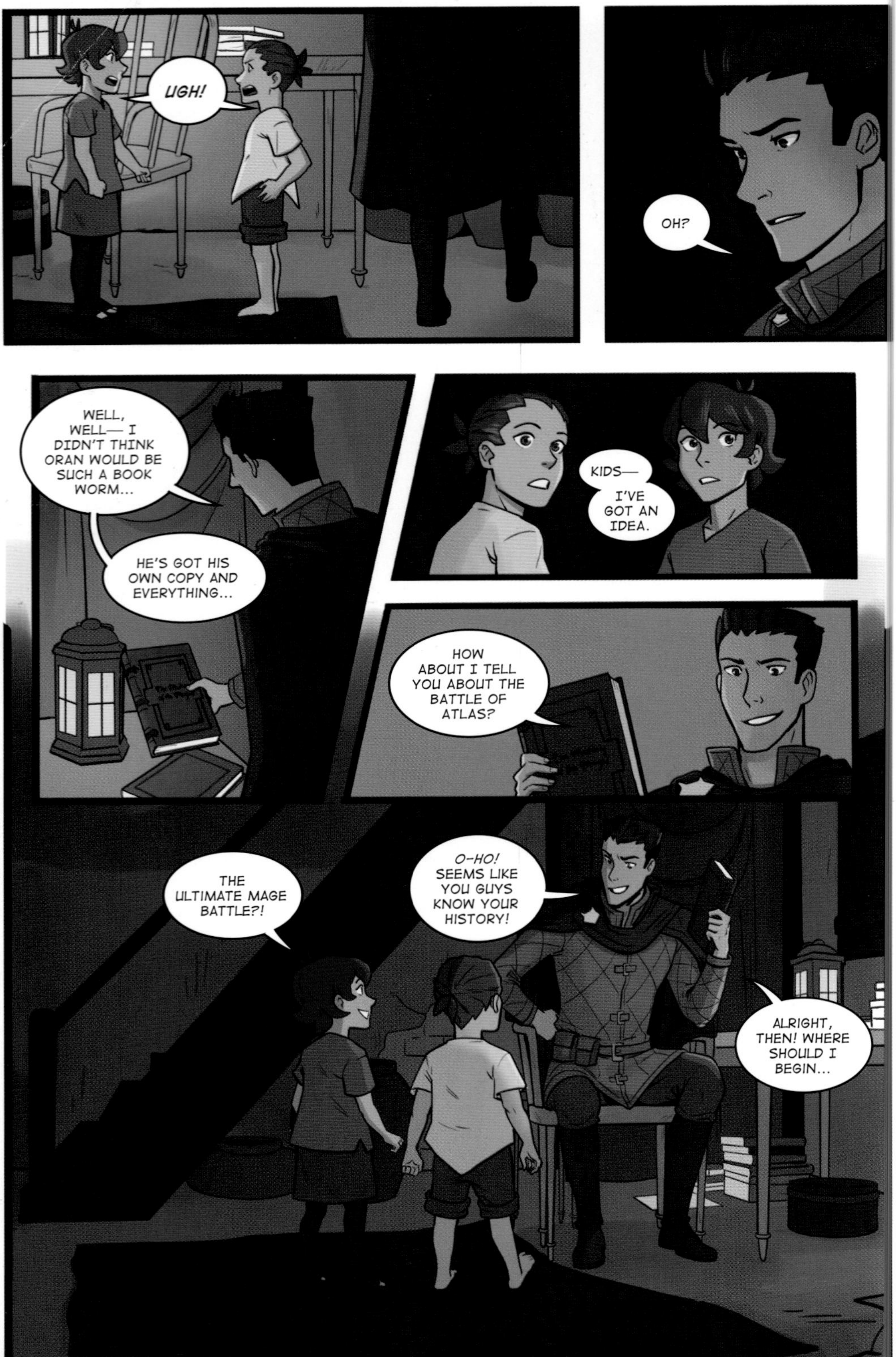
UGH!
OH?
WELL, WELL— I DIDN'T THINK ORAN WOULD BE SUCH A BOOK WORM...
HE'S GOT HIS OWN COPY AND EVERYTHING...
KIDS—
I'VE GOT AN IDEA.
HOW ABOUT I TELL YOU ABOUT THE BATTLE OF ATLAS?
THE ULTIMATE MAGE BATTLE?!
O-HO! SEEMS LIKE YOU GUYS KNOW YOUR HISTORY!
ALRIGHT, THEN! WHERE SHOULD I BEGIN...

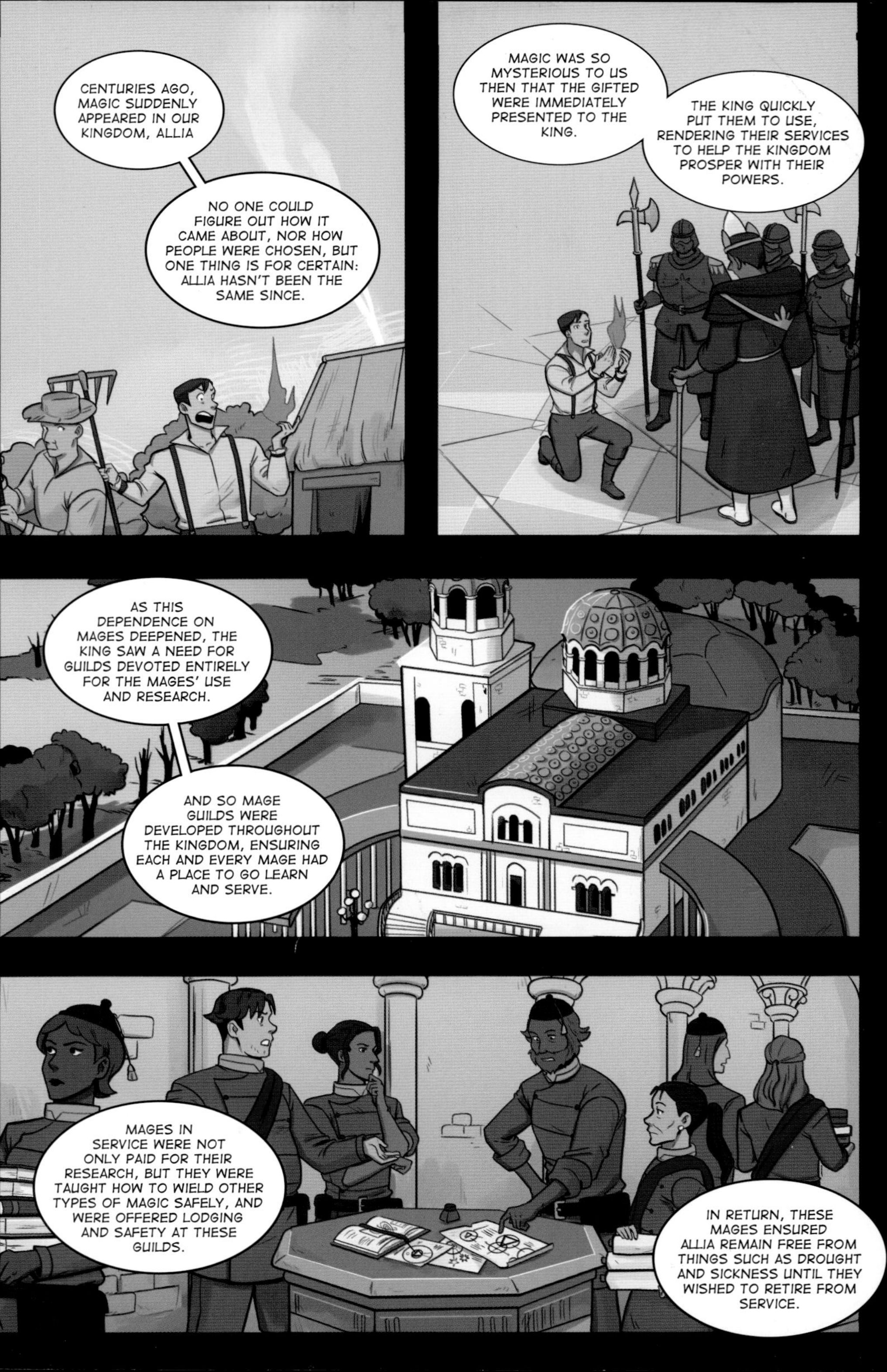
CENTURIES AGO, MAGIC SUDDENLY APPEARED IN OUR KINGDOM, ALLIA
NO ONE COULD FIGURE OUT HOW IT CAME ABOUT, NOR HOW PEOPLE WERE CHOSEN, BUT ONE THING IS FOR CERTAIN: ALLIA HASN'T BEEN THE SAME SINCE.
MAGIC WAS SO MYSTERIOUS TO US THEN THAT THE GIFTED WERE IMMEDIATELY PRESENTED TO THE KING.
THE KING QUICKLY PUT THEM TO USE, RENDERING THEIR SERVICES TO HELP THE KINGDOM PROSPER WITH THEIR POWERS.
AS THIS DEPENDENCE ON MAGES DEEPENED, THE KING SAW A NEED FOR GUILDS DEVOTED ENTIRELY FOR THE MAGES' USE AND RESEARCH.
AND SO MAGE GUILDS WERE DEVELOPED THROUGHOUT THE KINGDOM, ENSURING EACH AND EVERY MAGE HAD A PLACE TO GO LEARN AND SERVE.
MAGES IN SERVICE WERE NOT ONLY PAID FOR THEIR RESEARCH, BUT THEY WERE TAUGHT HOW TO WIELD OTHER TYPES OF MAGIC SAFELY, AND WERE OFFERED LODGING AND SAFETY AT THESE GUILDS.
IN RETURN, THESE MAGES ENSURED ALLIA REMAIN FREE FROM THINGS SUCH AS DROUGHT AND SICKNESS UNTIL THEY WISHED TO RETIRE FROM SERVICE.

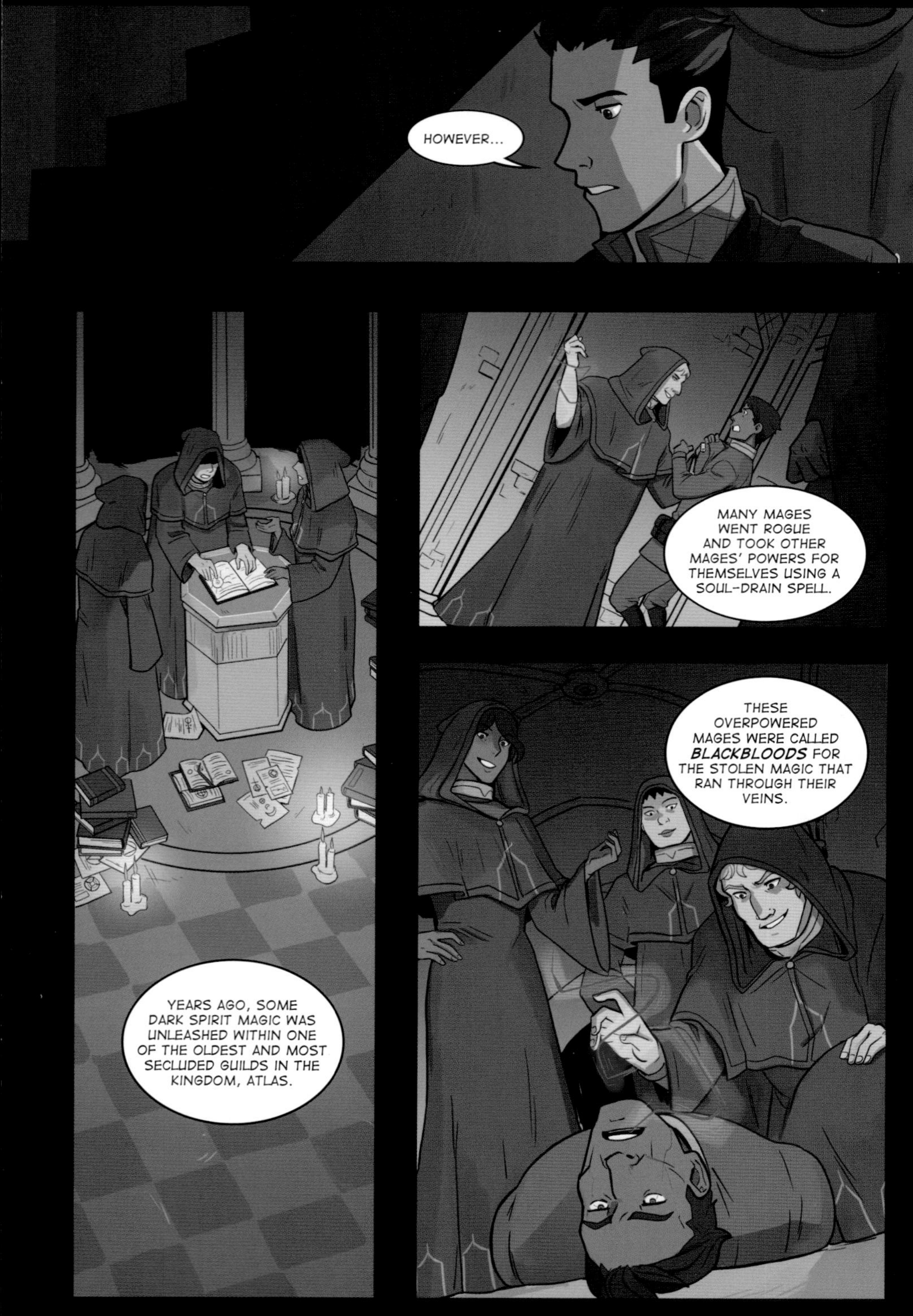
HOWEVER...
YEARS AGO, SOME DARK SPIRIT MAGIC WAS UNLEASHED WITHIN ONE OF THE OLDEST AND MOST SECLUDED GUILDS IN THE KINGDOM, ATLAS.
MANY MAGES WENT ROGUE AND TOOK OTHER MAGES' POWERS FOR THEMSELVES USING A SOUL-DRAIN SPELL.
THESE OVERPOWERED MAGES WERE CALLED BLACKBLOODS FOR THE STOLEN MAGIC THAT RAN THROUGH THEIR VEINS.

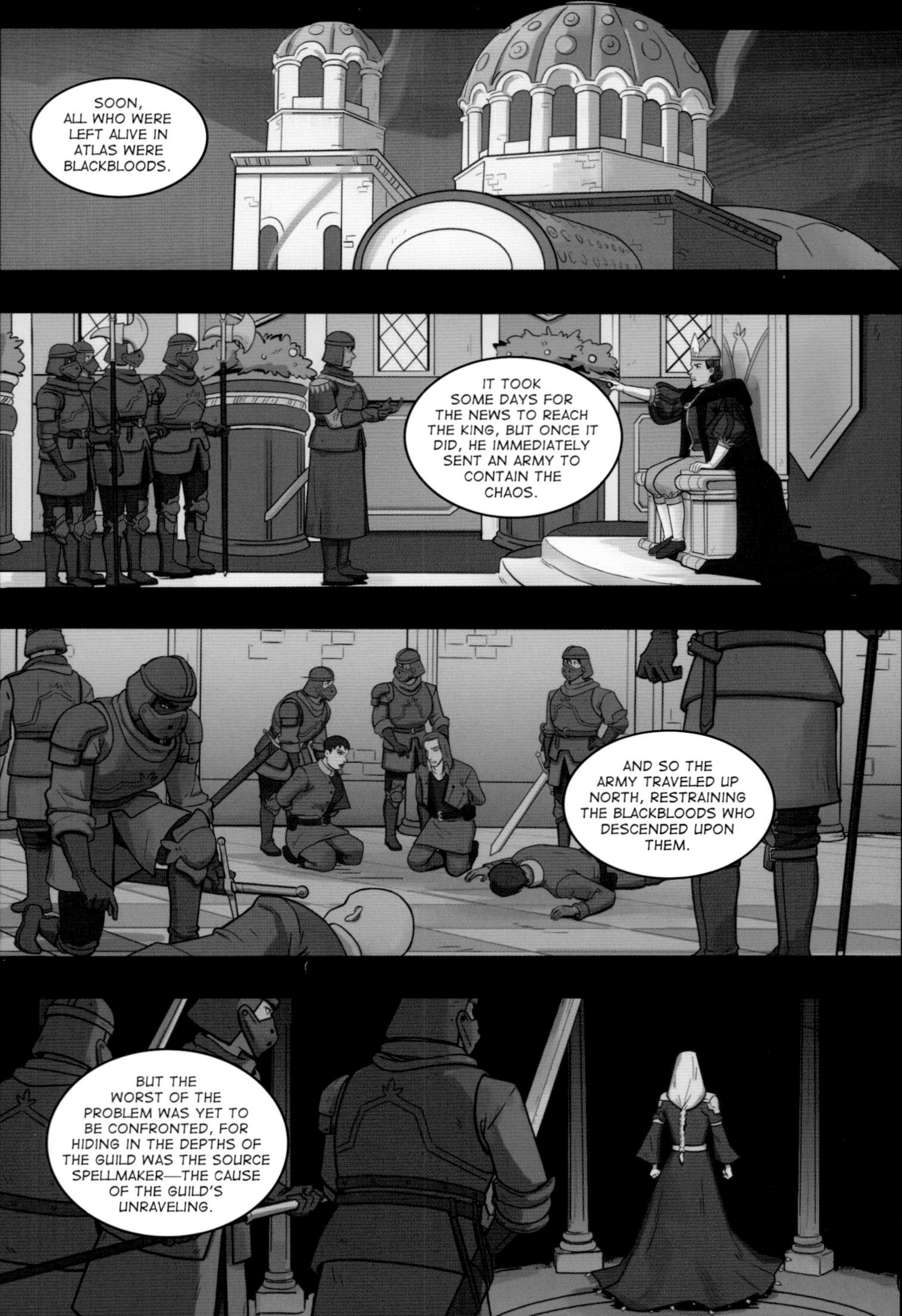
SOON, ALL WHO WERE LEFT ALIVE IN ATLAS WERE BLACKBLOODS.
IT TOOK SOME DAYS FOR THE NEWS TO REACH THE KING, BUT ONCE IT DID, HE IMMEDIATELY SENT AN ARMY TO CONTAIN THE CHAOS.
AND SO THE ARMY TRAVELED UP NORTH, RESTRAINING THE BLACKBLOODS WHO DESCENDED UPON THEM.
BUT THE WORST OF THE PROBLEM WAS YET TO BE CONFRONTED, FOR HIDING IN THE DEPTHS OF THE GUILD WAS THE SOURCE SPELLMAKER—THE CAUSE OF THE GUILD'S UNRAVELING.

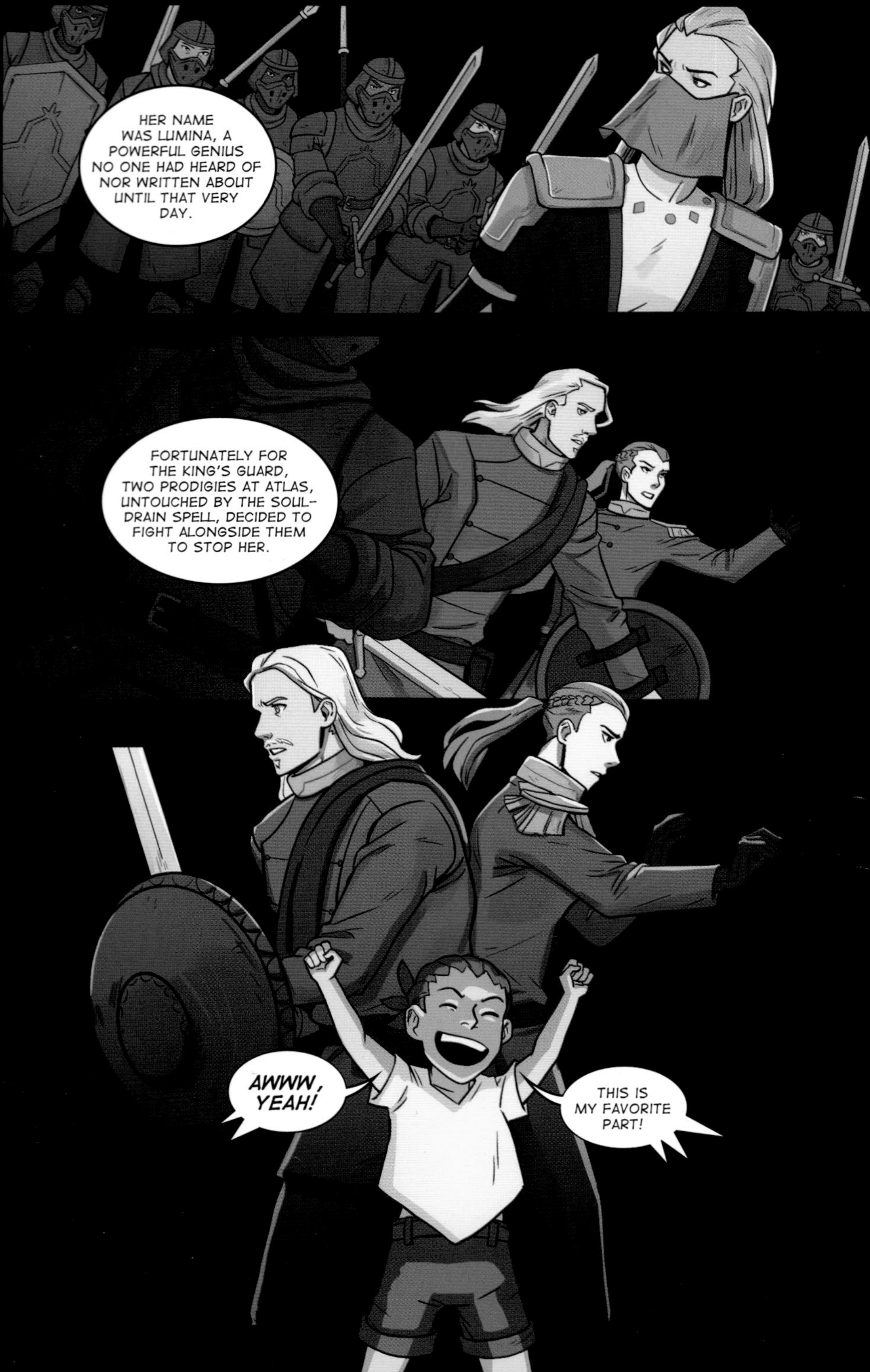
HER NAME WAS LUMINA, A POWERFUL GENIUS NO ONE HAD HEARD OF NOR WRITTEN ABOUT UNTIL THAT VERY DAY.
FORTUNATELY FOR THE KING'S GUARD, TWO PRODIGIES AT ATLAS, UNTOUCHED BY THE SOUL-DRAIN SPELL, DECIDED TO FIGHT ALONGSIDE THEM TO STOP HER.
AWWW, YEAH!
THIS IS MY FAVORITE PART!

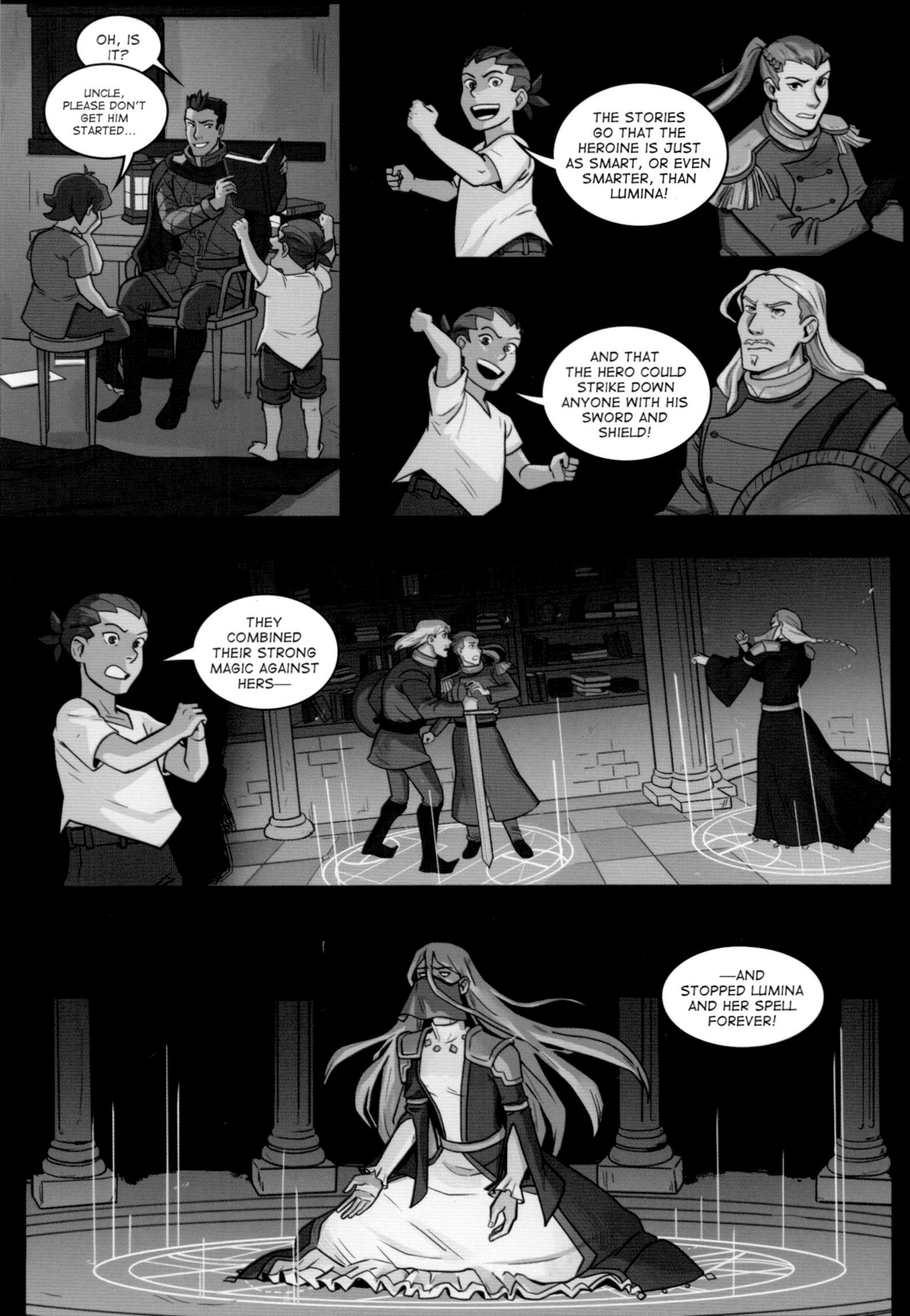
OH, IS IT?
UNCLE, PLEASE DON'T GET HIM STARTED...
THE STORIES GO THAT THE HEROINE IS JUST AS SMART, OR EVEN SMARTER, THAN LUMINA!
AND THAT THE HERO COULD STRIKE DOWN ANYONE WITH HIS SWORD AND SHIELD!
THEY COMBINED THEIR STRONG MAGIC AGAINST HERS—
—AND STOPPED LUMINA AND HER SPELL FOREVER!

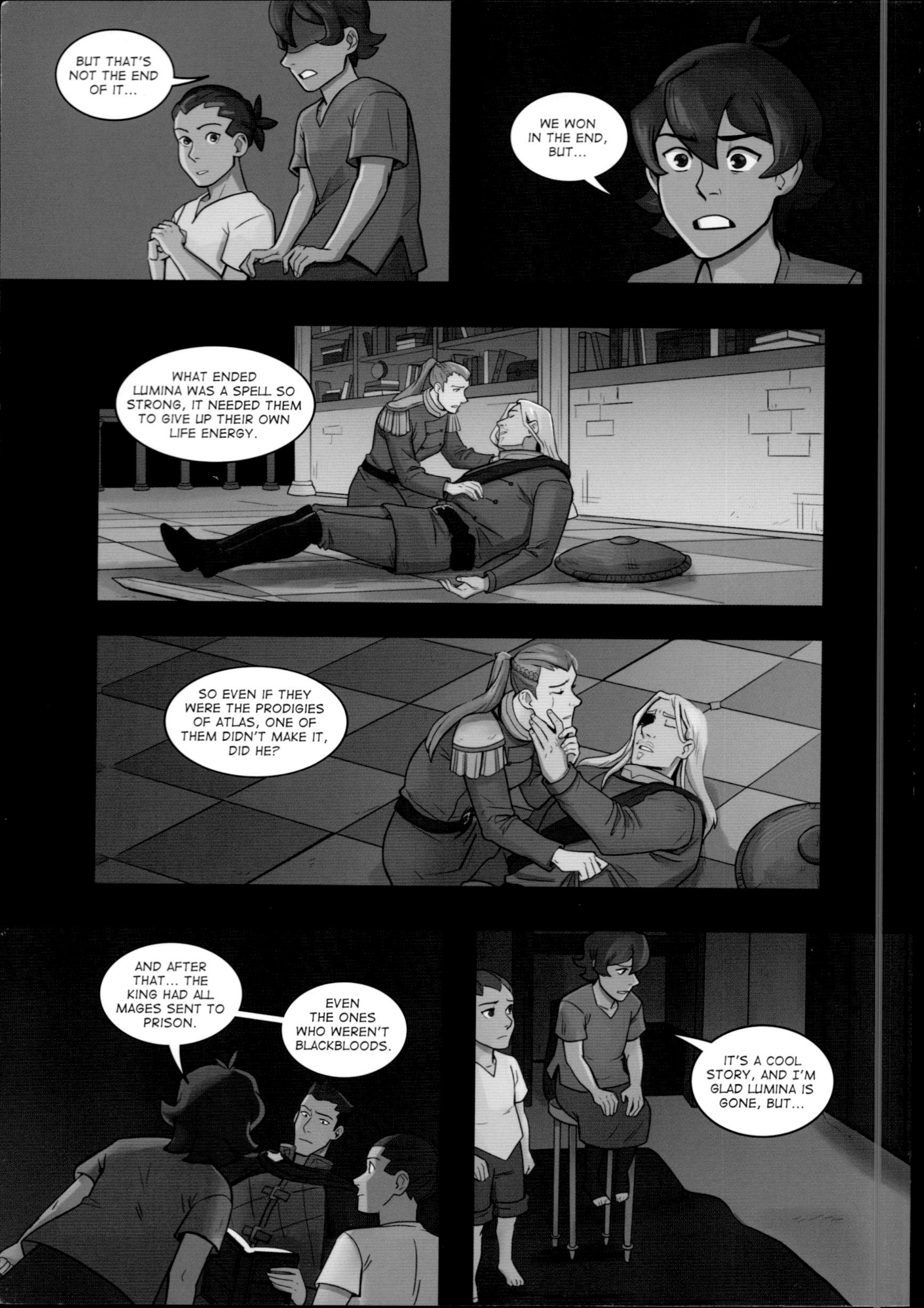
BUT THAT'S NOT THE END OF IT...
WE WON IN THE END, BUT...
WHAT ENDED LUMINA WAS A SPELL SO STRONG, IT NEEDED THEM TO GIVE UP THEIR OWN LIFE ENERGY.
SO EVEN IF THEY WERE THE PRODIGIES OF ATLAS, ONE OF THEM DIDN'T MAKE IT, DID HE?
AND AFTER THAT... THE KING HAD ALL MAGES SENT TO PRISON.
EVEN THE ONES WHO WEREN'T BLACKBLOODS.
IT'S A COOL STORY, AND I'M GLAD LUMINA IS GONE, BUT...

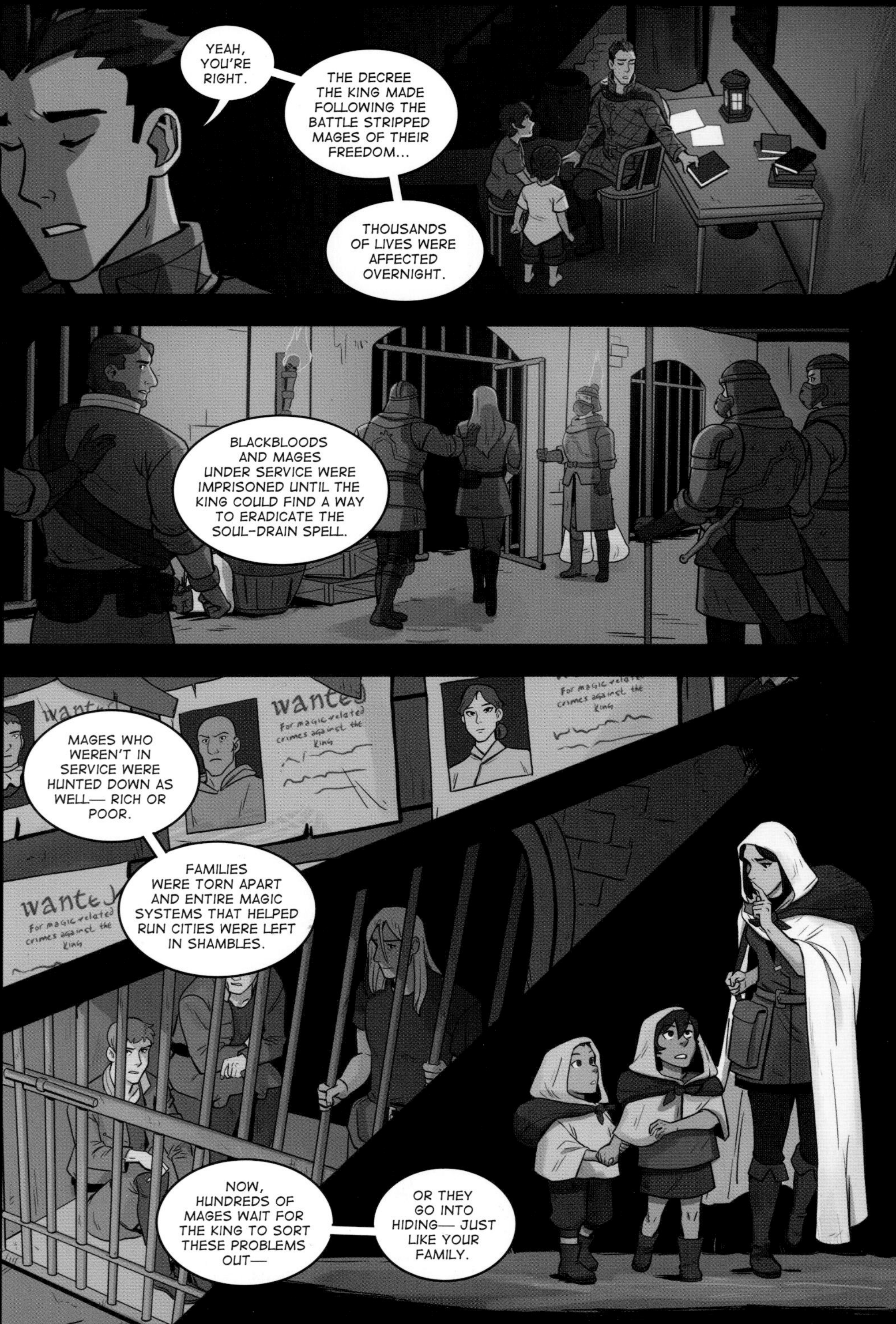
YEAH, YOU'RE RIGHT.
THE DECREE THE KING MADE FOLLOWING THE BATTLE STRIPPED MAGES OF THEIR FREEDOM...
THOUSANDS OF LIVES WERE AFFECTED OVERNIGHT.
BLACKBLOODS AND MAGES UNDER SERVICE WERE IMPRISONED UNTIL THE KING COULD FIND A WAY TO ERADICATE THE SOUL-DRAIN SPELL.
wanted
For magic-related crimes against the King
MAGES WHO WEREN'T IN SERVICE WERE HUNTED DOWN AS WELL— RICH OR POOR.
FAMILIES WERE TORN APART AND ENTIRE MAGIC SYSTEMS THAT HELPED RUN CITIES WERE LEFT IN SHAMBLES.
NOW, HUNDREDS OF MAGES WAIT FOR THE KING TO SORT THESE PROBLEMS OUT—
OR THEY GO INTO HIDING— JUST LIKE YOUR FAMILY.

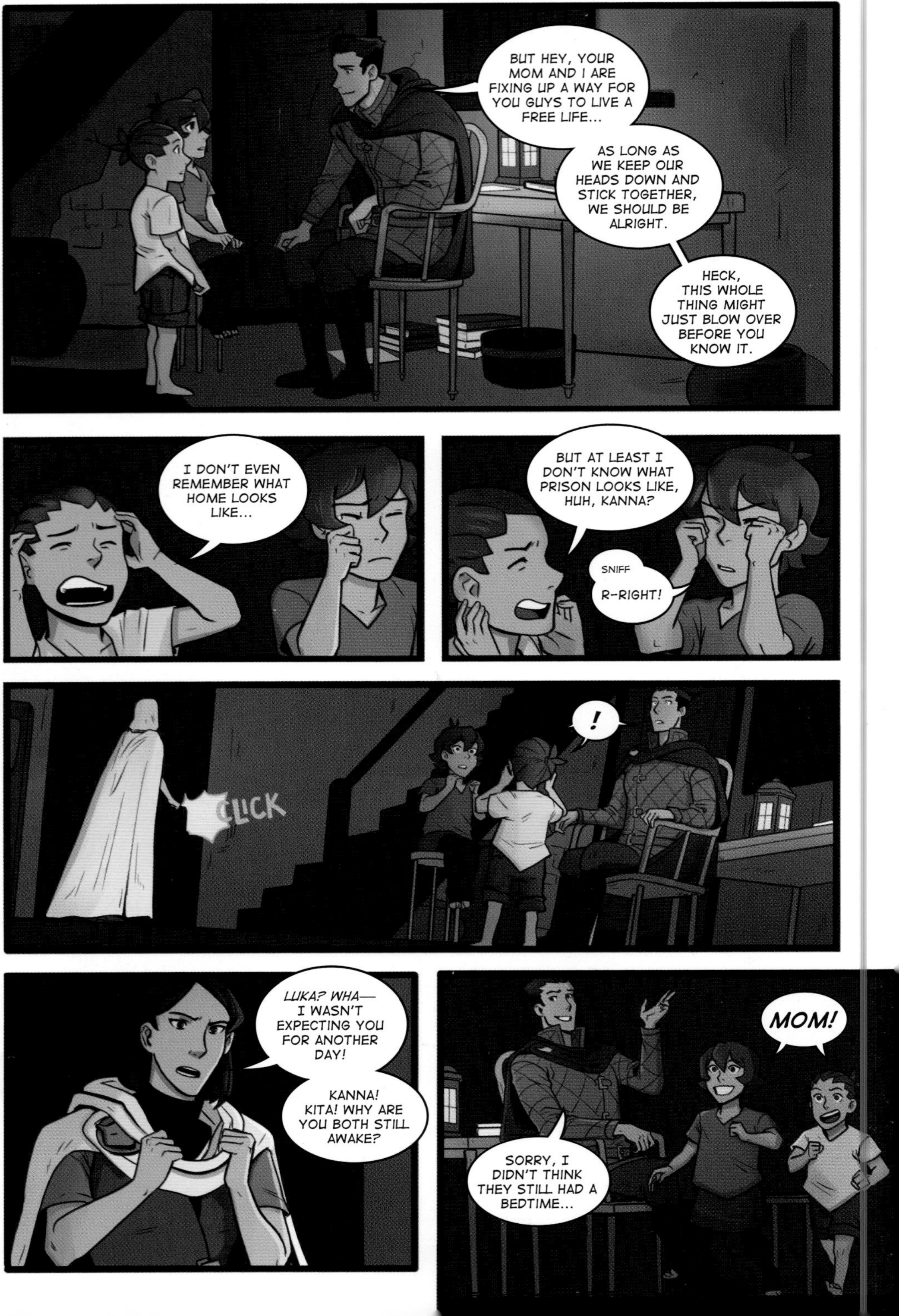
BUT HEY, YOUR MOM AND I ARE FIXING UP A WAY FOR YOU GUYS TO LIVE A FREE LIFE...
AS LONG AS WE KEEP OUR HEADS DOWN AND STICK TOGETHER, WE SHOULD BE ALRIGHT.
HECK, THIS WHOLE THING MIGHT JUST BLOW OVER BEFORE YOU KNOW IT.
I DON'T EVEN REMEMBER WHAT HOME LOOKS LIKE...
BUT AT LEAST I DON'T KNOW WHAT PRISON LOOKS LIKE, HUH, KANNA?
SNIFF
R-RIGHT!
!
CLICK
LUKA? WHA— I WASN'T EXPECTING YOU FOR ANOTHER DAY!
KANNA! KITA! WHY ARE YOU BOTH STILL AWAKE?
MOM!
SORRY, I DIDN'T THINK THEY STILL HAD A BEDTIME...

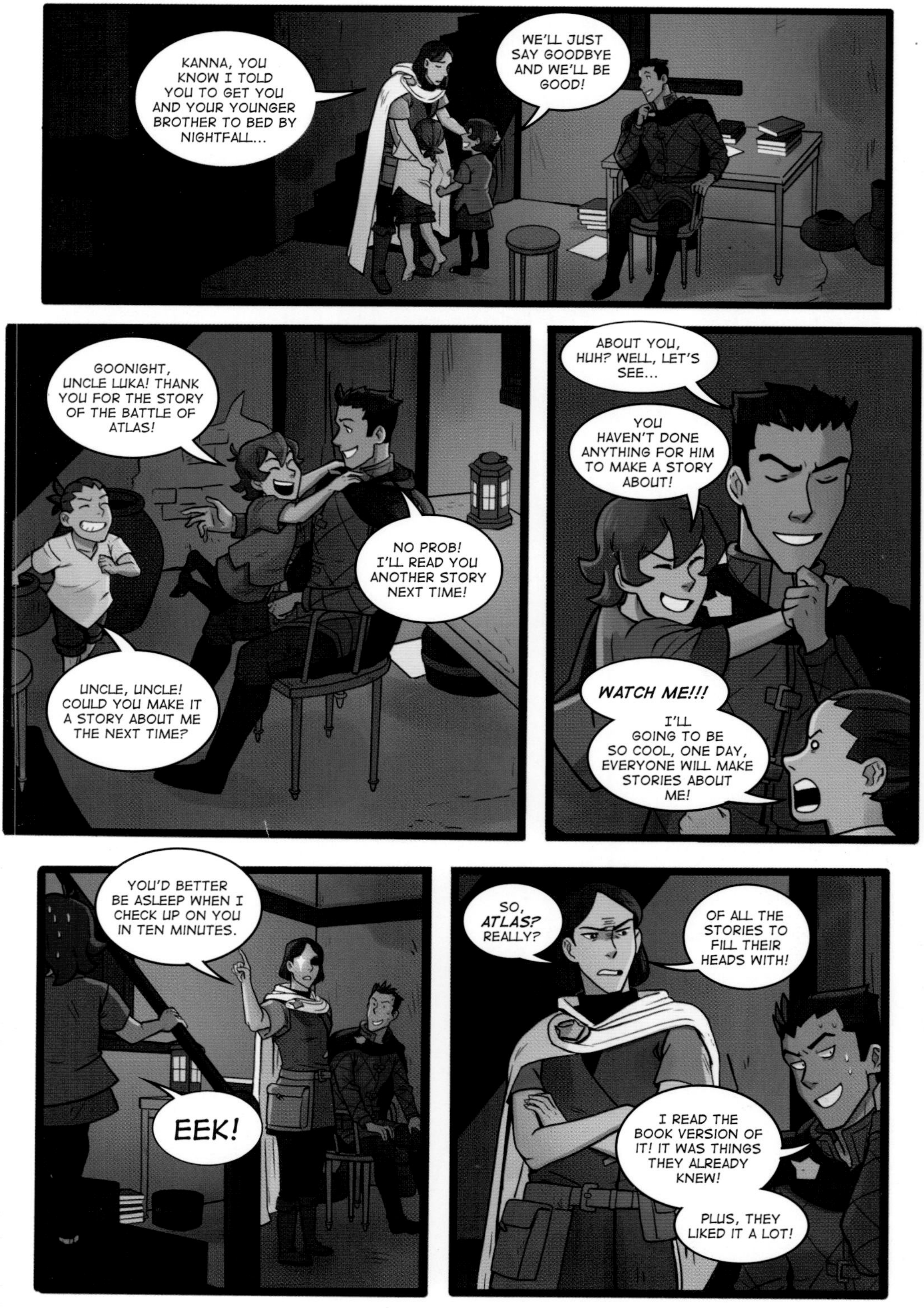
KANNA, YOU KNOW I TOLD YOU TO GET YOU AND YOUR YOUNGER BROTHER TO BED BY NIGHTFALL...
WE'LL JUST SAY GOODBYE AND WE'LL BE GOOD!
GOONIGHT, UNCLE LUKA! THANK YOU FOR THE STORY OF THE BATTLE OF ATLAS!
NO PROB! I'LL READ YOU ANOTHER STORY NEXT TIME!
UNCLE, UNCLE! COULD YOU MAKE IT A STORY ABOUT ME THE NEXT TIME?
ABOUT YOU, HUH? WELL, LET'S SEE...
YOU HAVEN'T DONE ANYTHING FOR HIM TO MAKE A STORY ABOUT!
WATCH ME!!!
I'LL GOING TO BE SO COOL, ONE DAY, EVERYONE WILL MAKE STORIES ABOUT ME!
YOU'D BETTER BE ASLEEP WHEN I CHECK UP ON YOU IN TEN MINUTES.
EEK!
SO, ATLAS? REALLY?
OF ALL THE STORIES TO FILL THEIR HEADS WITH!
I READ THE BOOK VERSION OF IT! IT WAS THINGS THEY ALREADY KNEW!
PLUS, THEY LIKED IT A LOT!

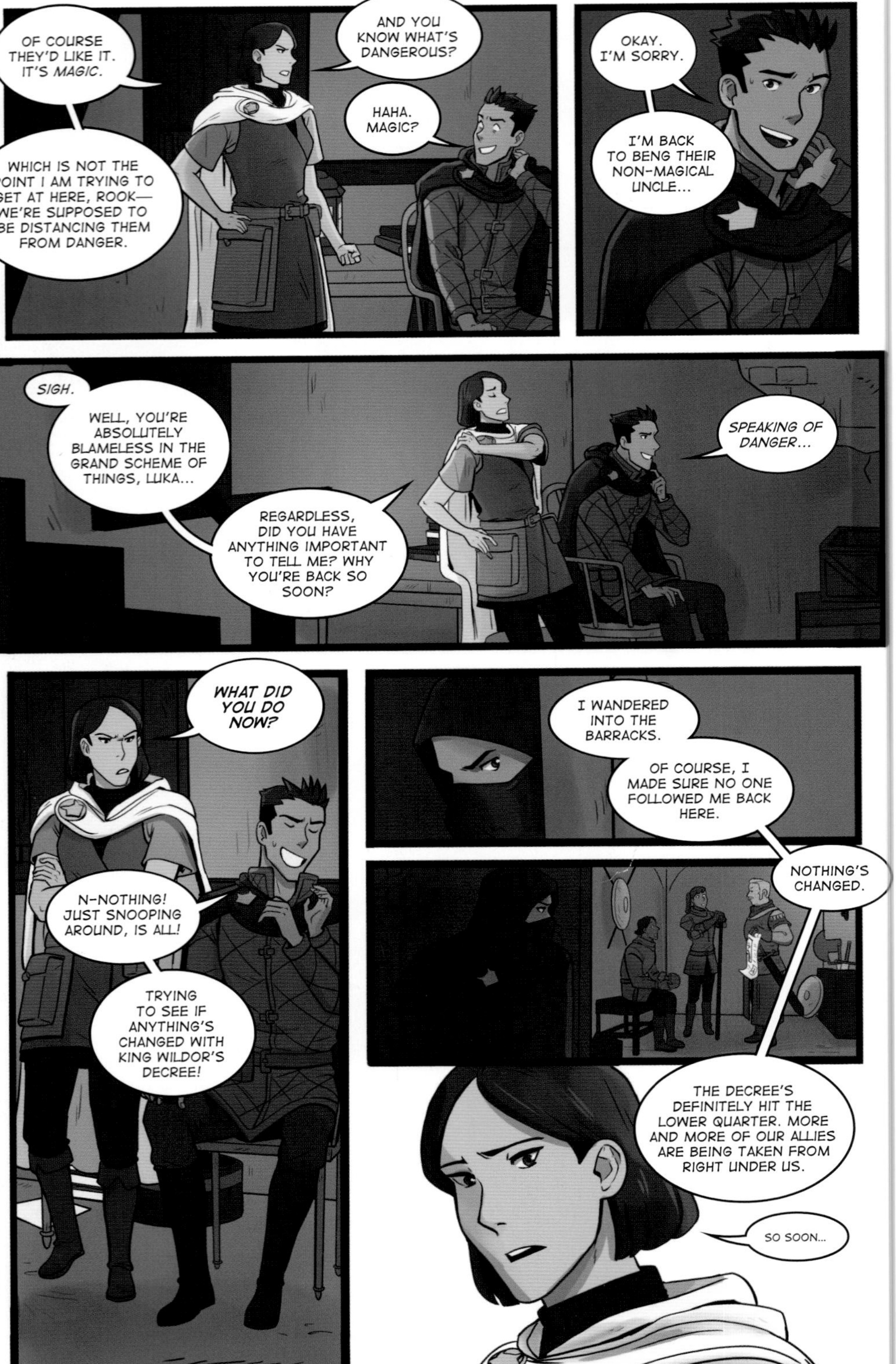

OF COURSE THEY'D LIKE IT. IT'S *MAGIC*.
WHICH IS NOT THE POINT I AM TRYING TO GET AT HERE, ROOK— WE'RE SUPPOSED TO BE DISTANCING THEM FROM DANGER.
AND YOU KNOW WHAT'S DANGEROUS?
HAHA. MAGIC?
OKAY. I'M SORRY.
I'M BACK TO BENG THEIR NON-MAGICAL UNCLE...
SIGH.
WELL, YOU'RE ABSOLUTELY BLAMELESS IN THE GRAND SCHEME OF THINGS, LUKA...
REGARDLESS, DID YOU HAVE ANYTHING IMPORTANT TO TELL ME? WHY YOU'RE BACK SO SOON?
SPEAKING OF DANGER...
WHAT DID YOU DO NOW?
N-NOTHING! JUST SNOOPING AROUND, IS ALL!
TRYING TO SEE IF ANYTHING'S CHANGED WITH KING WILDOR'S DECREE!
I WANDERED INTO THE BARRACKS.
OF COURSE, I MADE SURE NO ONE FOLLOWED ME BACK HERE.
NOTHING'S CHANGED.
THE DECREE'S DEFINITELY HIT THE LOWER QUARTER. MORE AND MORE OF OUR ALLIES ARE BEING TAKEN FROM RIGHT UNDER US.
SO SOON...

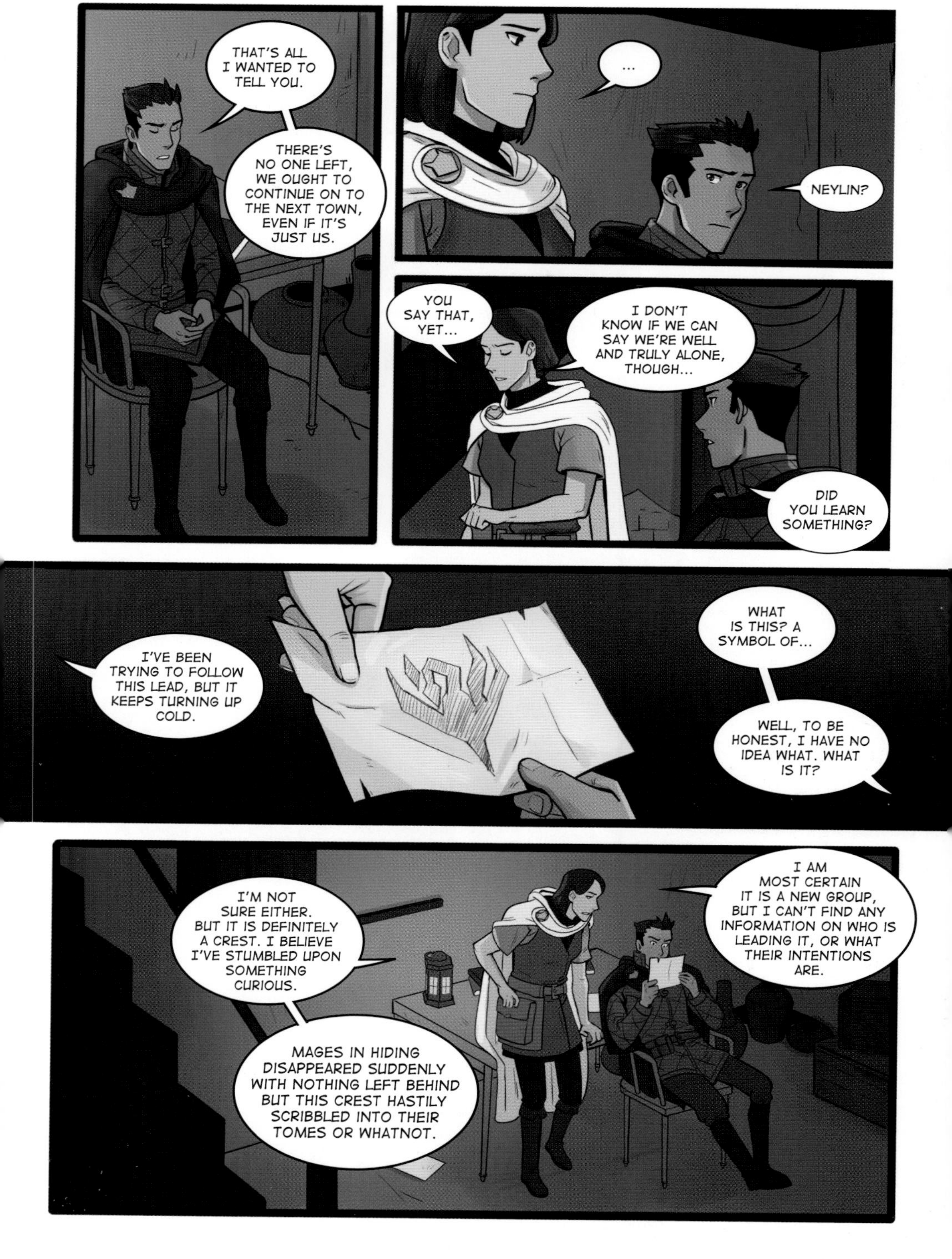
THAT'S ALL I WANTED TO TELL YOU.
THERE'S NO ONE LEFT, WE OUGHT TO CONTINUE ON TO THE NEXT TOWN, EVEN IF IT'S JUST US.
...
NEYLIN?
YOU SAY THAT, YET...
I DON'T KNOW IF WE CAN SAY WE'RE WELL AND TRULY ALONE, THOUGH...
DID YOU LEARN SOMETHING?
I'VE BEEN TRYING TO FOLLOW THIS LEAD, BUT IT KEEPS TURNING UP COLD.
WHAT IS THIS? A SYMBOL OF...
WELL, TO BE HONEST, I HAVE NO IDEA WHAT. WHAT IS IT?
I'M NOT SURE EITHER. BUT IT IS DEFINITELY A CREST. I BELIEVE I'VE STUMBLED UPON SOMETHING CURIOUS.
MAGES IN HIDING DISAPPEARED SUDDENLY WITH NOTHING LEFT BEHIND BUT THIS CREST HASTILY SCRIBBLED INTO THEIR TOMES OR WHATNOT.
I AM MOST CERTAIN IT IS A NEW GROUP, BUT I CAN'T FIND ANY INFORMATION ON WHO IS LEADING IT, OR WHAT THEIR INTENTIONS ARE.

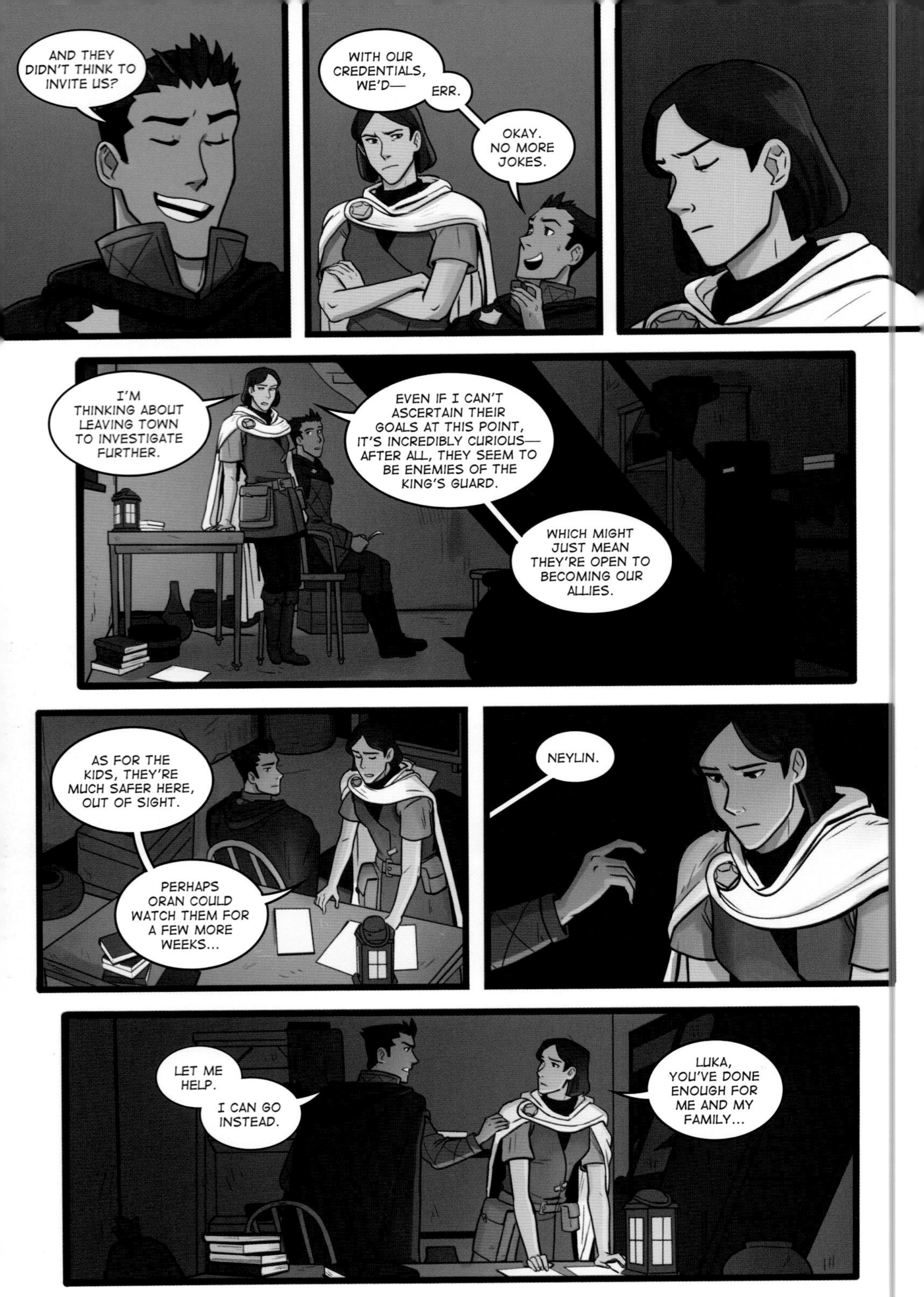
AND THEY DIDN'T THINK TO INVITE US?
WITH OUR CREDENTIALS, WE'D—
ERR.
OKAY. NO MORE JOKES.
I'M THINKING ABOUT LEAVING TOWN TO INVESTIGATE FURTHER.
EVEN IF I CAN'T ASCERTAIN THEIR GOALS AT THIS POINT, IT'S INCREDIBLY CURIOUS— AFTER ALL, THEY SEEM TO BE ENEMIES OF THE KING'S GUARD.
WHICH MIGHT JUST MEAN THEY'RE OPEN TO BECOMING OUR ALLIES.
AS FOR THE KIDS, THEY'RE MUCH SAFER HERE, OUT OF SIGHT.
PERHAPS ORAN COULD WATCH THEM FOR A FEW MORE WEEKS...
NEYLIN.
LET ME HELP.
I CAN GO INSTEAD.
LUKA, YOU'VE DONE ENOUGH FOR ME AND MY FAMILY...

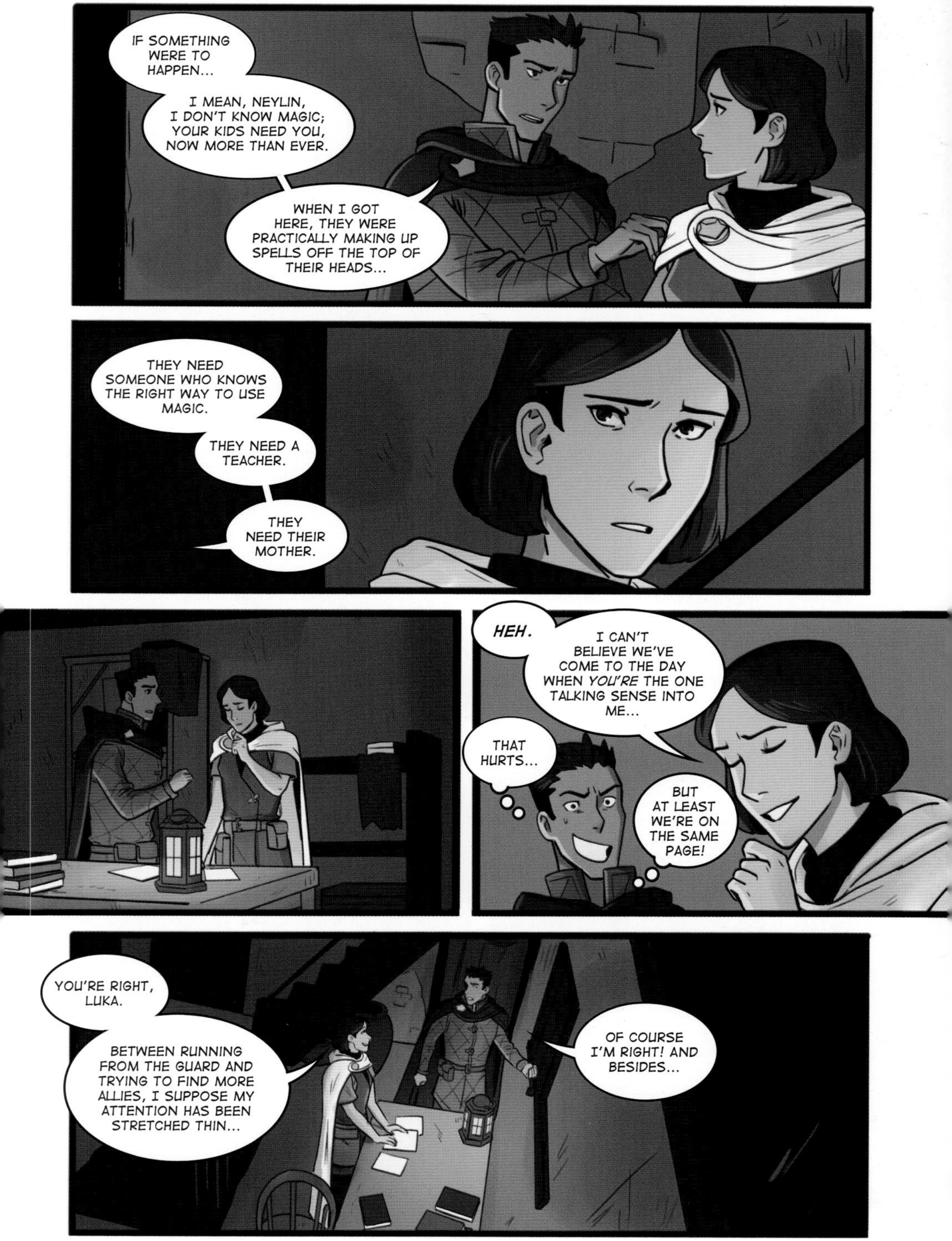
IF SOMETHING WERE TO HAPPEN...
I MEAN, NEYLIN, I DON'T KNOW MAGIC; YOUR KIDS NEED YOU, NOW MORE THAN EVER.
WHEN I GOT HERE, THEY WERE PRACTICALLY MAKING UP SPELLS OFF THE TOP OF THEIR HEADS...
THEY NEED SOMEONE WHO KNOWS THE RIGHT WAY TO USE MAGIC.
THEY NEED A TEACHER.
THEY NEED THEIR MOTHER.
HEH.
I CAN'T BELIEVE WE'VE COME TO THE DAY WHEN *YOU'RE* THE ONE TALKING SENSE INTO ME...
THAT HURTS...
BUT AT LEAST WE'RE ON THE SAME PAGE!
YOU'RE RIGHT, LUKA.
BETWEEN RUNNING FROM THE GUARD AND TRYING TO FIND MORE ALLIES, I SUPPOSE MY ATTENTION HAS BEEN STRETCHED THIN...
OF COURSE I'M RIGHT! AND BESIDES...

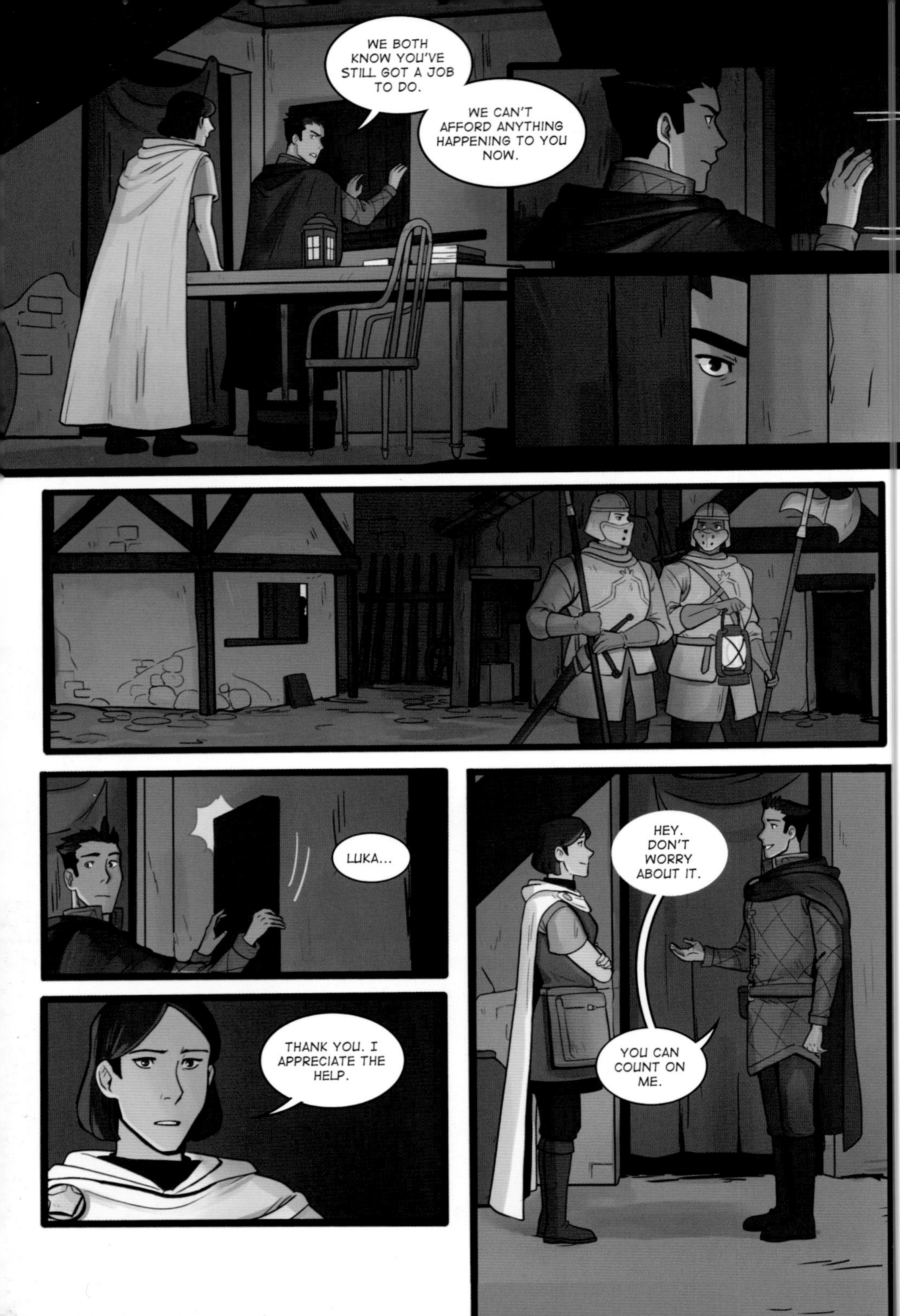
WE BOTH KNOW YOU'VE STILL GOT A JOB TO DO.
WE CAN'T AFFORD ANYTHING HAPPENING TO YOU NOW.
LUKA...
THANK YOU. I APPRECIATE THE HELP.
HEY. DON'T WORRY ABOUT IT.
YOU CAN COUNT ON ME.

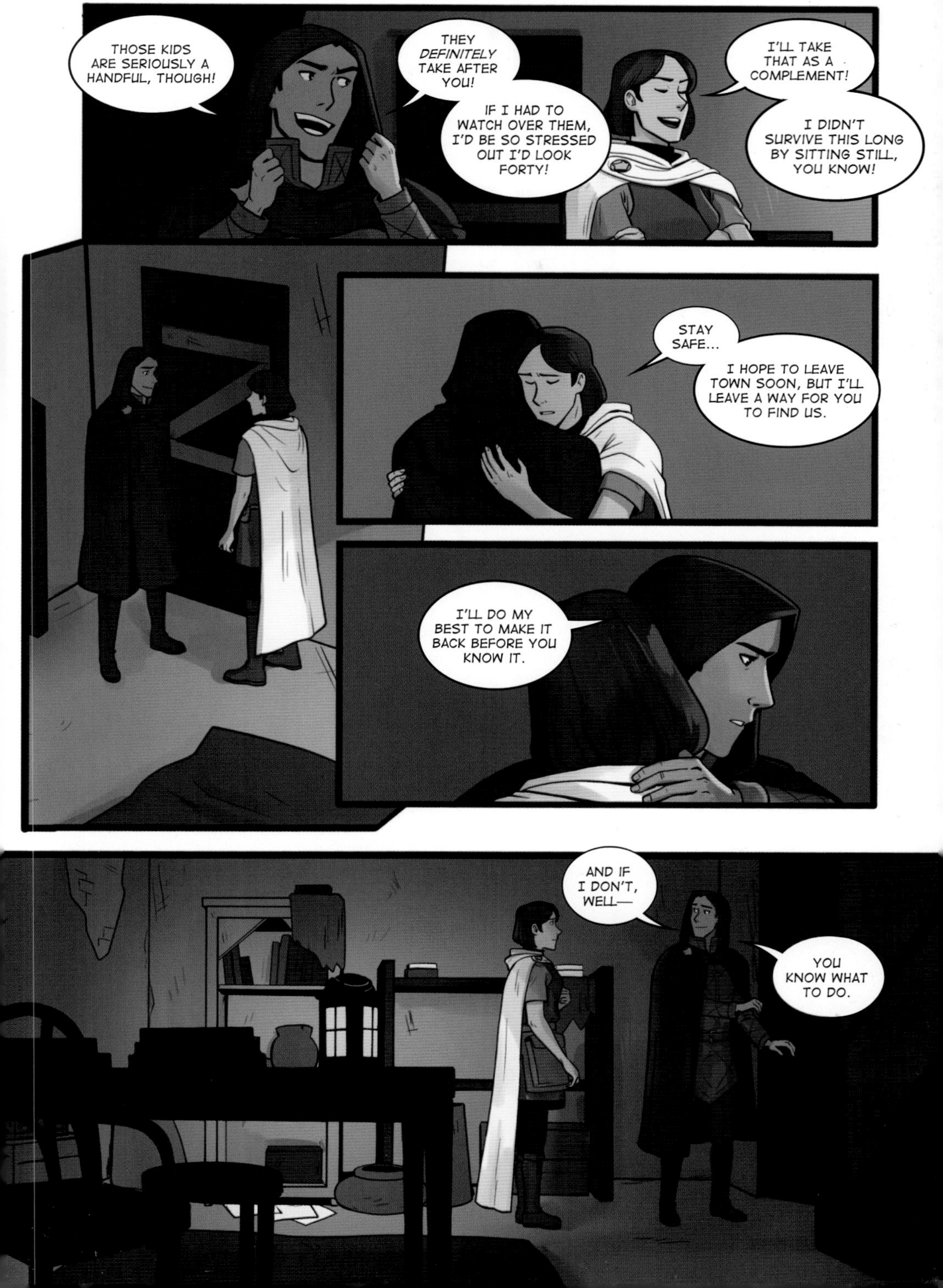
THOSE KIDS ARE SERIOUSLY A HANDFUL, THOUGH!
THEY *DEFINITELY* TAKE AFTER YOU!
IF I HAD TO WATCH OVER THEM, I'D BE SO STRESSED OUT I'D LOOK FORTY!
I'LL TAKE THAT AS A COMPLEMENT!
I DIDN'T SURVIVE THIS LONG BY SITTING STILL, YOU KNOW!
STAY SAFE...
I HOPE TO LEAVE TOWN SOON, BUT I'LL LEAVE A WAY FOR YOU TO FIND US.
I'LL DO MY BEST TO MAKE IT BACK BEFORE YOU KNOW IT.
AND IF I DON'T, WELL—
YOU KNOW WHAT TO DO.

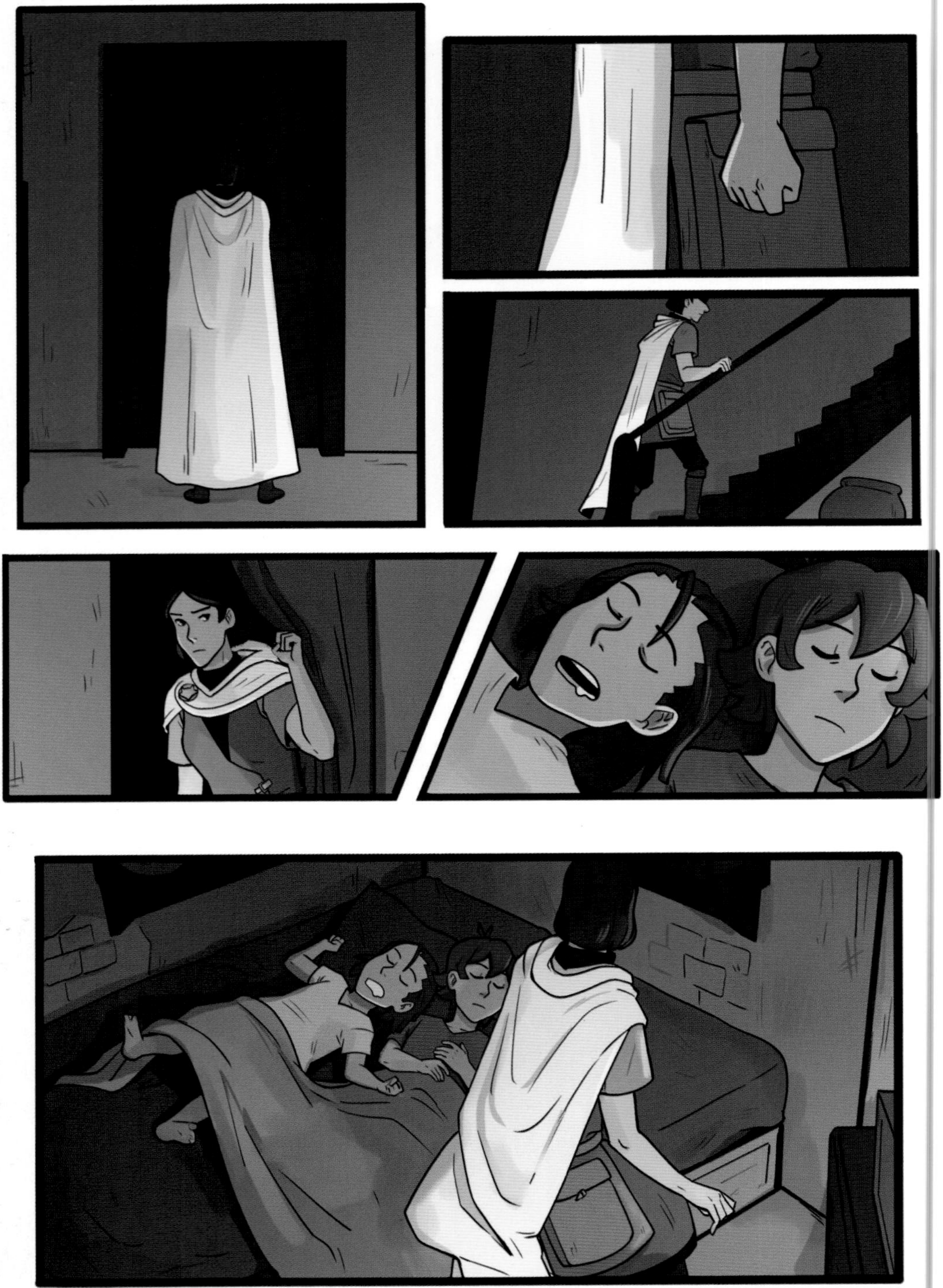

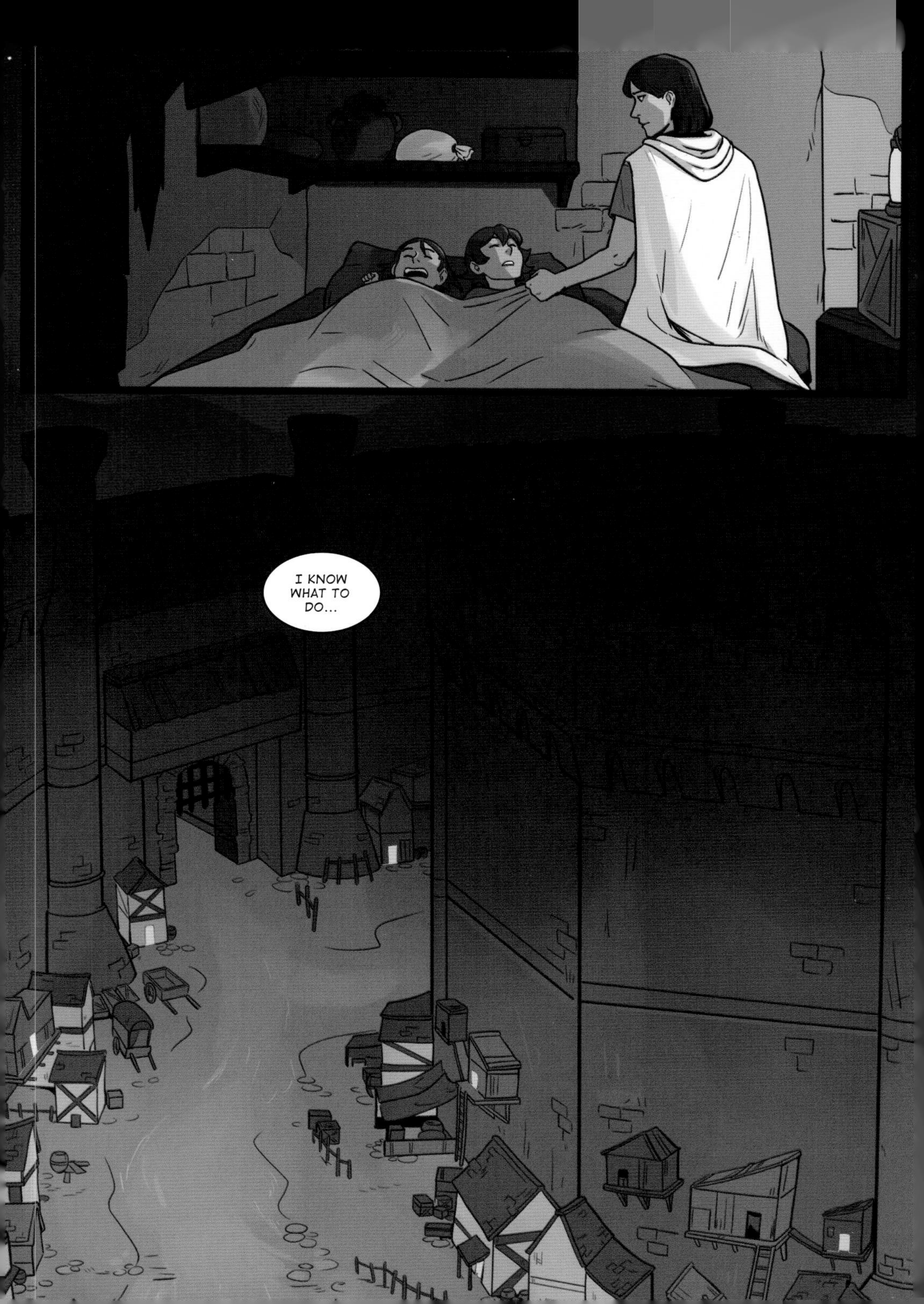
I KNOW WHAT TO DO...

CHAPTER 2:
THE DAY THAT TORE US APART

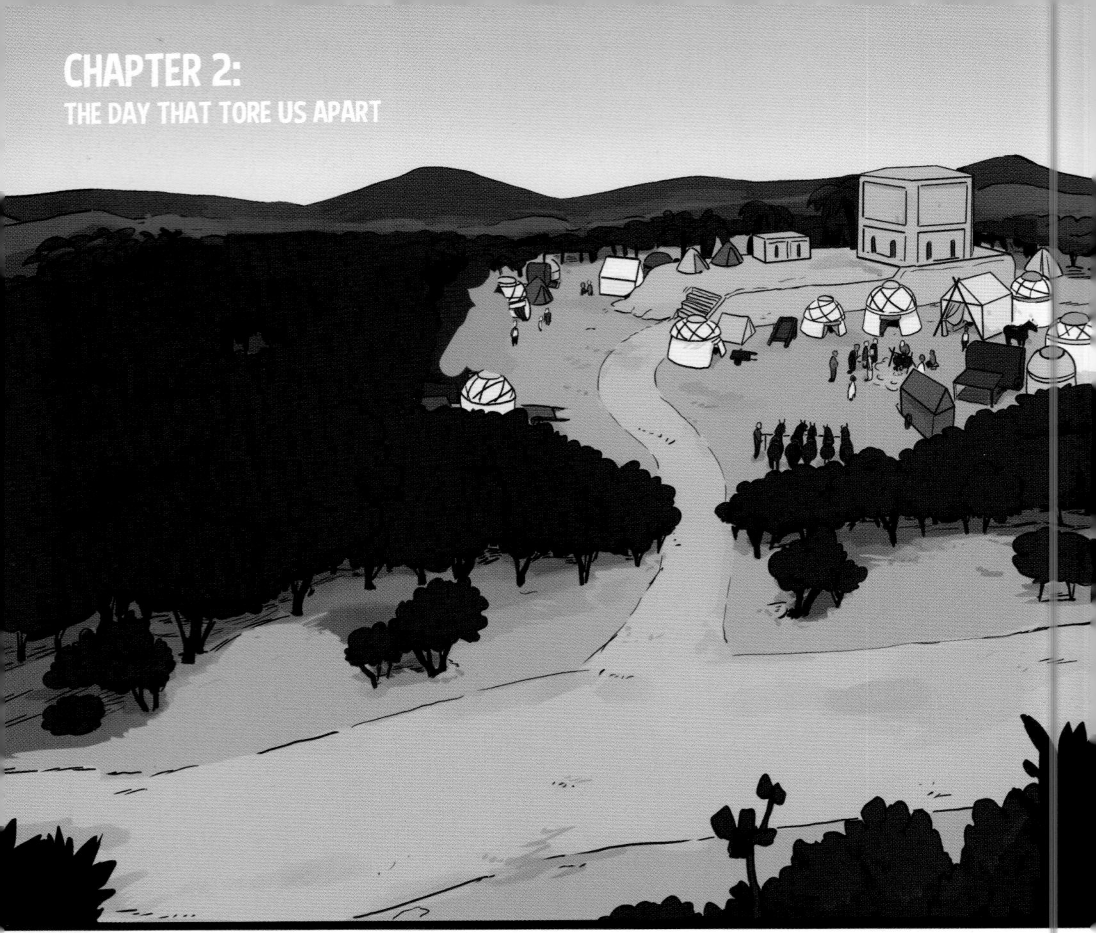

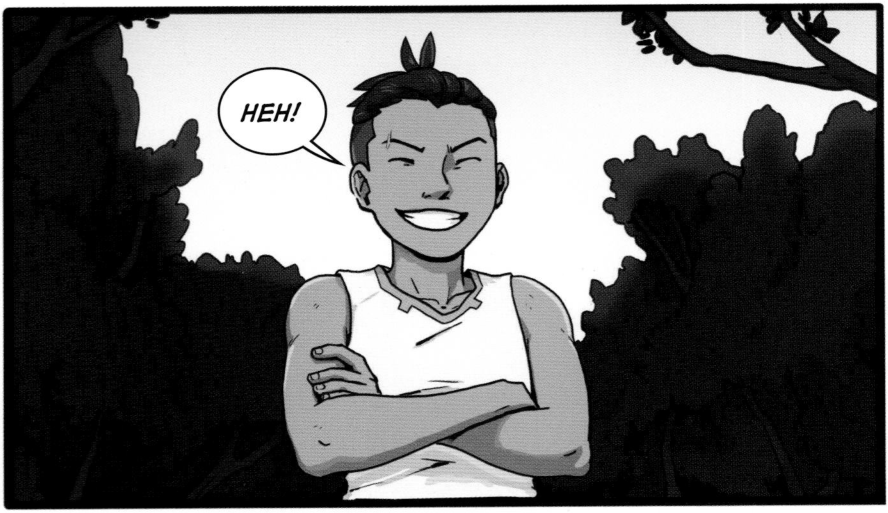
HEH!

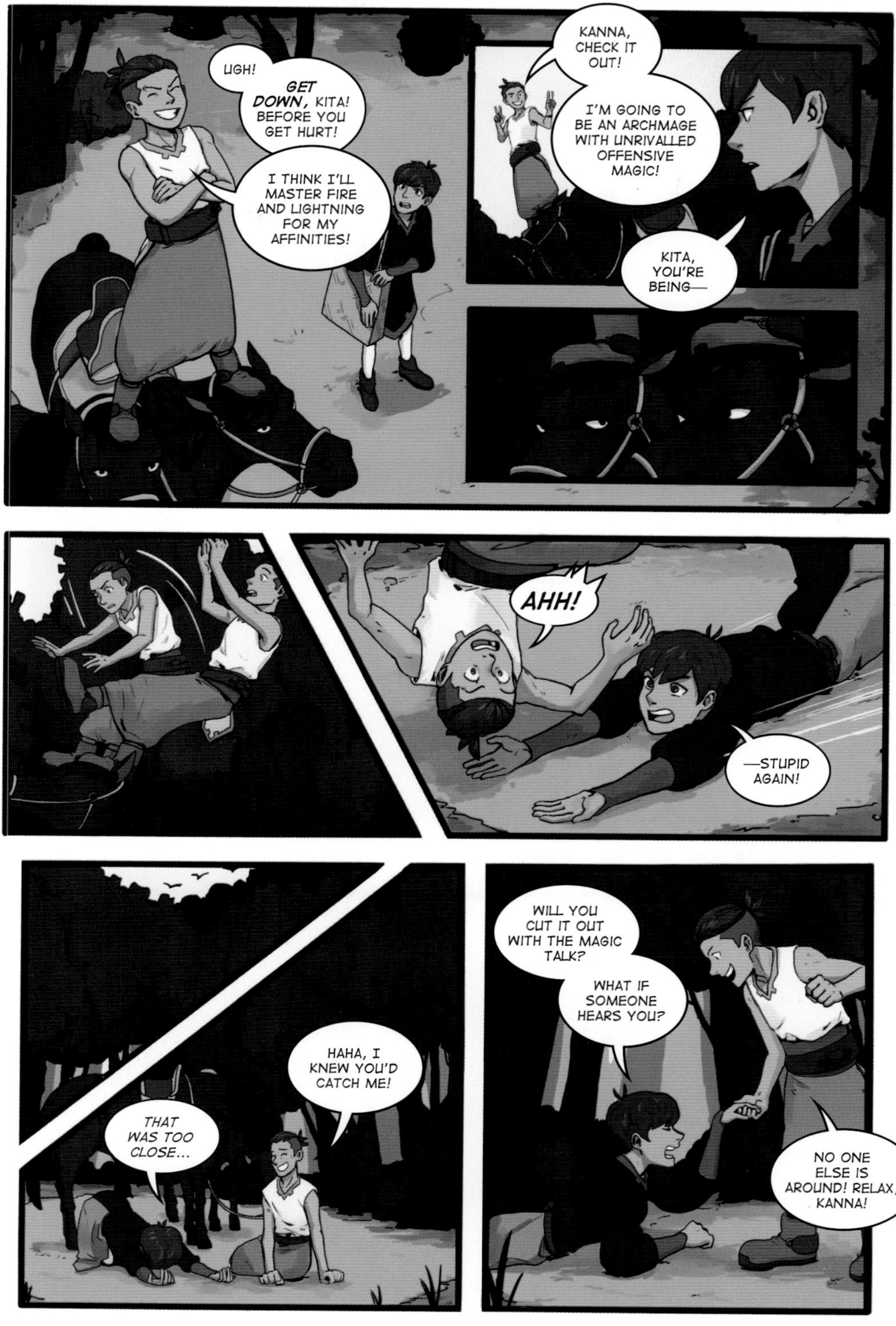
UGH!
GET DOWN, KITA! BEFORE YOU GET HURT!
I THINK I'LL MASTER FIRE AND LIGHTNING FOR MY AFFINITIES!
KANNA, CHECK IT OUT!
I'M GOING TO BE AN ARCHMAGE WITH UNRIVALLED OFFENSIVE MAGIC!
KITA, YOU'RE BEING—
AHH!
—STUPID AGAIN!
THAT WAS TOO CLOSE...
HAHA, I KNEW YOU'D CATCH ME!
WILL YOU CUT IT OUT WITH THE MAGIC TALK?
WHAT IF SOMEONE HEARS YOU?
NO ONE ELSE IS AROUND! RELAX, KANNA!

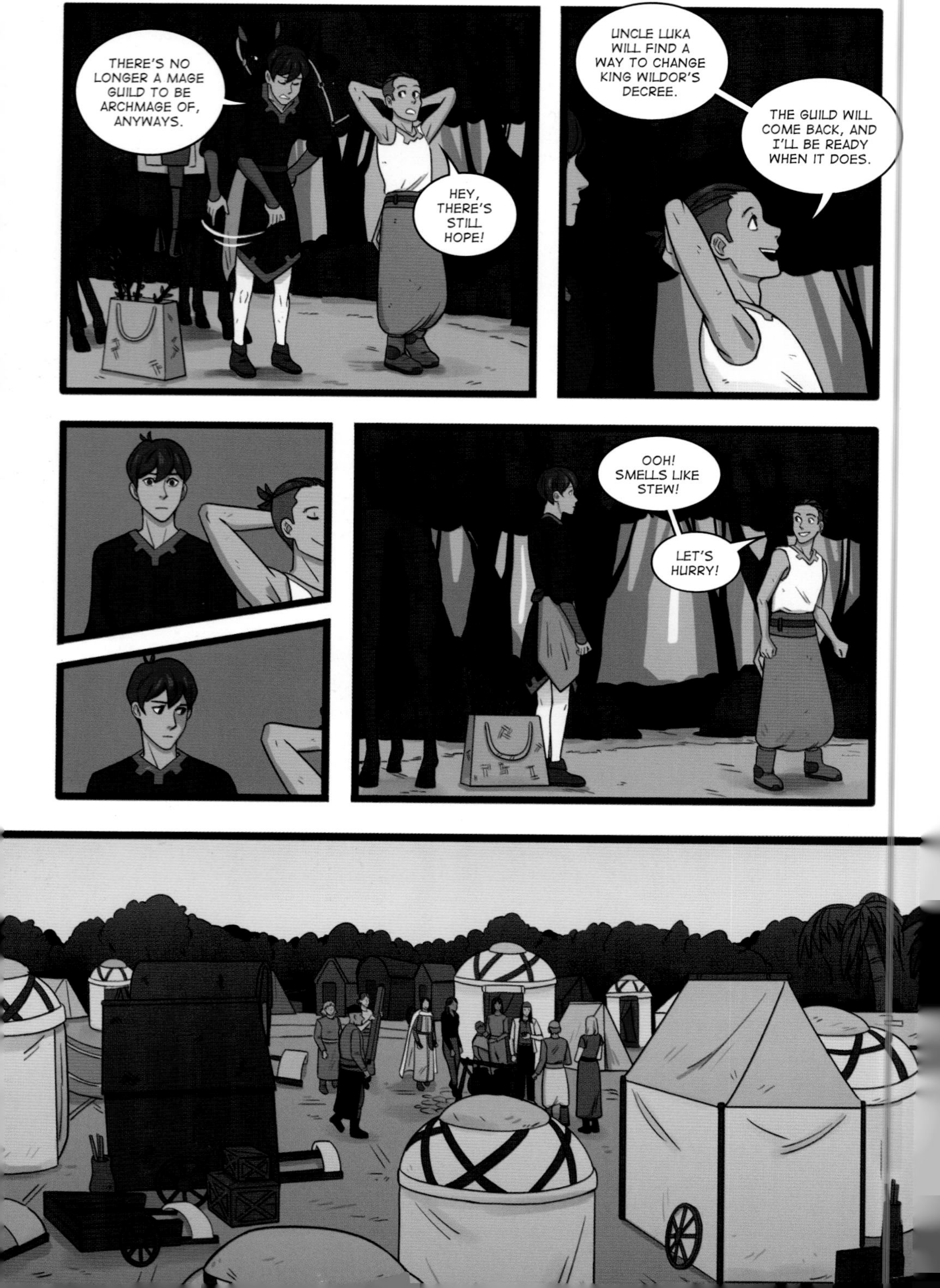
THERE'S NO LONGER A MAGE GUILD TO BE ARCHMAGE OF, ANYWAYS.
HEY, THERE'S STILL HOPE!
UNCLE LUKA WILL FIND A WAY TO CHANGE KING WILDOR'S DECREE.
THE GUILD WILL COME BACK, AND I'LL BE READY WHEN IT DOES.
OOH! SMELLS LIKE STEW!
LET'S HURRY!

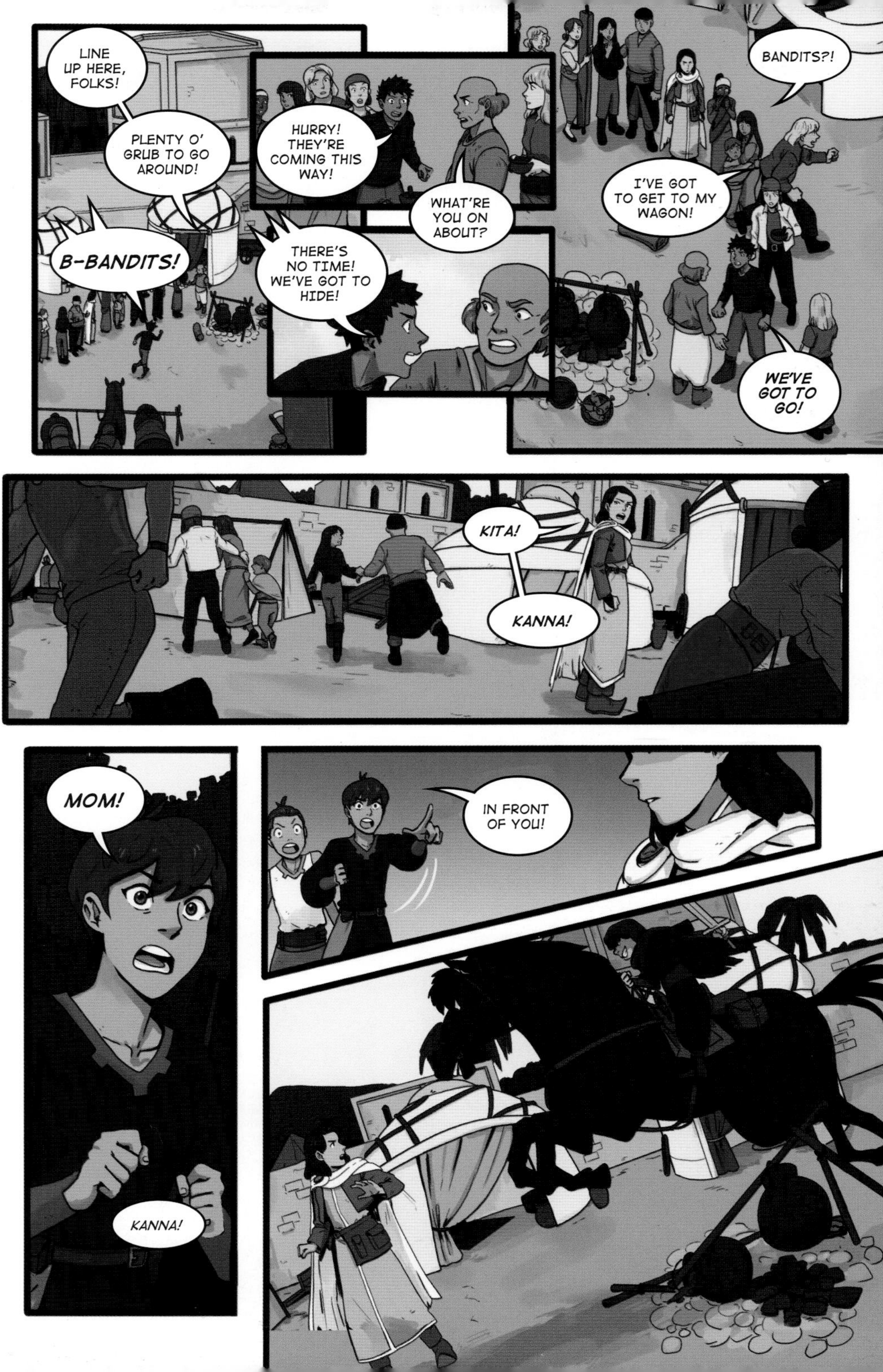
LINE UP HERE, FOLKS!
PLENTY O' GRUB TO GO AROUND!
B-BANDITS!
HURRY! THEY'RE COMING THIS WAY!
WHAT'RE YOU ON ABOUT?
THERE'S NO TIME! WE'VE GOT TO HIDE!
BANDITS?!
I'VE GOT TO GET TO MY WAGON!
WE'VE GOT TO GO!
KITA!
KANNA!
MOM!
KANNA!
IN FRONT OF YOU!

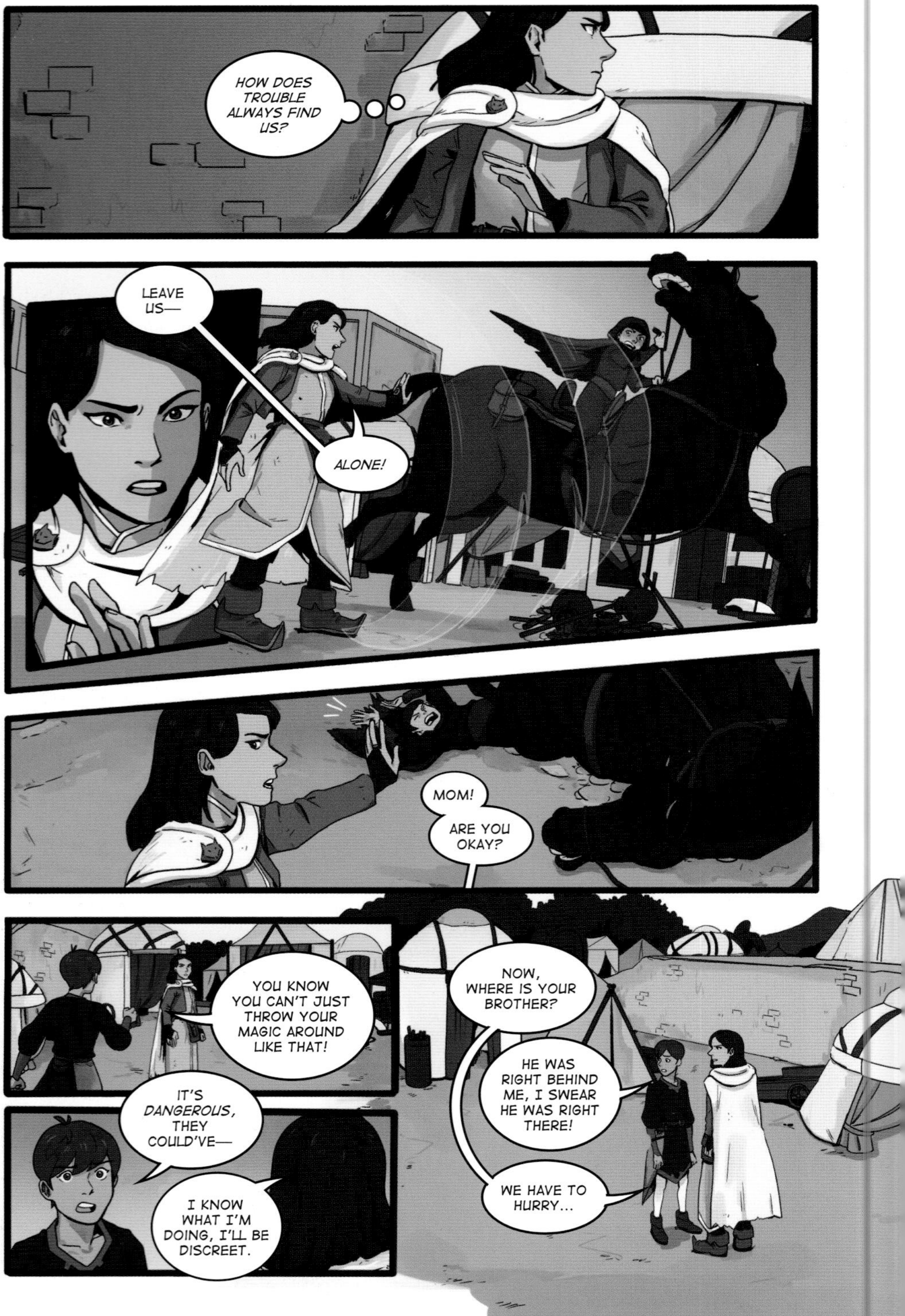
HOW DOES TROUBLE ALWAYS FIND US?
LEAVE US—
ALONE!
MOM!
ARE YOU OKAY?
YOU KNOW YOU CAN'T JUST THROW YOUR MAGIC AROUND LIKE THAT!
IT'S *DANGEROUS*, THEY COULD'VE—
I KNOW WHAT I'M DOING, I'LL BE DISCREET.
NOW, WHERE IS YOUR BROTHER?
HE WAS RIGHT BEHIND ME, I SWEAR HE WAS RIGHT THERE!
WE HAVE TO HURRY...

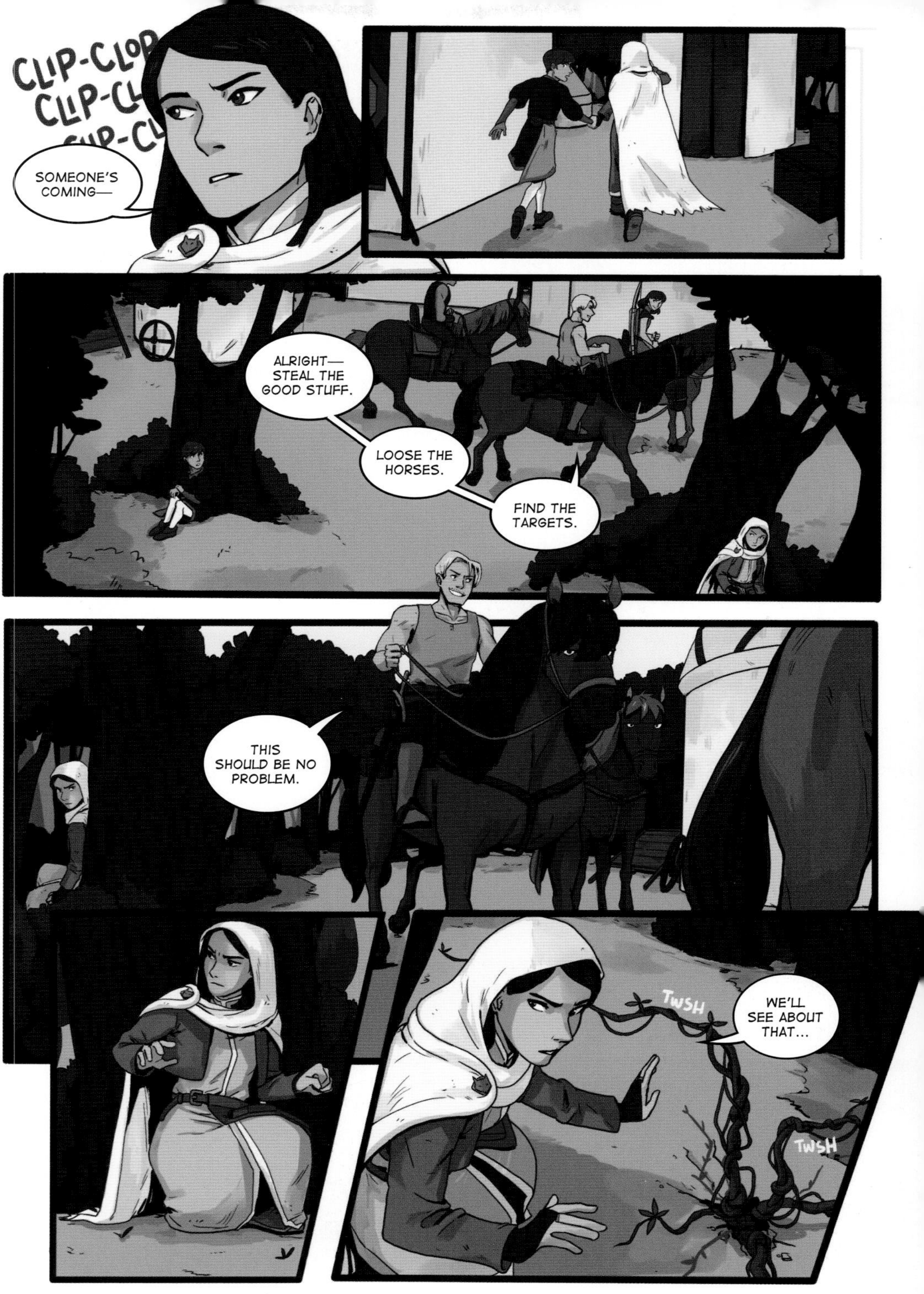
CLIP-CLOP
CLIP-CL
CLIP-CL
SOMEONE'S COMING—
ALRIGHT— STEAL THE GOOD STUFF.
LOOSE THE HORSES.
FIND THE TARGETS.
THIS SHOULD BE NO PROBLEM.
TWSH
WE'LL SEE ABOUT THAT...
TWSH

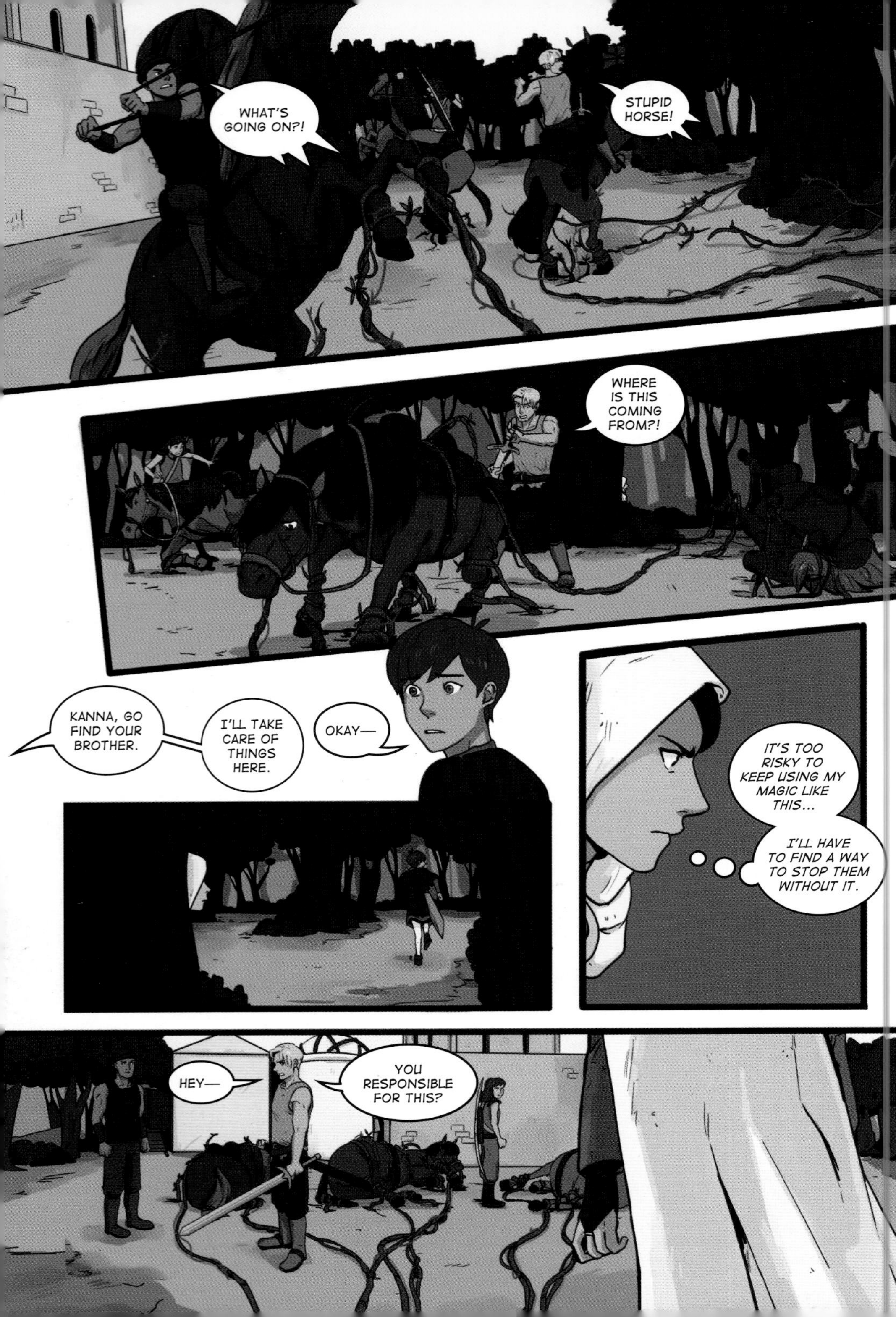
WHAT'S GOING ON?!
STUPID HORSE!
WHERE IS THIS COMING FROM?!
KANNA, GO FIND YOUR BROTHER.
I'LL TAKE CARE OF THINGS HERE.
OKAY—
IT'S TOO RISKY TO KEEP USING MY MAGIC LIKE THIS...
I'LL HAVE TO FIND A WAY TO STOP THEM WITHOUT IT.
HEY—
YOU RESPONSIBLE FOR THIS?

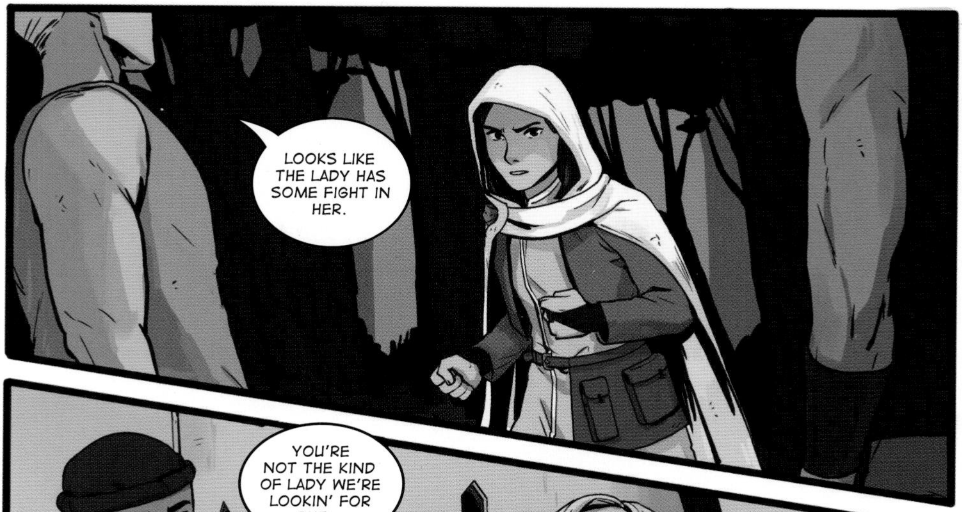
LOOKS LIKE THE LADY HAS SOME FIGHT IN HER.

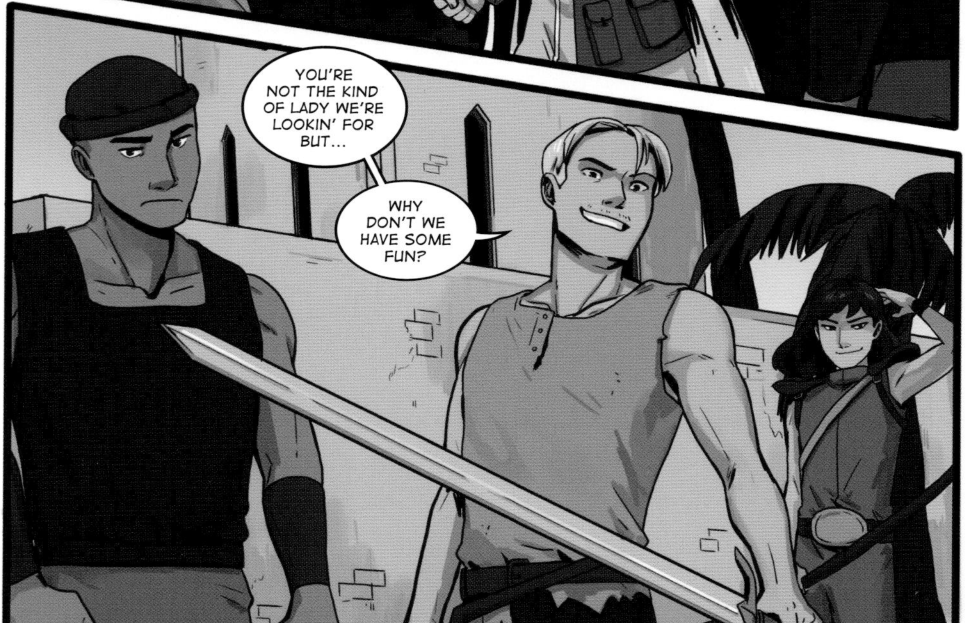
YOU'RE NOT THE KIND OF LADY WE'RE LOOKIN' FOR BUT...
WHY DON'T WE HAVE SOME FUN?

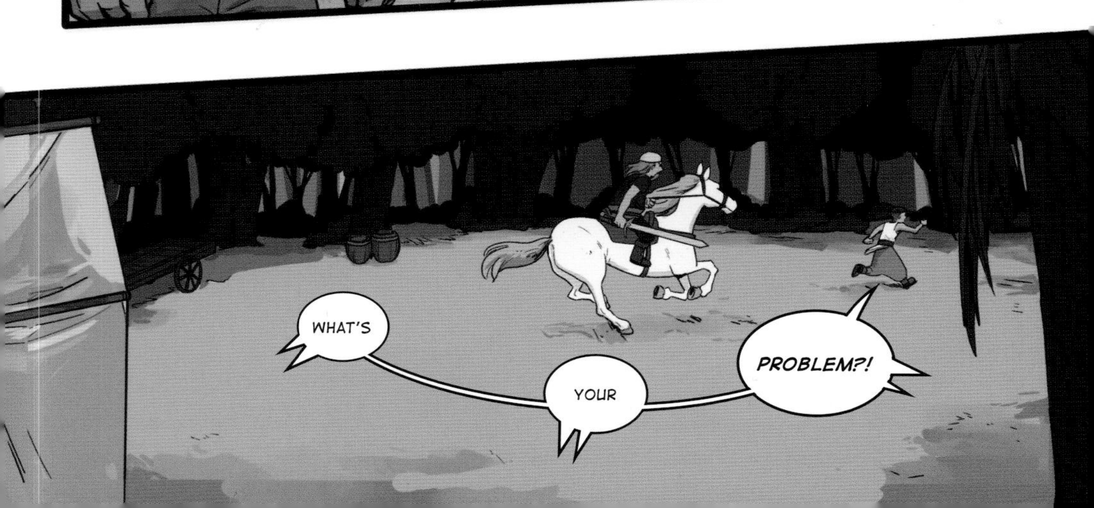
WHAT'S
YOUR
PROBLEM?!

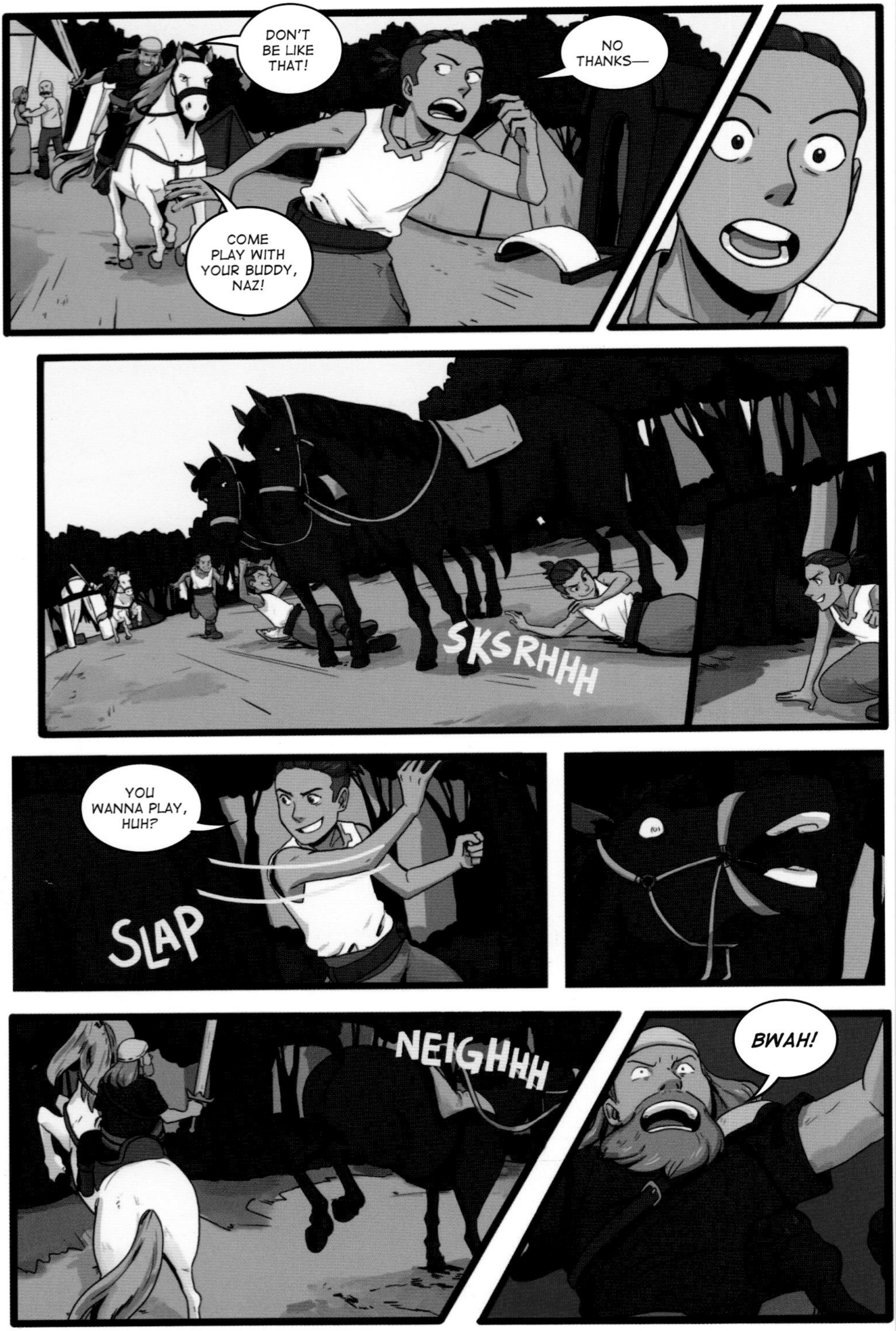
DON'T BE LIKE THAT!
NO THANKS—
COME PLAY WITH YOUR BUDDY, NAZ!
SKSRHHH
YOU WANNA PLAY, HUH?
SLAP
NEIGHHH
BWAH!

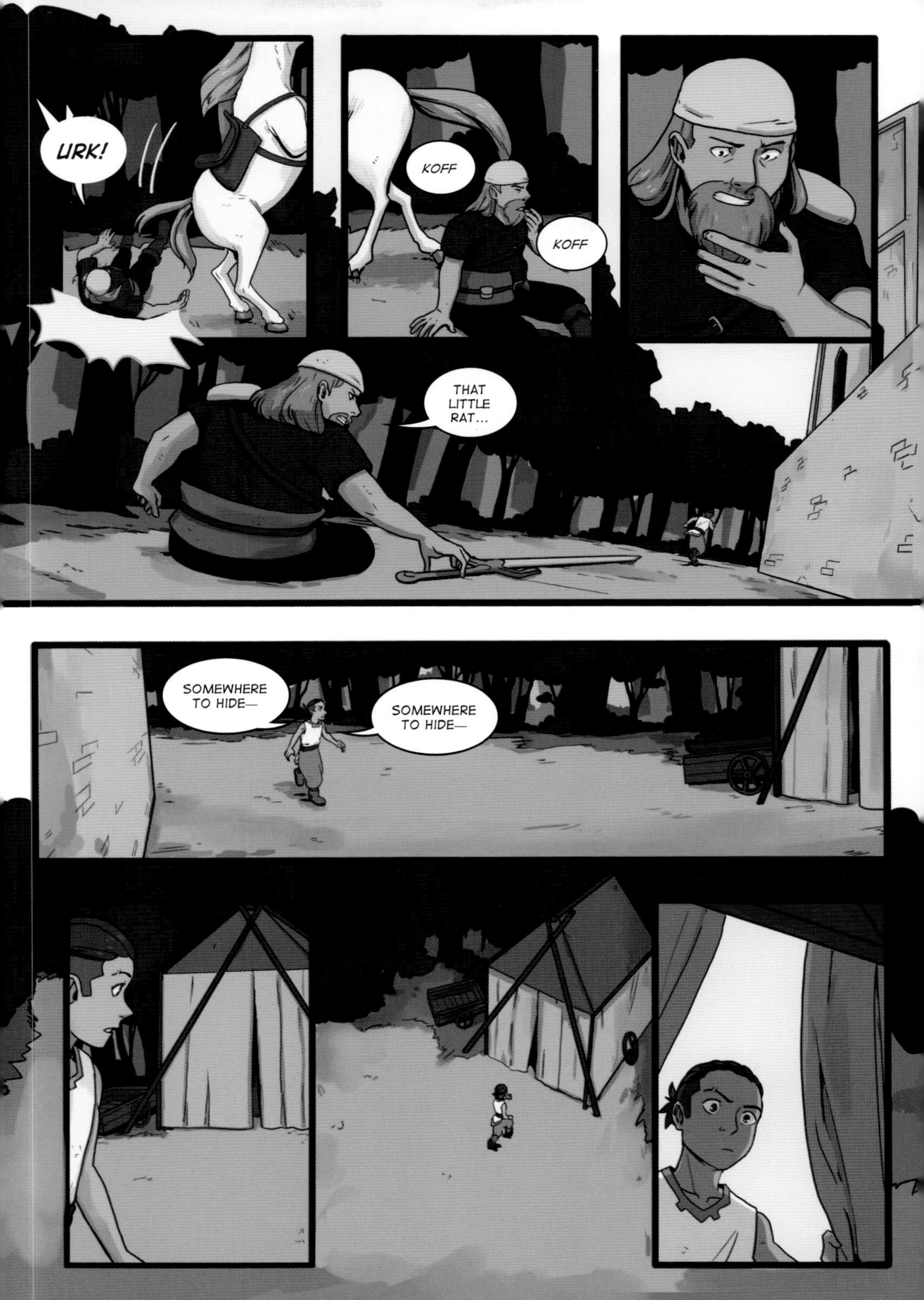
URK!
KOFF
KOFF
THAT LITTLE RAT...
SOMEWHERE TO HIDE—
SOMEWHERE TO HIDE—

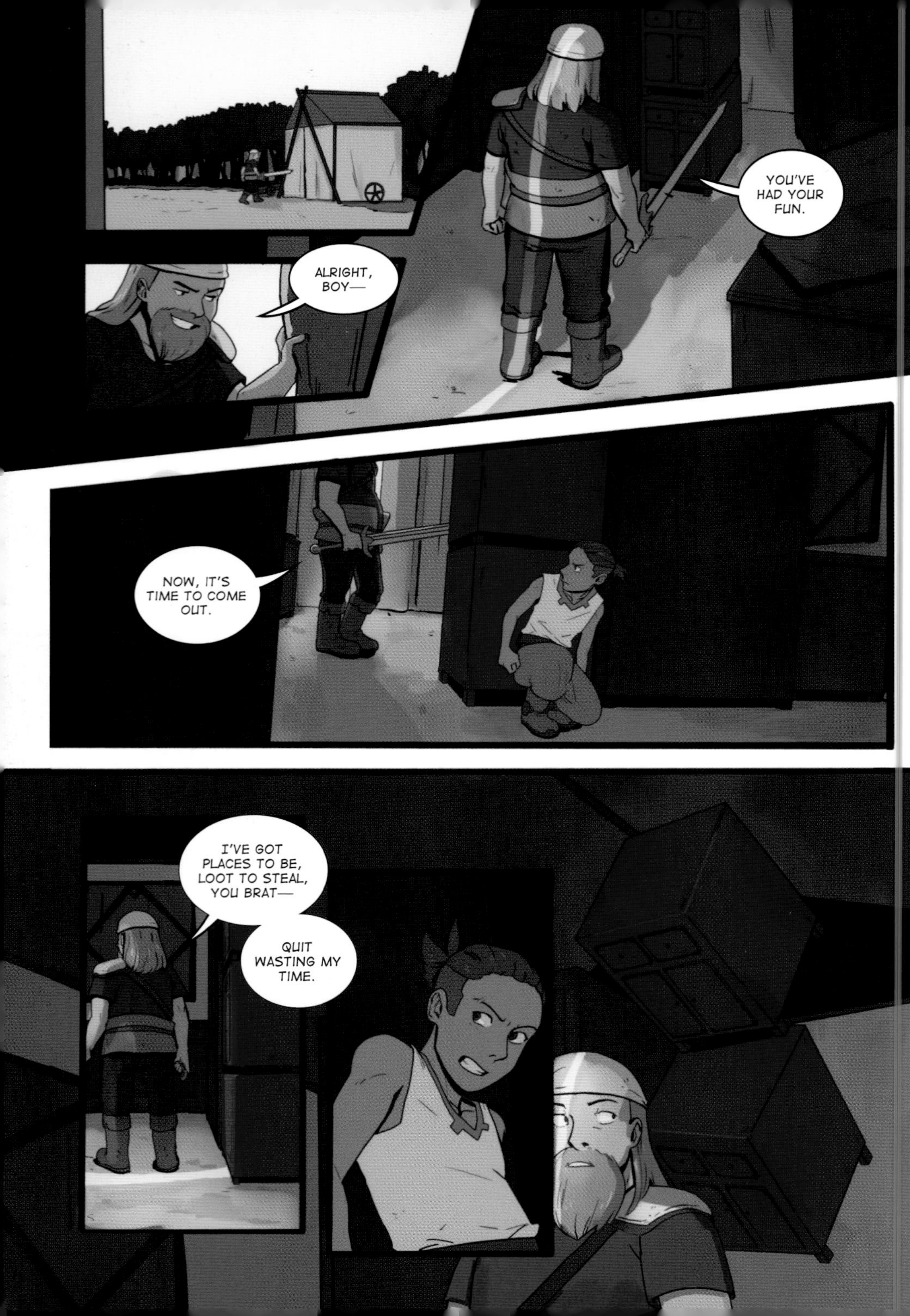
YOU'VE HAD YOUR FUN.
ALRIGHT, BOY—
NOW, IT'S TIME TO COME OUT.
I'VE GOT PLACES TO BE, LOOT TO STEAL, YOU BRAT—
QUIT WASTING MY TIME.

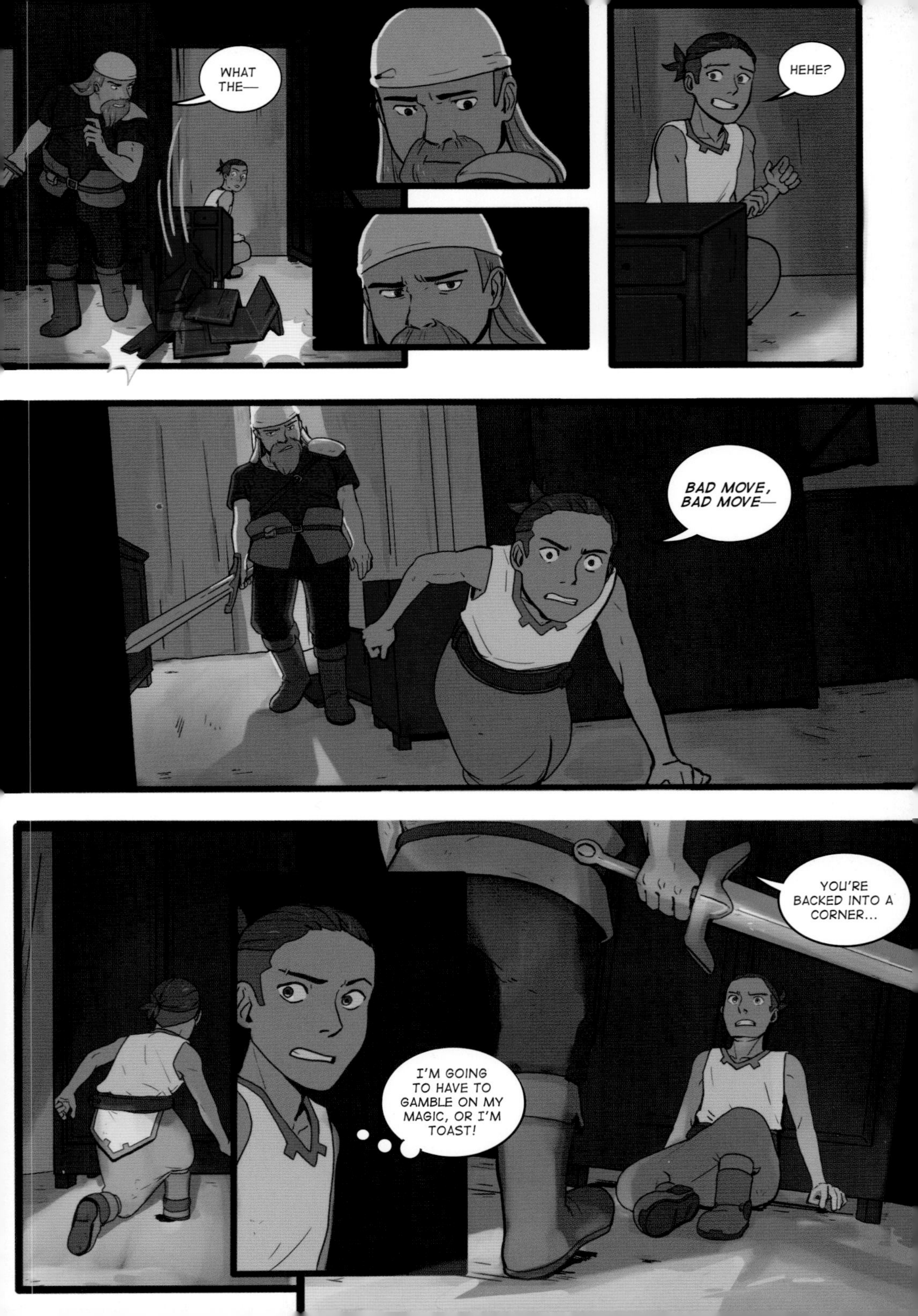
WHAT THE—
HEHE?
BAD MOVE, BAD MOVE—
YOU'RE BACKED INTO A CORNER...
I'M GOING TO HAVE TO GAMBLE ON MY MAGIC, OR I'M TOAST!

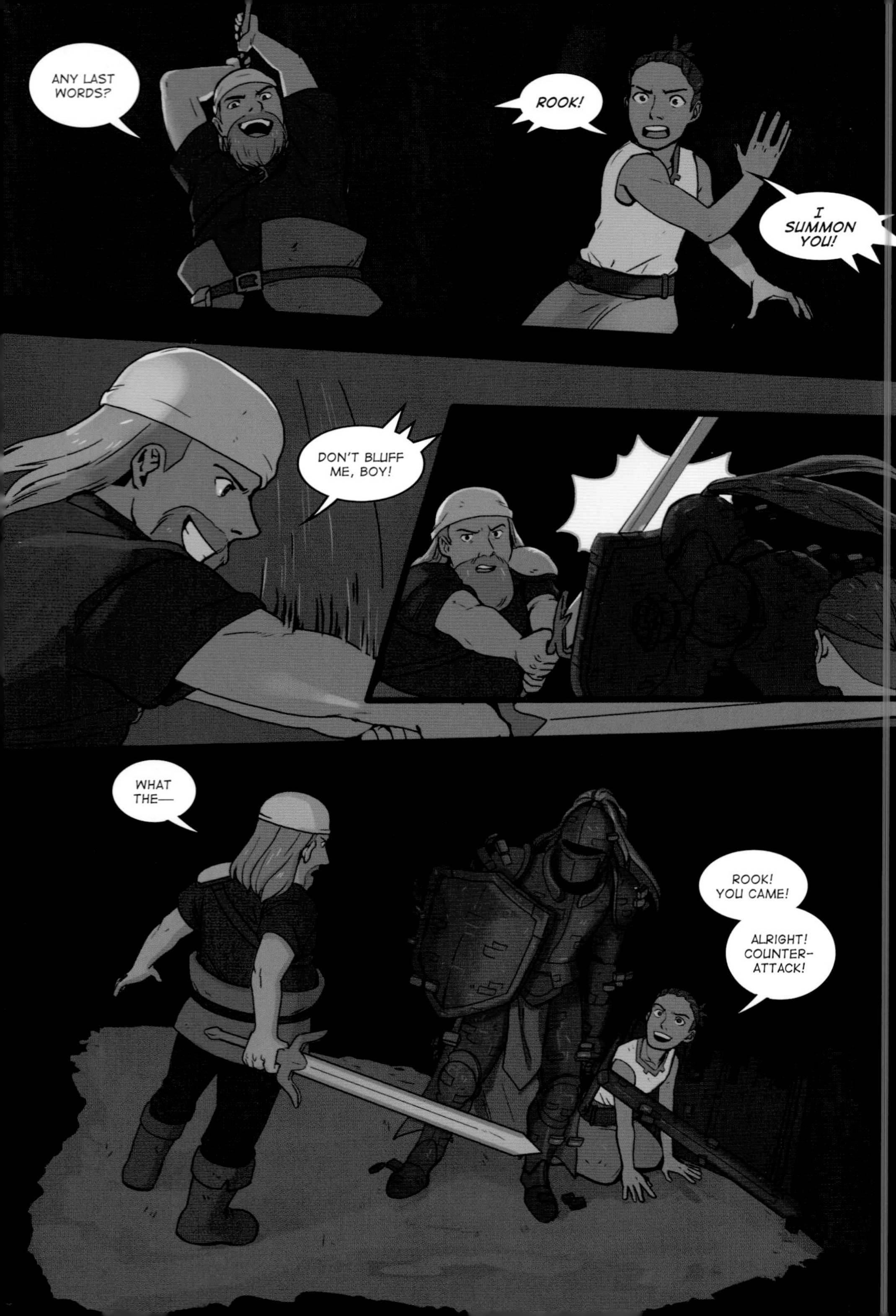

ANY LAST WORDS?
ROOK!
I SUMMON YOU!
DON'T BLUFF ME, BOY!
WHAT THE—
ROOK! YOU CAME!
ALRIGHT! COUNTER-ATTACK!

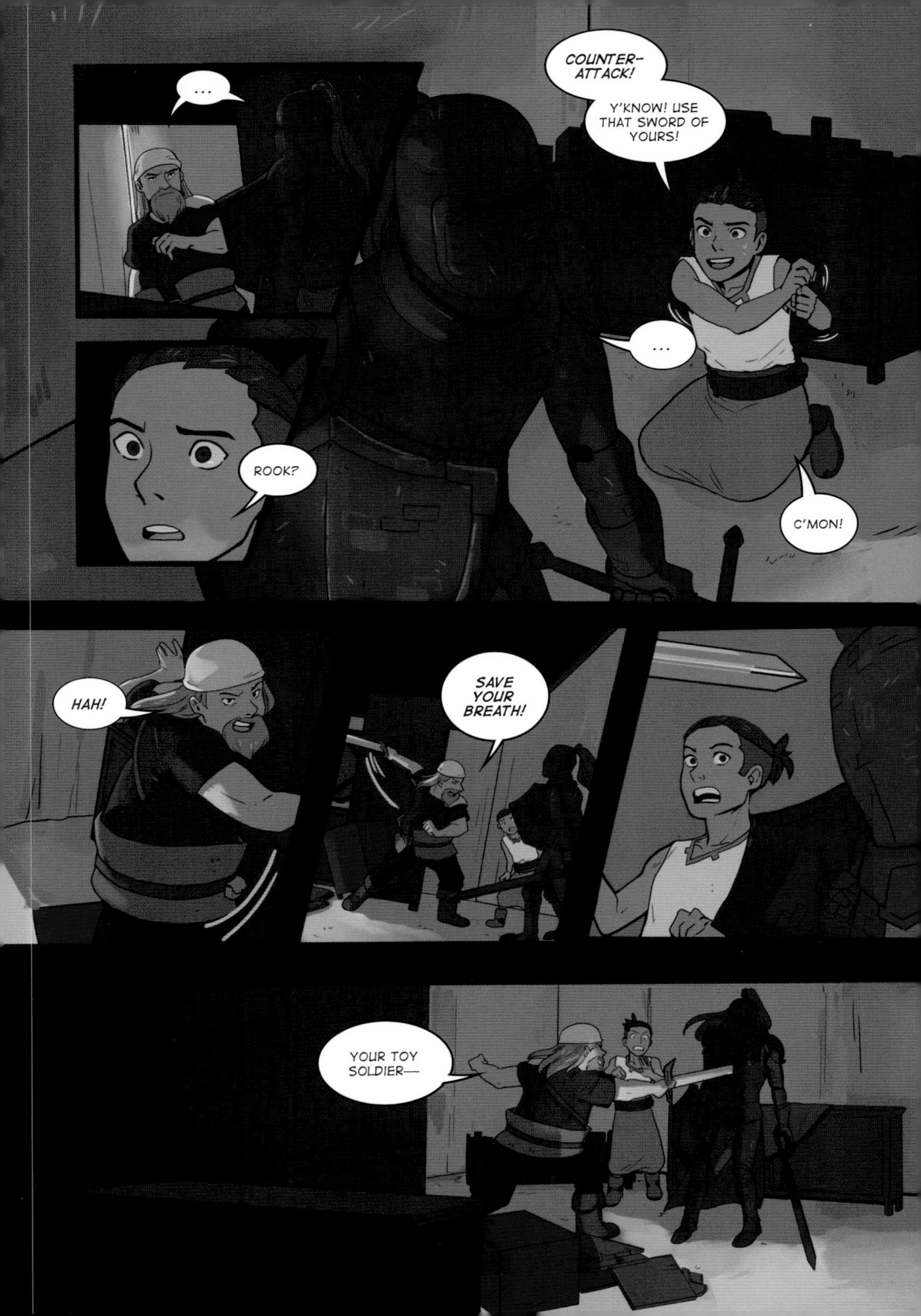
...
COUNTER-ATTACK!
Y'KNOW! USE THAT SWORD OF YOURS!
...
ROOK?
C'MON!
HAH!
SAVE YOUR BREATH!
YOUR TOY SOLDIER—

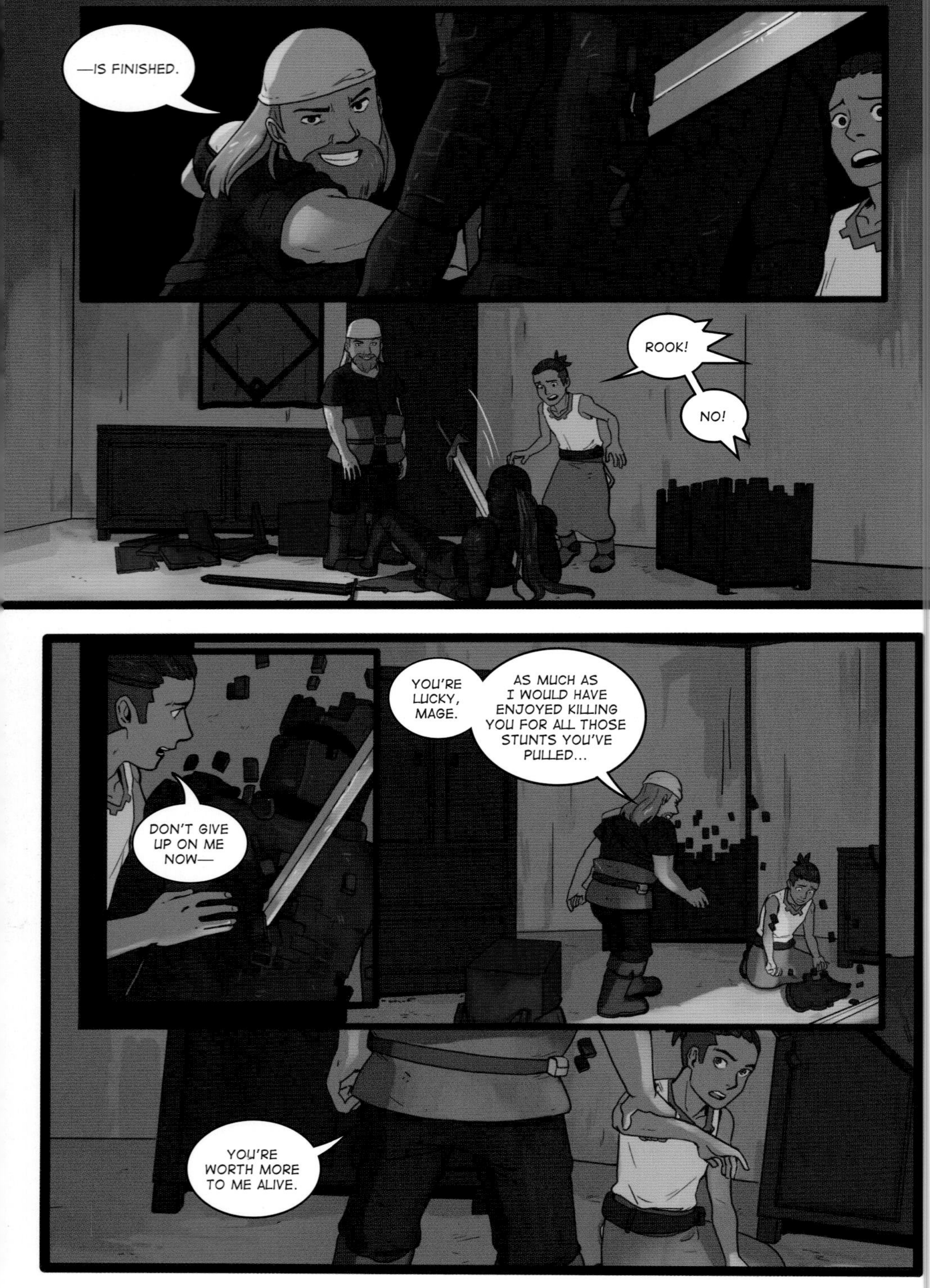
—IS FINISHED.
ROOK!
NO!
DON'T GIVE UP ON ME NOW—
YOU'RE LUCKY, MAGE.
AS MUCH AS I WOULD HAVE ENJOYED KILLING YOU FOR ALL THOSE STUNTS YOU'VE PULLED...
YOU'RE WORTH MORE TO ME ALIVE.

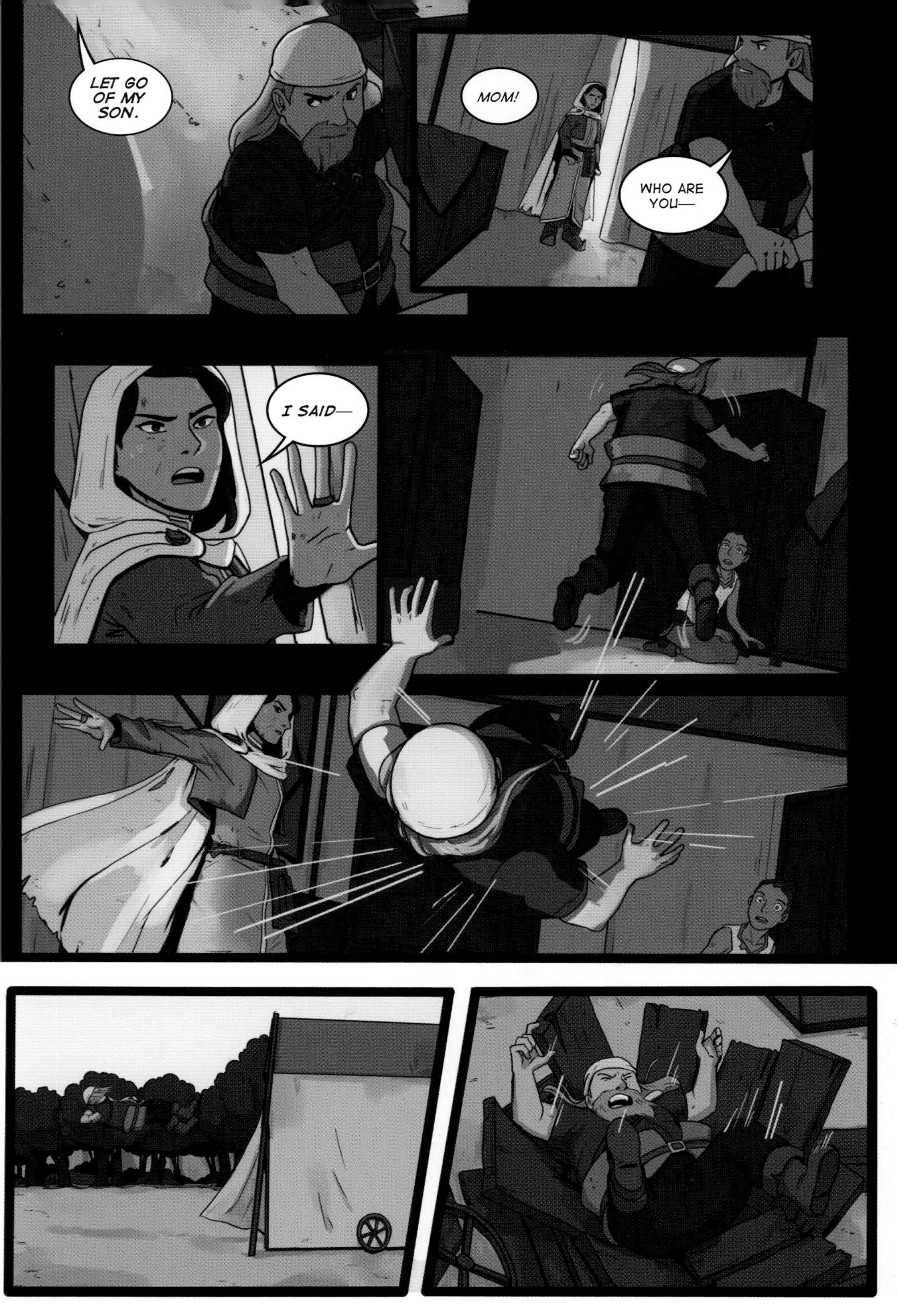
LET GO OF MY SON.
MOM!
WHO ARE YOU—
I SAID—

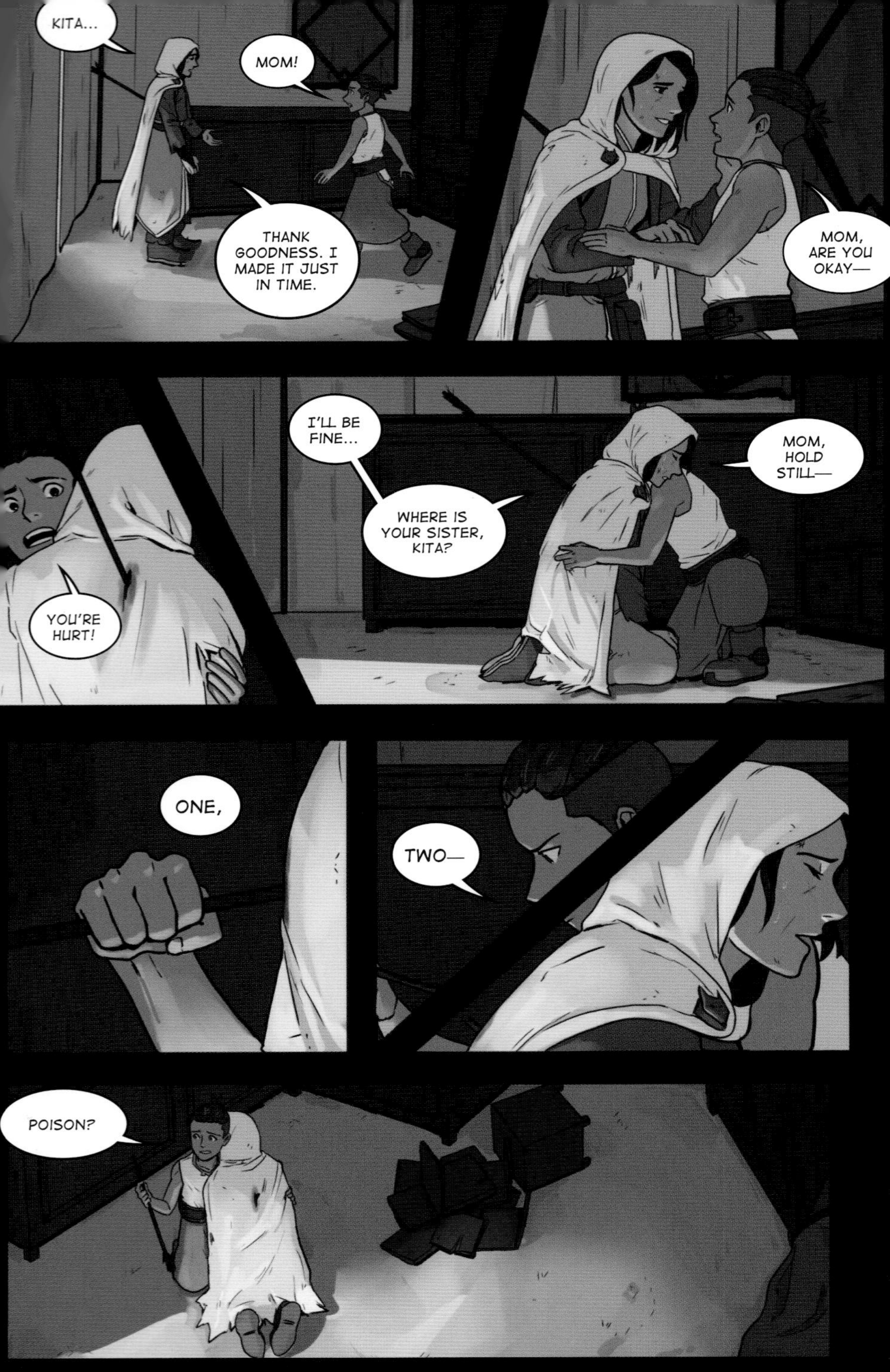
KITA...
MOM!
THANK GOODNESS. I MADE IT JUST IN TIME.
MOM, ARE YOU OKAY—
YOU'RE HURT!
I'LL BE FINE...
WHERE IS YOUR SISTER, KITA?
MOM, HOLD STILL—
ONE,
TWO—
POISON?

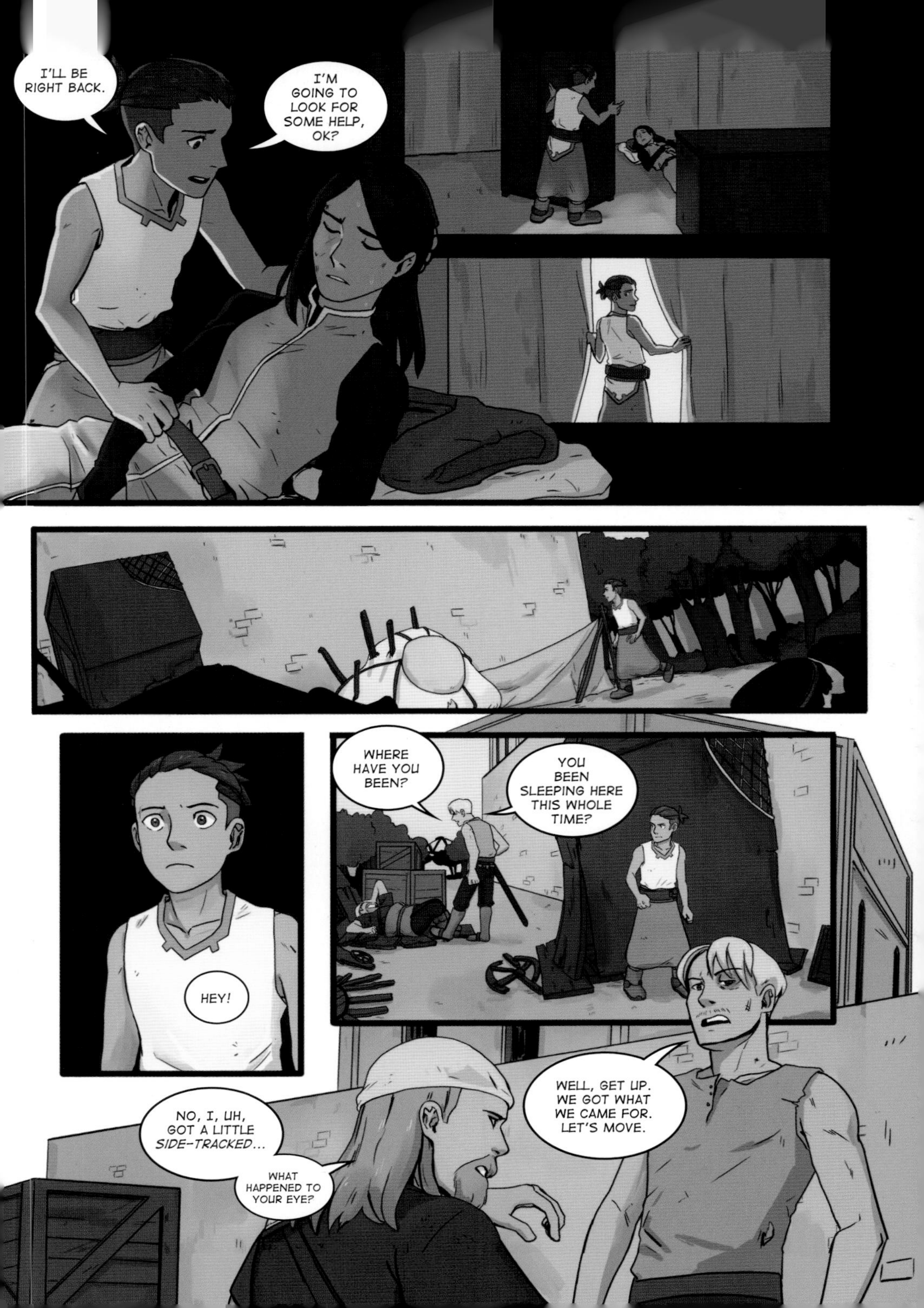
I'LL BE RIGHT BACK.
I'M GOING TO LOOK FOR SOME HELP, OK?
HEY!
WHERE HAVE YOU BEEN?
YOU BEEN SLEEPING HERE THIS WHOLE TIME?
NO, I, UH, GOT A LITTLE *SIDE-TRACKED*...
WHAT HAPPENED TO YOUR EYE?
WELL, GET UP. WE GOT WHAT WE CAME FOR. LET'S MOVE.

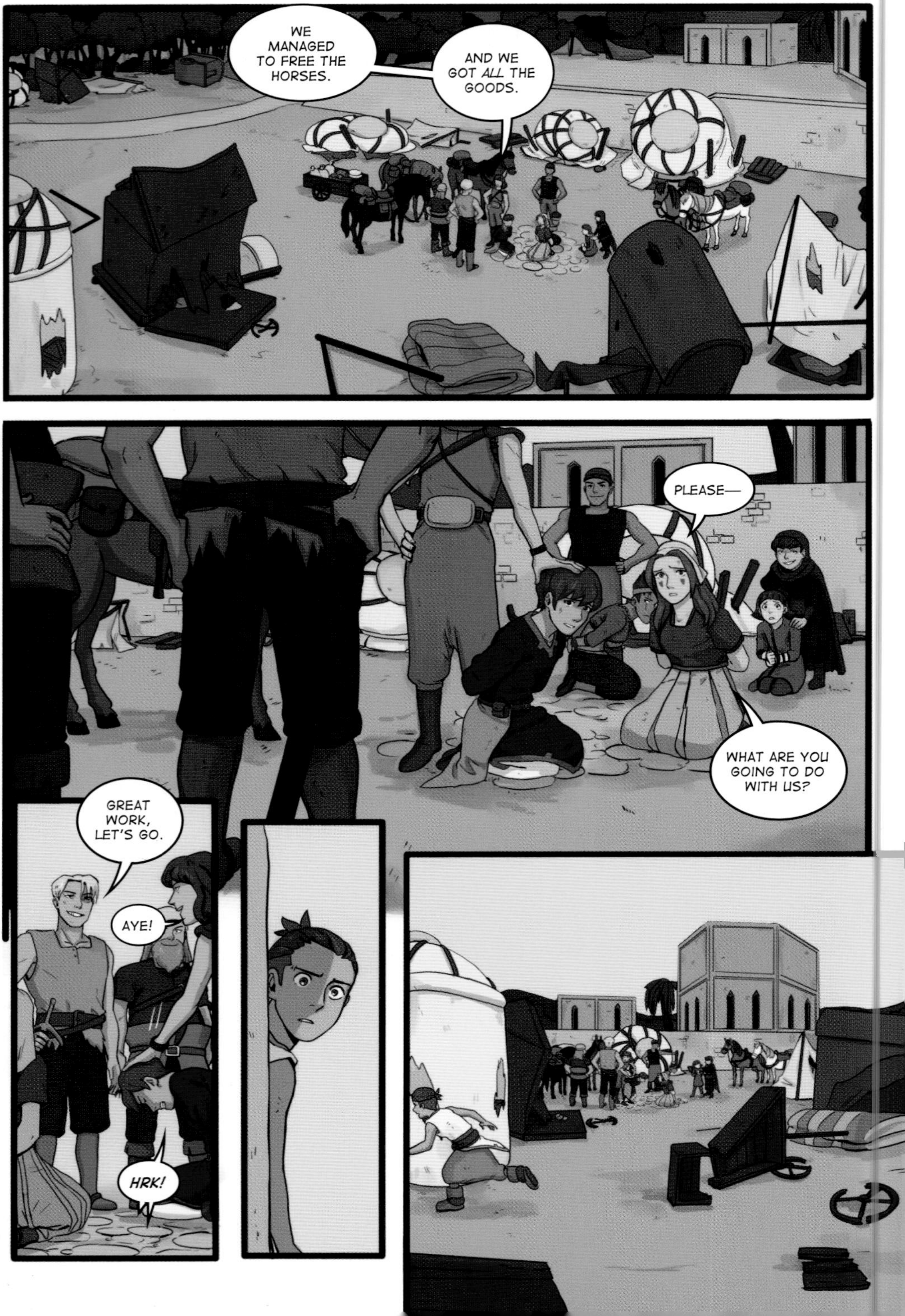

WE MANAGED TO FREE THE HORSES.
AND WE GOT *ALL* THE GOODS.
PLEASE—
WHAT ARE YOU GOING TO DO WITH US?
GREAT WORK, LET'S GO.
AYE!
HRK!

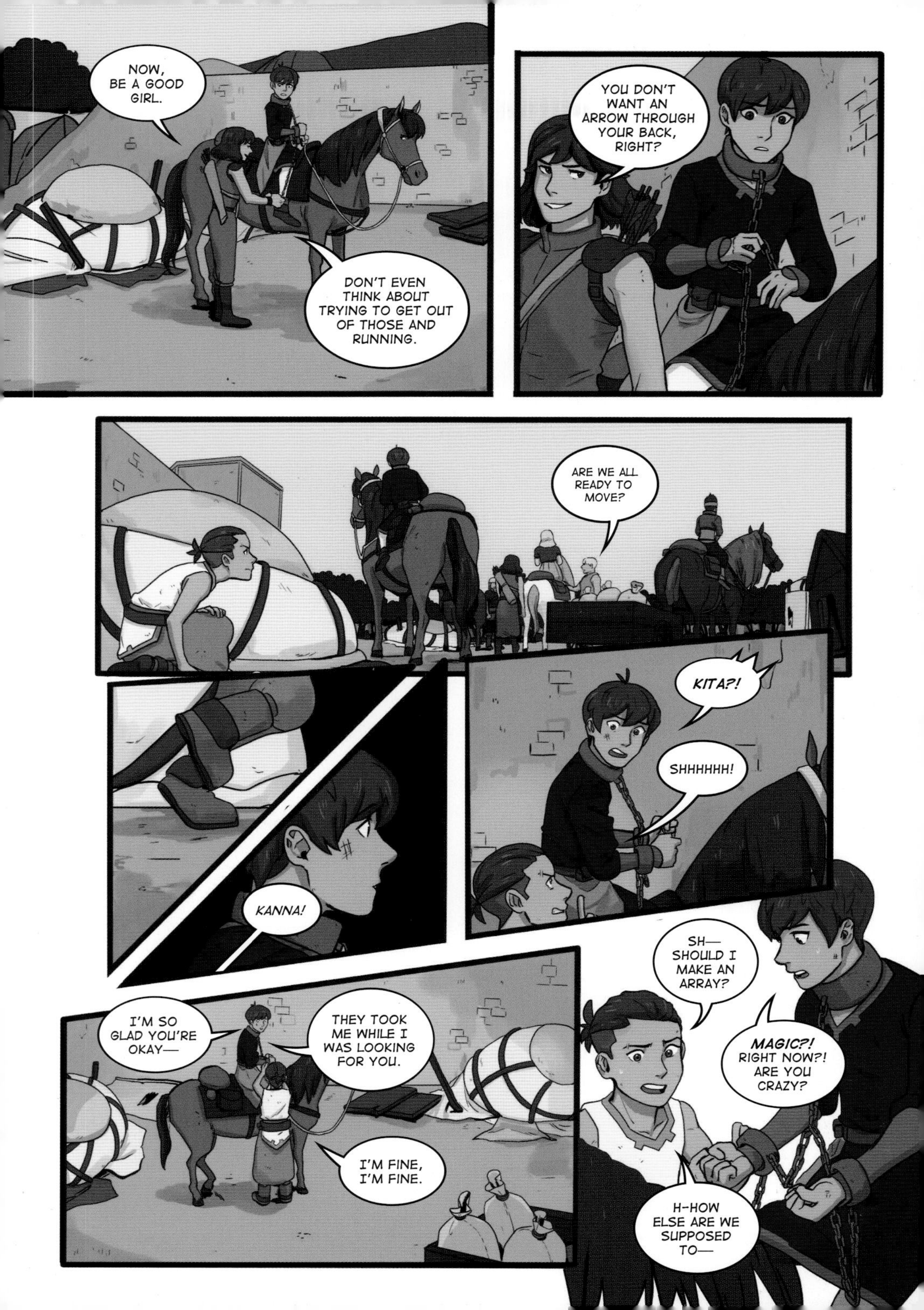
NOW, BE A GOOD GIRL.
DON'T EVEN THINK ABOUT TRYING TO GET OUT OF THOSE AND RUNNING.
YOU DON'T WANT AN ARROW THROUGH YOUR BACK, RIGHT?
ARE WE ALL READY TO MOVE?
KANNA!
KITA?!
SHHHHHH!
I'M SO GLAD YOU'RE OKAY—
THEY TOOK ME WHILE I WAS LOOKING FOR YOU.
I'M FINE, I'M FINE.
SH— SHOULD I MAKE AN ARRAY?
MAGIC?! RIGHT NOW?! ARE YOU CRAZY?
H-HOW ELSE ARE WE SUPPOSED TO—

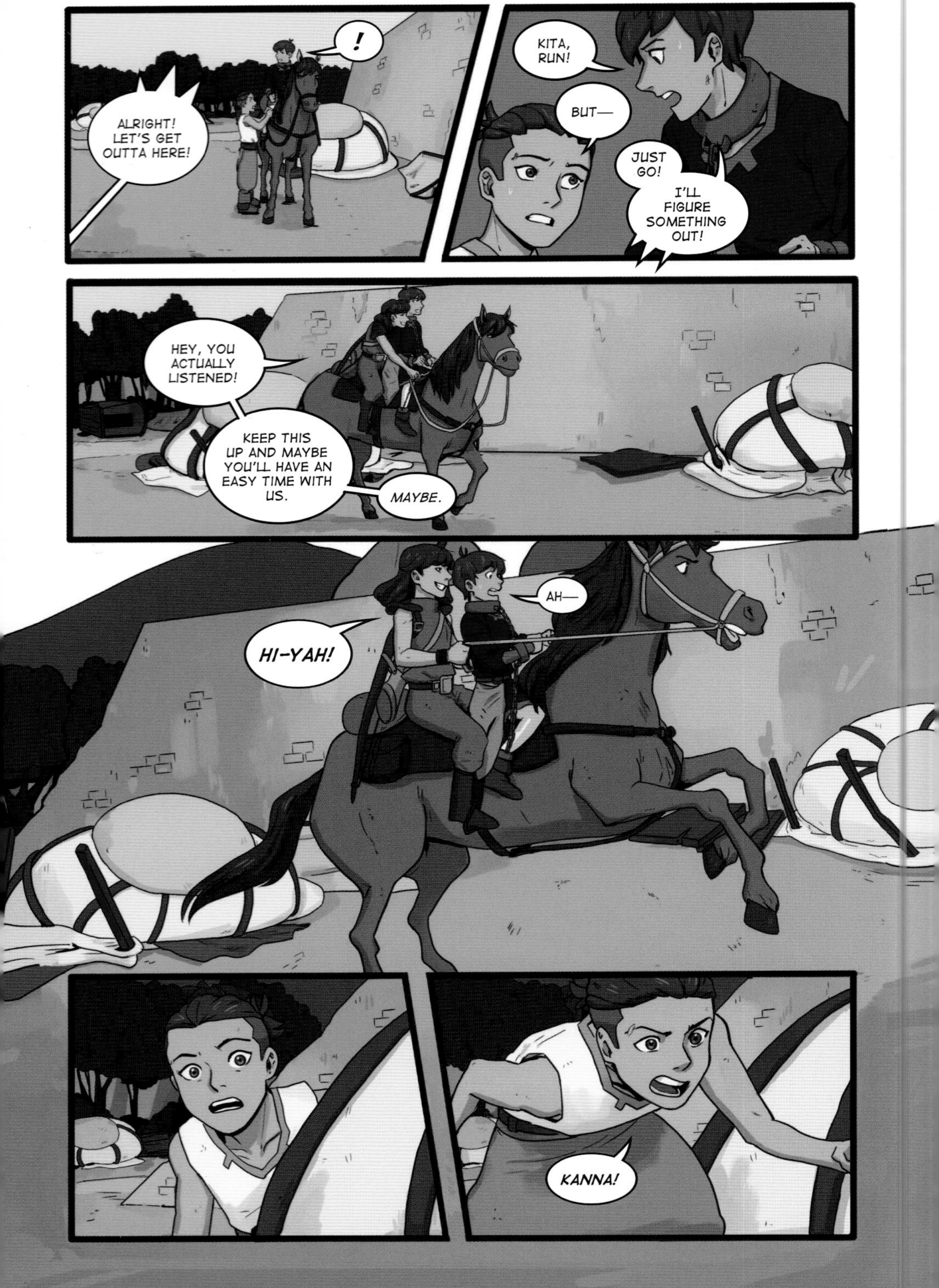
ALRIGHT! LET'S GET OUTTA HERE!
!
KITA, RUN!
BUT—
JUST GO!
I'LL FIGURE SOMETHING OUT!
HEY, YOU ACTUALLY LISTENED!
KEEP THIS UP AND MAYBE YOU'LL HAVE AN EASY TIME WITH US.
MAYBE.
AH—
HI-YAH!
KANNA!

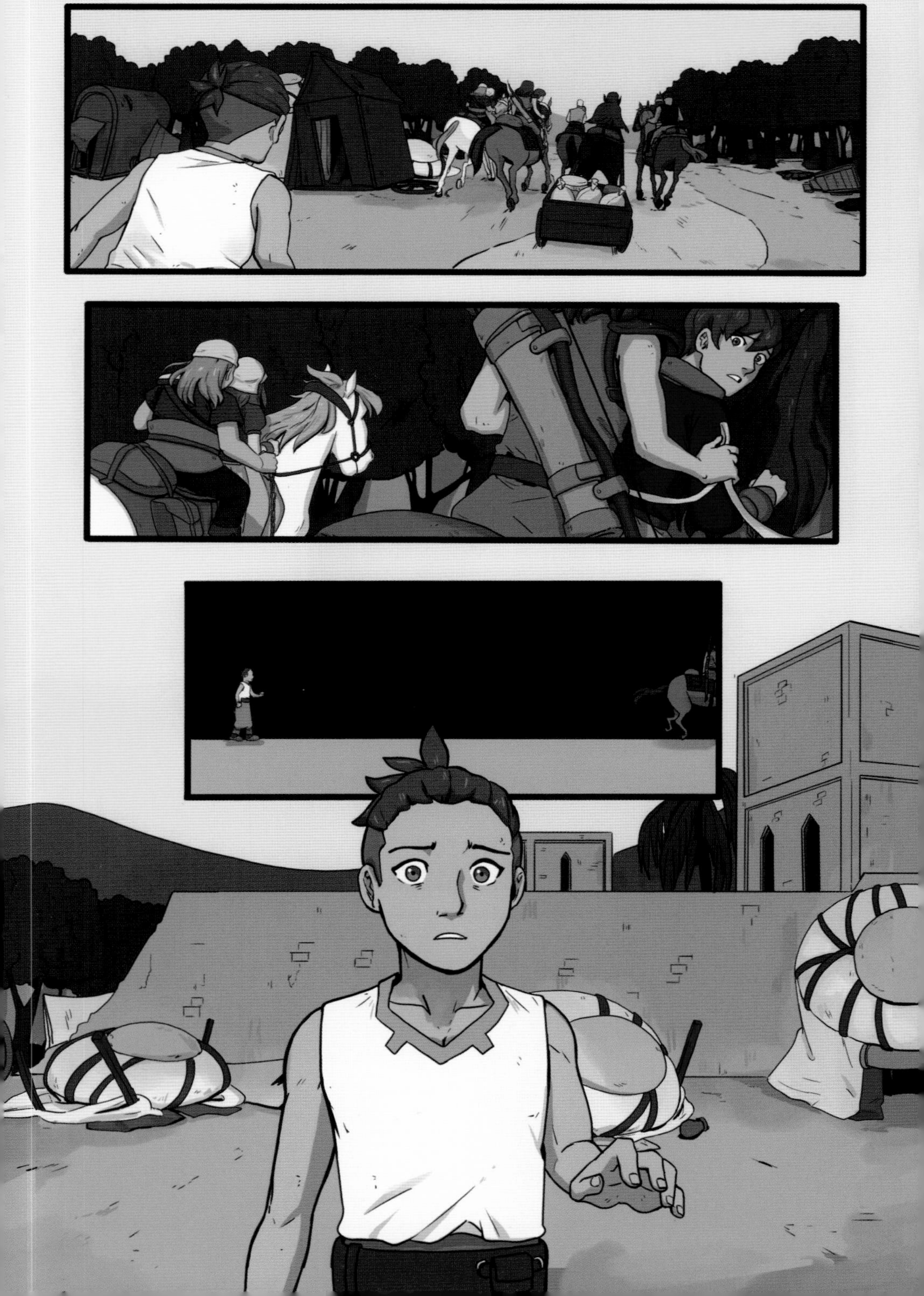

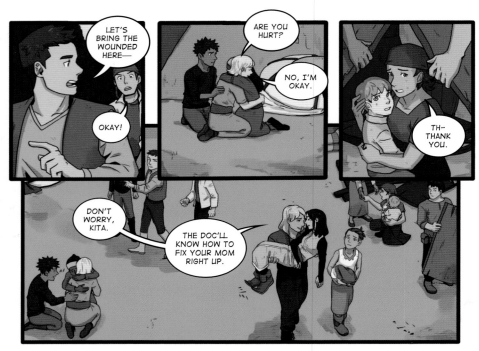

LET'S BRING THE WOUNDED HERE—

OKAY!

ARE YOU HURT?

NO, I'M OKAY.

TH—THANK YOU.

DON'T WORRY, KITA.

THE DOC'LL KNOW HOW TO FIX YOUR MOM RIGHT UP.

SHE HAS A FEVER.

THE POISON FROM THE ARROW SEEMS TO HAVE CAUSED IT. WE'VE SAFELY REMOVED THE ARROWHEAD, AT LEAST.

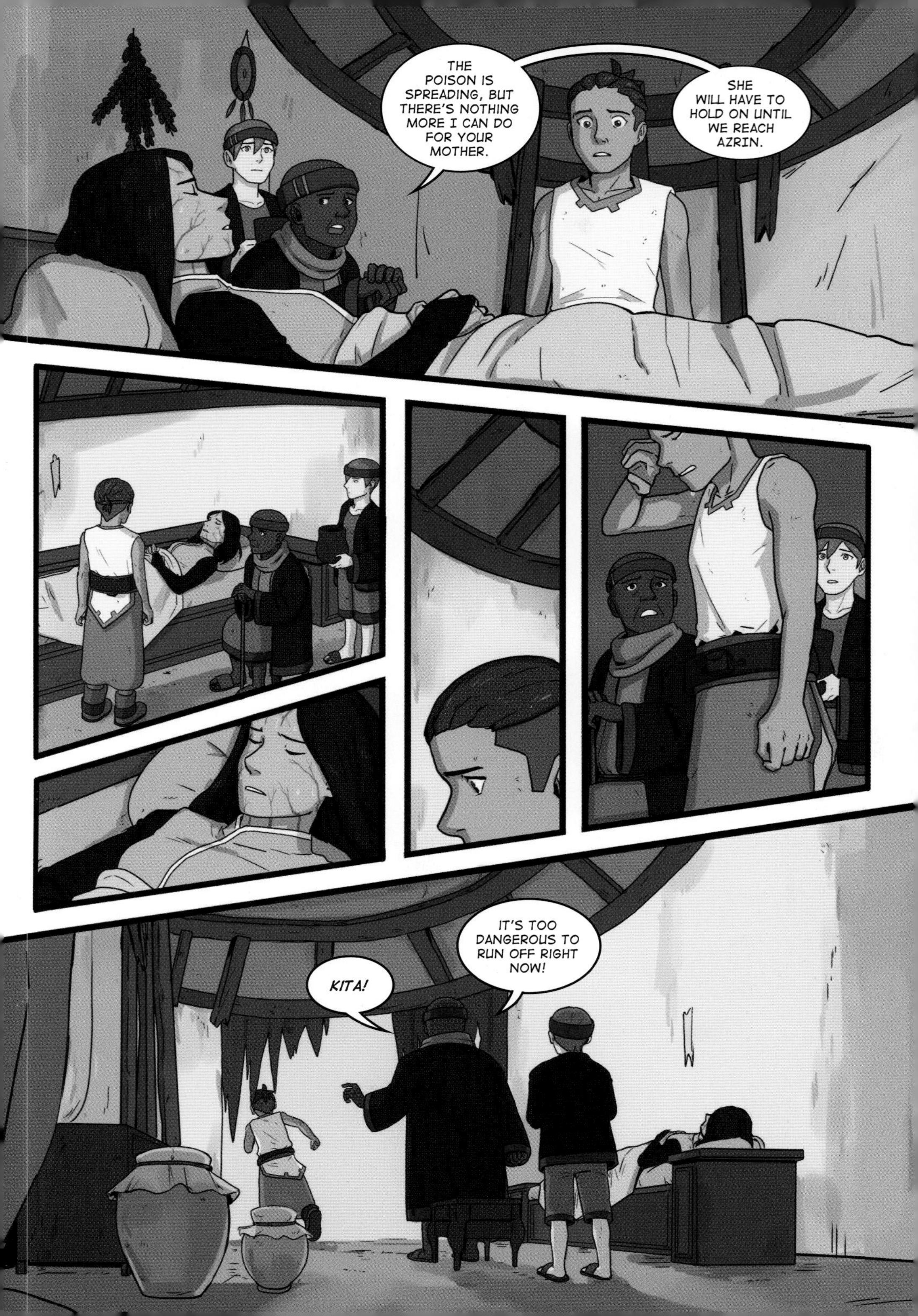
THE POISON IS SPREADING, BUT THERE'S NOTHING MORE I CAN DO FOR YOUR MOTHER.
SHE WILL HAVE TO HOLD ON UNTIL WE REACH AZRIN.
KITA!
IT'S TOO DANGEROUS TO RUN OFF RIGHT NOW!

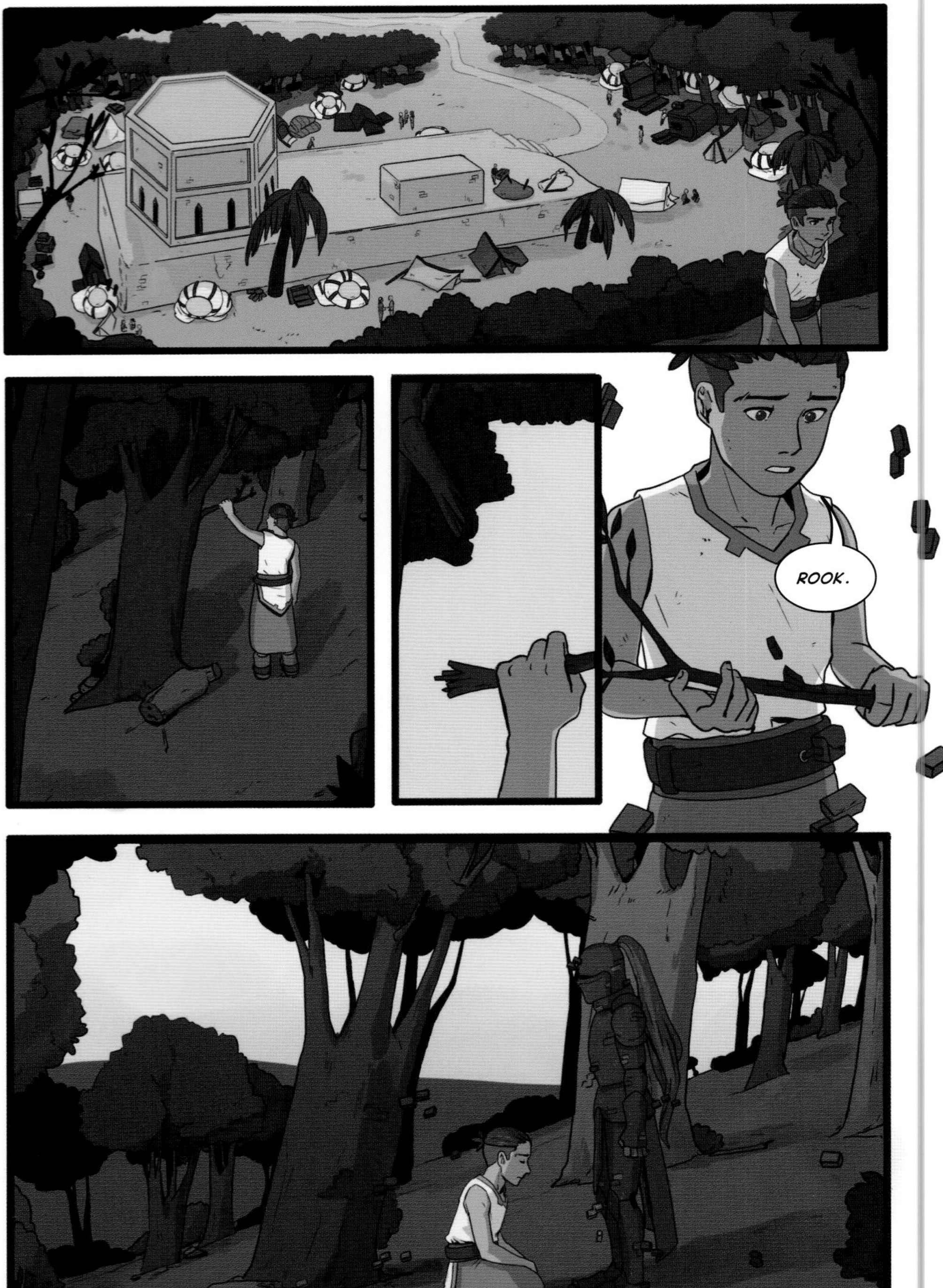
ROOK.

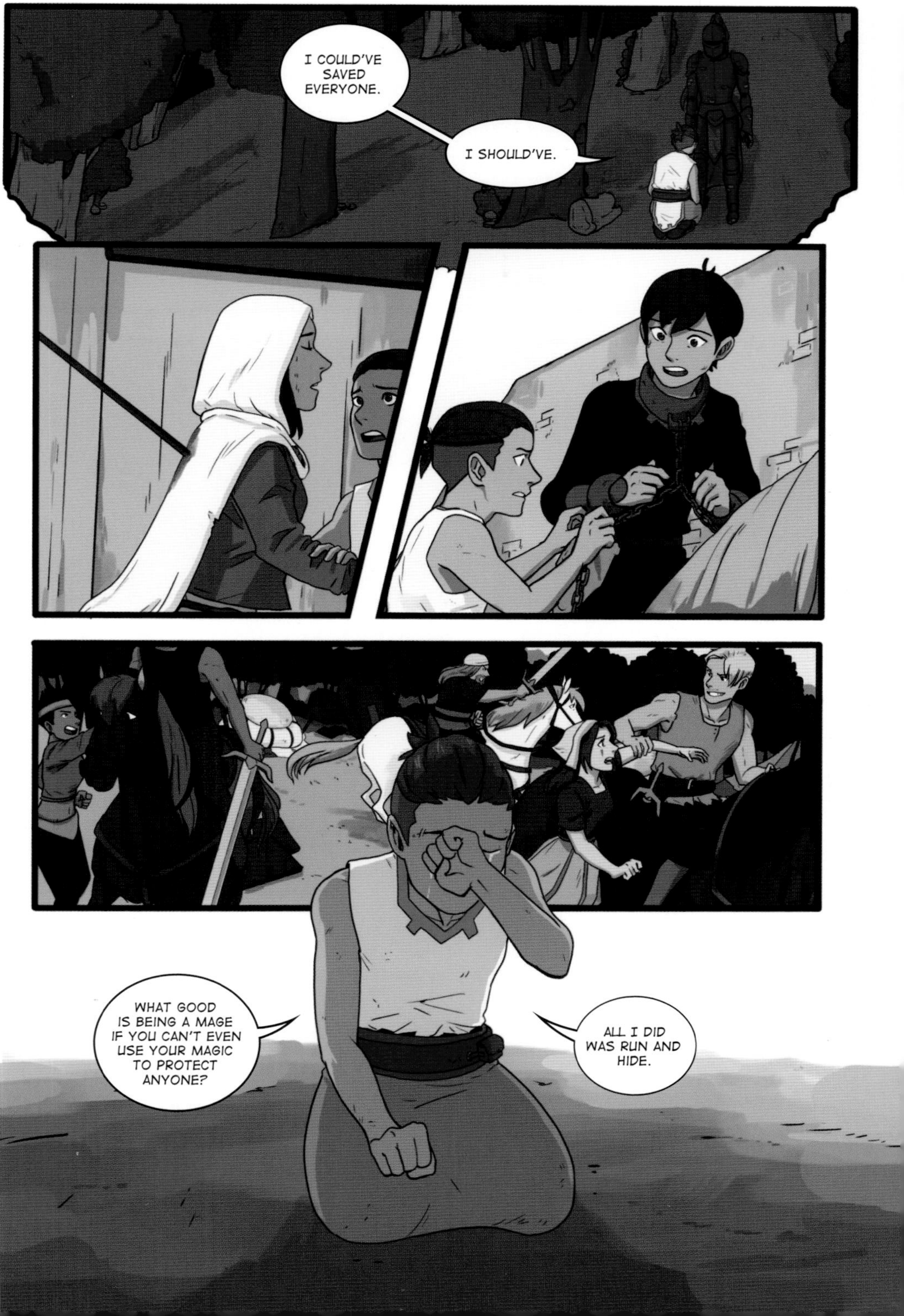
I COULD'VE SAVED EVERYONE.
I SHOULD'VE.
WHAT GOOD IS BEING A MAGE IF YOU CAN'T EVEN USE YOUR MAGIC TO PROTECT ANYONE?
ALL I DID WAS RUN AND HIDE.

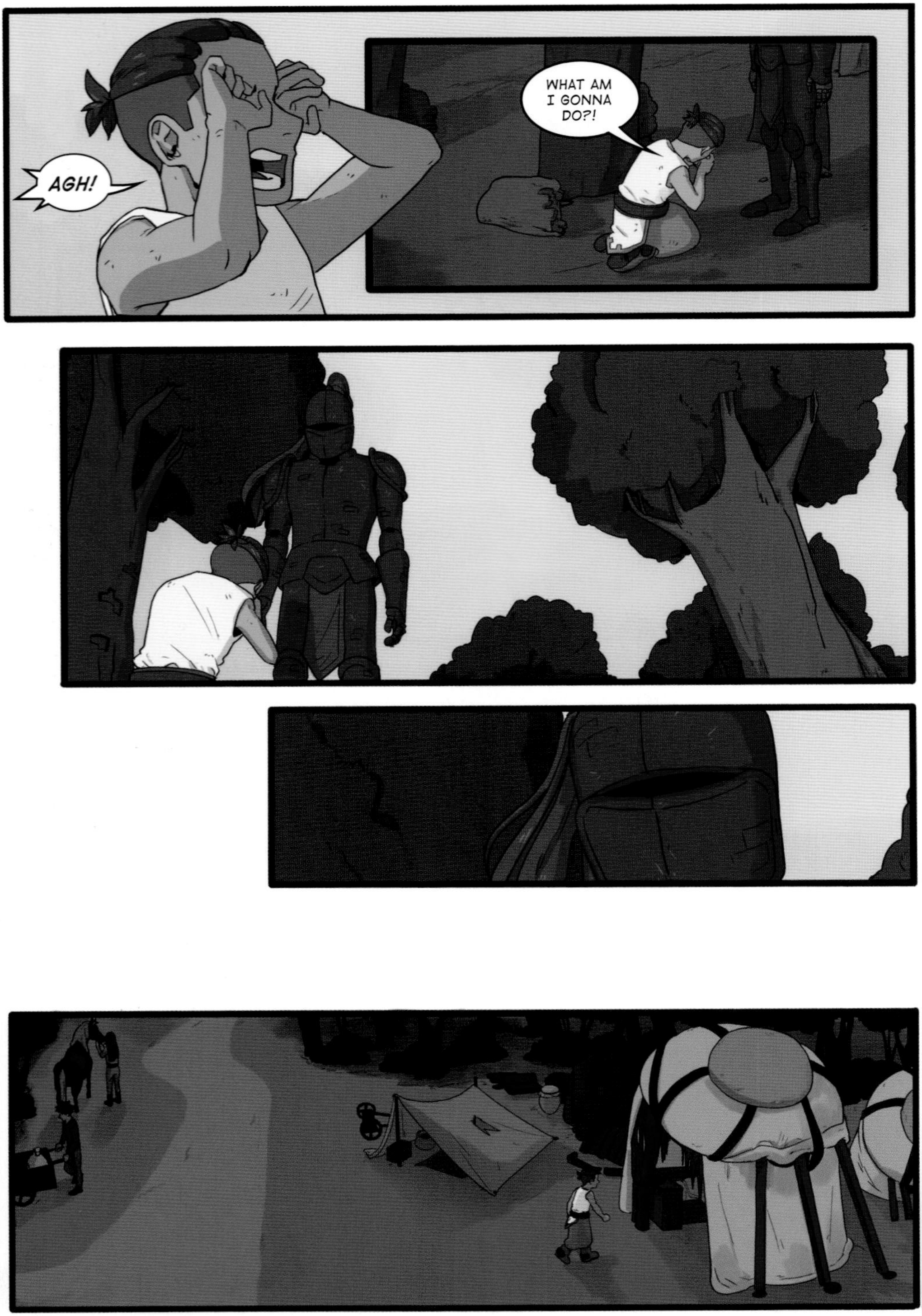
AGH!
WHAT AM I GONNA DO?!

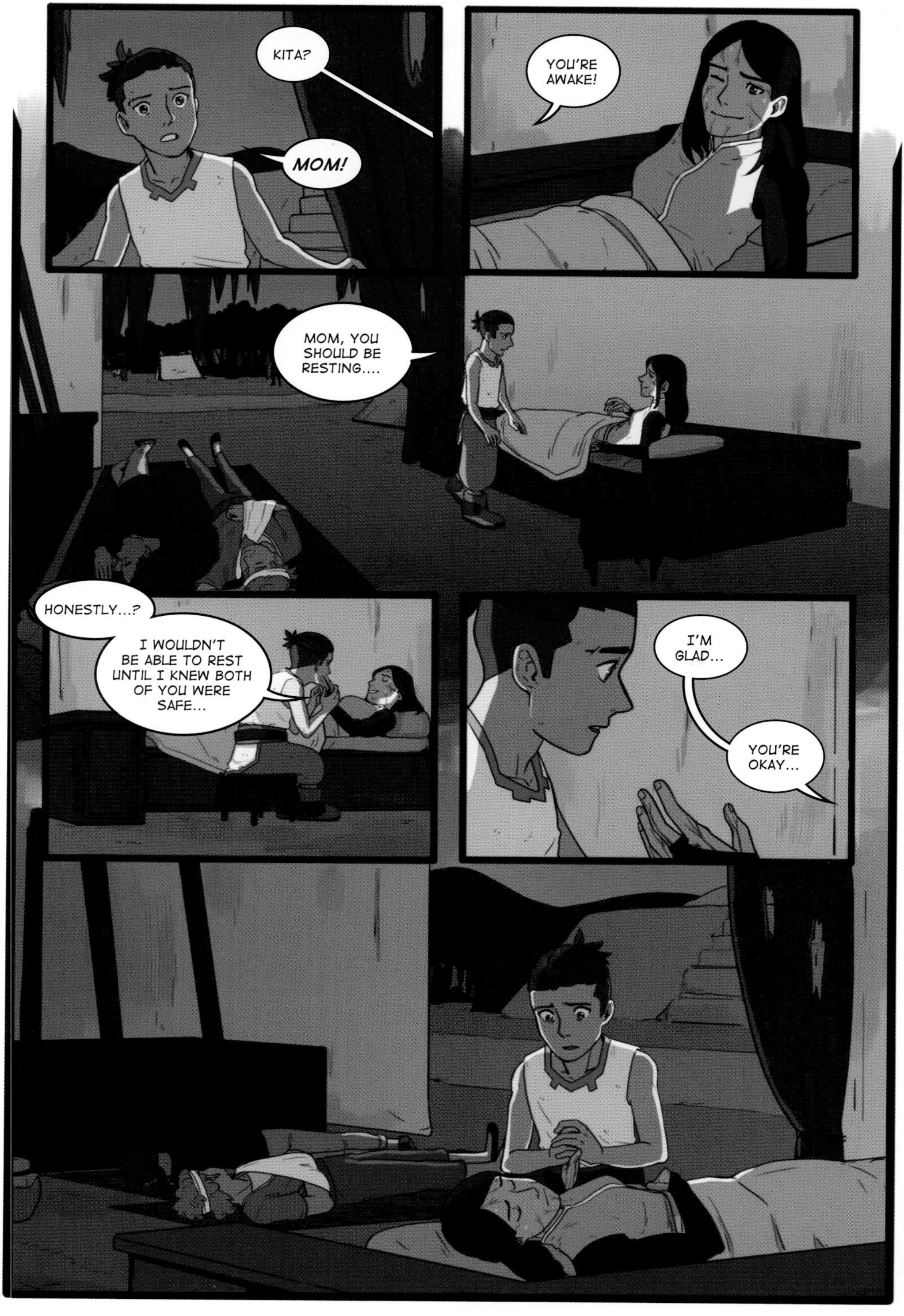
KITA?
MOM!
YOU'RE AWAKE!
MOM, YOU SHOULD BE RESTING....
HONESTLY...?
I WOULDN'T BE ABLE TO REST UNTIL I KNEW BOTH OF YOU WERE SAFE...
I'M GLAD...
YOU'RE OKAY...

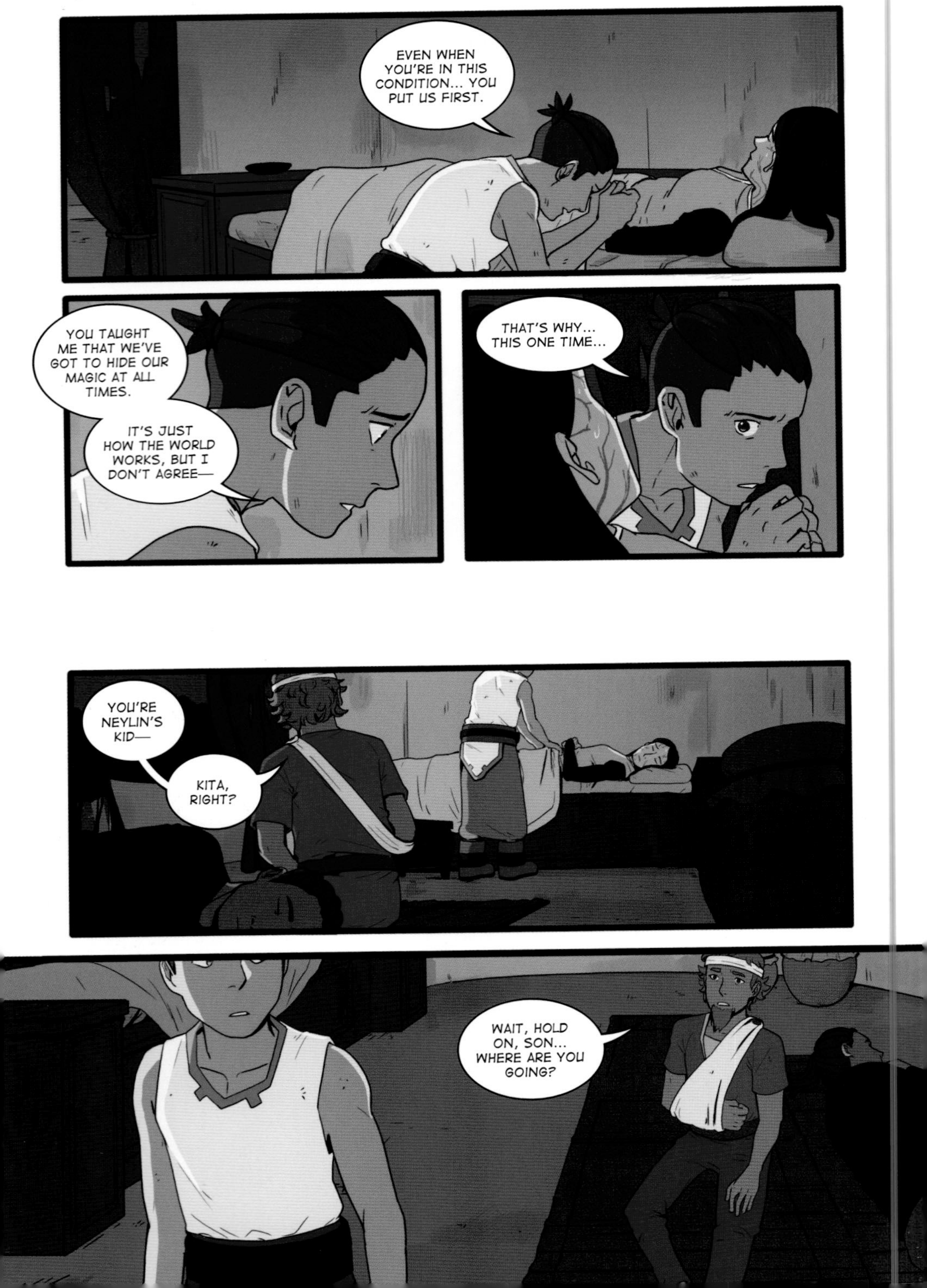
EVEN WHEN YOU'RE IN THIS CONDITION... YOU PUT US FIRST.
YOU TAUGHT ME THAT WE'VE GOT TO HIDE OUR MAGIC AT ALL TIMES.
IT'S JUST HOW THE WORLD WORKS, BUT I DON'T AGREE—
THAT'S WHY... THIS ONE TIME...
YOU'RE NEYLIN'S KID—
KITA, RIGHT?
WAIT, HOLD ON, SON... WHERE ARE YOU GOING?

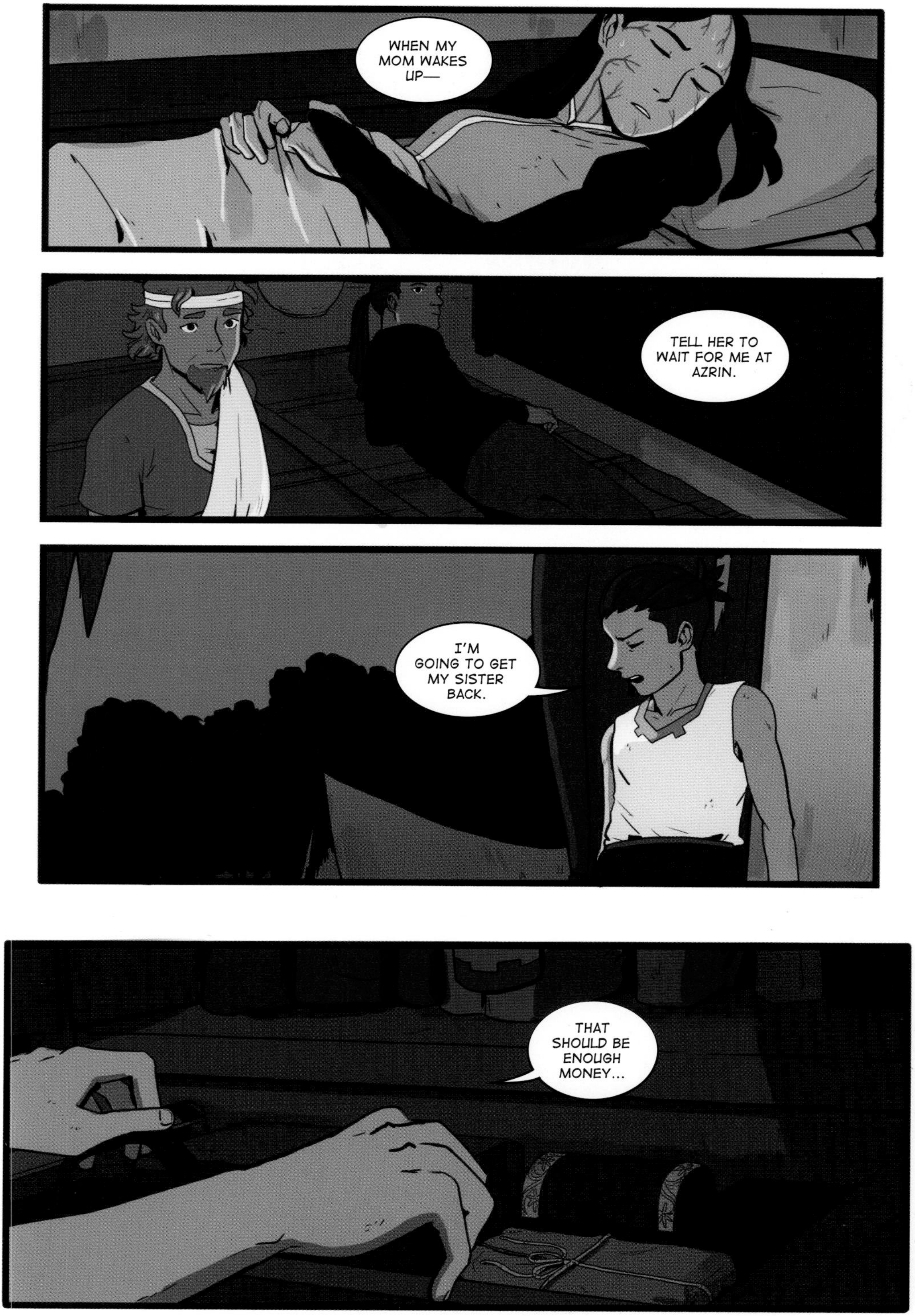
WHEN MY MOM WAKES UP—
TELL HER TO WAIT FOR ME AT AZRIN.
I'M GOING TO GET MY SISTER BACK.
THAT SHOULD BE ENOUGH MONEY...

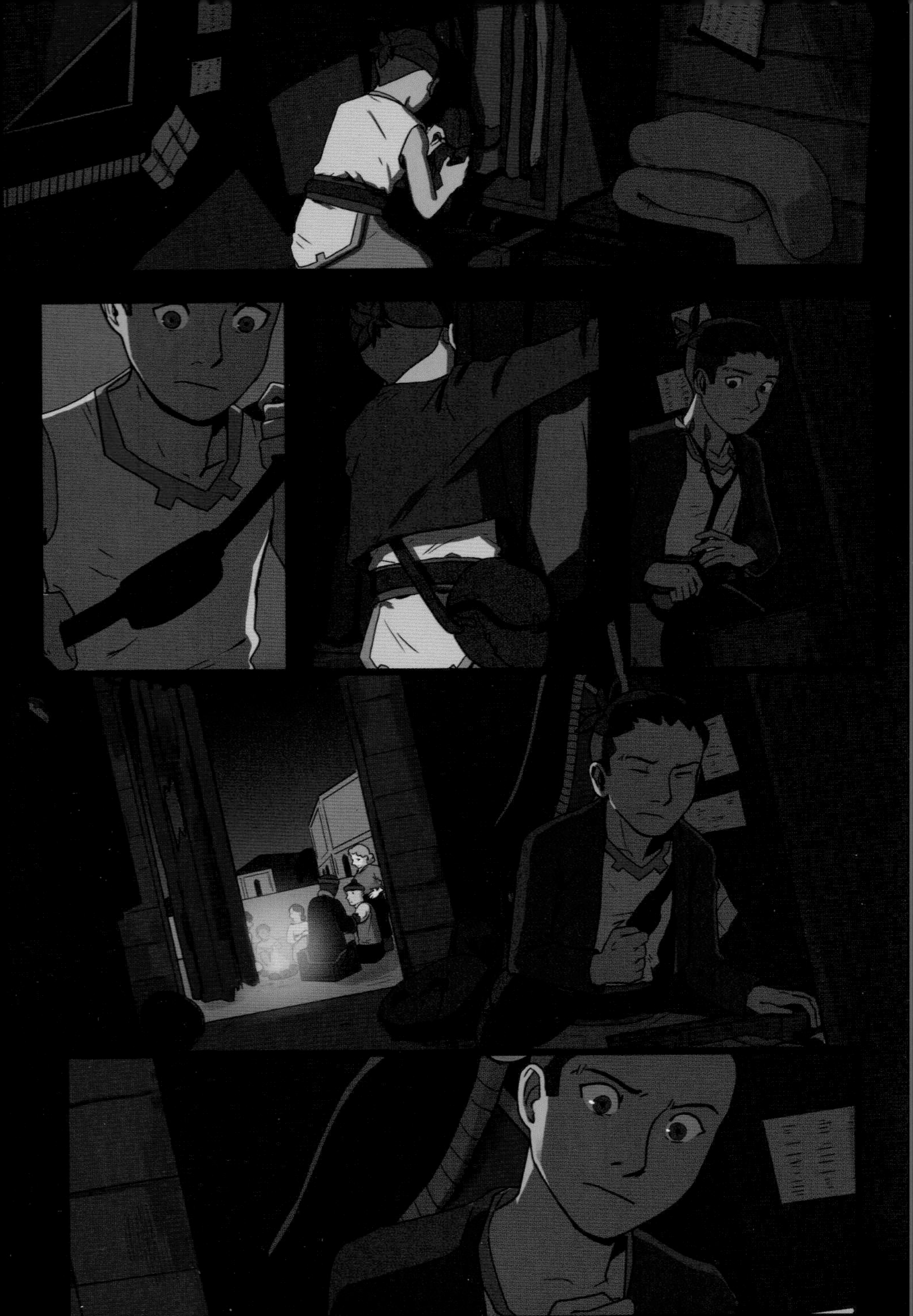

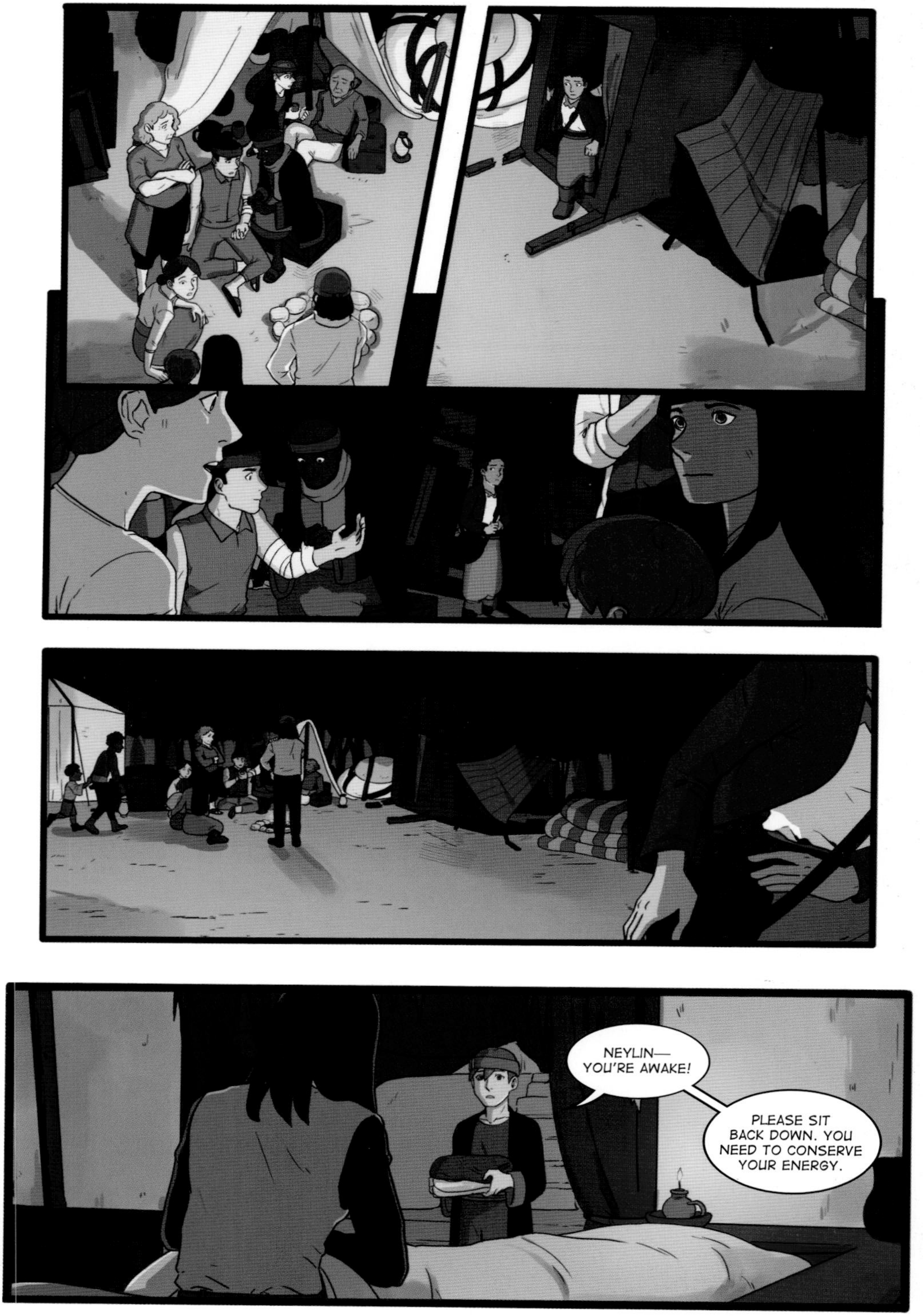
NEYLIN— YOU'RE AWAKE!
PLEASE SIT BACK DOWN. YOU NEED TO CONSERVE YOUR ENERGY.

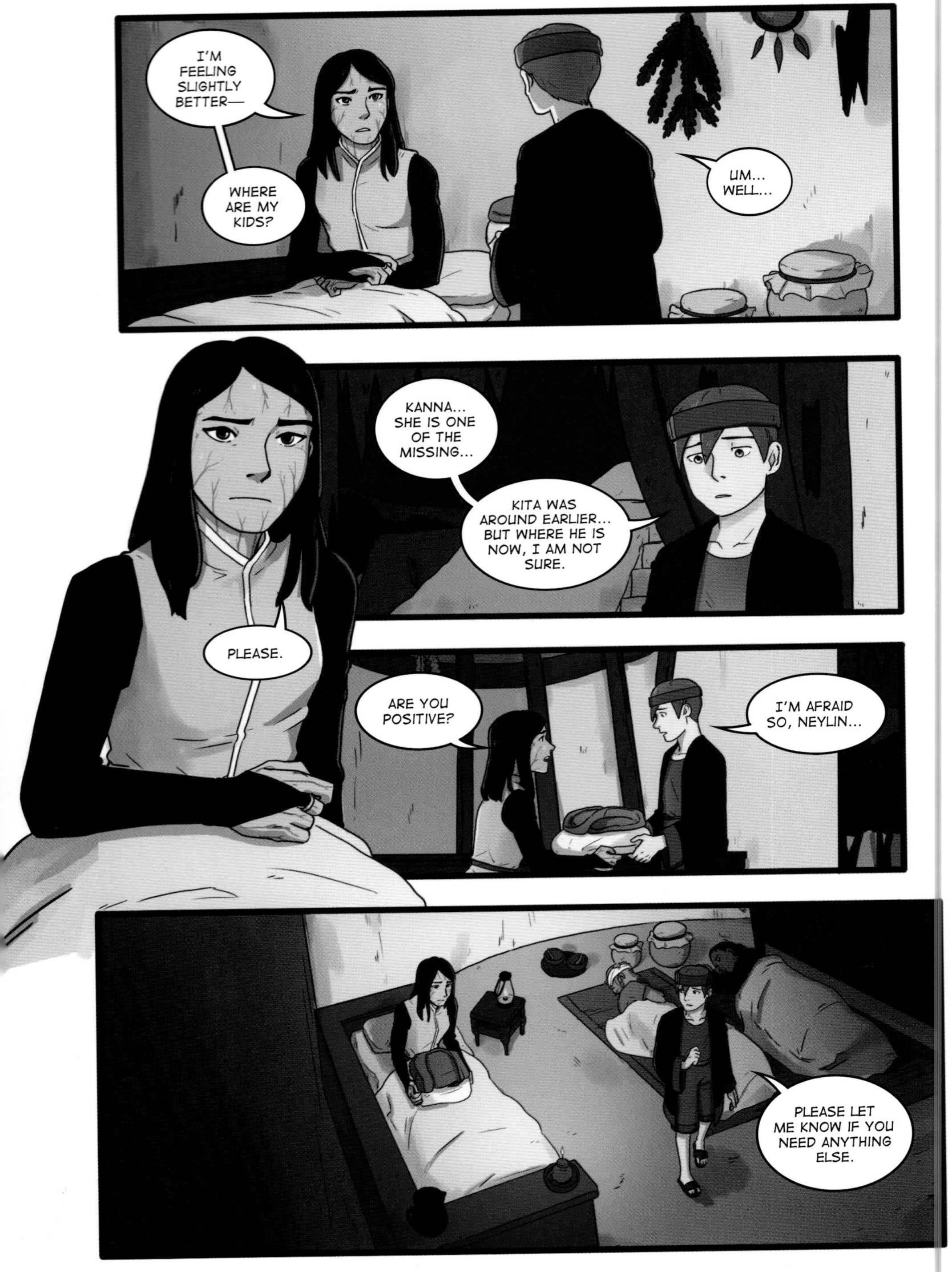
I'M FEELING SLIGHTLY BETTER—
WHERE ARE MY KIDS?
UM... WELL...
KANNA... SHE IS ONE OF THE MISSING...
KITA WAS AROUND EARLIER... BUT WHERE HE IS NOW, I AM NOT SURE.
PLEASE.
ARE YOU POSITIVE?
I'M AFRAID SO, NEYLIN...
PLEASE LET ME KNOW IF YOU NEED ANYTHING ELSE.

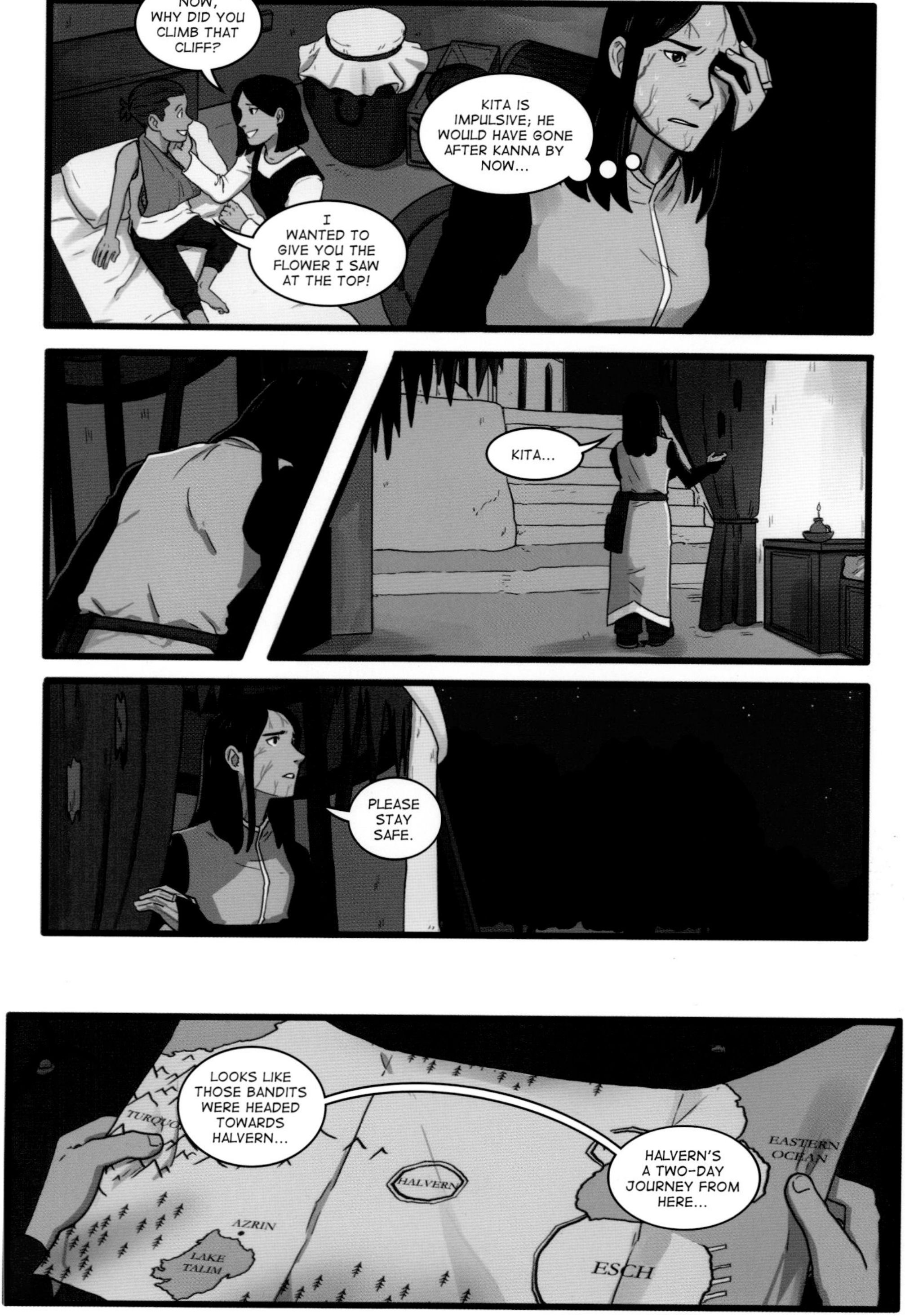
NOW, WHY DID YOU CLIMB THAT CLIFF?
I WANTED TO GIVE YOU THE FLOWER I SAW AT THE TOP!
KITA IS IMPULSIVE; HE WOULD HAVE GONE AFTER KANNA BY NOW...
KITA...
PLEASE STAY SAFE.
LOOKS LIKE THOSE BANDITS WERE HEADED TOWARDS HALVERN...
HALVERN'S A TWO-DAY JOURNEY FROM HERE...
HALVERN
EASTERN OCEAN
AZRIN
LAKE TALIM
ESCH

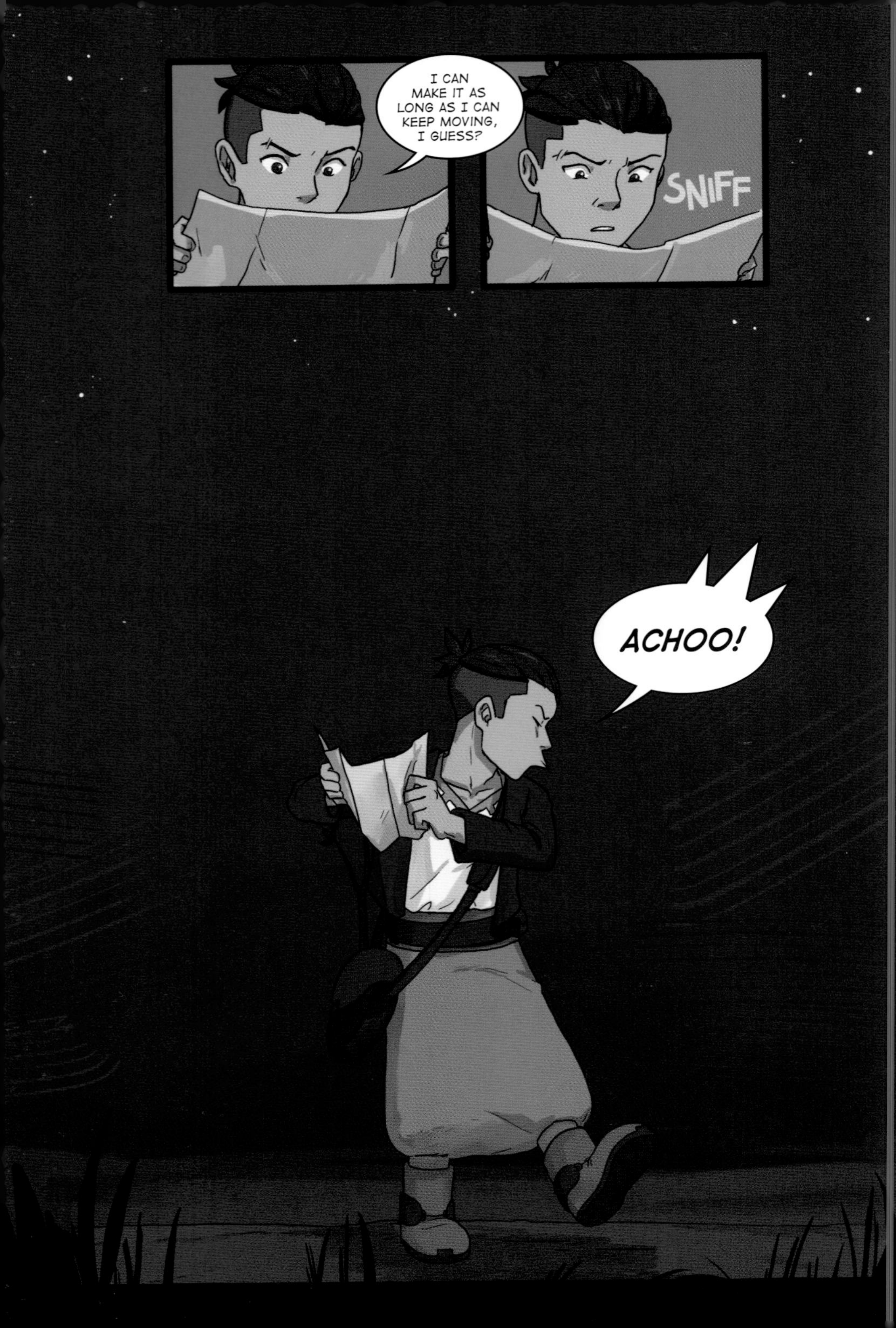
I CAN MAKE IT AS LONG AS I CAN KEEP MOVING, I GUESS?
SNIFF
ACHOO!

CHAPTER 3:
AN UNUSUAL CLIENT

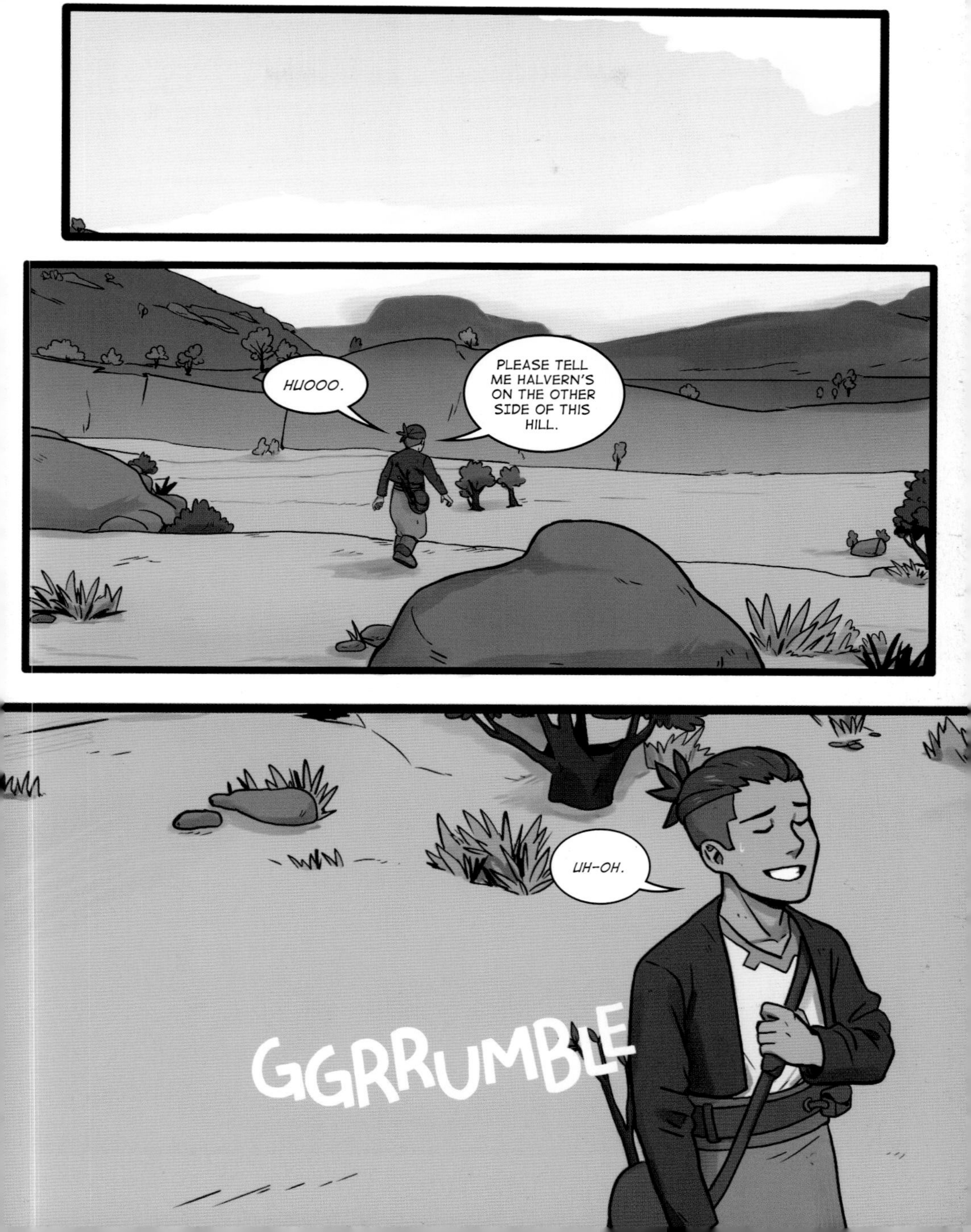
HUOOO.
PLEASE TELL ME HALVERN'S ON THE OTHER SIDE OF THIS HILL.
UH-OH.
GGRRUMBLE

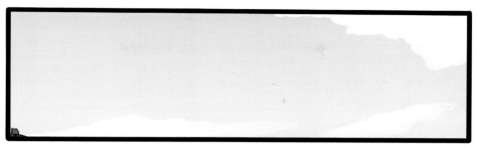

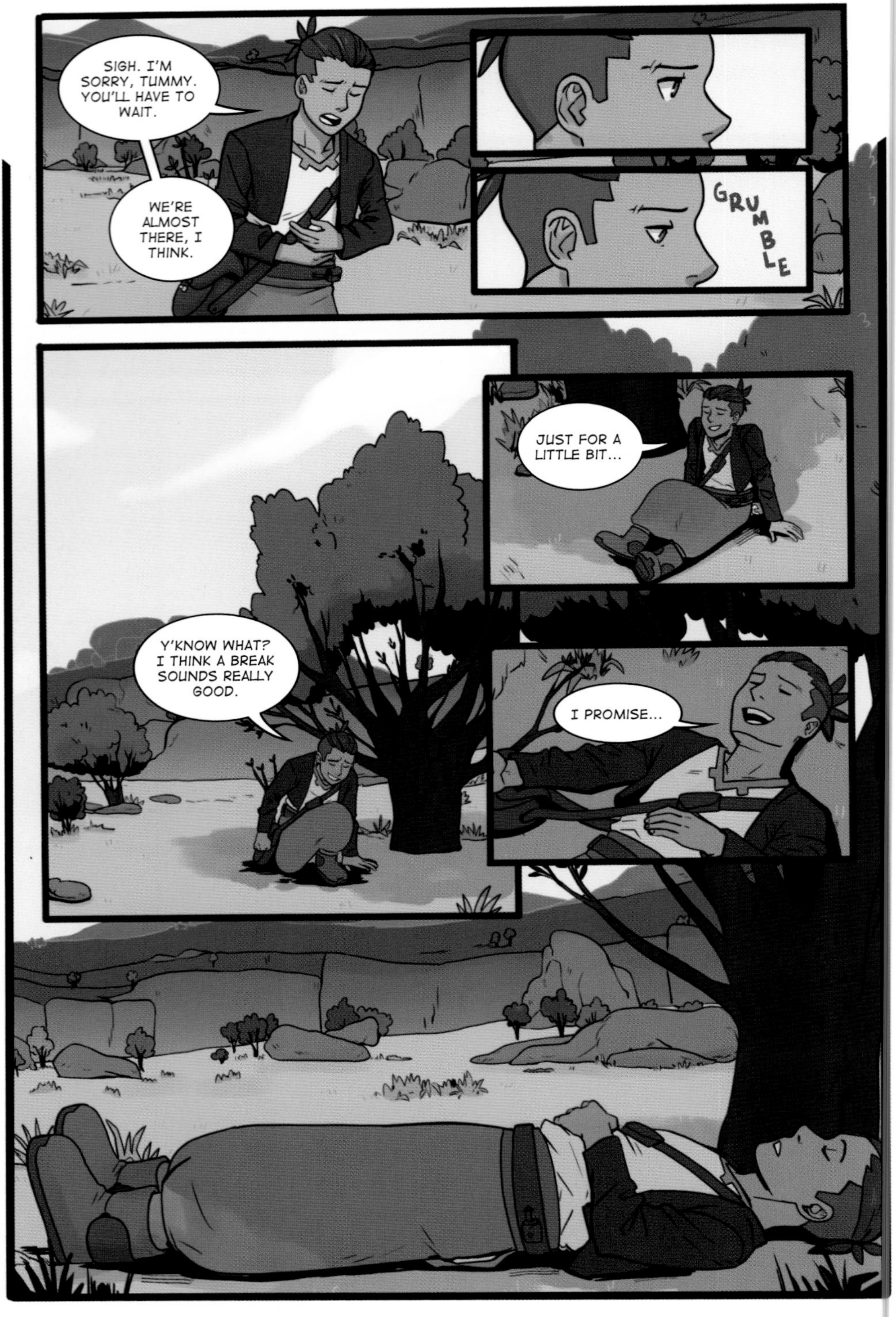
SIGH. I'M SORRY, TUMMY. YOU'LL HAVE TO WAIT.
WE'RE ALMOST THERE, I THINK.
GRUMBLE
Y'KNOW WHAT? I THINK A BREAK SOUNDS REALLY GOOD.
JUST FOR A LITTLE BIT...
I PROMISE...

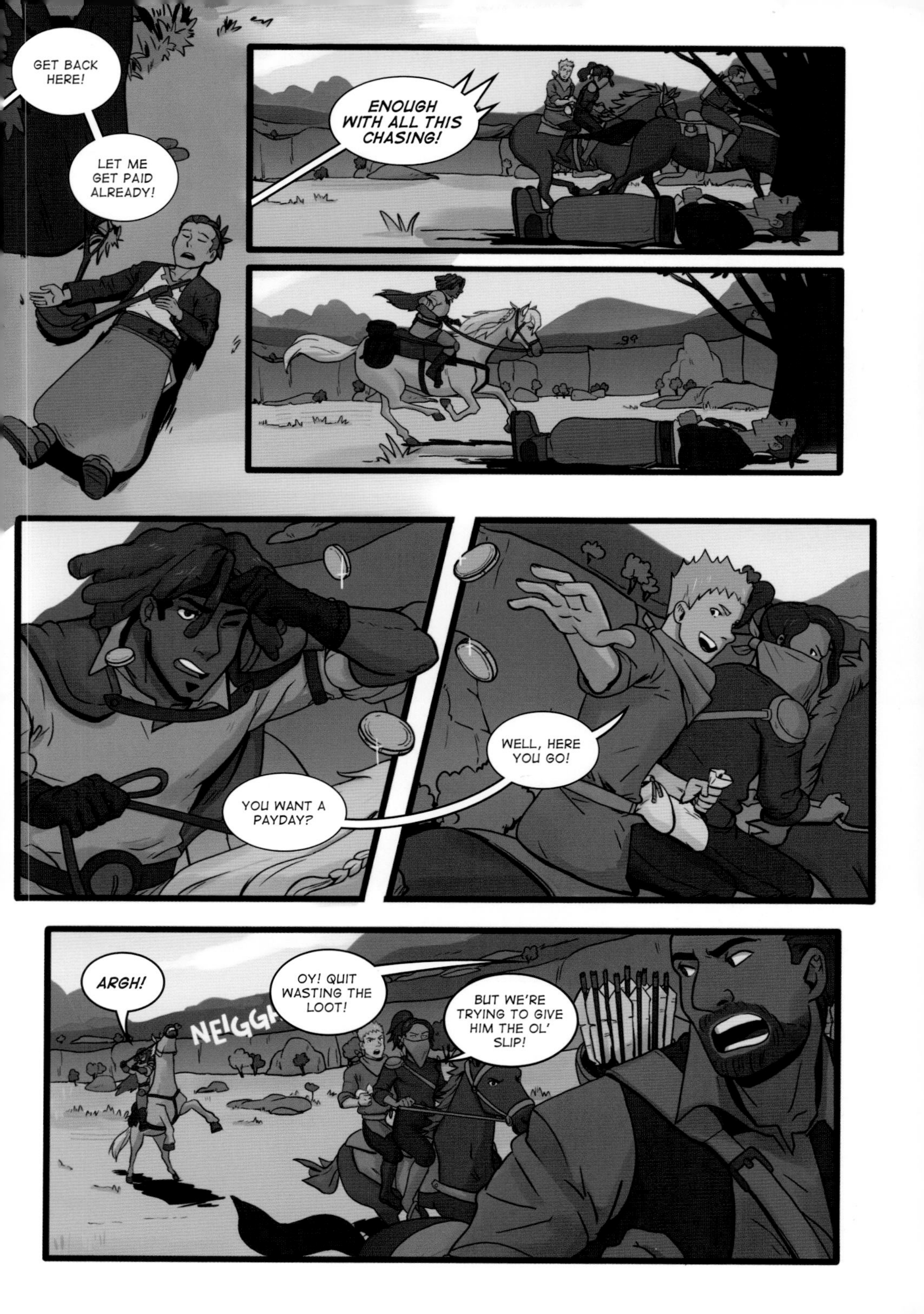
GET BACK HERE!
LET ME GET PAID ALREADY!
ENOUGH WITH ALL THIS CHASING!
YOU WANT A PAYDAY?
WELL, HERE YOU GO!
ARGH!
NEIGG
OY! QUIT WASTING THE LOOT!
BUT WE'RE TRYING TO GIVE HIM THE OL' SLIP!

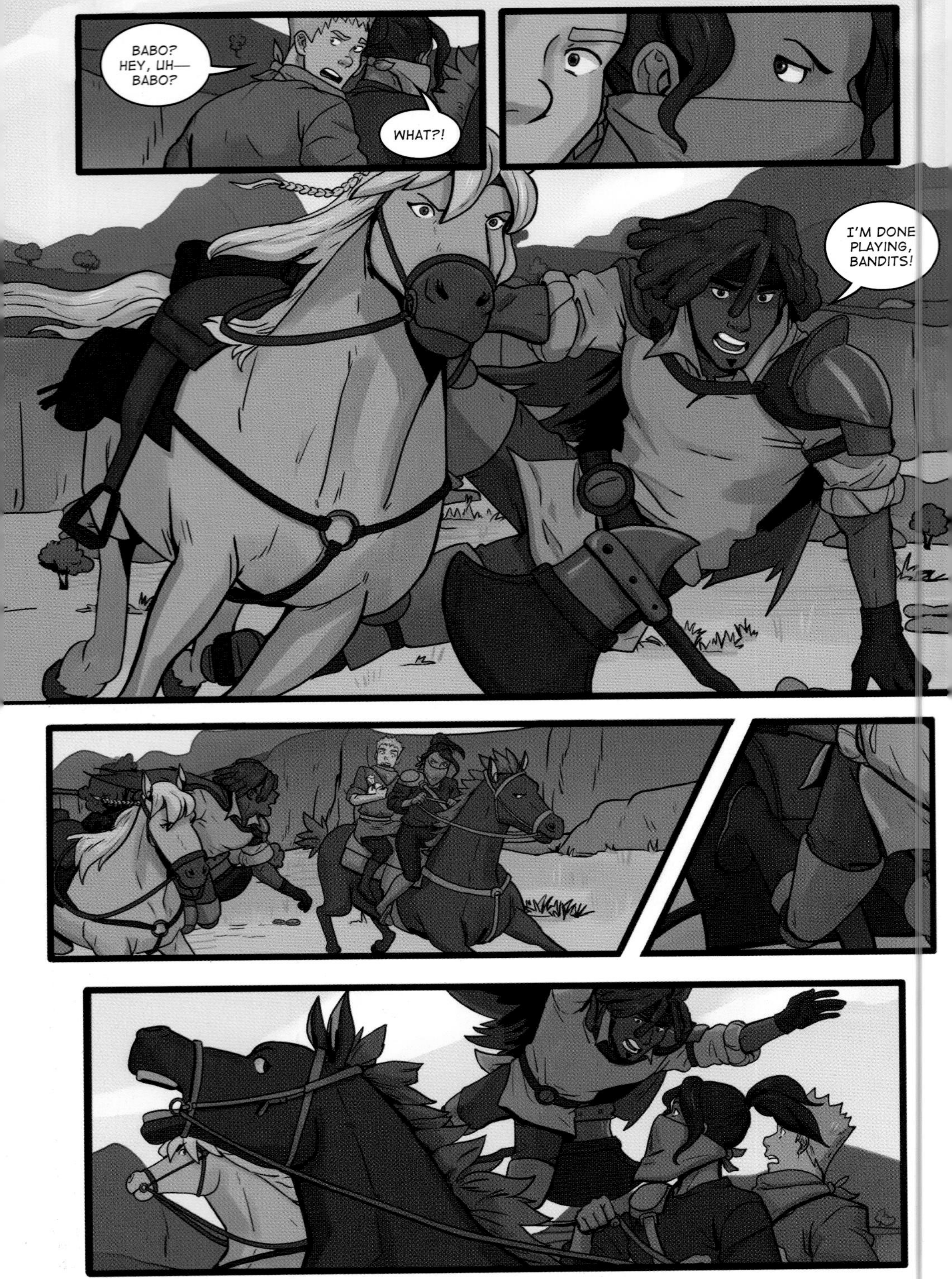
BABO? HEY, UH— BABO?
WHAT?!
I'M DONE PLAYING, BANDITS!

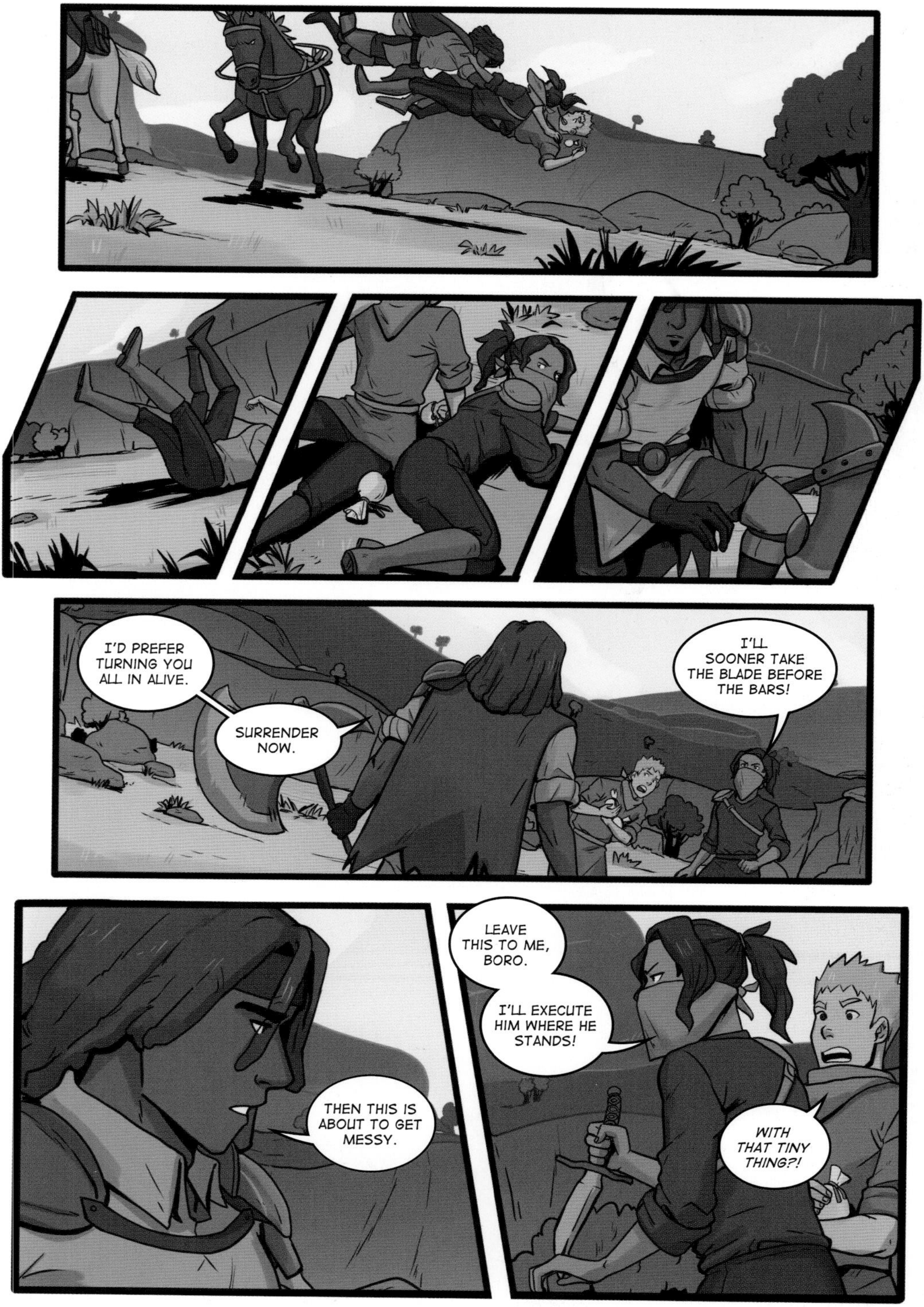
I'D PREFER TURNING YOU ALL IN ALIVE.
SURRENDER NOW.
I'LL SOONER TAKE THE BLADE BEFORE THE BARS!
THEN THIS IS ABOUT TO GET MESSY.
LEAVE THIS TO ME, BORO.
I'LL EXECUTE HIM WHERE HE STANDS!
WITH THAT TINY THING?!

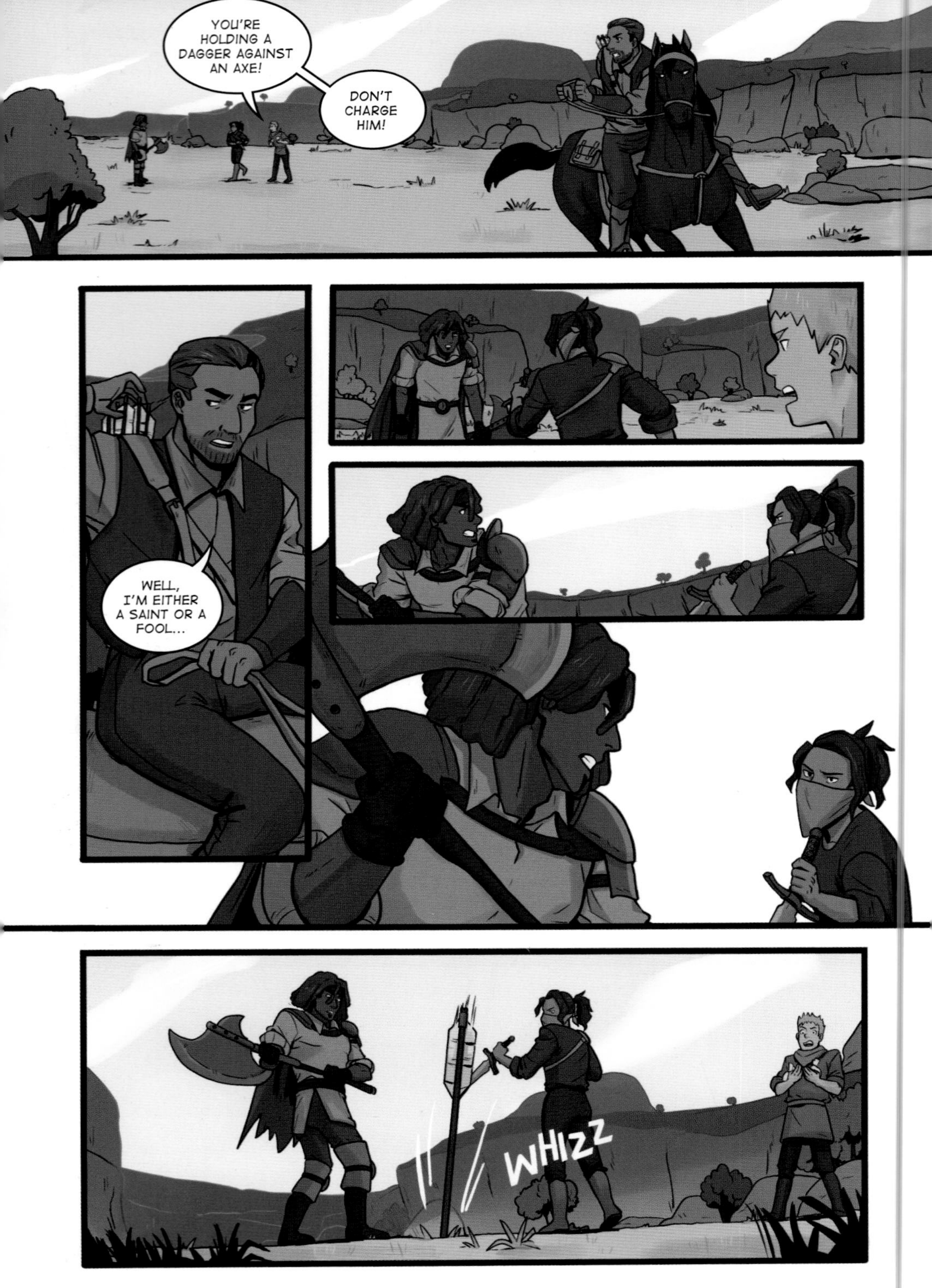
YOU'RE HOLDING A DAGGER AGAINST AN AXE!
DON'T CHARGE HIM!
WELL, I'M EITHER A SAINT OR A FOOL...
WHIZZ

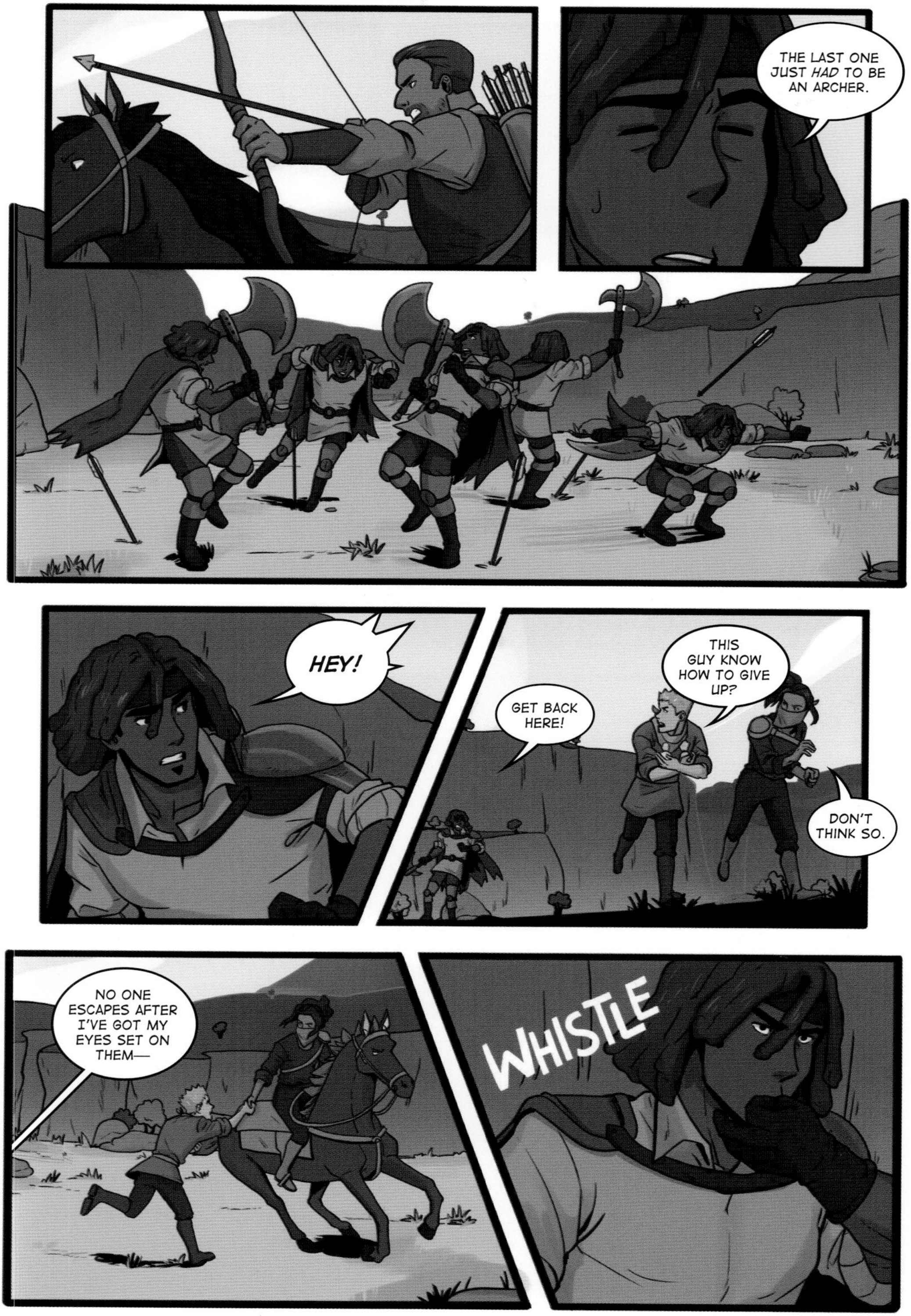
THE LAST ONE JUST *HAD* TO BE AN ARCHER.
HEY!
GET BACK HERE!
THIS GUY KNOW HOW TO GIVE UP?
DON'T THINK SO.
NO ONE ESCAPES AFTER I'VE GOT MY EYES SET ON THEM—
WHISTLE

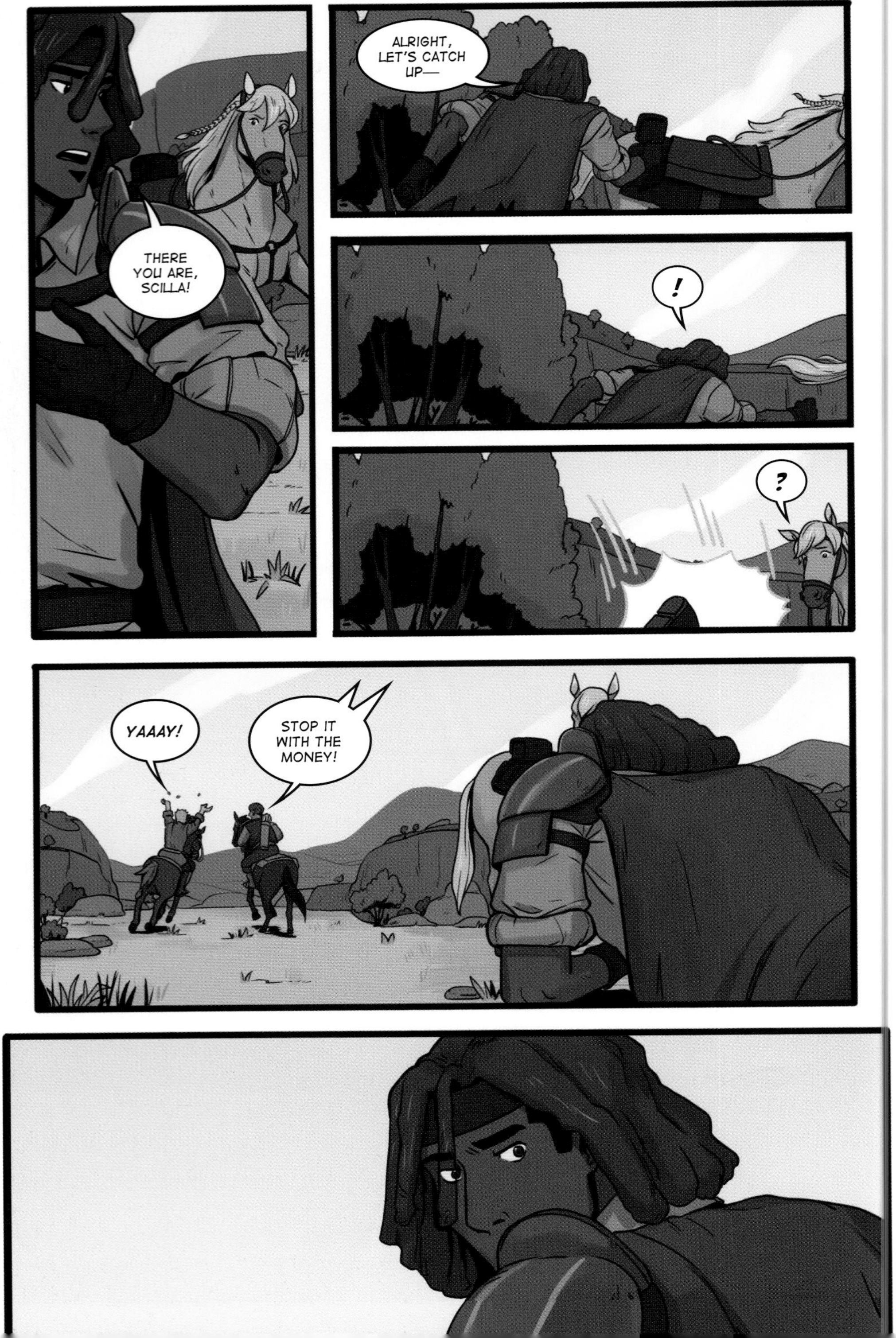
THERE YOU ARE, SCILLA!
ALRIGHT, LET'S CATCH UP—
!
?
YAAAY!
STOP IT WITH THE MONEY!

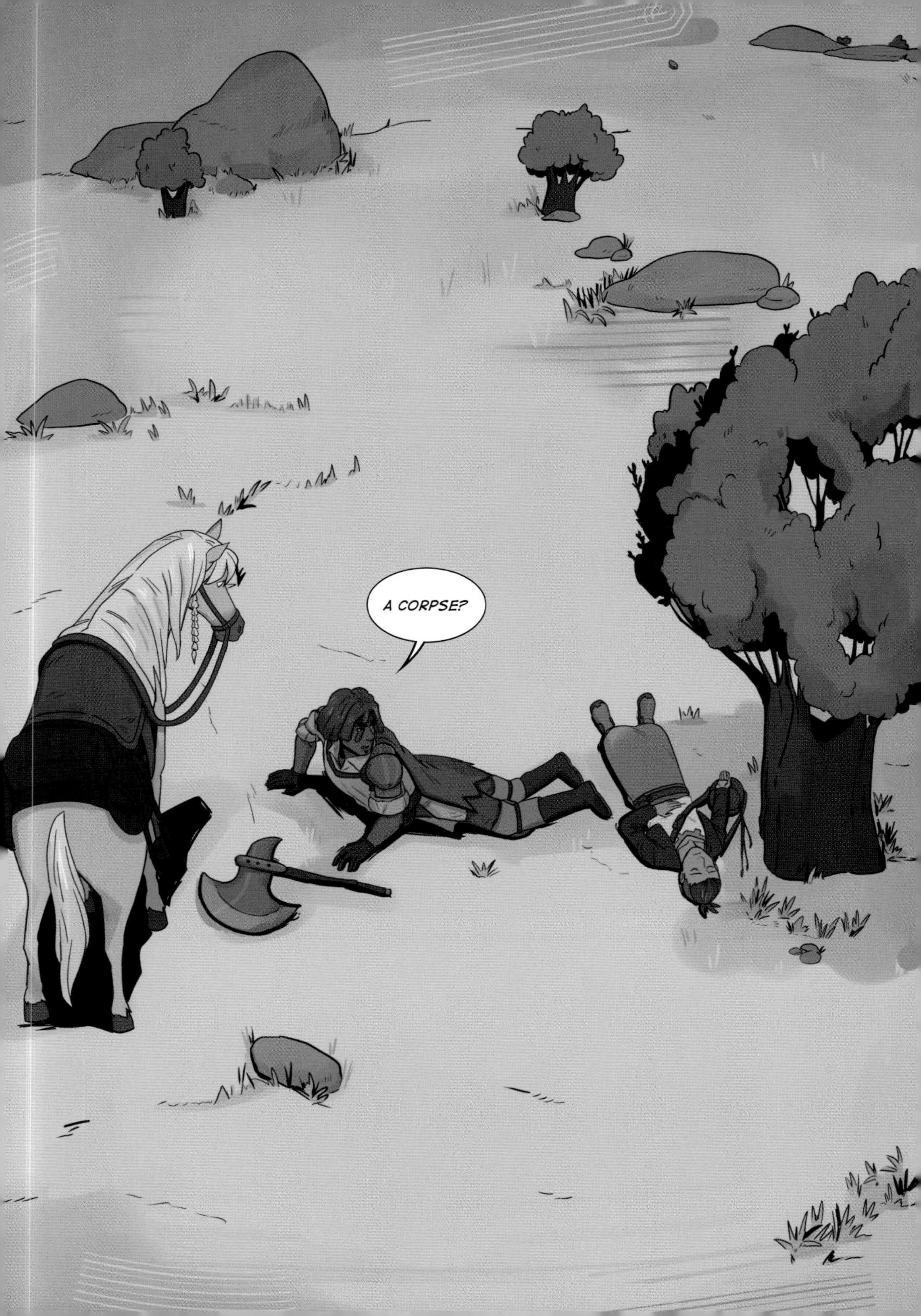
A CORPSE?

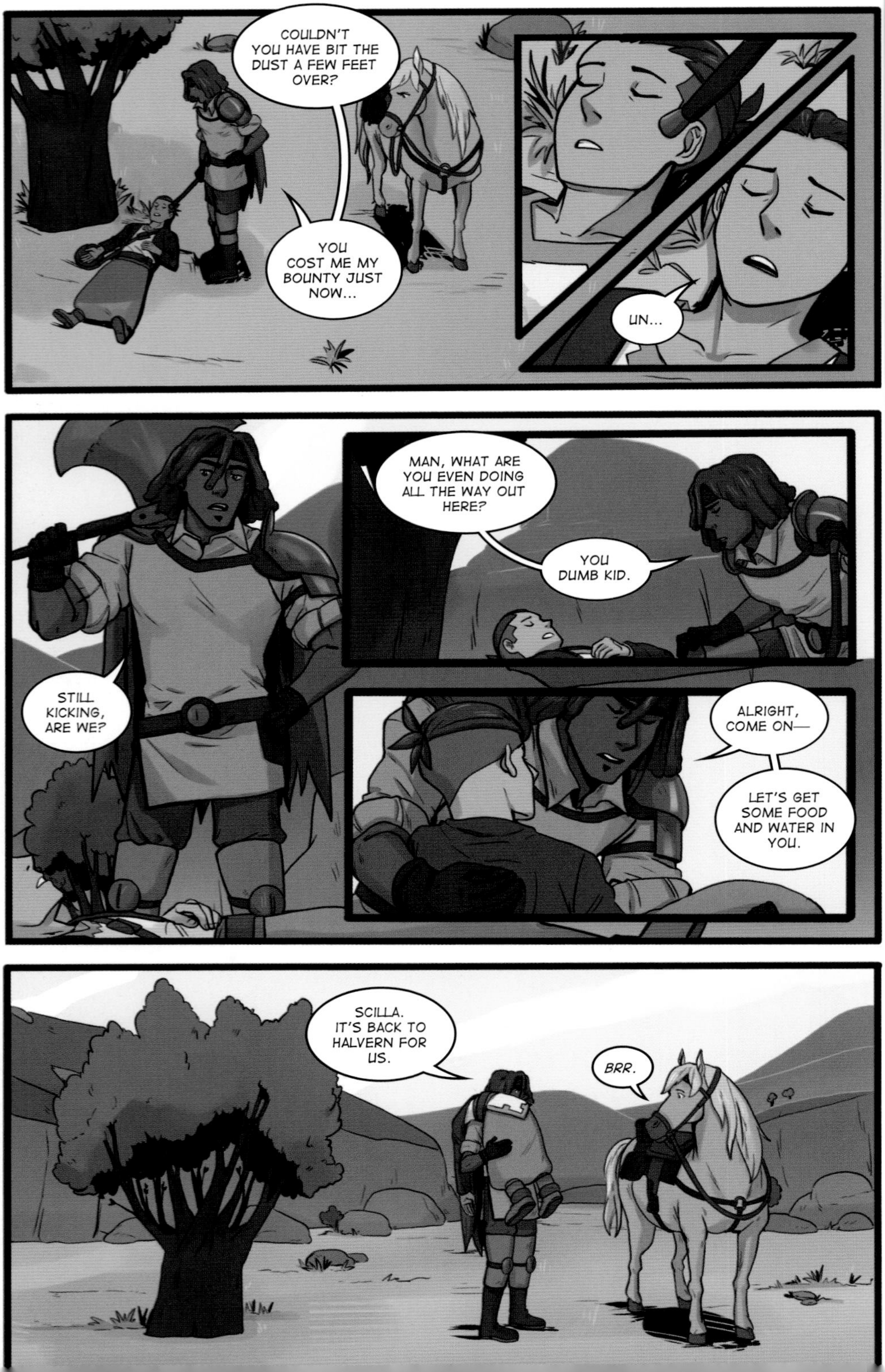
COULDN'T YOU HAVE BIT THE DUST A FEW FEET OVER?
YOU COST ME MY BOUNTY JUST NOW...
UN...
STILL KICKING, ARE WE?
MAN, WHAT ARE YOU EVEN DOING ALL THE WAY OUT HERE?
YOU DUMB KID.
ALRIGHT, COME ON—
LET'S GET SOME FOOD AND WATER IN YOU.
SCILLA. IT'S BACK TO HALVERN FOR US.
BRR.

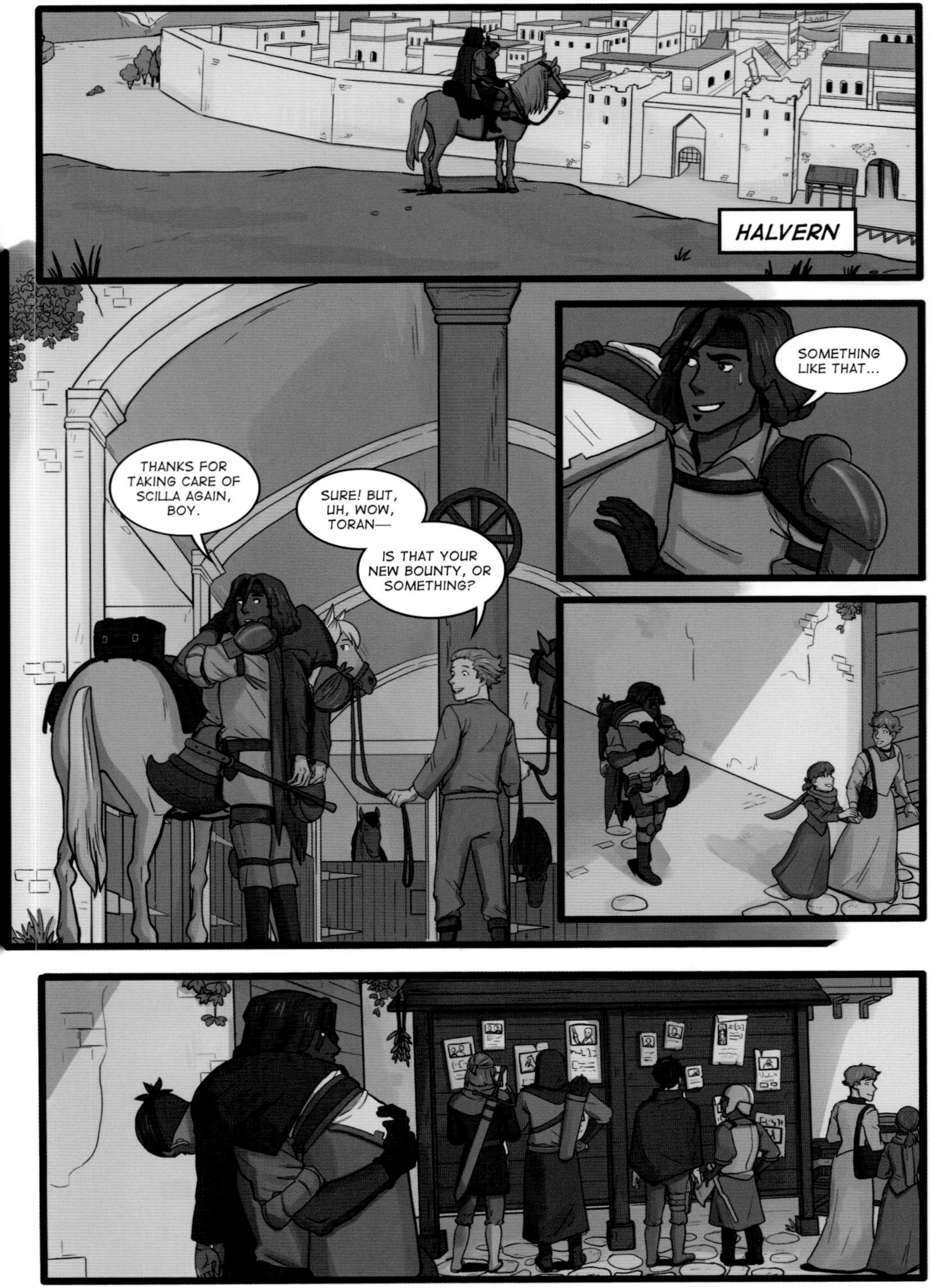
HALVERN
THANKS FOR TAKING CARE OF SCILLA AGAIN, BOY.
SURE! BUT, UH, WOW, TORAN—
IS THAT YOUR NEW BOUNTY, OR SOMETHING?
SOMETHING LIKE THAT...

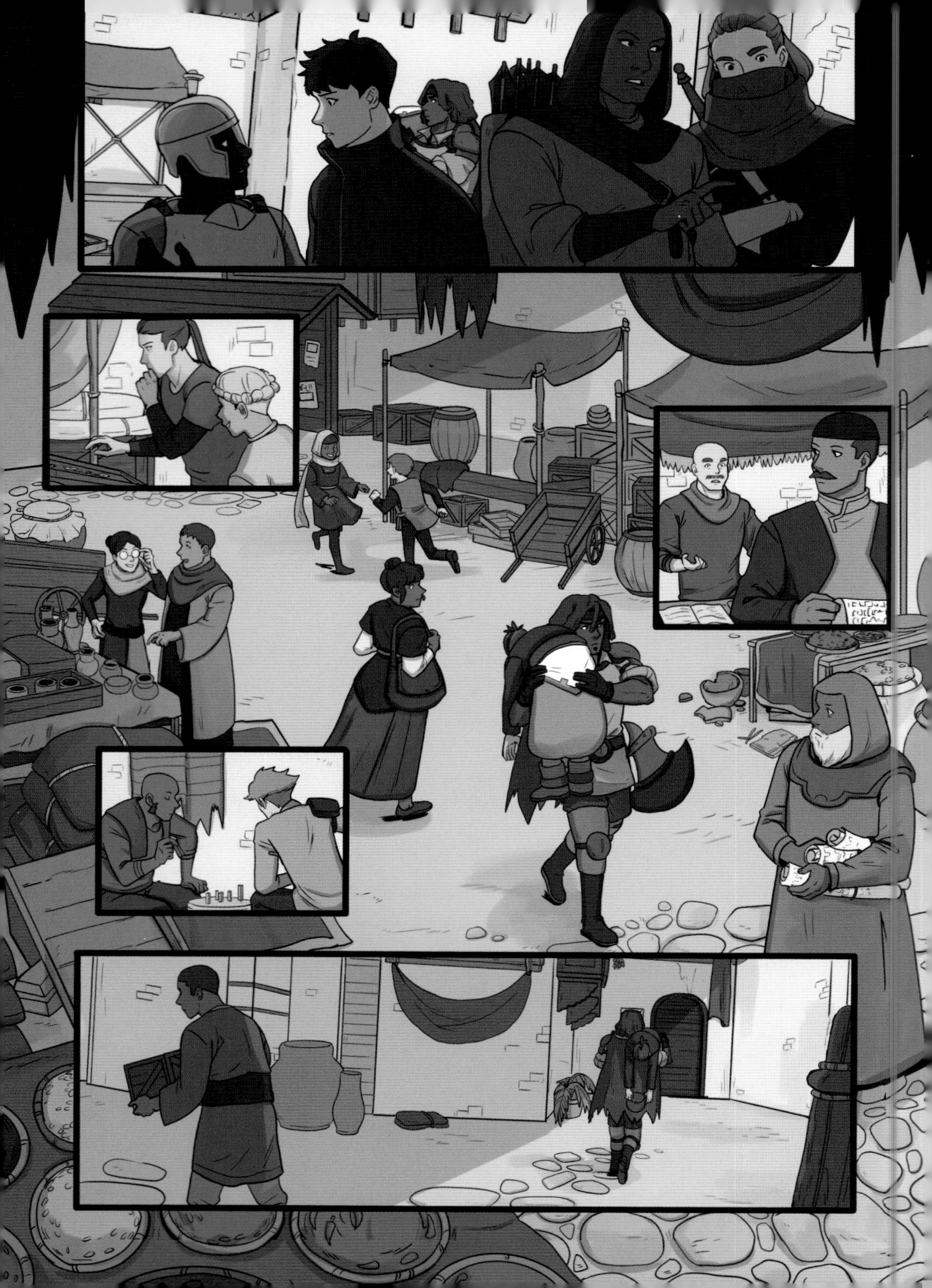

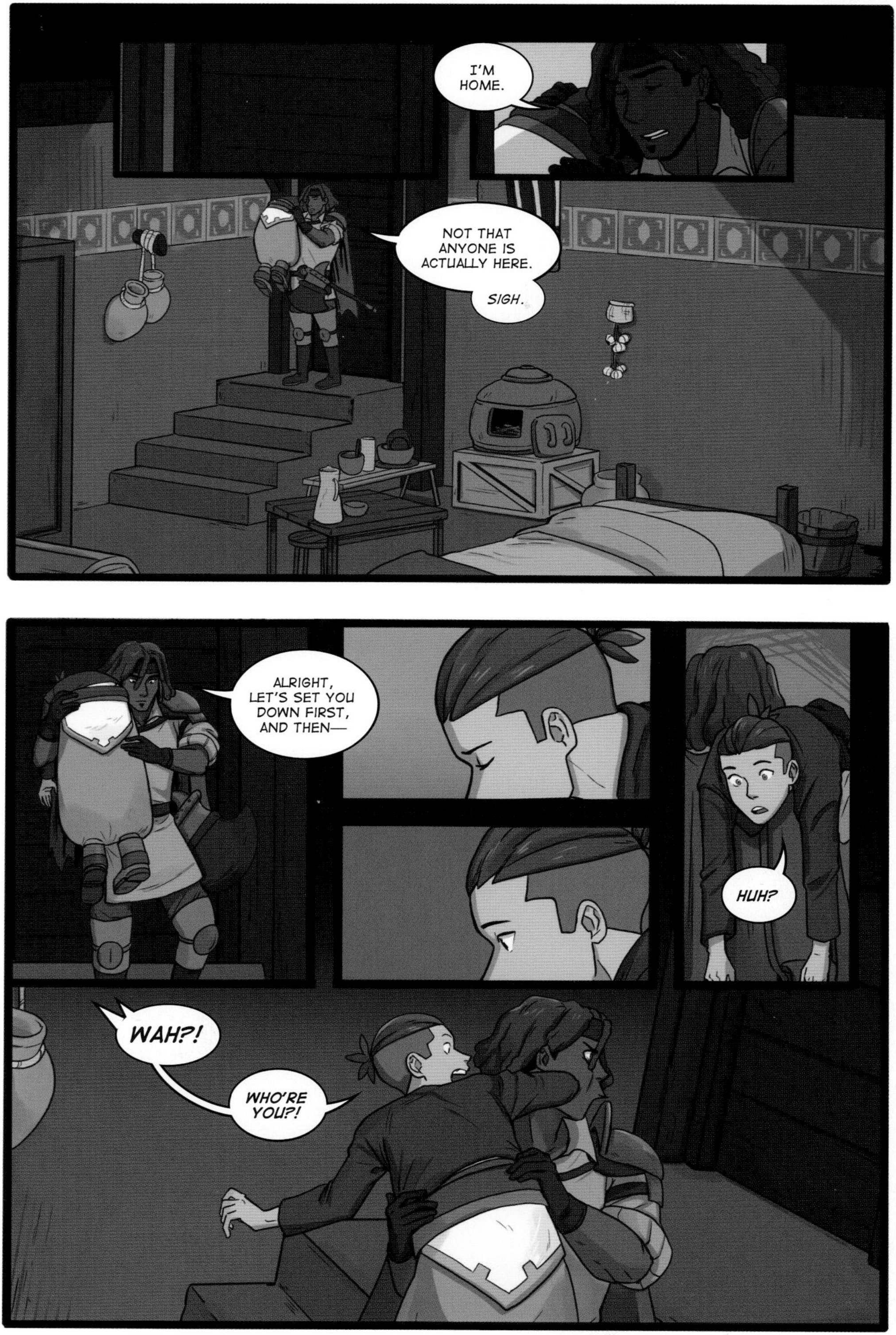
I'M HOME.
NOT THAT ANYONE IS ACTUALLY HERE.
SIGH.
ALRIGHT, LET'S SET YOU DOWN FIRST, AND THEN—
HUH?
WAH?!
WHO'RE YOU?!

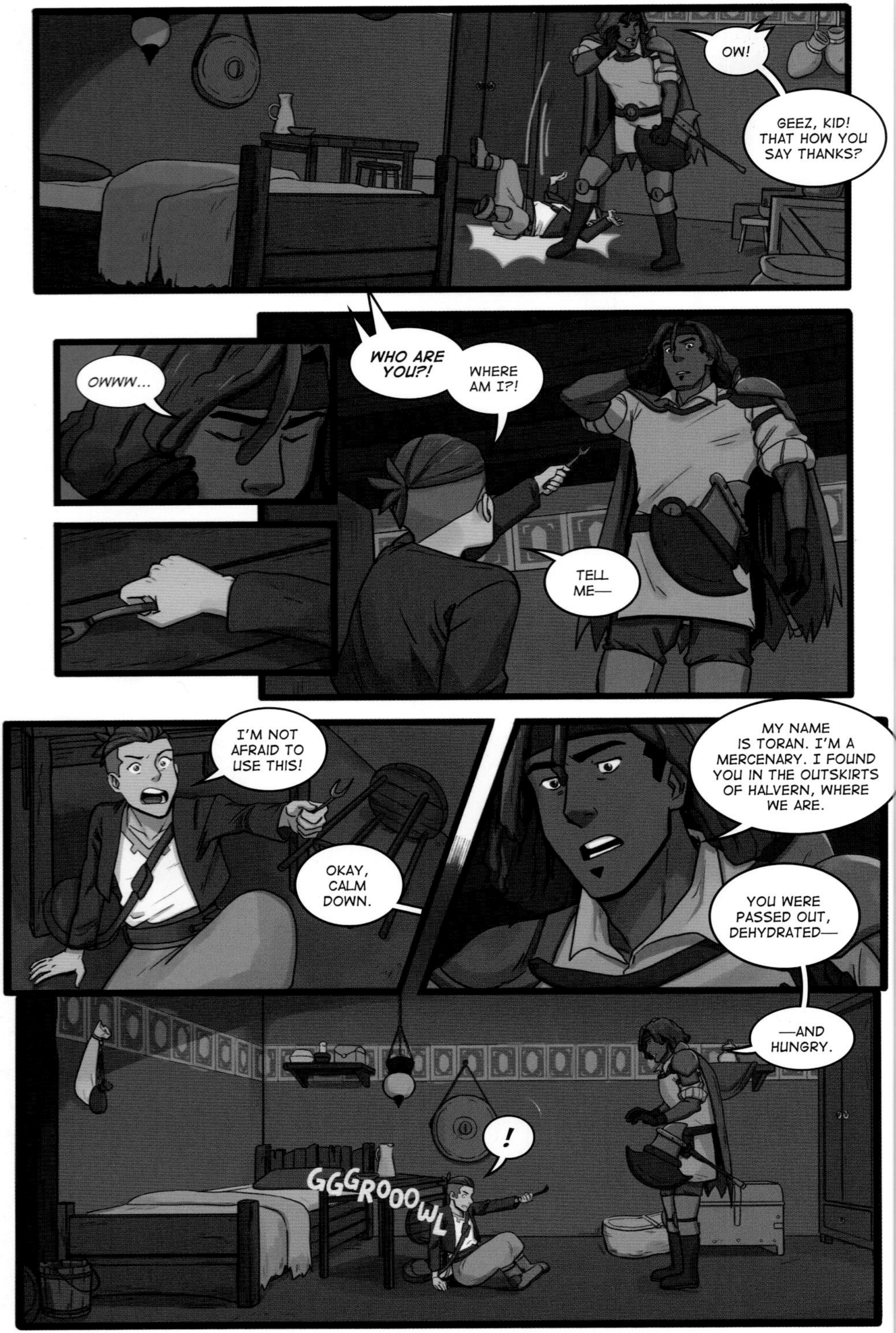
OW!
GEEZ, KID! THAT HOW YOU SAY THANKS?
OWWW...
WHO ARE YOU?!
WHERE AM I?!
TELL ME—
I'M NOT AFRAID TO USE THIS!
OKAY, CALM DOWN.
MY NAME IS TORAN. I'M A MERCENARY. I FOUND YOU IN THE OUTSKIRTS OF HALVERN, WHERE WE ARE.
YOU WERE PASSED OUT, DEHYDRATED—
—AND HUNGRY.
!
GGGROOOWL

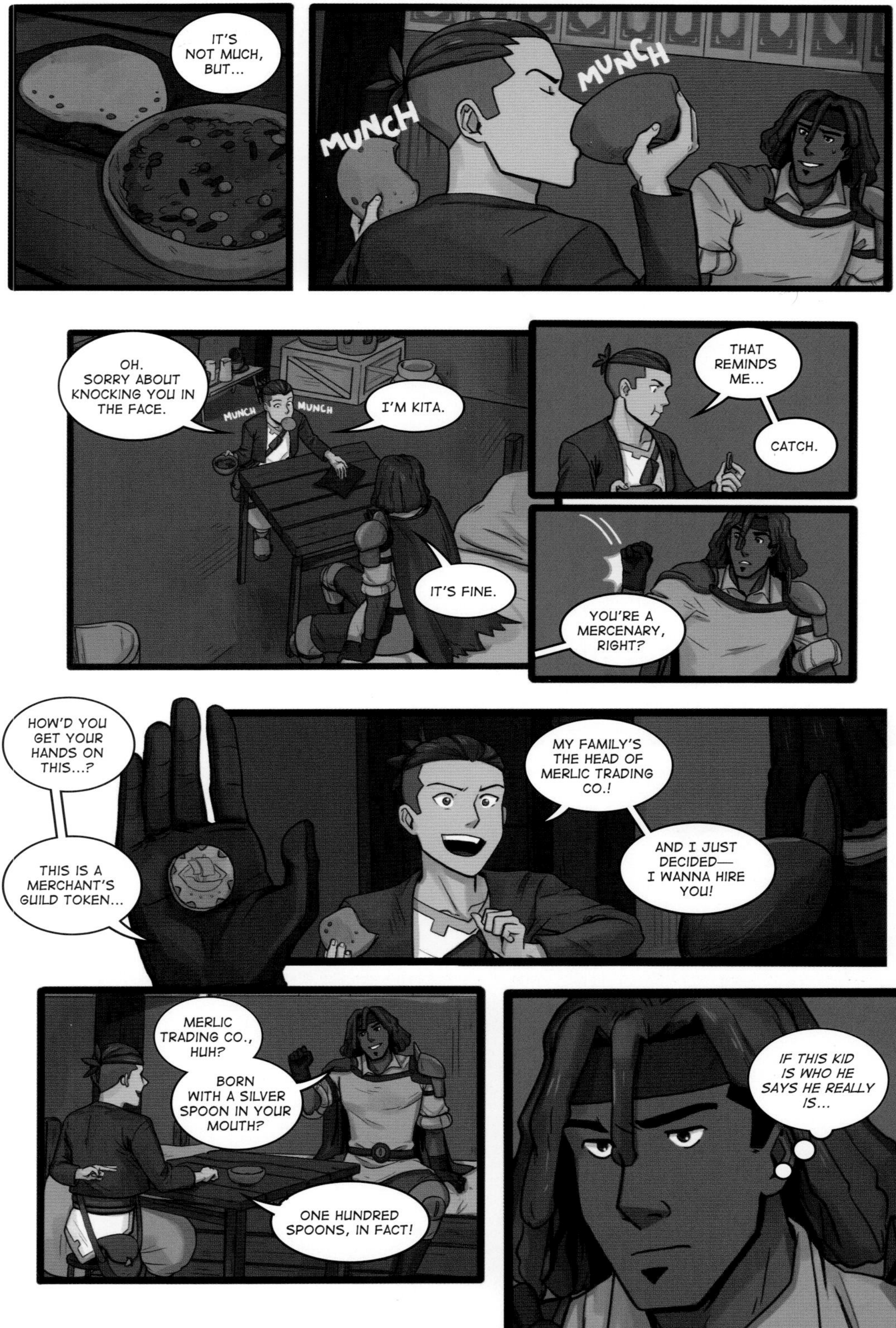
IT'S NOT MUCH, BUT...
MUNCH
MUNCH
OH. SORRY ABOUT KNOCKING YOU IN THE FACE.
MUNCH
MUNCH
I'M KITA.
IT'S FINE.
THAT REMINDS ME...
CATCH.
YOU'RE A MERCENARY, RIGHT?
HOW'D YOU GET YOUR HANDS ON THIS...?
THIS IS A MERCHANT'S GUILD TOKEN...
MY FAMILY'S THE HEAD OF MERLIC TRADING CO.!
AND I JUST DECIDED— I WANNA HIRE YOU!
MERLIC TRADING CO., HUH?
BORN WITH A SILVER SPOON IN YOUR MOUTH?
ONE HUNDRED SPOONS, IN FACT!
IF THIS KID IS WHO HE SAYS HE REALLY IS...

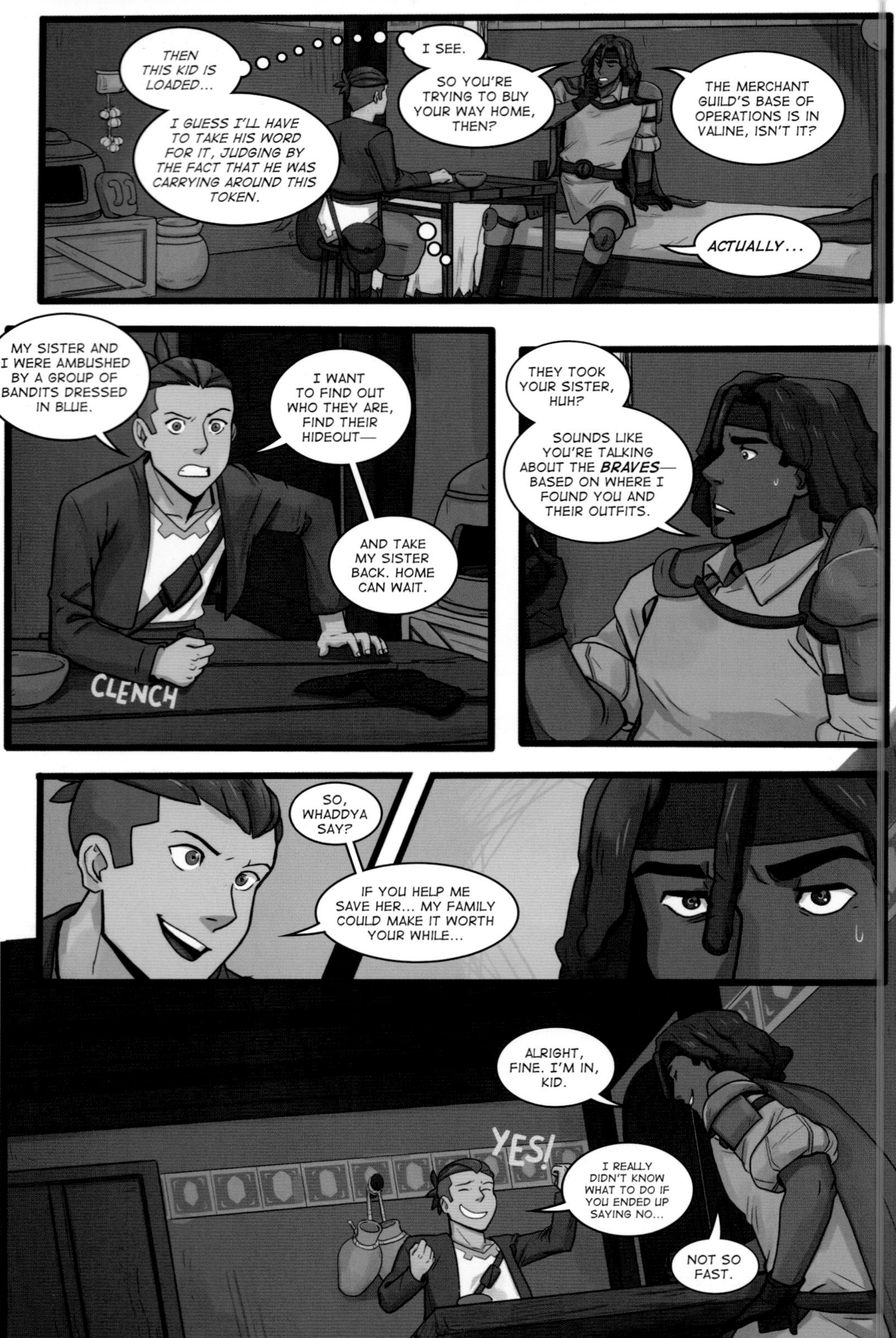

THEN THIS KID IS LOADED...
I GUESS I'LL HAVE TO TAKE HIS WORD FOR IT, JUDGING BY THE FACT THAT HE WAS CARRYING AROUND THIS TOKEN.
I SEE.
SO YOU'RE TRYING TO BUY YOUR WAY HOME, THEN?
THE MERCHANT GUILD'S BASE OF OPERATIONS IS IN VALINE, ISN'T IT?
ACTUALLY...
MY SISTER AND I WERE AMBUSHED BY A GROUP OF BANDITS DRESSED IN BLUE.
I WANT TO FIND OUT WHO THEY ARE, FIND THEIR HIDEOUT—
AND TAKE MY SISTER BACK. HOME CAN WAIT.
CLENCH
THEY TOOK YOUR SISTER, HUH?
SOUNDS LIKE YOU'RE TALKING ABOUT THE BRAVES— BASED ON WHERE I FOUND YOU AND THEIR OUTFITS.
SO, WHADDYA SAY?
IF YOU HELP ME SAVE HER... MY FAMILY COULD MAKE IT WORTH YOUR WHILE...
ALRIGHT, FINE. I'M IN, KID.
YES!
I REALLY DIDN'T KNOW WHAT TO DO IF YOU ENDED UP SAYING NO...
NOT SO FAST.

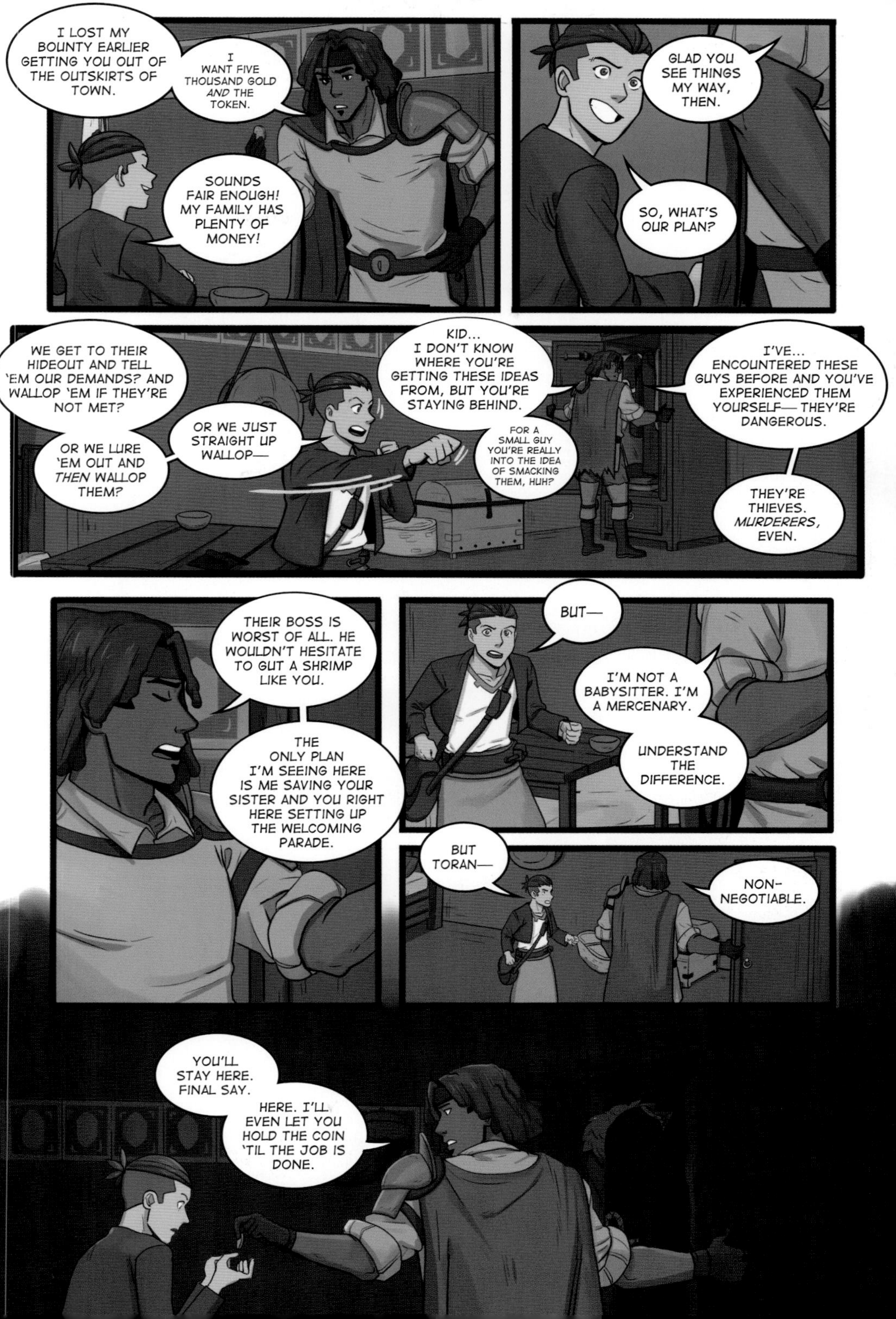
I LOST MY BOUNTY EARLIER GETTING YOU OUT OF THE OUTSKIRTS OF TOWN.
I WANT FIVE THOUSAND GOLD *AND* THE TOKEN.
SOUNDS FAIR ENOUGH! MY FAMILY HAS PLENTY OF MONEY!
GLAD YOU SEE THINGS MY WAY, THEN.
SO, WHAT'S OUR PLAN?
WE GET TO THEIR HIDEOUT AND TELL 'EM OUR DEMANDS? AND WALLOP 'EM IF THEY'RE NOT MET?
OR WE LURE 'EM OUT AND *THEN* WALLOP THEM?
OR WE JUST STRAIGHT UP WALLOP—
KID... I DON'T KNOW WHERE YOU'RE GETTING THESE IDEAS FROM, BUT YOU'RE STAYING BEHIND.
FOR A SMALL GUY YOU'RE REALLY INTO THE IDEA OF SMACKING THEM, HUH?
I'VE... ENCOUNTERED THESE GUYS BEFORE AND YOU'VE EXPERIENCED THEM YOURSELF— THEY'RE DANGEROUS.
THEY'RE THIEVES. *MURDERERS*, EVEN.
THEIR BOSS IS WORST OF ALL. HE WOULDN'T HESITATE TO GUT A SHRIMP LIKE YOU.
THE ONLY PLAN I'M SEEING HERE IS ME SAVING YOUR SISTER AND YOU RIGHT HERE SETTING UP THE WELCOMING PARADE.
BUT—
I'M NOT A BABYSITTER. I'M A MERCENARY.
UNDERSTAND THE DIFFERENCE.
BUT TORAN—
NON-NEGOTIABLE.
YOU'LL STAY HERE. FINAL SAY.
HERE. I'LL EVEN LET YOU HOLD THE COIN 'TIL THE JOB IS DONE.

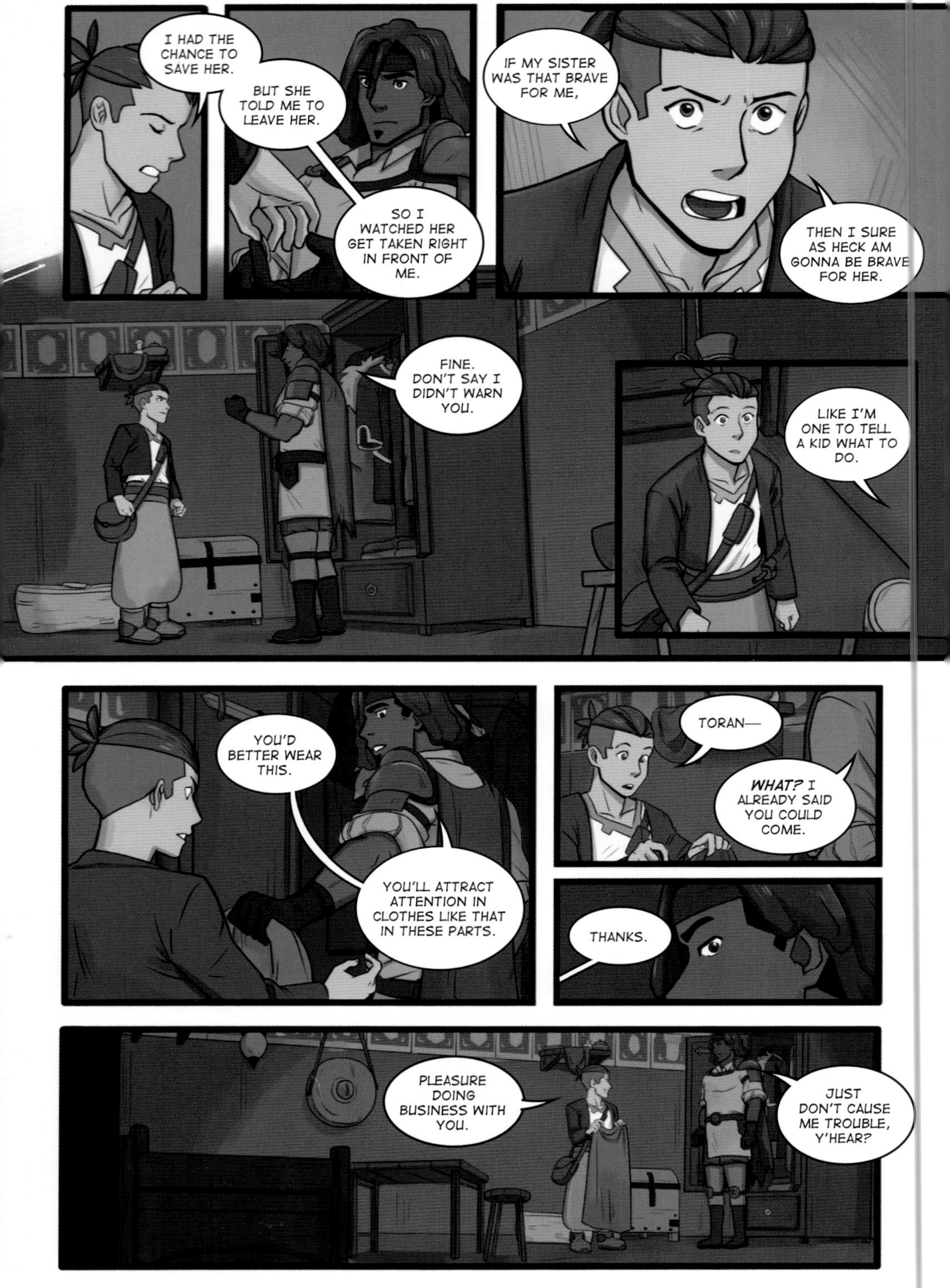
I HAD THE CHANCE TO SAVE HER.
BUT SHE TOLD ME TO LEAVE HER.
SO I WATCHED HER GET TAKEN RIGHT IN FRONT OF ME.
IF MY SISTER WAS THAT BRAVE FOR ME,
THEN I SURE AS HECK AM GONNA BE BRAVE FOR HER.
FINE. DON'T SAY I DIDN'T WARN YOU.
LIKE I'M ONE TO TELL A KID WHAT TO DO.
YOU'D BETTER WEAR THIS.
YOU'LL ATTRACT ATTENTION IN CLOTHES LIKE THAT IN THESE PARTS.
TORAN—
WHAT? I ALREADY SAID YOU COULD COME.
THANKS.
PLEASURE DOING BUSINESS WITH YOU.
JUST DON'T CAUSE ME TROUBLE, Y'HEAR?

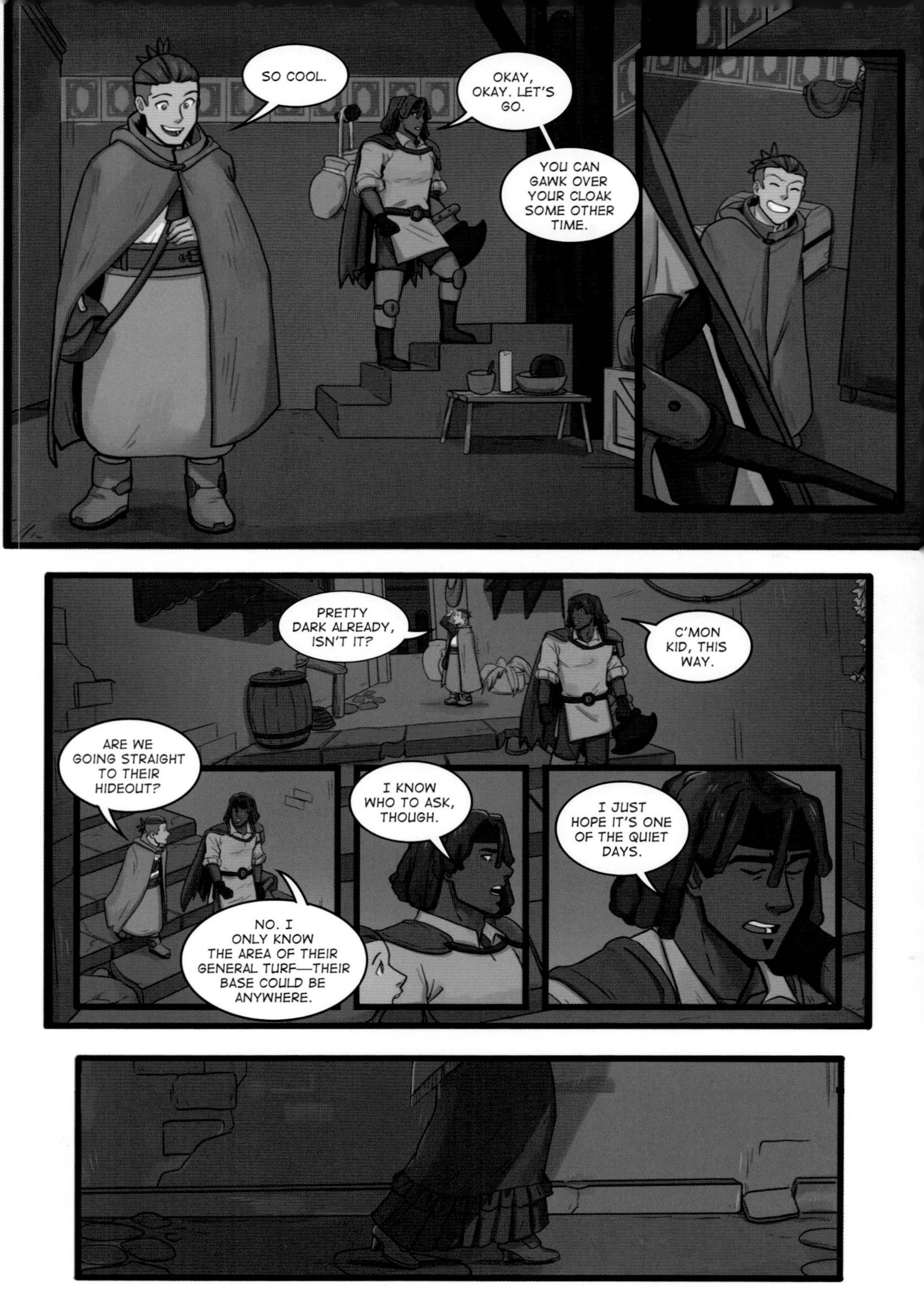
SO COOL.
OKAY, OKAY. LET'S GO.
YOU CAN GAWK OVER YOUR CLOAK SOME OTHER TIME.
PRETTY DARK ALREADY, ISN'T IT?
C'MON KID, THIS WAY.
ARE WE GOING STRAIGHT TO THEIR HIDEOUT?
NO. I ONLY KNOW THE AREA OF THEIR GENERAL TURF—THEIR BASE COULD BE ANYWHERE.
I KNOW WHO TO ASK, THOUGH.
I JUST HOPE IT'S ONE OF THE QUIET DAYS.

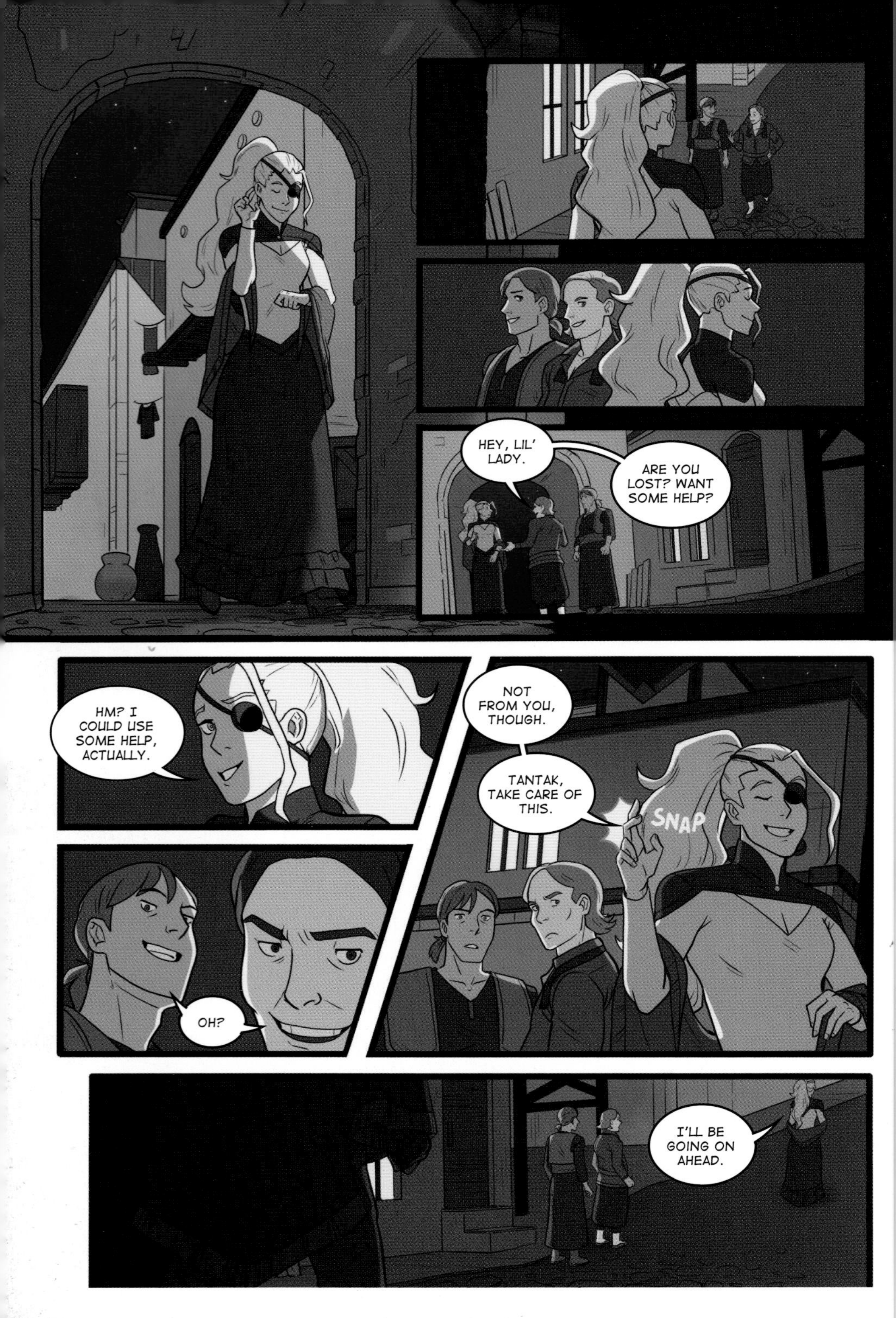
HEY, LIL' LADY.
ARE YOU LOST? WANT SOME HELP?
HM? I COULD USE SOME HELP, ACTUALLY.
OH?
NOT FROM YOU, THOUGH.
TANTAK, TAKE CARE OF THIS.
SNAP
I'LL BE GOING ON AHEAD.

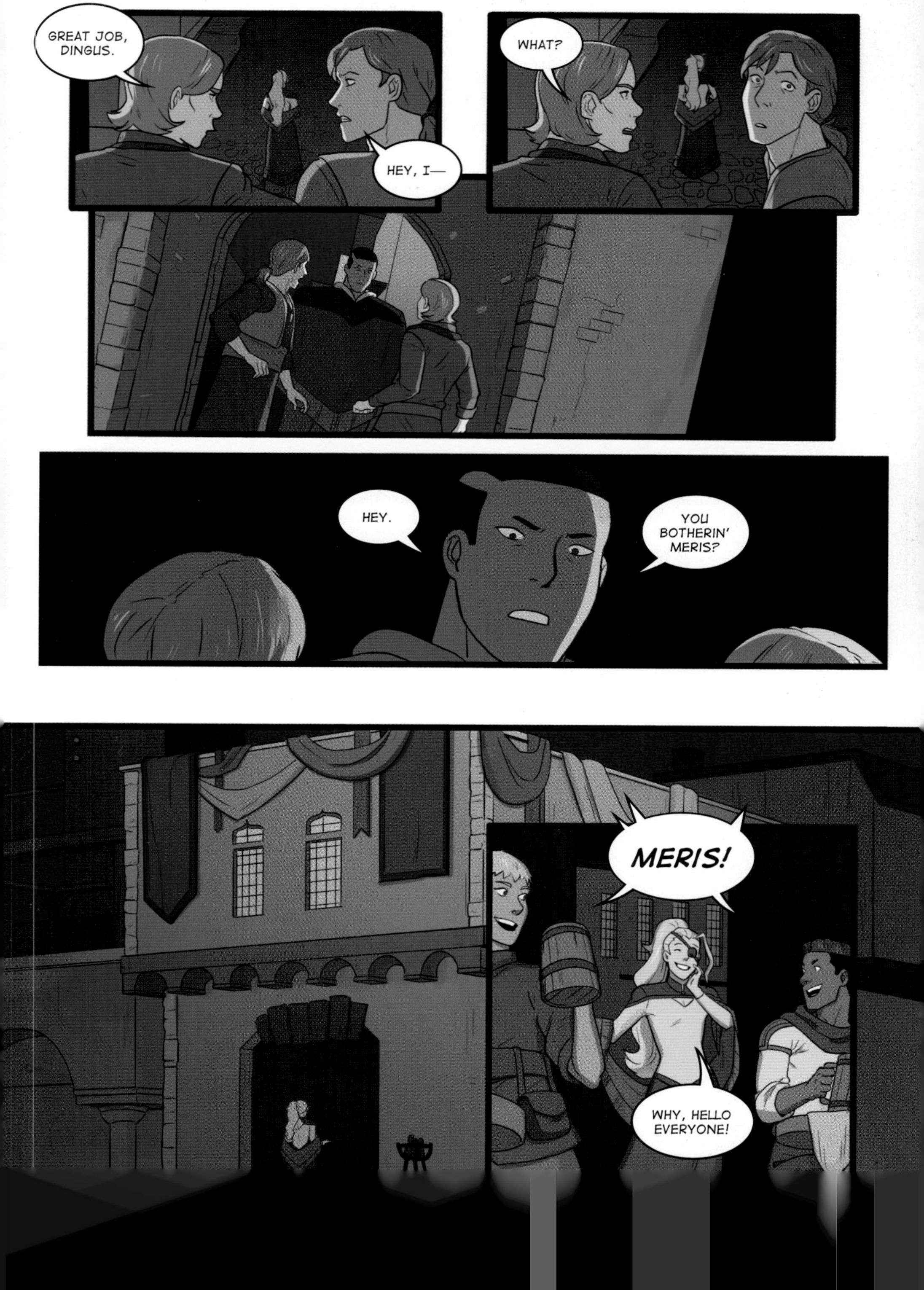
GREAT JOB, DINGUS.
HEY, I—
WHAT?
HEY.
YOU BOTHERIN' MERIS?
MERIS!
WHY, HELLO EVERYONE!

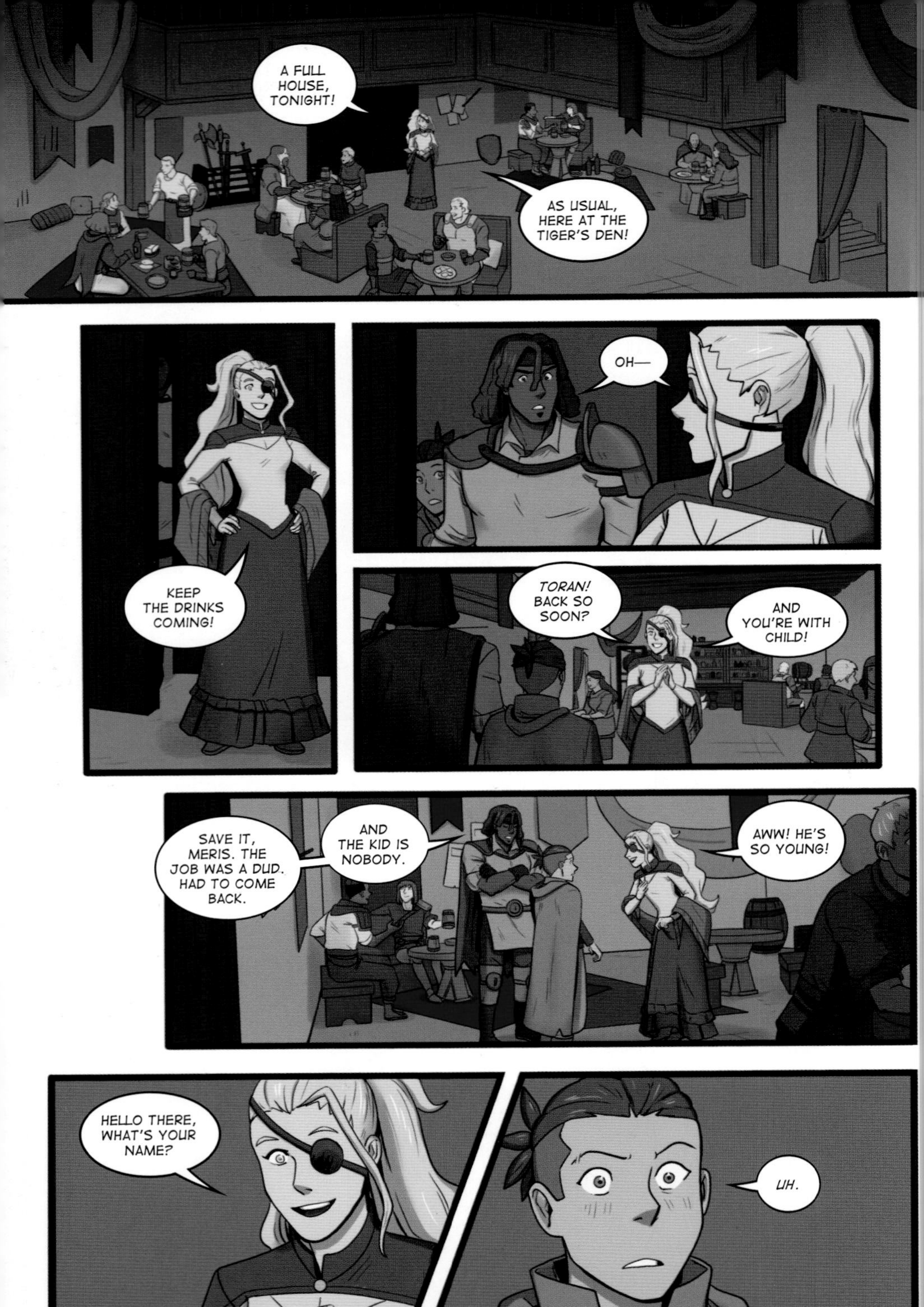
A FULL HOUSE, TONIGHT!
AS USUAL, HERE AT THE TIGER'S DEN!
KEEP THE DRINKS COMING!
OH—
TORAN! BACK SO SOON?
AND YOU'RE WITH CHILD!
SAVE IT, MERIS. THE JOB WAS A DUD. HAD TO COME BACK.
AND THE KID IS NOBODY.
AWW! HE'S SO YOUNG!
HELLO THERE, WHAT'S YOUR NAME?
UH.

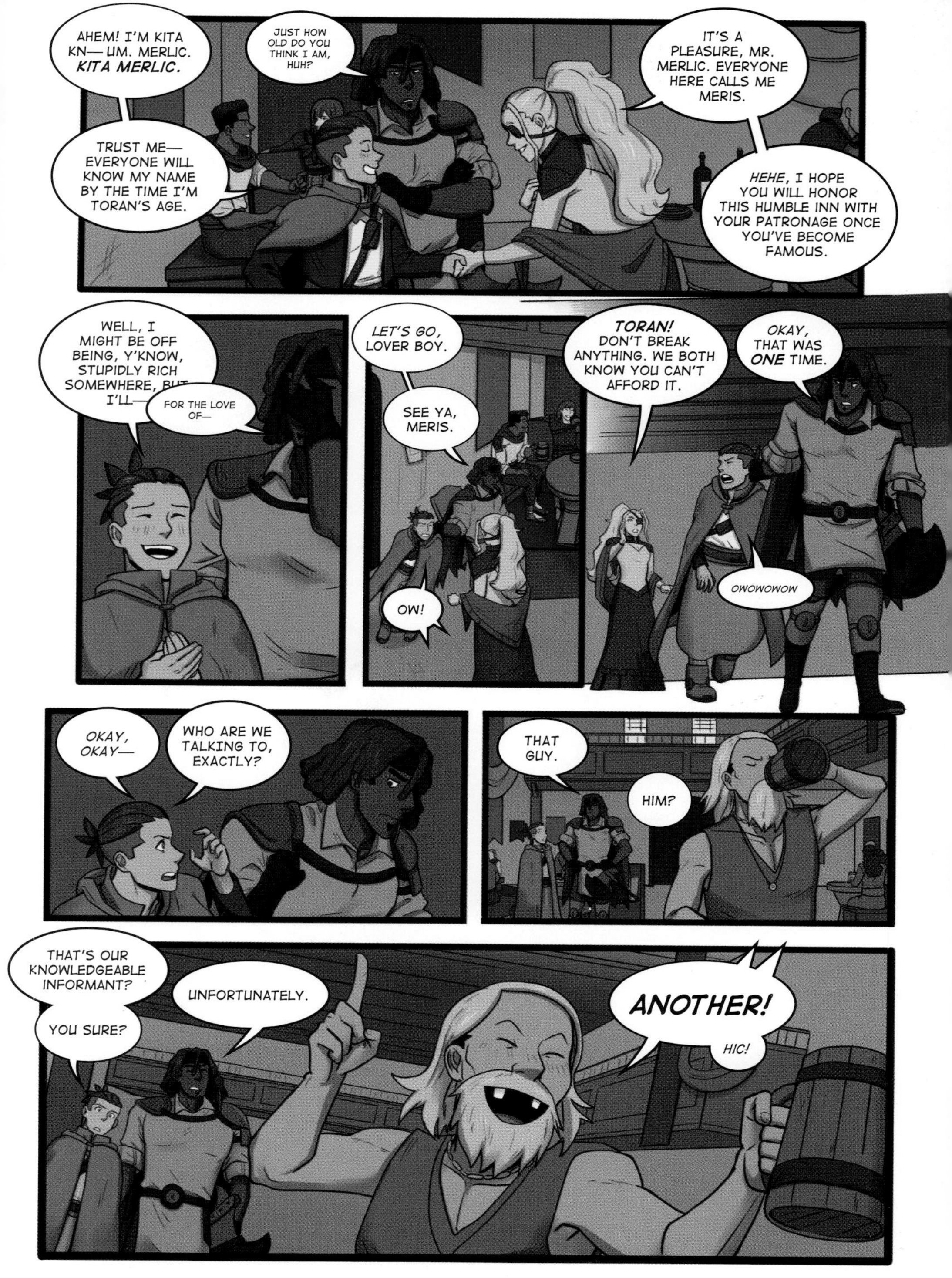
AHEM! I'M KITA KN— UM. MERLIC. KITA MERLIC.
TRUST ME— EVERYONE WILL KNOW MY NAME BY THE TIME I'M TORAN'S AGE.
JUST HOW OLD DO YOU THINK I AM, HUH?
IT'S A PLEASURE, MR. MERLIC. EVERYONE HERE CALLS ME MERIS.
HEHE, I HOPE YOU WILL HONOR THIS HUMBLE INN WITH YOUR PATRONAGE ONCE YOU'VE BECOME FAMOUS.
WELL, I MIGHT BE OFF BEING, Y'KNOW, STUPIDLY RICH SOMEWHERE, BUT I'LL—
FOR THE LOVE OF—
LET'S GO, LOVER BOY.
SEE YA, MERIS.
OW!
TORAN! DON'T BREAK ANYTHING. WE BOTH KNOW YOU CAN'T AFFORD IT.
OKAY, THAT WAS ONE TIME.
OWOWOWOW
OKAY, OKAY—
WHO ARE WE TALKING TO, EXACTLY?
THAT GUY.
HIM?
THAT'S OUR KNOWLEDGEABLE INFORMANT?
YOU SURE?
UNFORTUNATELY.
ANOTHER!
HIC!

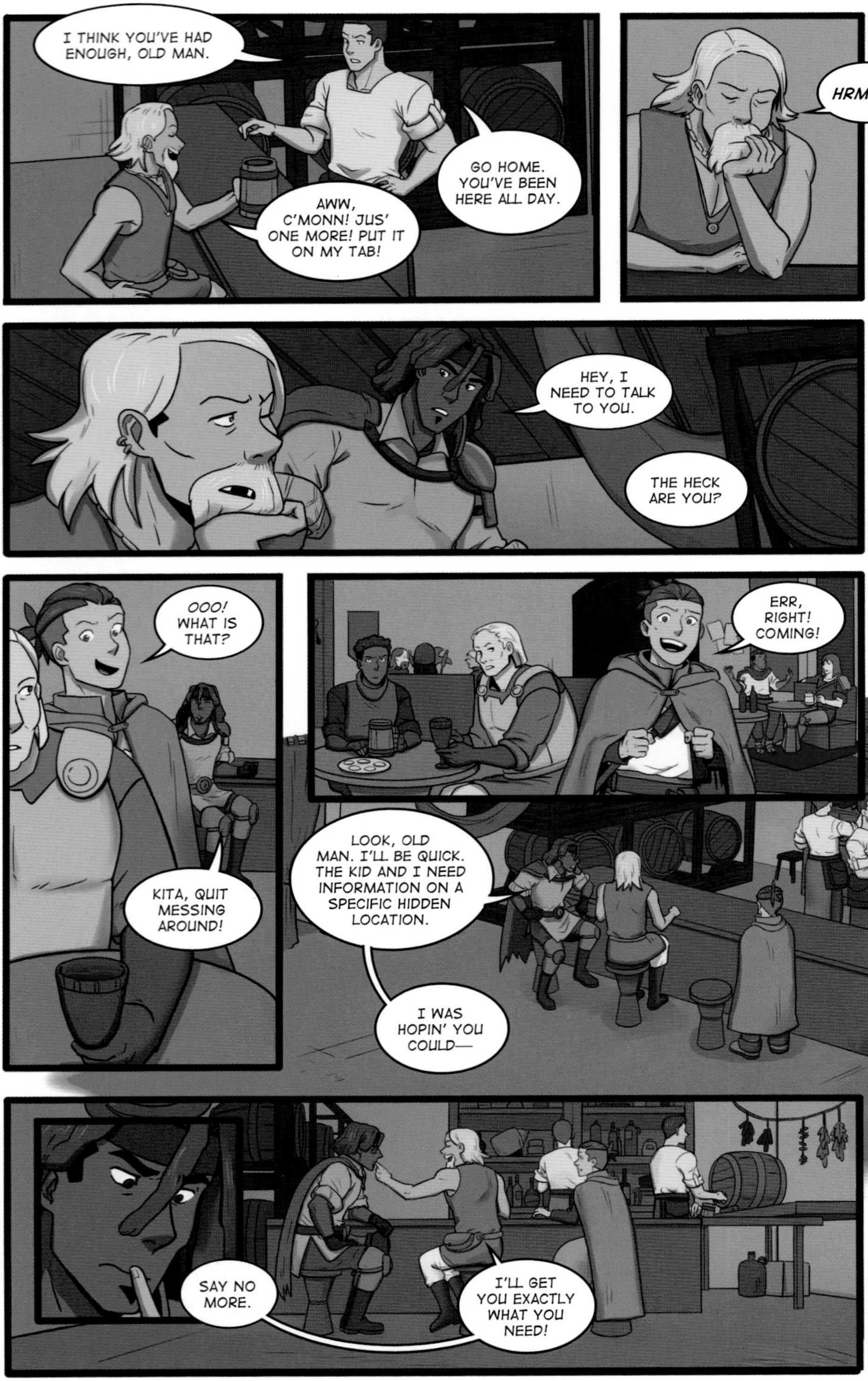
I THINK YOU'VE HAD ENOUGH, OLD MAN.
AWW, C'MONN! JUS' ONE MORE! PUT IT ON MY TAB!
GO HOME. YOU'VE BEEN HERE ALL DAY.
HRMPH.
HEY, I NEED TO TALK TO YOU.
THE HECK ARE YOU?
OOO! WHAT IS THAT?
KITA, QUIT MESSING AROUND!
ERR, RIGHT! COMING!
LOOK, OLD MAN. I'LL BE QUICK. THE KID AND I NEED INFORMATION ON A SPECIFIC HIDDEN LOCATION.
I WAS HOPIN' YOU COULD—
SAY NO MORE.
I'LL GET YOU EXACTLY WHAT YOU NEED!

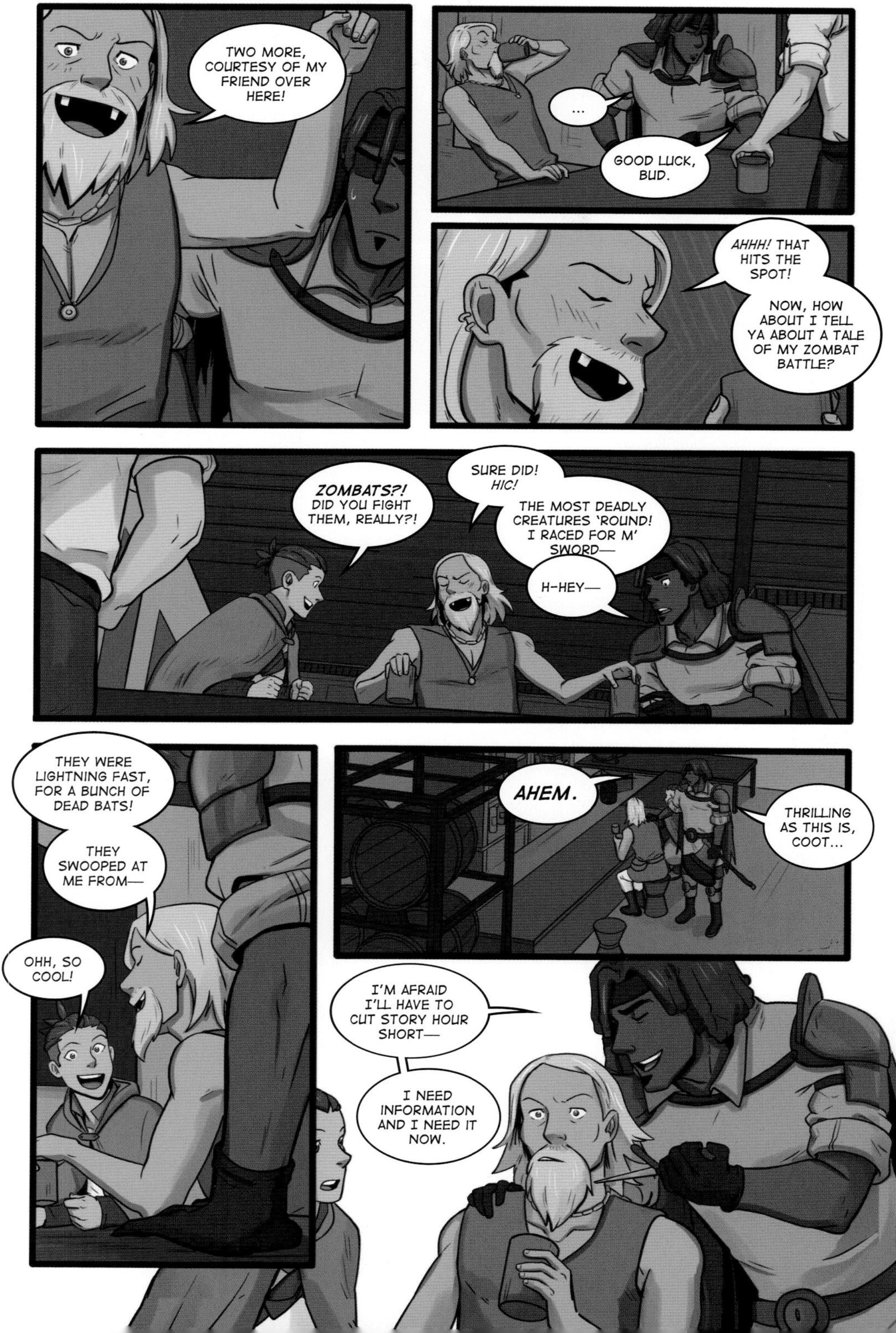
TWO MORE, COURTESY OF MY FRIEND OVER HERE!
...
GOOD LUCK, BUD.
AHHH! THAT HITS THE SPOT!
NOW, HOW ABOUT I TELL YA ABOUT A TALE OF MY ZOMBAT BATTLE?
ZOMBATS?! DID YOU FIGHT THEM, REALLY?!
SURE DID! *HIC!*
THE MOST DEADLY CREATURES 'ROUND! I RACED FOR M' SWORD—
H-HEY—
THEY WERE LIGHTNING FAST, FOR A BUNCH OF DEAD BATS!
THEY SWOOPED AT ME FROM—
OHH, SO COOL!
AHEM.
THRILLING AS THIS IS, COOT...
I'M AFRAID I'LL HAVE TO CUT STORY HOUR SHORT—
I NEED INFORMATION AND I NEED IT NOW.

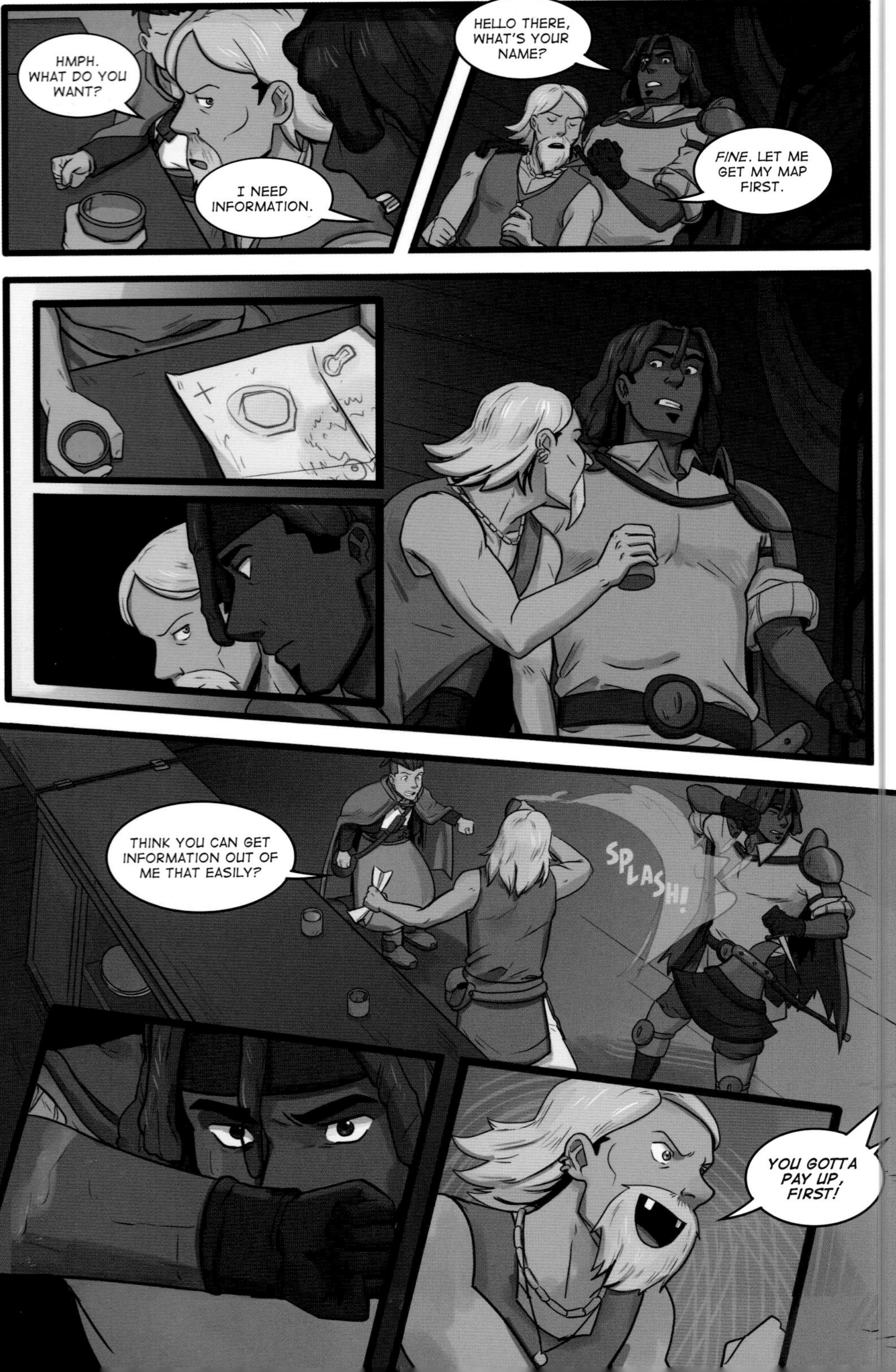
HMPH. WHAT DO YOU WANT?
I NEED INFORMATION.
HELLO THERE, WHAT'S YOUR NAME?
FINE. LET ME GET MY MAP FIRST.
THINK YOU CAN GET INFORMATION OUT OF ME THAT EASILY?
SPLASH!
YOU GOTTA PAY UP, FIRST!

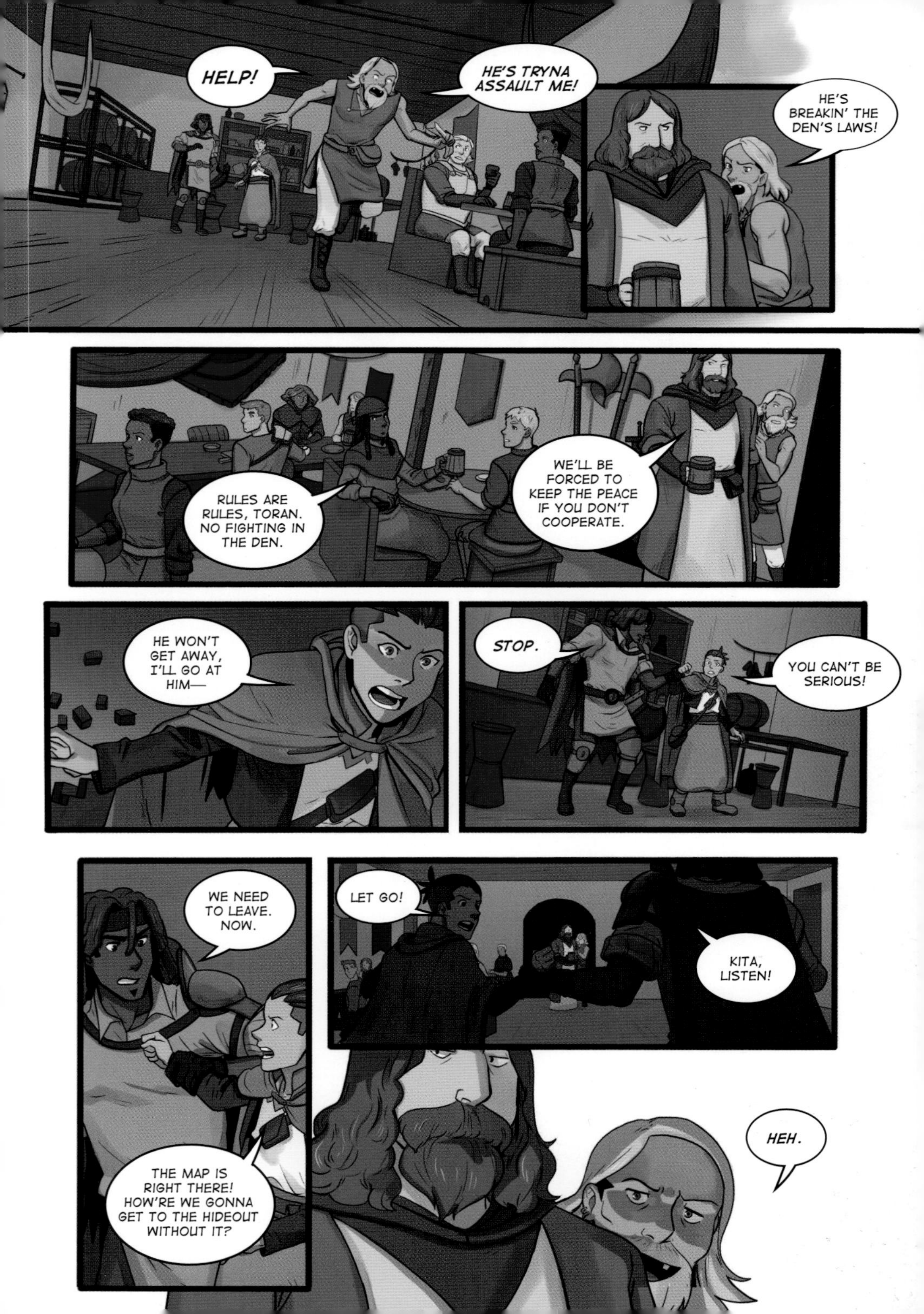
HELP!
HE'S TRYNA ASSAULT ME!
HE'S BREAKIN' THE DEN'S LAWS!
RULES ARE RULES, TORAN. NO FIGHTING IN THE DEN.
WE'LL BE FORCED TO KEEP THE PEACE IF YOU DON'T COOPERATE.
HE WON'T GET AWAY, I'LL GO AT HIM—
STOP.
YOU CAN'T BE SERIOUS!
WE NEED TO LEAVE. NOW.
LET GO!
KITA, LISTEN!
THE MAP IS RIGHT THERE! HOW'RE WE GONNA GET TO THE HIDEOUT WITHOUT IT?
HEH.

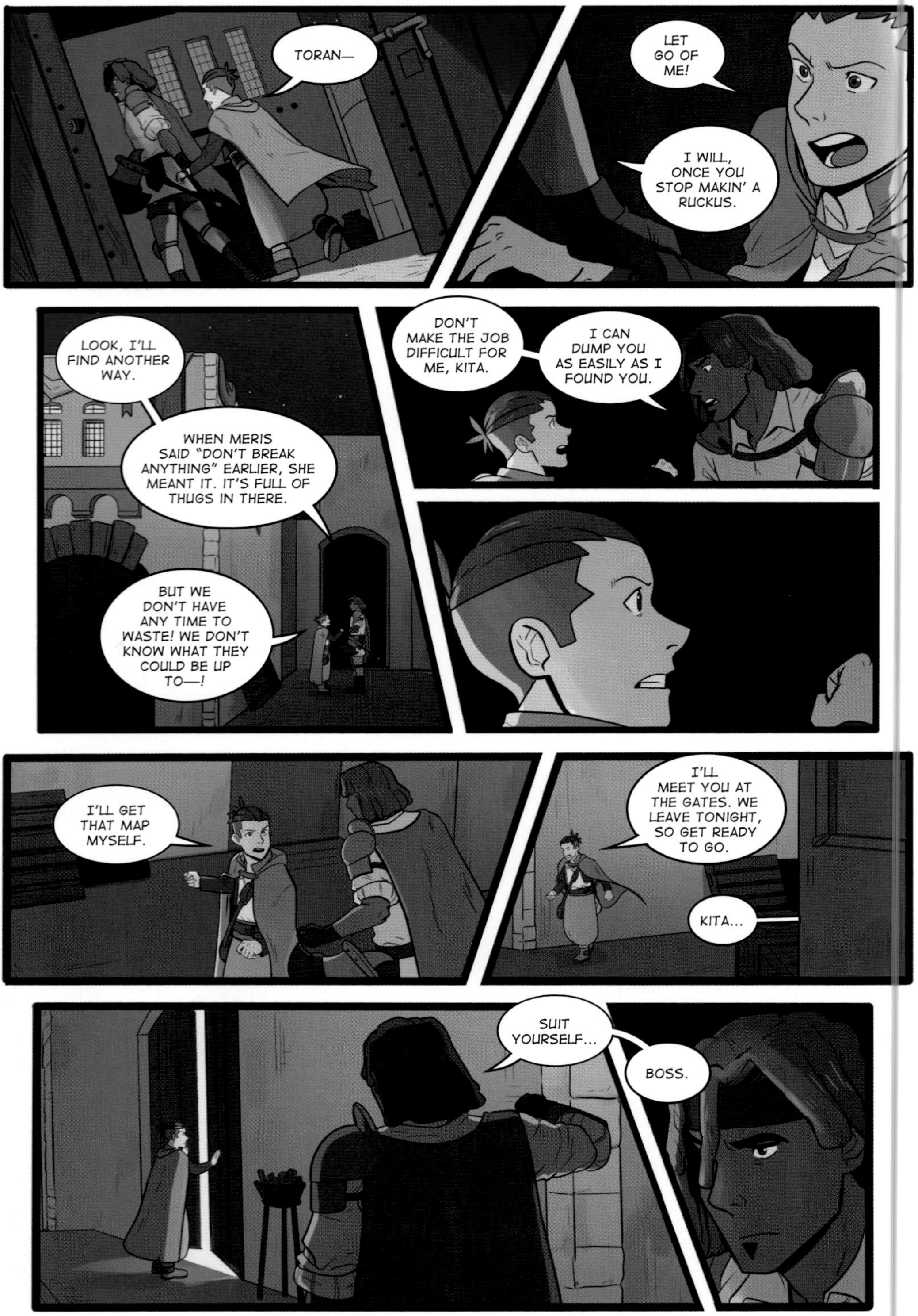
TORAN—
LET GO OF ME!
I WILL, ONCE YOU STOP MAKIN' A RUCKUS.
LOOK, I'LL FIND ANOTHER WAY.
WHEN MERIS SAID "DON'T BREAK ANYTHING" EARLIER, SHE MEANT IT. IT'S FULL OF THUGS IN THERE.
BUT WE DON'T HAVE ANY TIME TO WASTE! WE DON'T KNOW WHAT THEY COULD BE UP TO—!
DON'T MAKE THE JOB DIFFICULT FOR ME, KITA.
I CAN DUMP YOU AS EASILY AS I FOUND YOU.
I'LL GET THAT MAP MYSELF.
I'LL MEET YOU AT THE GATES. WE LEAVE TONIGHT, SO GET READY TO GO.
KITA...
SUIT YOURSELF...
BOSS.

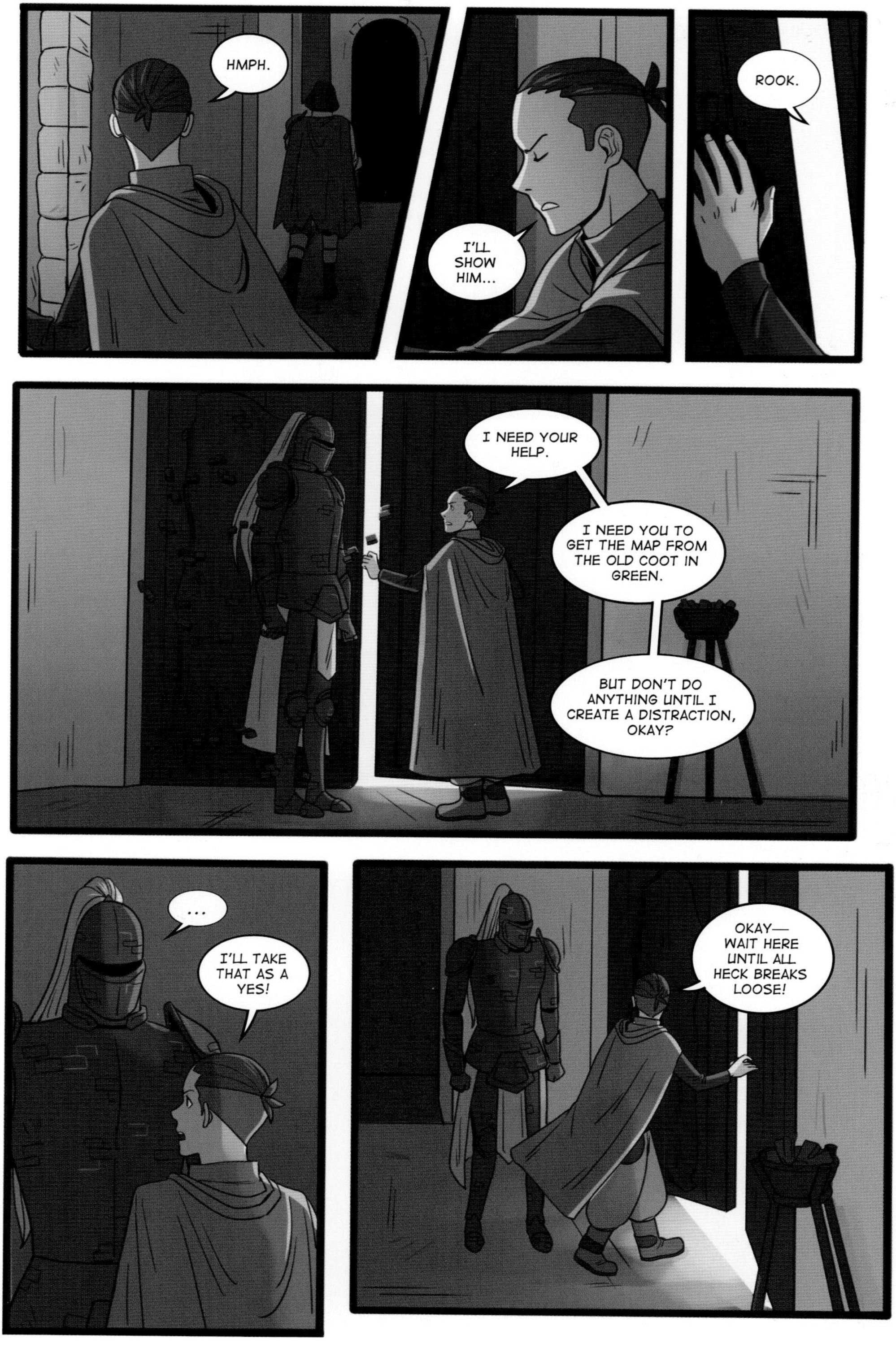
HMPH.
I'LL SHOW HIM...
ROOK.
I NEED YOUR HELP.
I NEED YOU TO GET THE MAP FROM THE OLD COOT IN GREEN.
BUT DON'T DO ANYTHING UNTIL I CREATE A DISTRACTION, OKAY?
...
I'LL TAKE THAT AS A YES!
OKAY— WAIT HERE UNTIL ALL HECK BREAKS LOOSE!

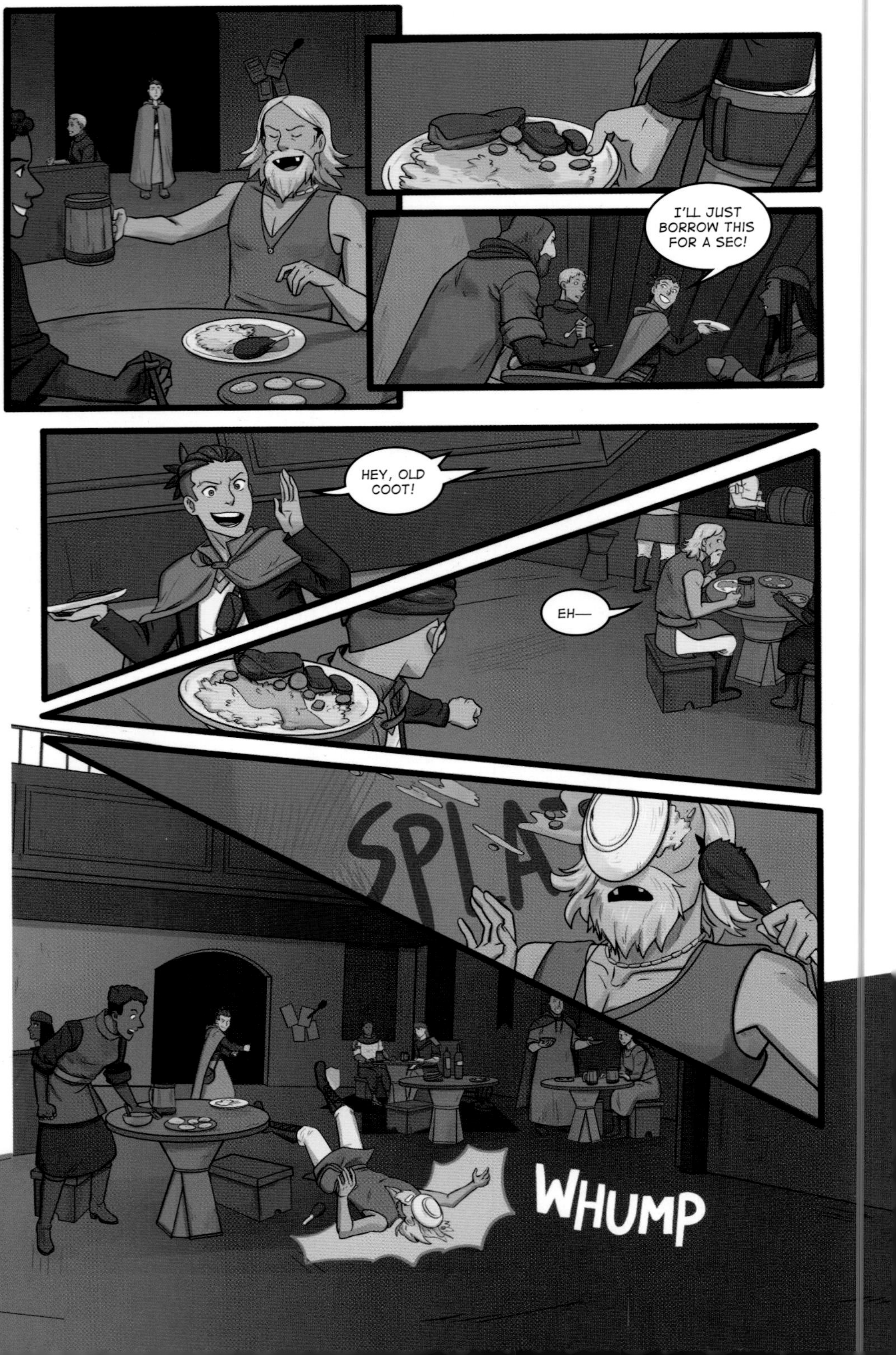
I'LL JUST BORROW THIS FOR A SEC!
HEY, OLD COOT!
EH—
SPLA
WHUMP

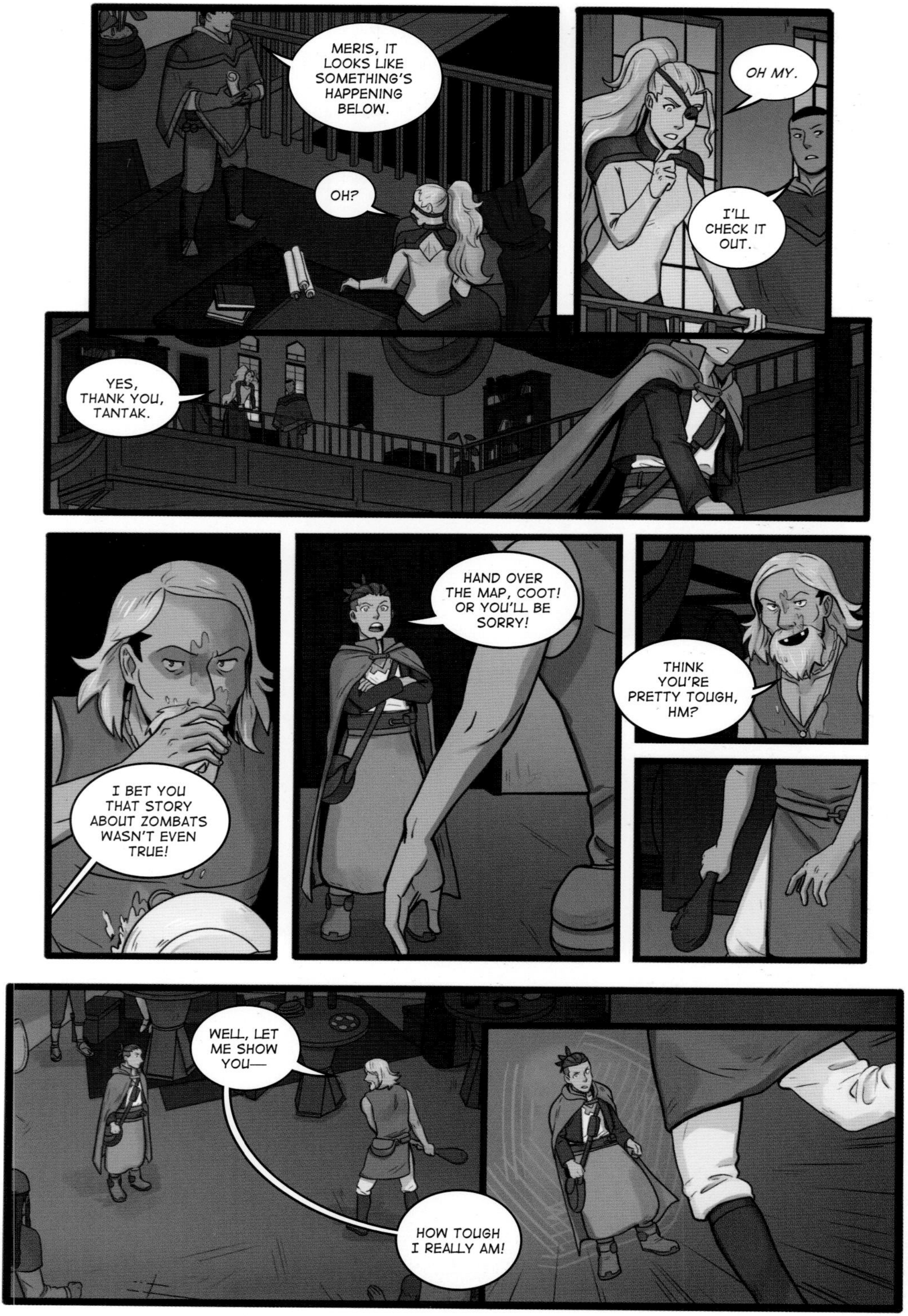
MERIS, IT LOOKS LIKE SOMETHING'S HAPPENING BELOW.
OH?
OH MY.
I'LL CHECK IT OUT.
YES, THANK YOU, TANTAK.
I BET YOU THAT STORY ABOUT ZOMBATS WASN'T EVEN TRUE!
HAND OVER THE MAP, COOT! OR YOU'LL BE SORRY!
THINK YOU'RE PRETTY TOUGH, HM?
WELL, LET ME SHOW YOU—
HOW TOUGH I REALLY AM!

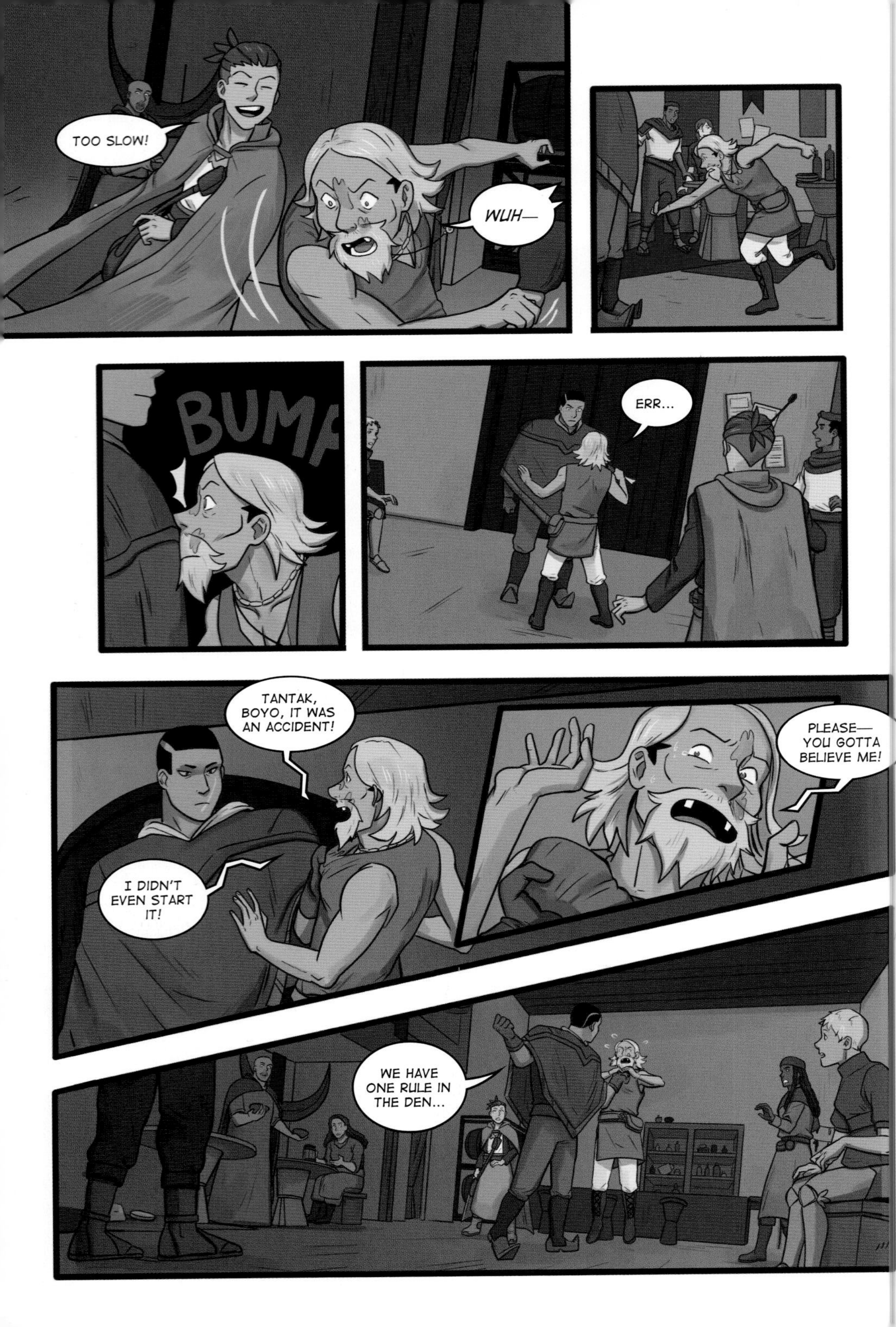
TOO SLOW!
WUH—
BUMP
ERR...
TANTAK, BOYO, IT WAS AN ACCIDENT!
I DIDN'T EVEN START IT!
PLEASE— YOU GOTTA BELIEVE ME!
WE HAVE ONE RULE IN THE DEN...

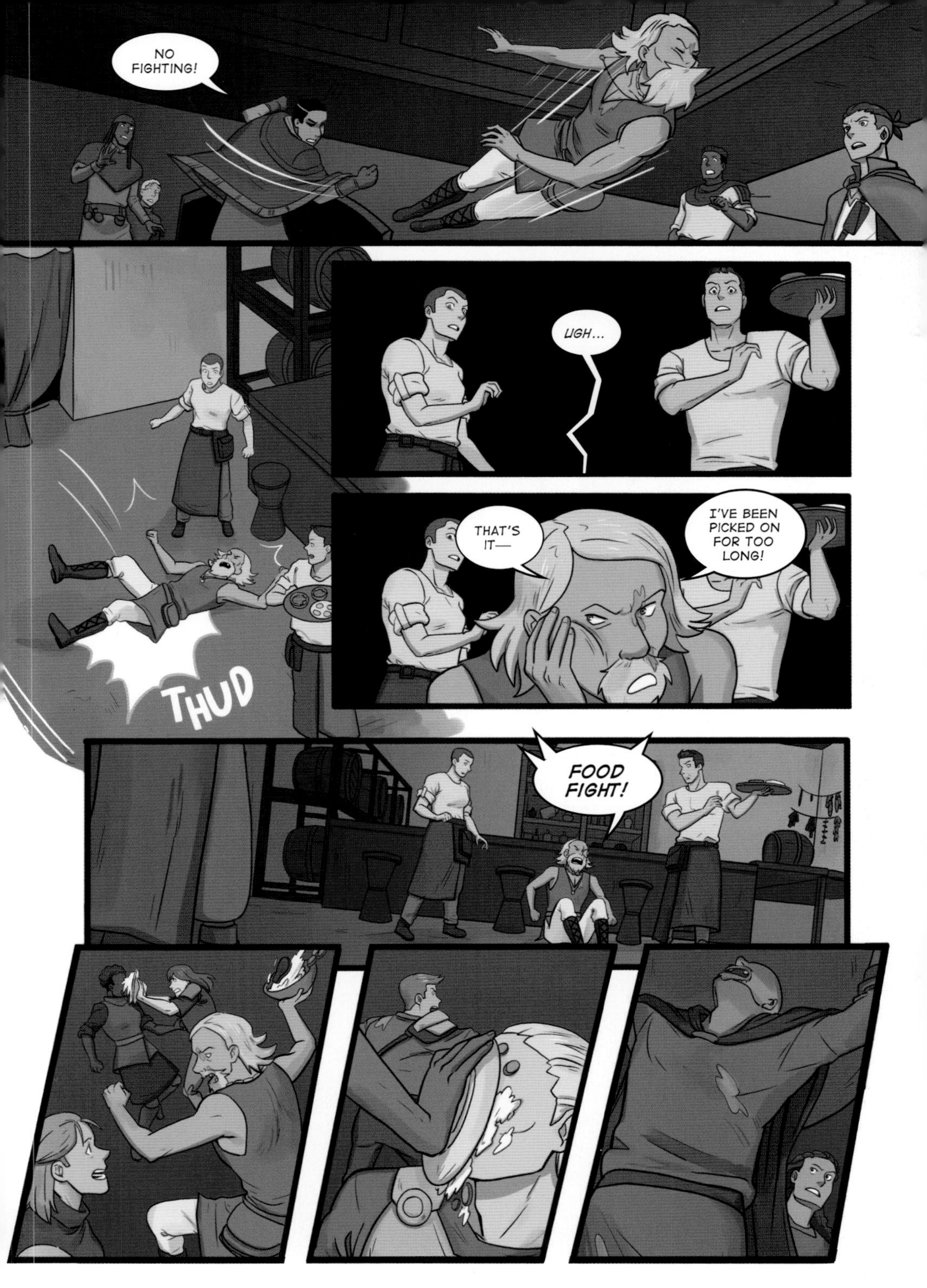
NO FIGHTING!
UGH...
THUD
THAT'S IT—
I'VE BEEN PICKED ON FOR TOO LONG!
FOOD FIGHT!

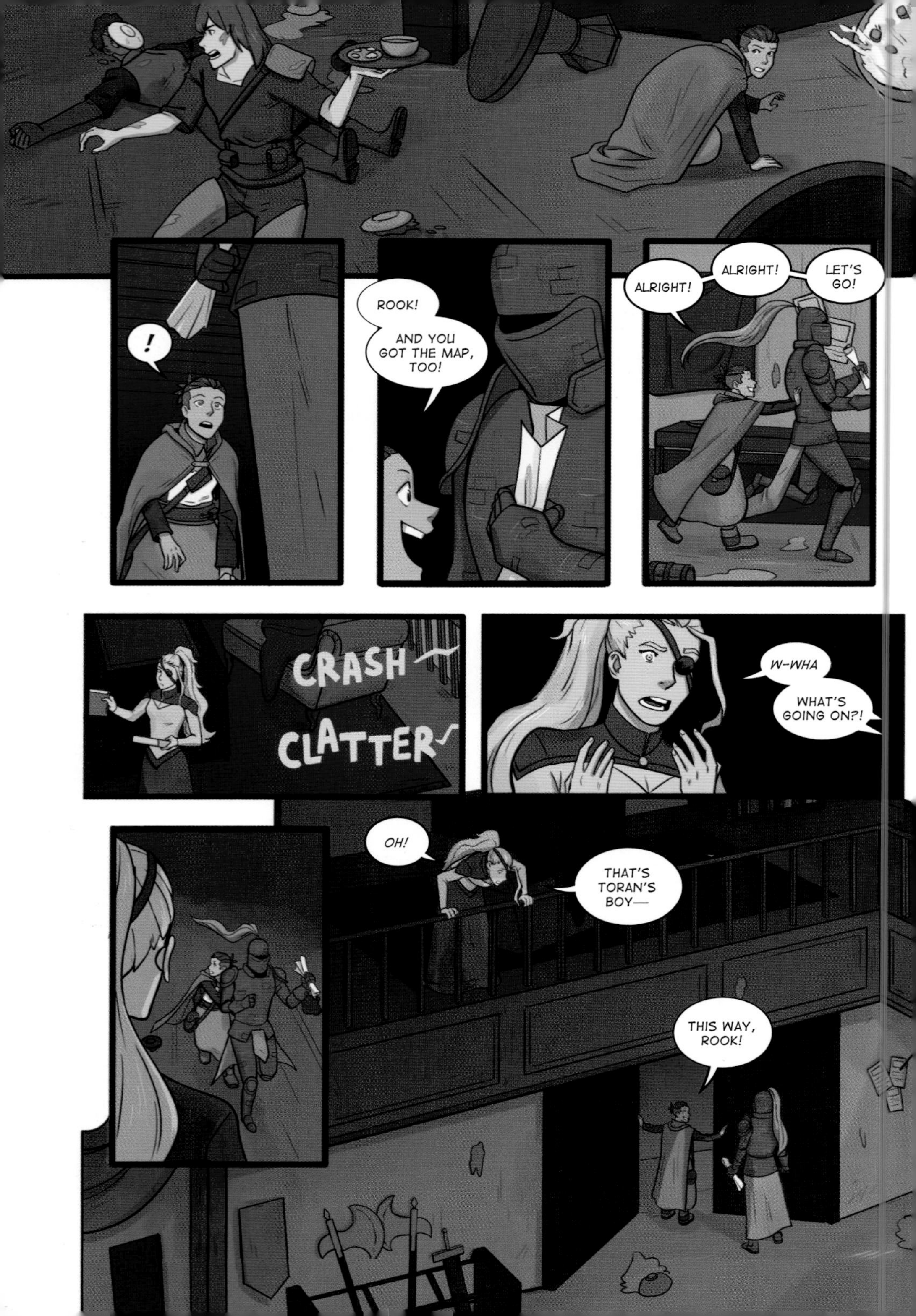
!
ROOK!
AND YOU GOT THE MAP, TOO!
ALRIGHT!
ALRIGHT!
LET'S GO!
CRASH
CLATTER
W-WHA
WHAT'S GOING ON?!
OH!
THAT'S TORAN'S BOY—
THIS WAY, ROOK!

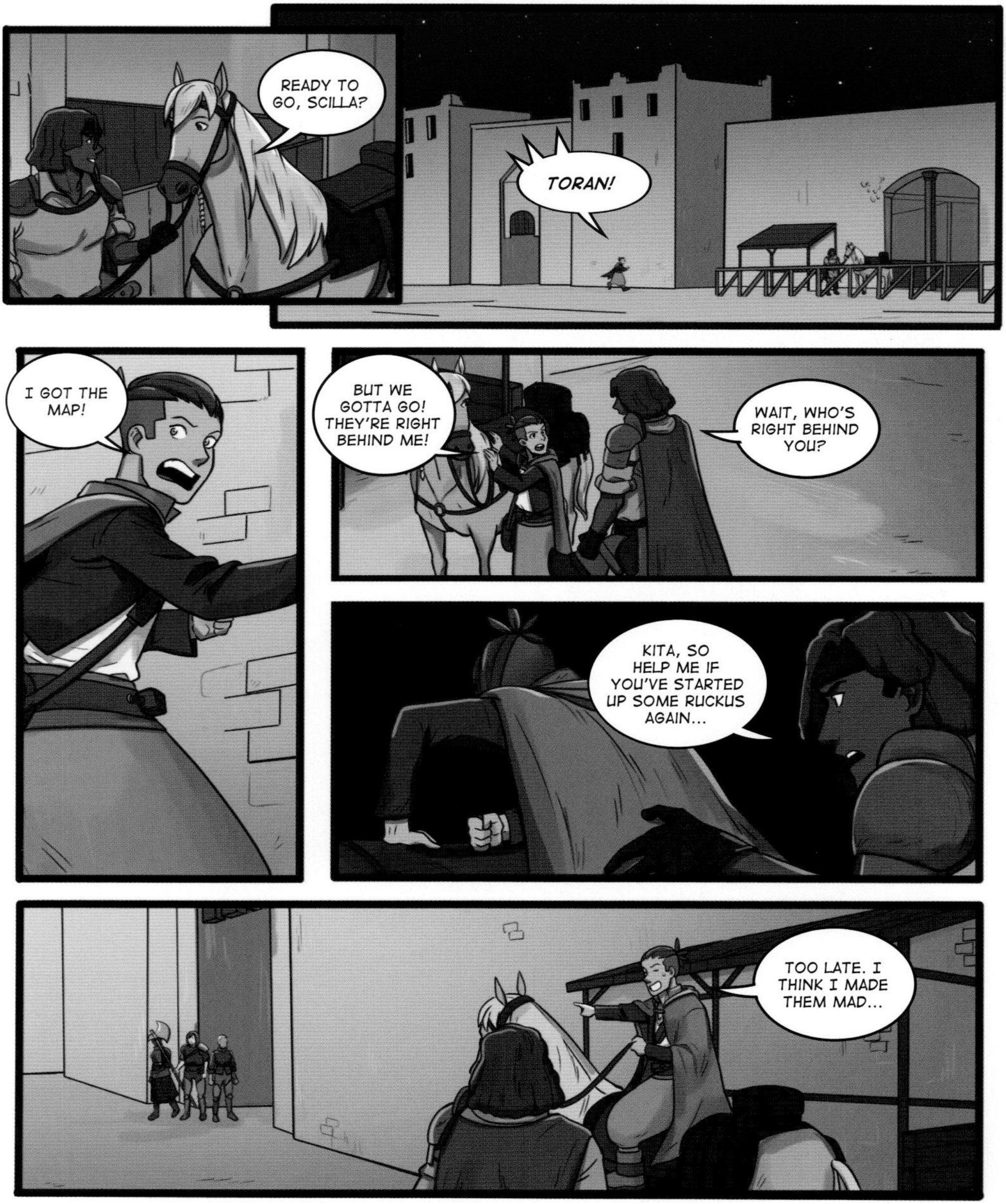
READY TO GO, SCILLA?
TORAN!
I GOT THE MAP!
BUT WE GOTTA GO! THEY'RE RIGHT BEHIND ME!
WAIT, WHO'S RIGHT BEHIND YOU?
KITA, SO HELP ME IF YOU'VE STARTED UP SOME RUCKUS AGAIN...
TOO LATE. I THINK I MADE THEM MAD...

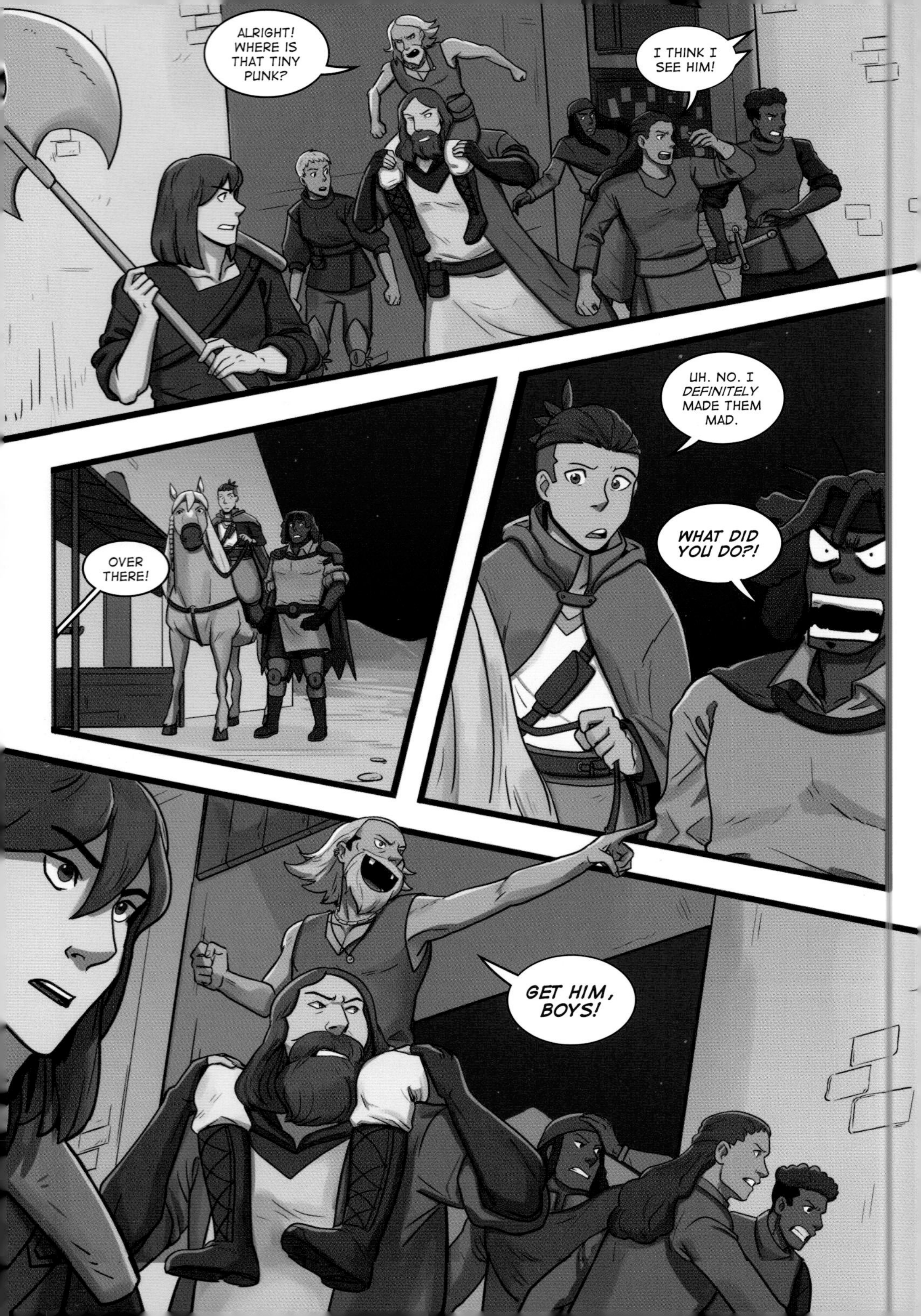
ALRIGHT! WHERE IS THAT TINY PUNK?
I THINK I SEE HIM!
OVER THERE!
UH. NO. I *DEFINITELY* MADE THEM MAD.
WHAT DID YOU DO?!
GET HIM, BOYS!

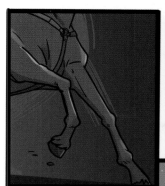

CHAPTER 4:
THE SILHOUETTE OF A MONSTER

HEY—

UM—

HEY, KEEP IT QUIET!

JUST WHERE ARE YOU TAKING US?!

YOU'VE TAKEN EVERYTHING WE HAD! WHAT MORE COULD WE POSSIBLY GIVE YOU?!

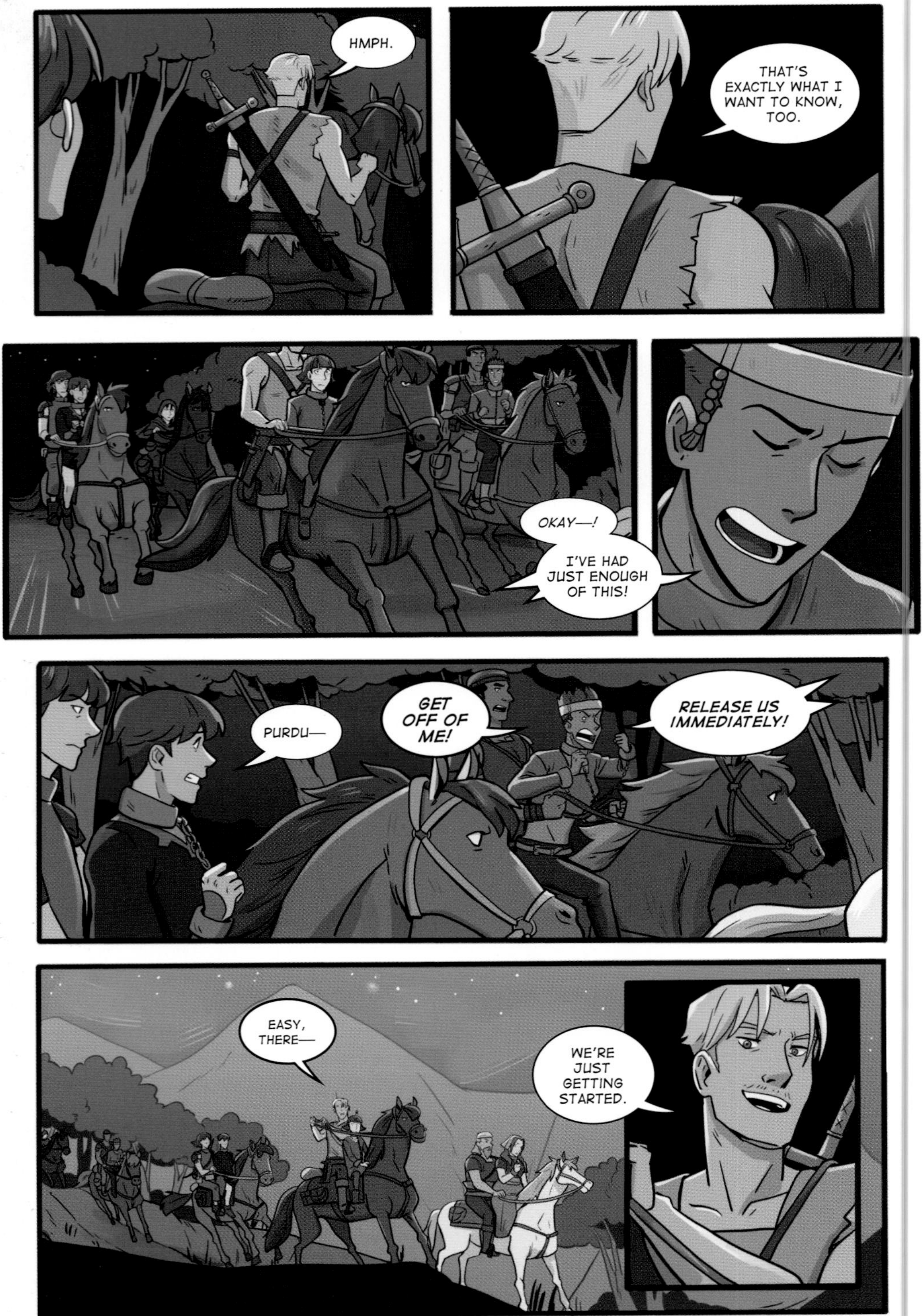
HMPH.
THAT'S EXACTLY WHAT I WANT TO KNOW, TOO.
OKAY—!
I'VE HAD JUST ENOUGH OF THIS!
PURDU—
GET OFF OF ME!
RELEASE US IMMEDIATELY!
EASY, THERE—
WE'RE JUST GETTING STARTED.

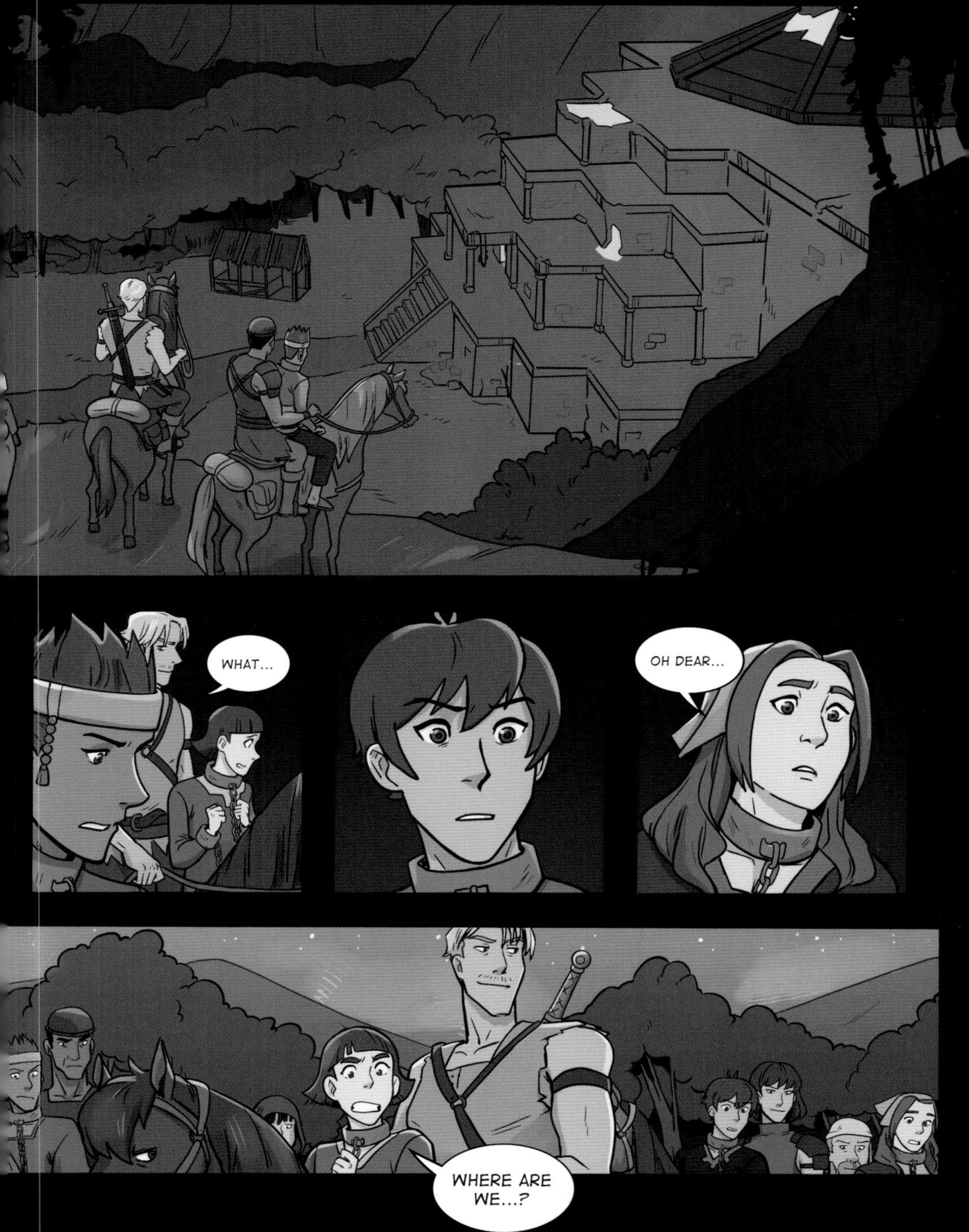
WHAT...
OH DEAR...
WHERE ARE WE...?

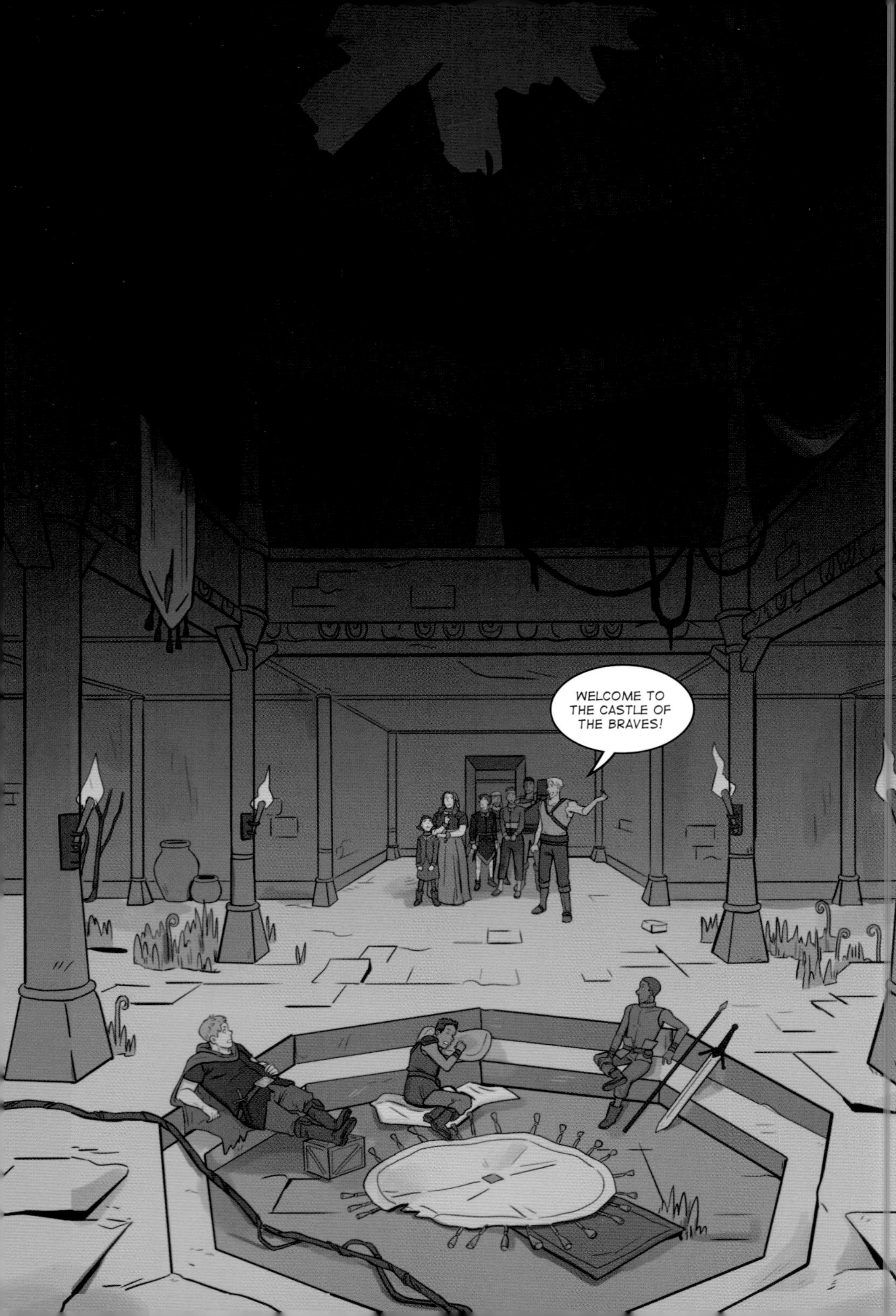
WELCOME TO THE CASTLE OF THE BRAVES!

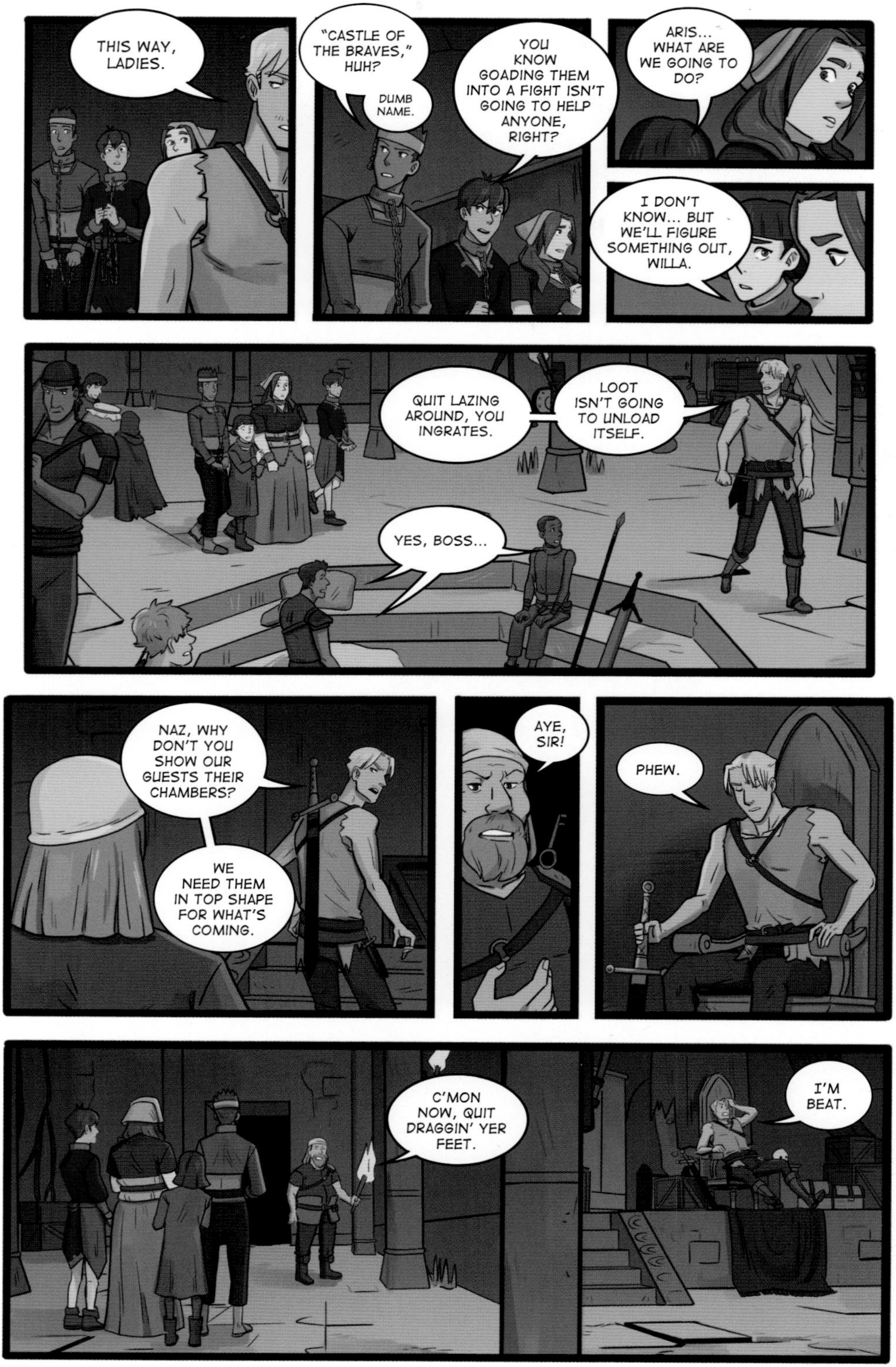
THIS WAY, LADIES.
"CASTLE OF THE BRAVES," HUH?
DUMB NAME.
YOU KNOW GOADING THEM INTO A FIGHT ISN'T GOING TO HELP ANYONE, RIGHT?
ARIS... WHAT ARE WE GOING TO DO?
I DON'T KNOW... BUT WE'LL FIGURE SOMETHING OUT, WILLA.
QUIT LAZING AROUND, YOU INGRATES.
LOOT ISN'T GOING TO UNLOAD ITSELF.
YES, BOSS...
NAZ, WHY DON'T YOU SHOW OUR GUESTS THEIR CHAMBERS?
WE NEED THEM IN TOP SHAPE FOR WHAT'S COMING.
AYE, SIR!
PHEW.
C'MON NOW, QUIT DRAGGIN' YER FEET.
I'M BEAT.

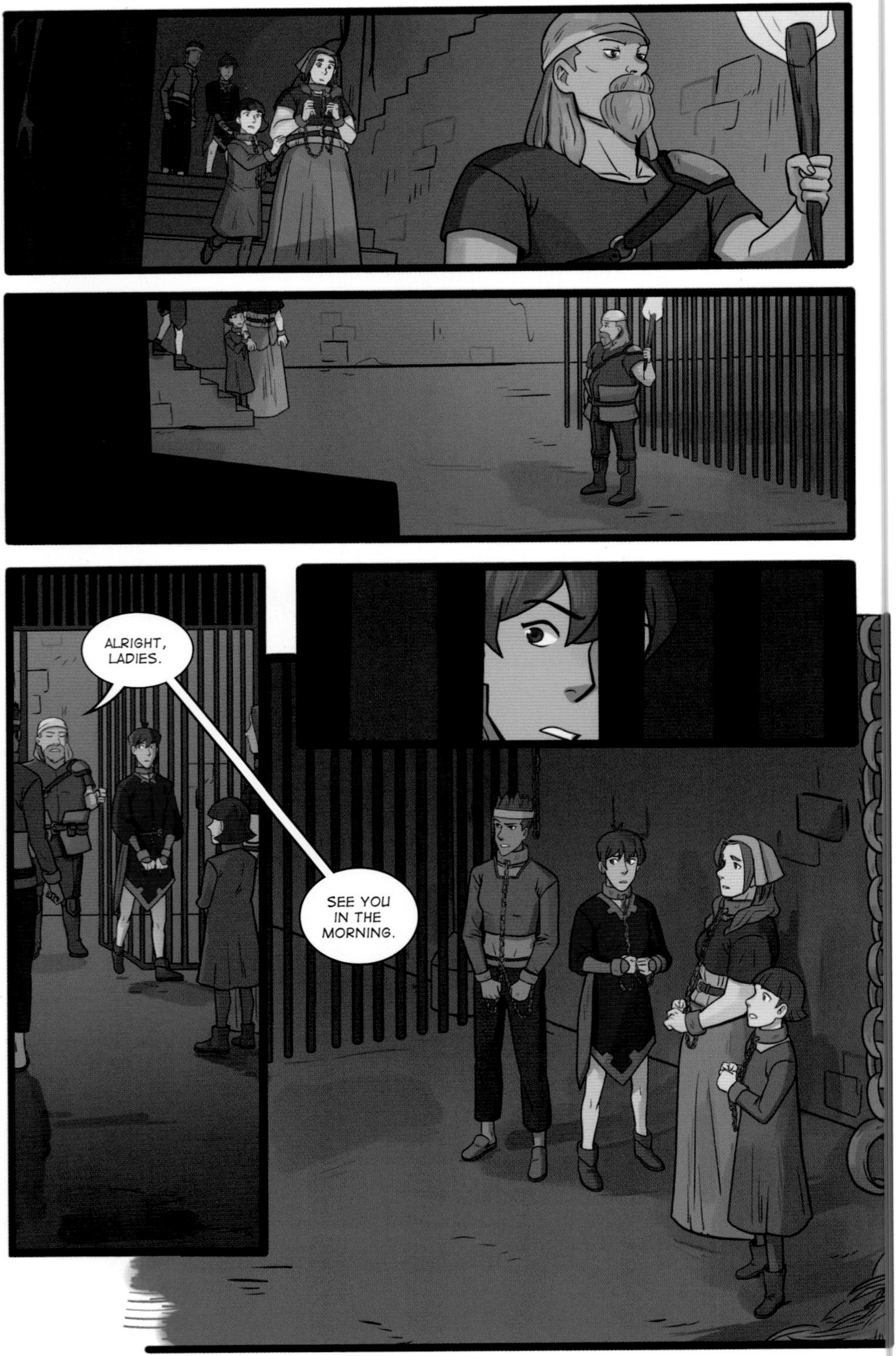
ALRIGHT, LADIES.
SEE YOU IN THE MORNING.

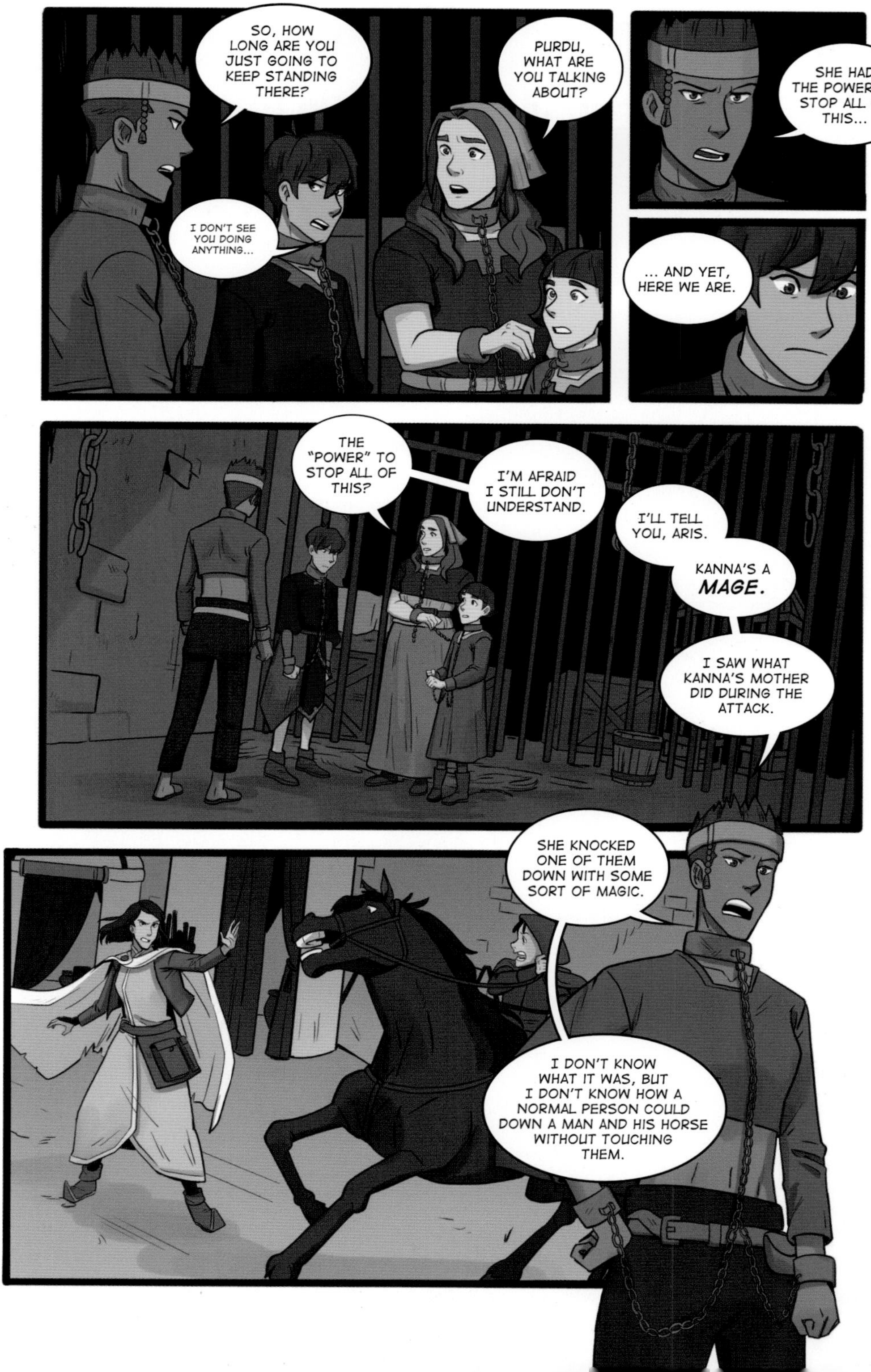
SO, HOW LONG ARE YOU JUST GOING TO KEEP STANDING THERE?
I DON'T SEE YOU DOING ANYTHING...
PURDU, WHAT ARE YOU TALKING ABOUT?
SHE HAD THE POWER TO STOP ALL OF THIS...
... AND YET, HERE WE ARE.
THE "POWER" TO STOP ALL OF THIS?
I'M AFRAID I STILL DON'T UNDERSTAND.
I'LL TELL YOU, ARIS.
KANNA'S A *MAGE.*
I SAW WHAT KANNA'S MOTHER DID DURING THE ATTACK.
SHE KNOCKED ONE OF THEM DOWN WITH SOME SORT OF MAGIC.
I DON'T KNOW WHAT IT WAS, BUT I DON'T KNOW HOW A NORMAL PERSON COULD DOWN A MAN AND HIS HORSE WITHOUT TOUCHING THEM.

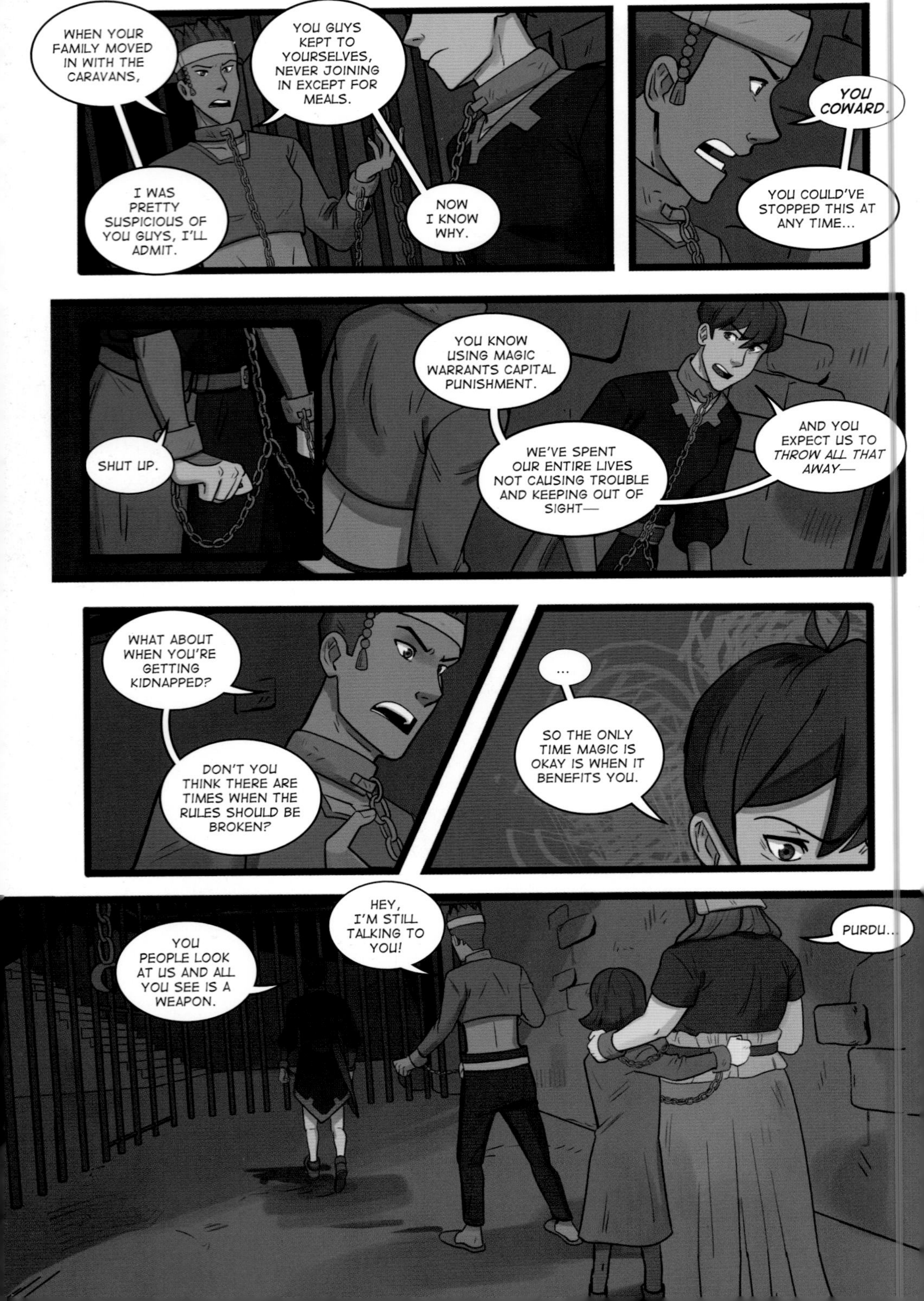
WHEN YOUR FAMILY MOVED IN WITH THE CARAVANS,
I WAS PRETTY SUSPICIOUS OF YOU GUYS, I'LL ADMIT.
YOU GUYS KEPT TO YOURSELVES, NEVER JOINING IN EXCEPT FOR MEALS.
NOW I KNOW WHY.
YOU COWARD.
YOU COULD'VE STOPPED THIS AT ANY TIME...
SHUT UP.
YOU KNOW USING MAGIC WARRANTS CAPITAL PUNISHMENT.
WE'VE SPENT OUR ENTIRE LIVES NOT CAUSING TROUBLE AND KEEPING OUT OF SIGHT—
AND YOU EXPECT US TO THROW ALL THAT AWAY—
WHAT ABOUT WHEN YOU'RE GETTING KIDNAPPED?
DON'T YOU THINK THERE ARE TIMES WHEN THE RULES SHOULD BE BROKEN?
...
SO THE ONLY TIME MAGIC IS OKAY IS WHEN IT BENEFITS YOU.
YOU PEOPLE LOOK AT US AND ALL YOU SEE IS A WEAPON.
HEY, I'M STILL TALKING TO YOU!
PURDU...

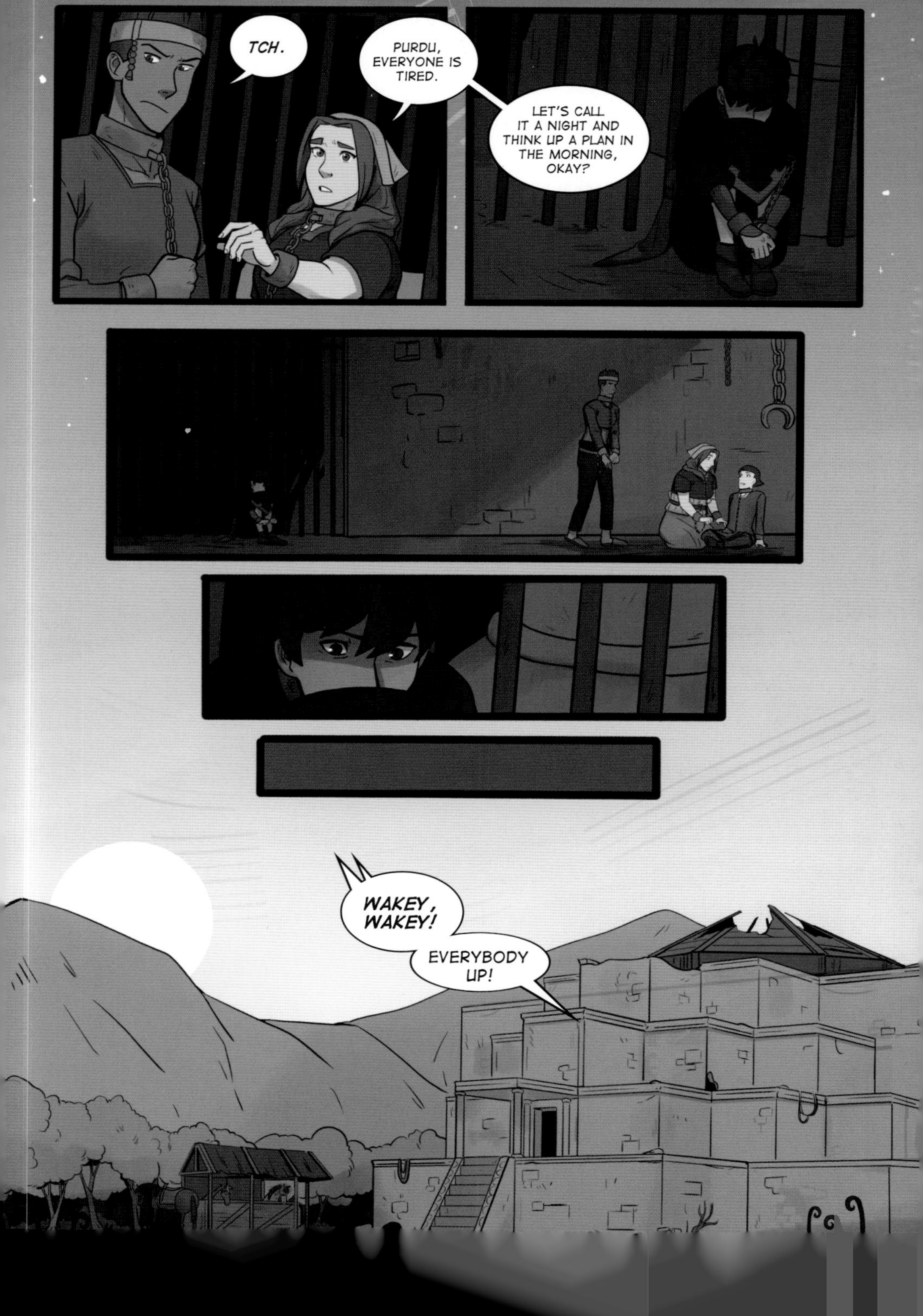
TCH.
PURDU, EVERYONE IS TIRED.
LET'S CALL IT A NIGHT AND THINK UP A PLAN IN THE MORNING, OKAY?
WAKEY, WAKEY!
EVERYBODY UP!

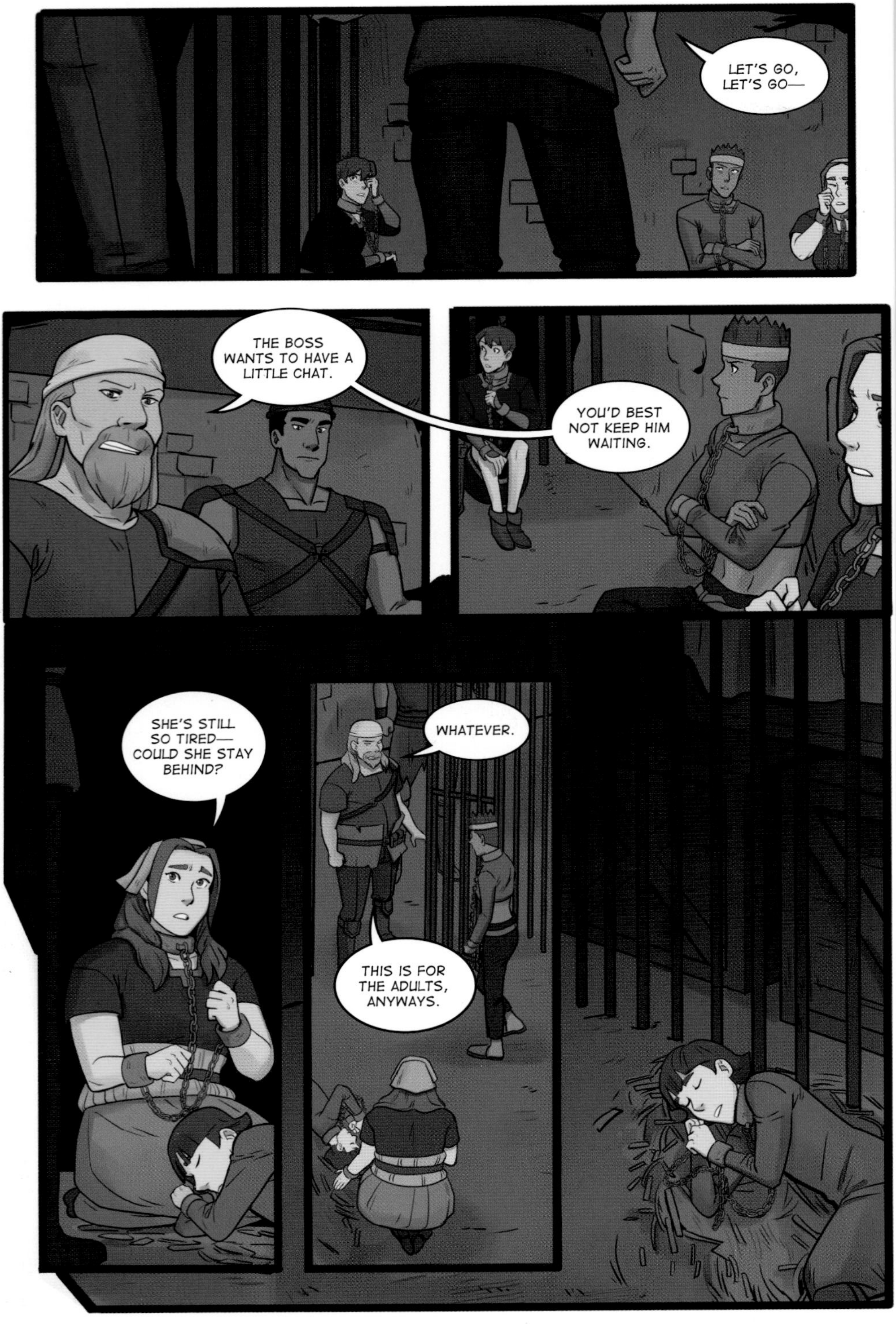
LET'S GO, LET'S GO—
THE BOSS WANTS TO HAVE A LITTLE CHAT.
YOU'D BEST NOT KEEP HIM WAITING.
SHE'S STILL SO TIRED— COULD SHE STAY BEHIND?
WHATEVER.
THIS IS FOR THE ADULTS, ANYWAYS.

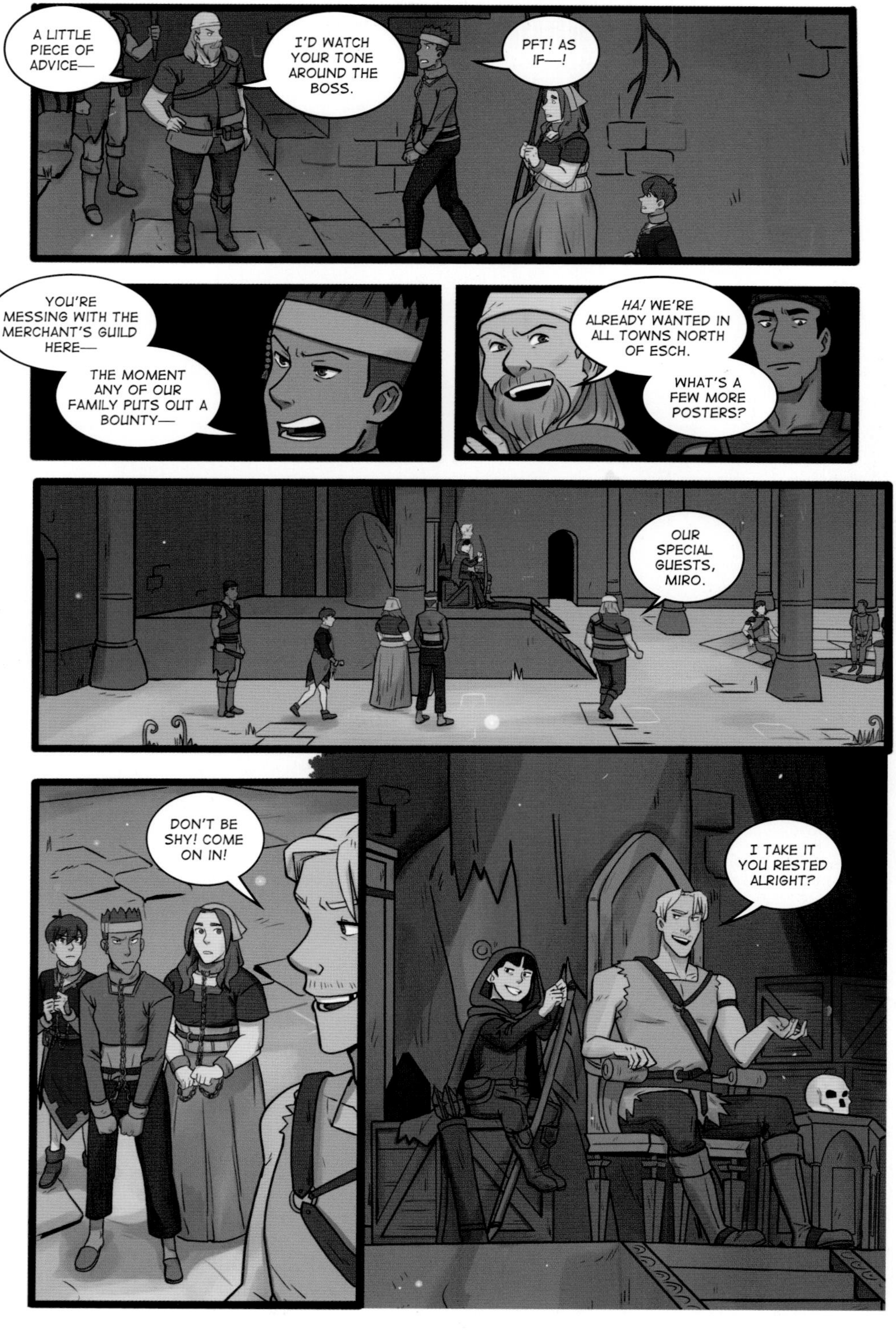
A LITTLE PIECE OF ADVICE—
I'D WATCH YOUR TONE AROUND THE BOSS.
PFT! AS IF—!
YOU'RE MESSING WITH THE MERCHANT'S GUILD HERE—
THE MOMENT ANY OF OUR FAMILY PUTS OUT A BOUNTY—
HA! WE'RE ALREADY WANTED IN ALL TOWNS NORTH OF ESCH.
WHAT'S A FEW MORE POSTERS?
OUR SPECIAL GUESTS, MIRO.
DON'T BE SHY! COME ON IN!
I TAKE IT YOU RESTED ALRIGHT?

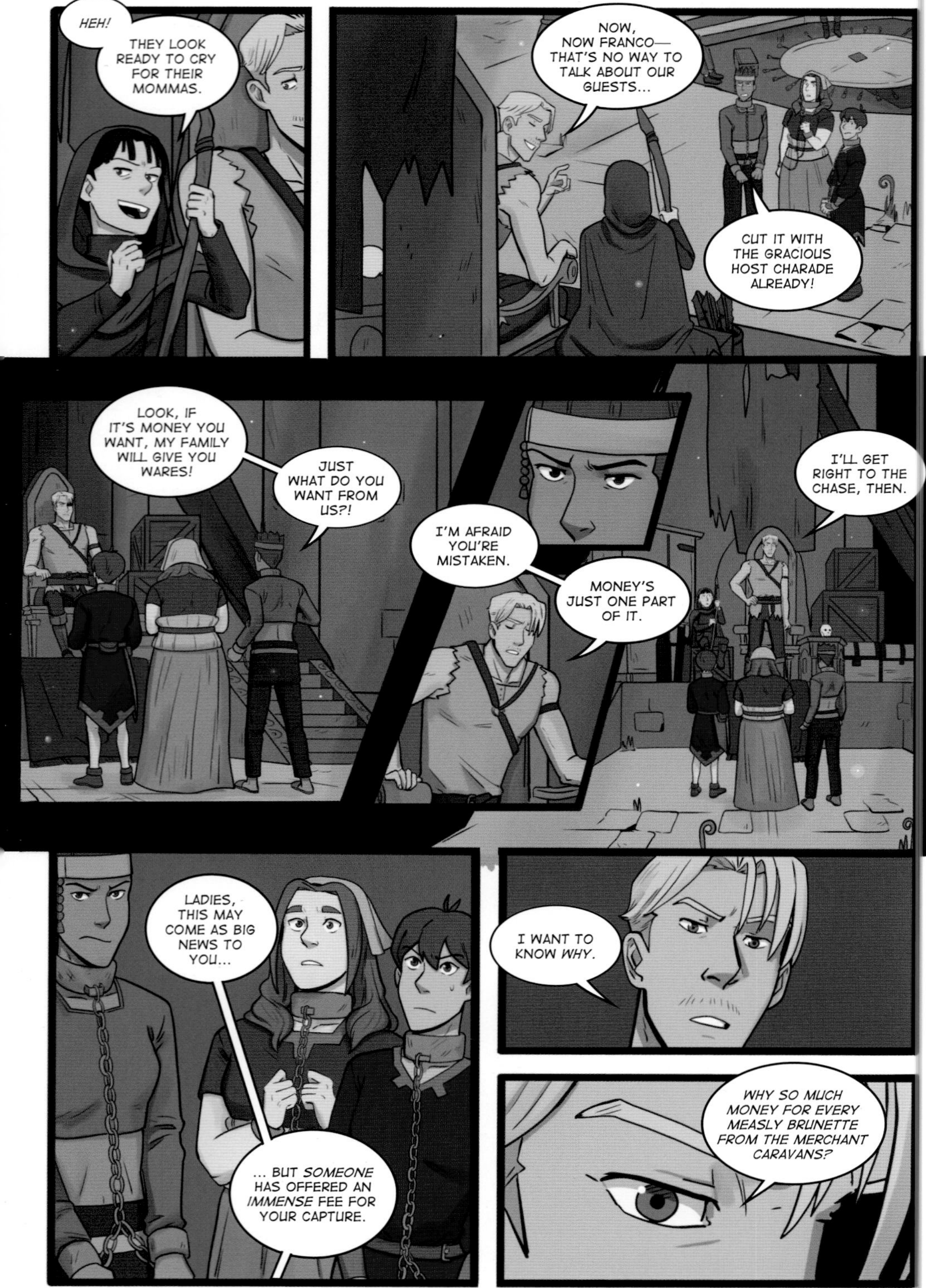
HEH!
THEY LOOK READY TO CRY FOR THEIR MOMMAS.
NOW, NOW FRANCO— THAT'S NO WAY TO TALK ABOUT OUR GUESTS...
CUT IT WITH THE GRACIOUS HOST CHARADE ALREADY!
LOOK, IF IT'S MONEY YOU WANT, MY FAMILY WILL GIVE YOU WARES!
JUST WHAT DO YOU WANT FROM US?!
I'M AFRAID YOU'RE MISTAKEN.
MONEY'S JUST ONE PART OF IT.
I'LL GET RIGHT TO THE CHASE, THEN.
LADIES, THIS MAY COME AS BIG NEWS TO YOU...
... BUT SOMEONE HAS OFFERED AN IMMENSE FEE FOR YOUR CAPTURE.
I WANT TO KNOW WHY.
WHY SO MUCH MONEY FOR EVERY MEASLY BRUNETTE FROM THE MERCHANT CARAVANS?

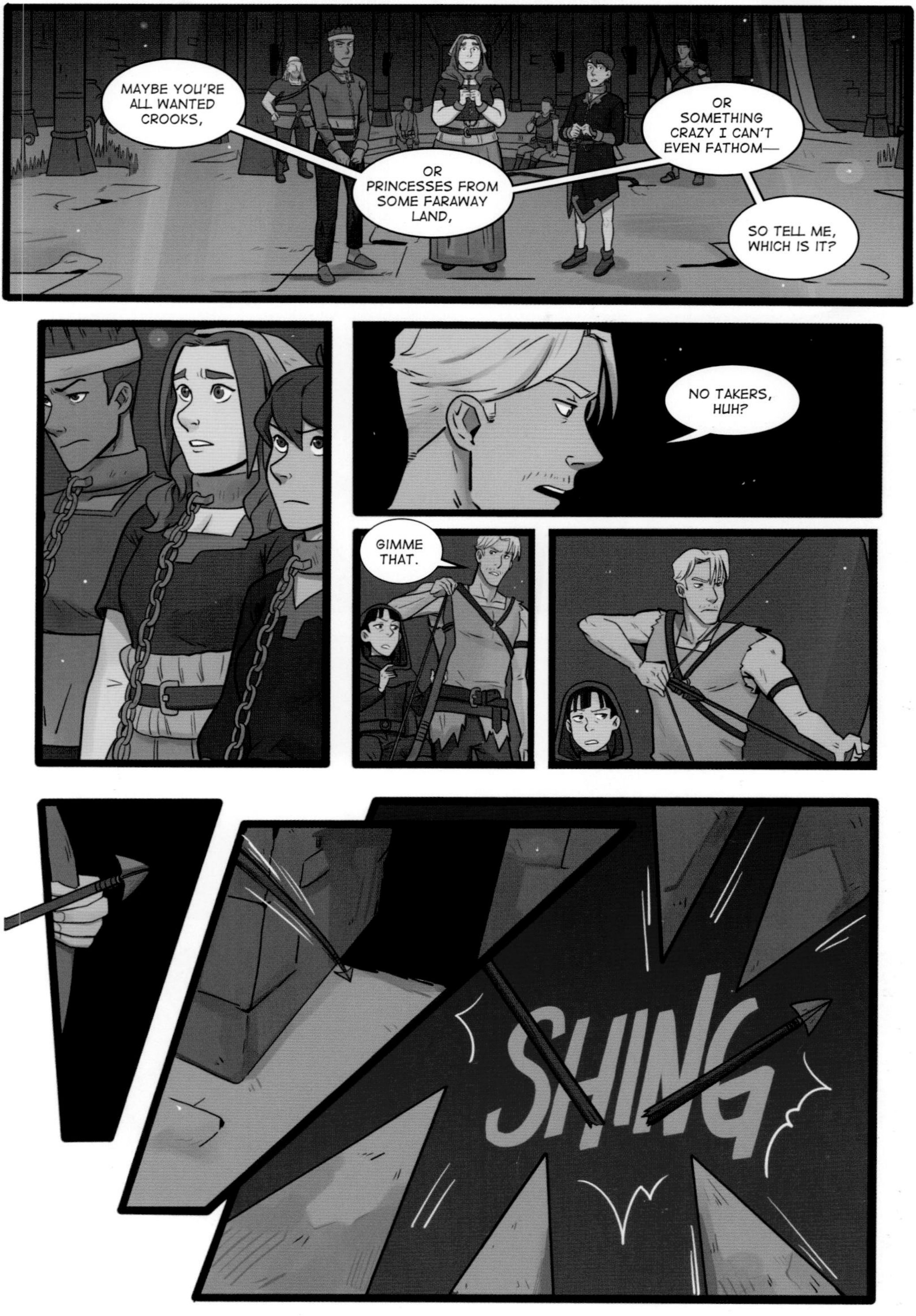
MAYBE YOU'RE ALL WANTED CROOKS,
OR PRINCESSES FROM SOME FARAWAY LAND,
OR SOMETHING CRAZY I CAN'T EVEN FATHOM—
SO TELL ME, WHICH IS IT?
NO TAKERS, HUH?
GIMME THAT.
SHING

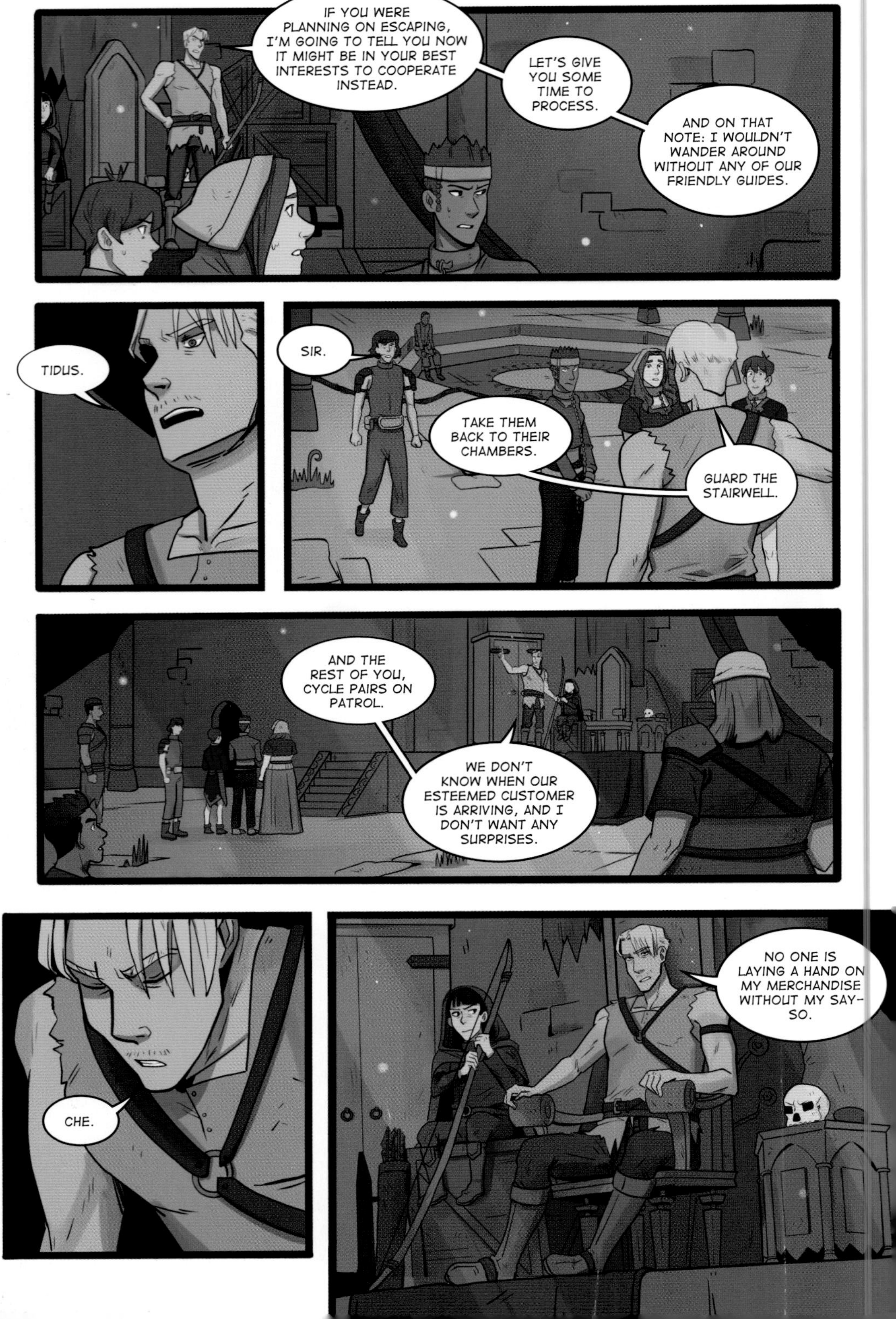
IF YOU WERE PLANNING ON ESCAPING, I'M GOING TO TELL YOU NOW IT MIGHT BE IN YOUR BEST INTERESTS TO COOPERATE INSTEAD.
LET'S GIVE YOU SOME TIME TO PROCESS.
AND ON THAT NOTE: I WOULDN'T WANDER AROUND WITHOUT ANY OF OUR FRIENDLY GUIDES.
TIDUS.
SIR.
TAKE THEM BACK TO THEIR CHAMBERS.
GUARD THE STAIRWELL.
AND THE REST OF YOU, CYCLE PAIRS ON PATROL.
WE DON'T KNOW WHEN OUR ESTEEMED CUSTOMER IS ARRIVING, AND I DON'T WANT ANY SURPRISES.
CHE.
NO ONE IS LAYING A HAND ON MY MERCHANDISE WITHOUT MY SAY-SO.

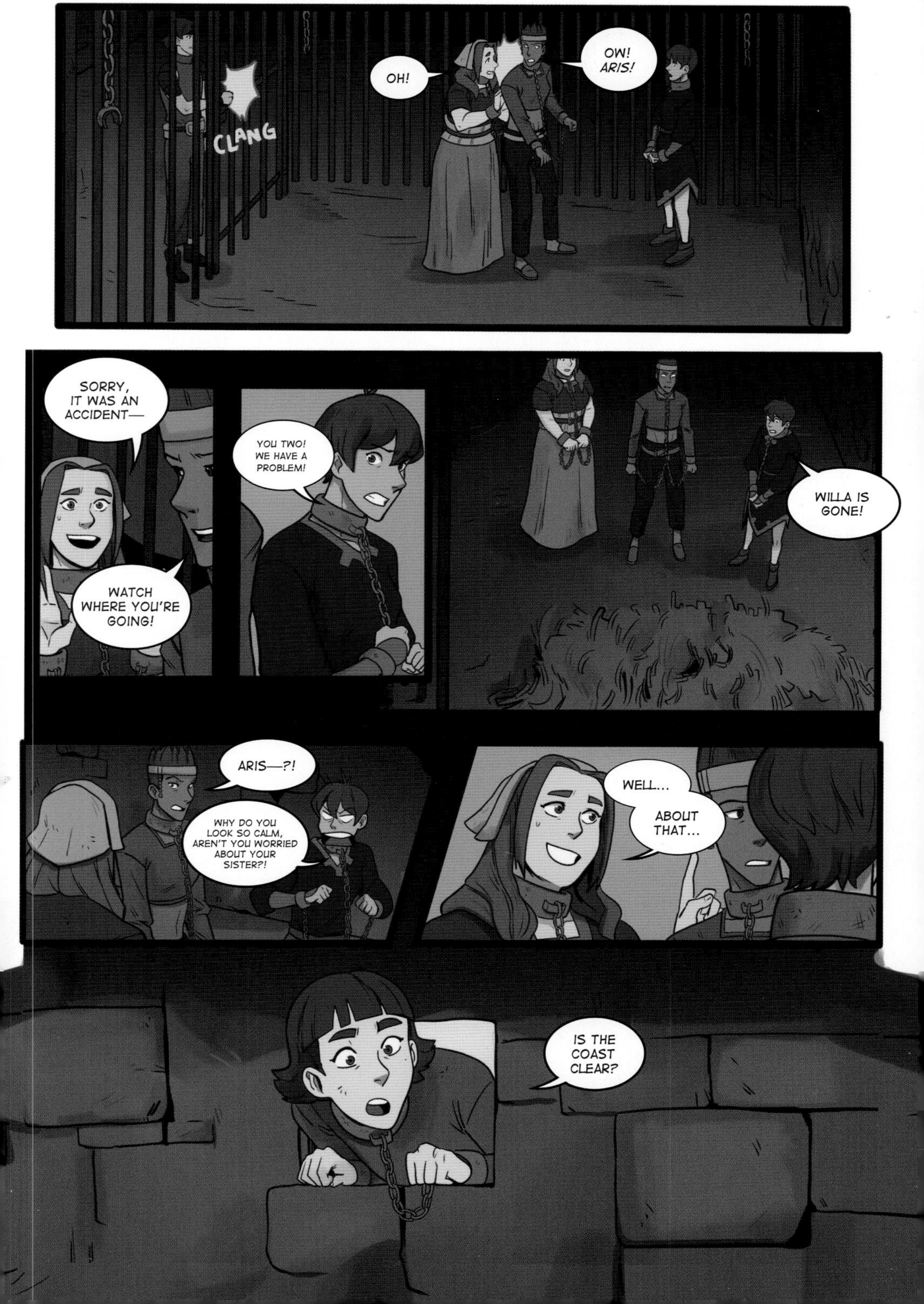
CLANG
OH!
OW! ARIS!
SORRY, IT WAS AN ACCIDENT—
WATCH WHERE YOU'RE GOING!
YOU TWO! WE HAVE A PROBLEM!
WILLA IS GONE!
ARIS—?!
WHY DO YOU LOOK SO CALM, AREN'T YOU WORRIED ABOUT YOUR SISTER?!
WELL...
ABOUT THAT...
IS THE COAST CLEAR?

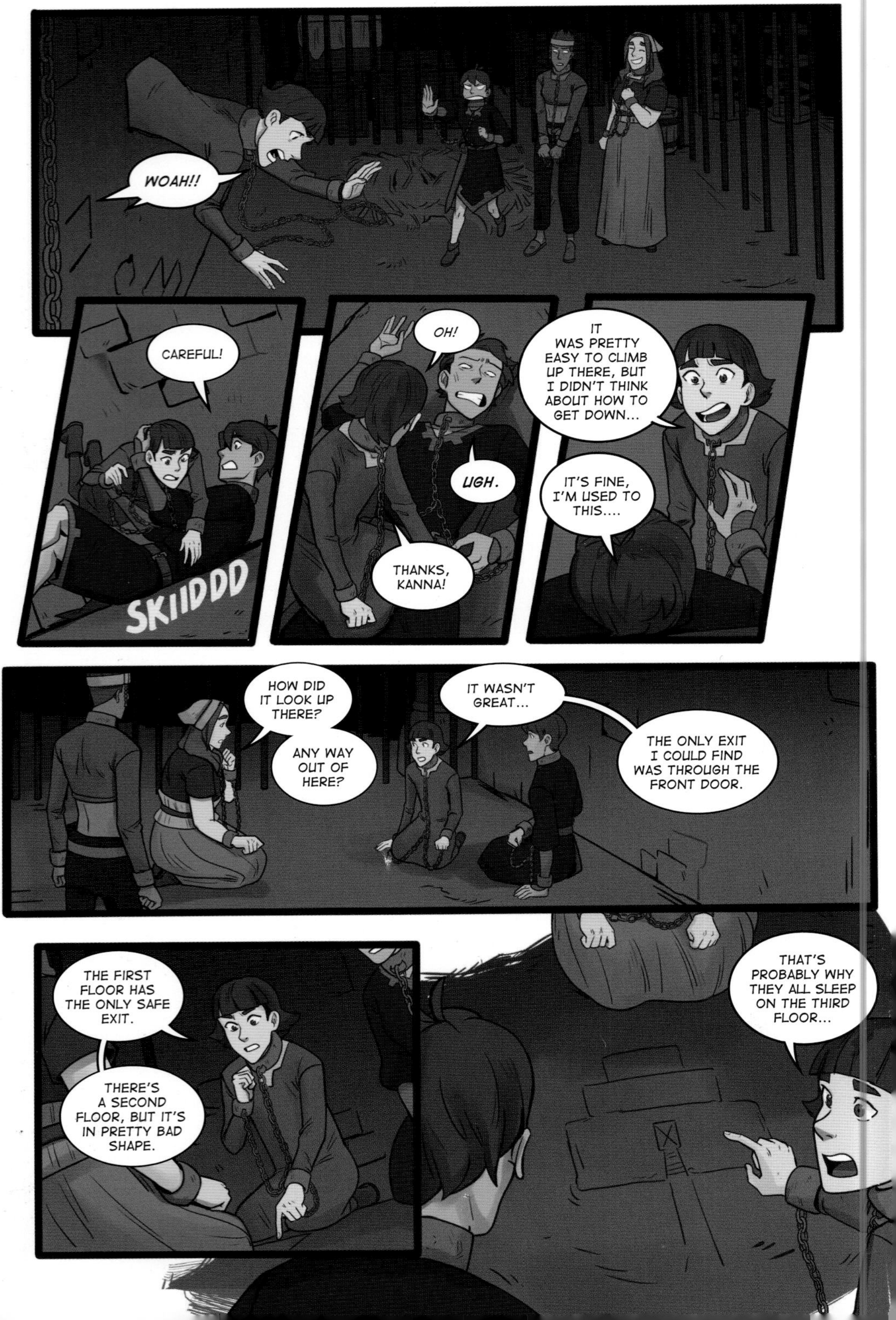
WOAH!!
CAREFUL!
SKIIDDD
OH!
UGH.
THANKS, KANNA!
IT WAS PRETTY EASY TO CLIMB UP THERE, BUT I DIDN'T THINK ABOUT HOW TO GET DOWN...
IT'S FINE, I'M USED TO THIS....
HOW DID IT LOOK UP THERE?
ANY WAY OUT OF HERE?
IT WASN'T GREAT...
THE ONLY EXIT I COULD FIND WAS THROUGH THE FRONT DOOR.
THE FIRST FLOOR HAS THE ONLY SAFE EXIT.
THERE'S A SECOND FLOOR, BUT IT'S IN PRETTY BAD SHAPE.
THAT'S PROBABLY WHY THEY ALL SLEEP ON THE THIRD FLOOR...

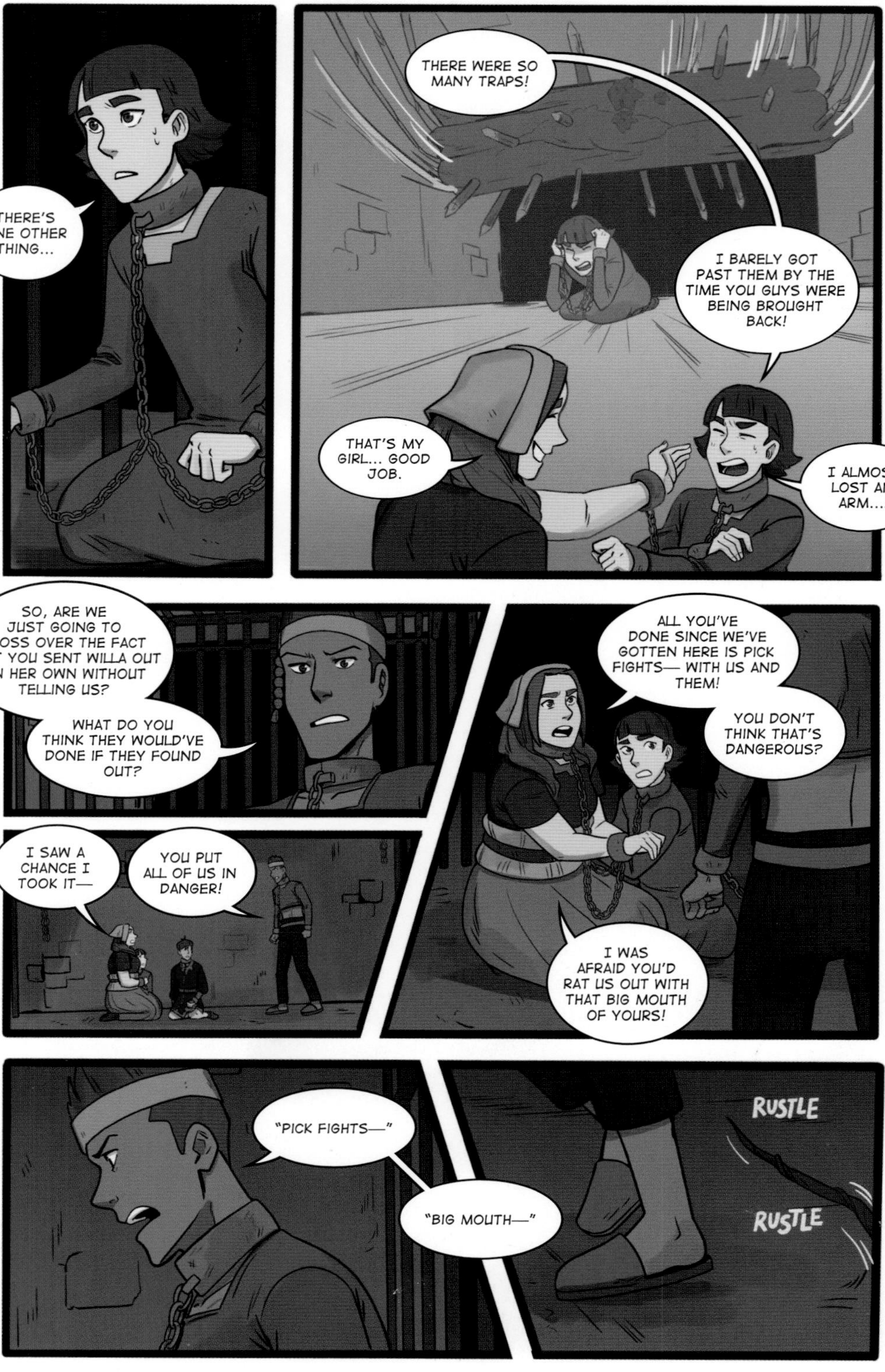
THERE'S ONE OTHER THING...
THERE WERE SO MANY TRAPS!
I BARELY GOT PAST THEM BY THE TIME YOU GUYS WERE BEING BROUGHT BACK!
THAT'S MY GIRL... GOOD JOB.
I ALMOST LOST AN ARM...!
SO, ARE WE JUST GOING TO GLOSS OVER THE FACT THAT YOU SENT WILLA OUT ON HER OWN WITHOUT TELLING US?
WHAT DO YOU THINK THEY WOULD'VE DONE IF THEY FOUND OUT?
I SAW A CHANCE I TOOK IT—
YOU PUT ALL OF US IN DANGER!
ALL YOU'VE DONE SINCE WE'VE GOTTEN HERE IS PICK FIGHTS— WITH US AND THEM!
YOU DON'T THINK THAT'S DANGEROUS?
I WAS AFRAID YOU'D RAT US OUT WITH THAT BIG MOUTH OF YOURS!
"PICK FIGHTS—"
"BIG MOUTH—"
RUSTLE
RUSTLE

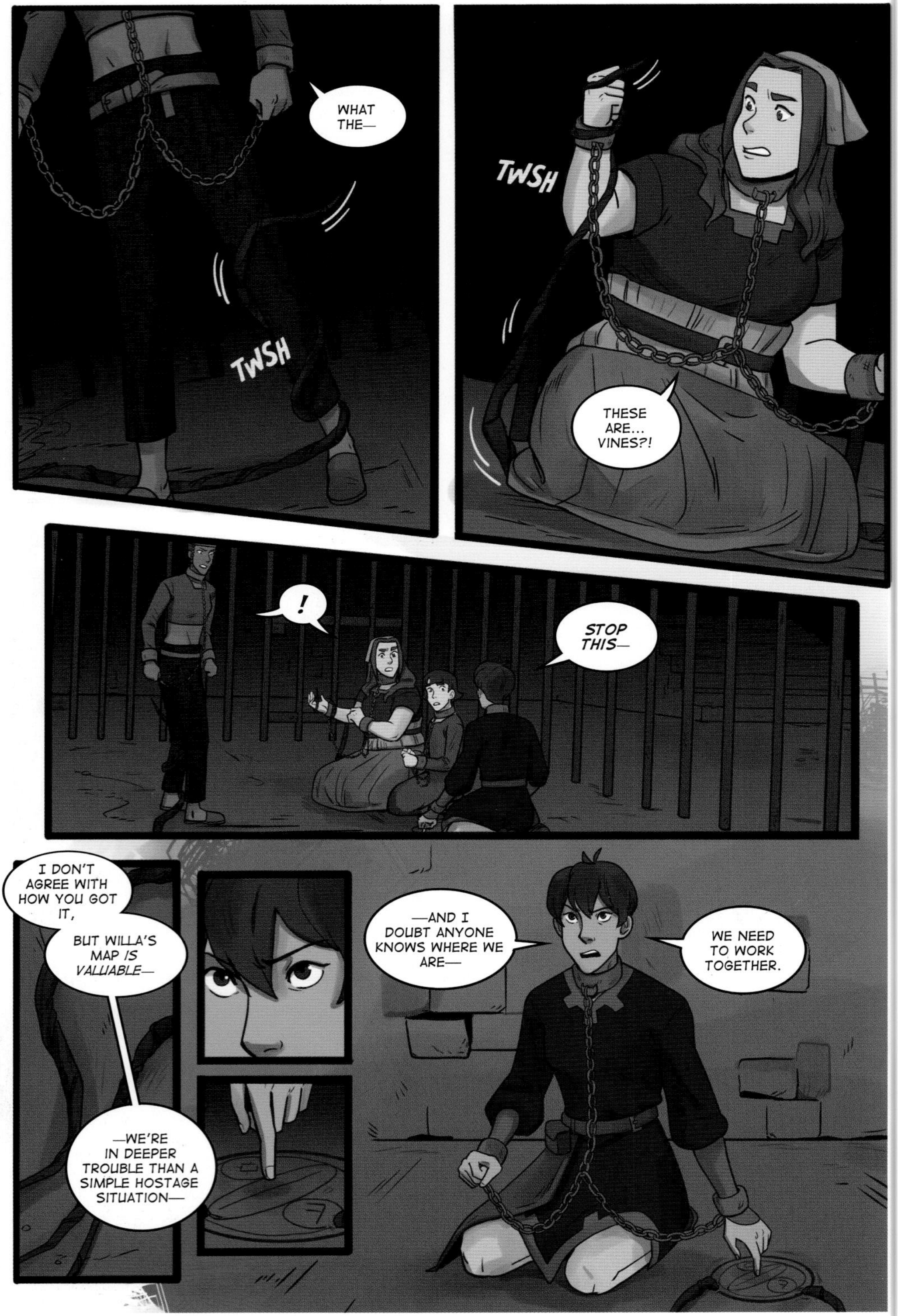
WHAT THE—
TWSH
TWSH
THESE ARE... VINES?!
!
STOP THIS—
I DON'T AGREE WITH HOW YOU GOT IT,
BUT WILLA'S MAP *IS* *VALUABLE*—
—WE'RE IN DEEPER TROUBLE THAN A SIMPLE HOSTAGE SITUATION—
—AND I DOUBT ANYONE KNOWS WHERE WE ARE—
WE NEED TO WORK TOGETHER.

HEY! GIRLS! KEEP IT DOWN IN THERE, WOULD YA?

M' TRYING TO RELAX UP HERE!

UGH.

GIRLS ARE STUPID.

THAT'S NOT VERY NICE NOW, IS IT?

SIGH.

I'M AFRAID WE DON'T HAVE MUCH TIME BEFORE WE'RE EITHER SOLD TO SOME CREEP OR WHO KNOWS WHAT ELSE.

EITHER WE WORK TOGETHER OR ACCEPT OUR FATE.

WHAT'S IT GOING TO BE?

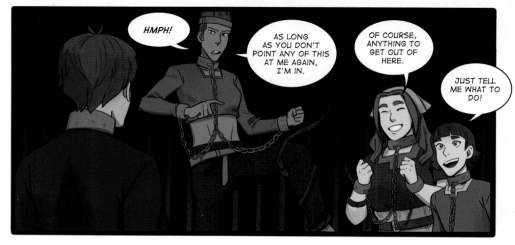

HMPH!

AS LONG AS YOU DON'T POINT ANY OF THIS AT ME AGAIN, I'M IN.

OF COURSE, ANYTHING TO GET OUT OF HERE.

JUST TELL ME WHAT TO DO!

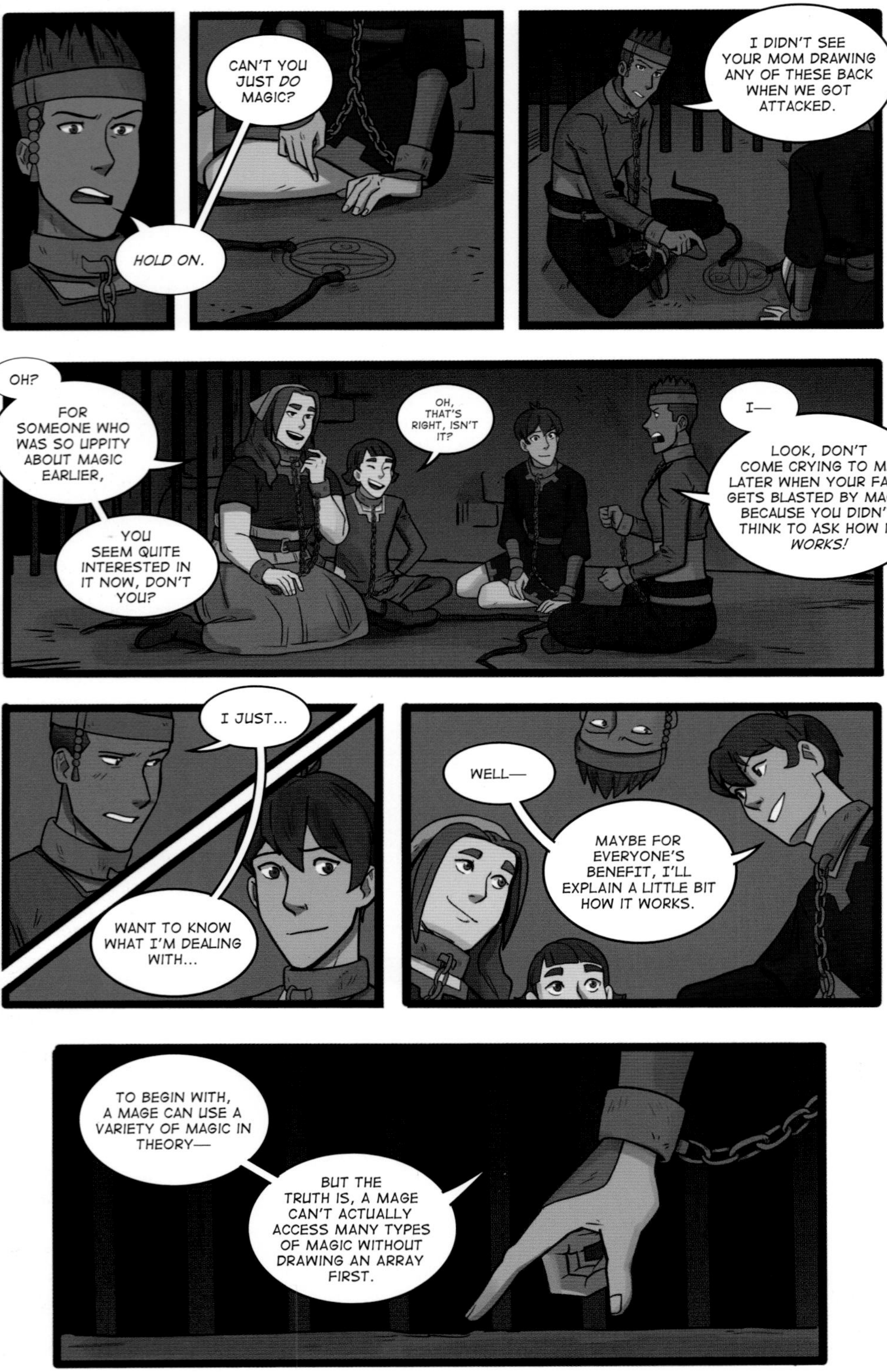
CAN'T YOU JUST DO MAGIC?
HOLD ON.
I DIDN'T SEE YOUR MOM DRAWING ANY OF THESE BACK WHEN WE GOT ATTACKED.
OH?
FOR SOMEONE WHO WAS SO UPPITY ABOUT MAGIC EARLIER,
YOU SEEM QUITE INTERESTED IN IT NOW, DON'T YOU?
OH, THAT'S RIGHT, ISN'T IT?
I—
LOOK, DON'T COME CRYING TO ME LATER WHEN YOUR FACE GETS BLASTED BY MAGIC BECAUSE YOU DIDN'T THINK TO ASK HOW IT WORKS!
I JUST...
WANT TO KNOW WHAT I'M DEALING WITH...
WELL—
MAYBE FOR EVERYONE'S BENEFIT, I'LL EXPLAIN A LITTLE BIT HOW IT WORKS.
TO BEGIN WITH, A MAGE CAN USE A VARIETY OF MAGIC IN THEORY—
BUT THE TRUTH IS, A MAGE CAN'T ACTUALLY ACCESS MANY TYPES OF MAGIC WITHOUT DRAWING AN ARRAY FIRST.

THAT'S DIFFERENT FOR *INHERITED MAGIC.*

MAGIC YOU'VE INHERITED FROM YOUR PREDECESSORS DOESN'T NEED ARRAYS—

IT'S THE SORT OF MAGIC MOST MAGES RELY ON, ESPECIALLY IN A PINCH.

THE SECOND TYPE OF MAGIC IS INNATE MAGIC, THAT WHICH YOU HAVE A NATURAL AFFINITY FOR.

IT TAKES A LOT OF TRIAL AND ERROR TO FIND YOUR AFFINITY, ON TOP OF HAVING TO DRAW AN ARRAY FOR IT.

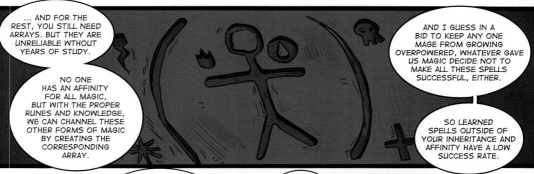

... AND FOR THE REST, YOU STILL NEED ARRAYS. BUT THEY ARE UNRELIABLE WITHOUT YEARS OF STUDY.

NO ONE HAS AN AFFINITY FOR ALL MAGIC, BUT WITH THE PROPER RUNES AND KNOWLEDGE, WE CAN CHANNEL THESE OTHER FORMS OF MAGIC BY CREATING THE CORRESPONDING ARRAY.

AND I GUESS IN A BID TO KEEP ANY ONE MAGE FROM GROWING OVERPOWERED, WHATEVER GAVE US MAGIC DECIDE NOT TO MAKE ALL THESE SPELLS SUCCESSFUL, EITHER.

SO LEARNED SPELLS OUTSIDE OF YOUR INHERITANCE AND AFFINITY HAVE A LOW SUCCESS RATE.

SO IF YOUR MOM WASN'T USING DRAWINGS FOR HER SPELL BACK AT THE ATTACK...

YOU'RE A FAMILY OF WIND MAGES?

ACTUALLY—

HEY, I GOT IT! S'NOT SO HARD!

I DON'T KNOW WHAT ANY OF THEM MEAN, BUT...

OH, SORRY... AM I NOT ALLOWED TO COPY IT?

NO, I JUST...

KANNA...?

WAIT!

I'VE GOT IT!

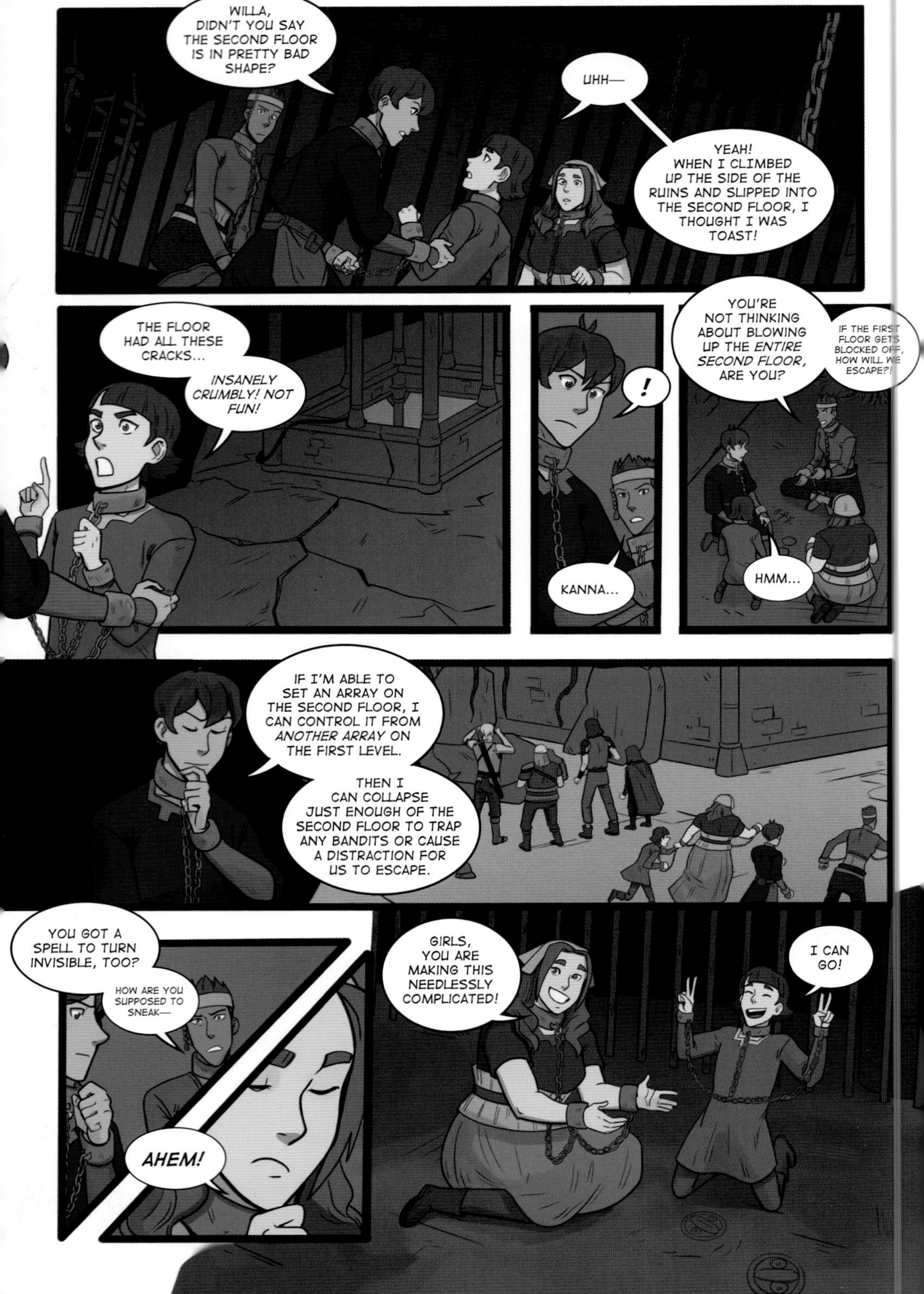
WILLA, DIDN'T YOU SAY THE SECOND FLOOR IS IN PRETTY BAD SHAPE?
UHH—
YEAH! WHEN I CLIMBED UP THE SIDE OF THE RUINS AND SLIPPED INTO THE SECOND FLOOR, I THOUGHT I WAS TOAST!
THE FLOOR HAD ALL THESE CRACKS...
INSANELY CRUMBLY! NOT FUN!
!
KANNA...
YOU'RE NOT THINKING ABOUT BLOWING UP THE ENTIRE SECOND FLOOR, ARE YOU?
IF THE FIRST FLOOR GETS BLOCKED OFF, HOW WILL WE ESCAPE?!
HMM...
IF I'M ABLE TO SET AN ARRAY ON THE SECOND FLOOR, I CAN CONTROL IT FROM ANOTHER ARRAY ON THE FIRST LEVEL.
THEN I CAN COLLAPSE JUST ENOUGH OF THE SECOND FLOOR TO TRAP ANY BANDITS OR CAUSE A DISTRACTION FOR US TO ESCAPE.
YOU GOT A SPELL TO TURN INVISIBLE, TOO?
HOW ARE YOU SUPPOSED TO SNEAK—
AHEM!
GIRLS, YOU ARE MAKING THIS NEEDLESSLY COMPLICATED!
I CAN GO!

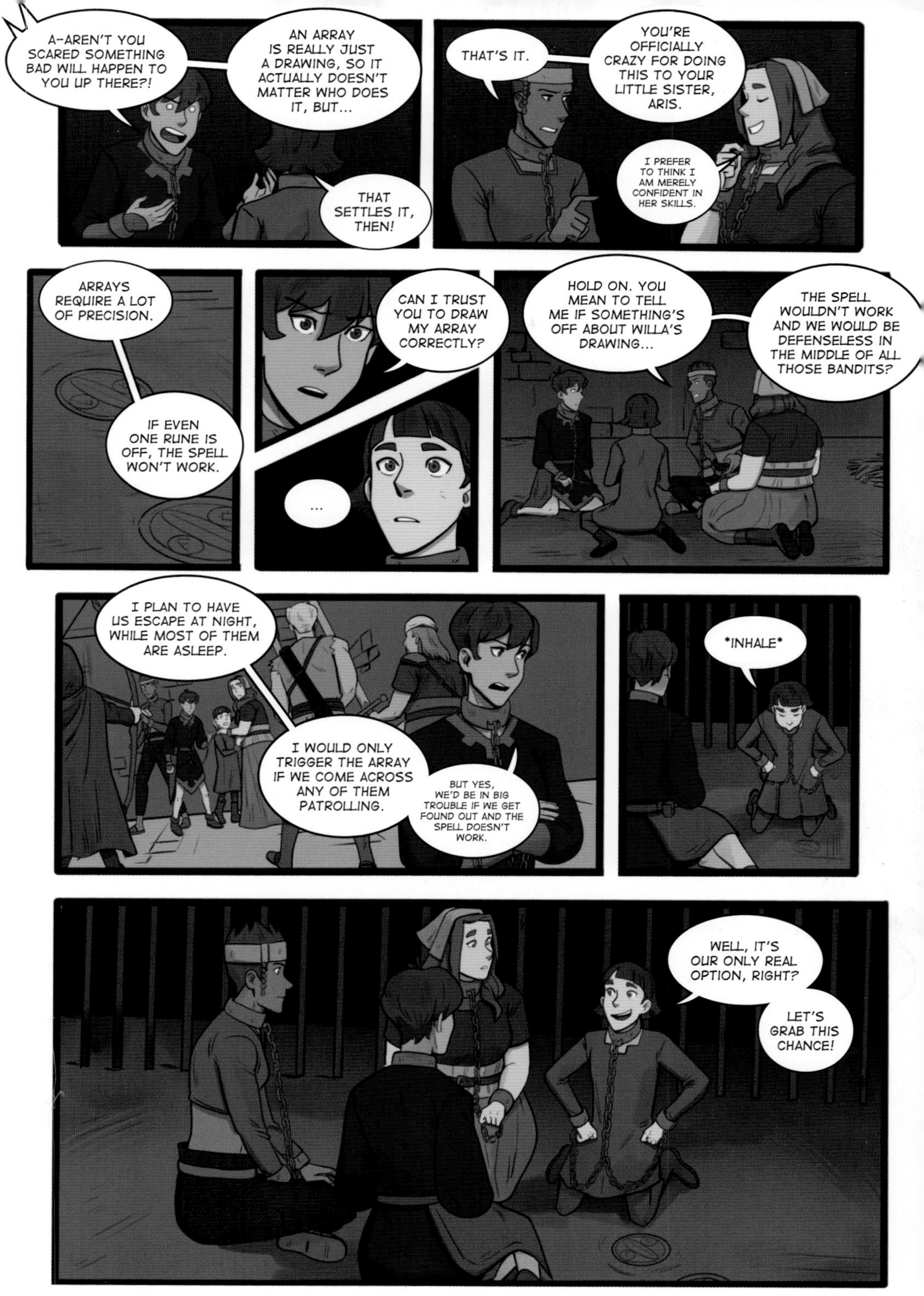
A-AREN'T YOU SCARED SOMETHING BAD WILL HAPPEN TO YOU UP THERE?!
AN ARRAY IS REALLY JUST A DRAWING, SO IT ACTUALLY DOESN'T MATTER WHO DOES IT, BUT...
THAT SETTLES IT, THEN!
THAT'S IT.
YOU'RE OFFICIALLY CRAZY FOR DOING THIS TO YOUR LITTLE SISTER, ARIS.
I PREFER TO THINK I AM MERELY CONFIDENT IN HER SKILLS.
ARRAYS REQUIRE A LOT OF PRECISION.
IF EVEN ONE RUNE IS OFF, THE SPELL WON'T WORK.
CAN I TRUST YOU TO DRAW MY ARRAY CORRECTLY?
...
HOLD ON. YOU MEAN TO TELL ME IF SOMETHING'S OFF ABOUT WILLA'S DRAWING...
THE SPELL WOULDN'T WORK AND WE WOULD BE DEFENSELESS IN THE MIDDLE OF ALL THOSE BANDITS?
I PLAN TO HAVE US ESCAPE AT NIGHT, WHILE MOST OF THEM ARE ASLEEP.
I WOULD ONLY TRIGGER THE ARRAY IF WE COME ACROSS ANY OF THEM PATROLLING.
BUT YES, WE'D BE IN BIG TROUBLE IF WE GET FOUND OUT AND THE SPELL DOESN'T WORK.
INHALE
WELL, IT'S OUR ONLY REAL OPTION, RIGHT?
LET'S GRAB THIS CHANCE!

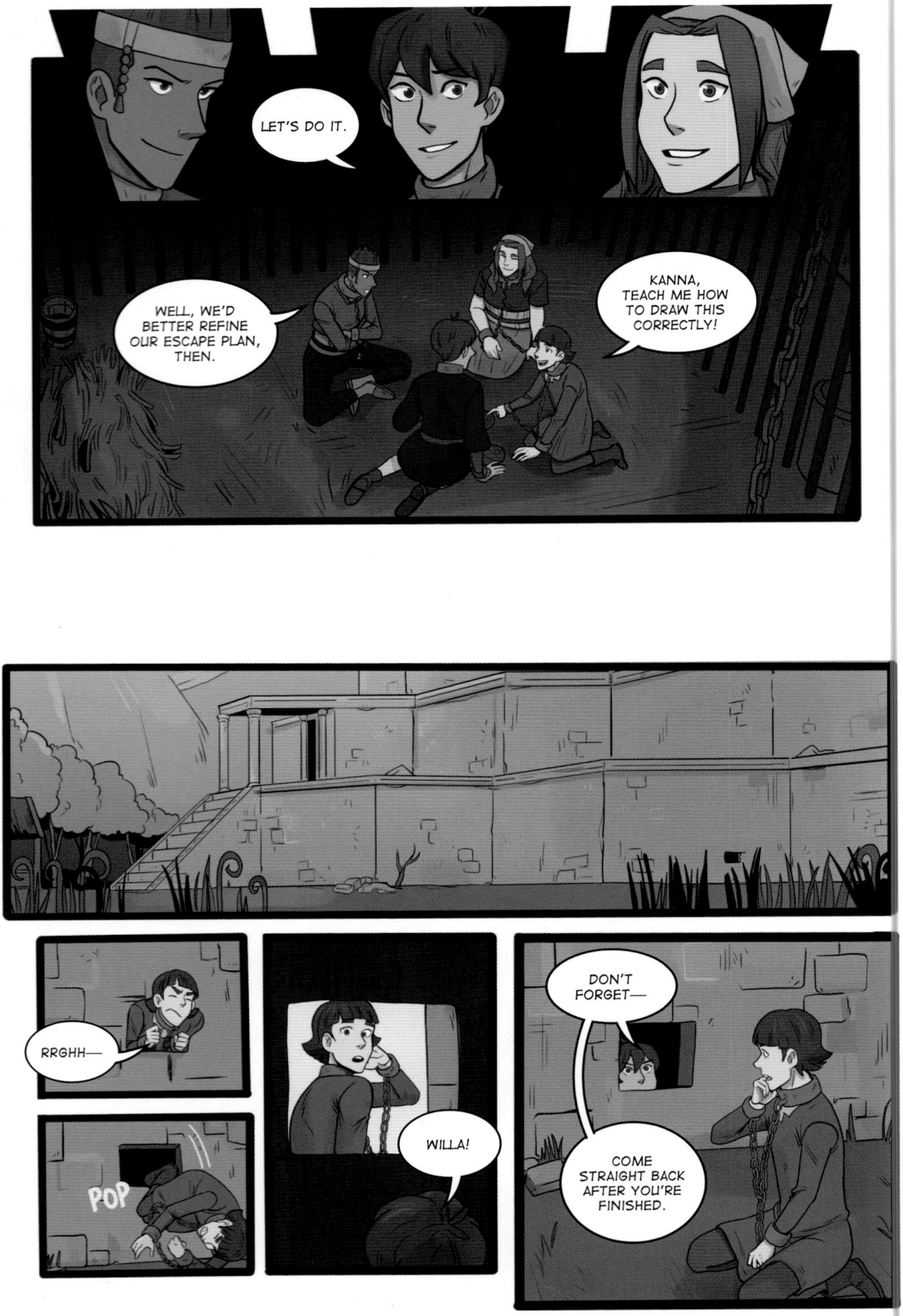
LET'S DO IT.
WELL, WE'D BETTER REFINE OUR ESCAPE PLAN, THEN.
KANNA, TEACH ME HOW TO DRAW THIS CORRECTLY!
RRGHH—
POP
WILLA!
DON'T FORGET—
COME STRAIGHT BACK AFTER YOU'RE FINISHED.

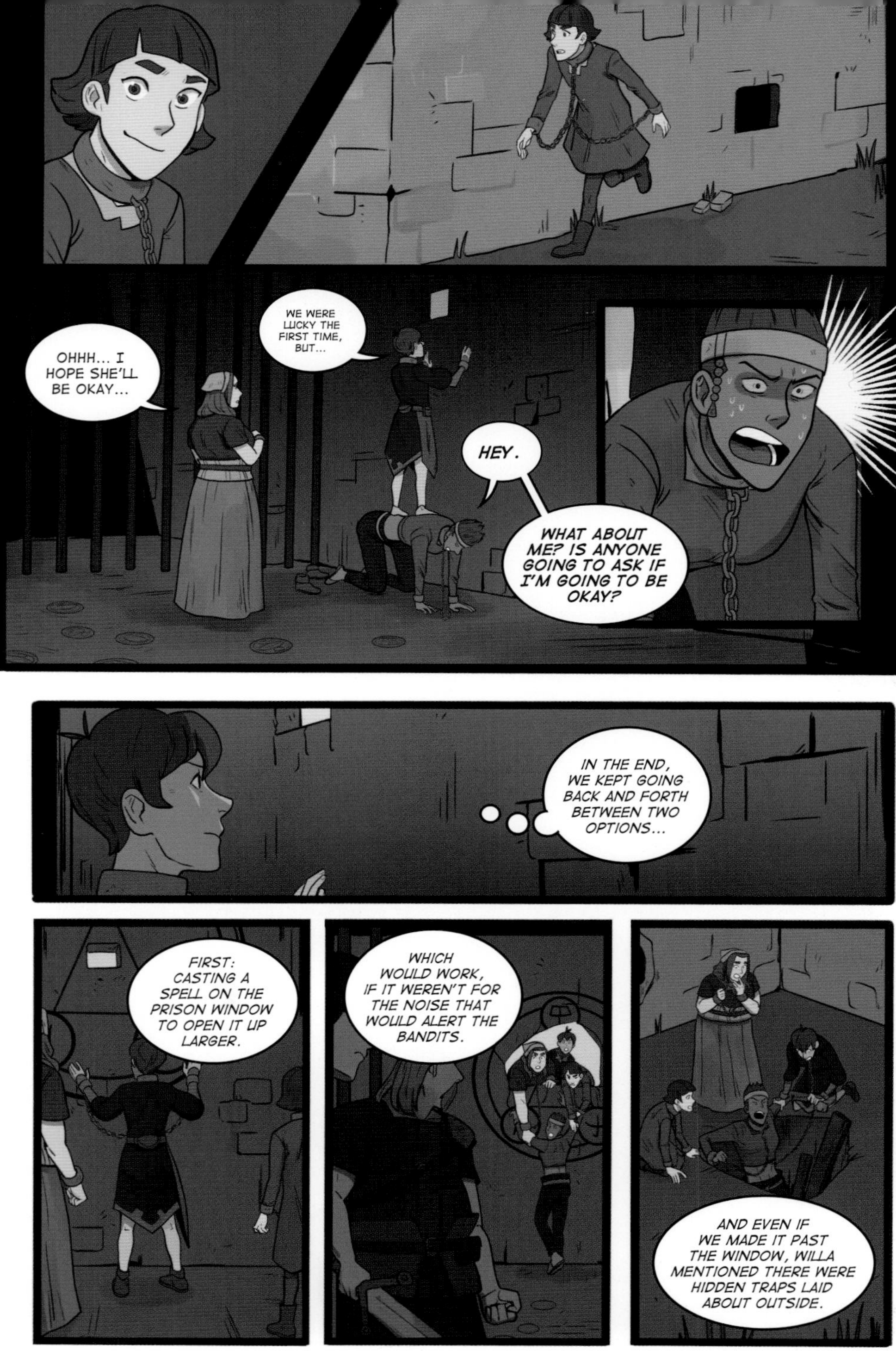

OHHH... I HOPE SHE'LL BE OKAY...
WE WERE LUCKY THE FIRST TIME, BUT...
HEY.
WHAT ABOUT ME? IS ANYONE GOING TO ASK IF I'M GOING TO BE OKAY?
IN THE END, WE KEPT GOING BACK AND FORTH BETWEEN TWO OPTIONS...
FIRST: CASTING A SPELL ON THE PRISON WINDOW TO OPEN IT UP LARGER.
WHICH WOULD WORK, IF IT WEREN'T FOR THE NOISE THAT WOULD ALERT THE BANDITS.
AND EVEN IF WE MADE IT PAST THE WINDOW, WILLA MENTIONED THERE WERE HIDDEN TRAPS LAID ABOUT OUTSIDE.

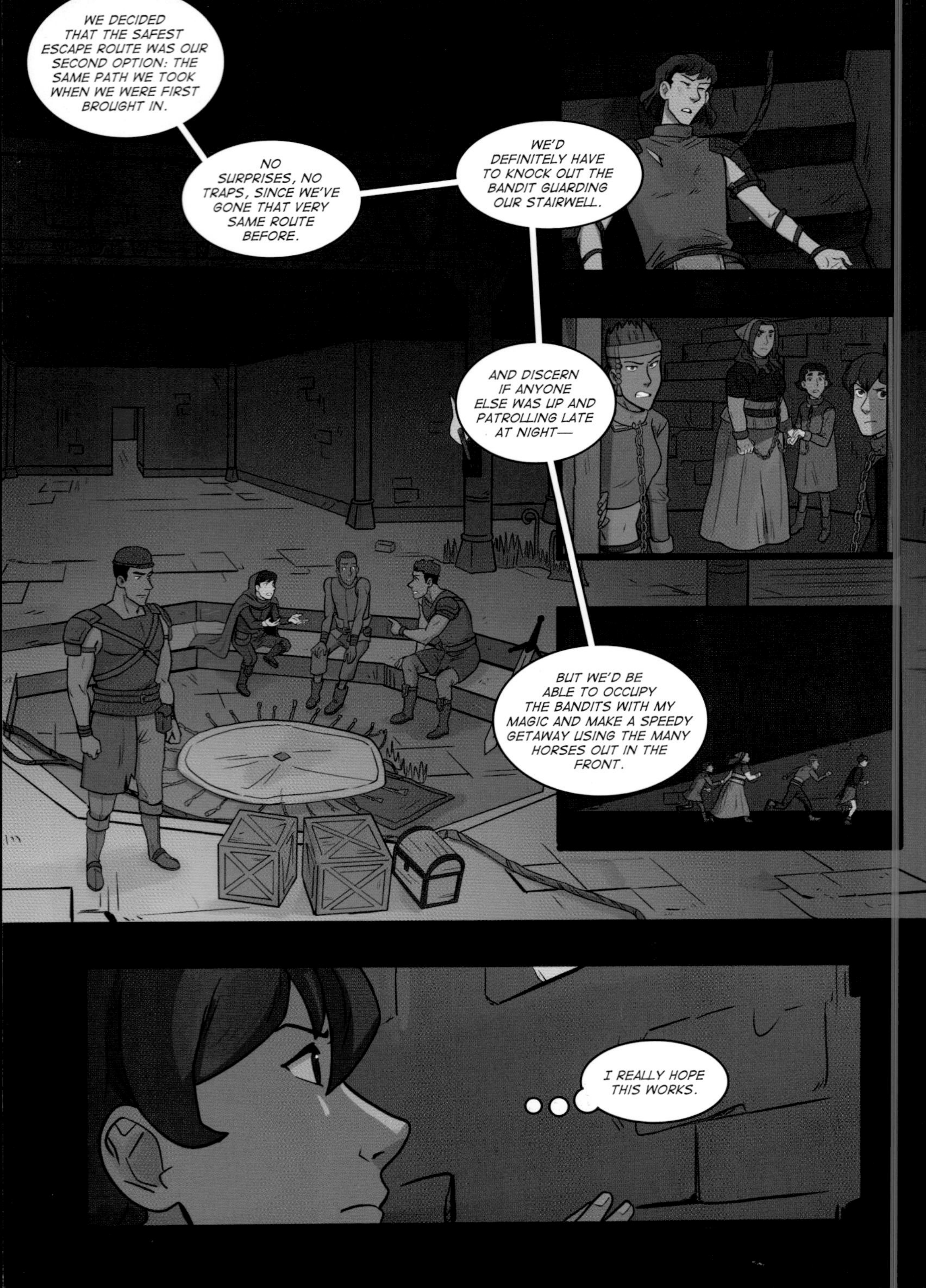
WE DECIDED THAT THE SAFEST ESCAPE ROUTE WAS OUR SECOND OPTION: THE SAME PATH WE TOOK WHEN WE WERE FIRST BROUGHT IN.
NO SURPRISES, NO TRAPS, SINCE WE'VE GONE THAT VERY SAME ROUTE BEFORE.
WE'D DEFINITELY HAVE TO KNOCK OUT THE BANDIT GUARDING OUR STAIRWELL.
AND DISCERN IF ANYONE ELSE WAS UP AND PATROLLING LATE AT NIGHT—
BUT WE'D BE ABLE TO OCCUPY THE BANDITS WITH MY MAGIC AND MAKE A SPEEDY GETAWAY USING THE MANY HORSES OUT IN THE FRONT.
I REALLY HOPE THIS WORKS.

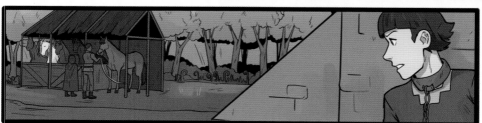

I MEAN, SERIOUSLY, I HEARD THERE WAS A LOT OF LOOTING BACK IN THE WAR...

MUST'VE BEEN NICE...

WITH EVERYONE ON THEIR TOES THESE DAYS, IT'S HARD TO BE A BANDIT...

I WOULDN'T KNOW, DUDE. I'M NOT *THAT* OLD.

NEITHER AM I!

I'M JUST SAYING, IT MUST'VE BEEN NICE!

INSTEAD OF BOSS MIRO TAKING WEIRD AND SHADY DEALS LIKE THIS...

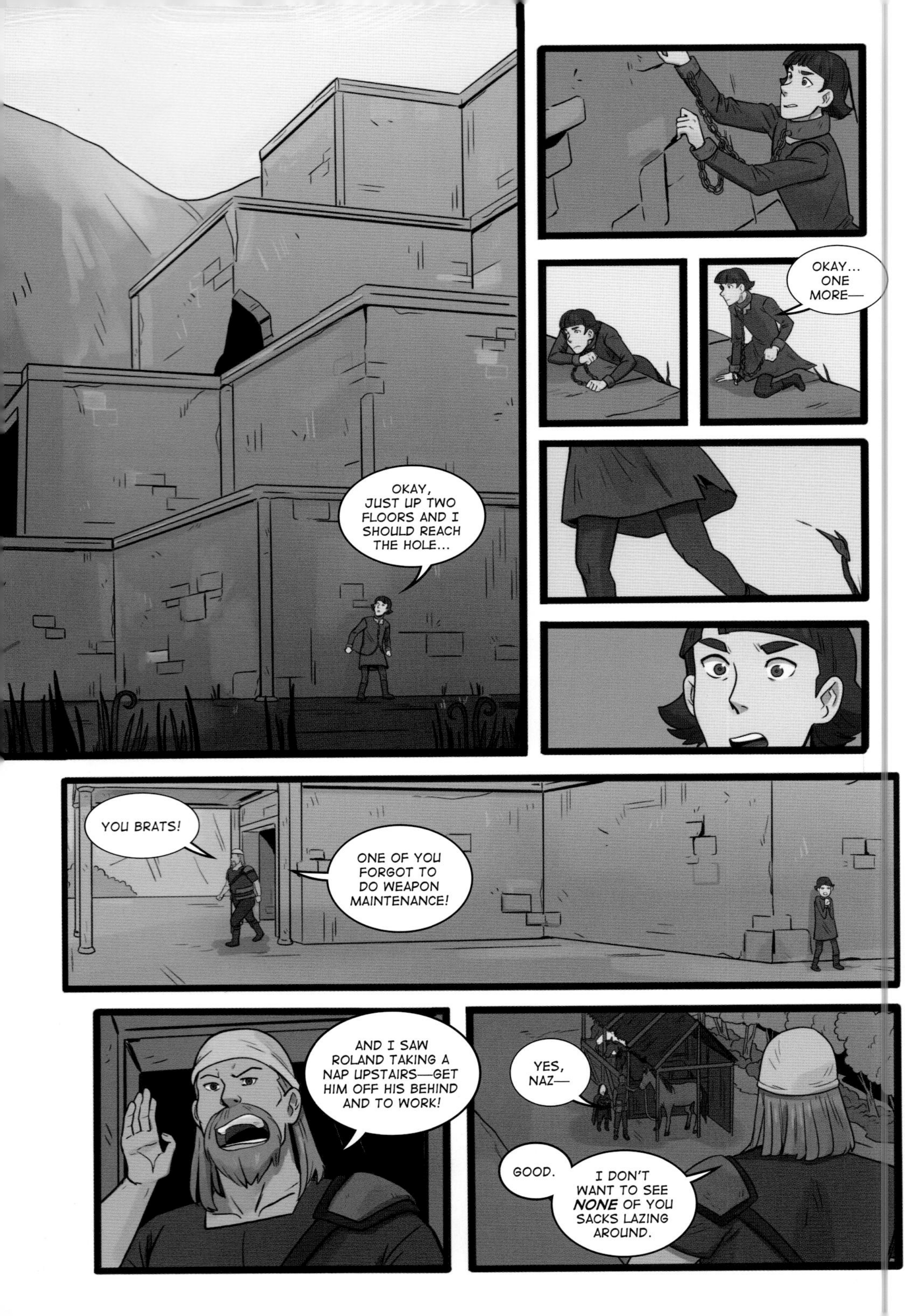
OKAY, JUST UP TWO FLOORS AND I SHOULD REACH THE HOLE...
OKAY... ONE MORE—
YOU BRATS!
ONE OF YOU FORGOT TO DO WEAPON MAINTENANCE!
AND I SAW ROLAND TAKING A NAP UPSTAIRS—GET HIM OFF HIS BEHIND AND TO WORK!
YES, NAZ—
GOOD.
I DON'T WANT TO SEE *NONE* OF YOU SACKS LAZING AROUND.

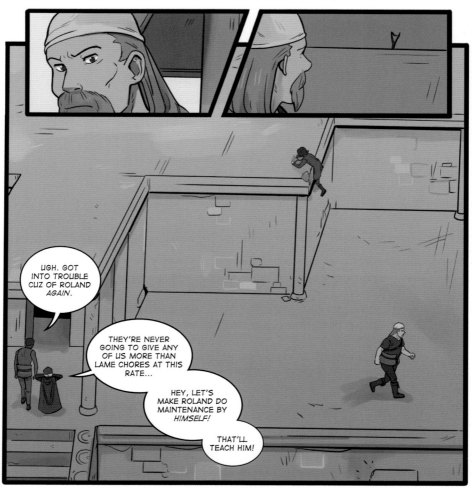

UGH. GOT INTO TROUBLE CUZ OF ROLAND *AGAIN.*

THEY'RE NEVER GOING TO GIVE ANY OF US MORE THAN LAME CHORES AT THIS RATE...

HEY, LET'S MAKE ROLAND DO MAINTENANCE BY *HIMSELF!*

THAT'LL TEACH HIM!

THIS IS...

MADE IT!

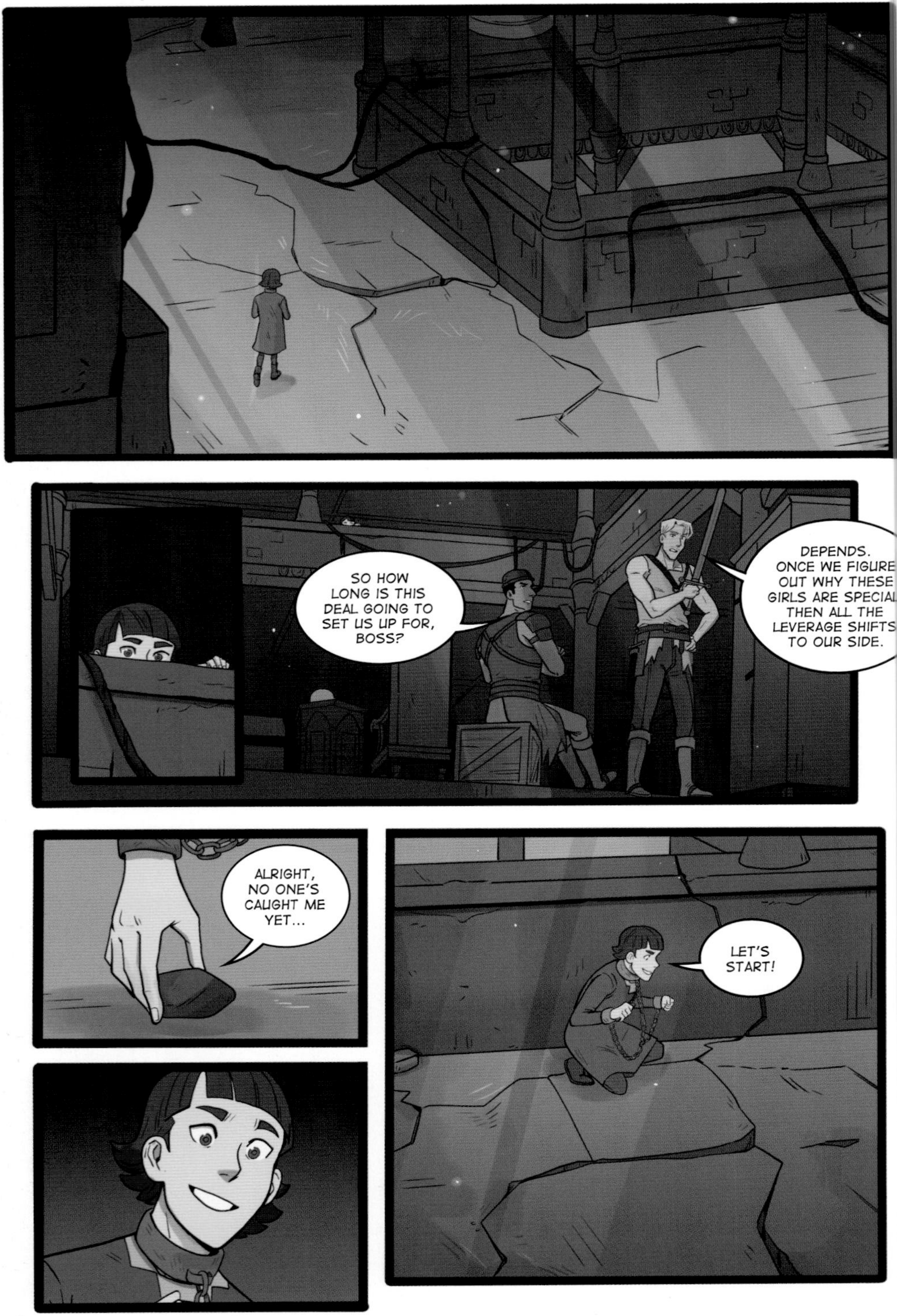

SO HOW LONG IS THIS DEAL GOING TO SET US UP FOR, BOSS?
DEPENDS. ONCE WE FIGURE OUT WHY THESE GIRLS ARE SPECIAL, THEN ALL THE LEVERAGE SHIFTS TO OUR SIDE.
ALRIGHT, NO ONE'S CAUGHT ME YET...
LET'S START!

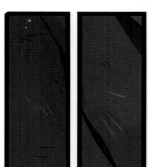

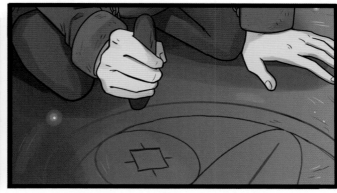

DONE!

I SHOULD HEAD BACK—

UNLESS...

IF THERE WAS ONLY A WAY TO FIGURE OUT WHEN THE STAIRWELL WASN'T BEING PATROLLED...

IT WON'T HURT TO CHECK...

RIGHT...?

AHHHHHHHH!

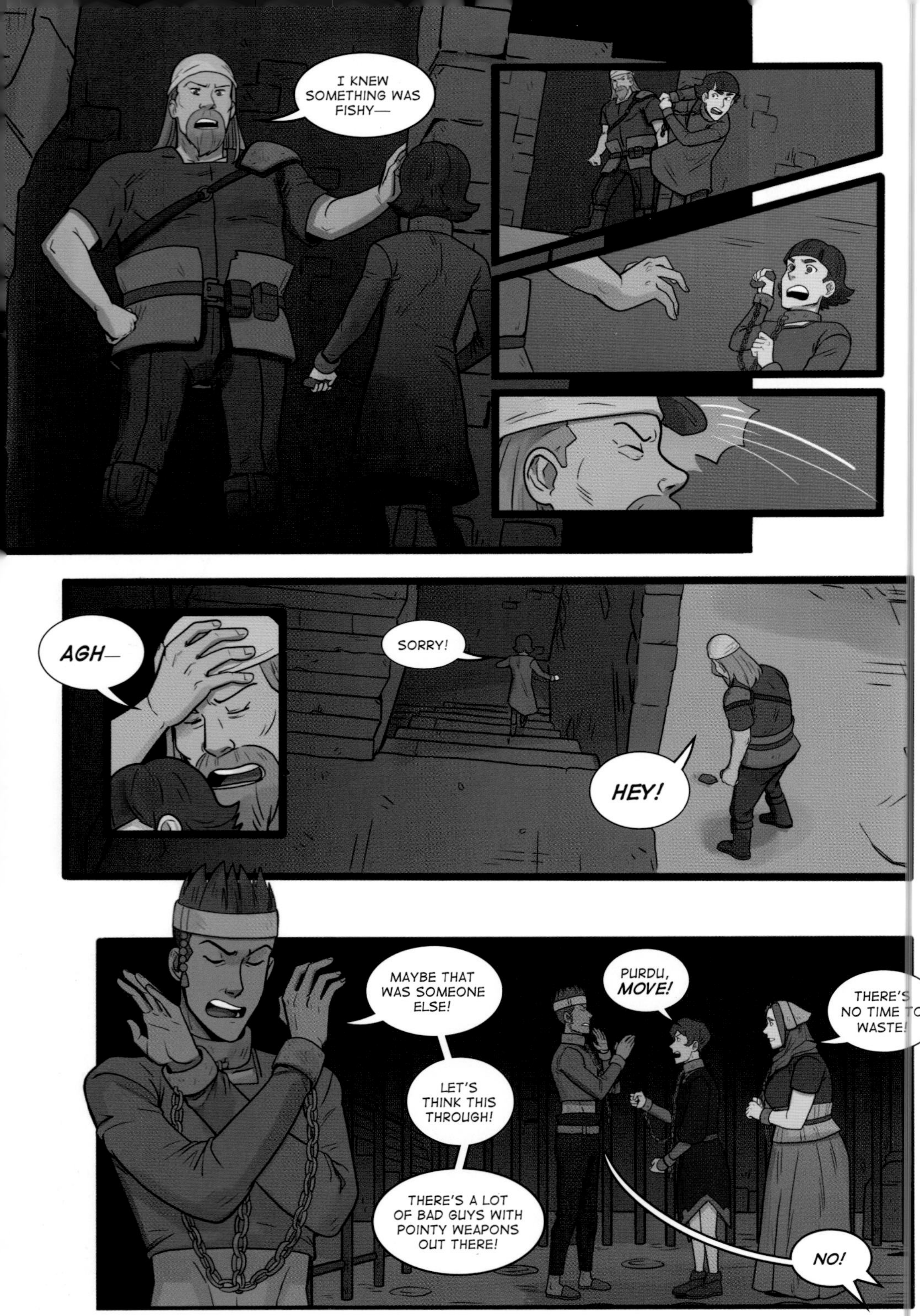
I KNEW SOMETHING WAS FISHY—
AGH—
SORRY!
HEY!
MAYBE THAT WAS SOMEONE ELSE!
LET'S THINK THIS THROUGH!
THERE'S A LOT OF BAD GUYS WITH POINTY WEAPONS OUT THERE!
PURDU, MOVE!
THERE'S NO TIME TO WASTE!
NO!

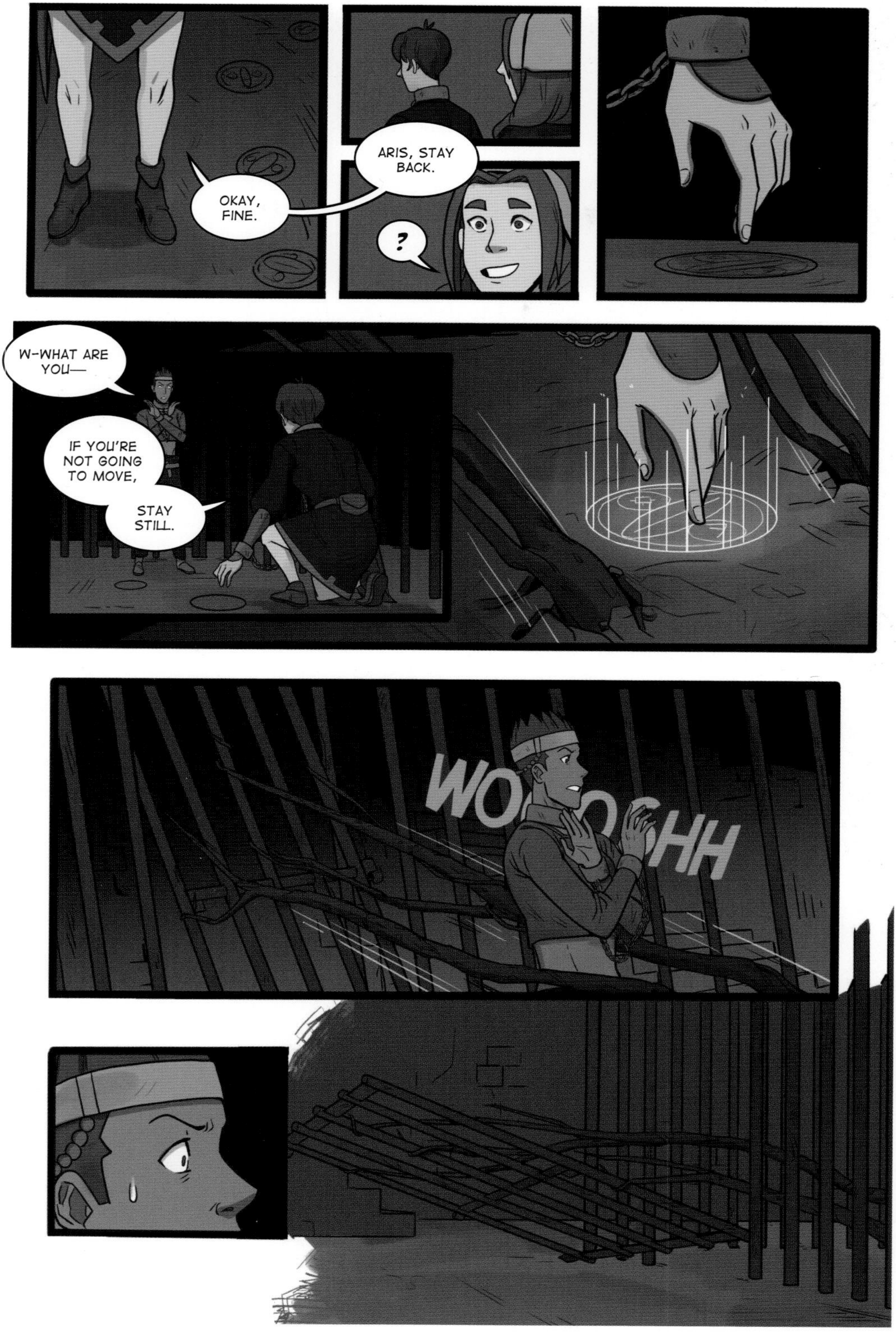
OKAY, FINE.
ARIS, STAY BACK.
?
W-WHAT ARE YOU—
IF YOU'RE NOT GOING TO MOVE,
STAY STILL.
WOOOSHH

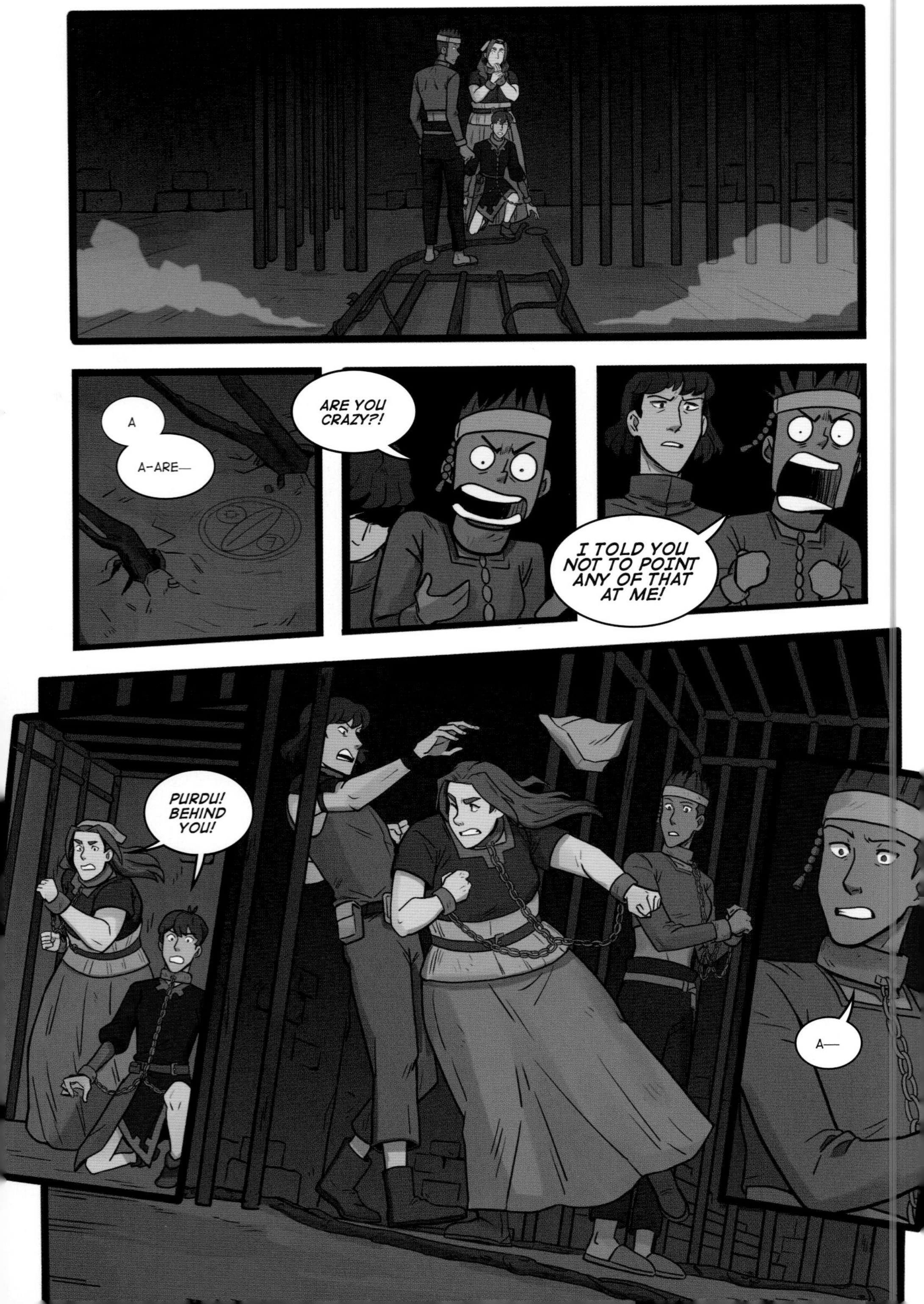
A
A-ARE—
ARE YOU CRAZY?!
I TOLD YOU NOT TO POINT ANY OF THAT AT ME!
PURDU! BEHIND YOU!
A—

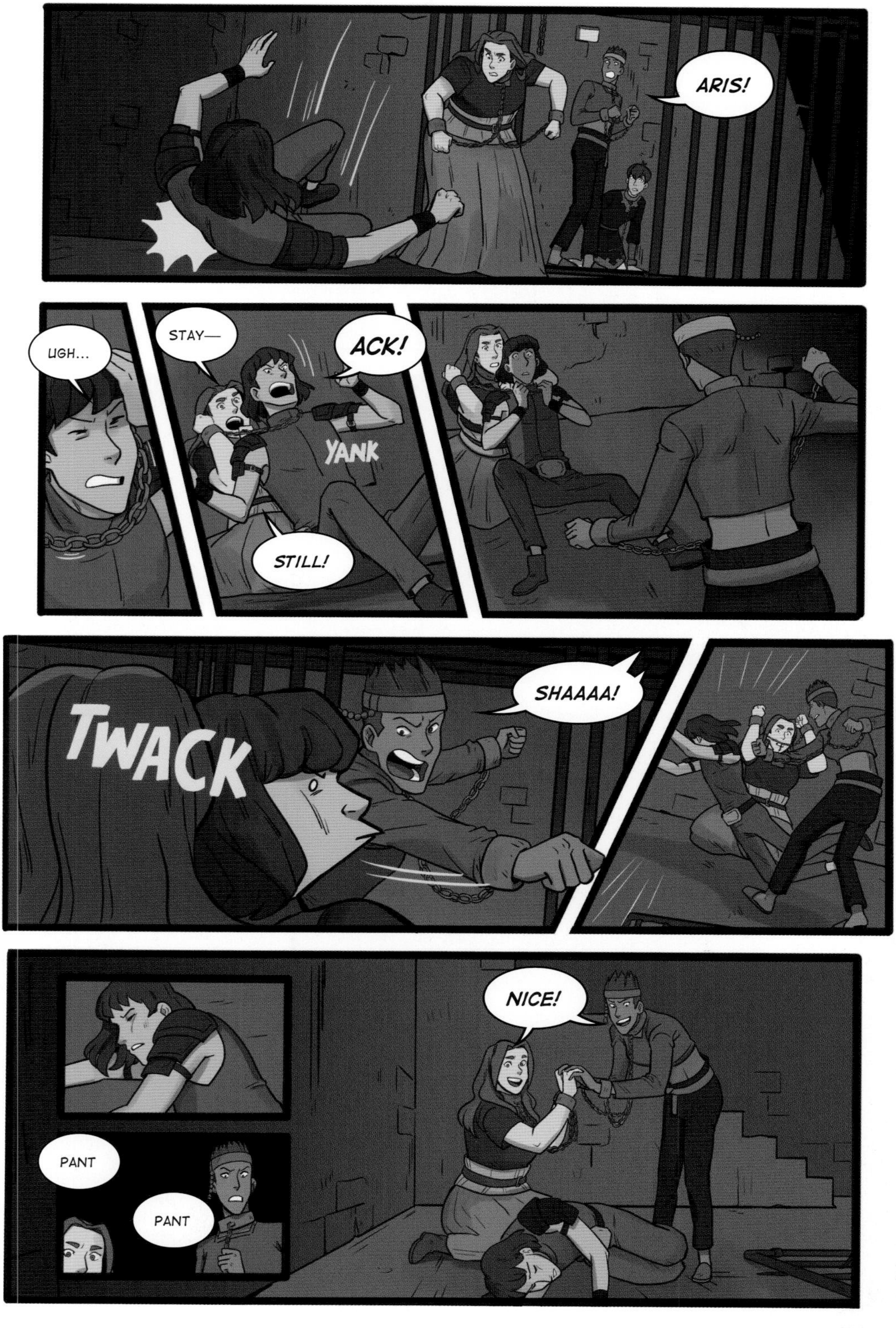
ARIS!
UGH...
STAY—
ACK!
YANK
STILL!
TWACK
SHAAAA!
NICE!
PANT
PANT

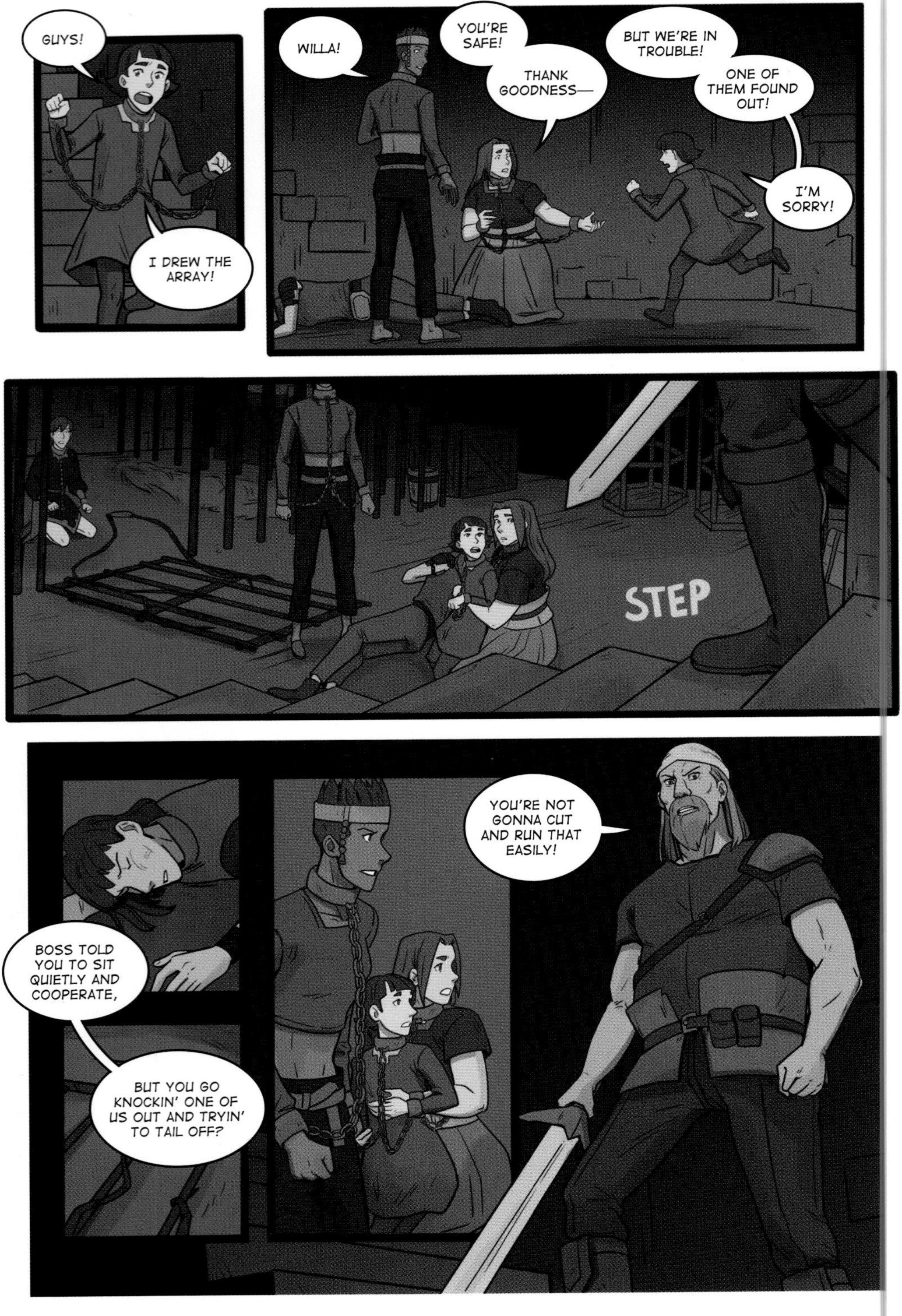
GUYS!
I DREW THE ARRAY!
WILLA!
YOU'RE SAFE!
THANK GOODNESS—
BUT WE'RE IN TROUBLE!
ONE OF THEM FOUND OUT!
I'M SORRY!
STEP
YOU'RE NOT GONNA CUT AND RUN THAT EASILY!
BOSS TOLD YOU TO SIT QUIETLY AND COOPERATE,
BUT YOU GO KNOCKIN' ONE OF US OUT AND TRYIN' TO TAIL OFF?

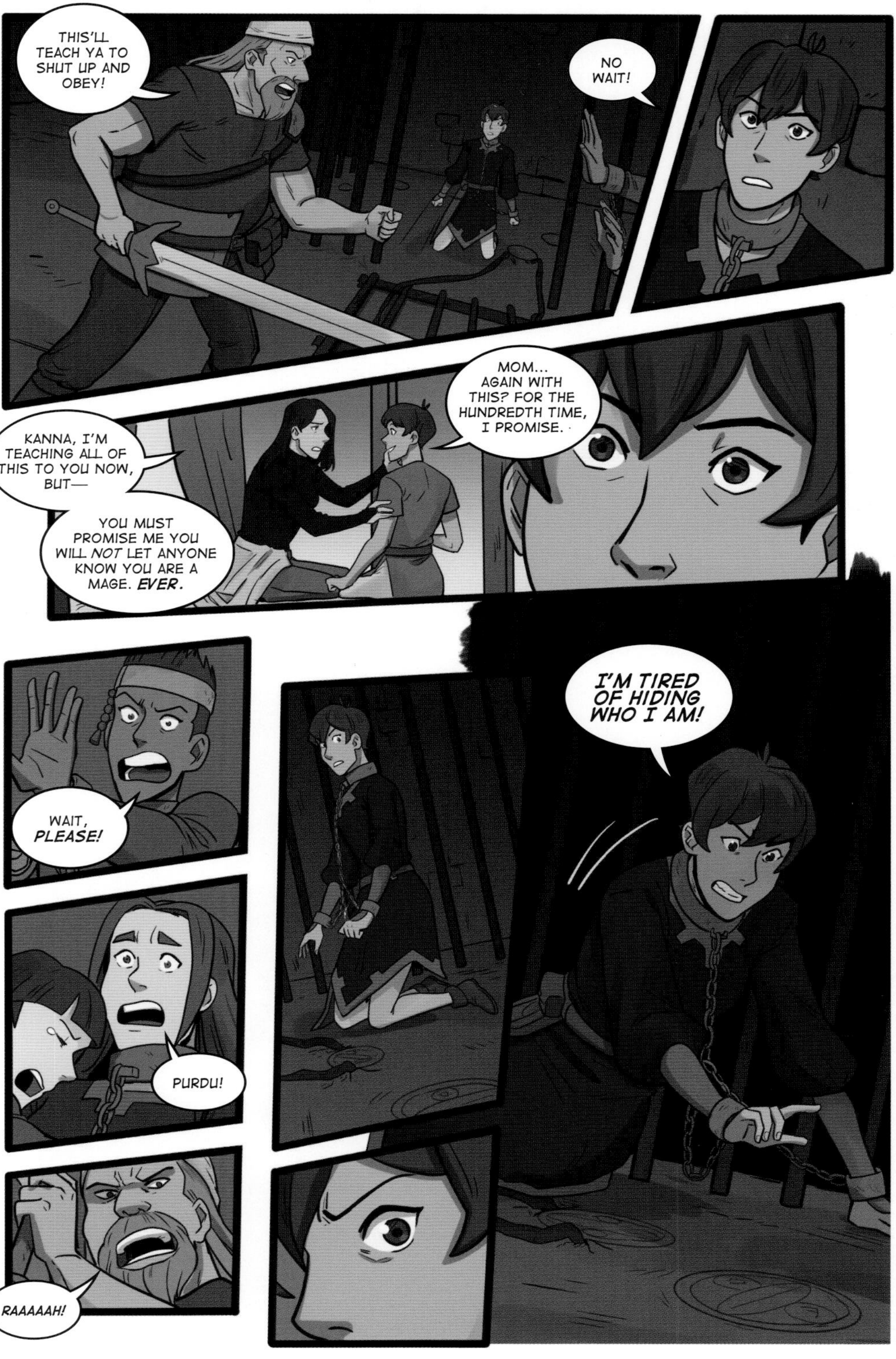

THIS'LL TEACH YA TO SHUT UP AND OBEY!
NO WAIT!
KANNA, I'M TEACHING ALL OF THIS TO YOU NOW, BUT—
YOU MUST PROMISE ME YOU WILL *NOT* LET ANYONE KNOW YOU ARE A MAGE. ***EVER.***
MOM... AGAIN WITH THIS? FOR THE HUNDREDTH TIME, I PROMISE.
WAIT, **PLEASE!**
PURDU!
RAAAAAH!
I'M TIRED OF HIDING WHO I AM!

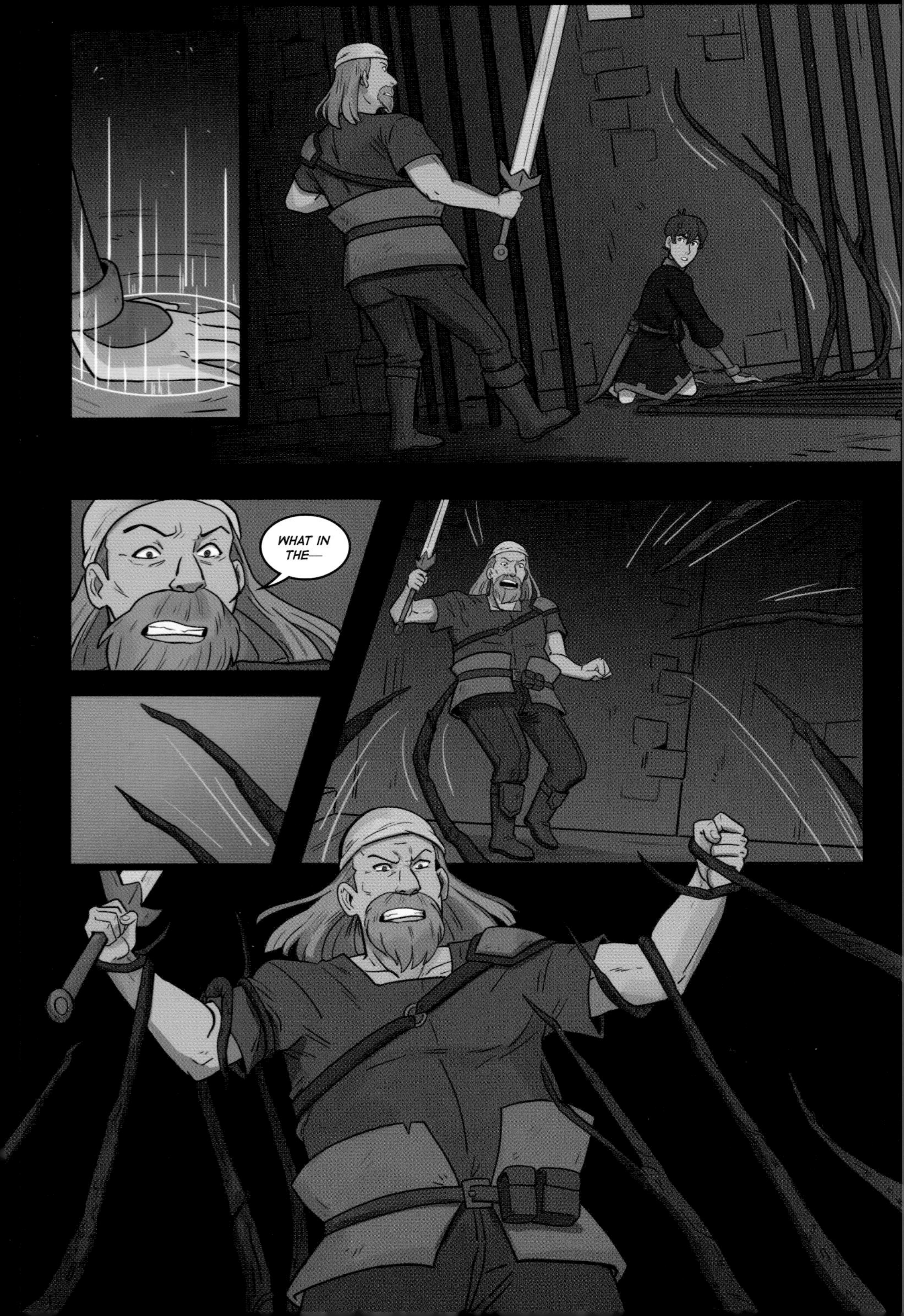
WHAT IN THE—

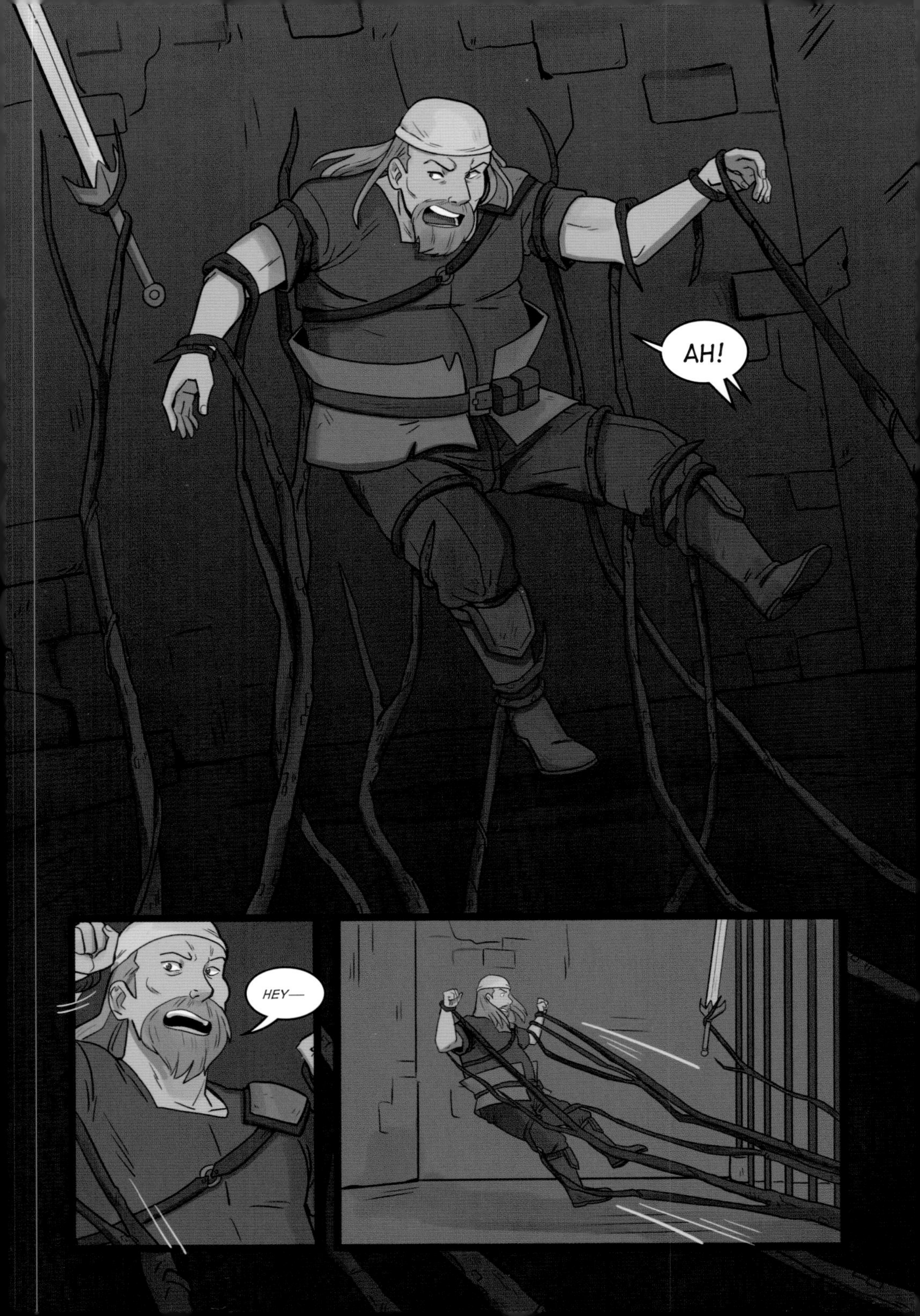
AH!
HEY—

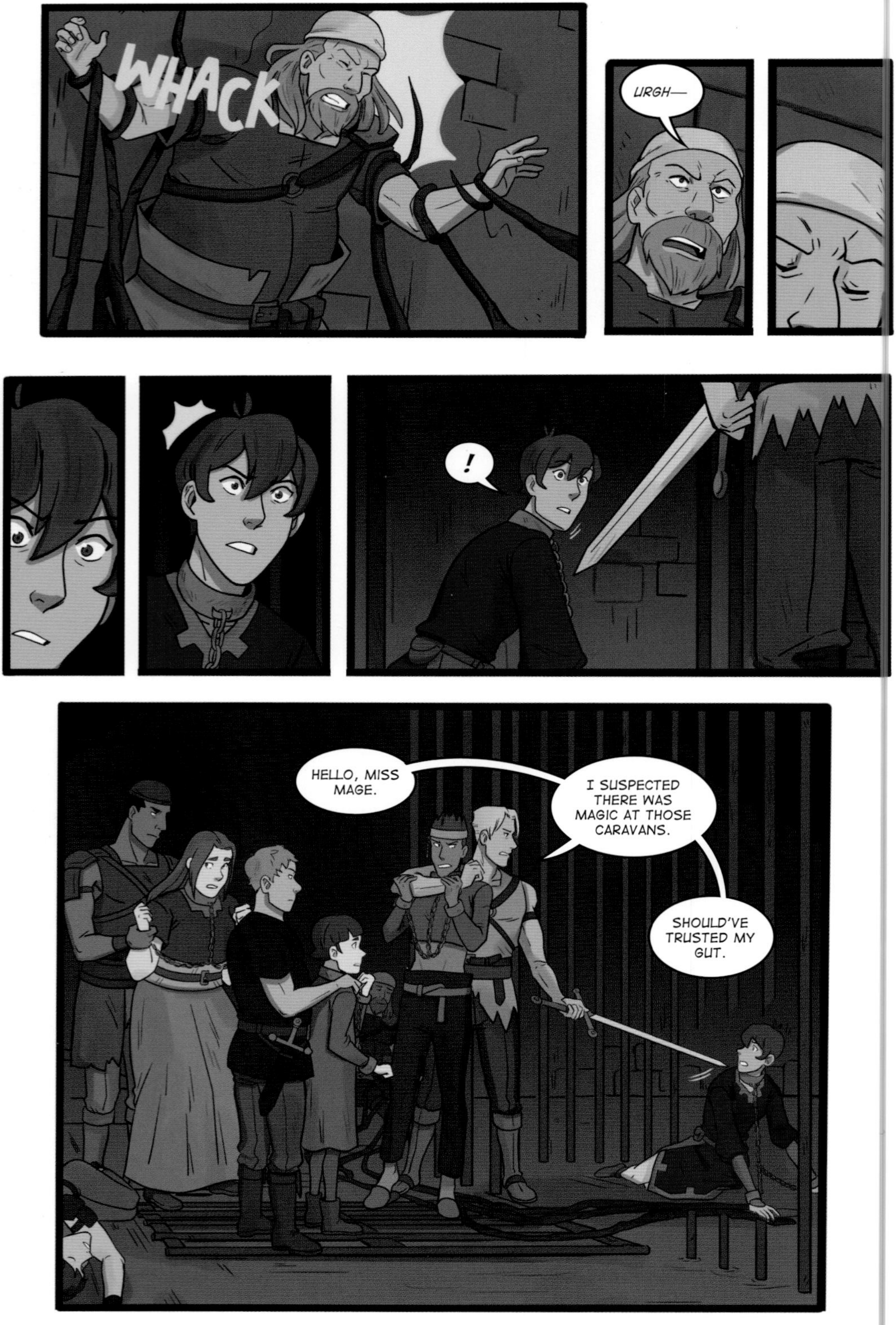
WHACK
URGH—
!
HELLO, MISS MAGE.
I SUSPECTED THERE WAS MAGIC AT THOSE CARAVANS.
SHOULD'VE TRUSTED MY GUT.

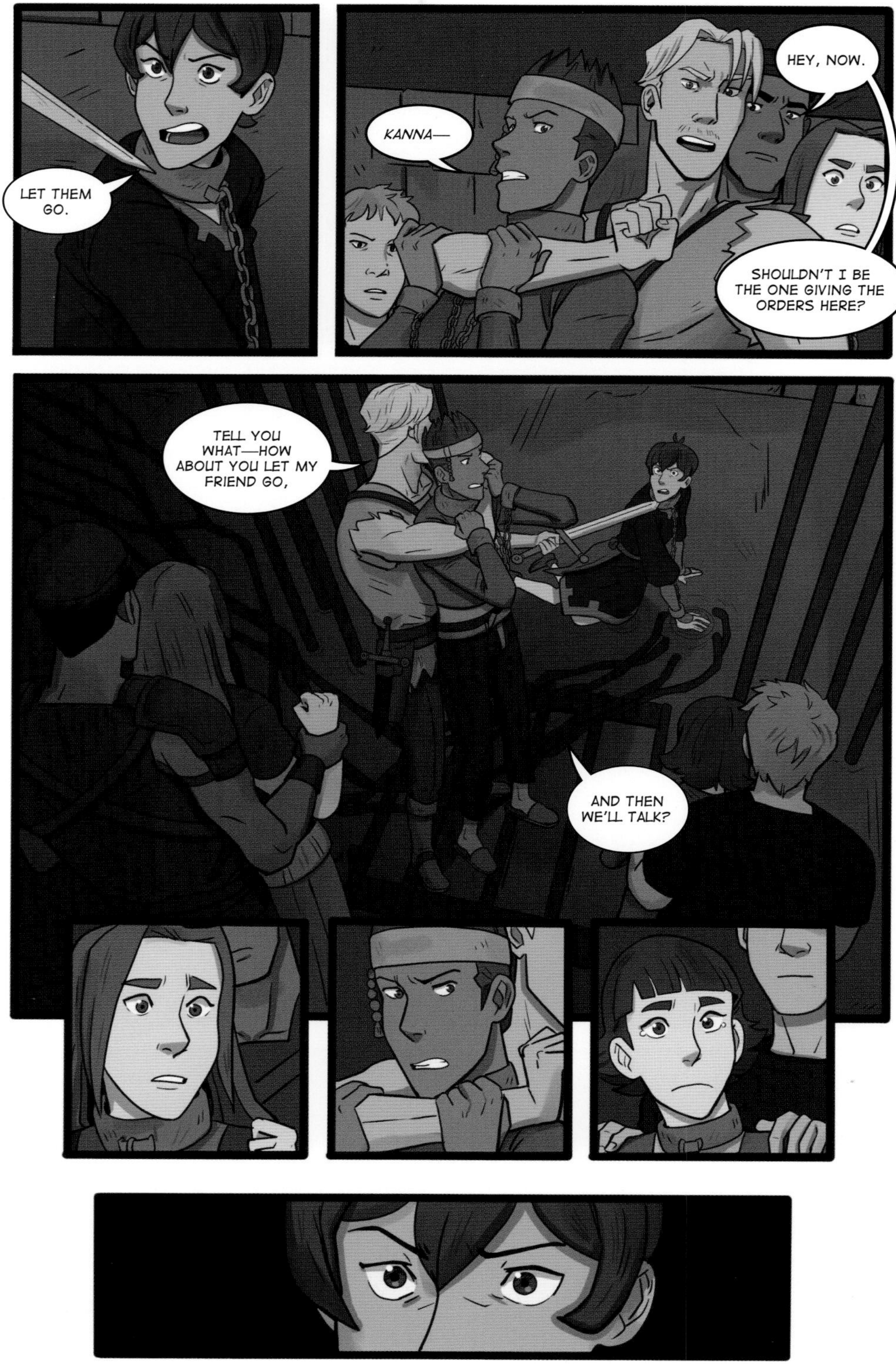
LET THEM GO.
KANNA—
HEY, NOW.
SHOULDN'T I BE THE ONE GIVING THE ORDERS HERE?
TELL YOU WHAT—HOW ABOUT YOU LET MY FRIEND GO,
AND THEN WE'LL TALK?

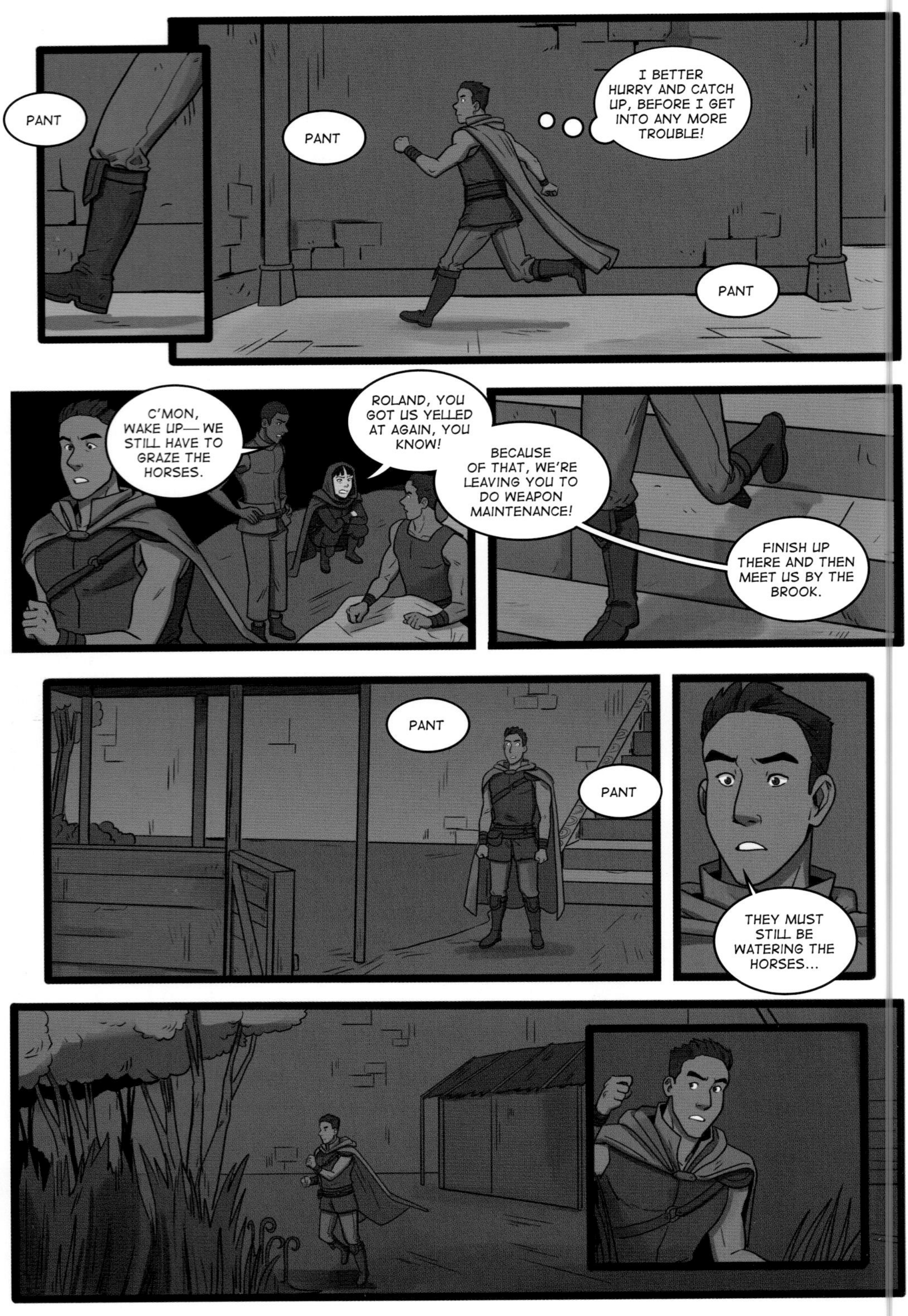
PANT
PANT
I BETTER HURRY AND CATCH UP, BEFORE I GET INTO ANY MORE TROUBLE!
PANT
C'MON, WAKE UP— WE STILL HAVE TO GRAZE THE HORSES.
ROLAND, YOU GOT US YELLED AT AGAIN, YOU KNOW!
BECAUSE OF THAT, WE'RE LEAVING YOU TO DO WEAPON MAINTENANCE!
FINISH UP THERE AND THEN MEET US BY THE BROOK.
PANT
PANT
THEY MUST STILL BE WATERING THE HORSES...

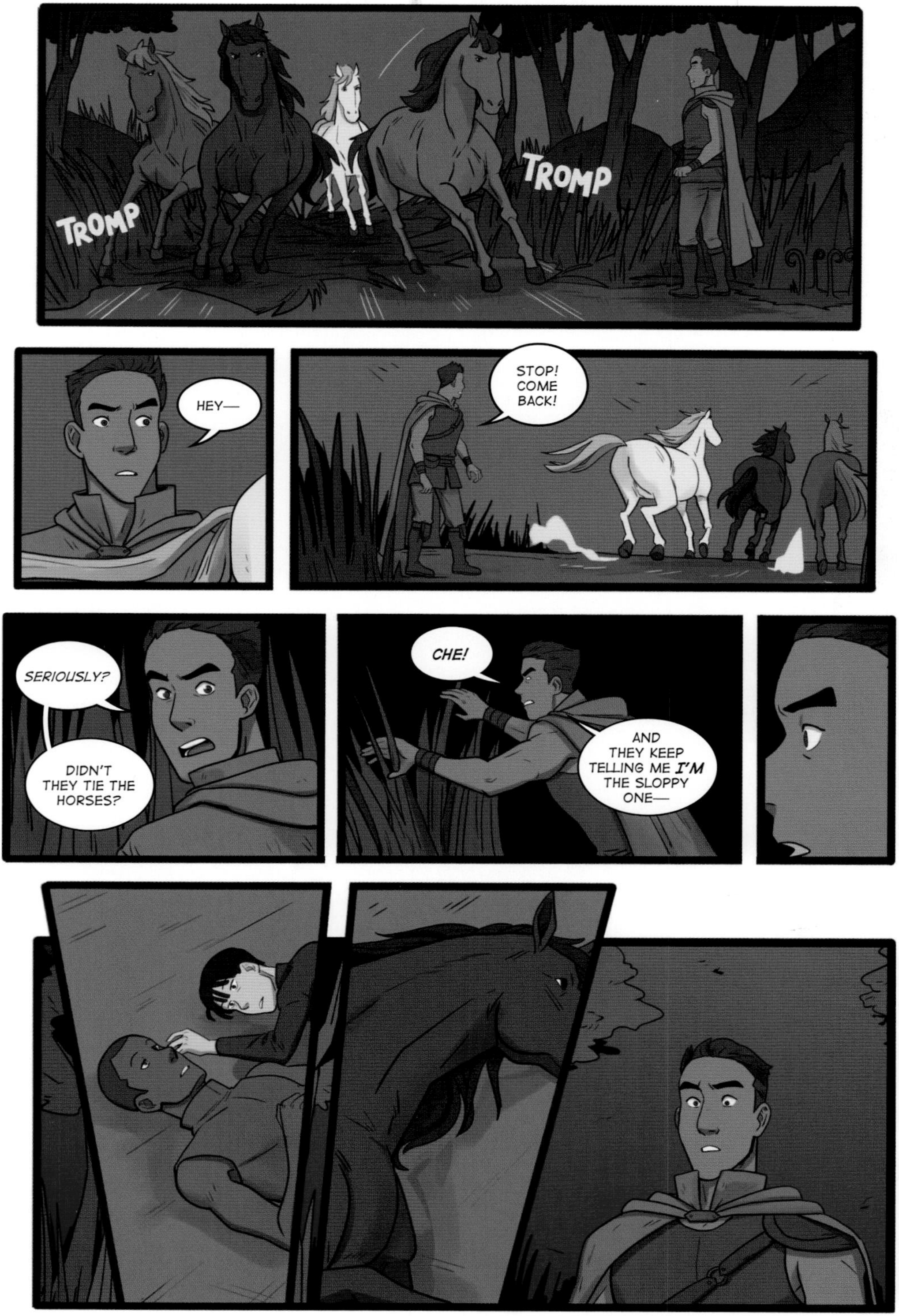
TROMP
TROMP
HEY—
STOP! COME BACK!
SERIOUSLY?
DIDN'T THEY TIE THE HORSES?
CHE!
AND THEY KEEP TELLING ME *I'M* THE SLOPPY ONE—

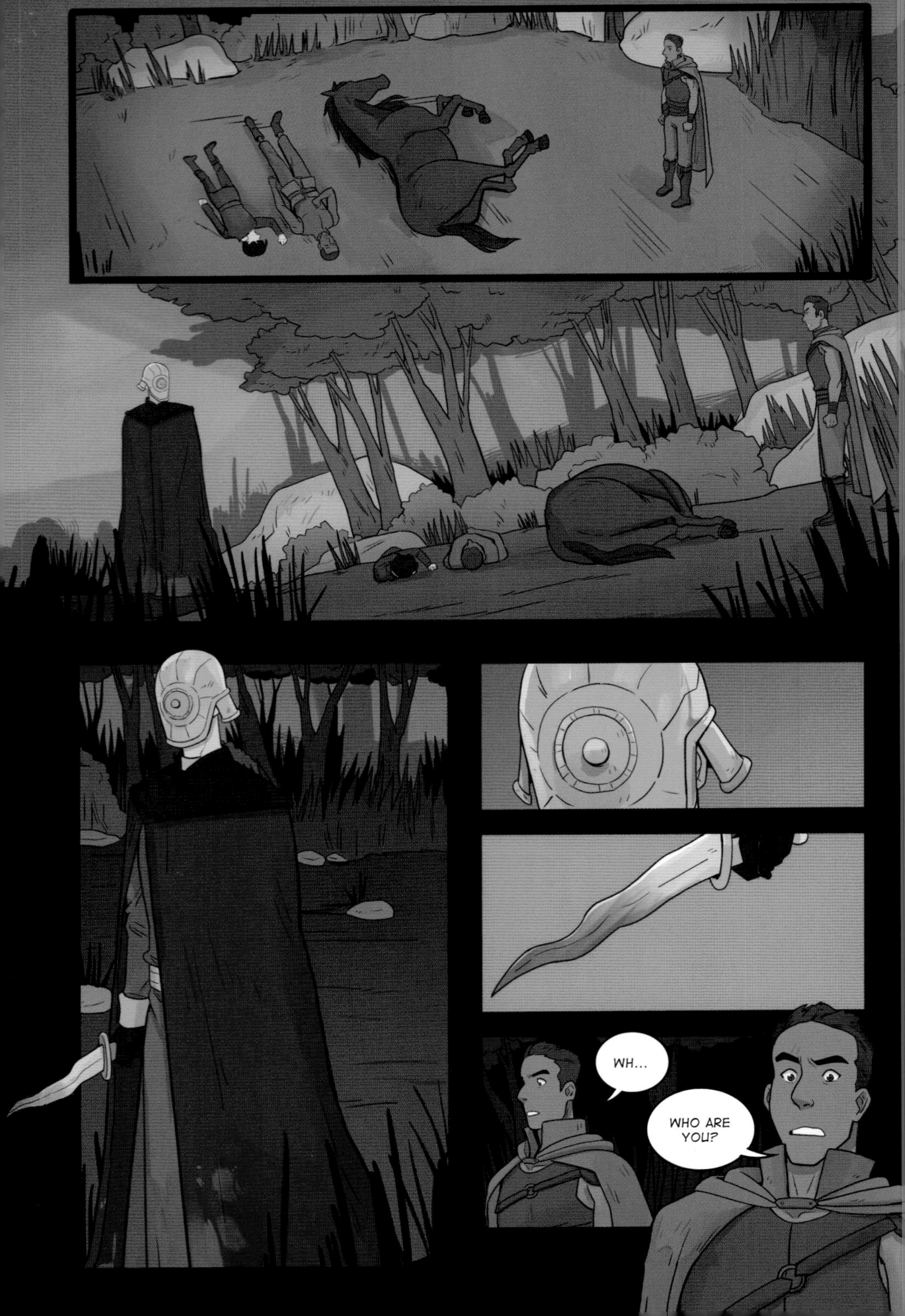
WH...
WHO ARE YOU?

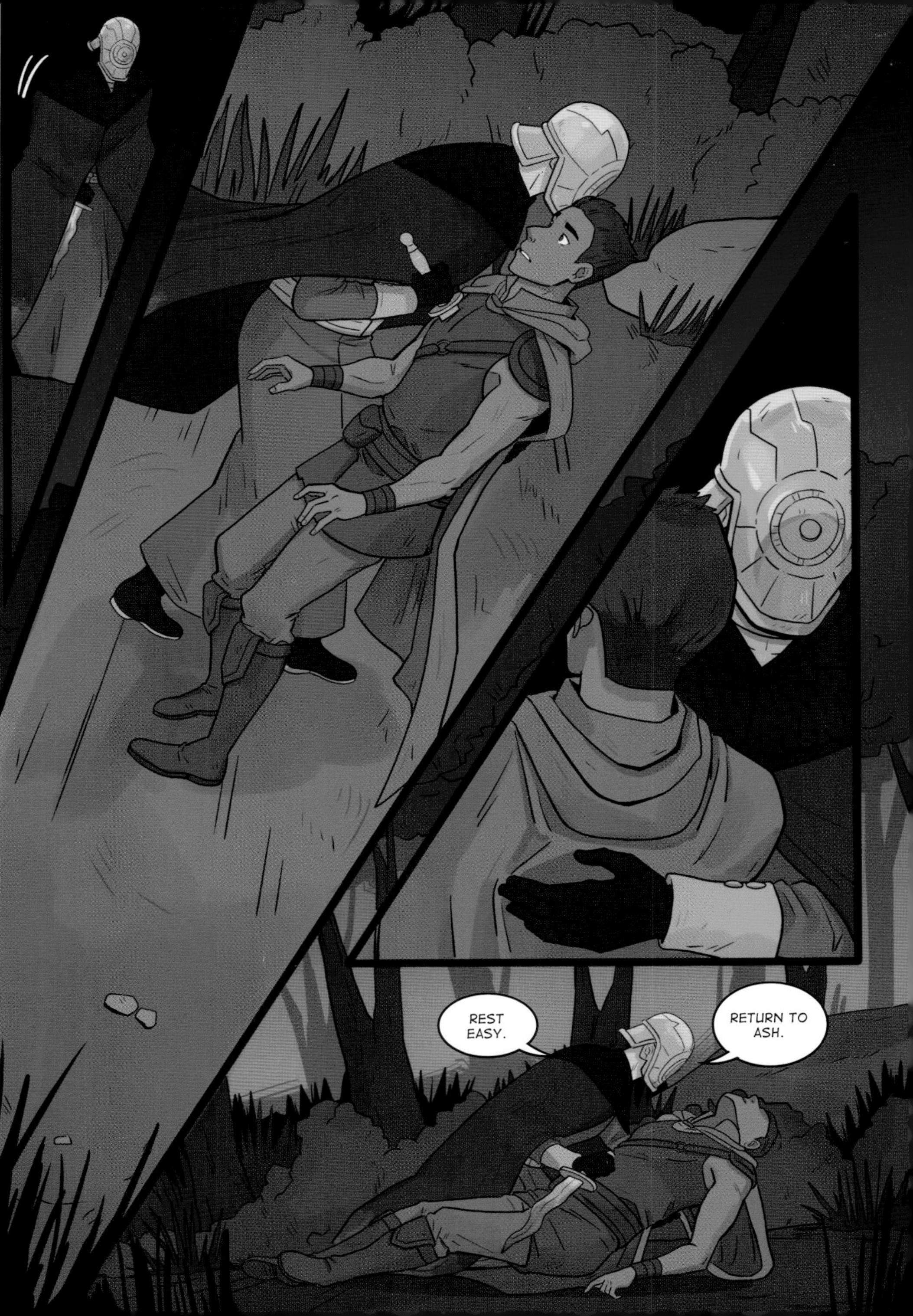
REST EASY.
RETURN TO ASH.

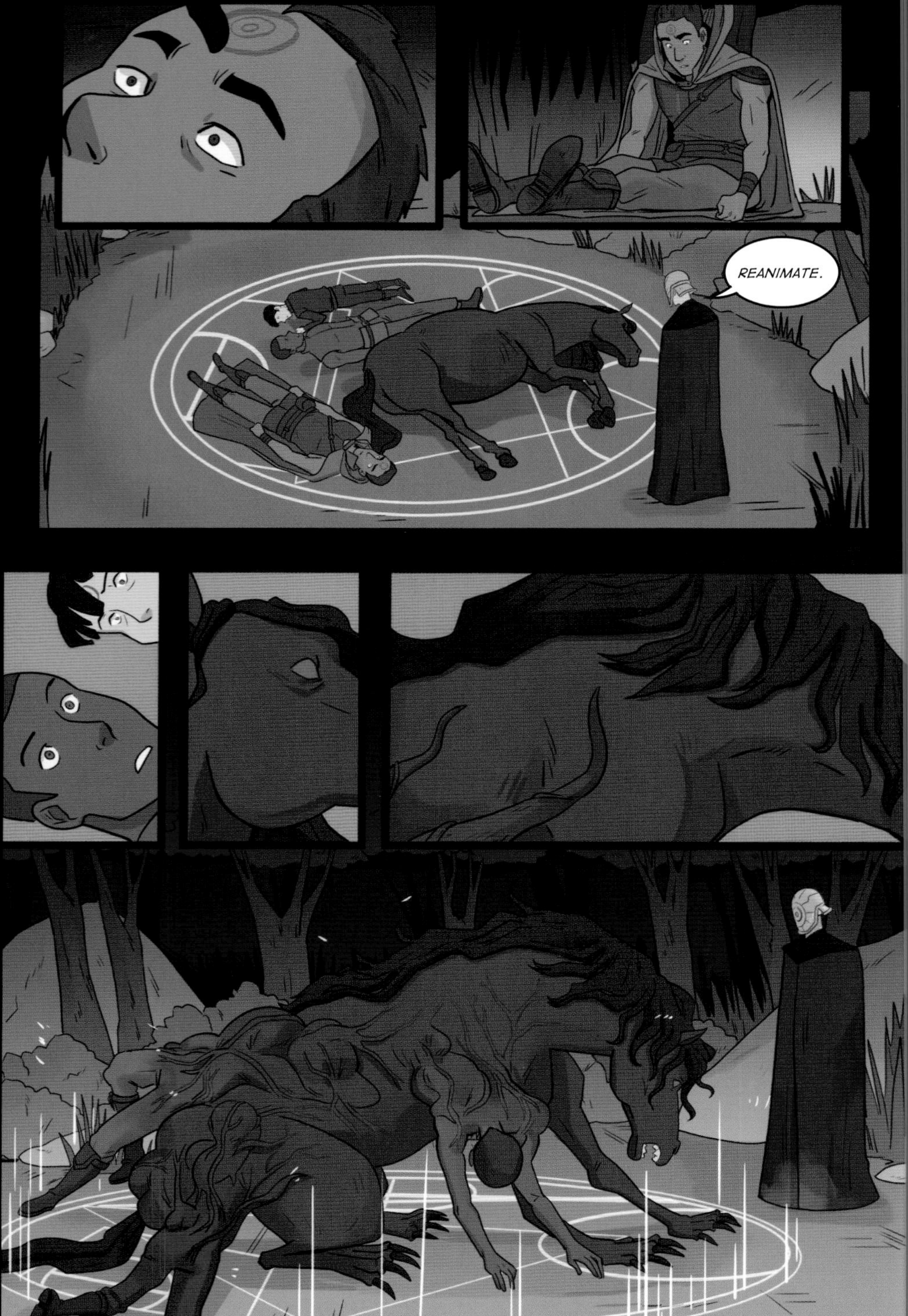
REANIMATE.

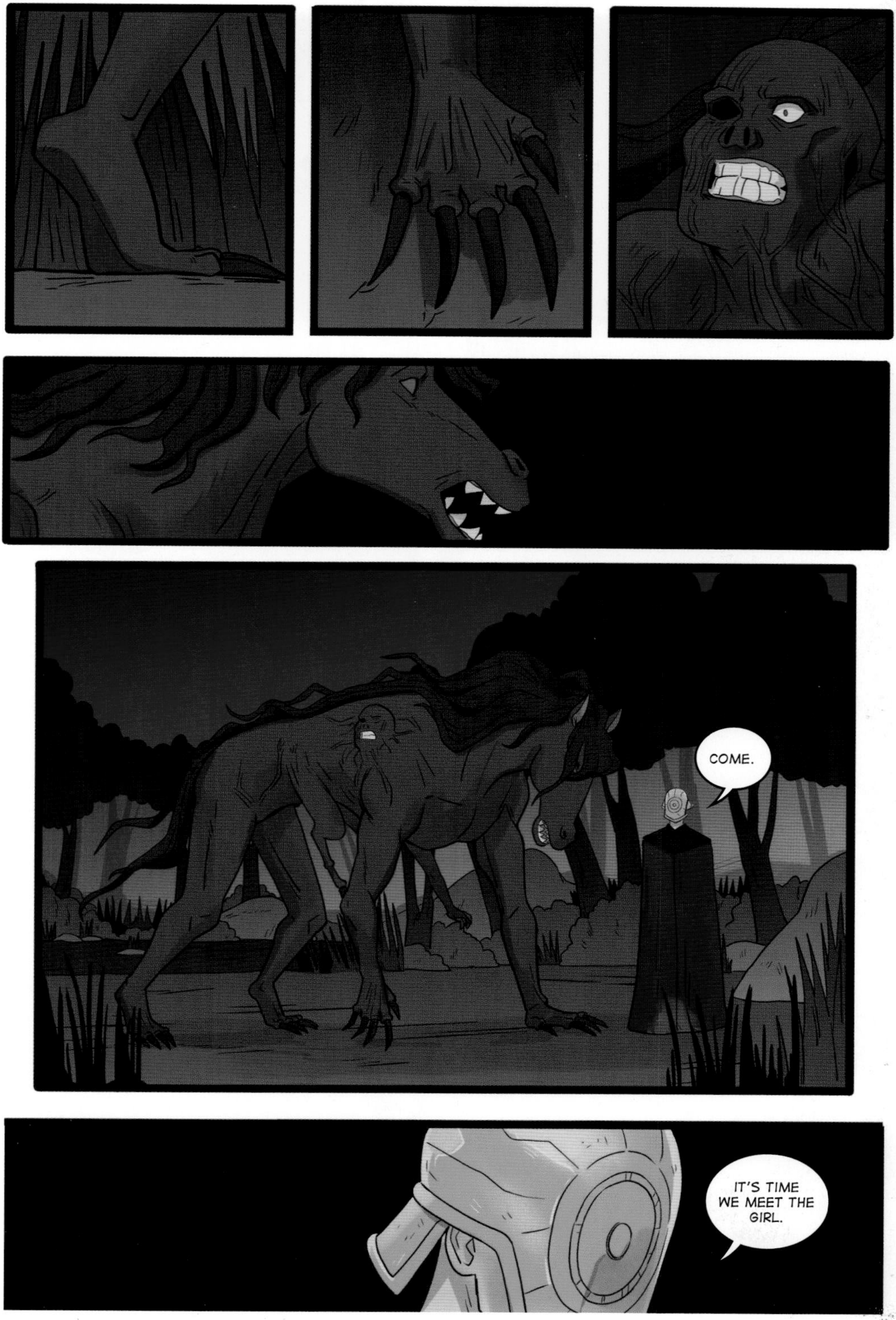
COME.
IT'S TIME WE MEET THE GIRL.

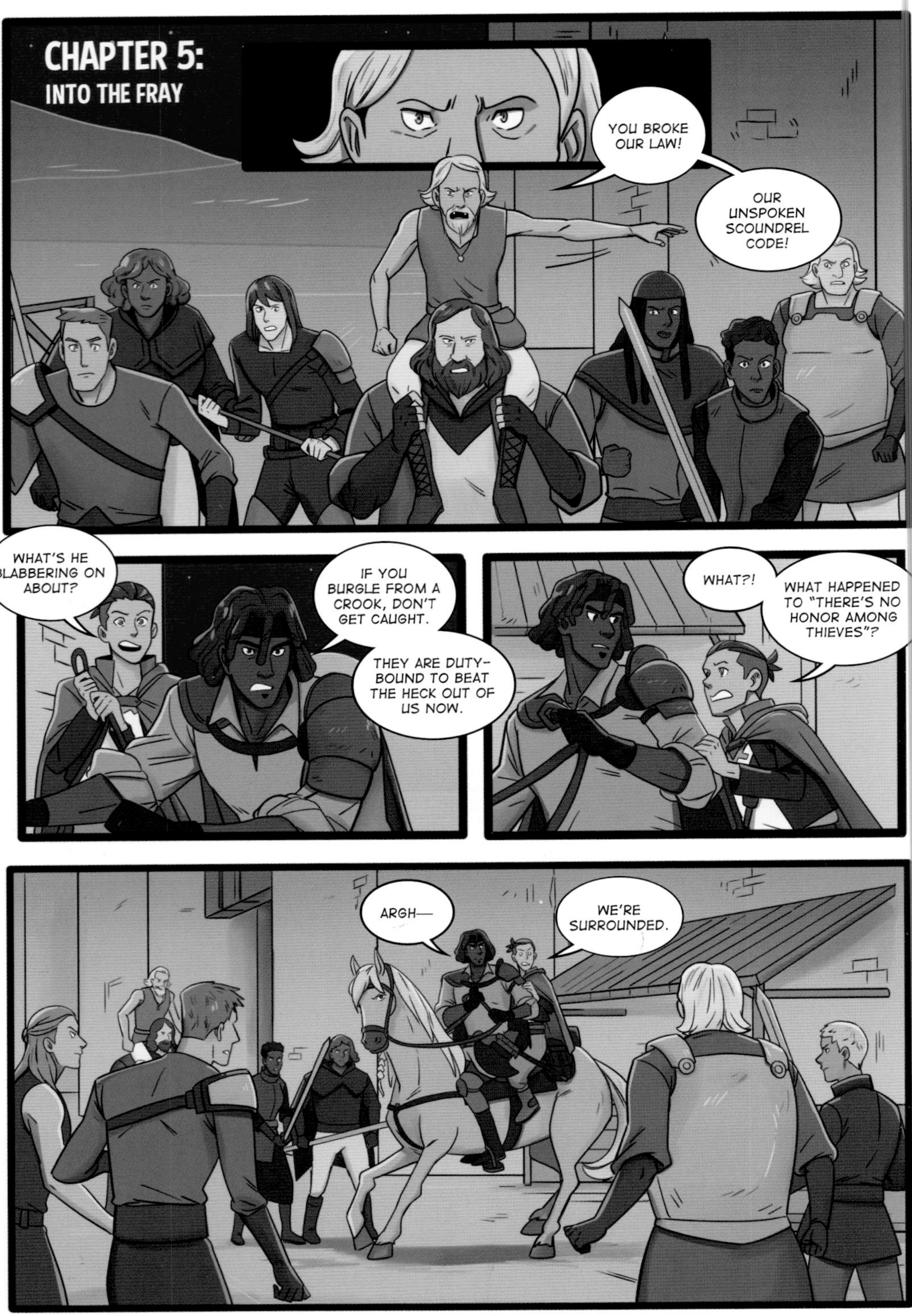
CHAPTER 5:
INTO THE FRAY
YOU BROKE OUR LAW!
OUR UNSPOKEN SCOUNDREL CODE!
WHAT'S HE BLABBERING ON ABOUT?
IF YOU BURGLE FROM A CROOK, DON'T GET CAUGHT.
THEY ARE DUTY-BOUND TO BEAT THE HECK OUT OF US NOW.
WHAT?!
WHAT HAPPENED TO "THERE'S NO HONOR AMONG THIEVES"?
ARGH—
WE'RE SURROUNDED.

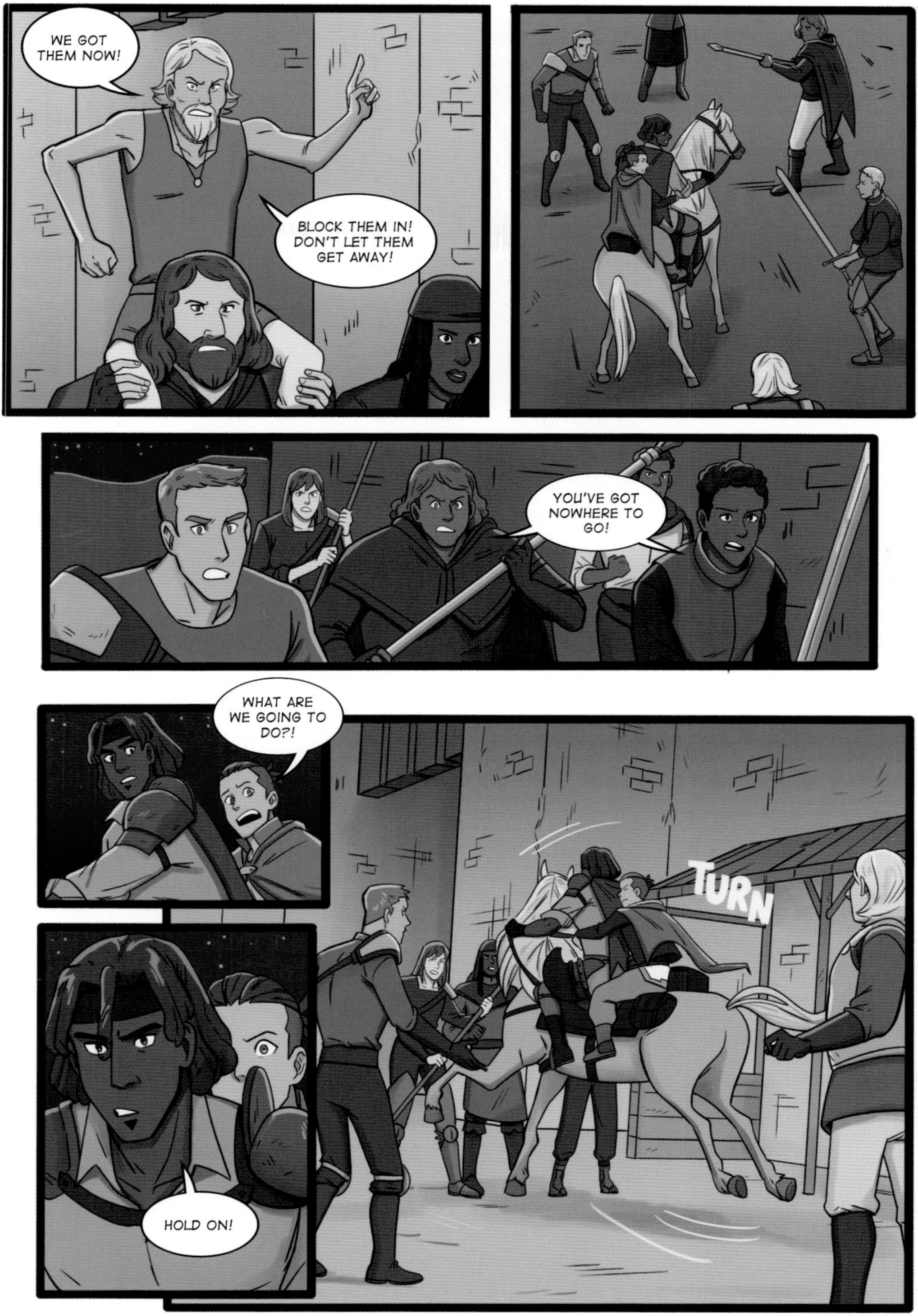
WE GOT THEM NOW!
BLOCK THEM IN! DON'T LET THEM GET AWAY!
YOU'VE GOT NOWHERE TO GO!
WHAT ARE WE GOING TO DO?!
HOLD ON!
TURN

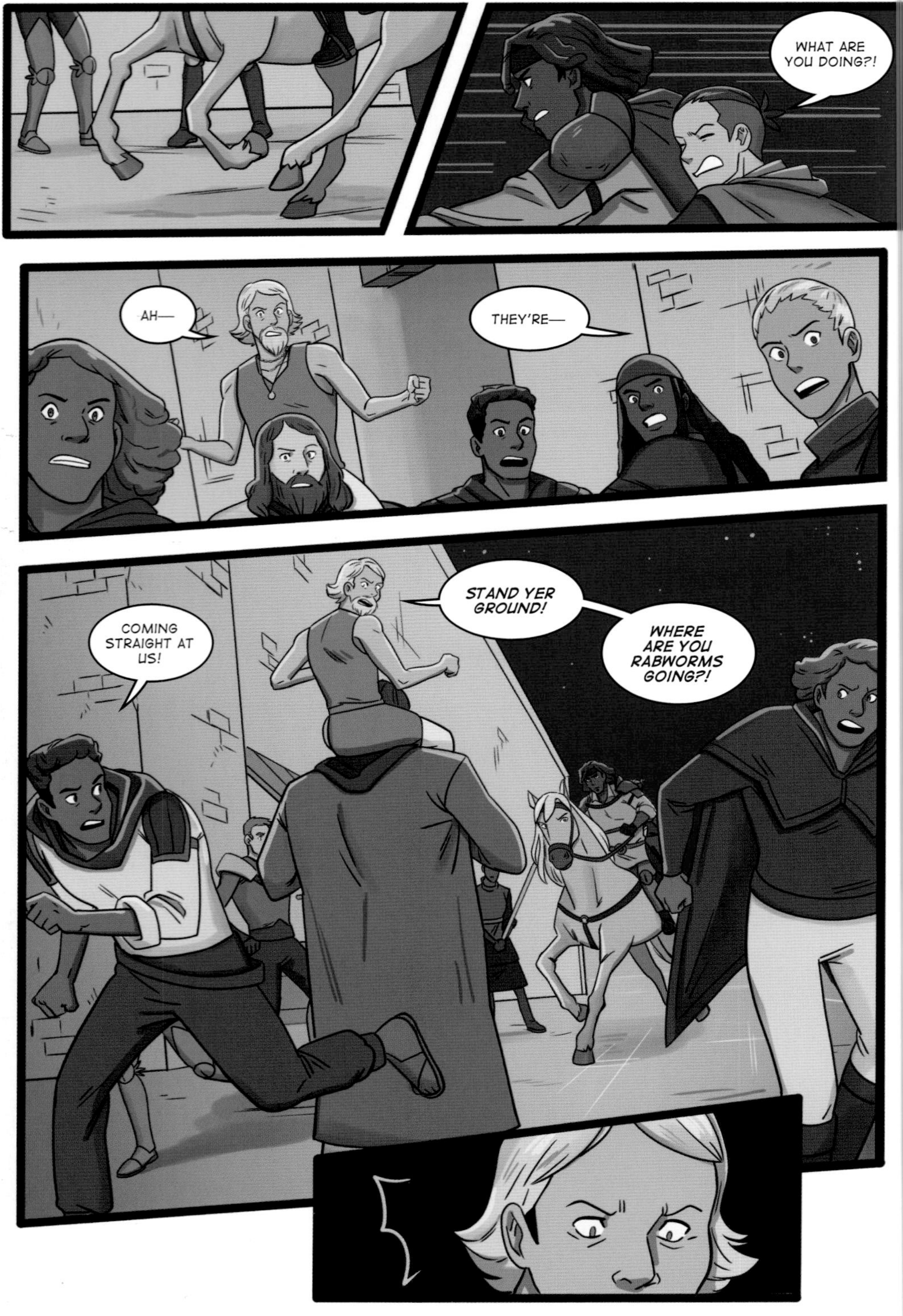
WHAT ARE YOU DOING?!
AH—
THEY'RE—
COMING STRAIGHT AT US!
STAND YER GROUND!
WHERE ARE YOU RABWORMS GOING?!

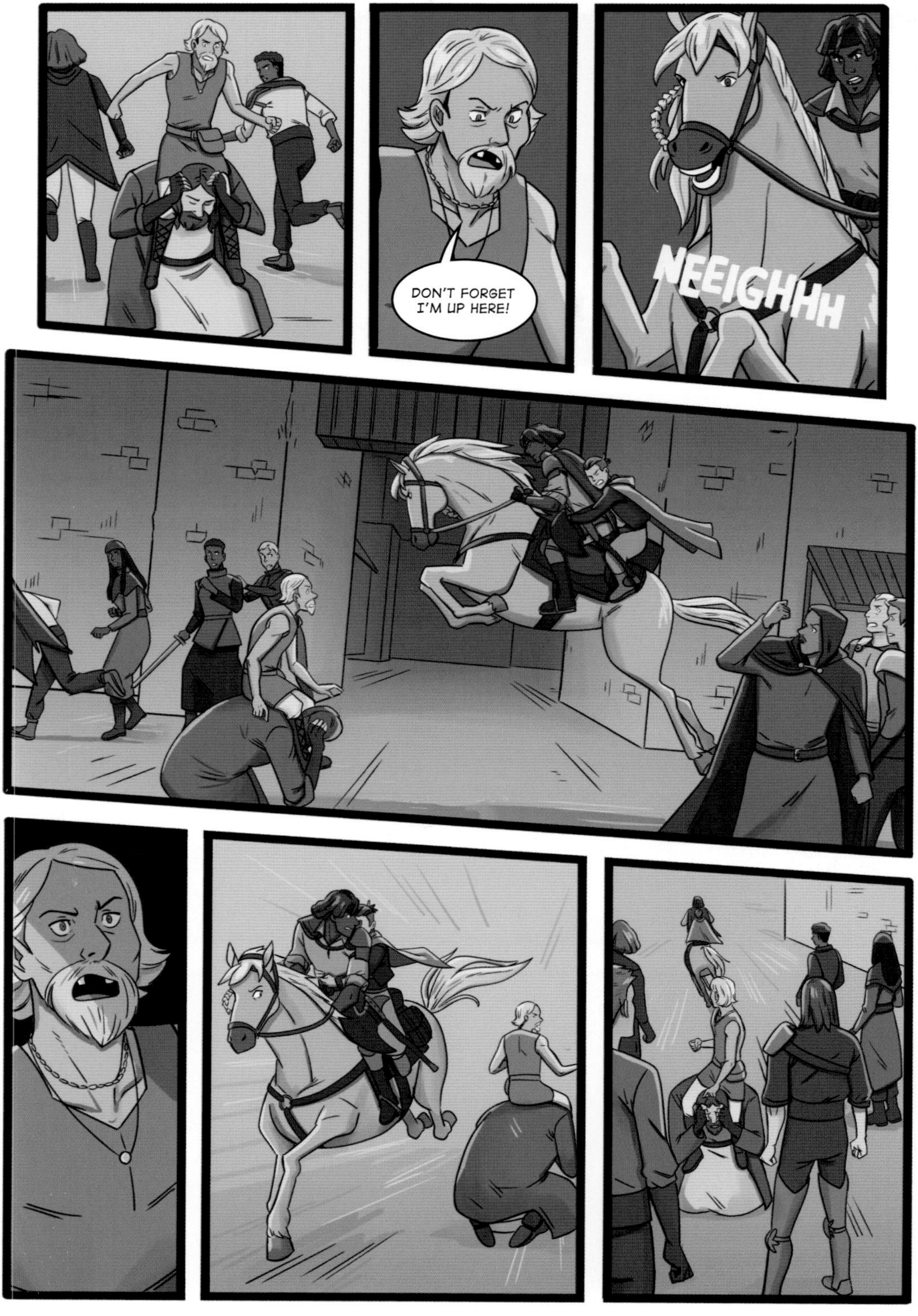
DON'T FORGET I'M UP HERE!
NEEIGHHH

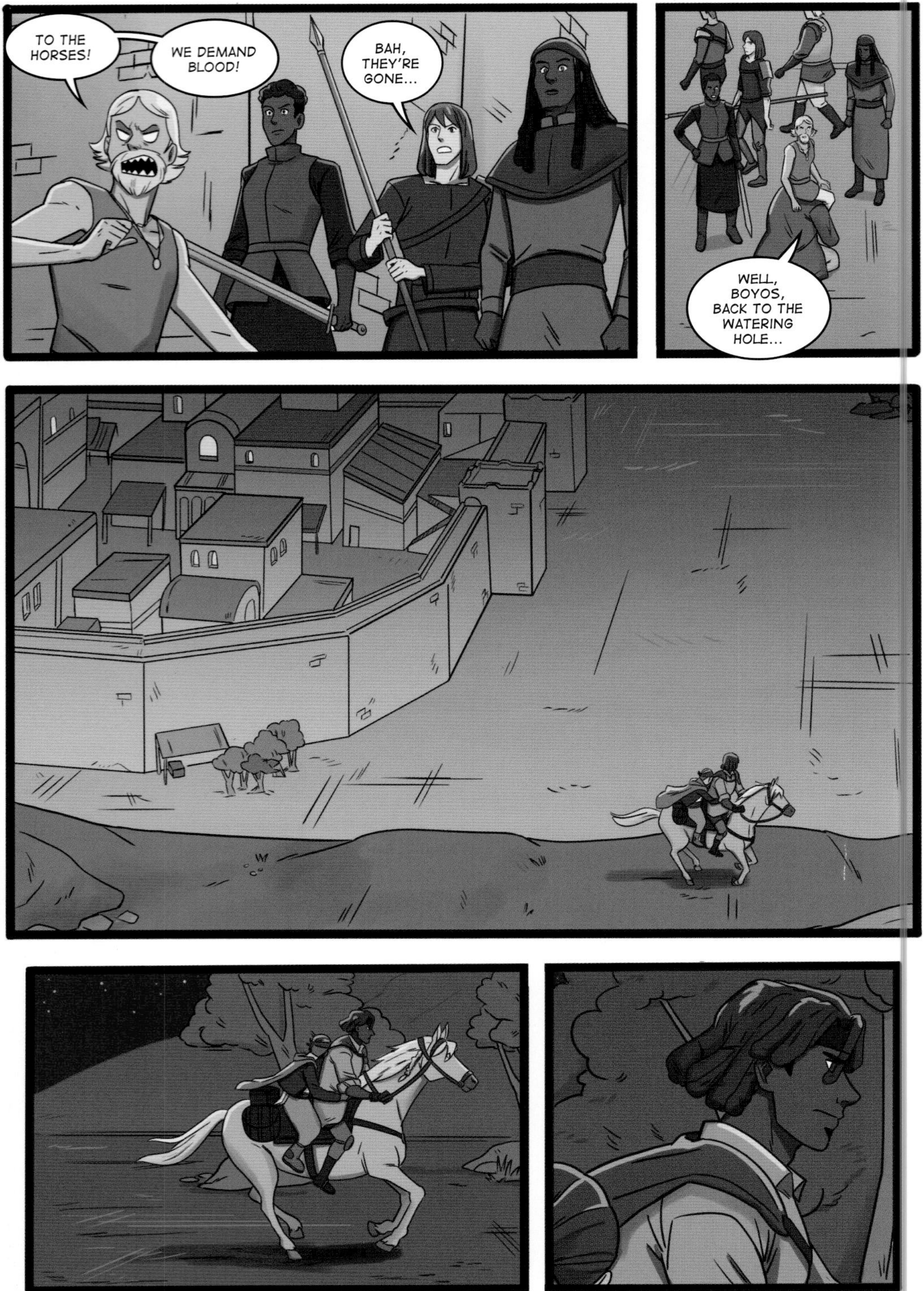
TO THE HORSES!
WE DEMAND BLOOD!
BAH, THEY'RE GONE...
WELL, BOYOS, BACK TO THE WATERING HOLE...

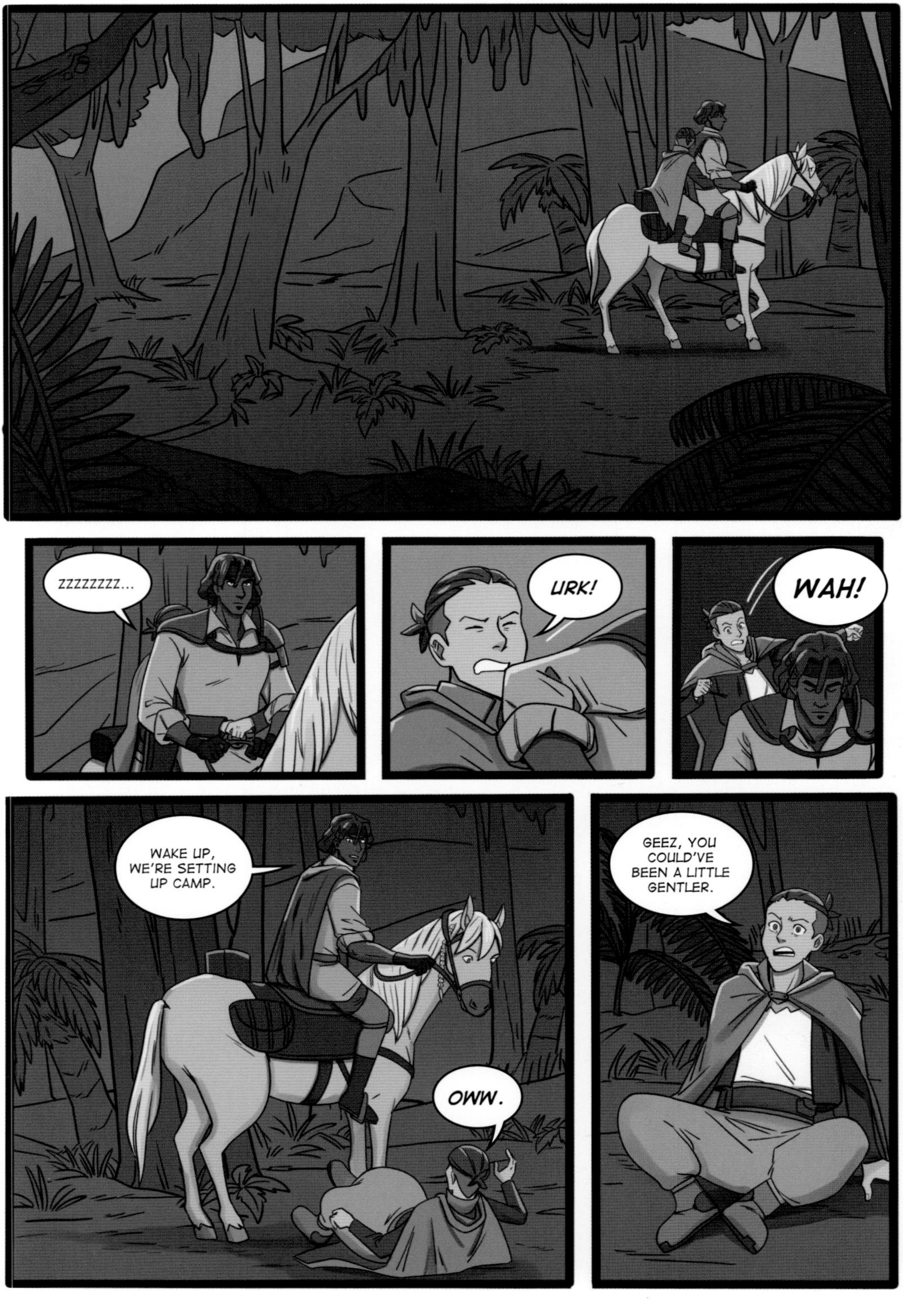
ZZZZZZZZ...
URK!
WAH!
WAKE UP, WE'RE SETTING UP CAMP.
OWW.
GEEZ, YOU COULD'VE BEEN A LITTLE GENTLER.

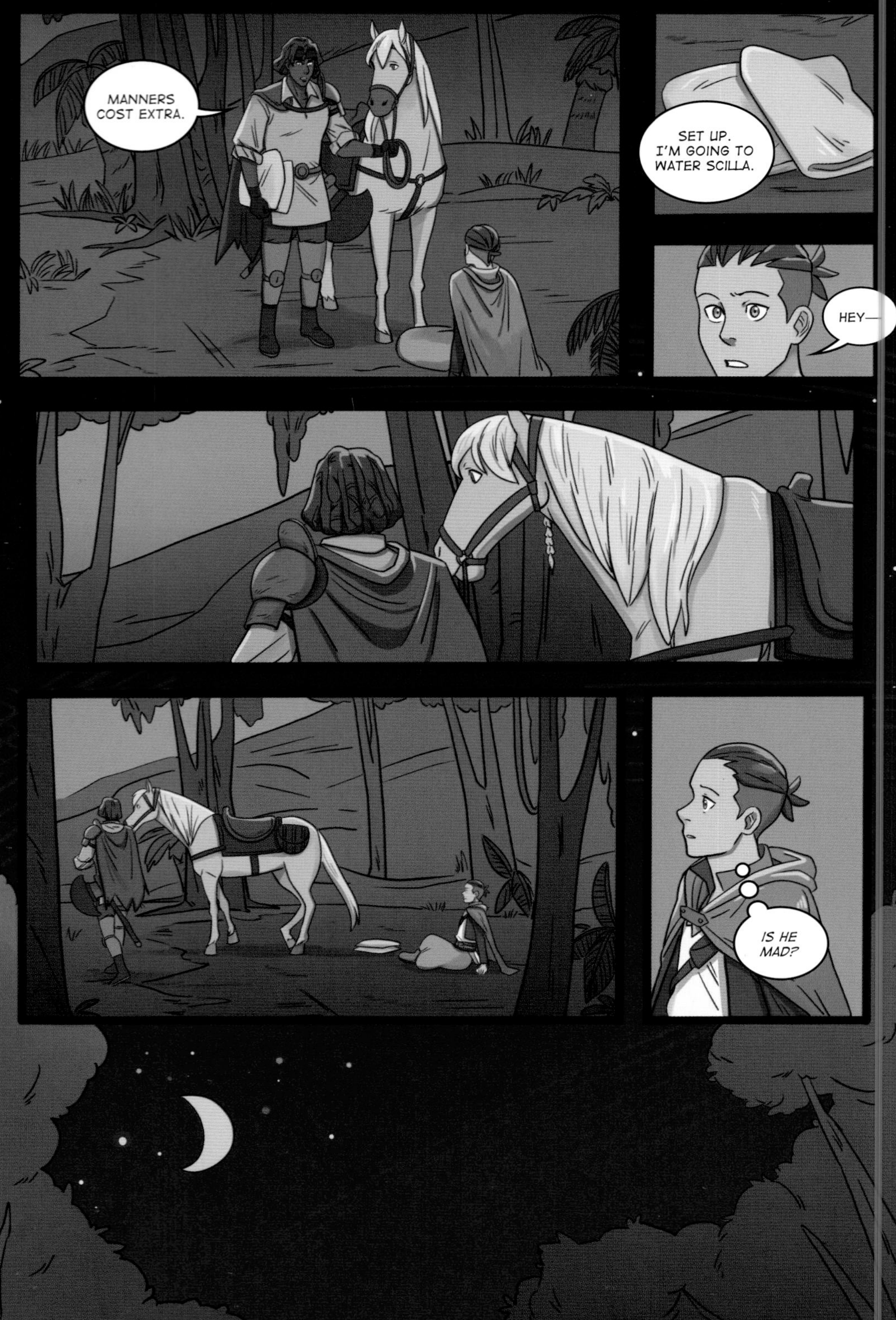
MANNERS COST EXTRA.
SET UP. I'M GOING TO WATER SCILLA.
HEY—
IS HE MAD?

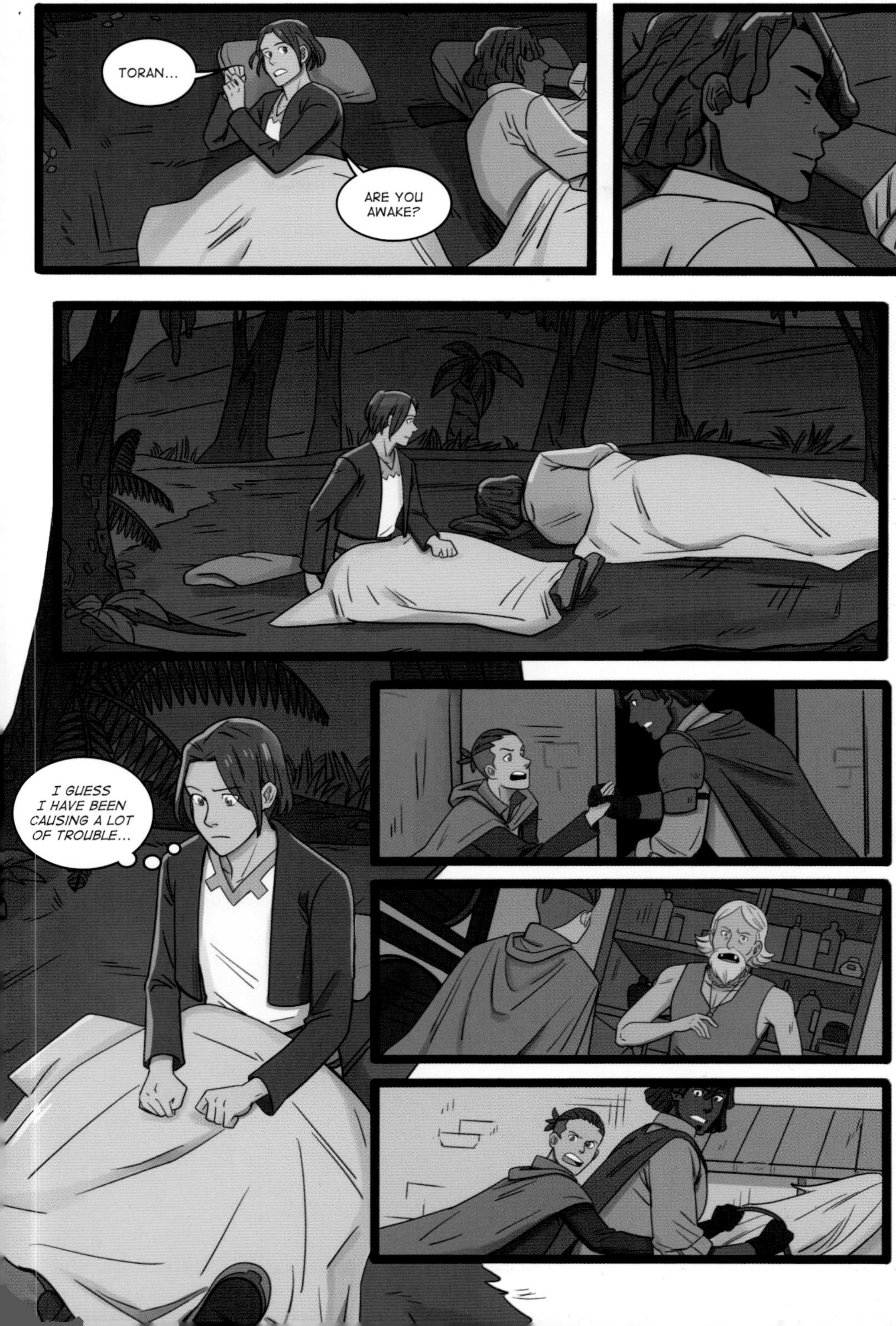
TORAN...
ARE YOU AWAKE?
I GUESS I HAVE BEEN CAUSING A LOT OF TROUBLE...

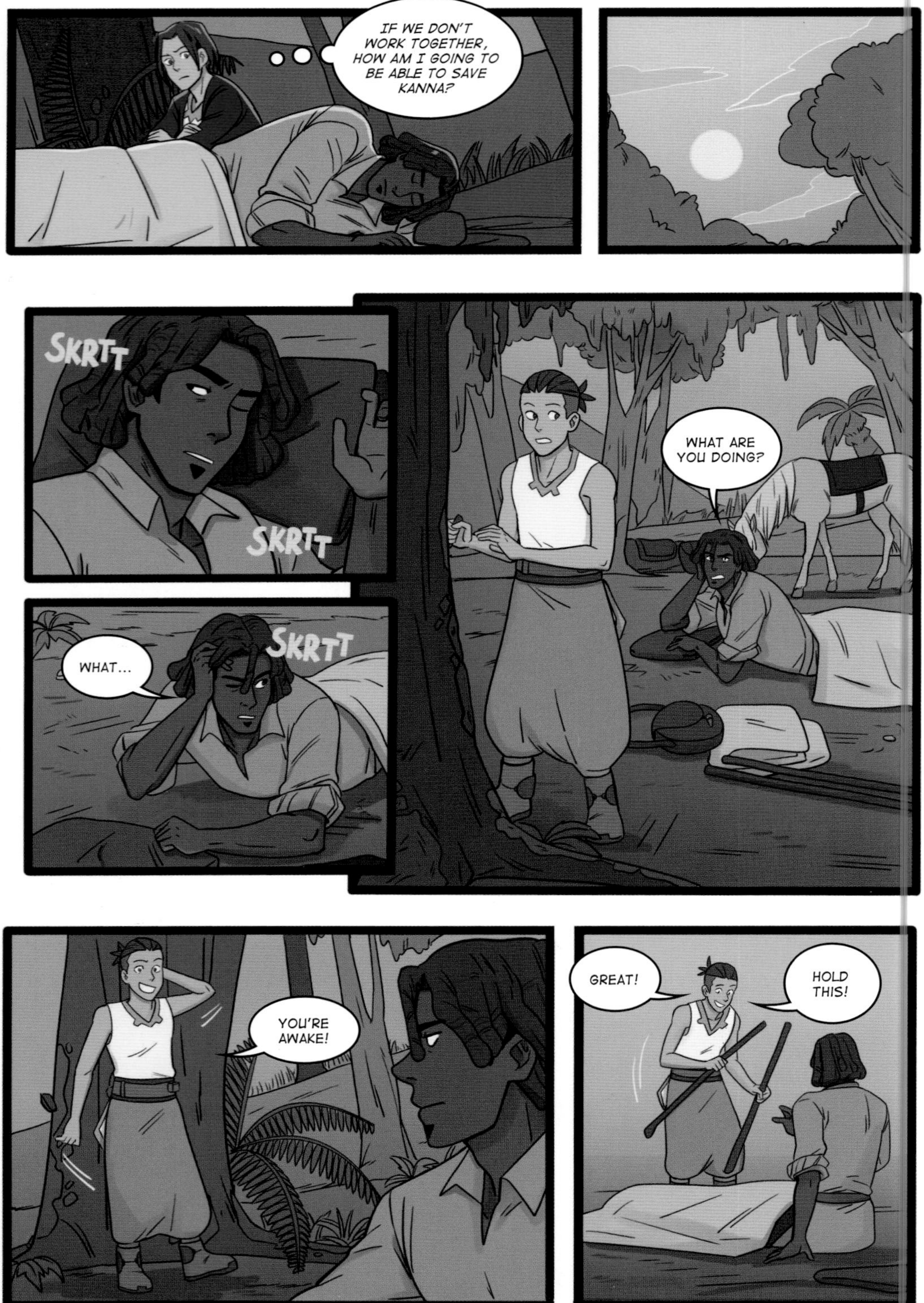
IF WE DON'T WORK TOGETHER, HOW AM I GOING TO BE ABLE TO SAVE KANNA?
SKRTT
SKRTT
SKRTT
WHAT...
WHAT ARE YOU DOING?
YOU'RE AWAKE!
GREAT!
HOLD THIS!

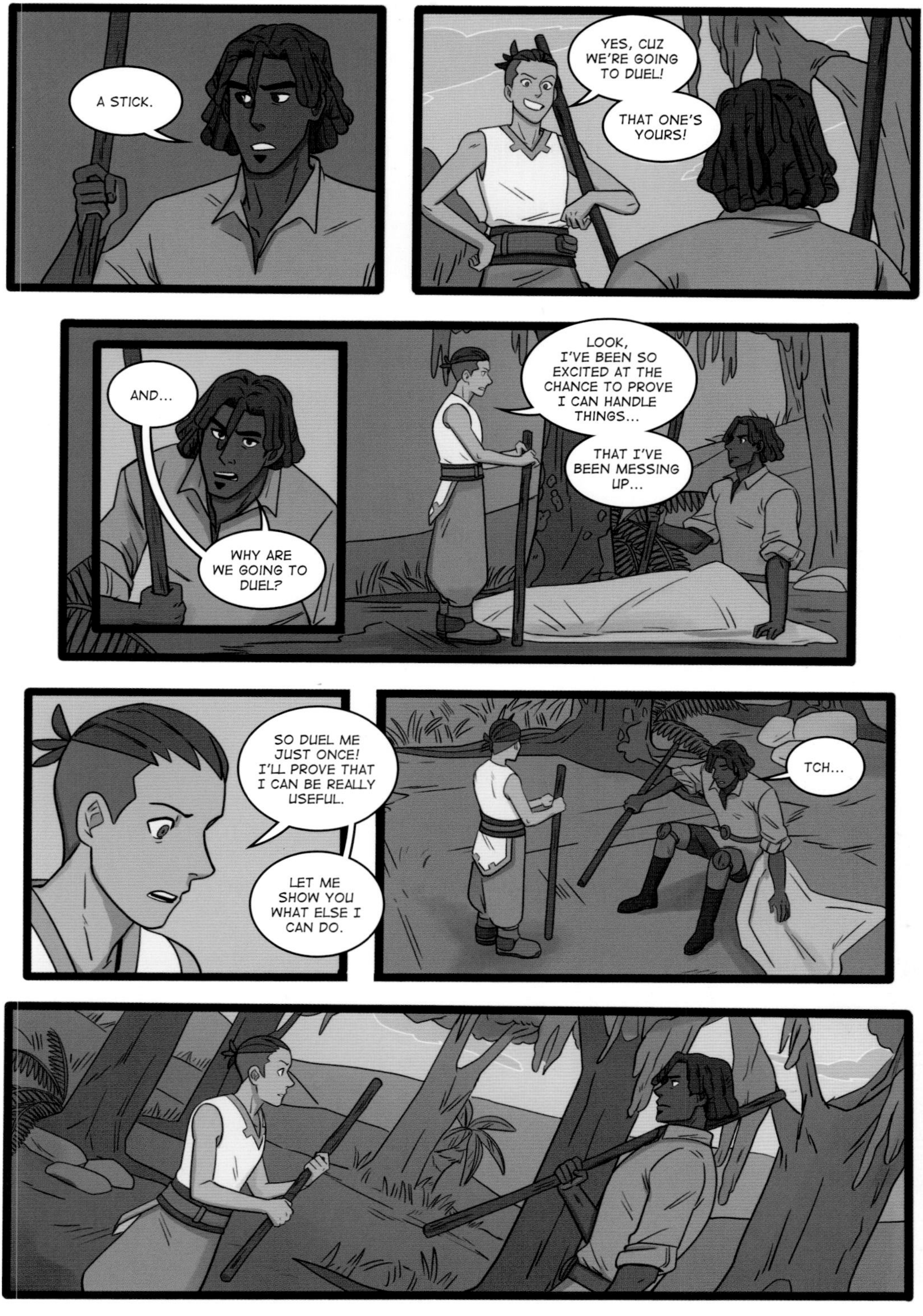
A STICK.
YES, CUZ WE'RE GOING TO DUEL!
THAT ONE'S YOURS!
AND...
WHY ARE WE GOING TO DUEL?
LOOK, I'VE BEEN SO EXCITED AT THE CHANCE TO PROVE I CAN HANDLE THINGS...
THAT I'VE BEEN MESSING UP...
SO DUEL ME JUST ONCE! I'LL PROVE THAT I CAN BE REALLY USEFUL.
LET ME SHOW YOU WHAT ELSE I CAN DO.
TCH...

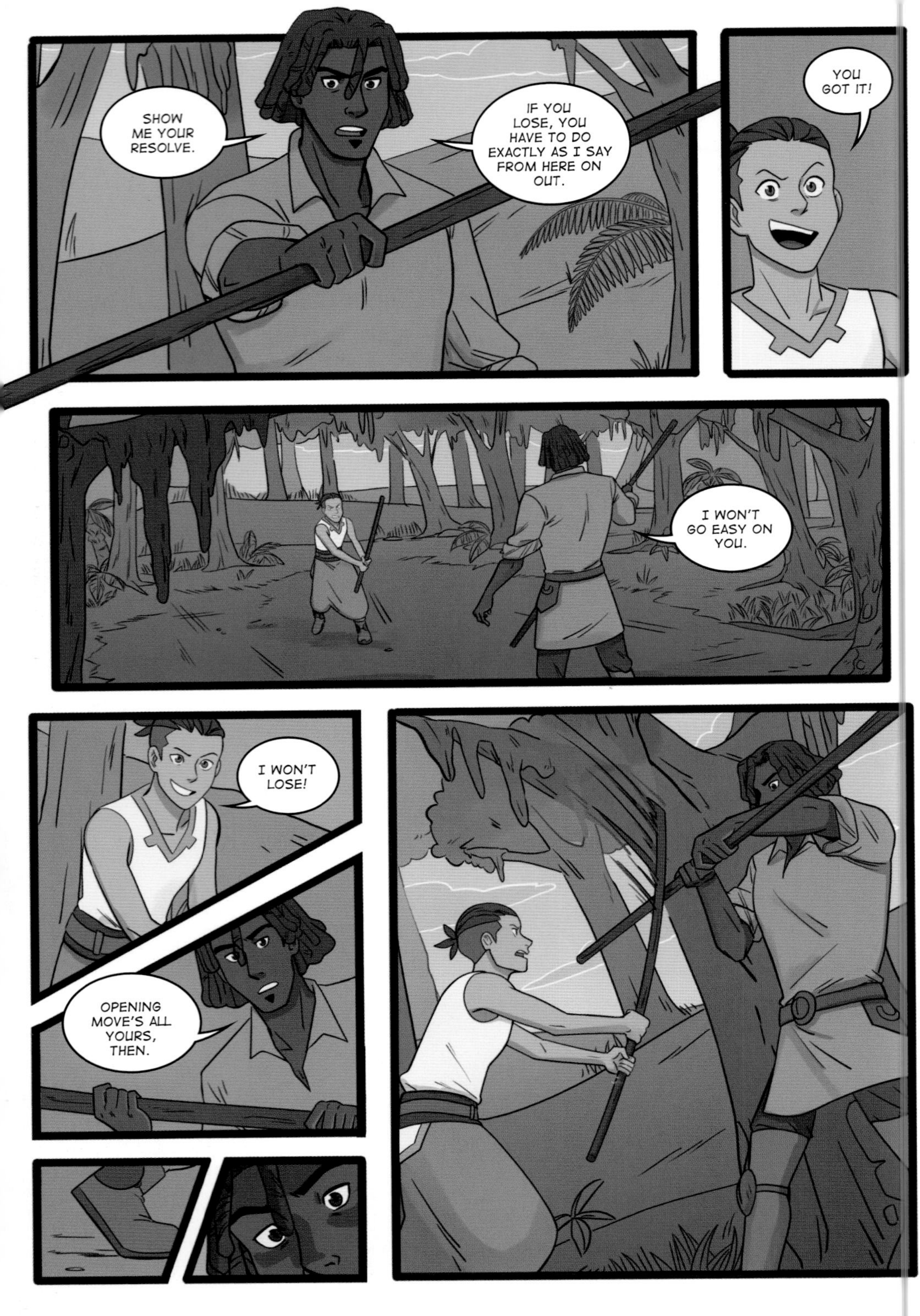
SHOW ME YOUR RESOLVE.
IF YOU LOSE, YOU HAVE TO DO EXACTLY AS I SAY FROM HERE ON OUT.
YOU GOT IT!
I WON'T GO EASY ON YOU.
I WON'T LOSE!
OPENING MOVE'S ALL YOURS, THEN.

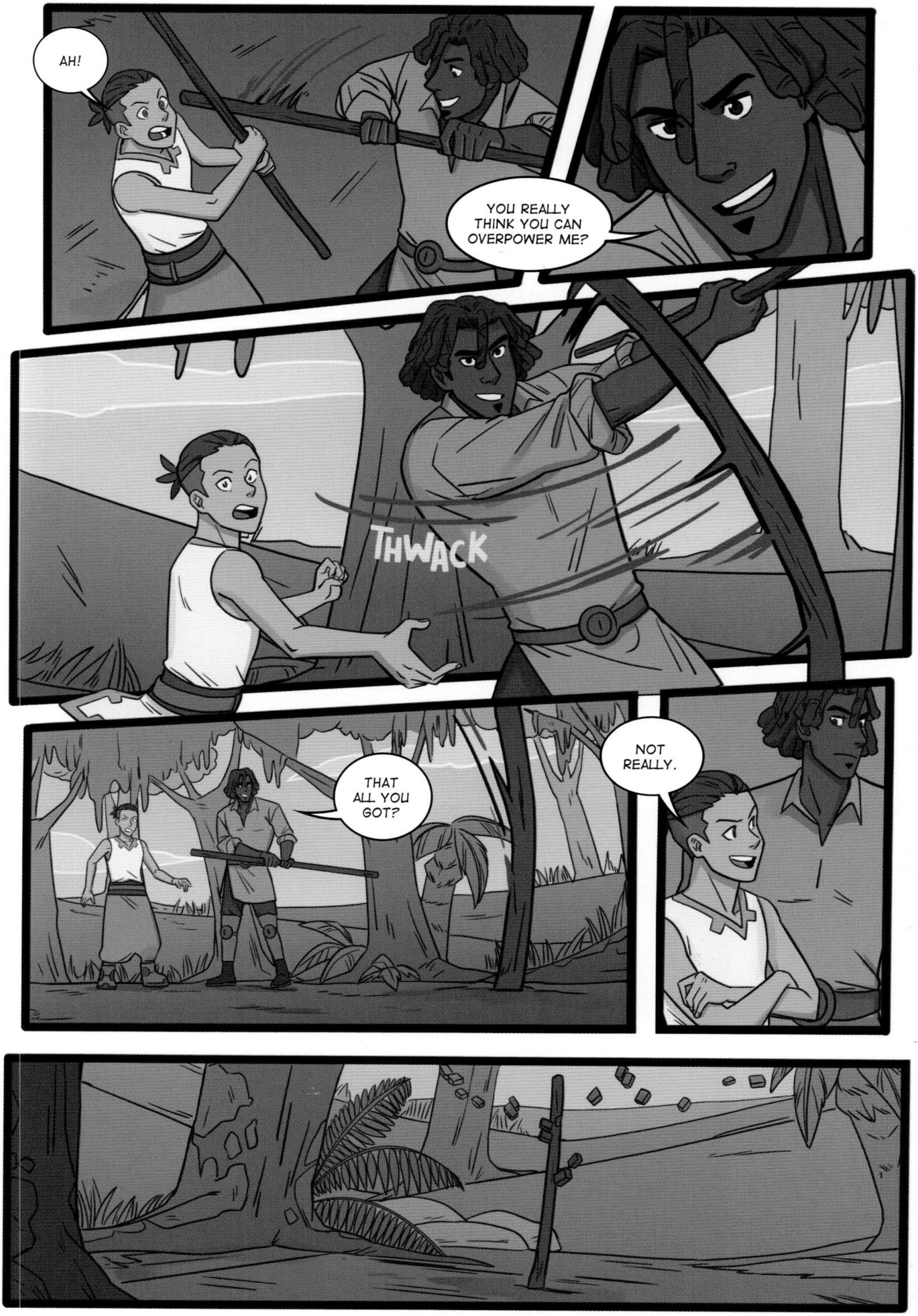
AH!
YOU REALLY THINK YOU CAN OVERPOWER ME?
THWACK
THAT ALL YOU GOT?
NOT REALLY.

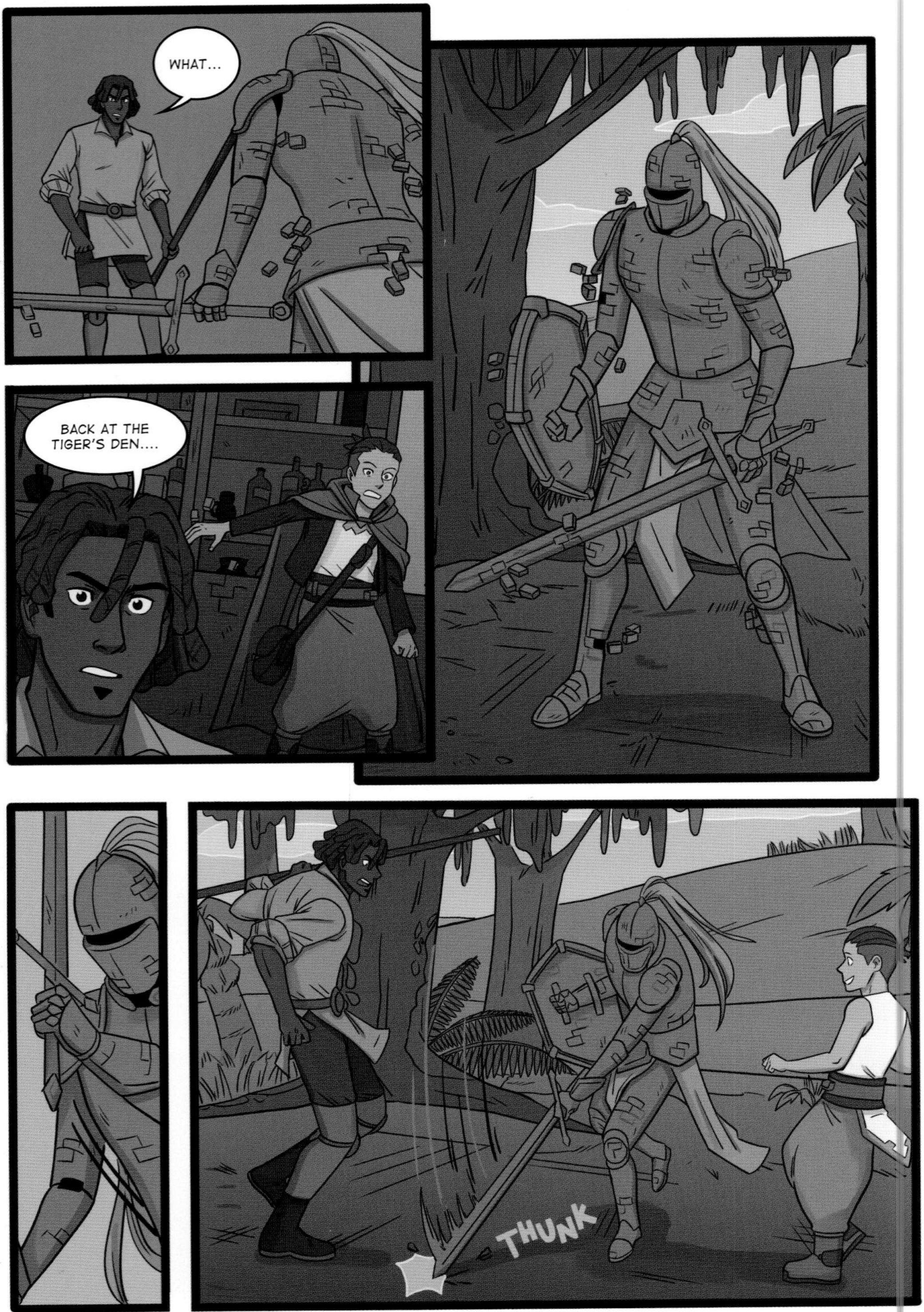
WHAT...
BACK AT THE TIGER'S DEN....
THUNK

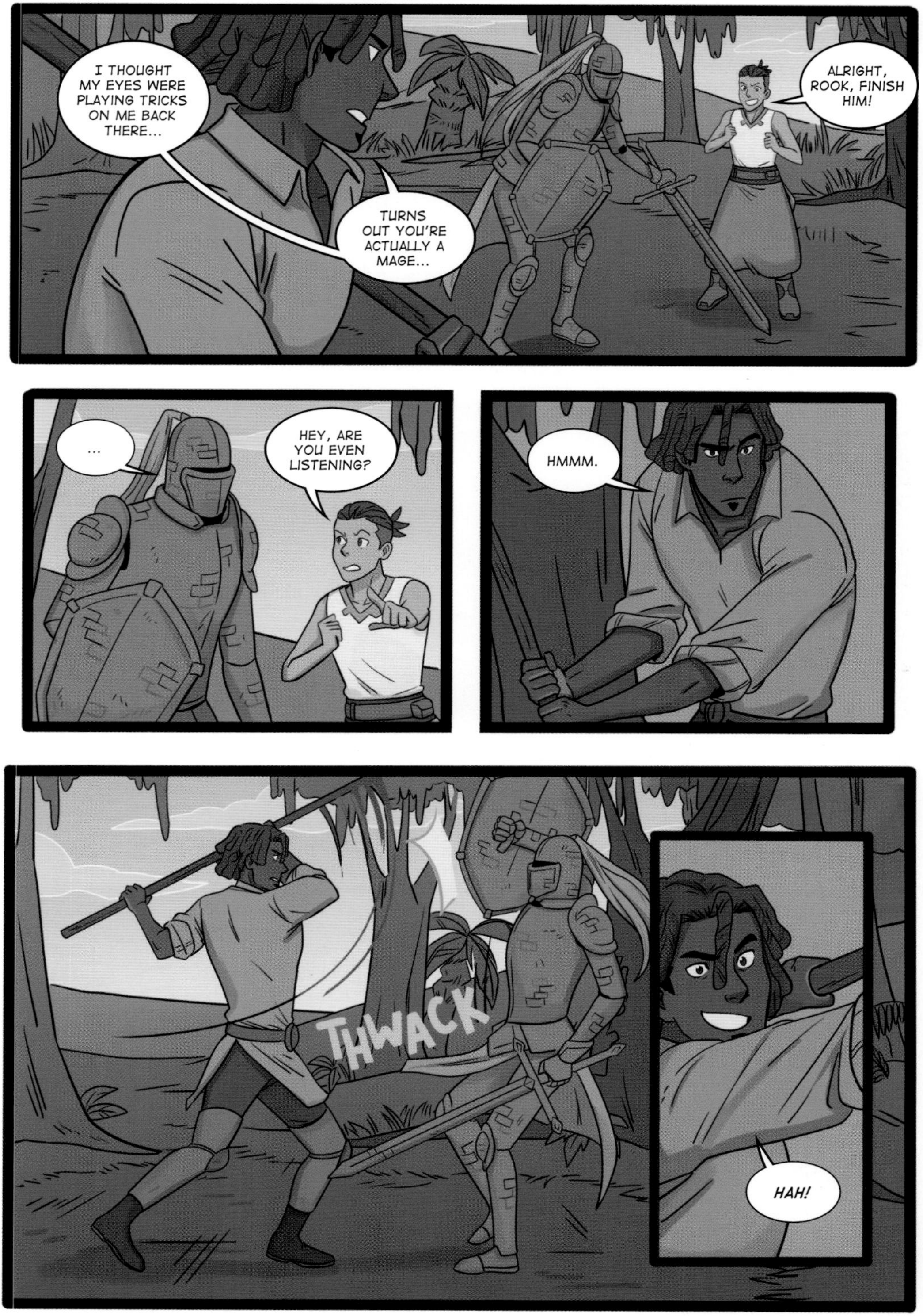
I THOUGHT MY EYES WERE PLAYING TRICKS ON ME BACK THERE...
TURNS OUT YOU'RE ACTUALLY A MAGE...
ALRIGHT, ROOK, FINISH HIM!
...
HEY, ARE YOU EVEN LISTENING?
HMMM.
THWACK
HAH!

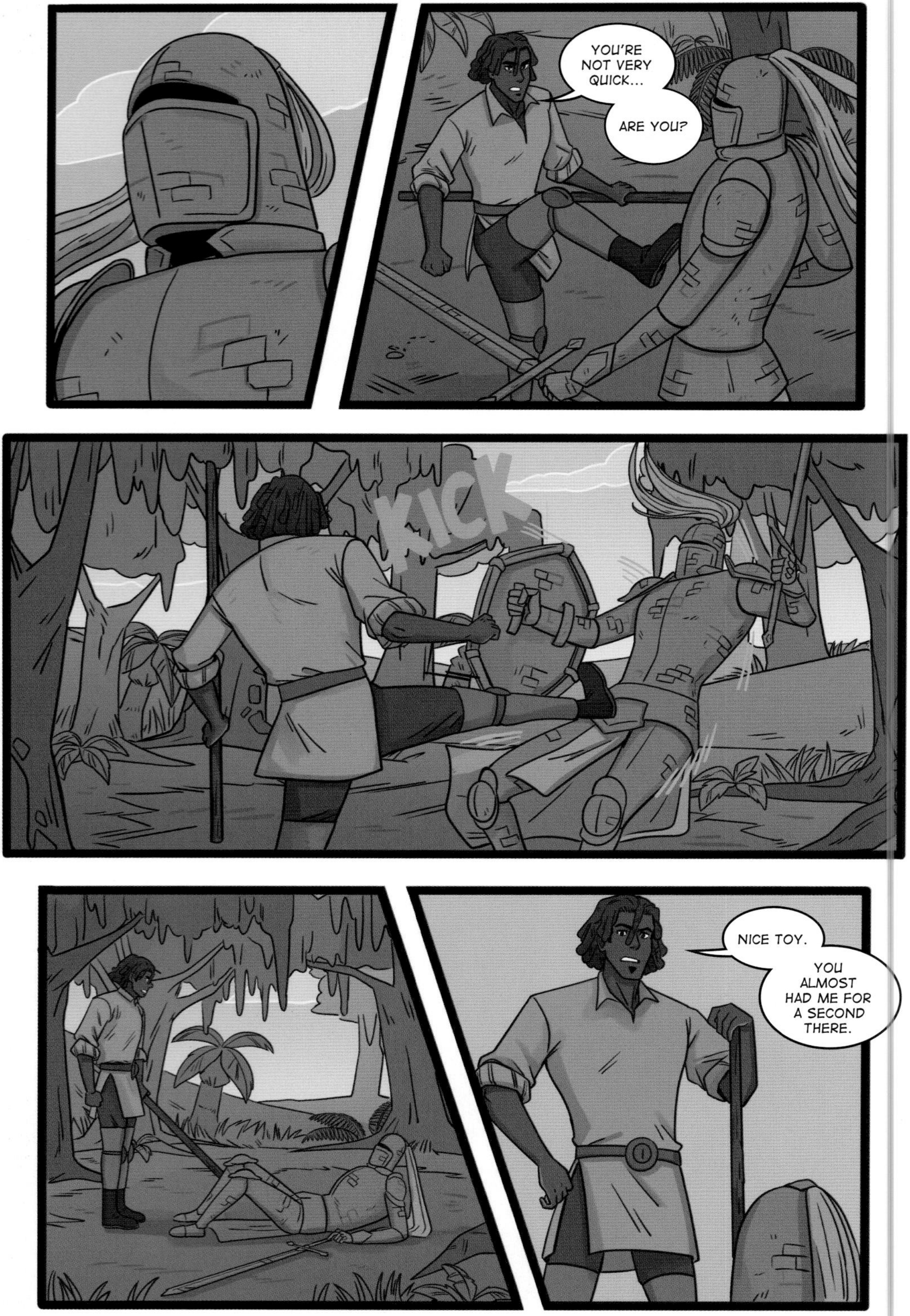
YOU'RE NOT VERY QUICK...
ARE YOU?
KICK
NICE TOY.
YOU ALMOST HAD ME FOR A SECOND THERE.

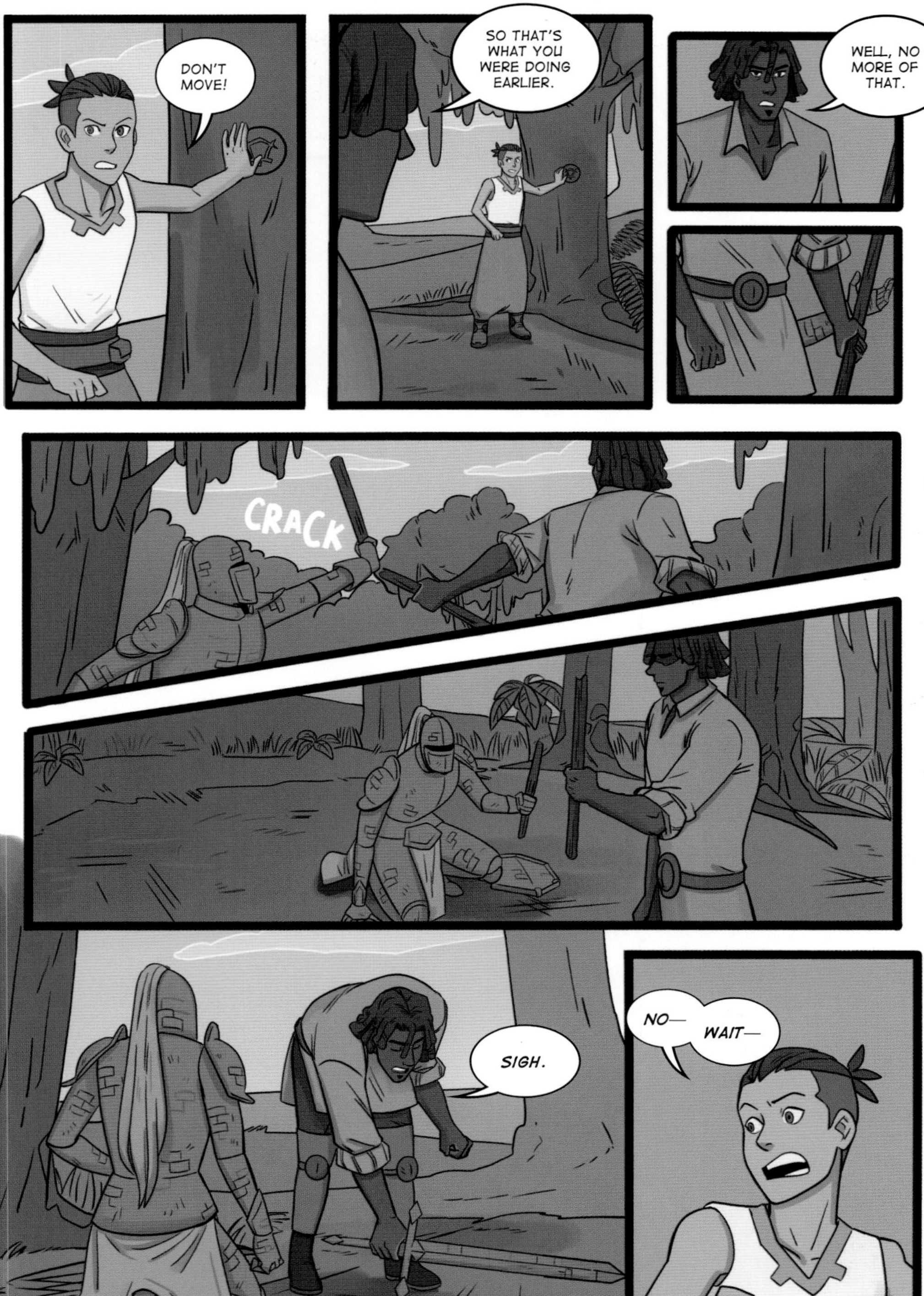
DON'T MOVE!
SO THAT'S WHAT YOU WERE DOING EARLIER.
WELL, NO MORE OF THAT.
CRACK
SIGH.
NO—
WAIT—

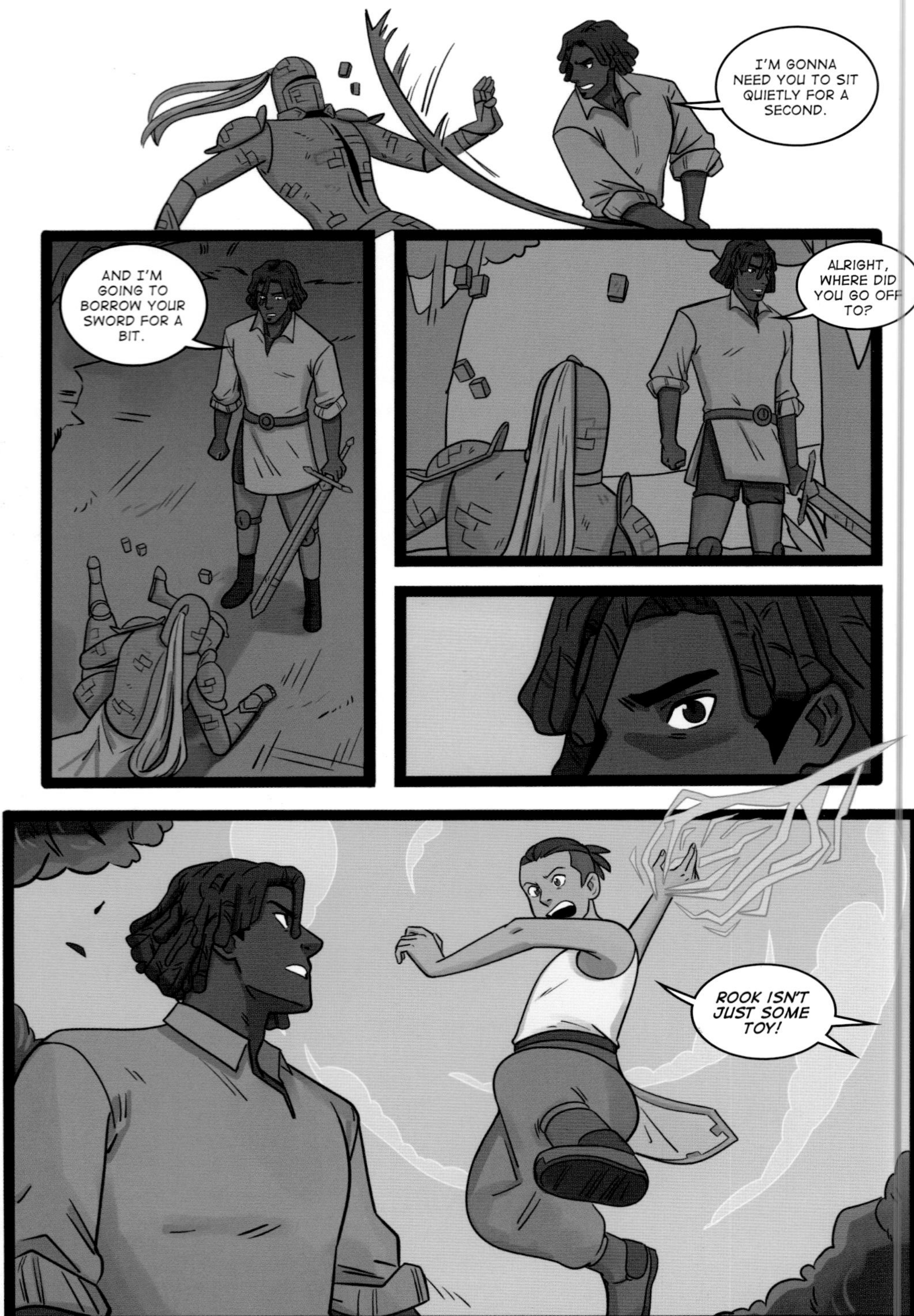
I'M GONNA NEED YOU TO SIT QUIETLY FOR A SECOND.
AND I'M GOING TO BORROW YOUR SWORD FOR A BIT.
ALRIGHT, WHERE DID YOU GO OFF TO?
ROOK ISN'T JUST SOME TOY!

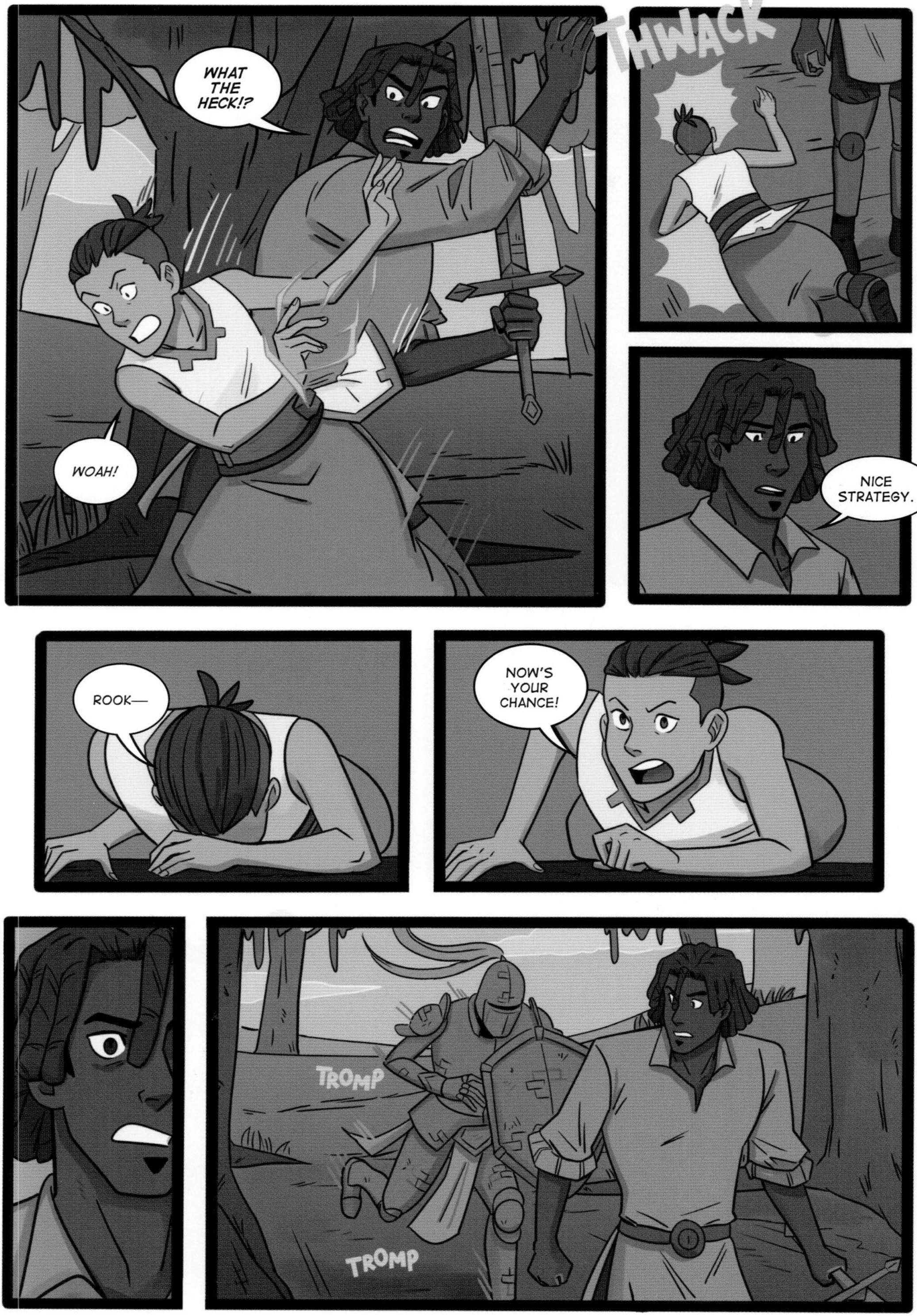
WHAT THE HECK!?
WOAH!
THWACK
NICE STRATEGY.
ROOK—
NOW'S YOUR CHANCE!
TROMP
TROMP

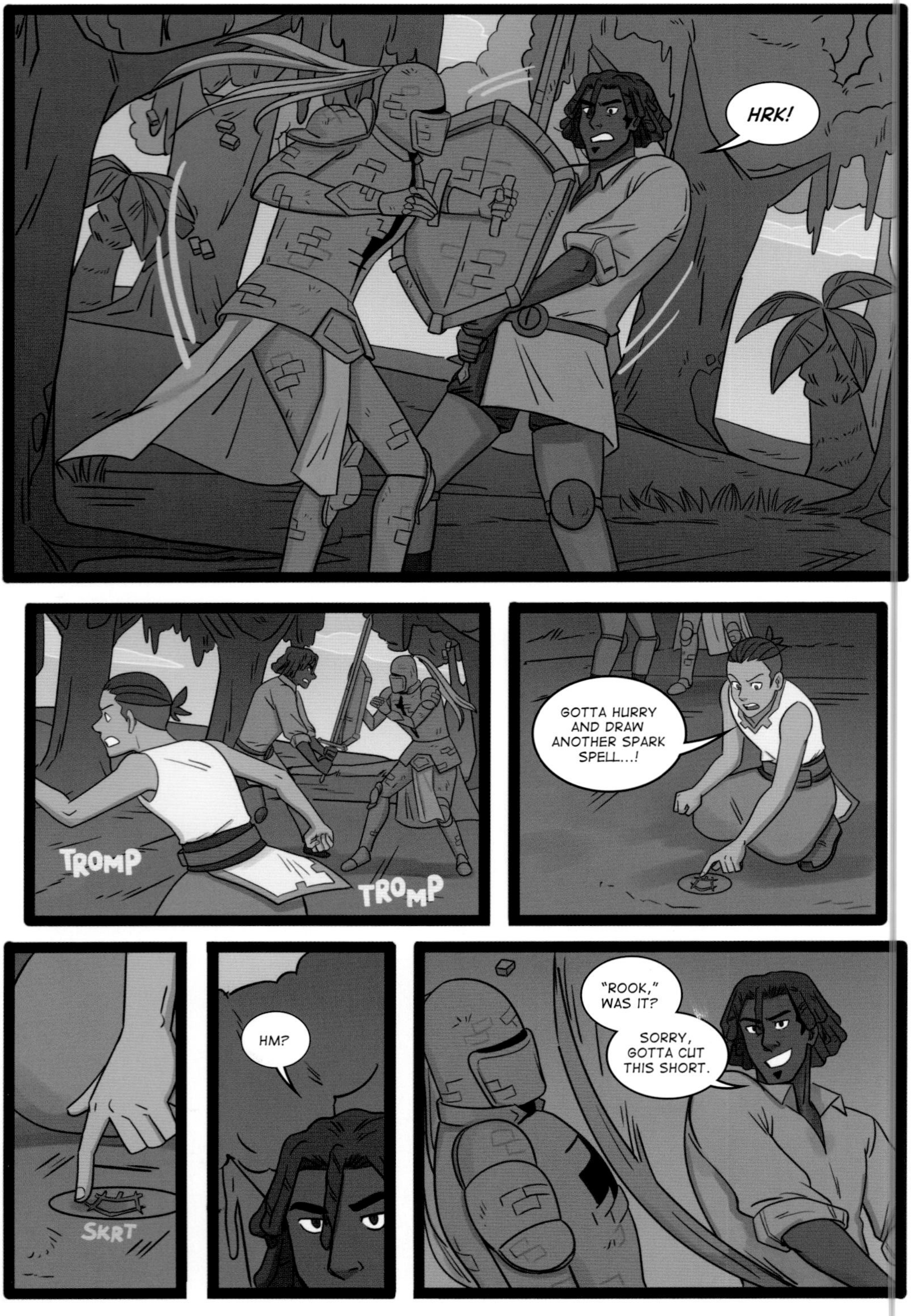
HRK!
TROMP
TROMP
GOTTA HURRY AND DRAW ANOTHER SPARK SPELL...!
SKRT
HM?
"ROOK," WAS IT?
SORRY, GOTTA CUT THIS SHORT.

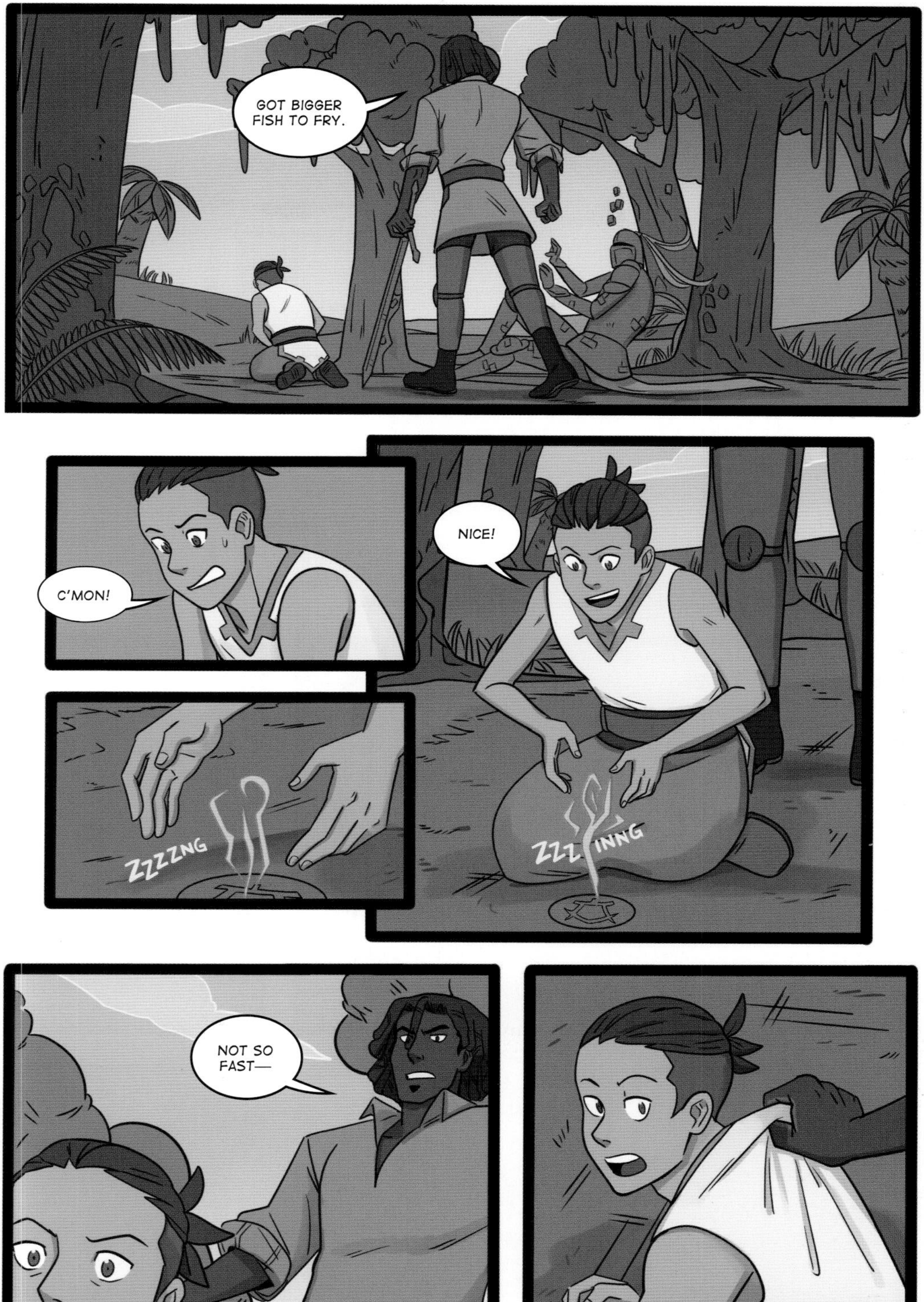
GOT BIGGER FISH TO FRY.
C'MON!
ZZZZNG
NICE!
ZZZ INNG
NOT SO FAST—

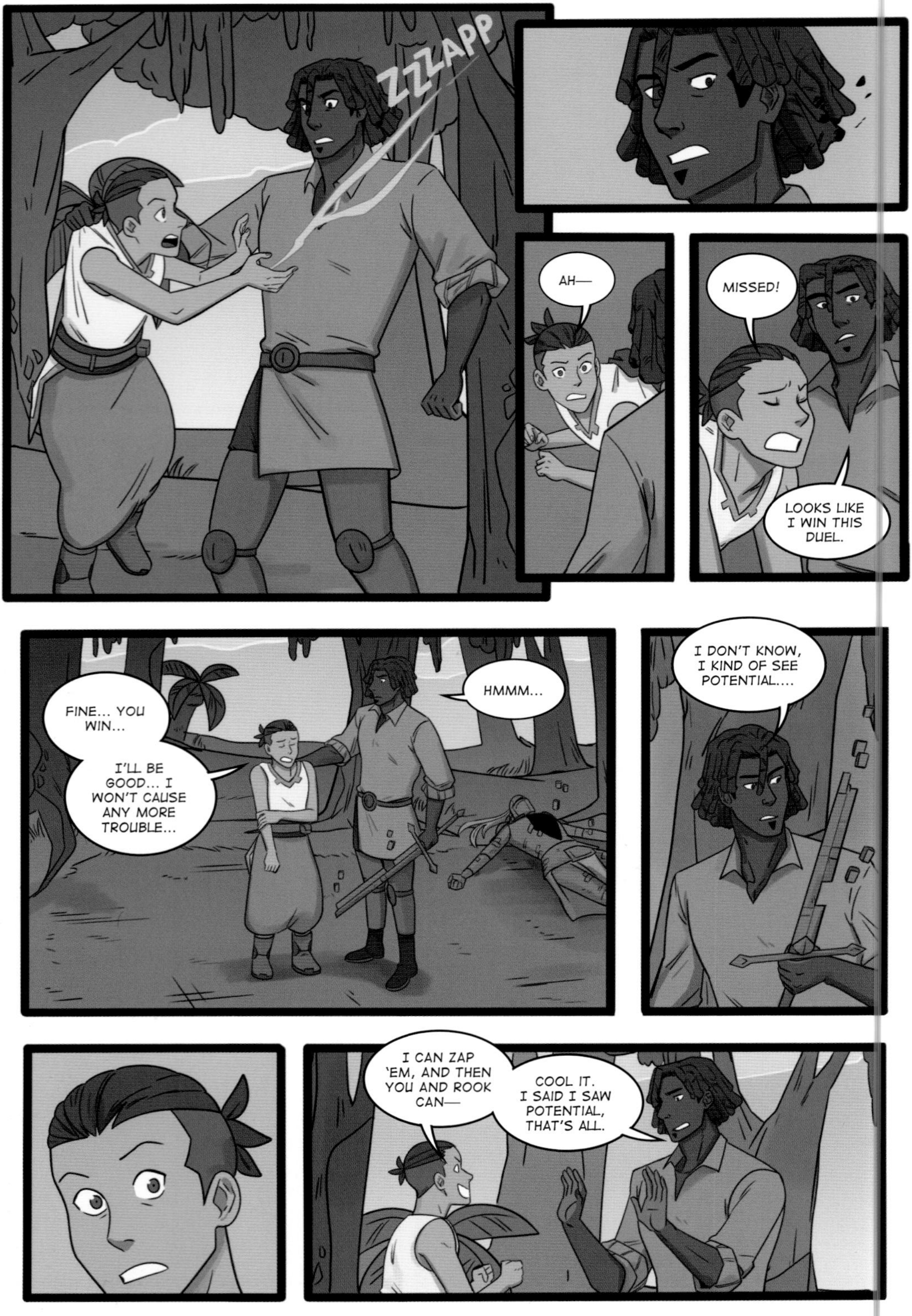
ZZZAPP
AH—
MISSED!
LOOKS LIKE I WIN THIS DUEL.
FINE... YOU WIN...
I'LL BE GOOD... I WON'T CAUSE ANY MORE TROUBLE...
HMMM...
I DON'T KNOW, I KIND OF SEE POTENTIAL....
I CAN ZAP 'EM, AND THEN YOU AND ROOK CAN—
COOL IT. I SAID I SAW POTENTIAL, THAT'S ALL.

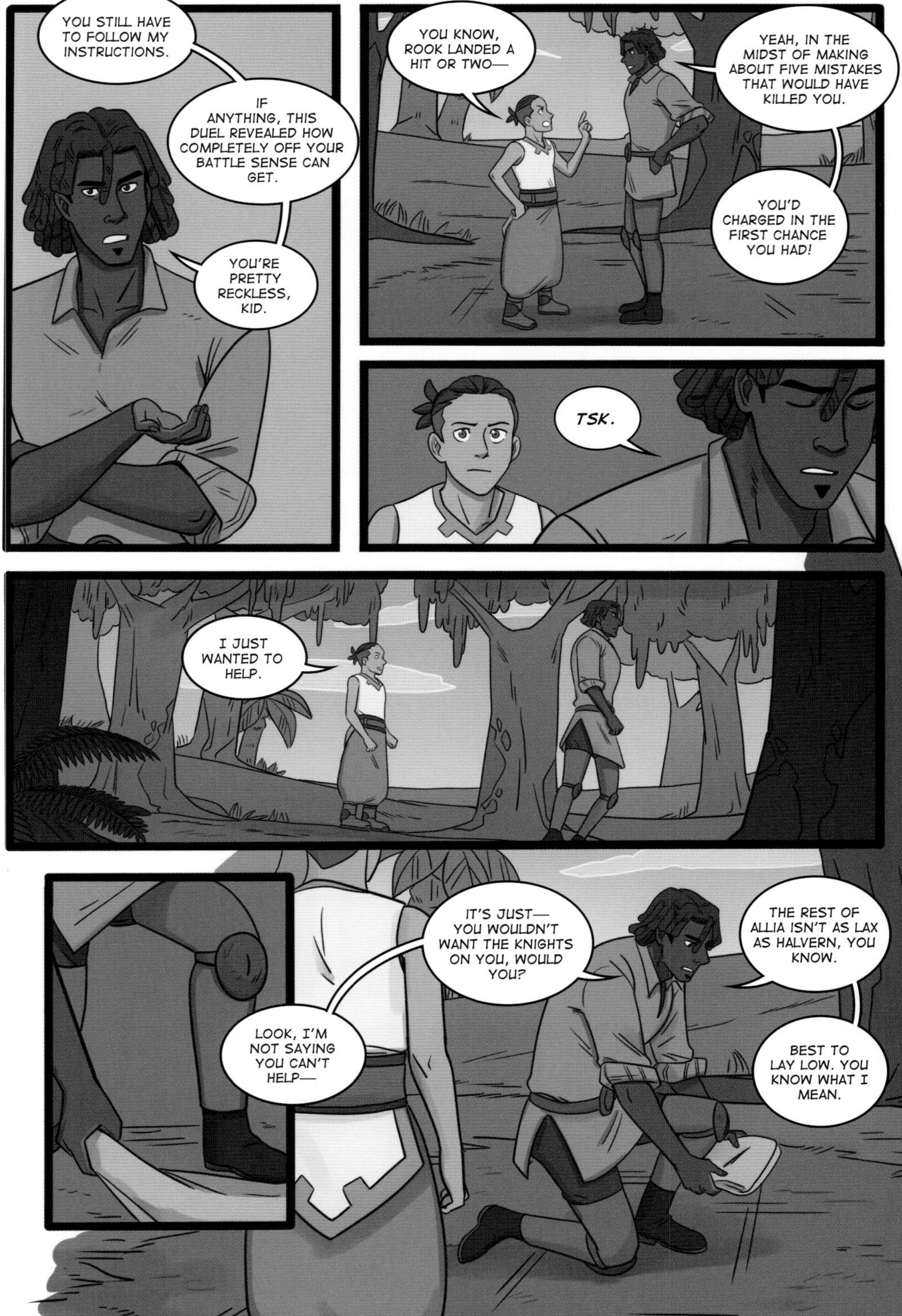
YOU STILL HAVE TO FOLLOW MY INSTRUCTIONS.
IF ANYTHING, THIS DUEL REVEALED HOW COMPLETELY OFF YOUR BATTLE SENSE CAN GET.
YOU'RE PRETTY RECKLESS, KID.
YOU KNOW, ROOK LANDED A HIT OR TWO—
YEAH, IN THE MIDST OF MAKING ABOUT FIVE MISTAKES THAT WOULD HAVE KILLED YOU.
YOU'D CHARGED IN THE FIRST CHANCE YOU HAD!
TSK.
I JUST WANTED TO HELP.
LOOK, I'M NOT SAYING YOU CAN'T HELP—
IT'S JUST— YOU WOULDN'T WANT THE KNIGHTS ON YOU, WOULD YOU?
THE REST OF ALLIA ISN'T AS LAX AS HALVERN, YOU KNOW.
BEST TO LAY LOW. YOU KNOW WHAT I MEAN.

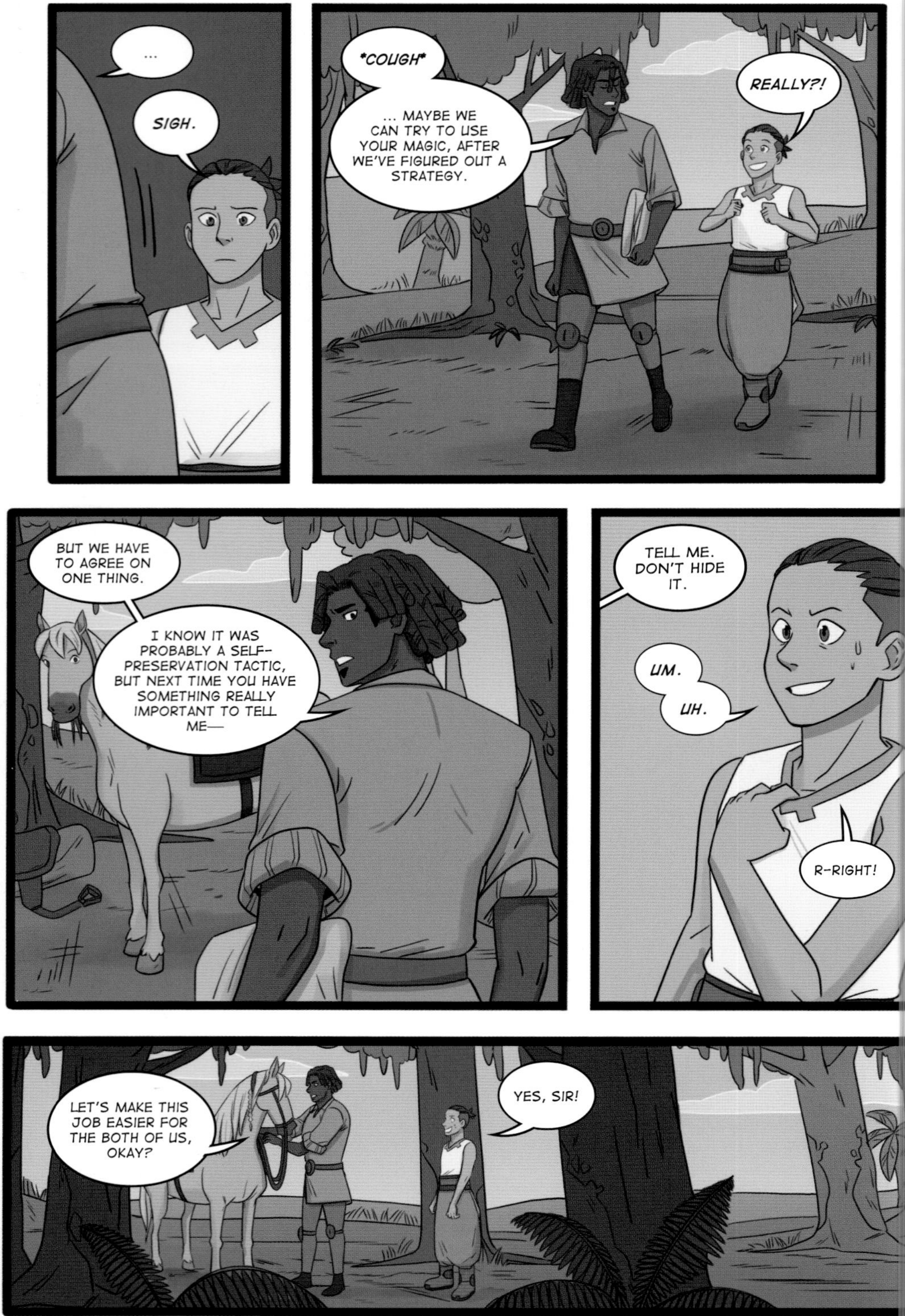
...
SIGH.
COUGH
... MAYBE WE CAN TRY TO USE YOUR MAGIC, AFTER WE'VE FIGURED OUT A STRATEGY.
REALLY?!
BUT WE HAVE TO AGREE ON ONE THING.
I KNOW IT WAS PROBABLY A SELF-PRESERVATION TACTIC, BUT NEXT TIME YOU HAVE SOMETHING REALLY IMPORTANT TO TELL ME—
TELL ME. DON'T HIDE IT.
UM.
UH.
R-RIGHT!
LET'S MAKE THIS JOB EASIER FOR THE BOTH OF US, OKAY?
YES, SIR!

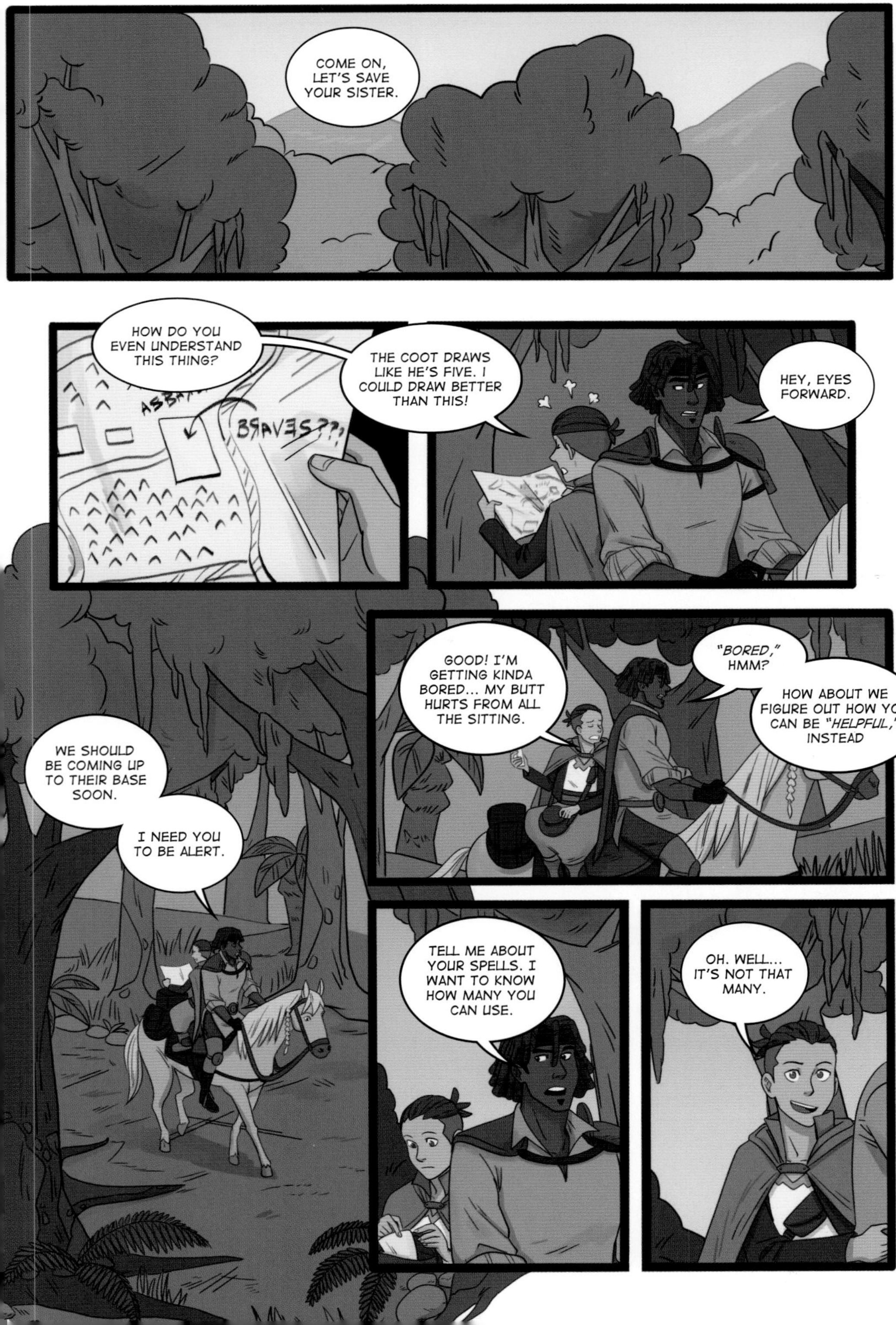
COME ON, LET'S SAVE YOUR SISTER.
HOW DO YOU EVEN UNDERSTAND THIS THING?
THE COOT DRAWS LIKE HE'S FIVE. I COULD DRAW BETTER THAN THIS!
BRAVES???
HEY, EYES FORWARD.
GOOD! I'M GETTING KINDA BORED... MY BUTT HURTS FROM ALL THE SITTING.
"BORED," HMM?
HOW ABOUT WE FIGURE OUT HOW YOU CAN BE "HELPFUL," INSTEAD
WE SHOULD BE COMING UP TO THEIR BASE SOON.
I NEED YOU TO BE ALERT.
TELL ME ABOUT YOUR SPELLS. I WANT TO KNOW HOW MANY YOU CAN USE.
OH. WELL... IT'S NOT THAT MANY.

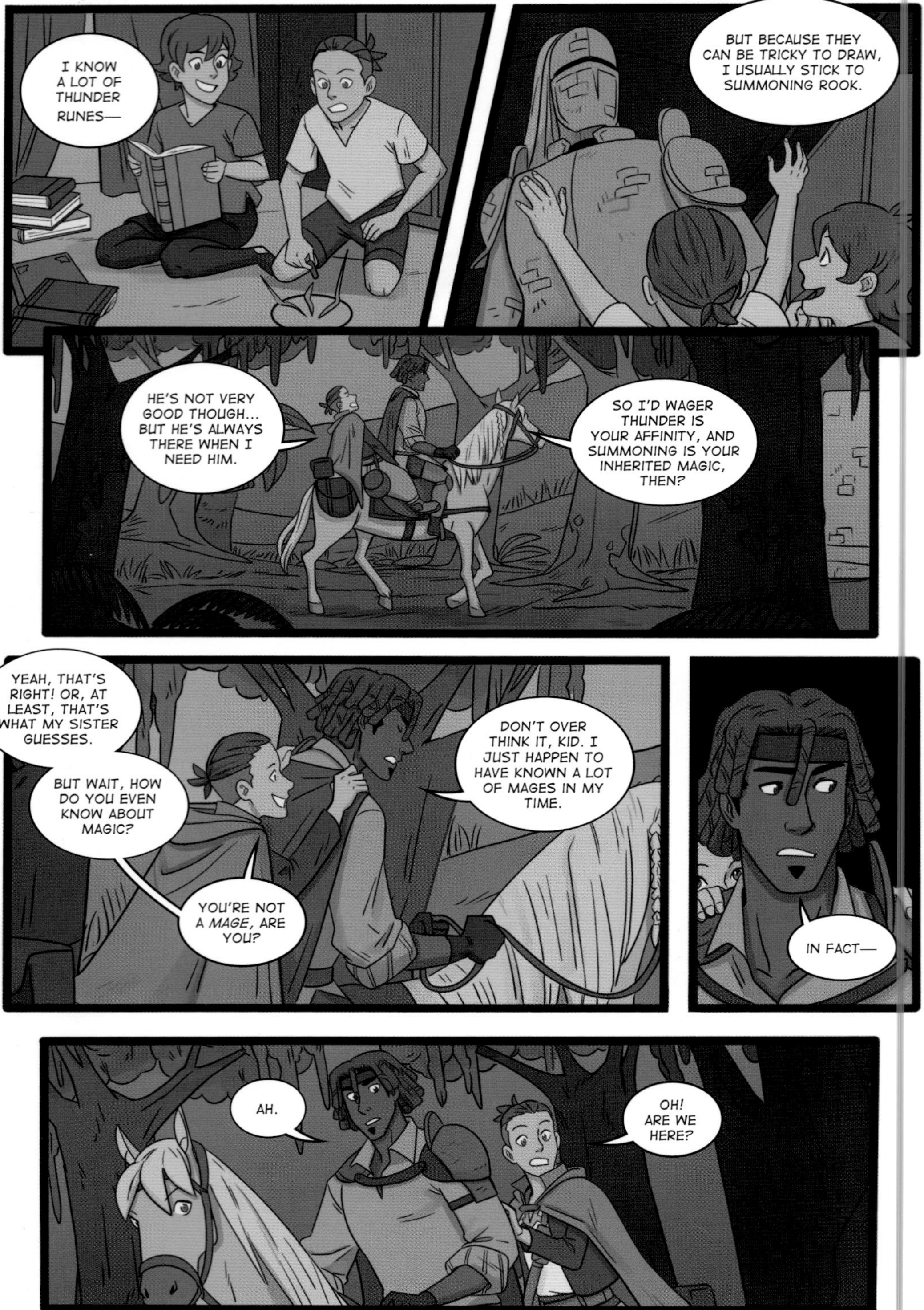

I KNOW A LOT OF THUNDER RUNES—
BUT BECAUSE THEY CAN BE TRICKY TO DRAW, I USUALLY STICK TO SUMMONING ROOK.
HE'S NOT VERY GOOD THOUGH... BUT HE'S ALWAYS THERE WHEN I NEED HIM.
SO I'D WAGER THUNDER IS YOUR AFFINITY, AND SUMMONING IS YOUR INHERITED MAGIC, THEN?
YEAH, THAT'S RIGHT! OR, AT LEAST, THAT'S WHAT MY SISTER GUESSES.
BUT WAIT, HOW DO YOU EVEN KNOW ABOUT MAGIC?
YOU'RE NOT A *MAGE*, ARE YOU?
DON'T OVER THINK IT, KID. I JUST HAPPEN TO HAVE KNOWN A LOT OF MAGES IN MY TIME.
IN FACT—
AH.
OH! ARE WE HERE?

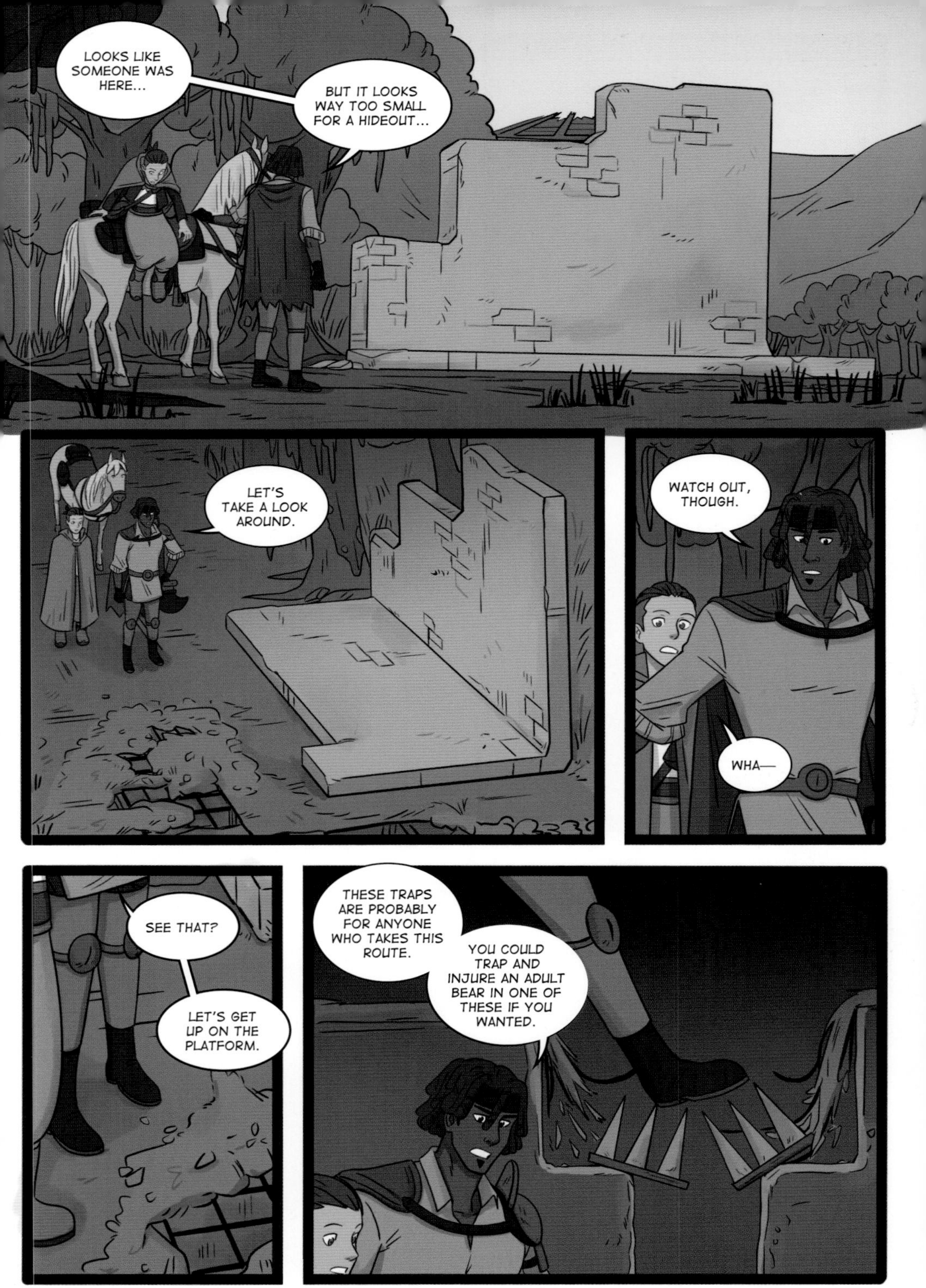
LOOKS LIKE SOMEONE WAS HERE...
BUT IT LOOKS WAY TOO SMALL FOR A HIDEOUT...
LET'S TAKE A LOOK AROUND.
WATCH OUT, THOUGH.
WHA—
SEE THAT?
LET'S GET UP ON THE PLATFORM.
THESE TRAPS ARE PROBABLY FOR ANYONE WHO TAKES THIS ROUTE.
YOU COULD TRAP AND INJURE AN ADULT BEAR IN ONE OF THESE IF YOU WANTED.

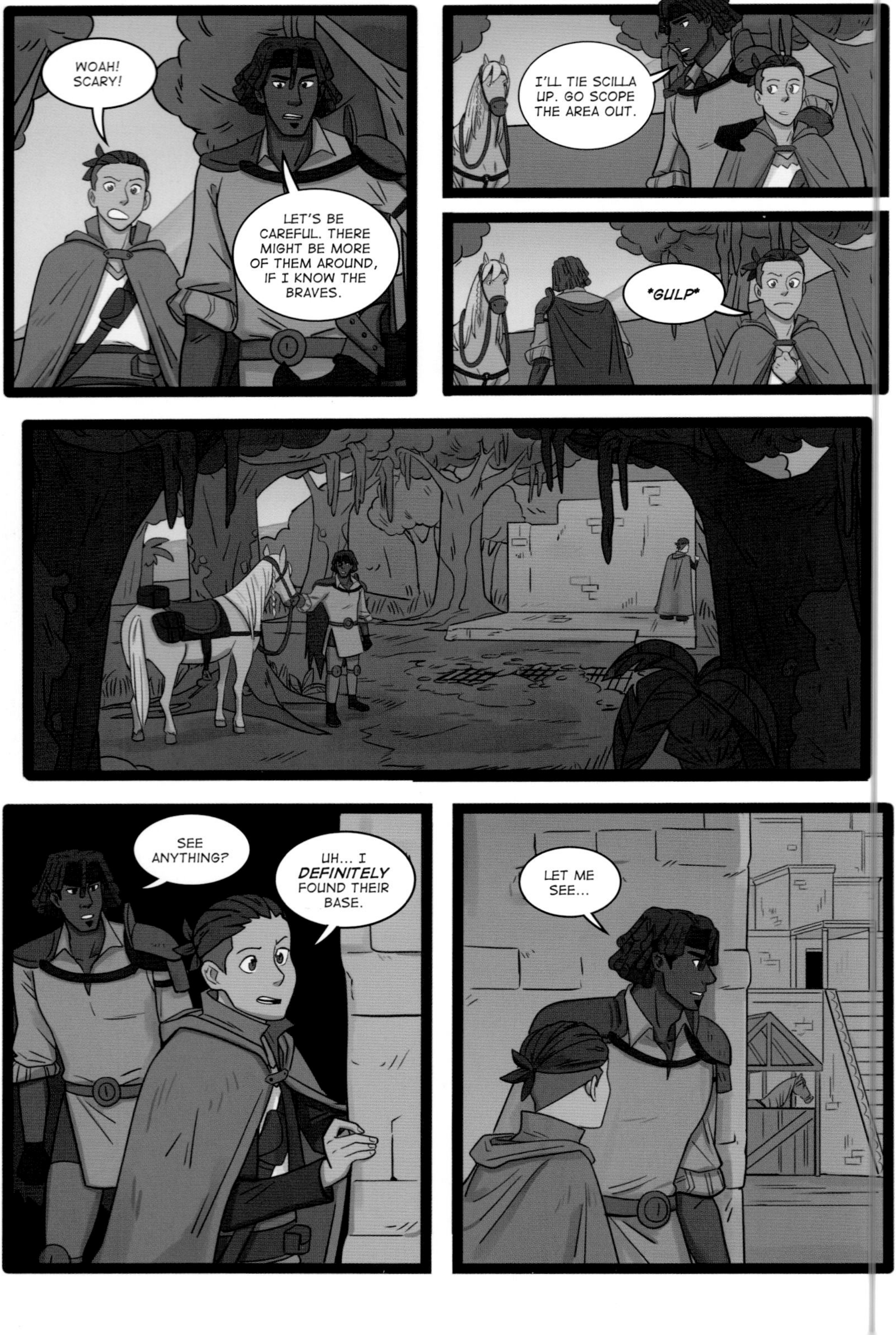
WOAH! SCARY!
LET'S BE CAREFUL. THERE MIGHT BE MORE OF THEM AROUND, IF I KNOW THE BRAVES.
I'LL TIE SCILLA UP. GO SCOPE THE AREA OUT.
GULP
SEE ANYTHING?
UH... I *DEFINITELY* FOUND THEIR BASE.
LET ME SEE...

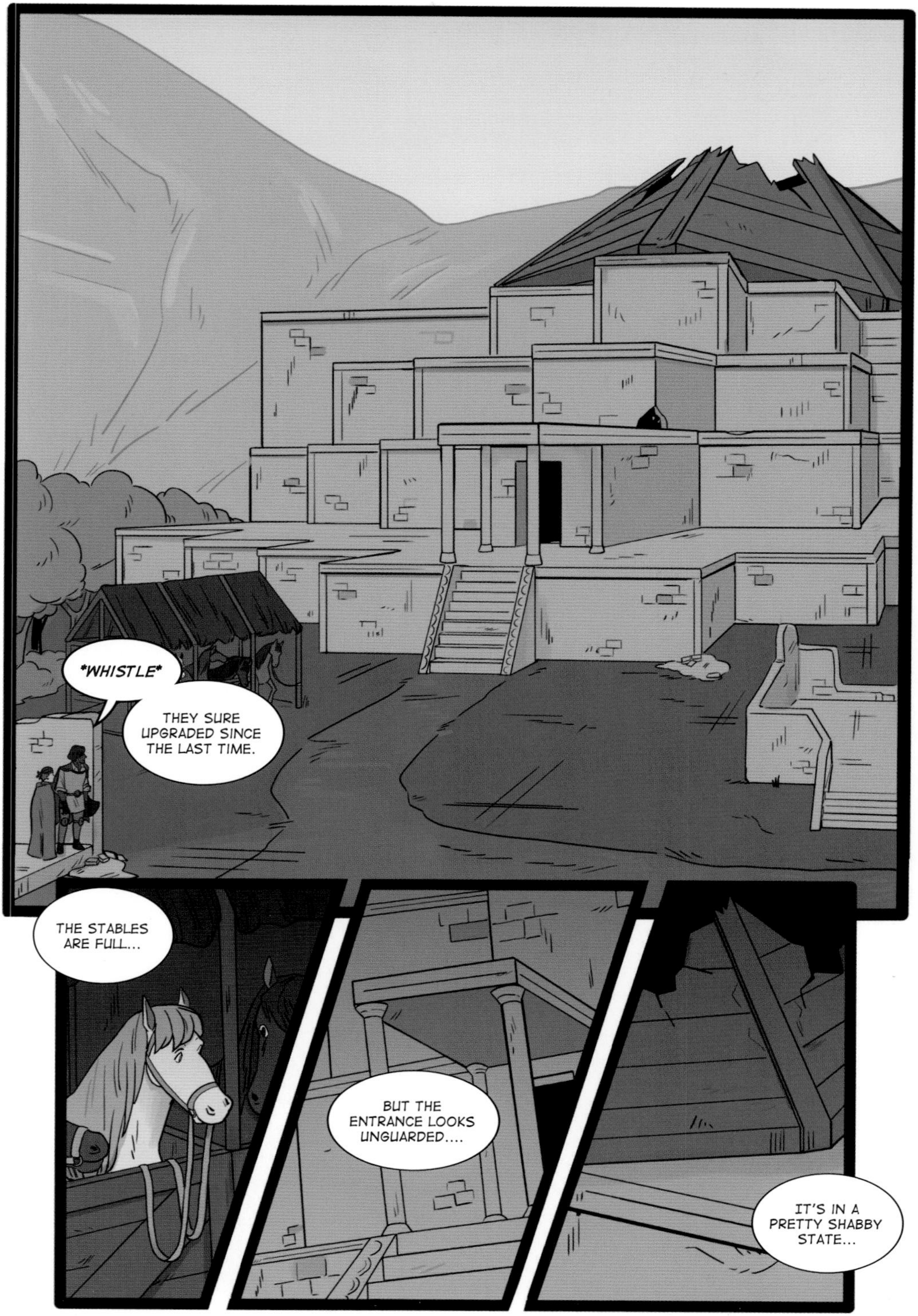
WHISTLE
THEY SURE UPGRADED SINCE THE LAST TIME.
THE STABLES ARE FULL...
BUT THE ENTRANCE LOOKS UNGUARDED....
IT'S IN A PRETTY SHABBY STATE...

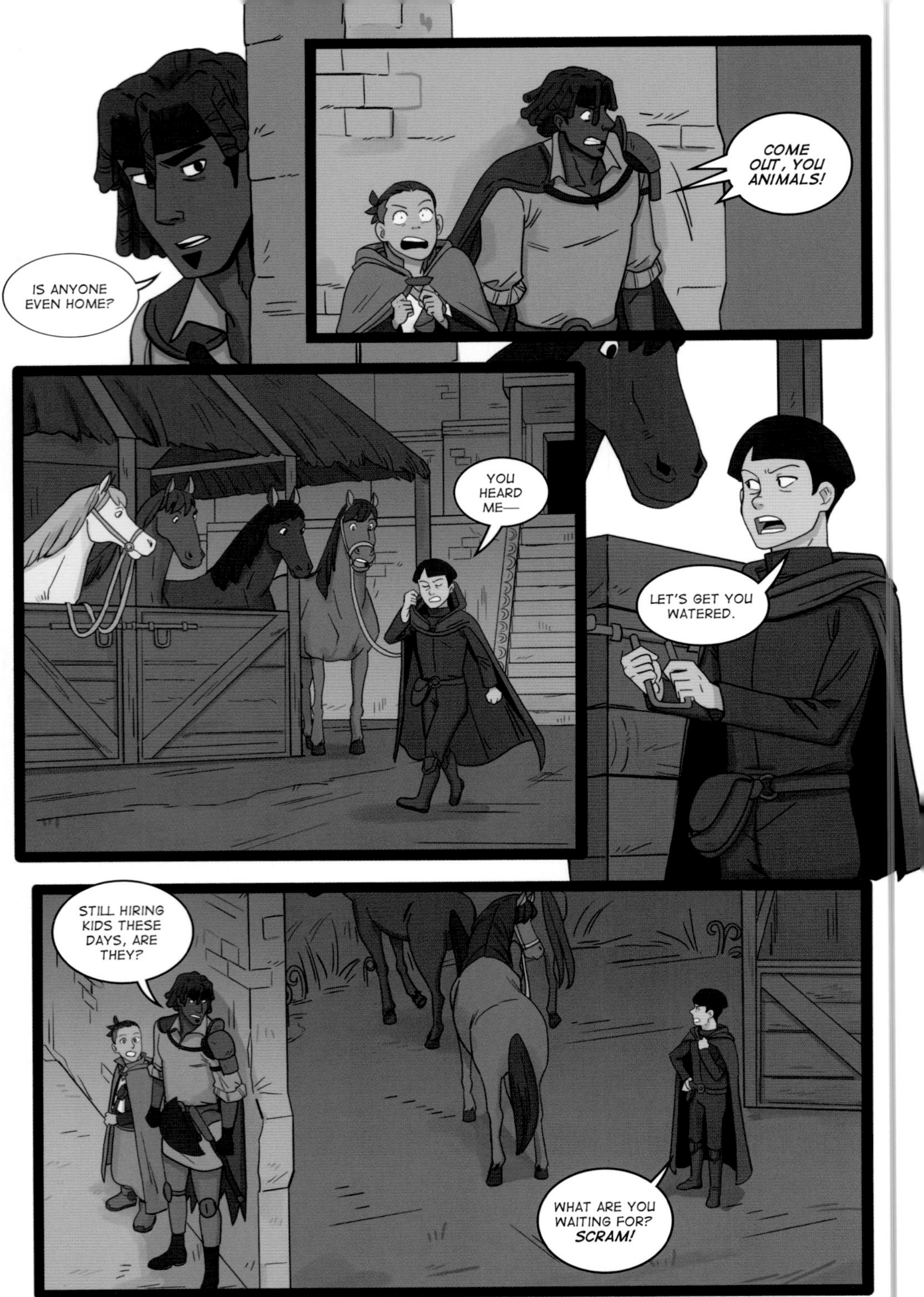
IS ANYONE EVEN HOME?
COME OUT, YOU ANIMALS!
YOU HEARD ME—
LET'S GET YOU WATERED.
STILL HIRING KIDS THESE DAYS, ARE THEY?
WHAT ARE YOU WAITING FOR? *SCRAM!*

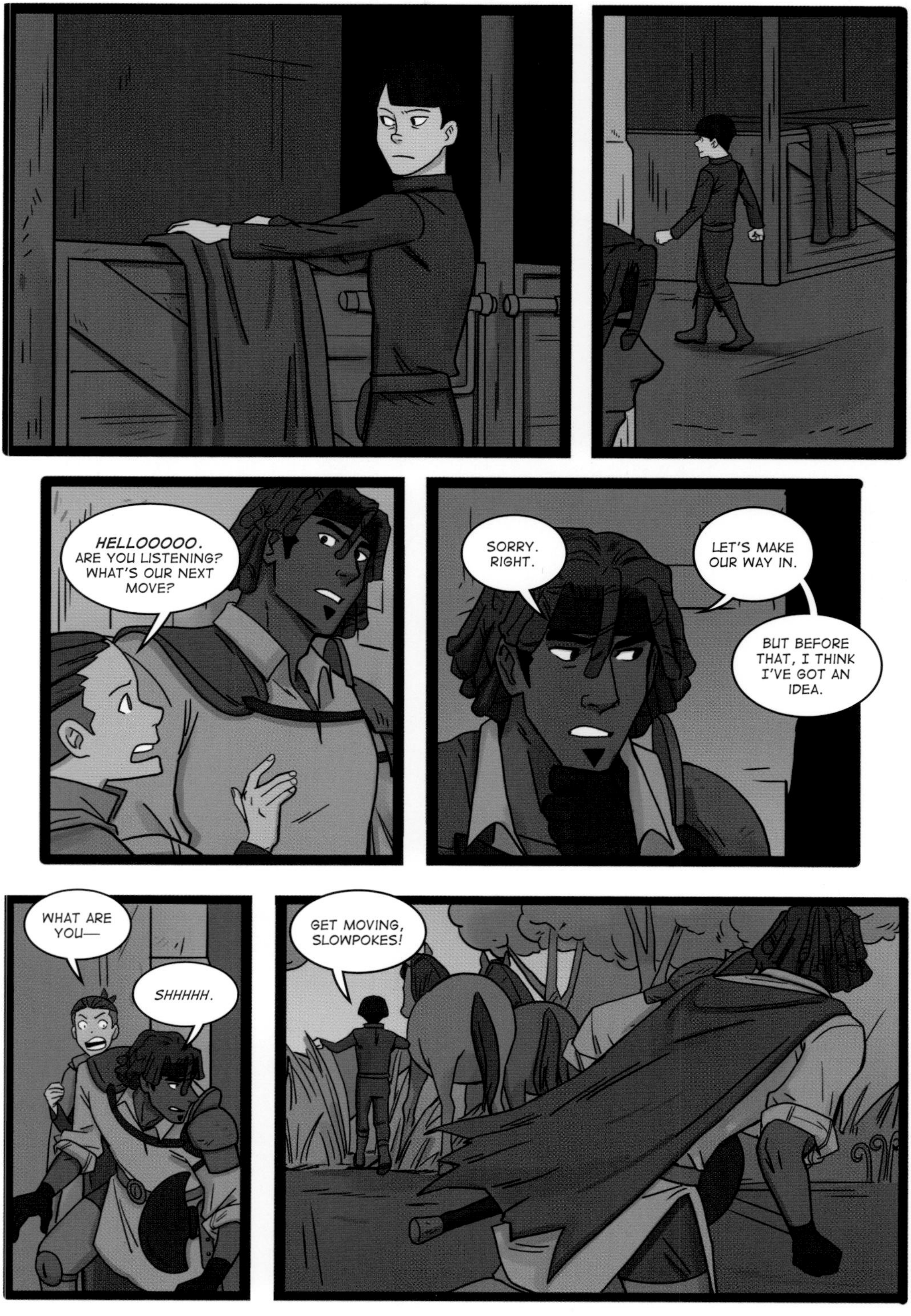
HELLOOOOO.
ARE YOU LISTENING? WHAT'S OUR NEXT MOVE?
SORRY. RIGHT.
LET'S MAKE OUR WAY IN.
BUT BEFORE THAT, I THINK I'VE GOT AN IDEA.
WHAT ARE YOU—
SHHHHH.
GET MOVING, SLOWPOKES!

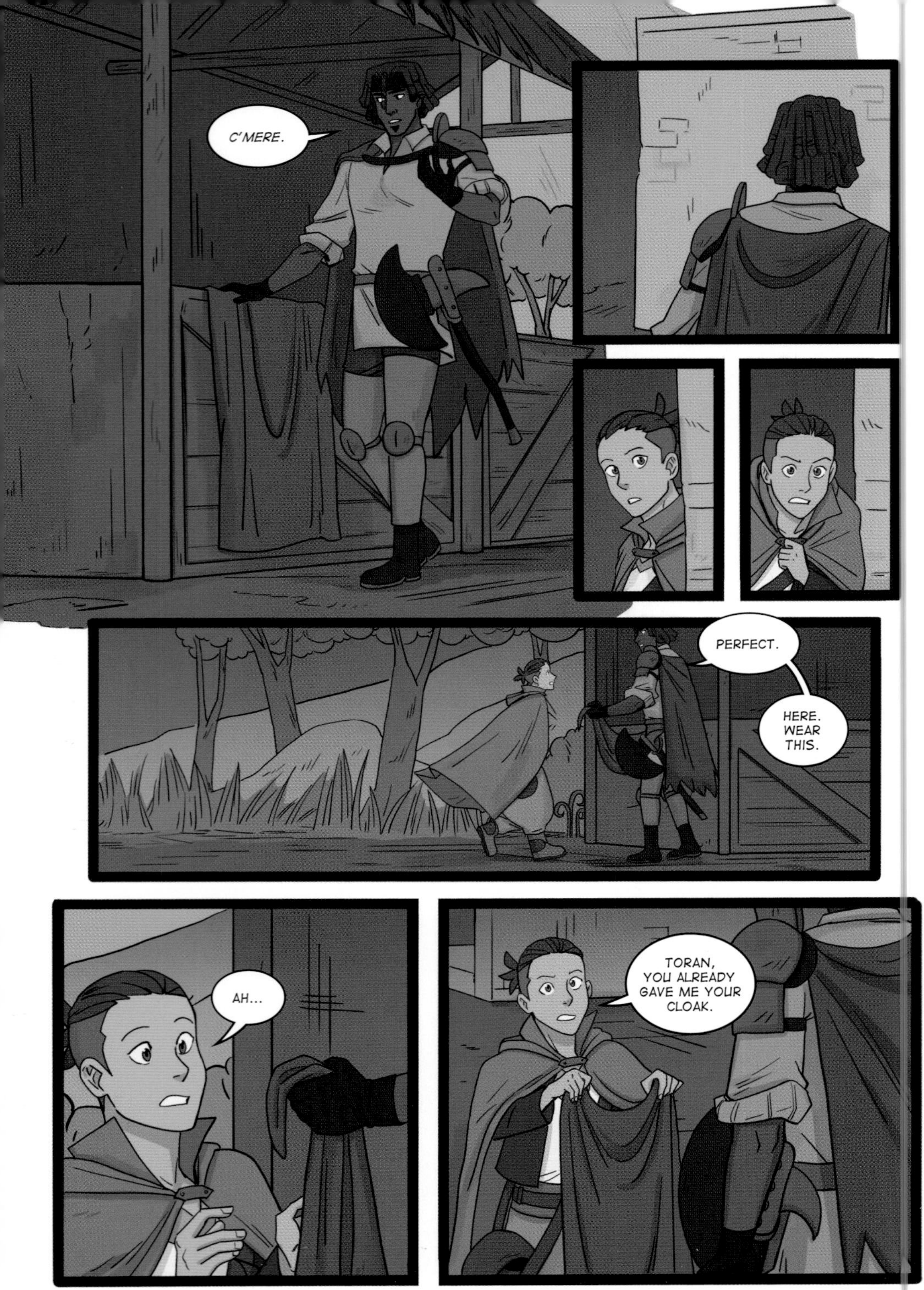
C'MERE.
PERFECT.
HERE. WEAR THIS.
AH...
TORAN, YOU ALREADY GAVE ME YOUR CLOAK.

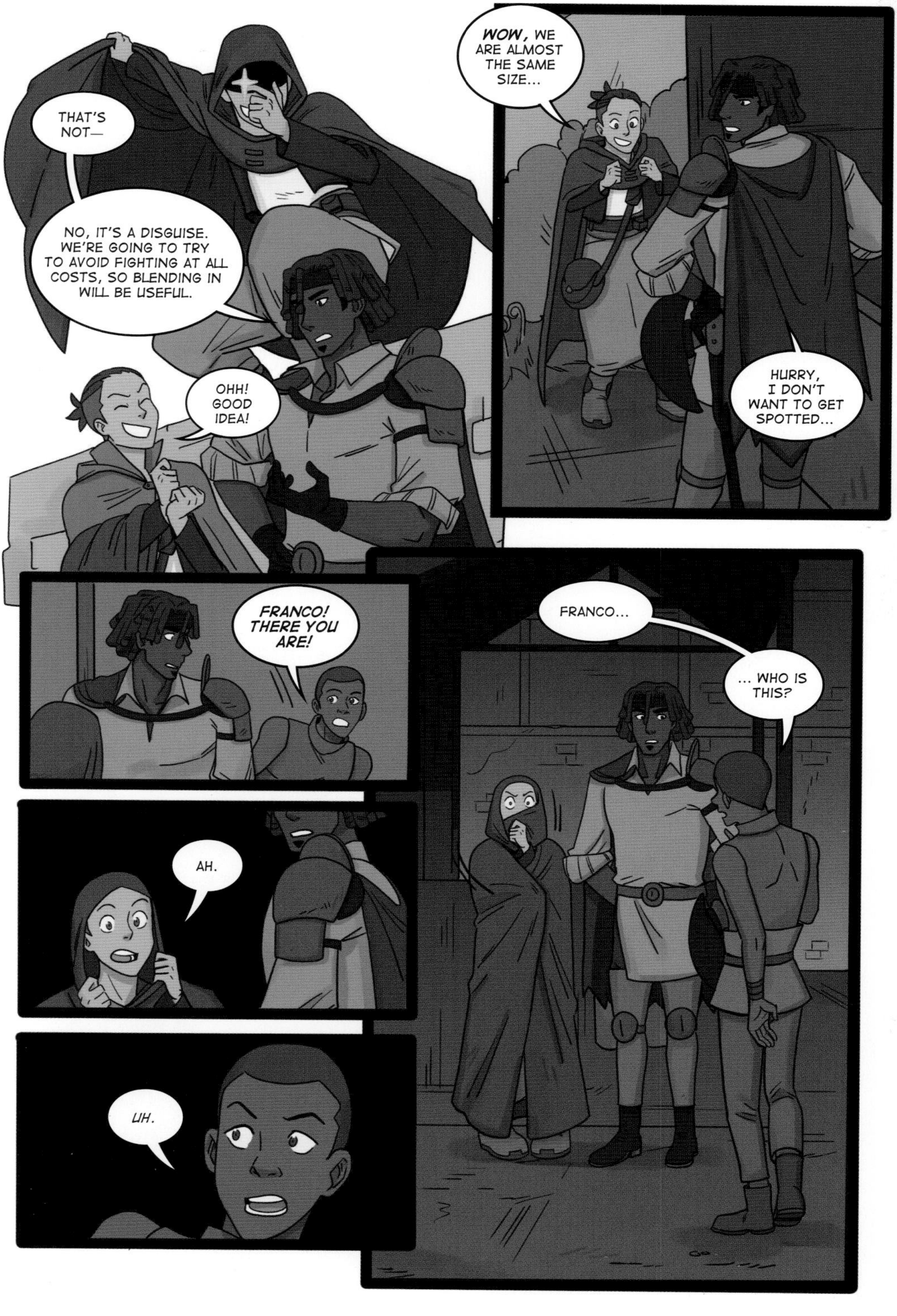
THAT'S NOT—
NO, IT'S A DISGUISE. WE'RE GOING TO TRY TO AVOID FIGHTING AT ALL COSTS, SO BLENDING IN WILL BE USEFUL.
OHH! GOOD IDEA!
WOW, WE ARE ALMOST THE SAME SIZE...
HURRY, I DON'T WANT TO GET SPOTTED...
FRANCO! THERE YOU ARE!
AH.
UH.
FRANCO...
... WHO IS THIS?

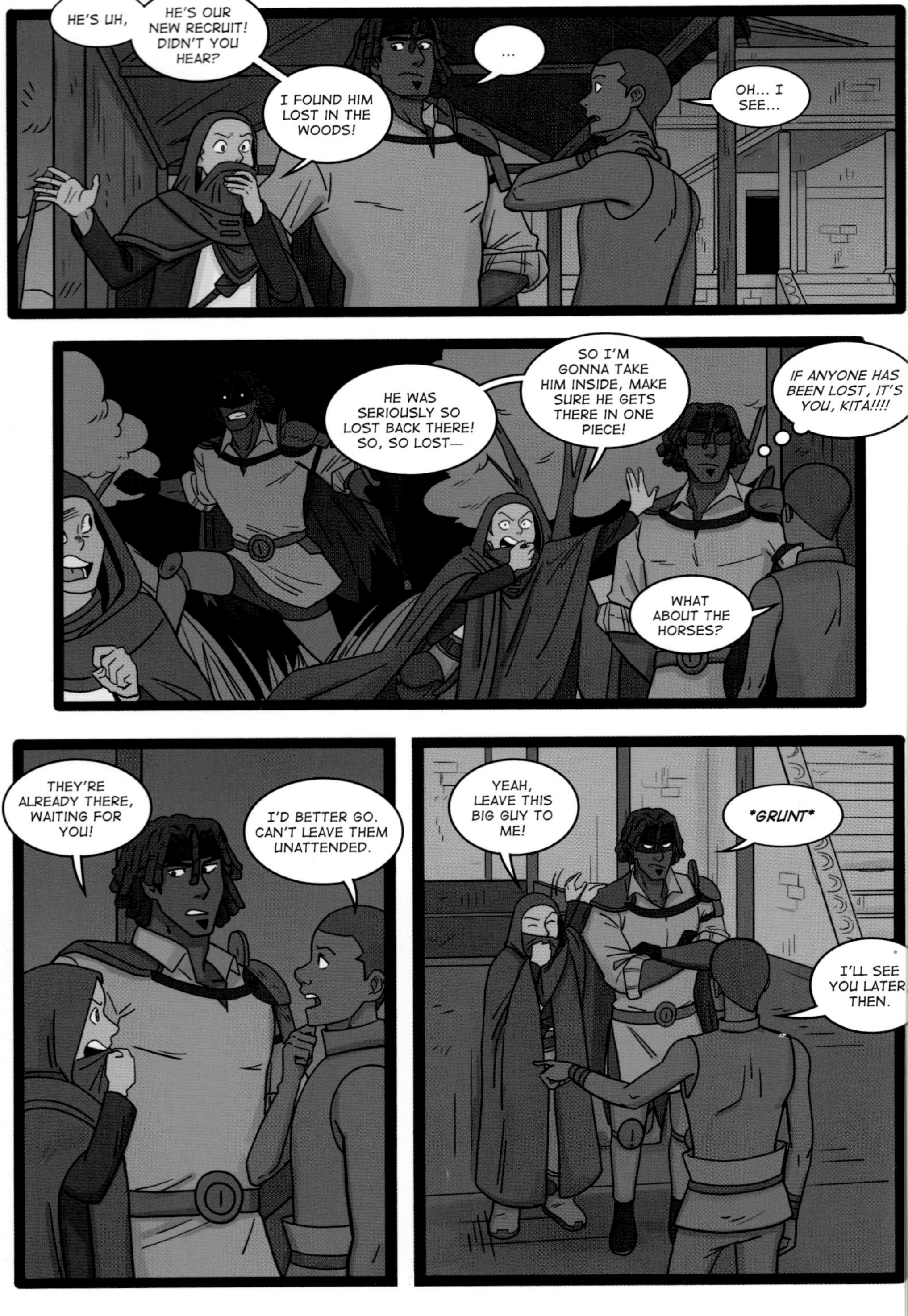
HE'S UH,
HE'S OUR NEW RECRUIT! DIDN'T YOU HEAR?
I FOUND HIM LOST IN THE WOODS!
...
OH... I SEE...
HE WAS SERIOUSLY SO LOST BACK THERE! SO, SO LOST—
SO I'M GONNA TAKE HIM INSIDE, MAKE SURE HE GETS THERE IN ONE PIECE!
IF ANYONE HAS BEEN LOST, IT'S YOU, KITA!!!!
WHAT ABOUT THE HORSES?
THEY'RE ALREADY THERE, WAITING FOR YOU!
I'D BETTER GO. CAN'T LEAVE THEM UNATTENDED.
YEAH, LEAVE THIS BIG GUY TO ME!
GRUNT
I'LL SEE YOU LATER, THEN.

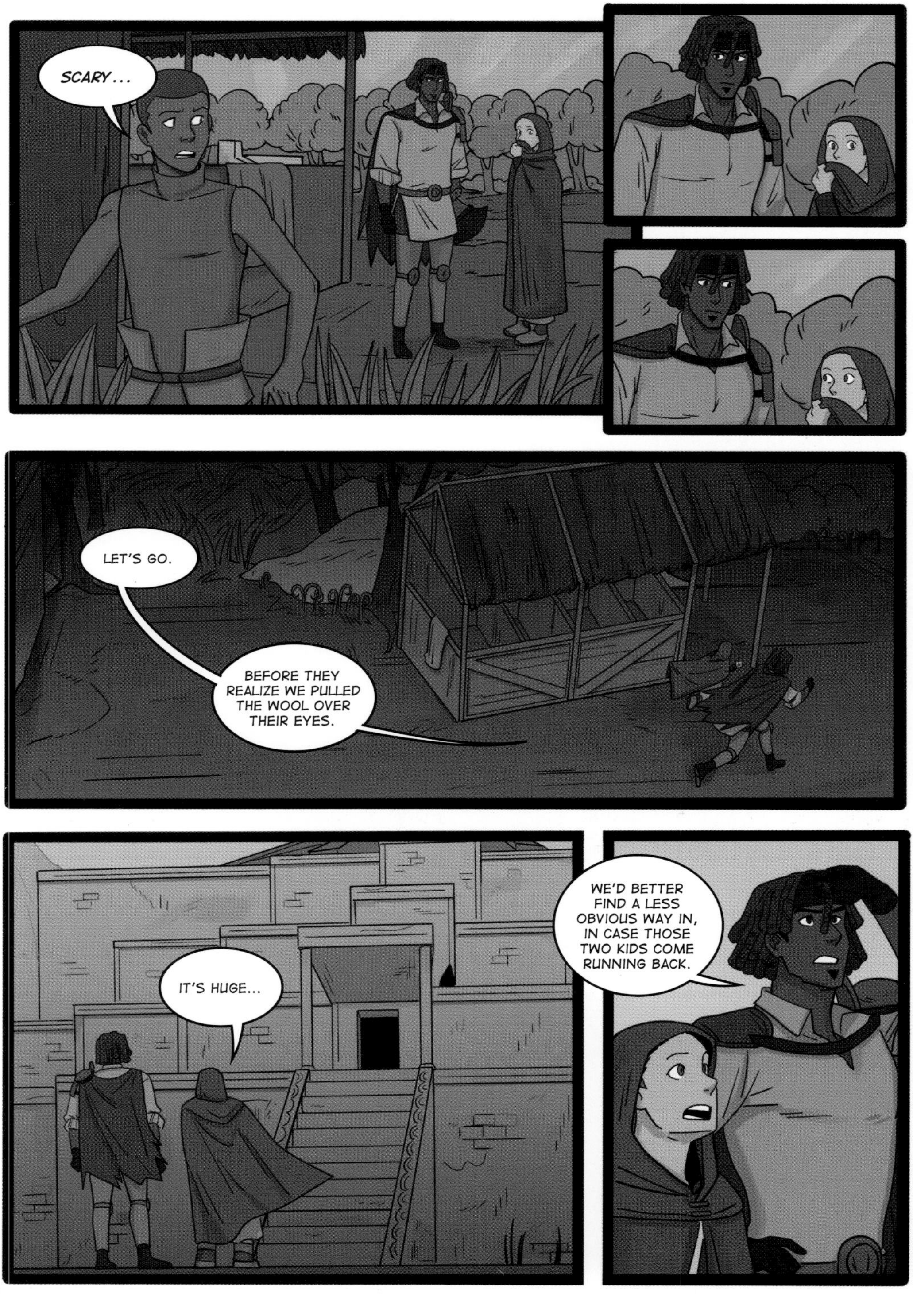
SCARY...
LET'S GO.
BEFORE THEY REALIZE WE PULLED THE WOOL OVER THEIR EYES.
IT'S HUGE...
WE'D BETTER FIND A LESS OBVIOUS WAY IN, IN CASE THOSE TWO KIDS COME RUNNING BACK.

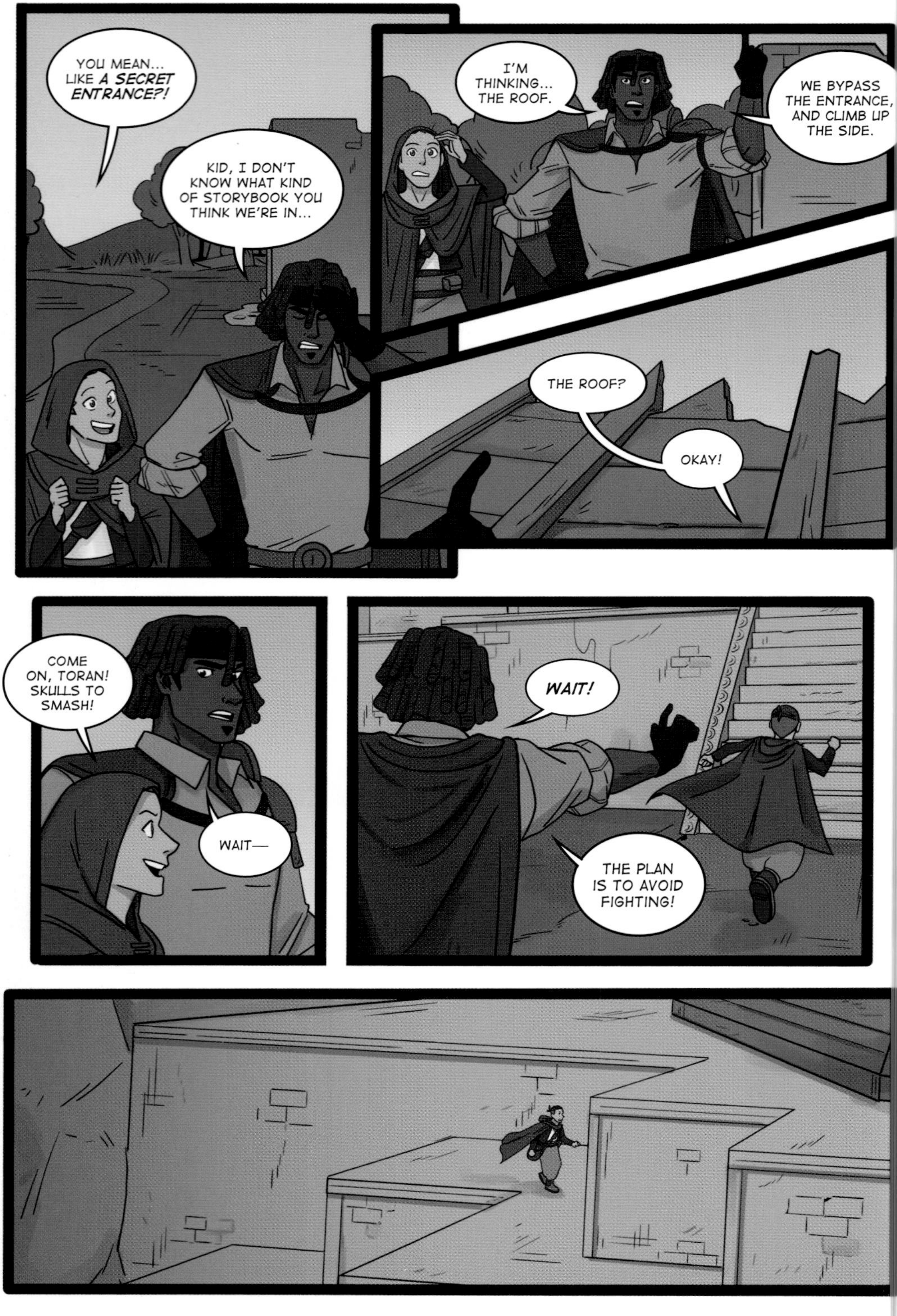
YOU MEAN... LIKE A SECRET ENTRANCE?!
KID, I DON'T KNOW WHAT KIND OF STORYBOOK YOU THINK WE'RE IN...
I'M THINKING... THE ROOF.
WE BYPASS THE ENTRANCE, AND CLIMB UP THE SIDE.
THE ROOF?
OKAY!
COME ON, TORAN! SKULLS TO SMASH!
WAIT—
WAIT!
THE PLAN IS TO AVOID FIGHTING!

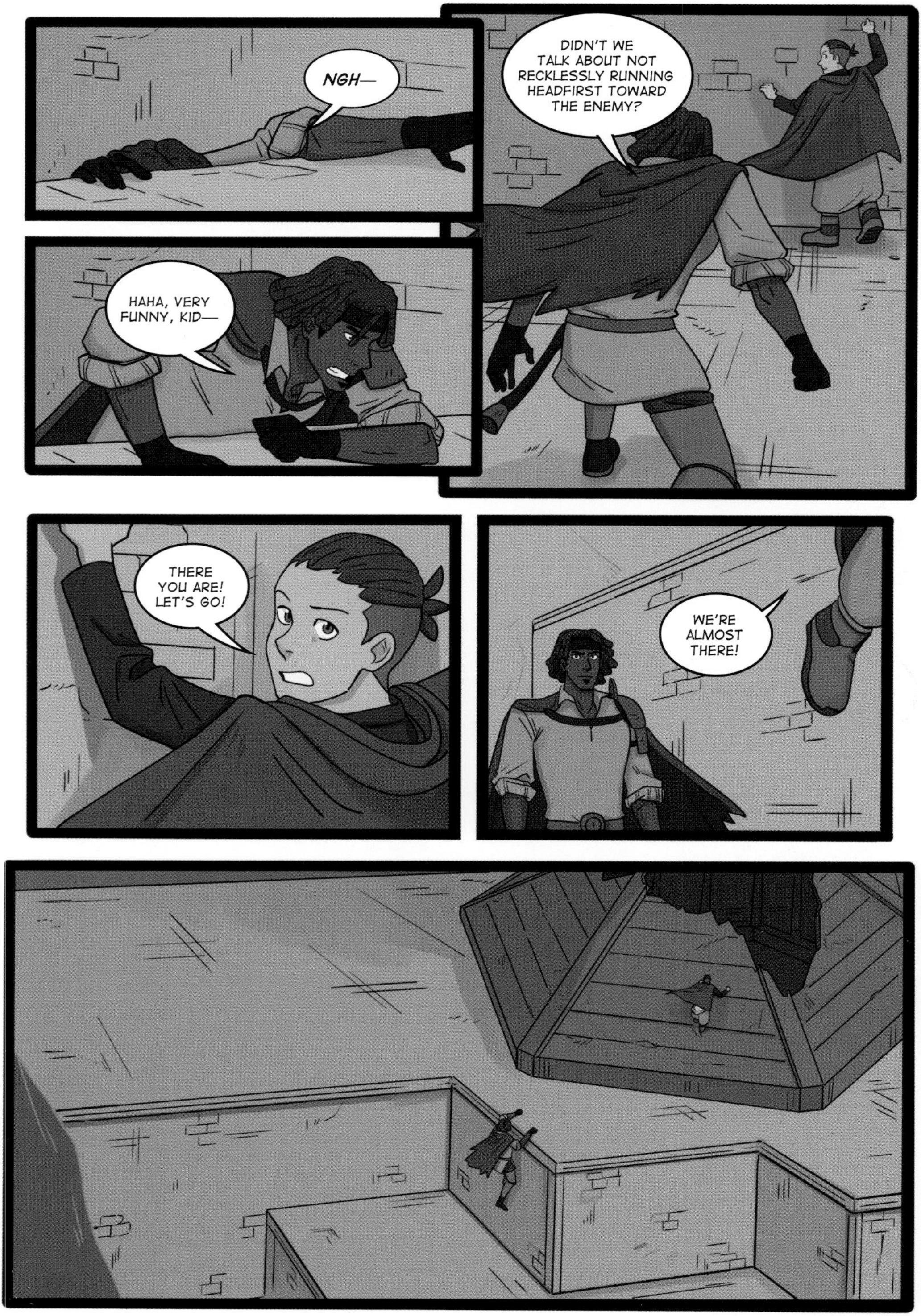
NGH—
DIDN'T WE TALK ABOUT NOT RECKLESSLY RUNNING HEADFIRST TOWARD THE ENEMY?
HAHA, VERY FUNNY, KID—
THERE YOU ARE! LET'S GO!
WE'RE ALMOST THERE!

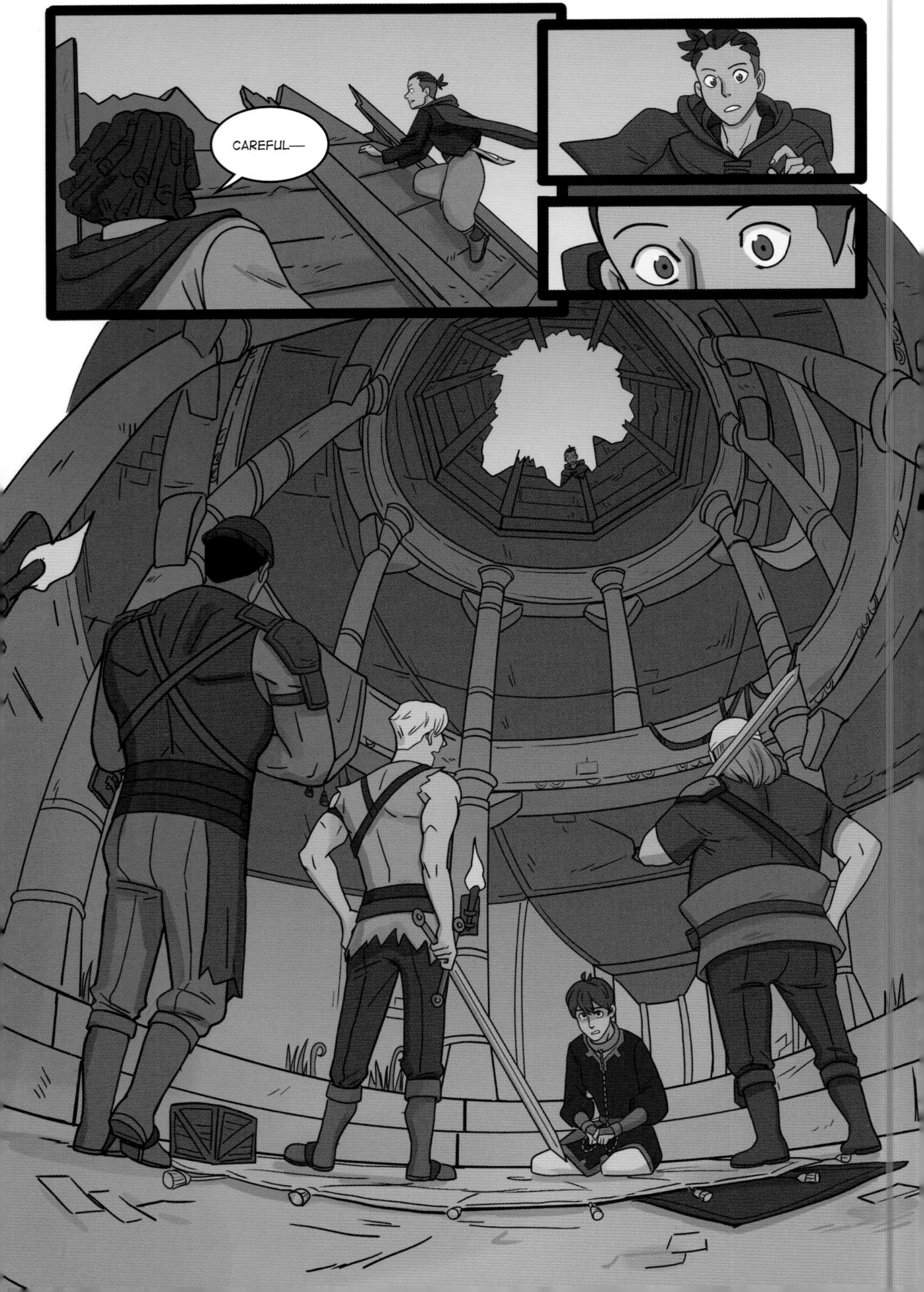
CAREFUL—

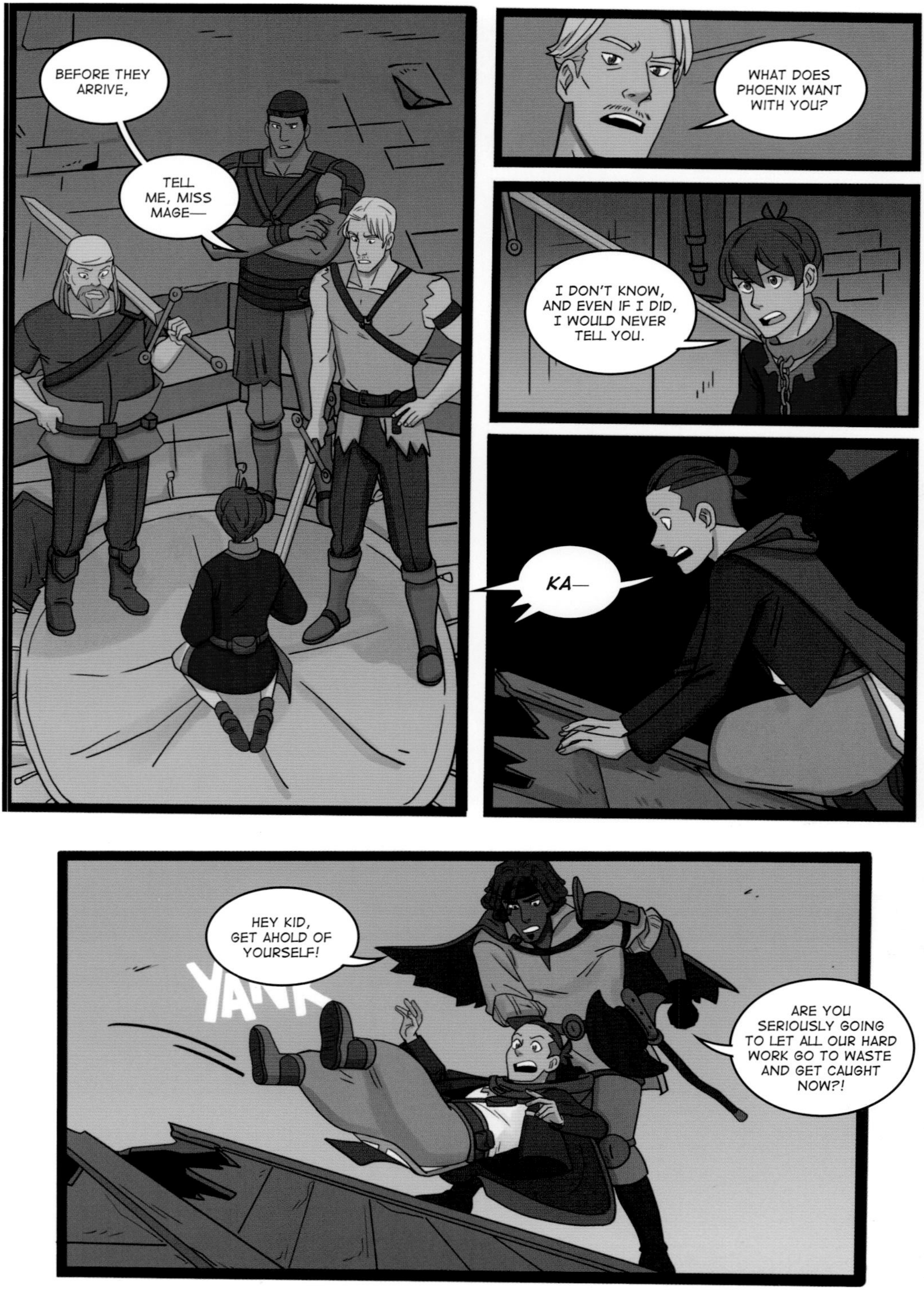
BEFORE THEY ARRIVE,
TELL ME, MISS MAGE—
WHAT DOES PHOENIX WANT WITH YOU?
I DON'T KNOW, AND EVEN IF I DID, I WOULD NEVER TELL YOU.
KA—
YANK
HEY KID, GET AHOLD OF YOURSELF!
ARE YOU SERIOUSLY GOING TO LET ALL OUR HARD WORK GO TO WASTE AND GET CAUGHT NOW?!

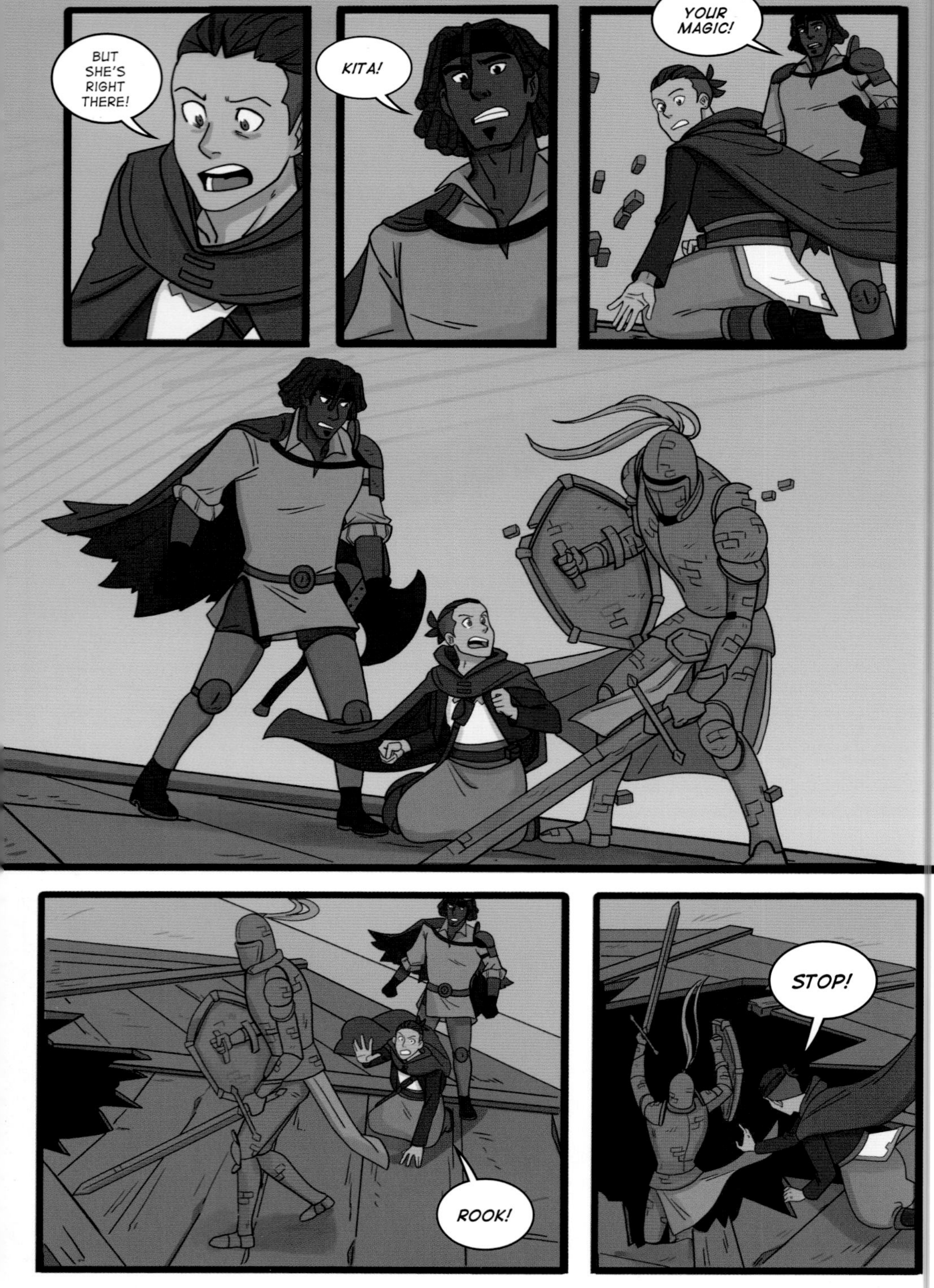
BUT SHE'S RIGHT THERE!
KITA!
YOUR MAGIC!
ROOK!
STOP!

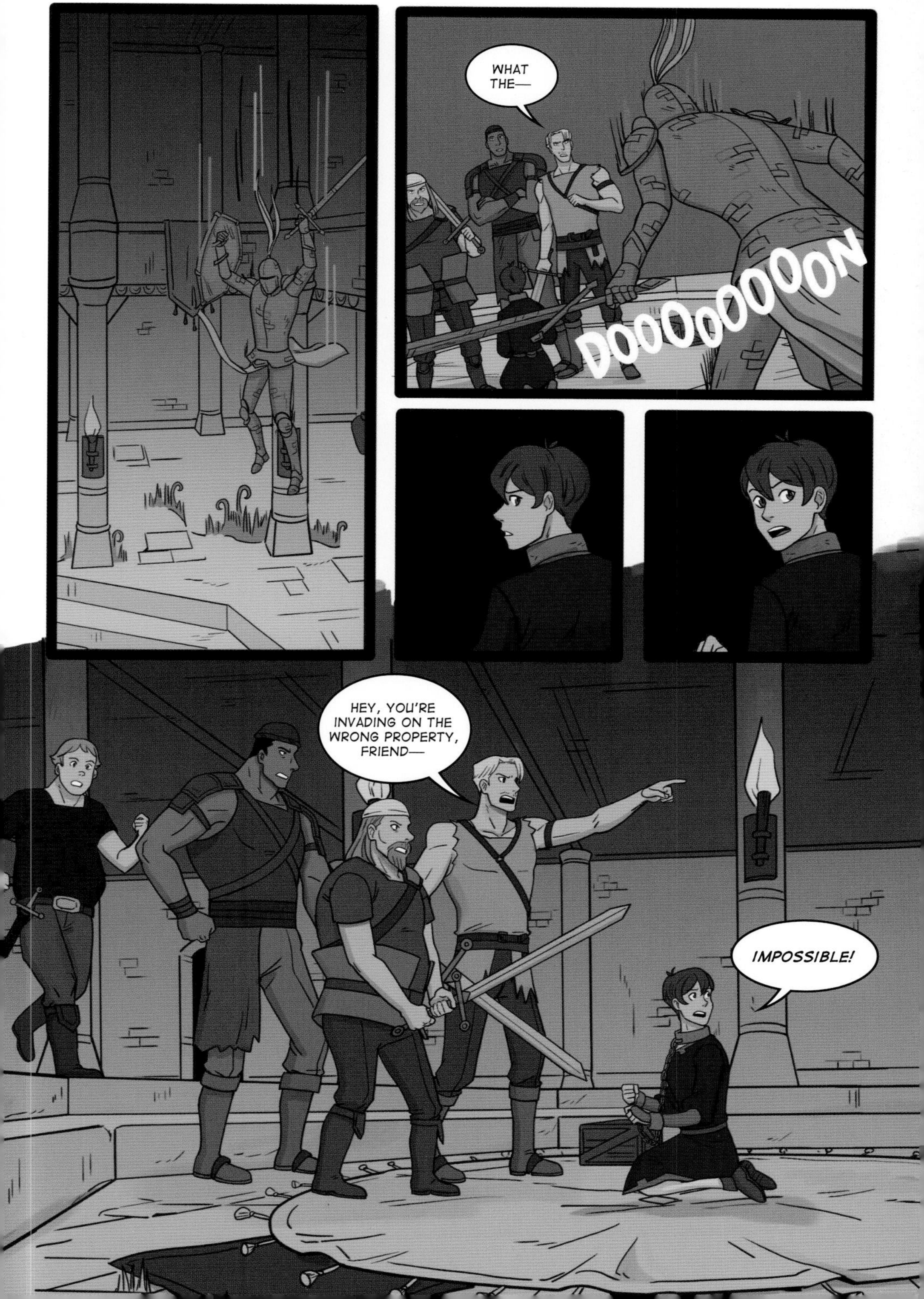
WHAT THE—
DOOOOOOOOON
HEY, YOU'RE INVADING ON THE WRONG PROPERTY, FRIEND—
IMPOSSIBLE!

CHAPTER 6:
AN ENEMY OF AN ENEMY

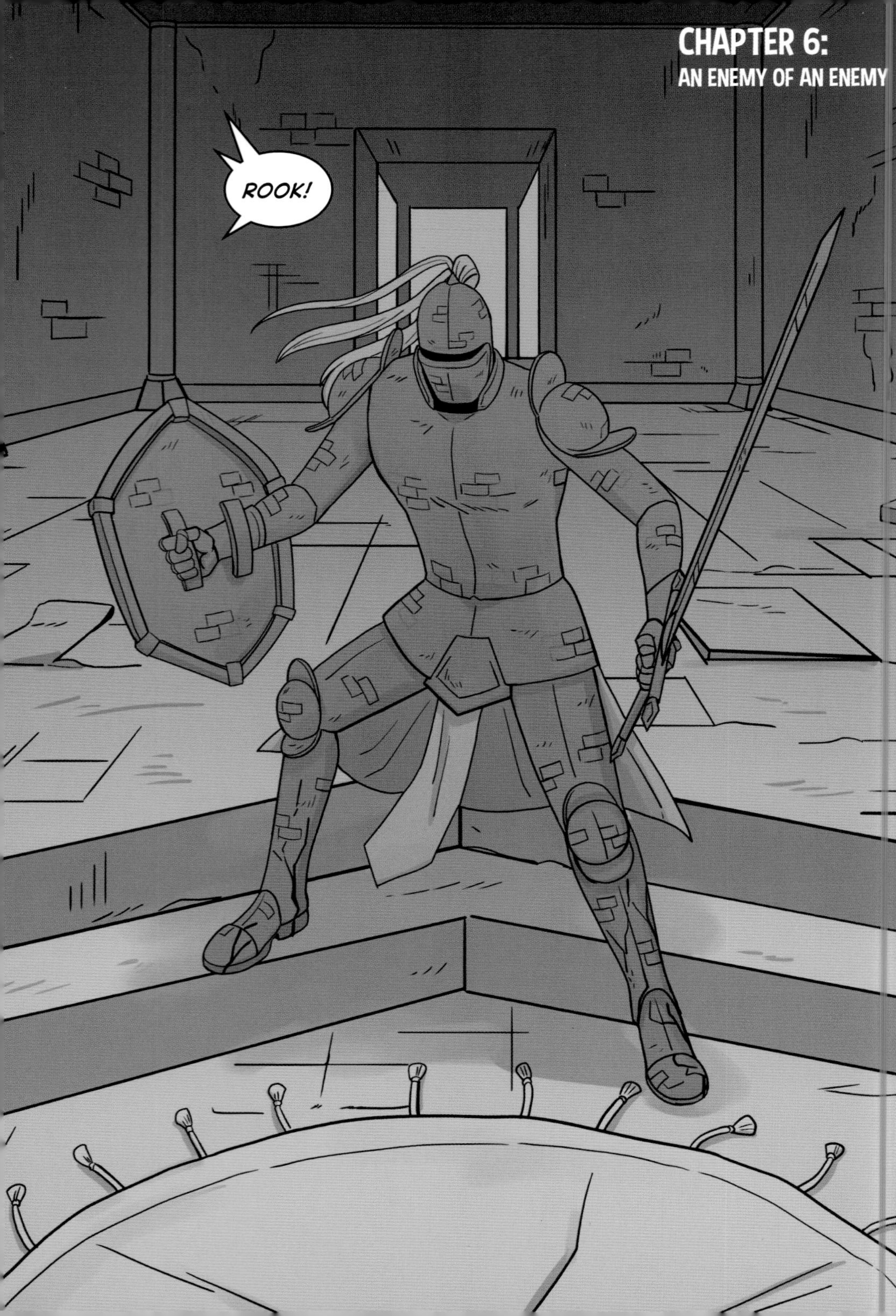
ROOK!

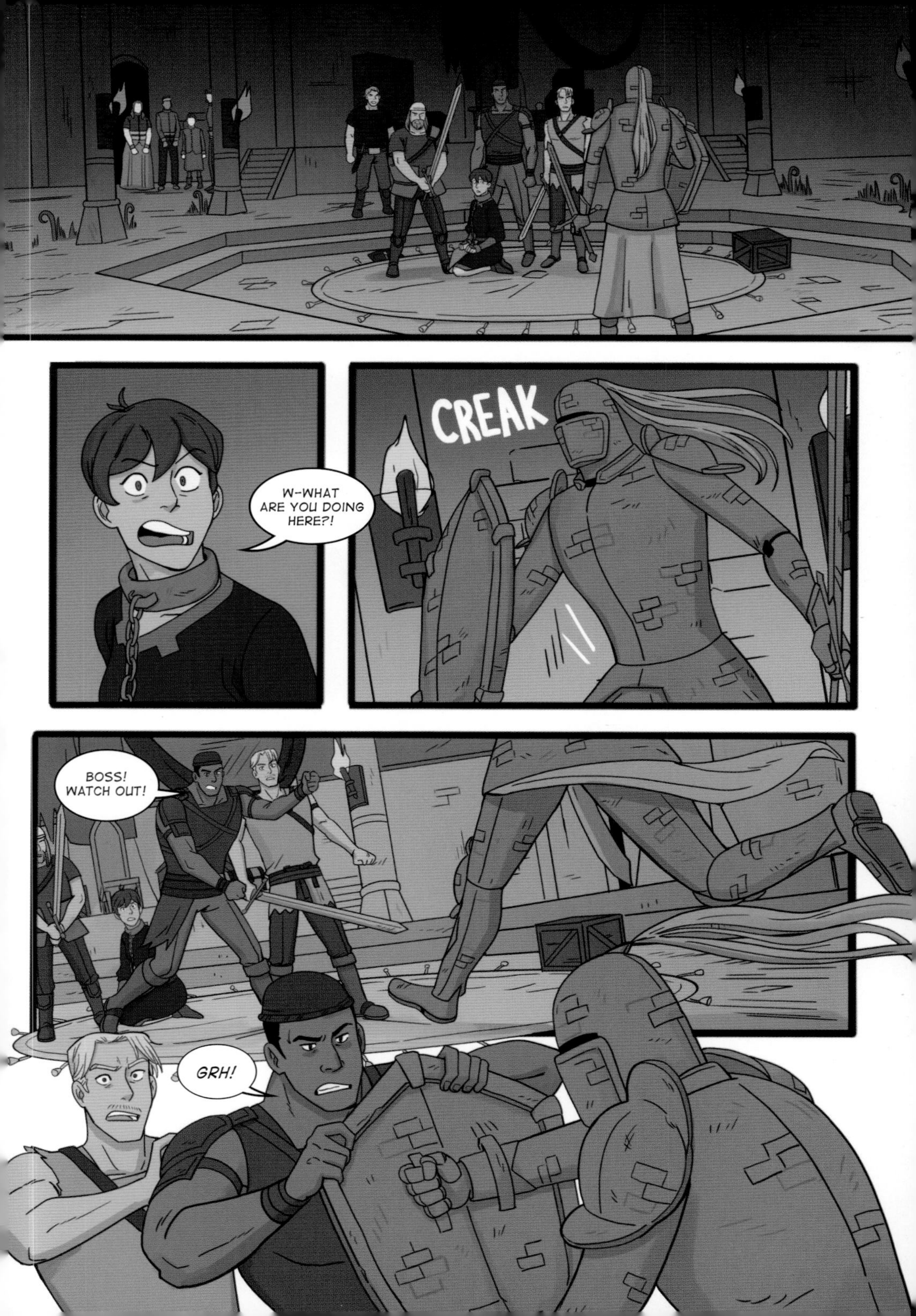
W-WHAT ARE YOU DOING HERE?!
CREAK
BOSS! WATCH OUT!
GRH!

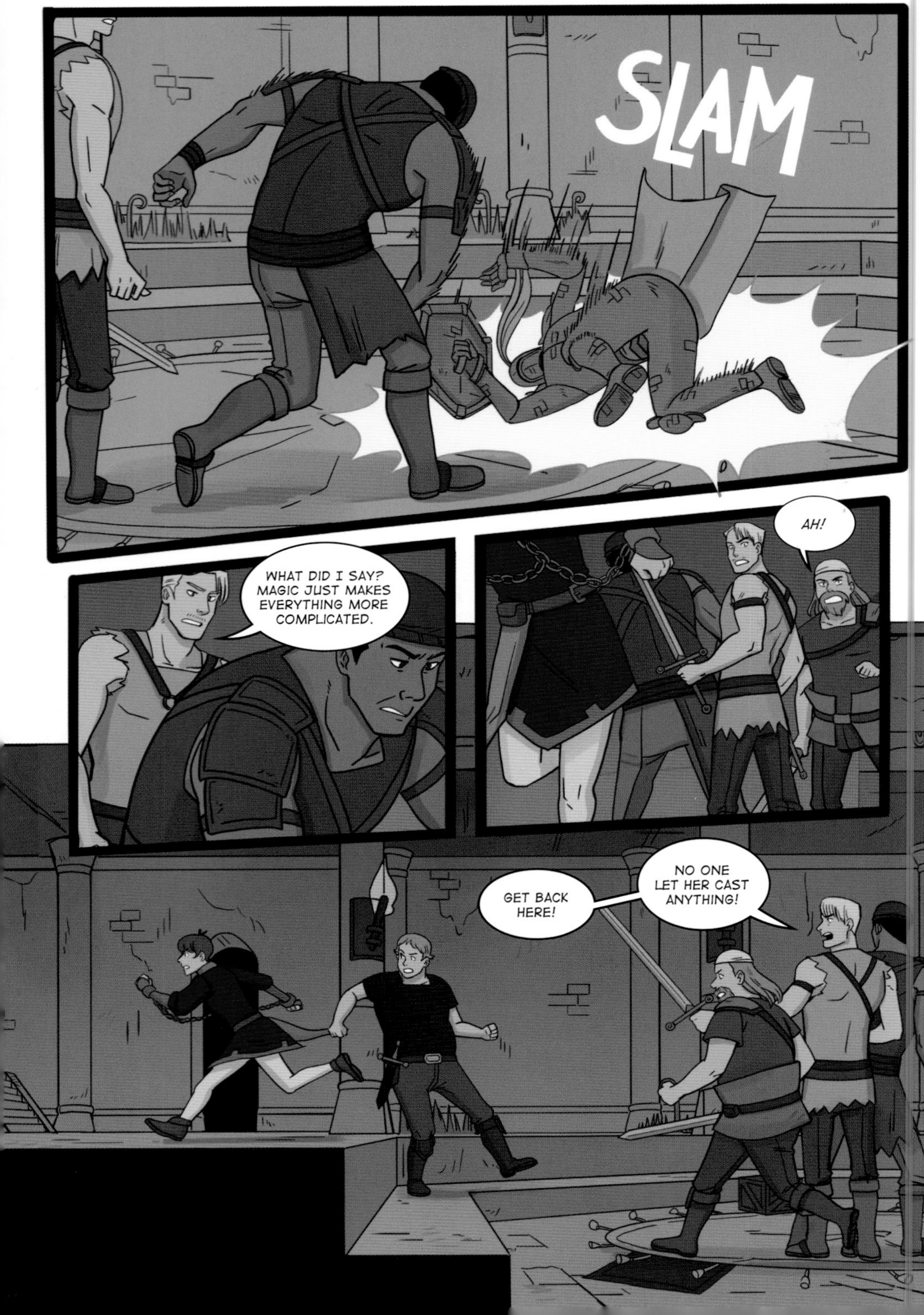
SLAM
WHAT DID I SAY? MAGIC JUST MAKES EVERYTHING MORE COMPLICATED.
AH!
GET BACK HERE!
NO ONE LET HER CAST ANYTHING!

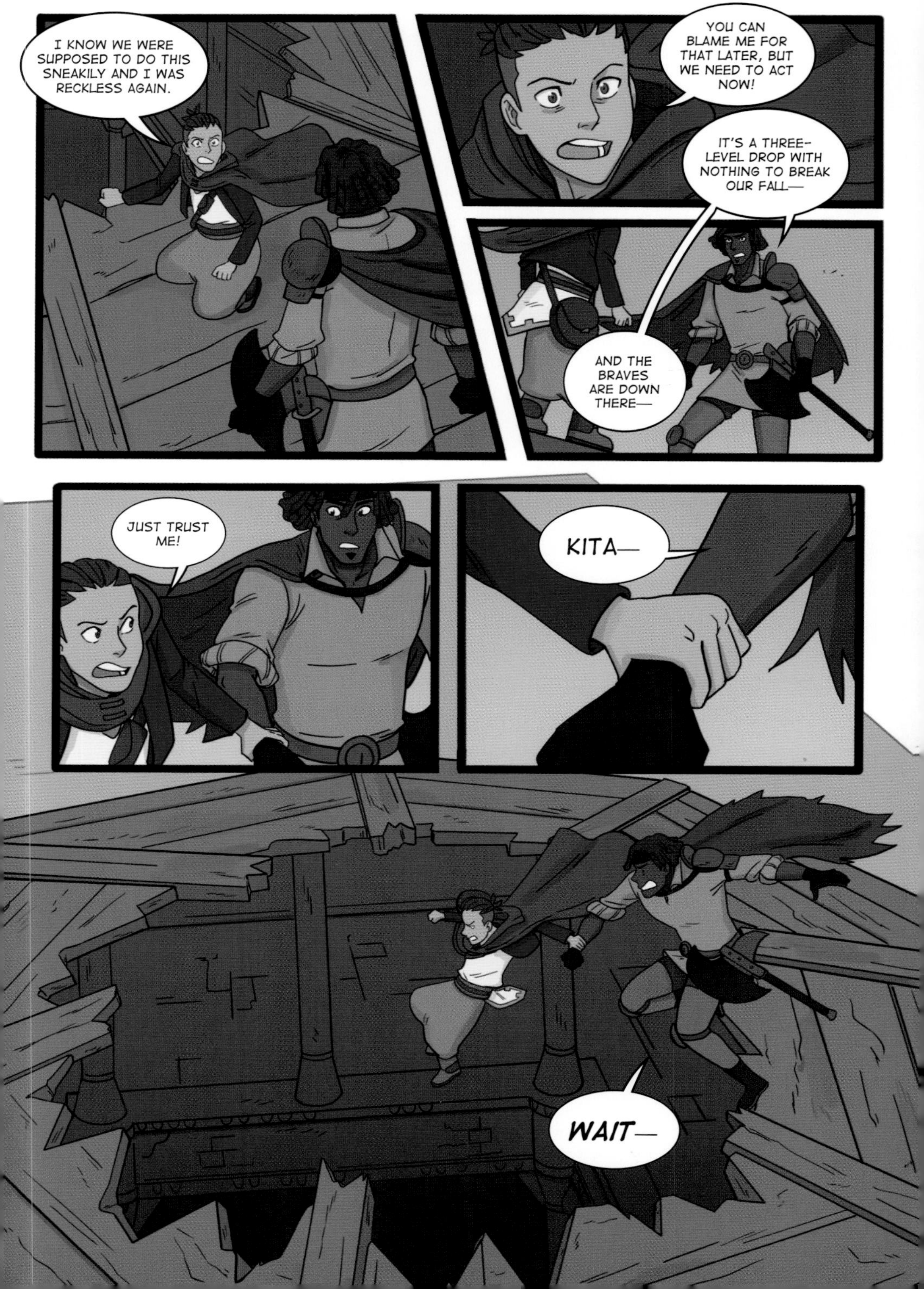
I KNOW WE WERE SUPPOSED TO DO THIS SNEAKILY AND I WAS RECKLESS AGAIN.
YOU CAN BLAME ME FOR THAT LATER, BUT WE NEED TO ACT NOW!
IT'S A THREE-LEVEL DROP WITH NOTHING TO BREAK OUR FALL—
AND THE BRAVES ARE DOWN THERE—
JUST TRUST ME!
KITA—
WAIT—

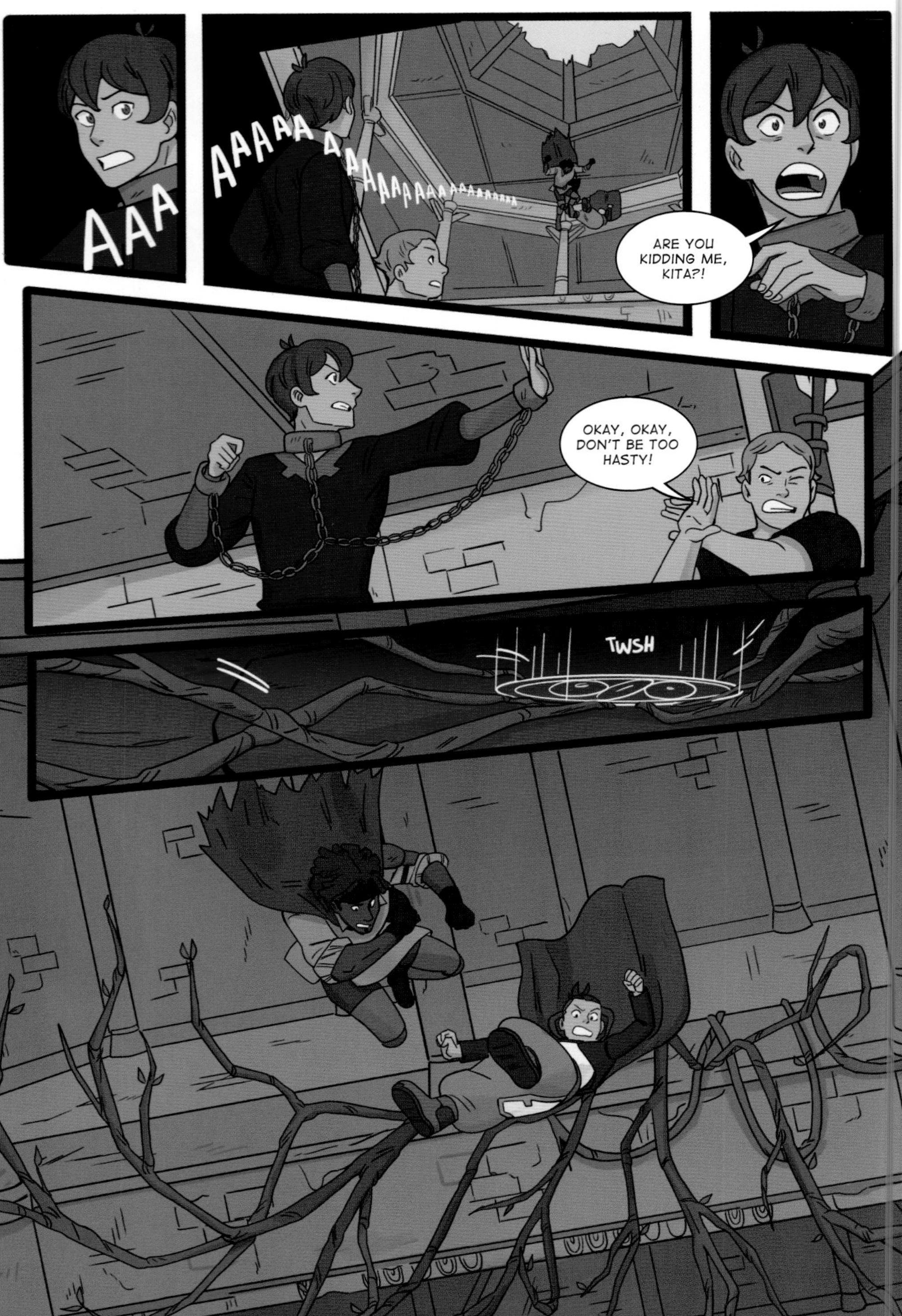
AAAAAAAAAAAAAAAAAAAAAAAAA
ARE YOU KIDDING ME, KITA?!
OKAY, OKAY, DON'T BE TOO HASTY!
TWSH

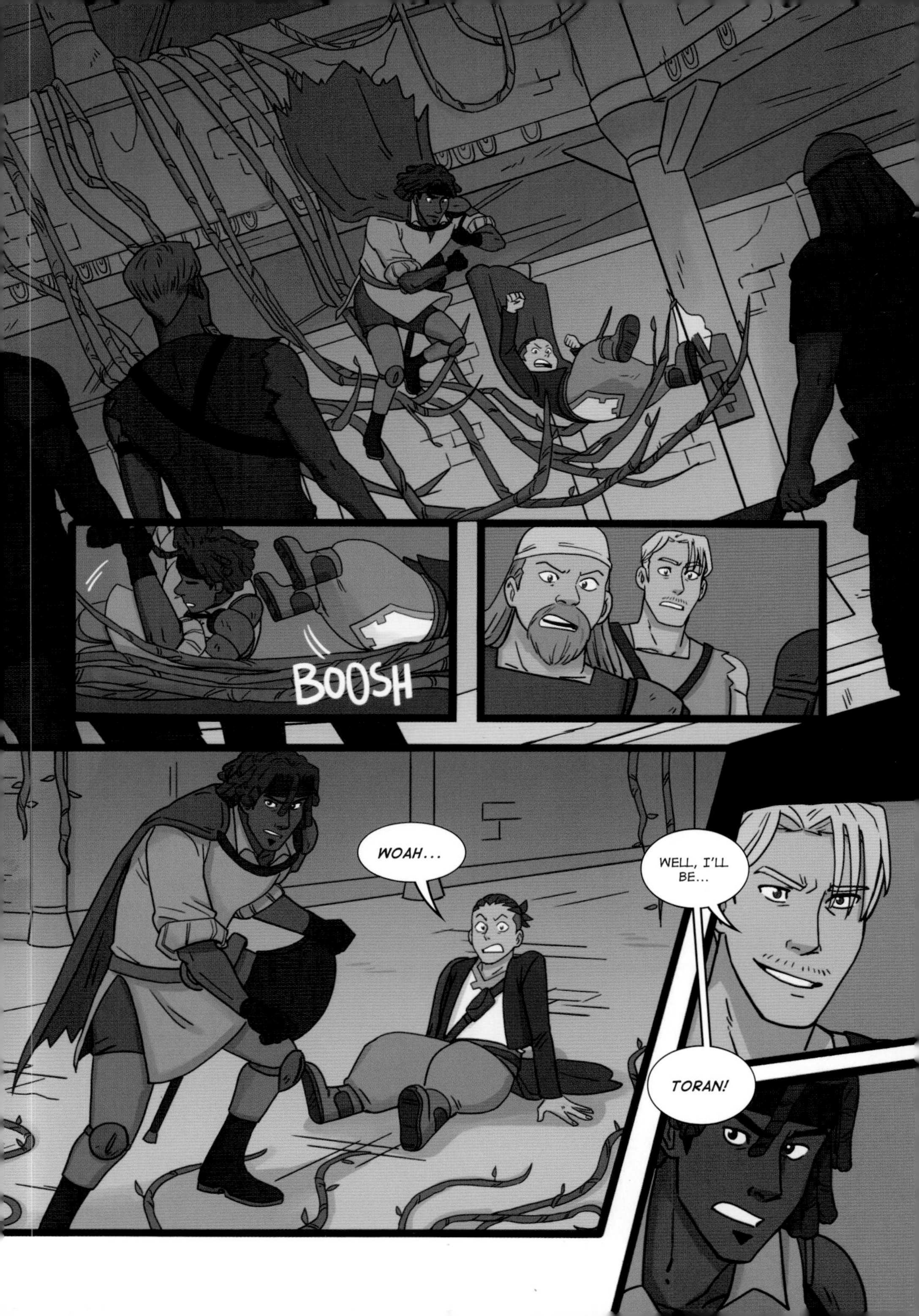

BOOSH
WOAH...
WELL, I'LL BE...
TORAN!

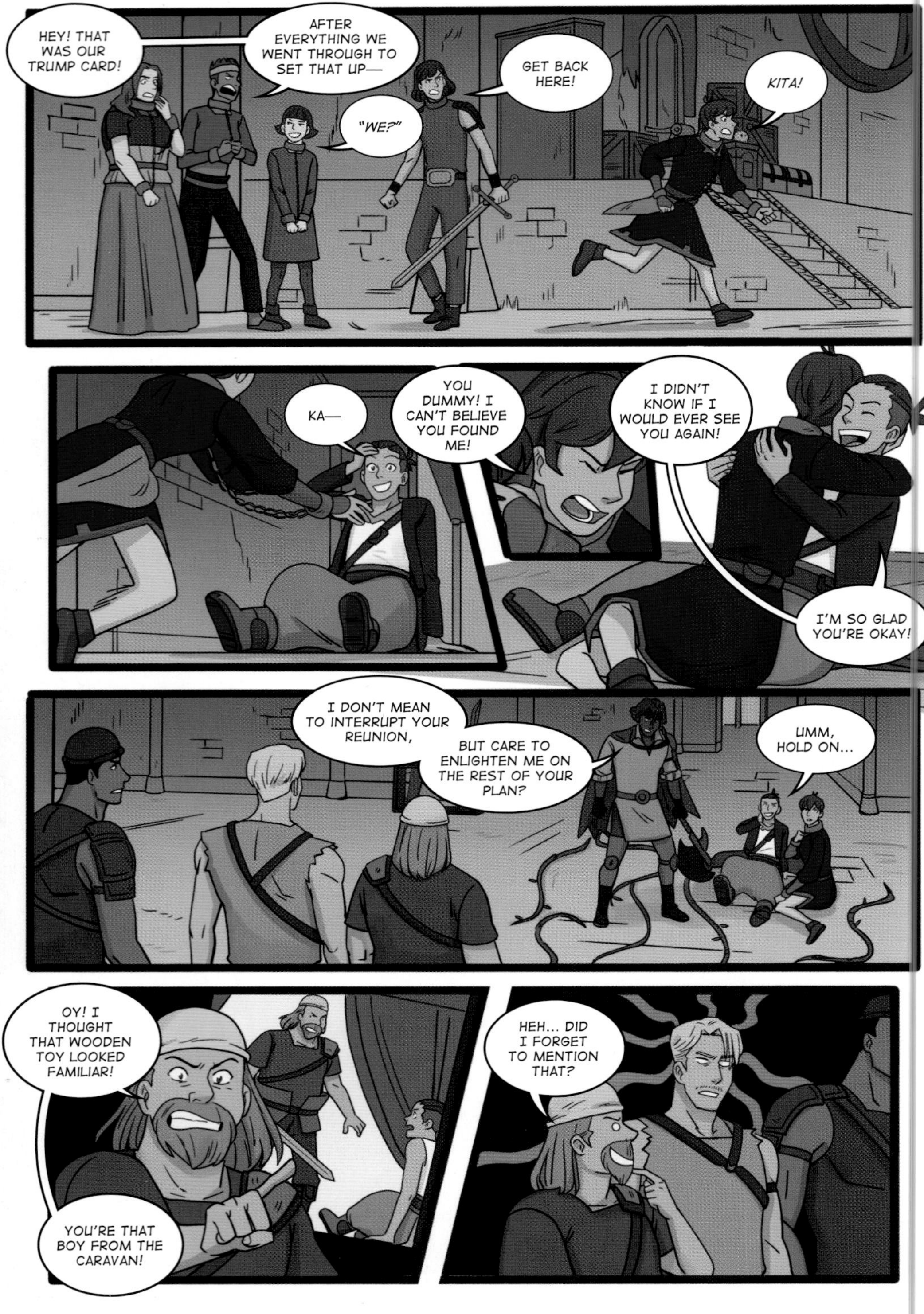
HEY! THAT WAS OUR TRUMP CARD!
AFTER EVERYTHING WE WENT THROUGH TO SET THAT UP—
"WE?"
GET BACK HERE!
KITA!
KA—
YOU DUMMY! I CAN'T BELIEVE YOU FOUND ME!
I DIDN'T KNOW IF I WOULD EVER SEE YOU AGAIN!
I'M SO GLAD YOU'RE OKAY!
I DON'T MEAN TO INTERRUPT YOUR REUNION,
BUT CARE TO ENLIGHTEN ME ON THE REST OF YOUR PLAN?
UMM, HOLD ON...
OY! I THOUGHT THAT WOODEN TOY LOOKED FAMILIAR!
YOU'RE THAT BOY FROM THE CARAVAN!
HEH... DID I FORGET TO MENTION THAT?

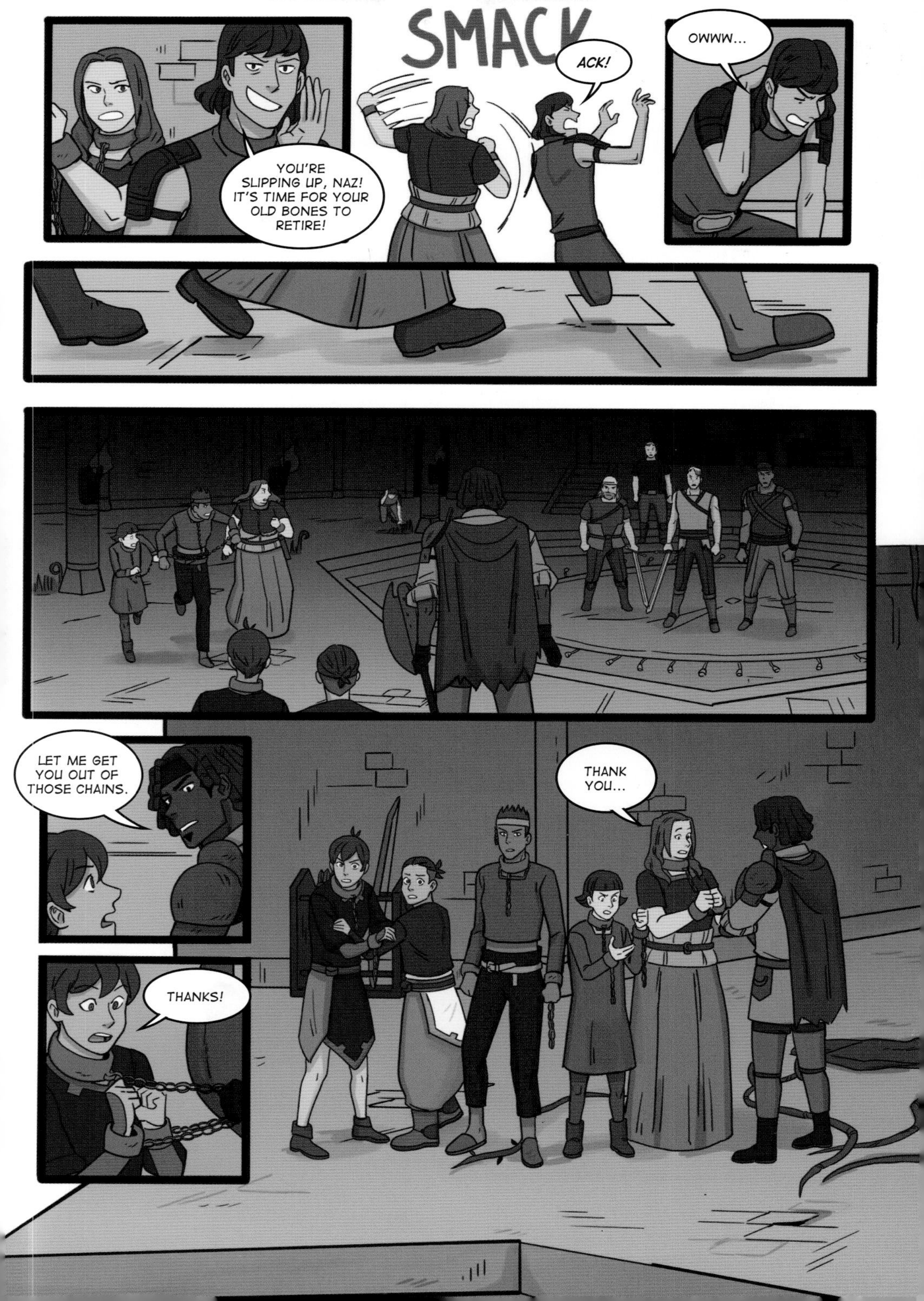
YOU'RE SLIPPING UP, NAZ! IT'S TIME FOR YOUR OLD BONES TO RETIRE!
SMACK
ACK!
OWWW...
LET ME GET YOU OUT OF THOSE CHAINS.
THANKS!
THANK YOU...

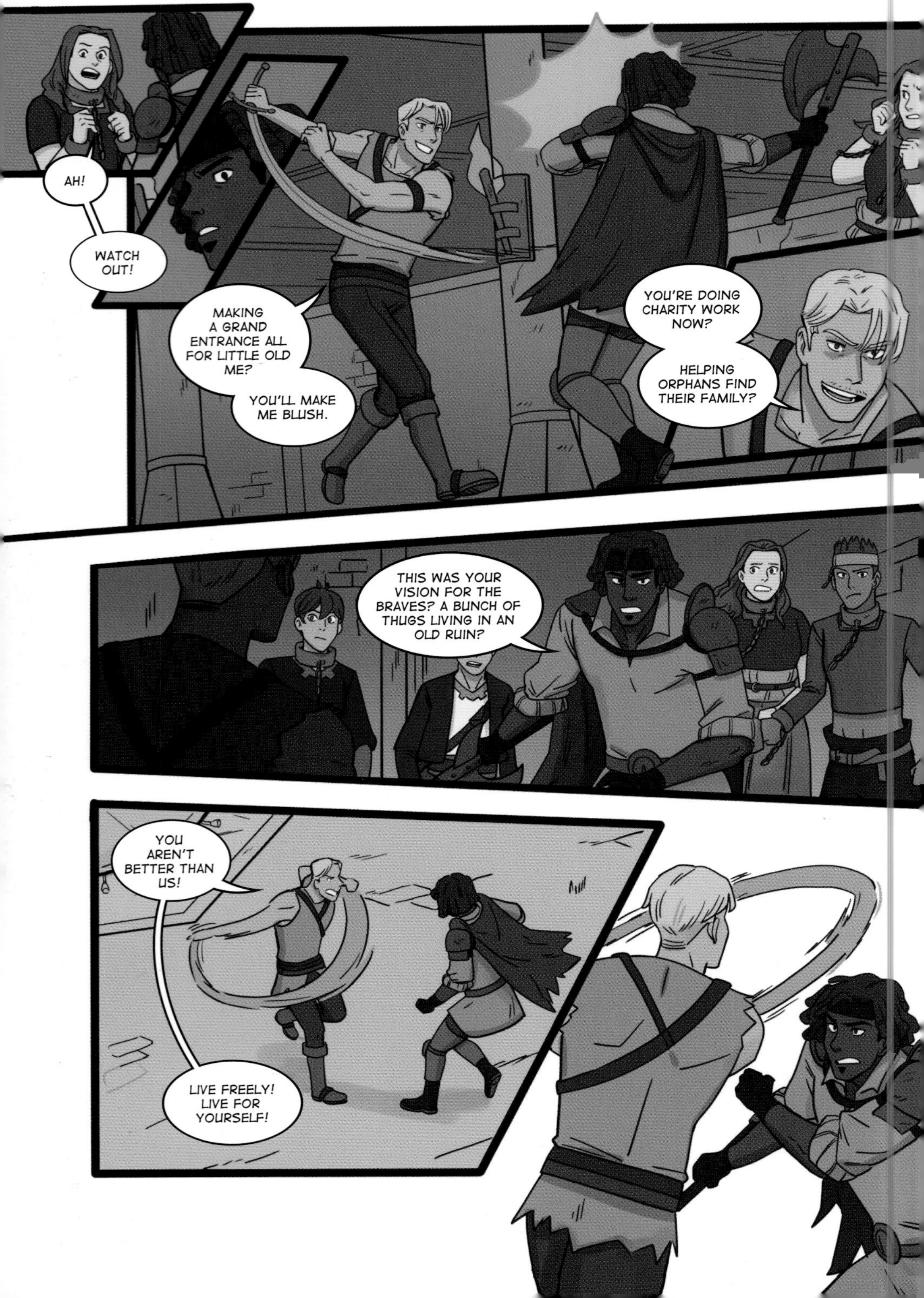
AH!
WATCH OUT!
MAKING A GRAND ENTRANCE ALL FOR LITTLE OLD ME?
YOU'LL MAKE ME BLUSH.
YOU'RE DOING CHARITY WORK NOW?
HELPING ORPHANS FIND THEIR FAMILY?
THIS WAS YOUR VISION FOR THE BRAVES? A BUNCH OF THUGS LIVING IN AN OLD RUIN?
YOU AREN'T BETTER THAN US!
LIVE FREELY! LIVE FOR YOURSELF!

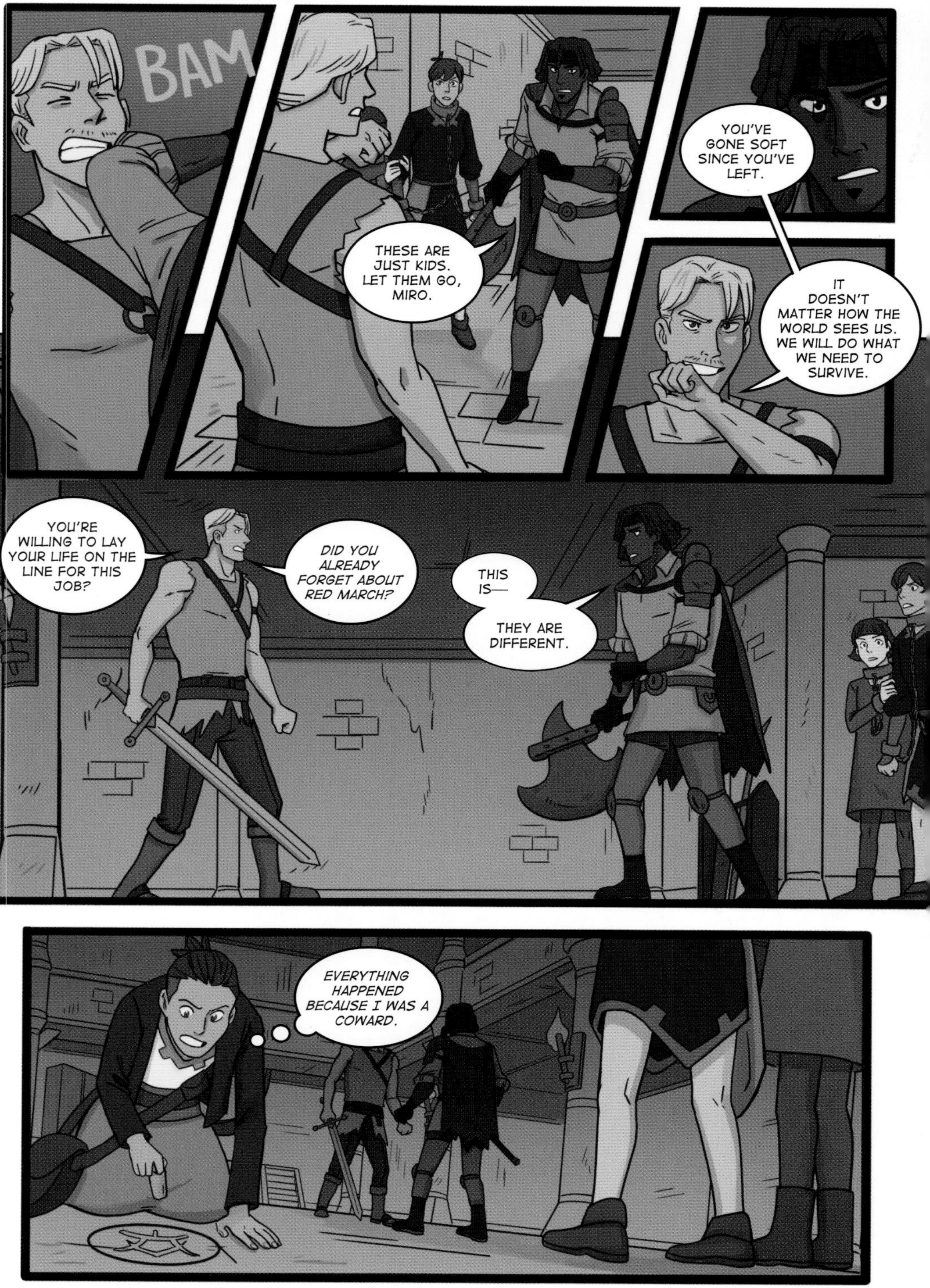
BAM
THESE ARE JUST KIDS. LET THEM GO, MIRO.
YOU'VE GONE SOFT SINCE YOU'VE LEFT.
IT DOESN'T MATTER HOW THE WORLD SEES US. WE WILL DO WHAT WE NEED TO SURVIVE.
YOU'RE WILLING TO LAY YOUR LIFE ON THE LINE FOR THIS JOB?
DID YOU ALREADY FORGET ABOUT RED MARCH?
THIS IS—
THEY ARE DIFFERENT.
EVERYTHING HAPPENED BECAUSE I WAS A COWARD.

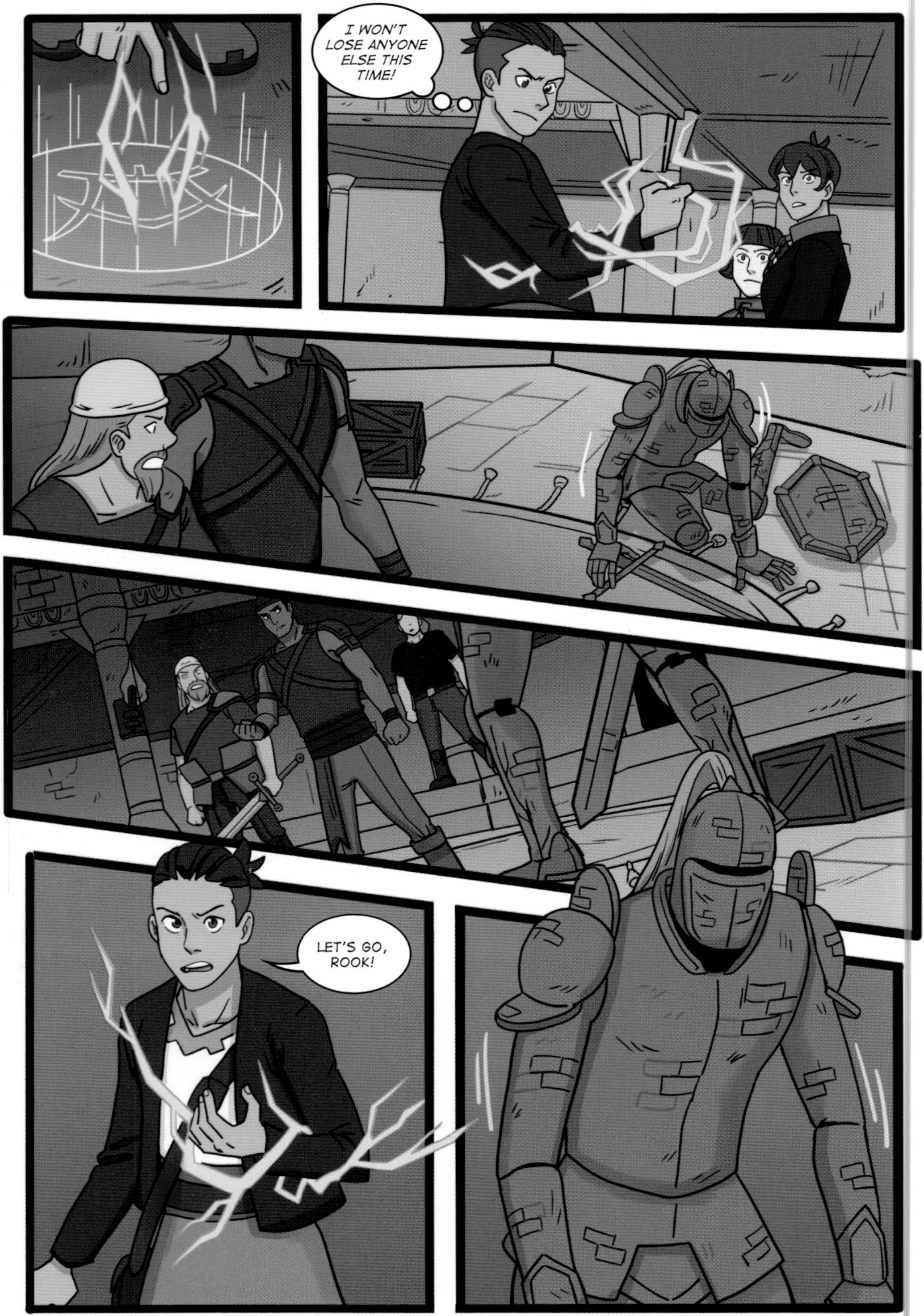
I WON'T LOSE ANYONE ELSE THIS TIME!
LET'S GO, ROOK!

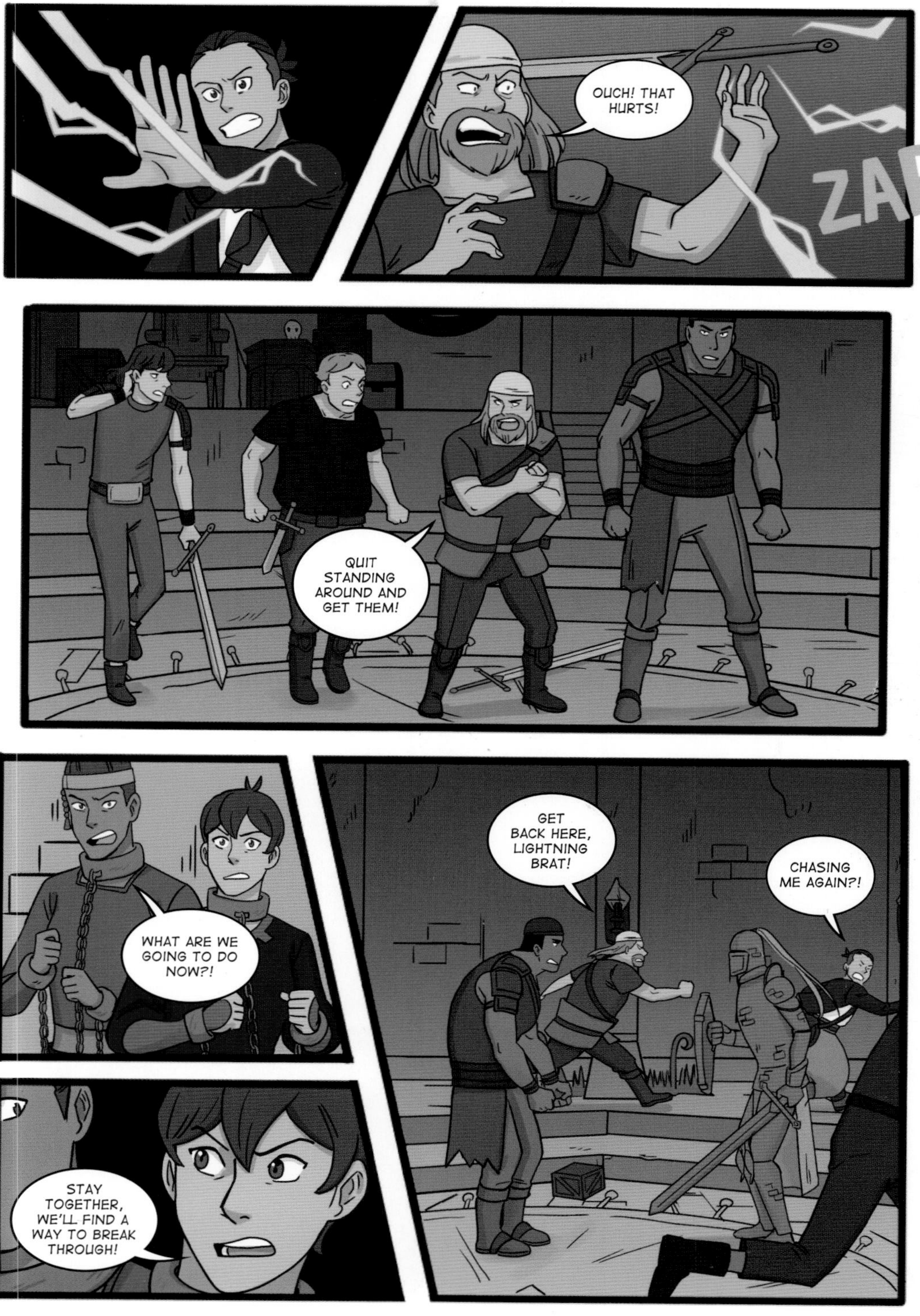
OUCH! THAT HURTS!
ZAP
QUIT STANDING AROUND AND GET THEM!
WHAT ARE WE GOING TO DO NOW?!
STAY TOGETHER, WE'LL FIND A WAY TO BREAK THROUGH!
GET BACK HERE, LIGHTNING BRAT!
CHASING ME AGAIN?!

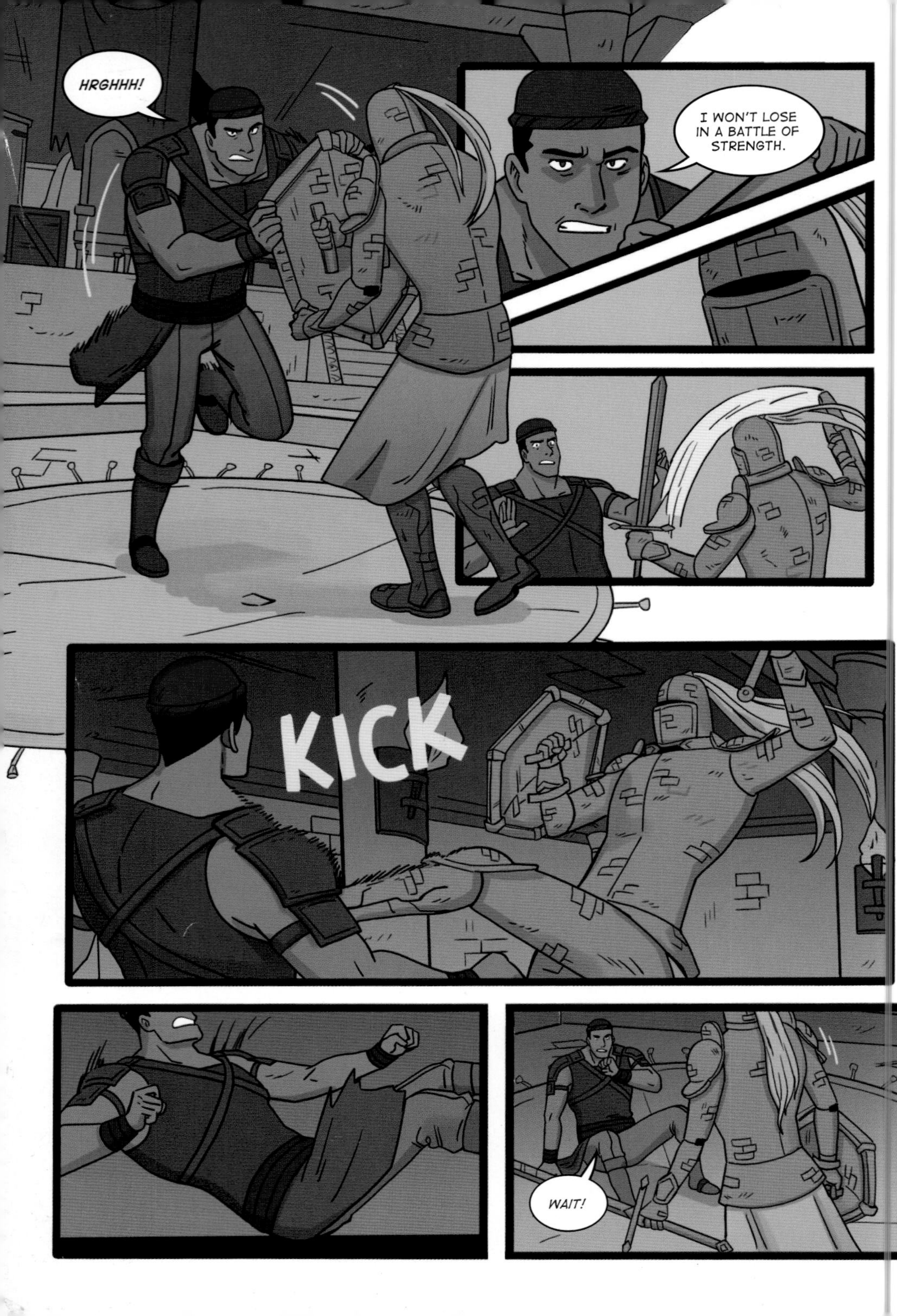
HRGHHH!
I WON'T LOSE IN A BATTLE OF STRENGTH.
KICK
WAIT!

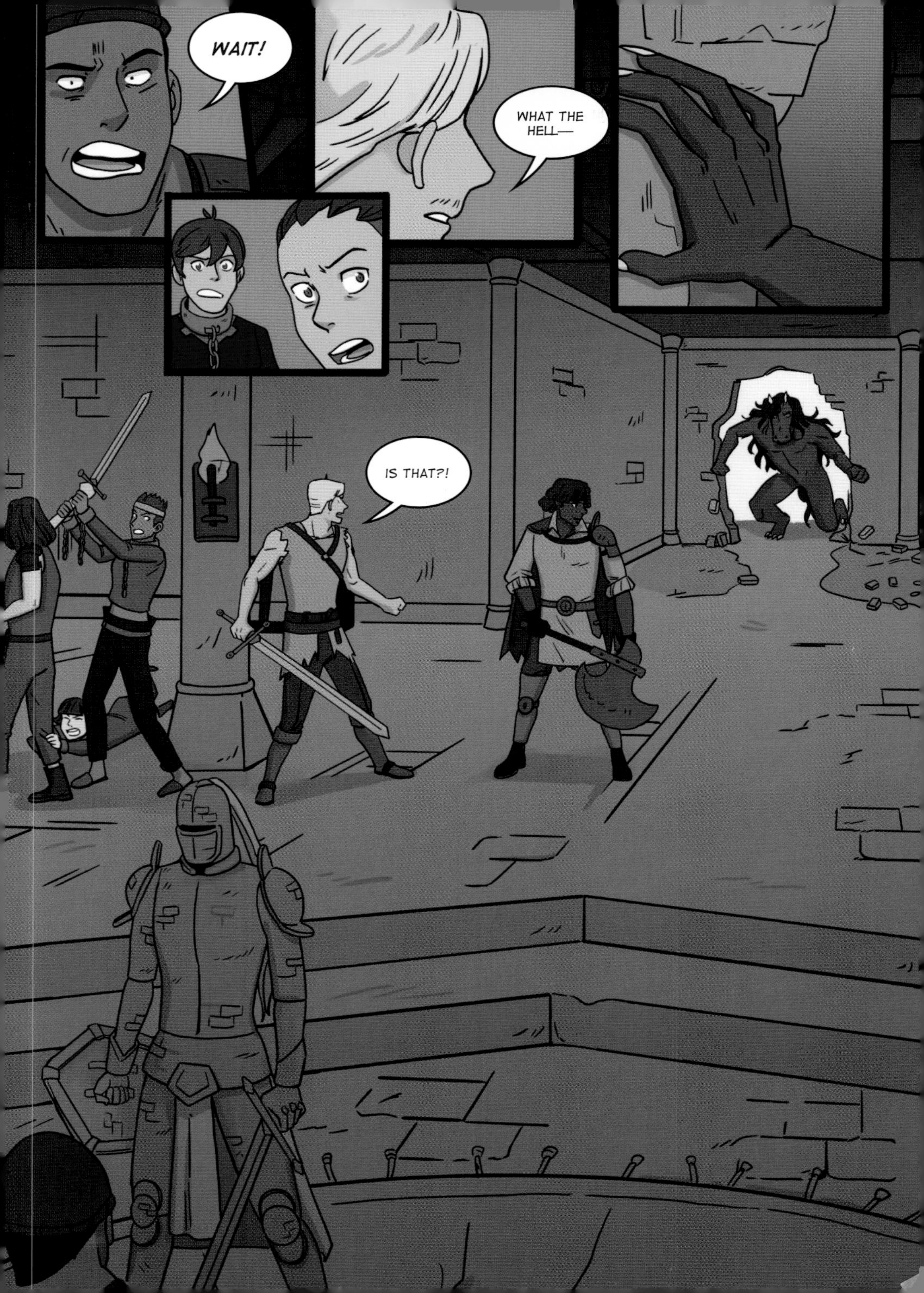
WAIT!
WHAT THE HELL—
IS THAT?!

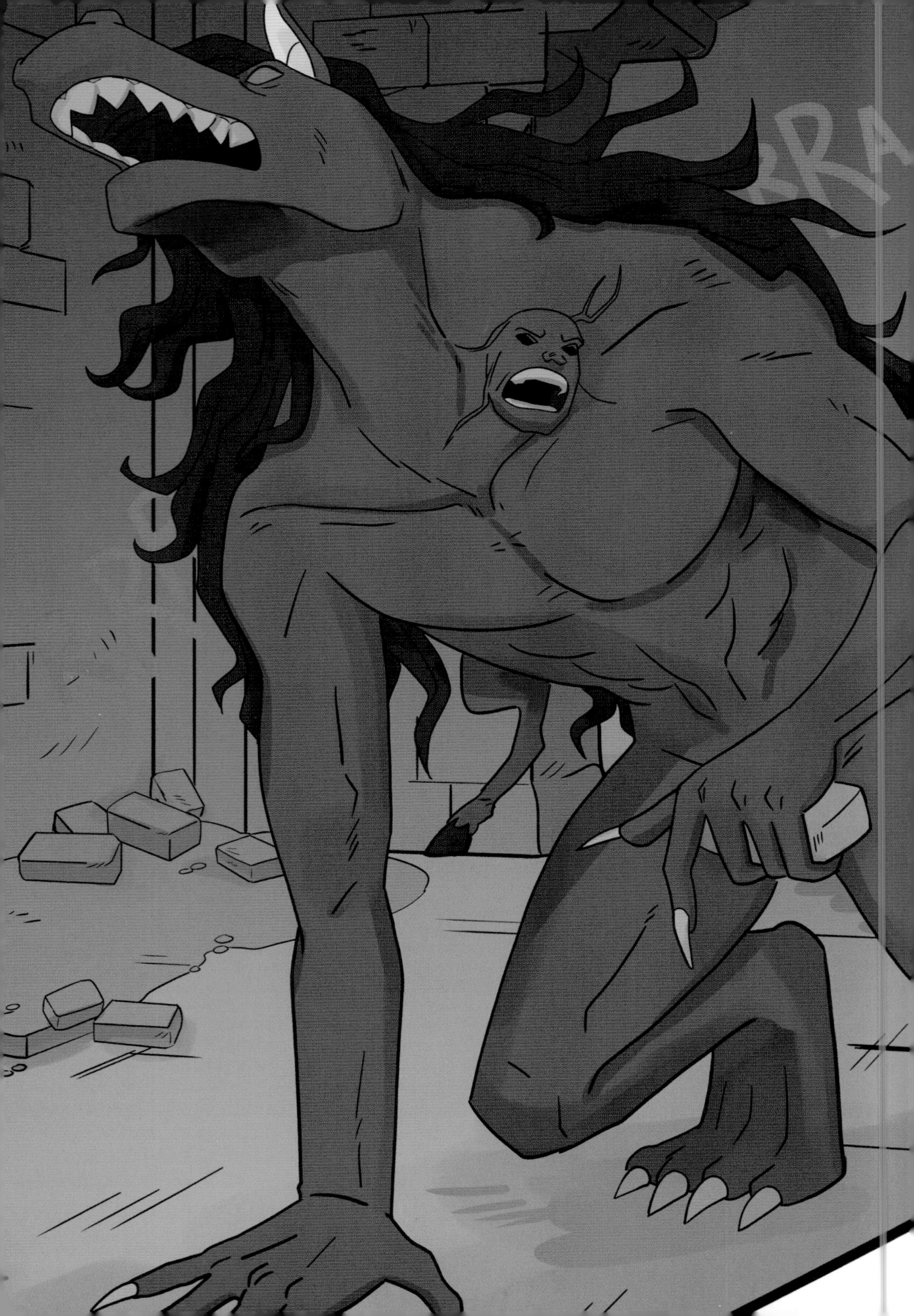

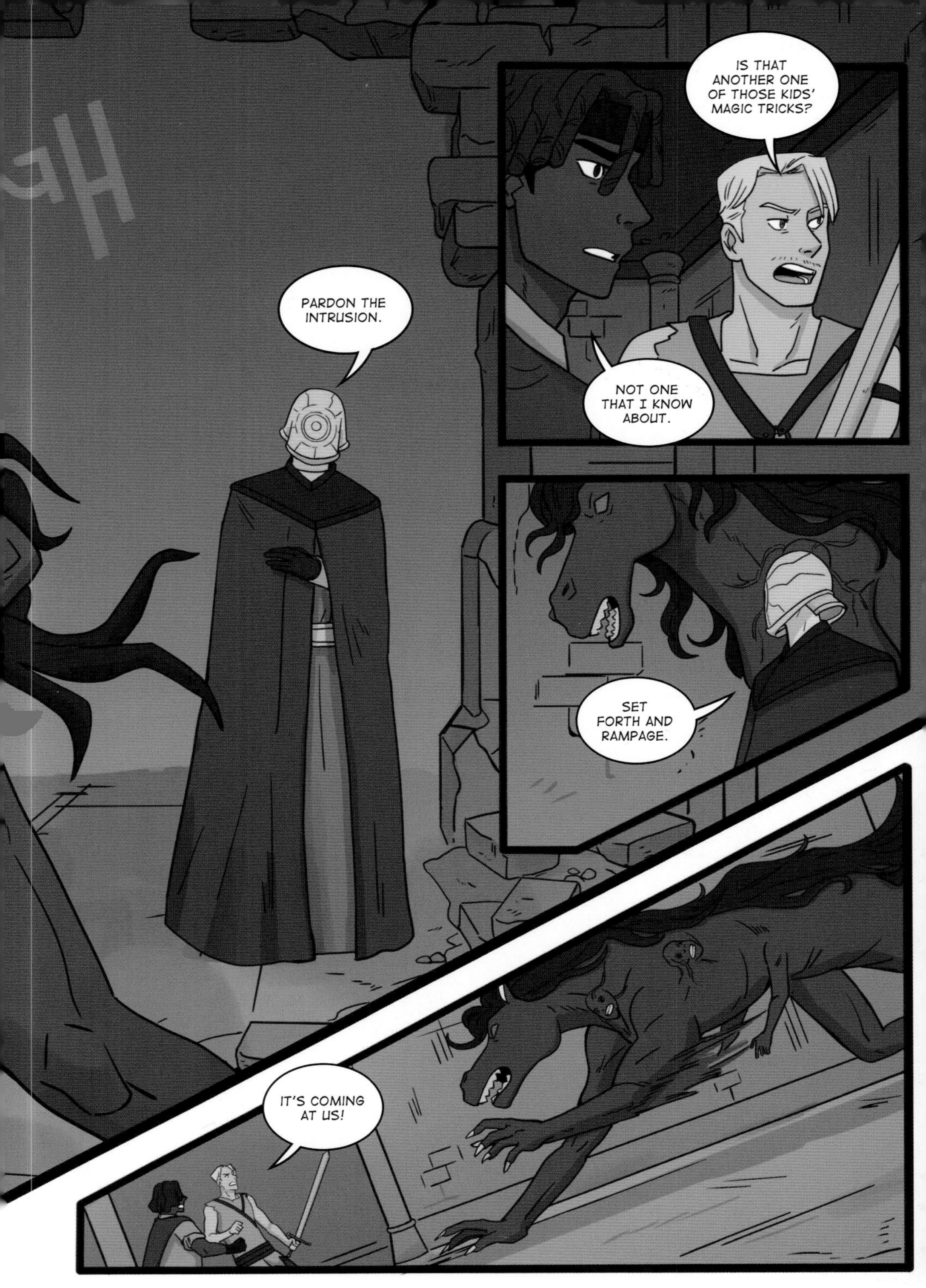
PARDON THE INTRUSION.
IS THAT ANOTHER ONE OF THOSE KIDS' MAGIC TRICKS?
NOT ONE THAT I KNOW ABOUT.
SET FORTH AND RAMPAGE.
IT'S COMING AT US!

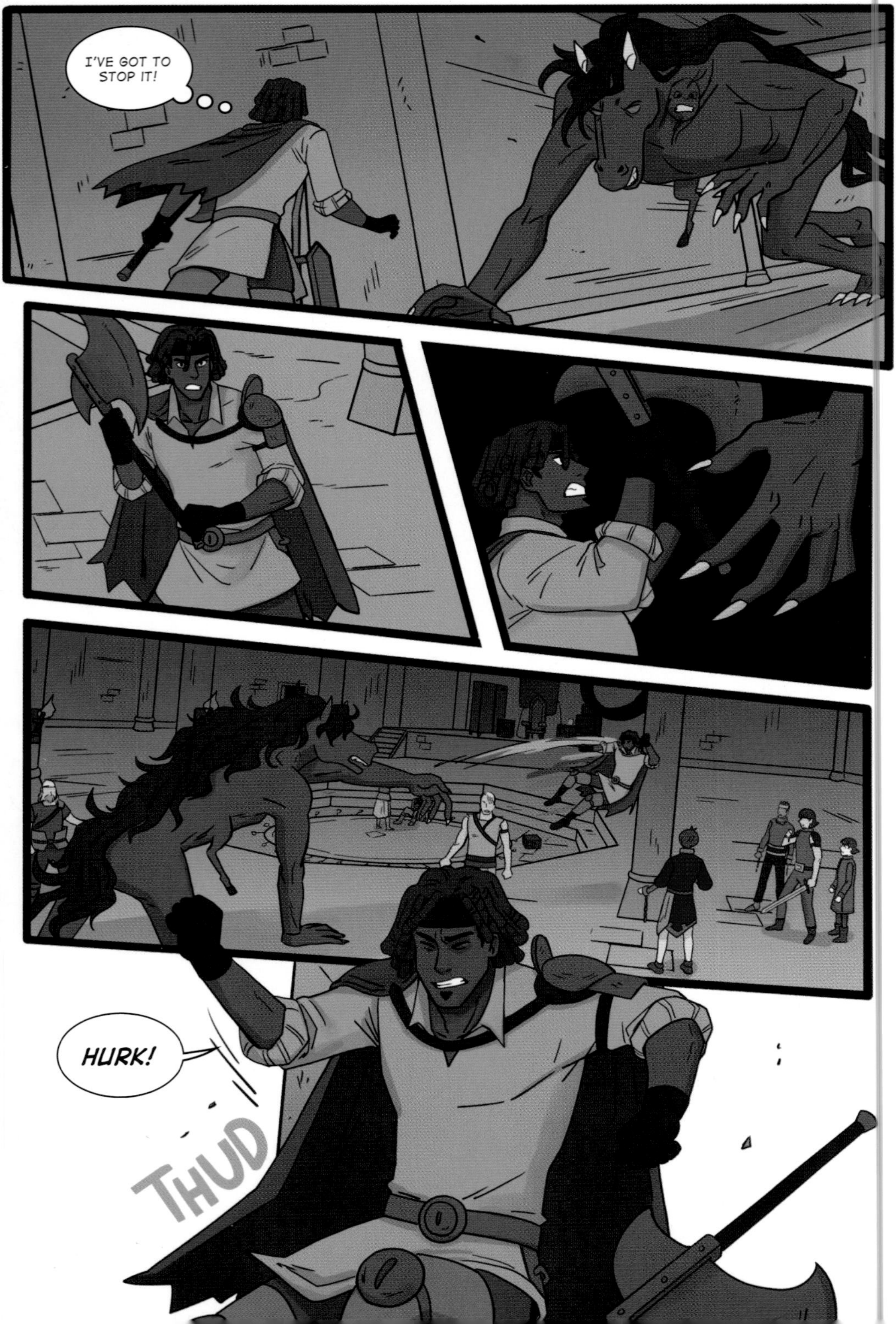
I'VE GOT TO STOP IT!
HURK!
THUD

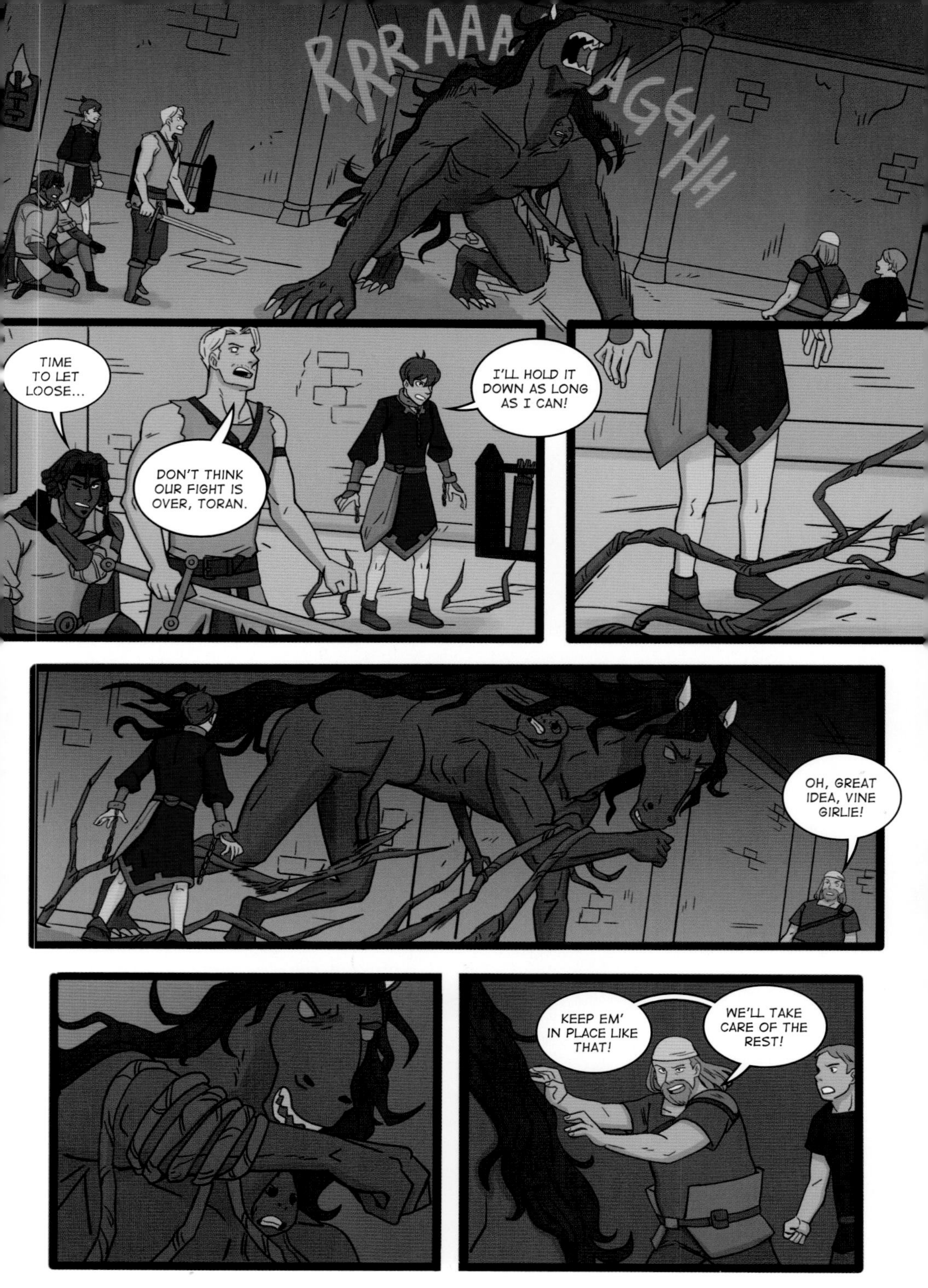
RRRAAAAGGHH
TIME TO LET LOOSE...
DON'T THINK OUR FIGHT IS OVER, TORAN.
I'LL HOLD IT DOWN AS LONG AS I CAN!
OH, GREAT IDEA, VINE GIRLIE!
KEEP EM' IN PLACE LIKE THAT!
WE'LL TAKE CARE OF THE REST!

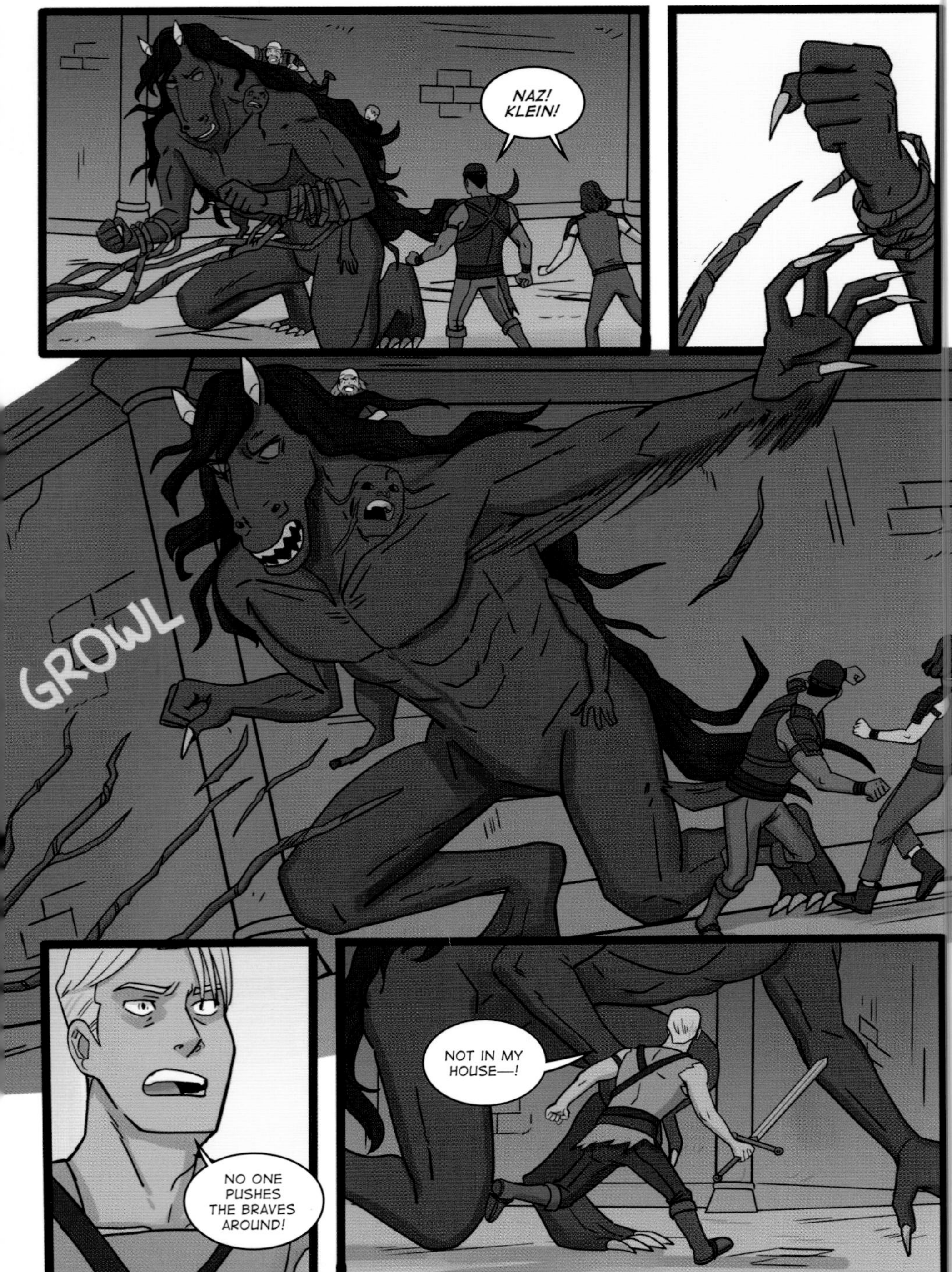
NAZ! KLEIN!
GROWL
NO ONE PUSHES THE BRAVES AROUND!
NOT IN MY HOUSE—!

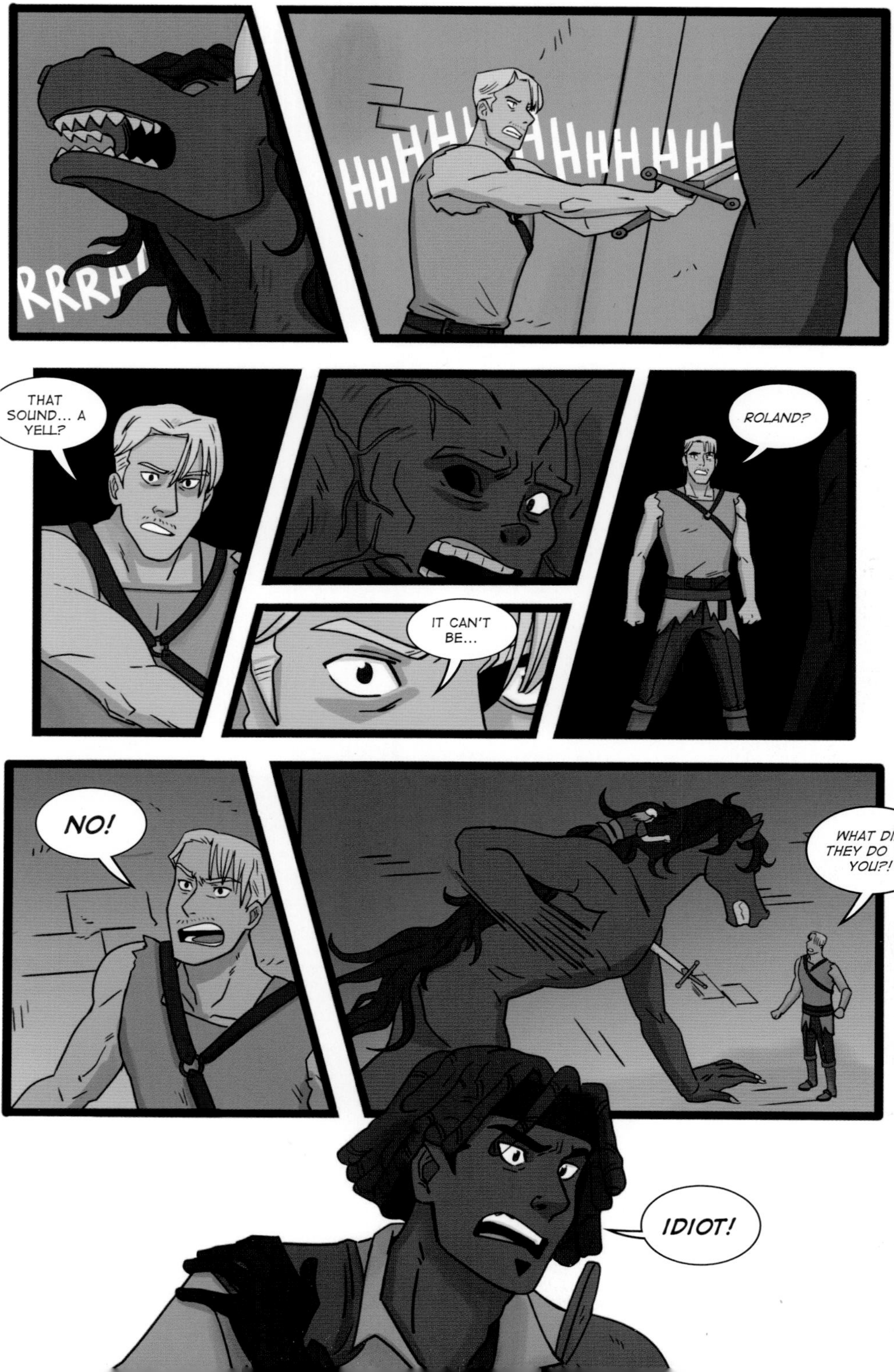
RRRA
HHHHHHHHHHHH
THAT SOUND... A YELL?
ROLAND?
IT CAN'T BE...
NO!
WHAT DID THEY DO TO YOU?!
IDIOT!

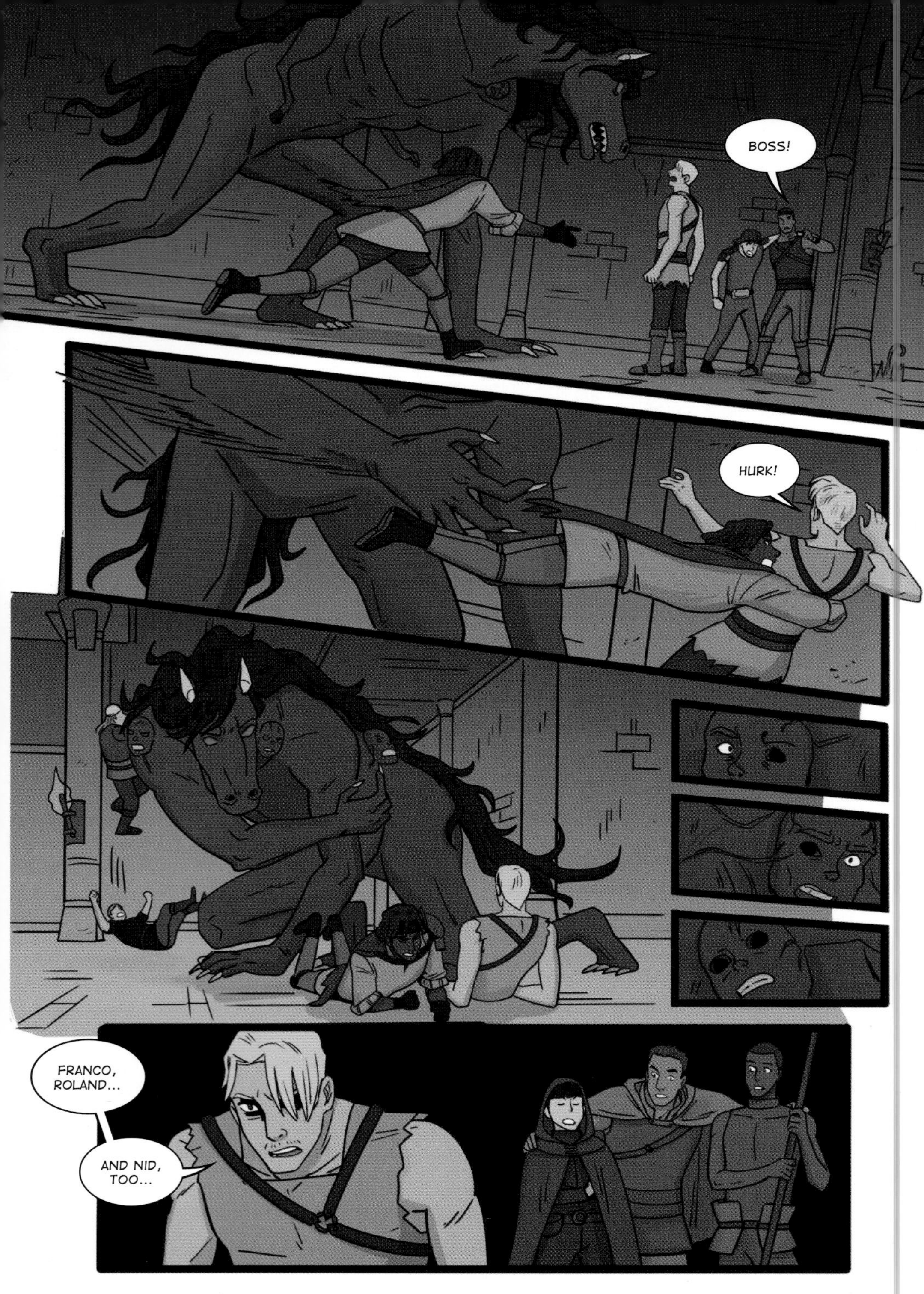
BOSS!
HURK!
FRANCO, ROLAND...
AND NID, TOO...

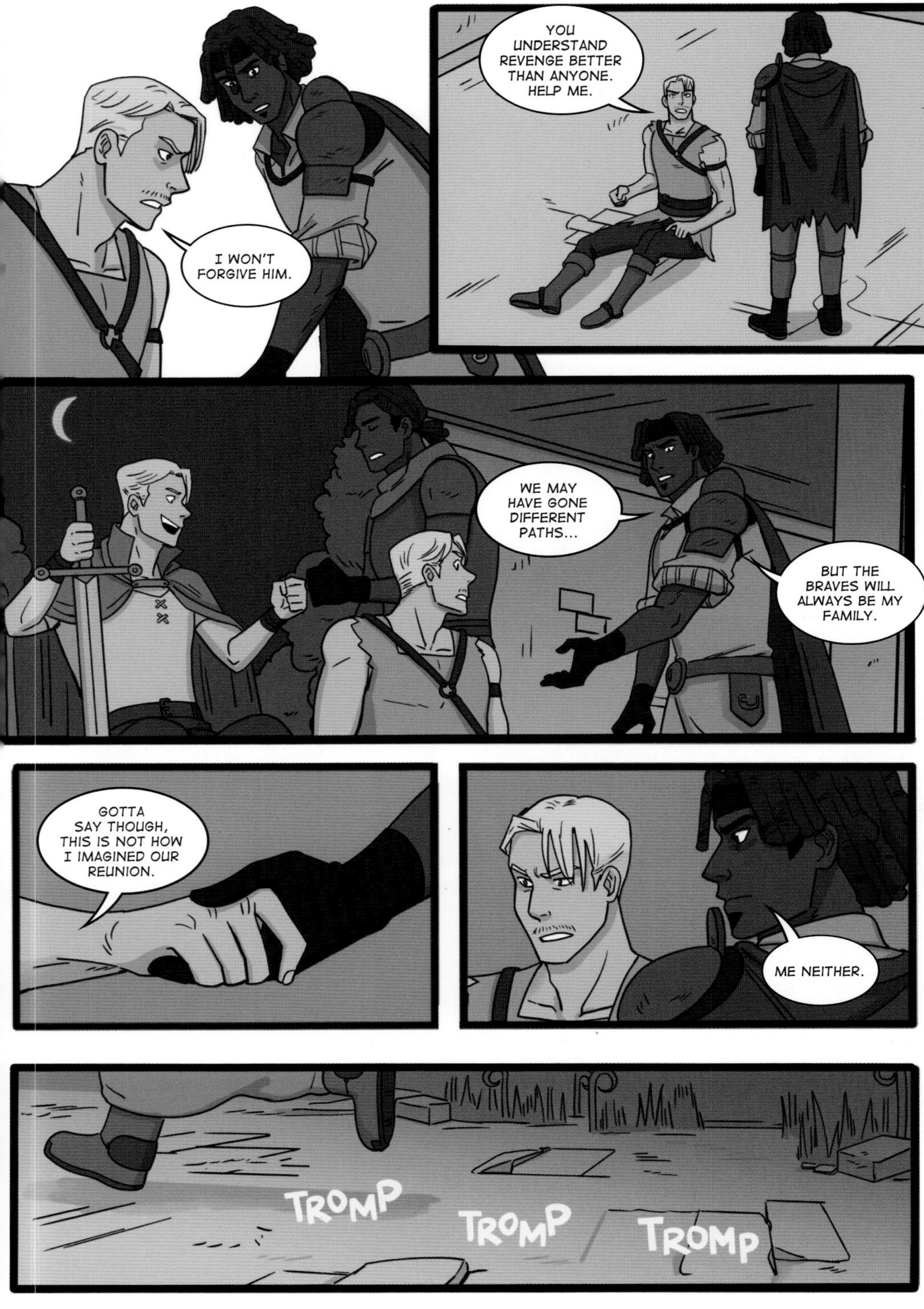

I WON'T FORGIVE HIM.
YOU UNDERSTAND REVENGE BETTER THAN ANYONE. HELP ME.
WE MAY HAVE GONE DIFFERENT PATHS...
BUT THE BRAVES WILL ALWAYS BE MY FAMILY.
GOTTA SAY THOUGH, THIS IS NOT HOW I IMAGINED OUR REUNION.
ME NEITHER.
TROMP
TROMP
TROMP

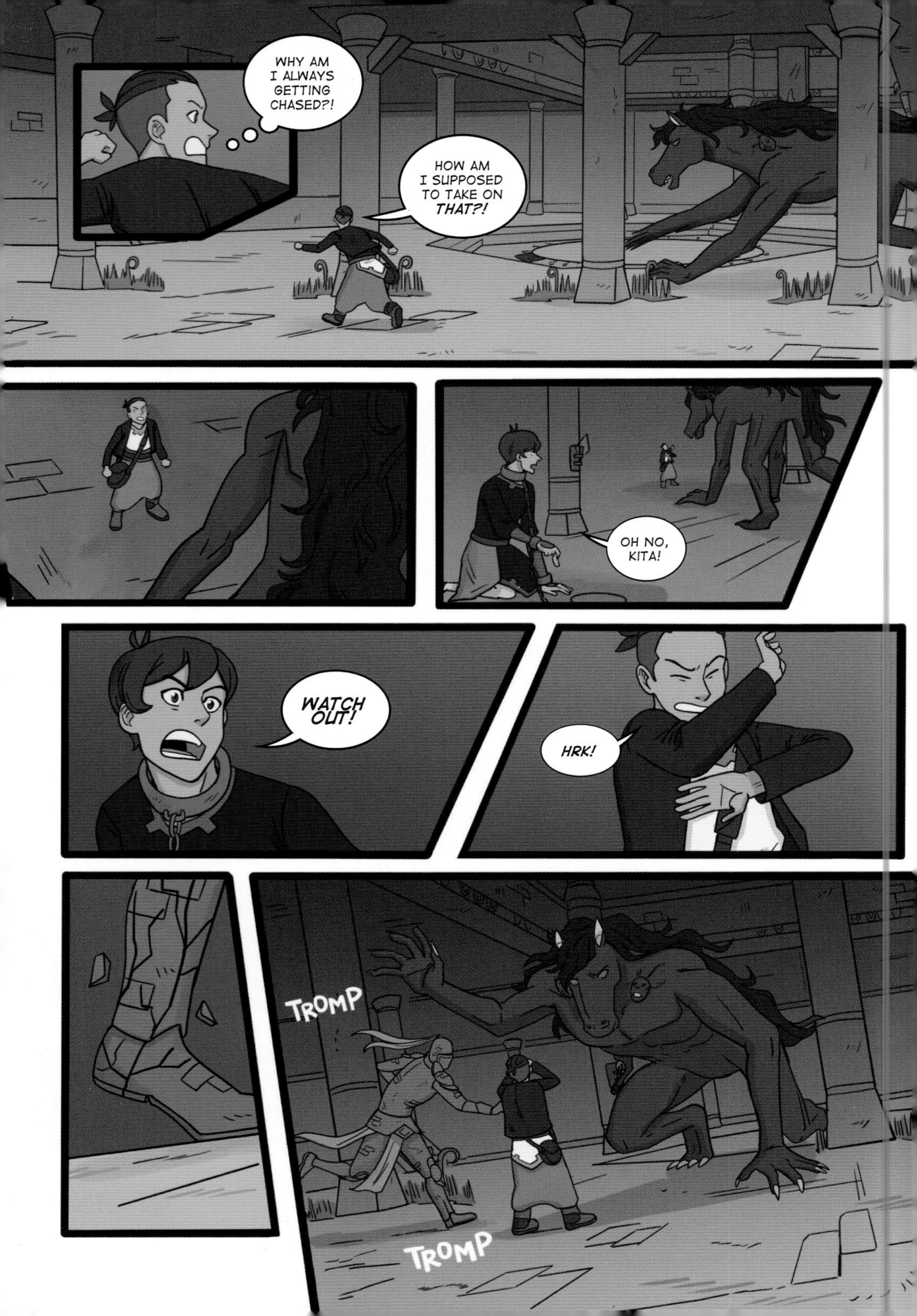
WHY AM I ALWAYS GETTING CHASED?!
HOW AM I SUPPOSED TO TAKE ON *THAT?!*
OH NO, KITA!
WATCH OUT!
HRK!
TROMP
TROMP

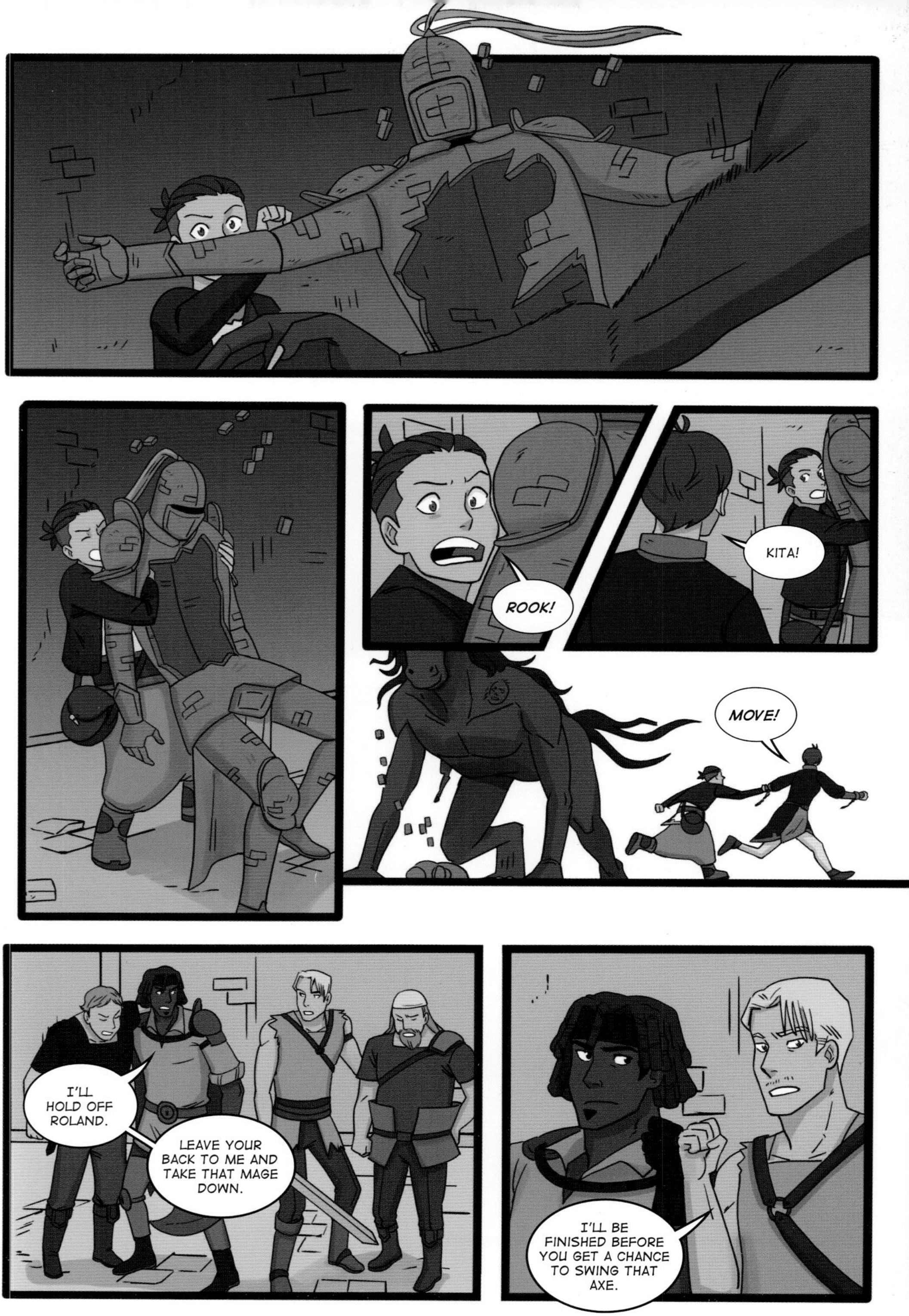
ROOK!
KITA!
MOVE!
I'LL HOLD OFF ROLAND.
LEAVE YOUR BACK TO ME AND TAKE THAT MAGE DOWN.
I'LL BE FINISHED BEFORE YOU GET A CHANCE TO SWING THAT AXE.

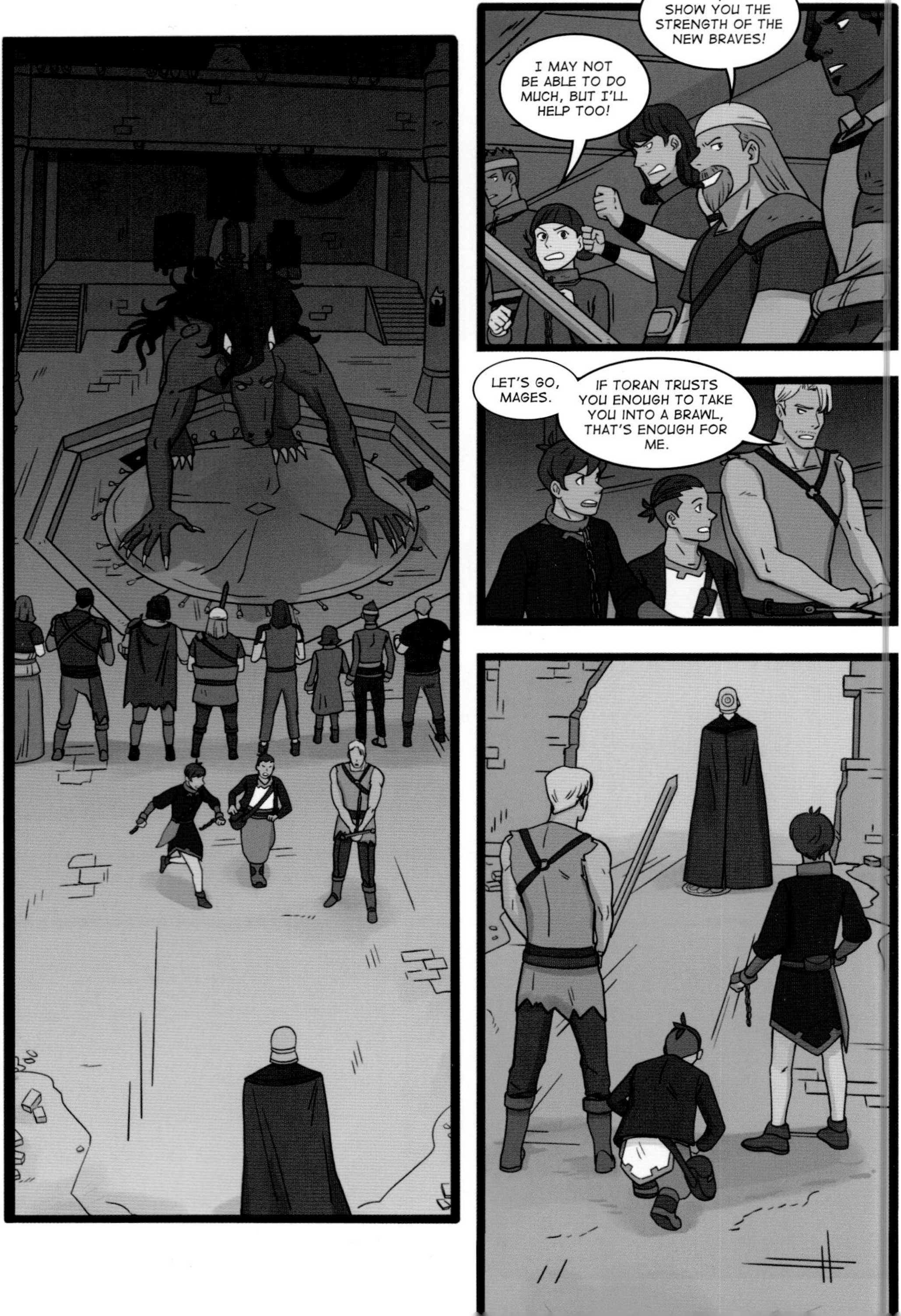
TORAN, WE'LL SHOW YOU THE STRENGTH OF THE NEW BRAVES!
I MAY NOT BE ABLE TO DO MUCH, BUT I'LL HELP TOO!
LET'S GO, MAGES.
IF TORAN TRUSTS YOU ENOUGH TO TAKE YOU INTO A BRAWL, THAT'S ENOUGH FOR ME.

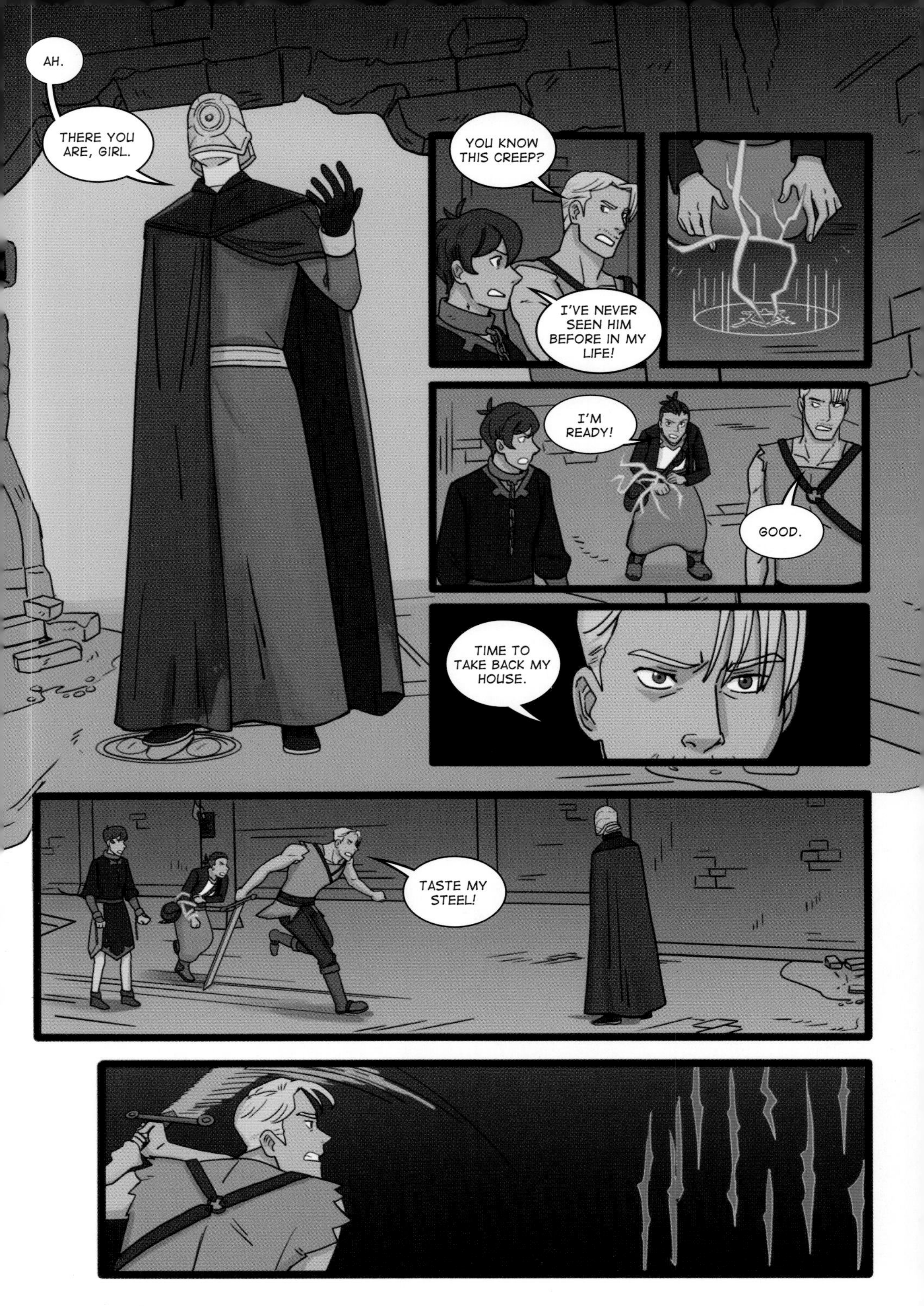
AH.
THERE YOU ARE, GIRL.
YOU KNOW THIS CREEP?
I'VE NEVER SEEN HIM BEFORE IN MY LIFE!
I'M READY!
GOOD.
TIME TO TAKE BACK MY HOUSE.
TASTE MY STEEL!

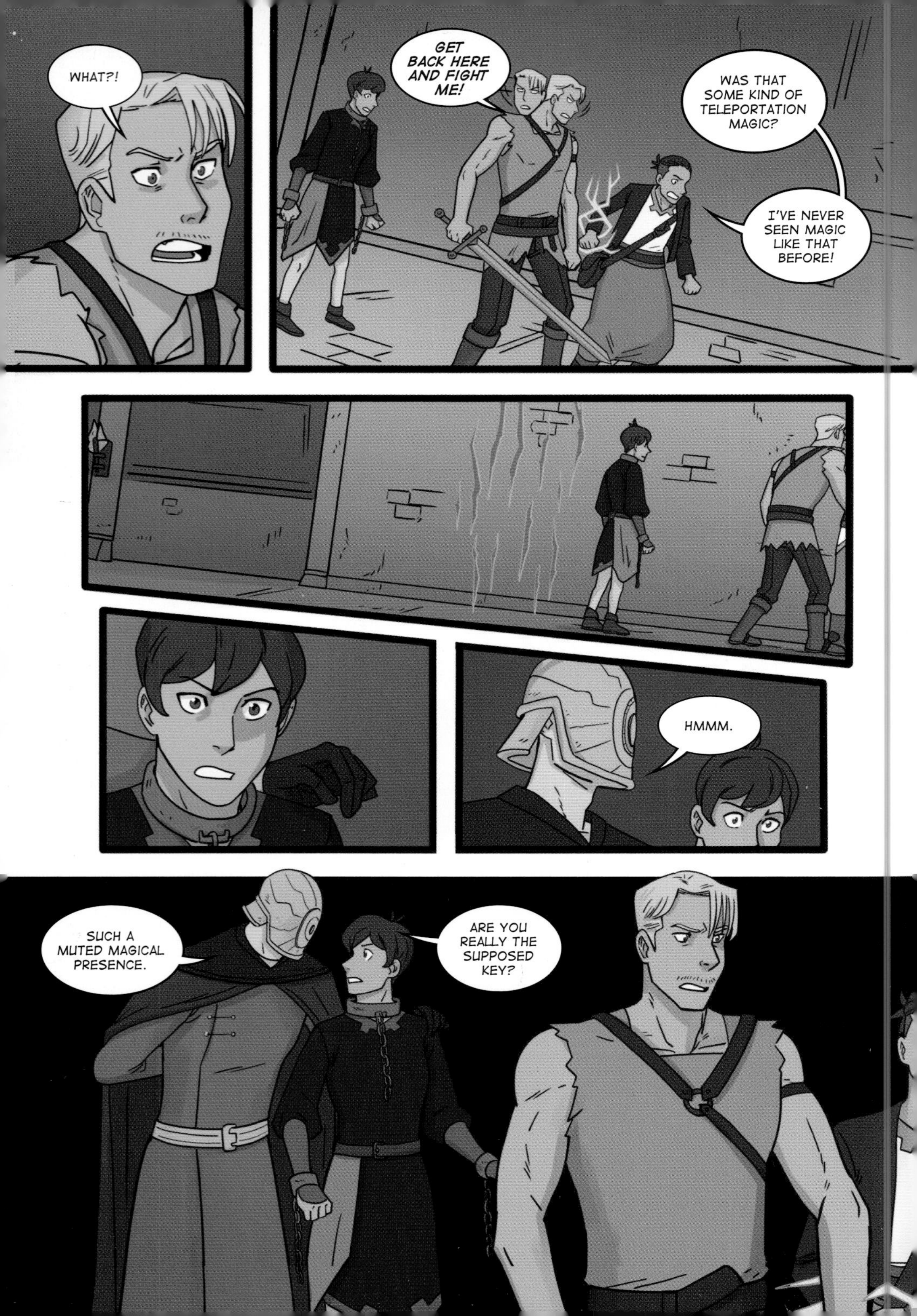
WHAT?!
GET BACK HERE AND FIGHT ME!
WAS THAT SOME KIND OF TELEPORTATION MAGIC?
I'VE NEVER SEEN MAGIC LIKE THAT BEFORE!
HMMM.
SUCH A MUTED MAGICAL PRESENCE.
ARE YOU REALLY THE SUPPOSED KEY?

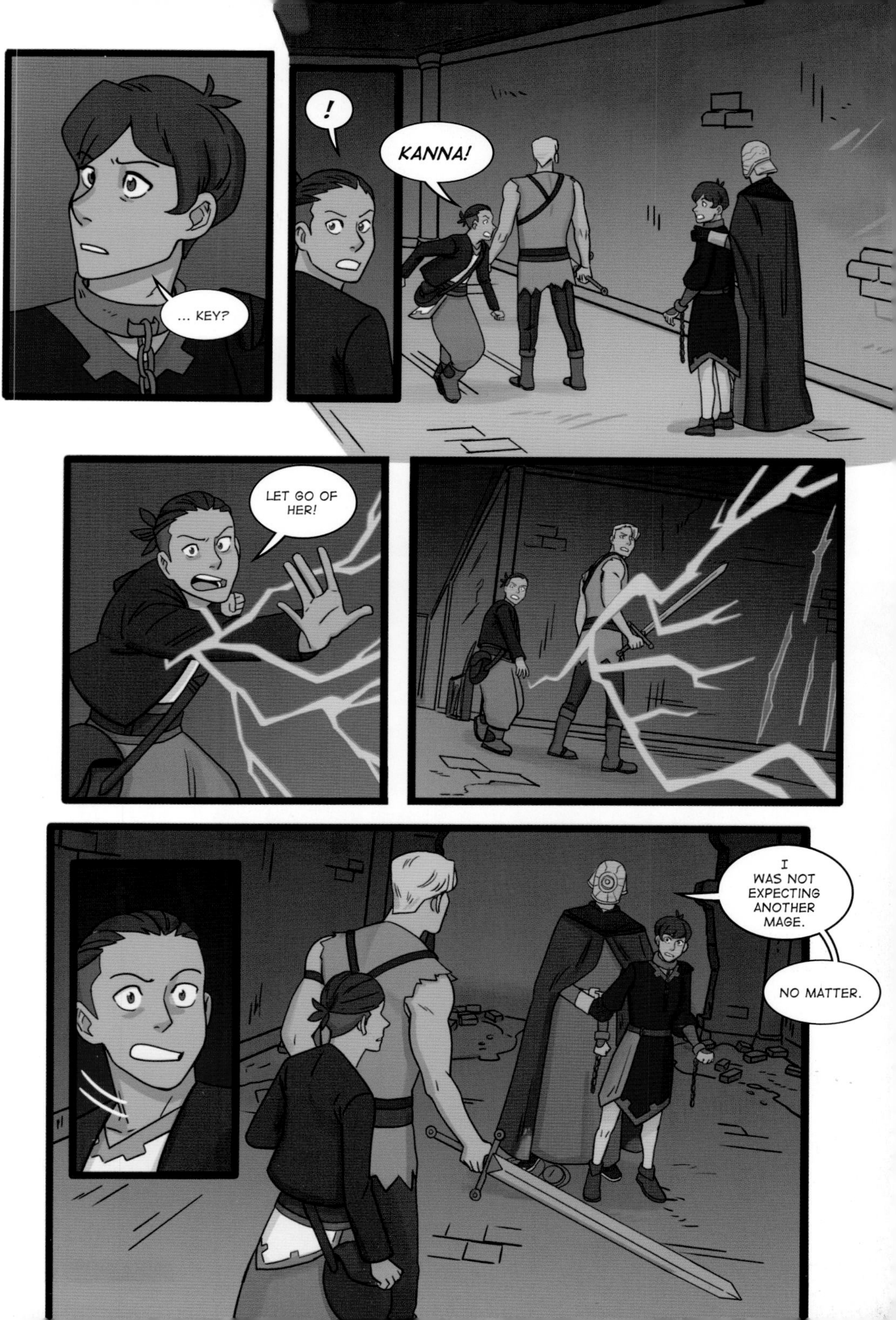

... KEY?
!
KANNA!
LET GO OF HER!
I WAS NOT EXPECTING ANOTHER MAGE.
NO MATTER.

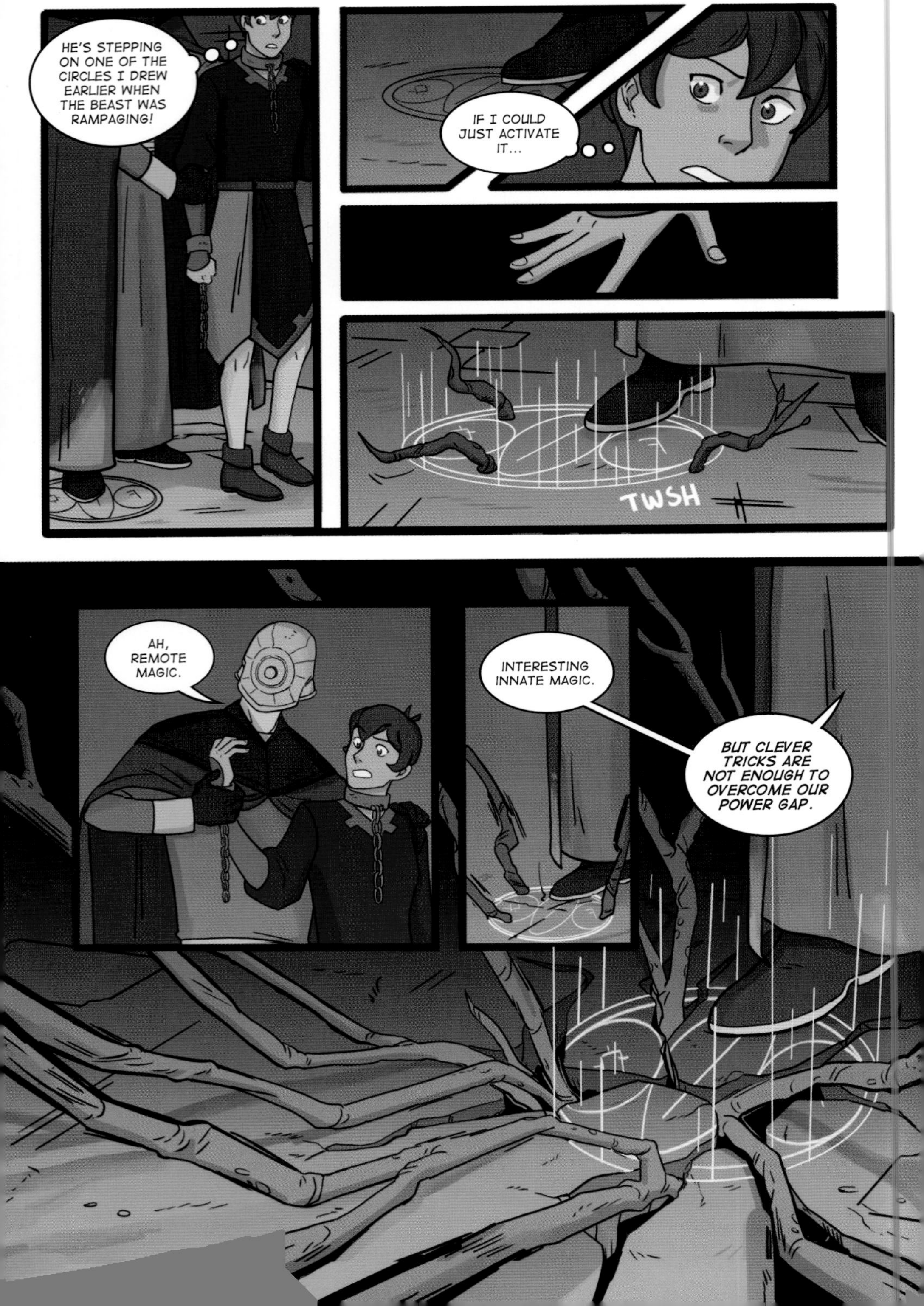
HE'S STEPPING ON ONE OF THE CIRCLES I DREW EARLIER WHEN THE BEAST WAS RAMPAGING!
IF I COULD JUST ACTIVATE IT...
TWSH
AH, REMOTE MAGIC.
INTERESTING INNATE MAGIC.
BUT CLEVER TRICKS ARE NOT ENOUGH TO OVERCOME OUR POWER GAP.

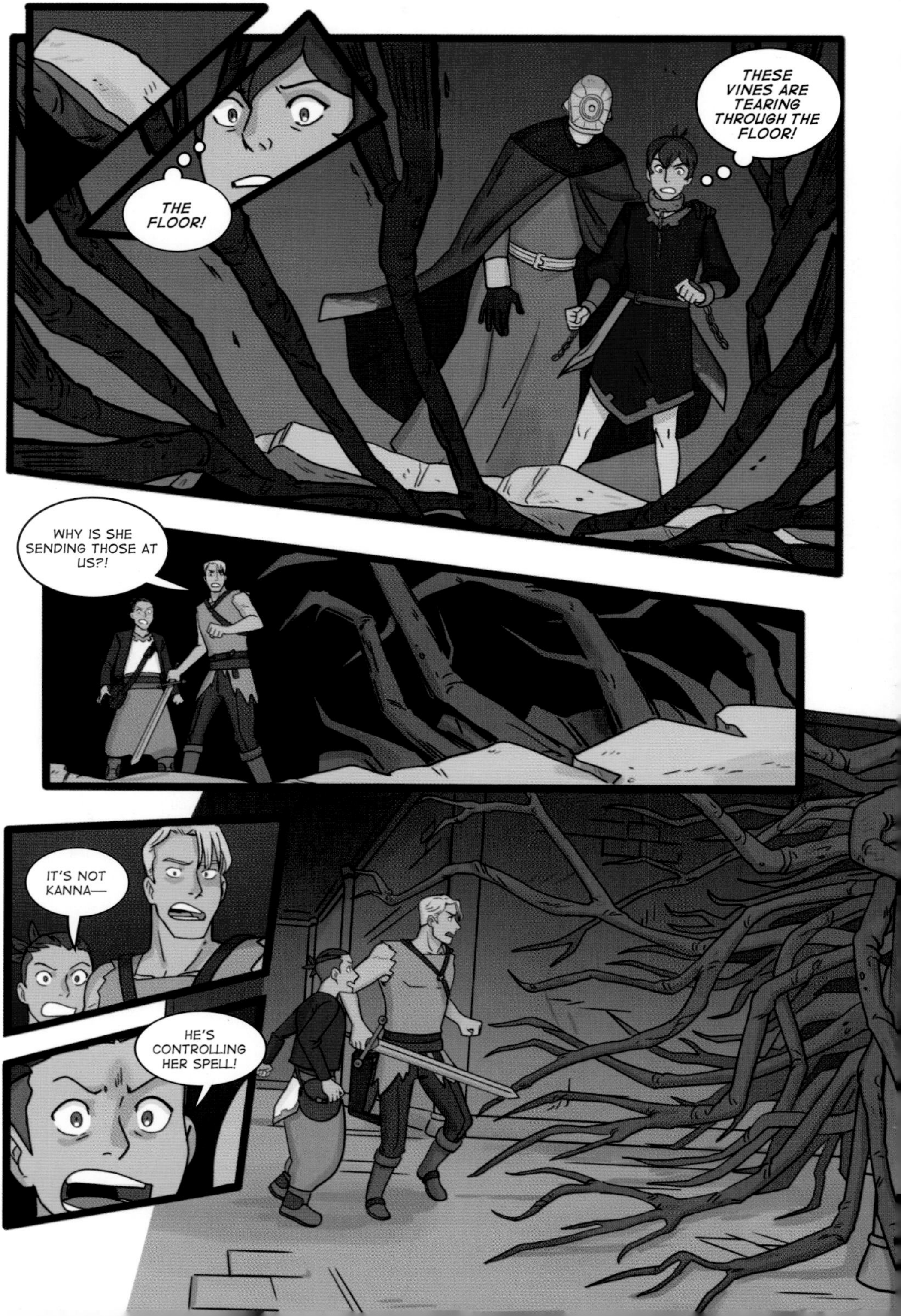
THE FLOOR!
THESE VINES ARE TEARING THROUGH THE FLOOR!
WHY IS SHE SENDING THOSE AT US?!
IT'S NOT KANNA—
HE'S CONTROLLING HER SPELL!

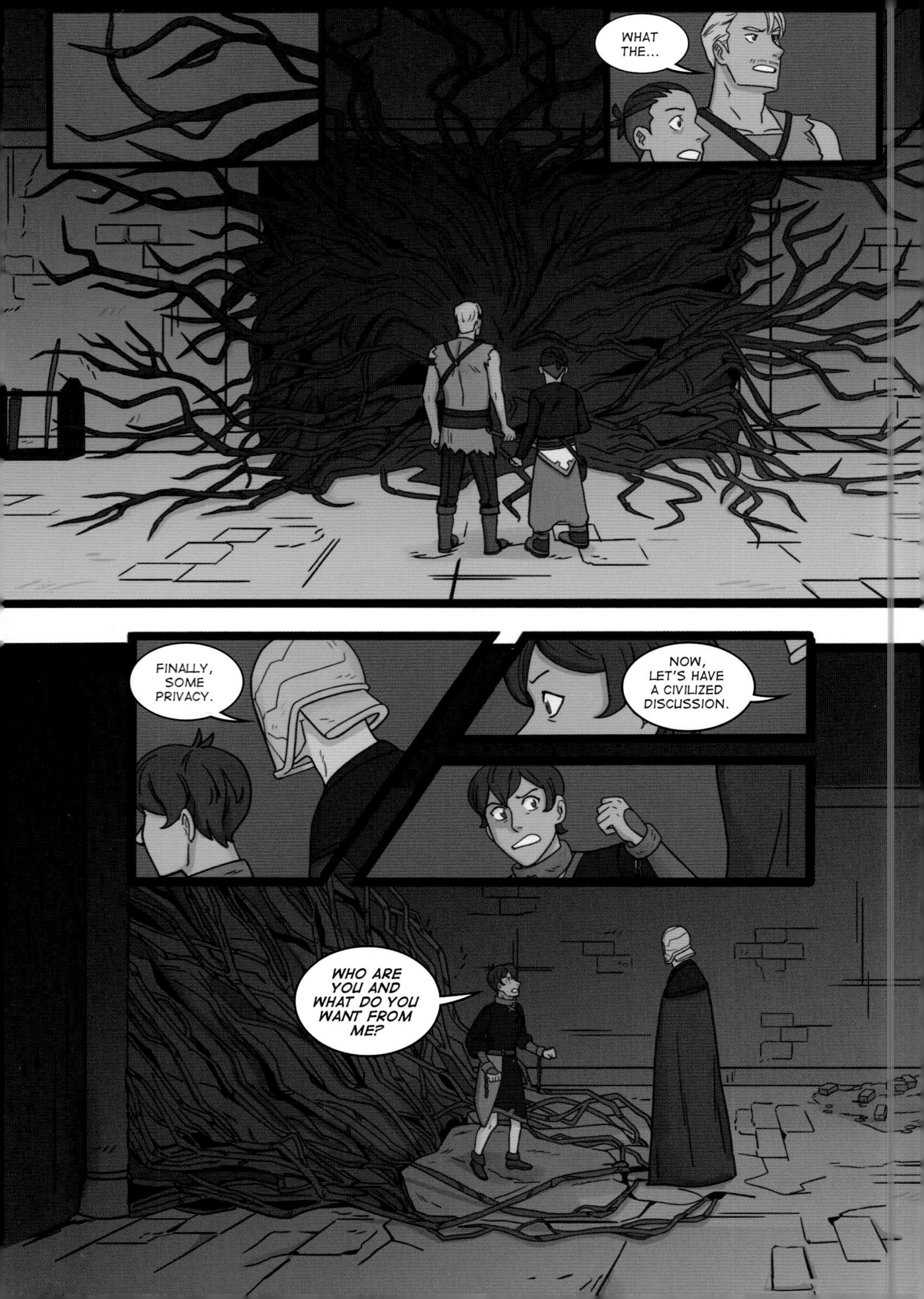
WHAT THE...
FINALLY, SOME PRIVACY.
NOW, LET'S HAVE A CIVILIZED DISCUSSION.
WHO ARE YOU AND WHAT DO YOU WANT FROM ME?

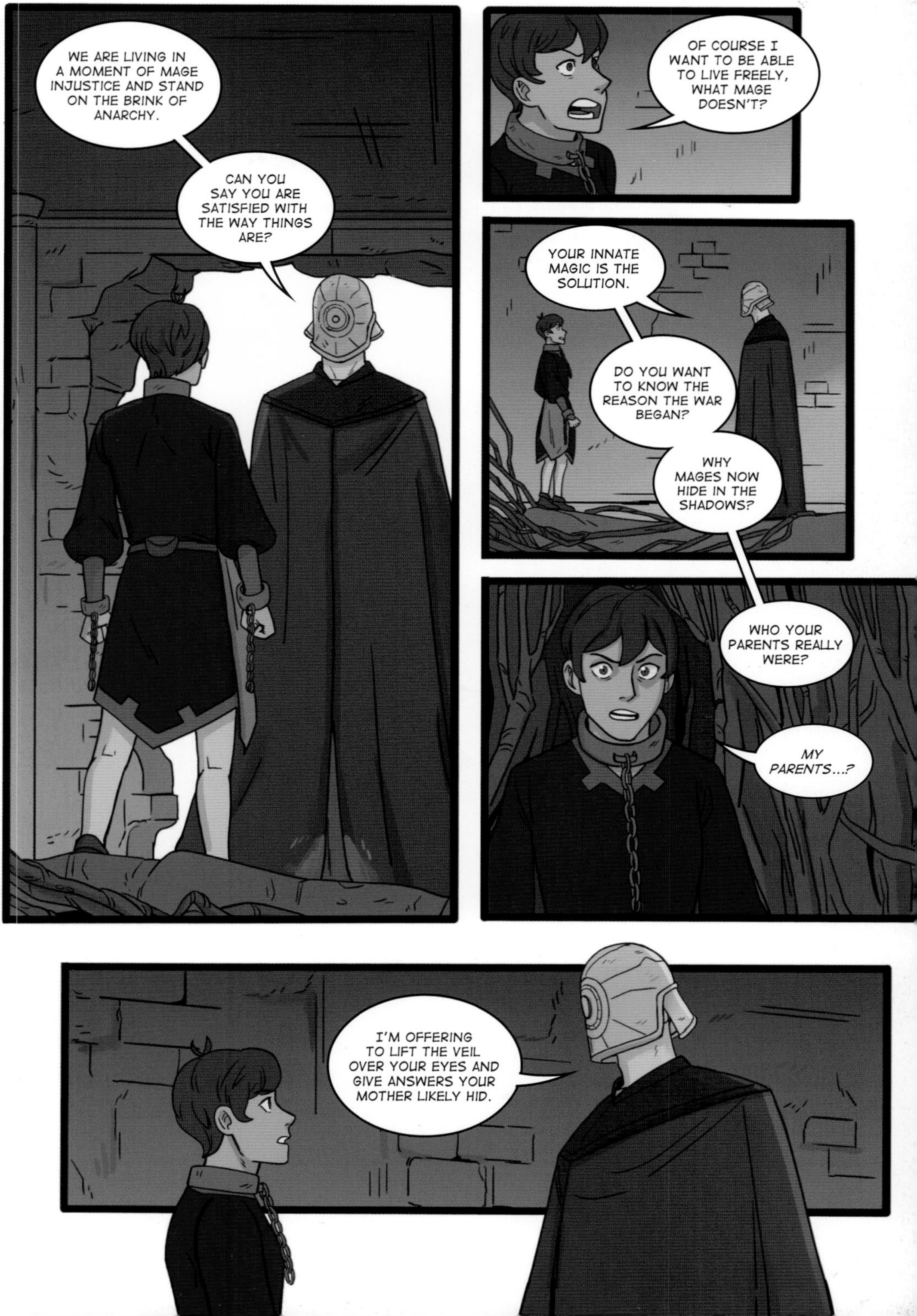
WE ARE LIVING IN A MOMENT OF MAGE INJUSTICE AND STAND ON THE BRINK OF ANARCHY.
CAN YOU SAY YOU ARE SATISFIED WITH THE WAY THINGS ARE?
OF COURSE I WANT TO BE ABLE TO LIVE FREELY, WHAT MAGE DOESN'T?
YOUR INNATE MAGIC IS THE SOLUTION.
DO YOU WANT TO KNOW THE REASON THE WAR BEGAN?
WHY MAGES NOW HIDE IN THE SHADOWS?
WHO YOUR PARENTS REALLY WERE?
MY PARENTS...?
I'M OFFERING TO LIFT THE VEIL OVER YOUR EYES AND GIVE ANSWERS YOUR MOTHER LIKELY HID.

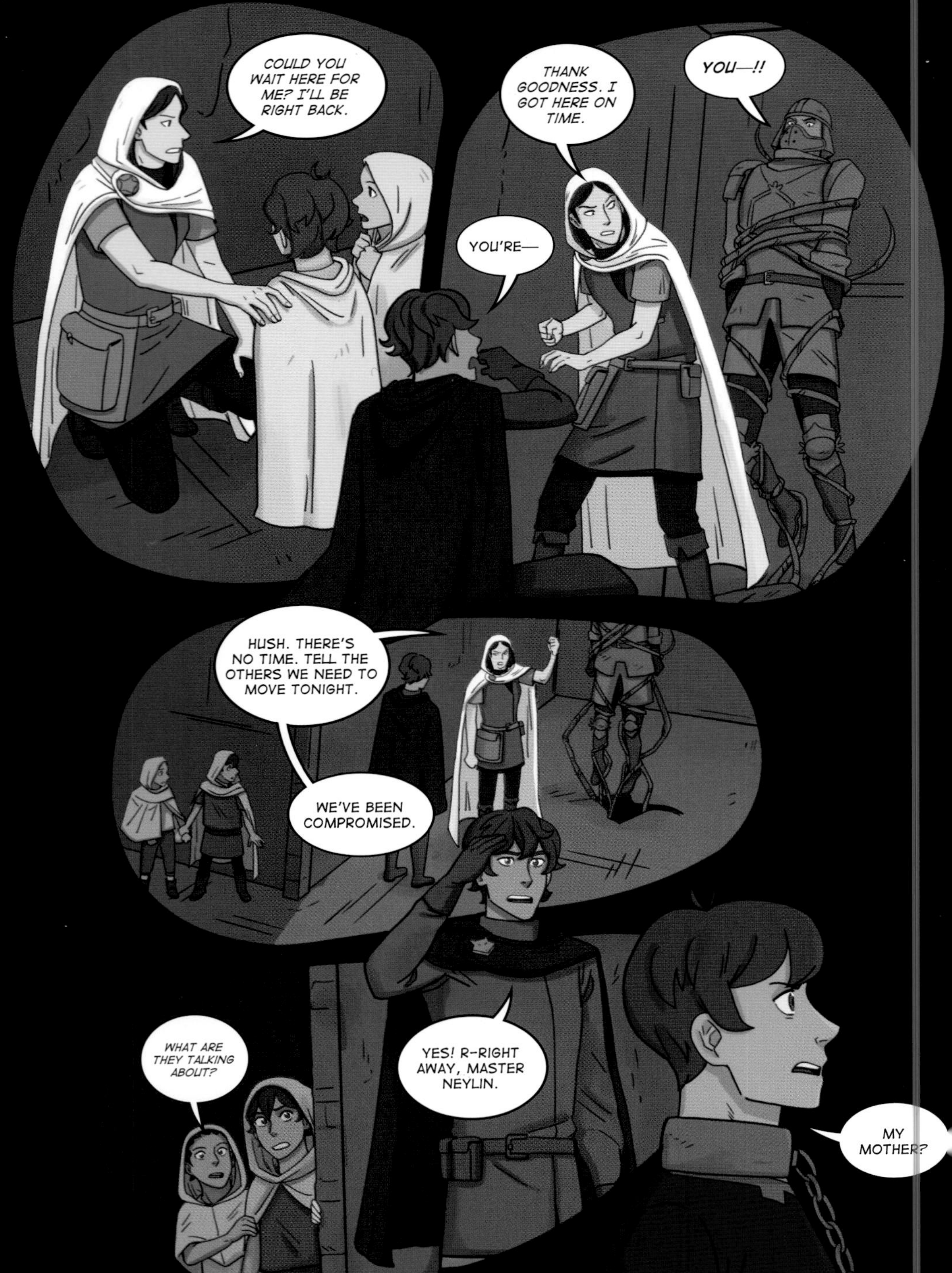
COULD YOU WAIT HERE FOR ME? I'LL BE RIGHT BACK.
THANK GOODNESS. I GOT HERE ON TIME.
YOU—!!
YOU'RE—
HUSH. THERE'S NO TIME. TELL THE OTHERS WE NEED TO MOVE TONIGHT.
WE'VE BEEN COMPROMISED.
WHAT ARE THEY TALKING ABOUT?
YES! R-RIGHT AWAY, MASTER NEYLIN.
MY MOTHER?

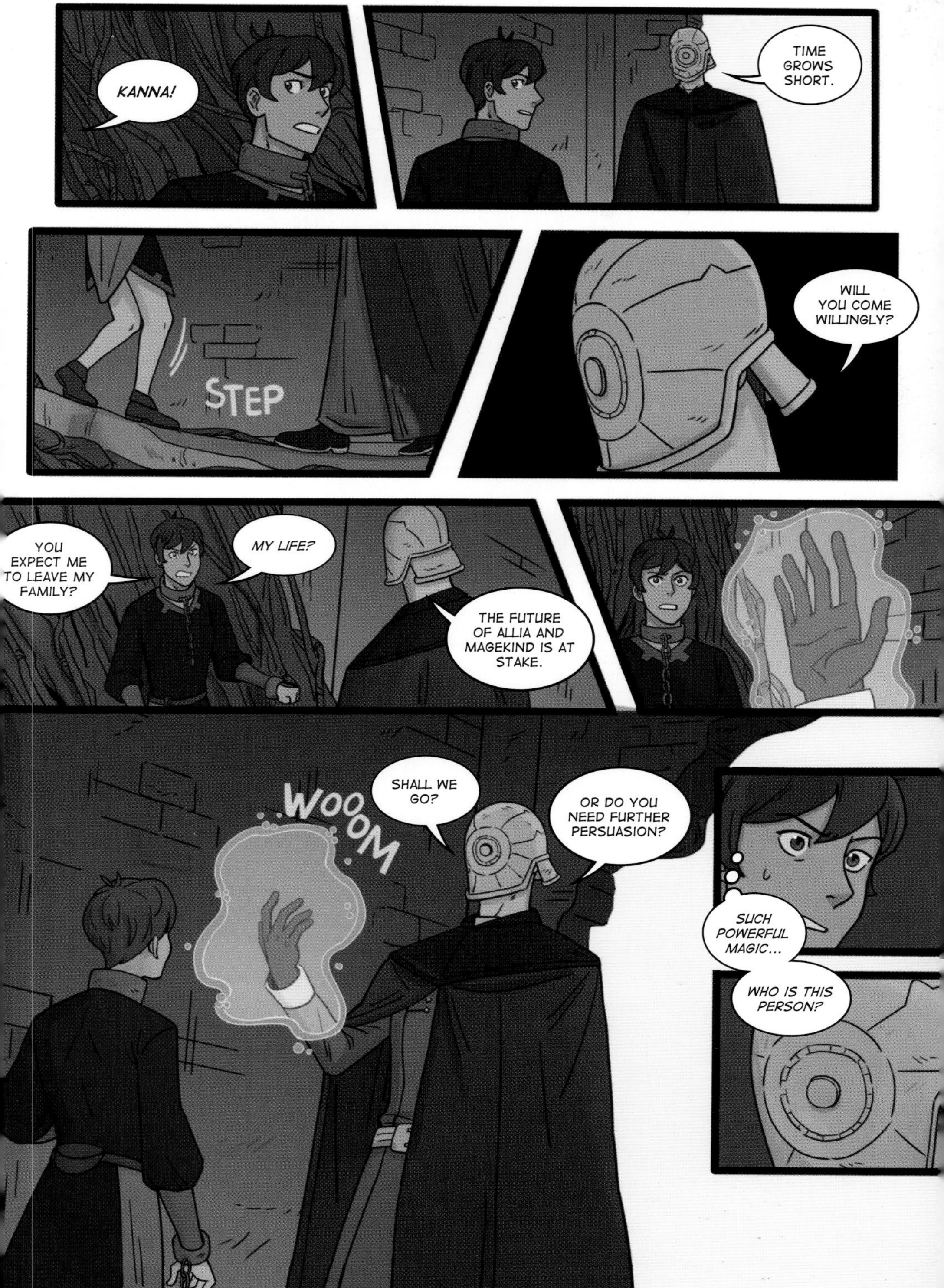
KANNA!
TIME GROWS SHORT.
STEP
WILL YOU COME WILLINGLY?
YOU EXPECT ME TO LEAVE MY FAMILY?
MY LIFE?
THE FUTURE OF ALLIA AND MAGEKIND IS AT STAKE.
WOOOM
SHALL WE GO?
OR DO YOU NEED FURTHER PERSUASION?
SUCH POWERFUL MAGIC...
WHO IS THIS PERSON?

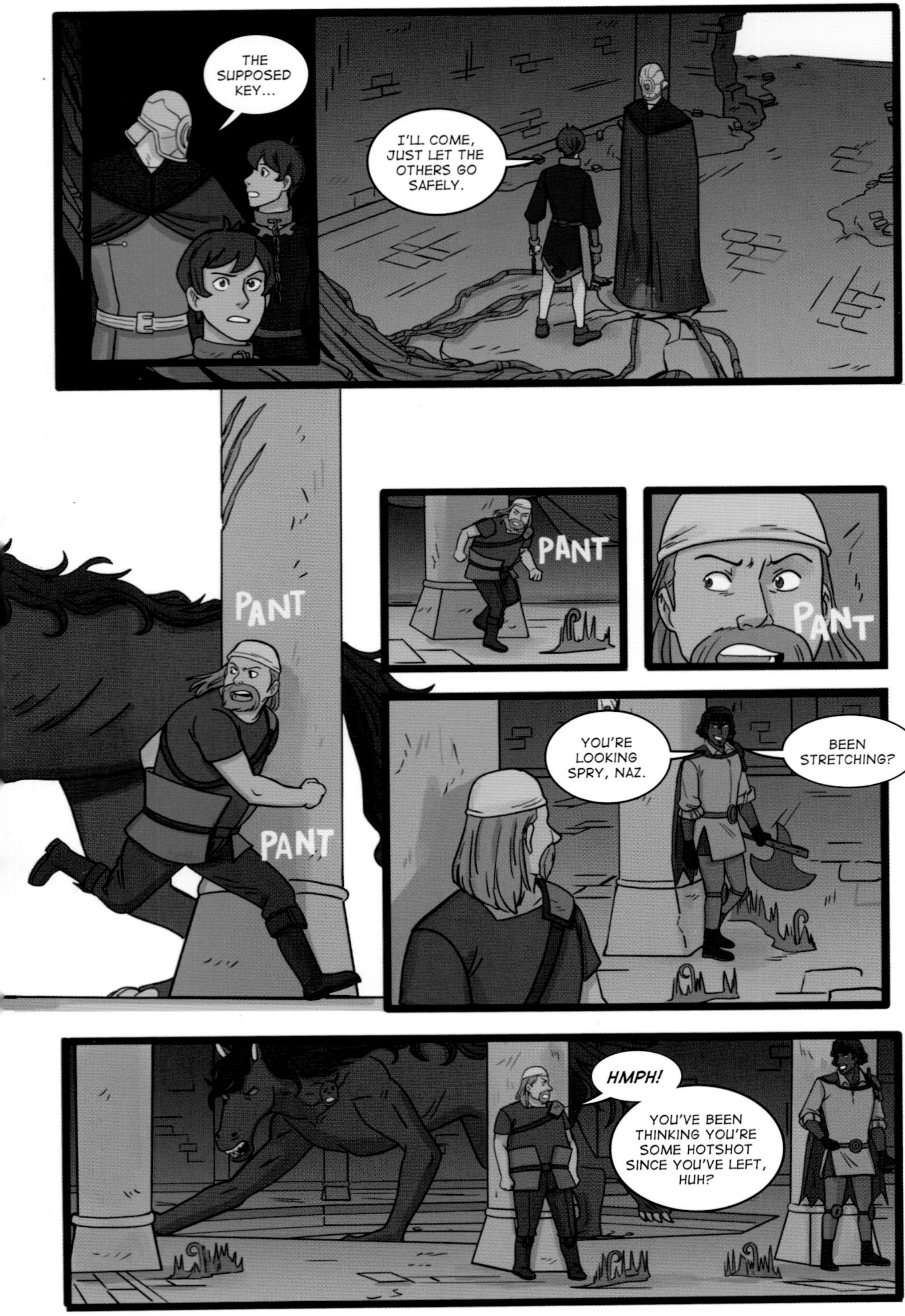
THE SUPPOSED KEY...
I'LL COME, JUST LET THE OTHERS GO SAFELY.
PANT
PANT
PANT
PANT
YOU'RE LOOKING SPRY, NAZ.
BEEN STRETCHING?
HMPH!
YOU'VE BEEN THINKING YOU'RE SOME HOTSHOT SINCE YOU'VE LEFT, HUH?

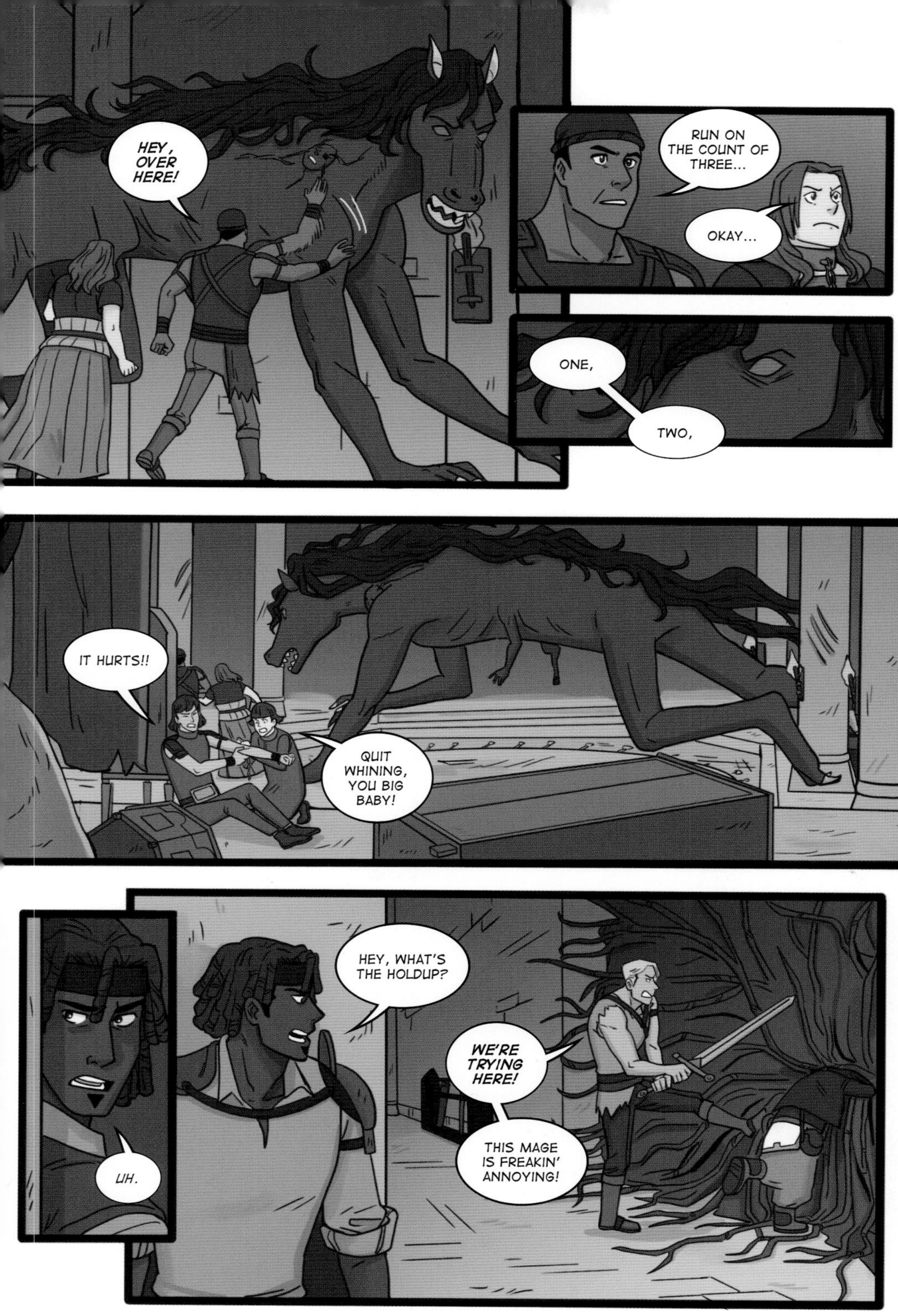
HEY, OVER HERE!
RUN ON THE COUNT OF THREE...
OKAY...
ONE,
TWO,
IT HURTS!!
QUIT WHINING, YOU BIG BABY!
HEY, WHAT'S THE HOLDUP?
WE'RE TRYING HERE!
THIS MAGE IS FREAKIN' ANNOYING!
UH.

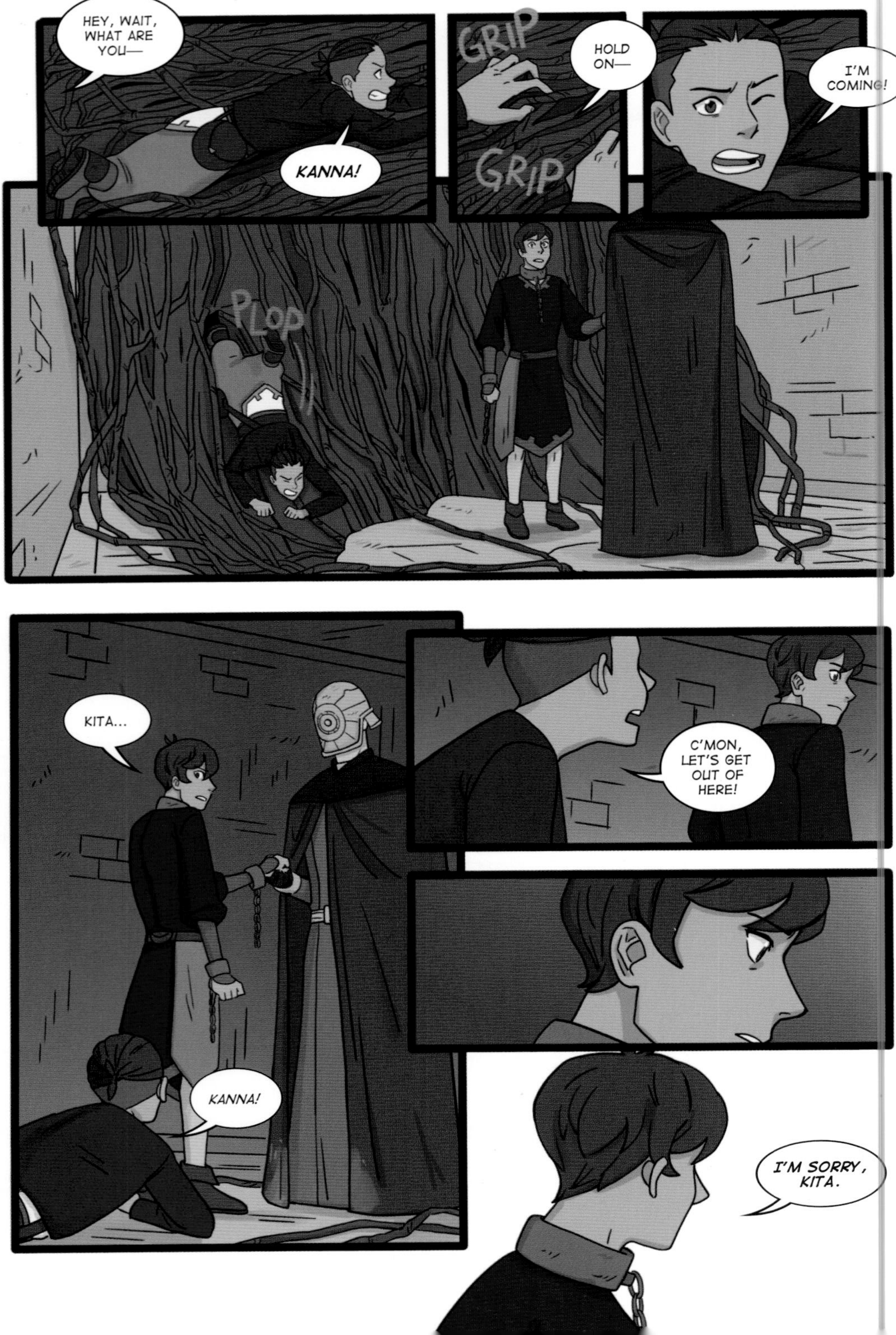
HEY, WAIT, WHAT ARE YOU—
KANNA!
GRIP
HOLD ON—
GRIP
I'M COMING!
PLOP
KITA...
C'MON, LET'S GET OUT OF HERE!
KANNA!
I'M SORRY, KITA.

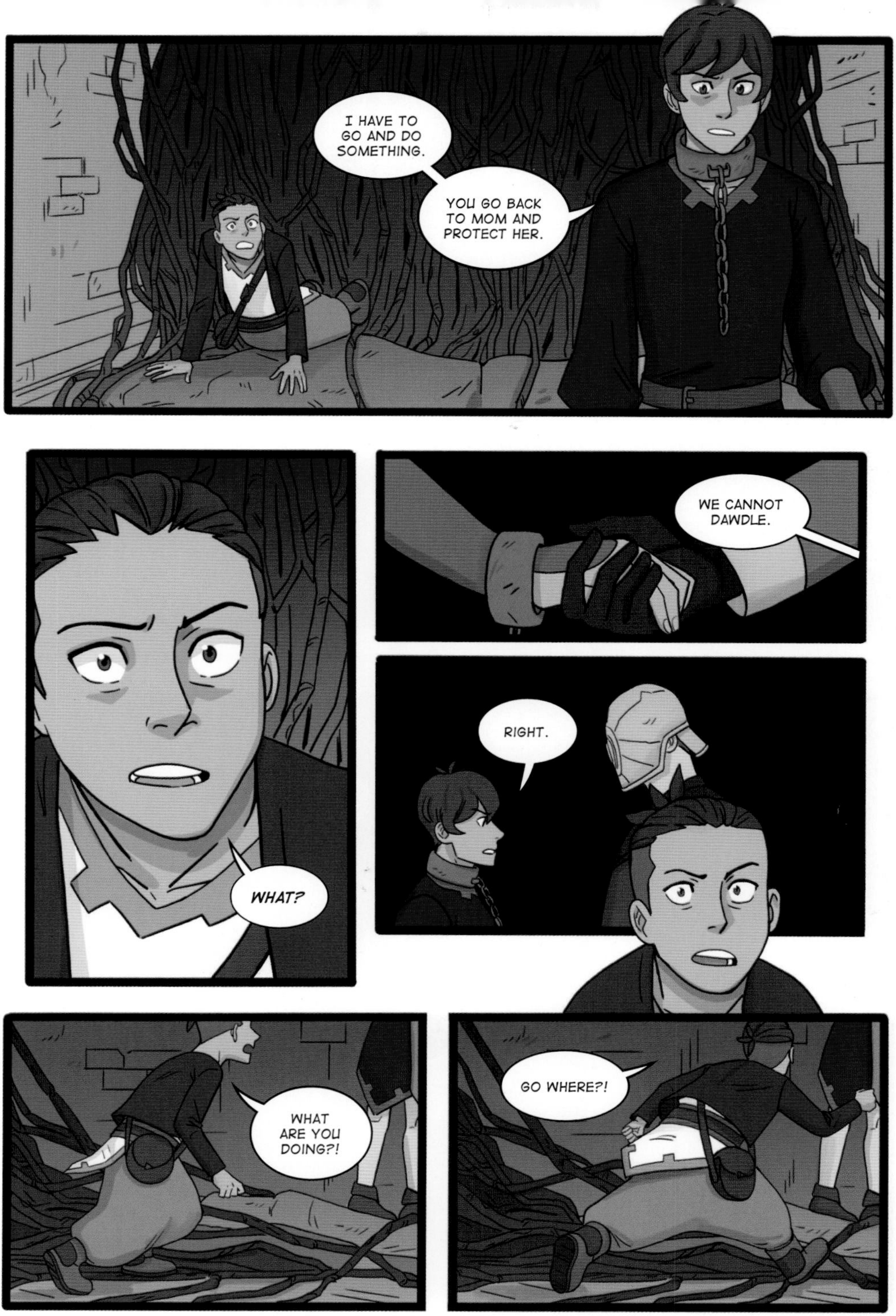
I HAVE TO GO AND DO SOMETHING.
YOU GO BACK TO MOM AND PROTECT HER.
WHAT?
WE CANNOT DAWDLE.
RIGHT.
WHAT ARE YOU DOING?!
GO WHERE?!

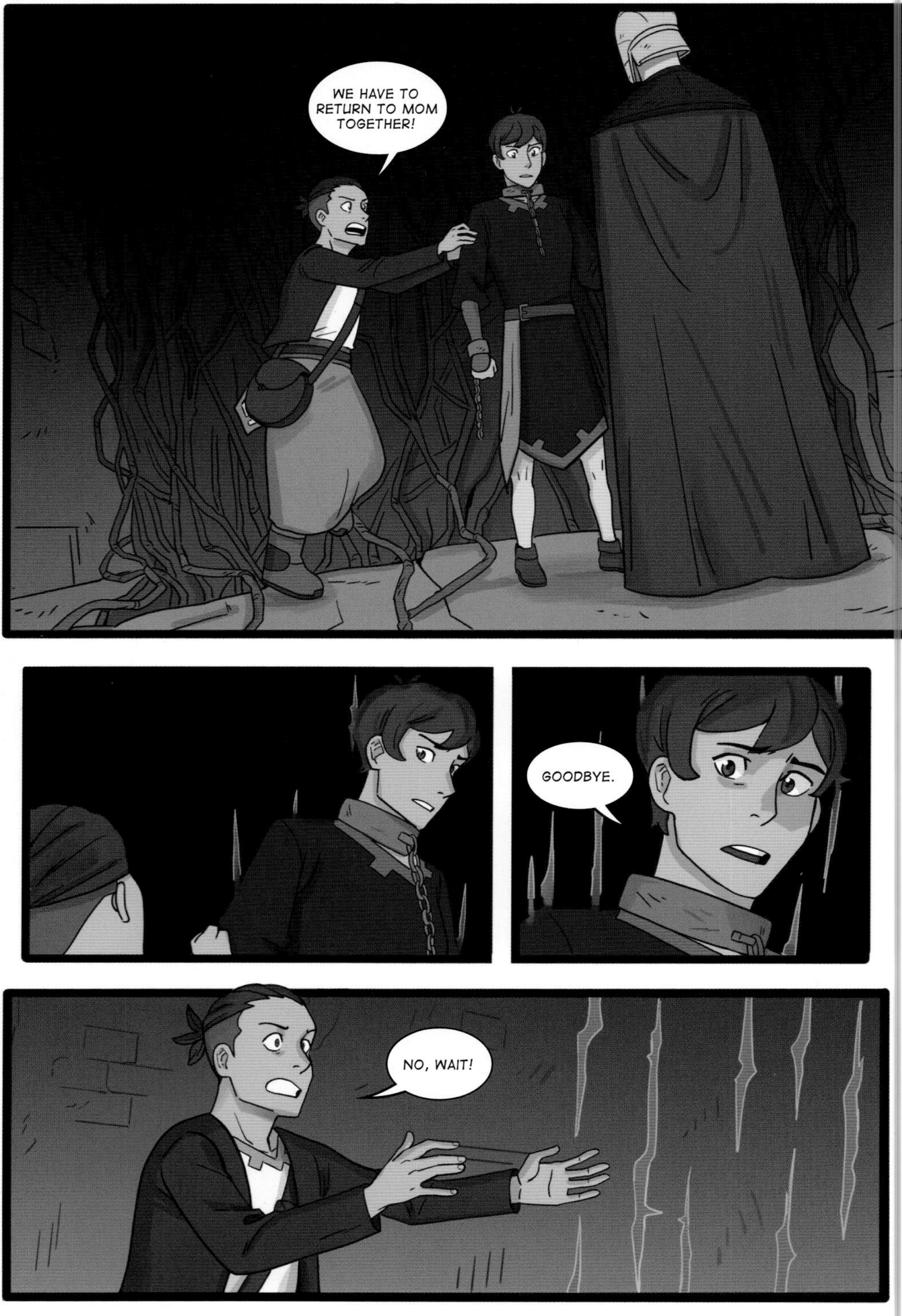
WE HAVE TO RETURN TO MOM TOGETHER!
GOODBYE.
NO, WAIT!

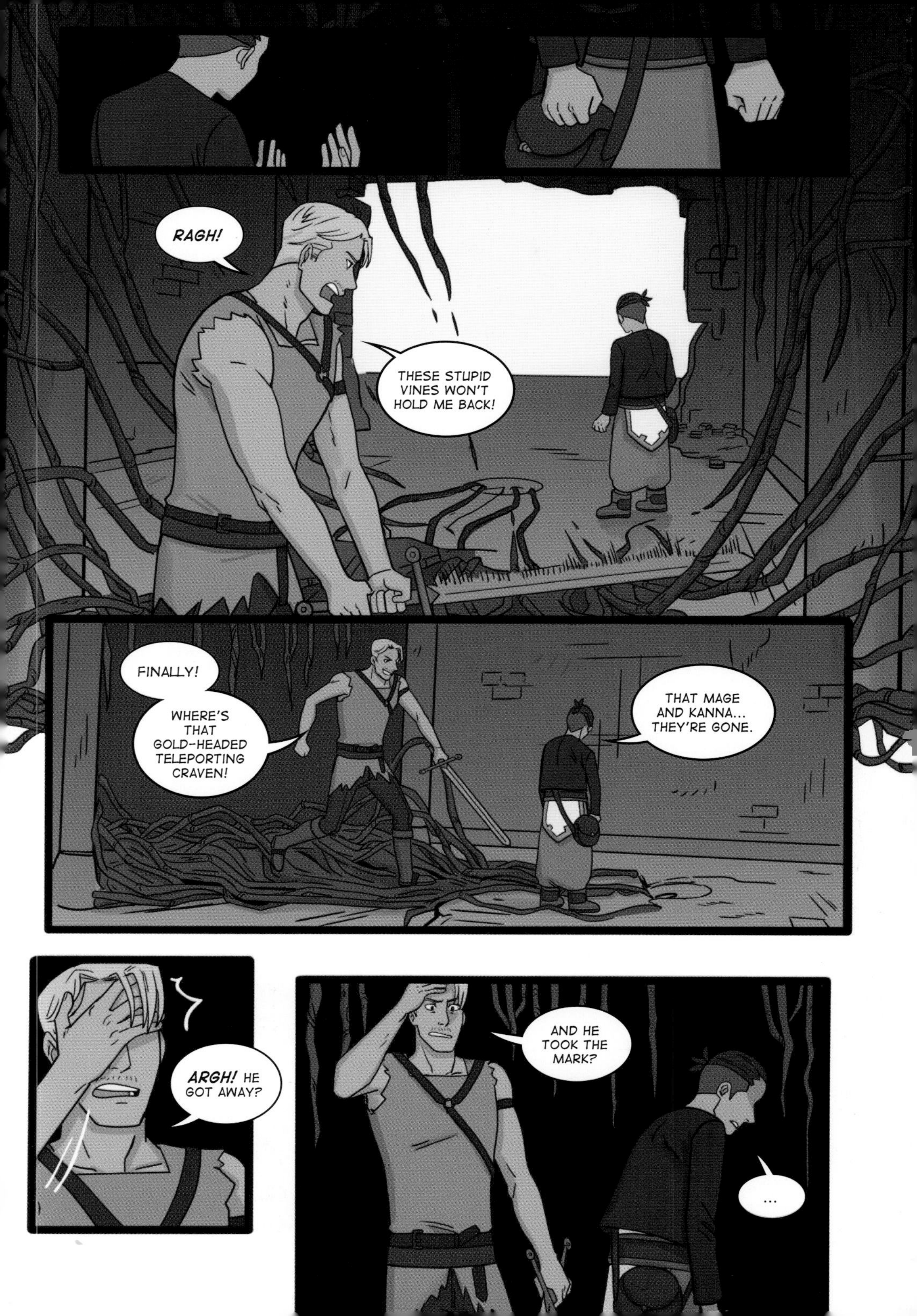
RAGH!
THESE STUPID VINES WON'T HOLD ME BACK!
FINALLY!
WHERE'S THAT GOLD-HEADED TELEPORTING CRAVEN!
THAT MAGE AND KANNA... THEY'RE GONE.
ARGH! HE GOT AWAY?
AND HE TOOK THE MARK?
...

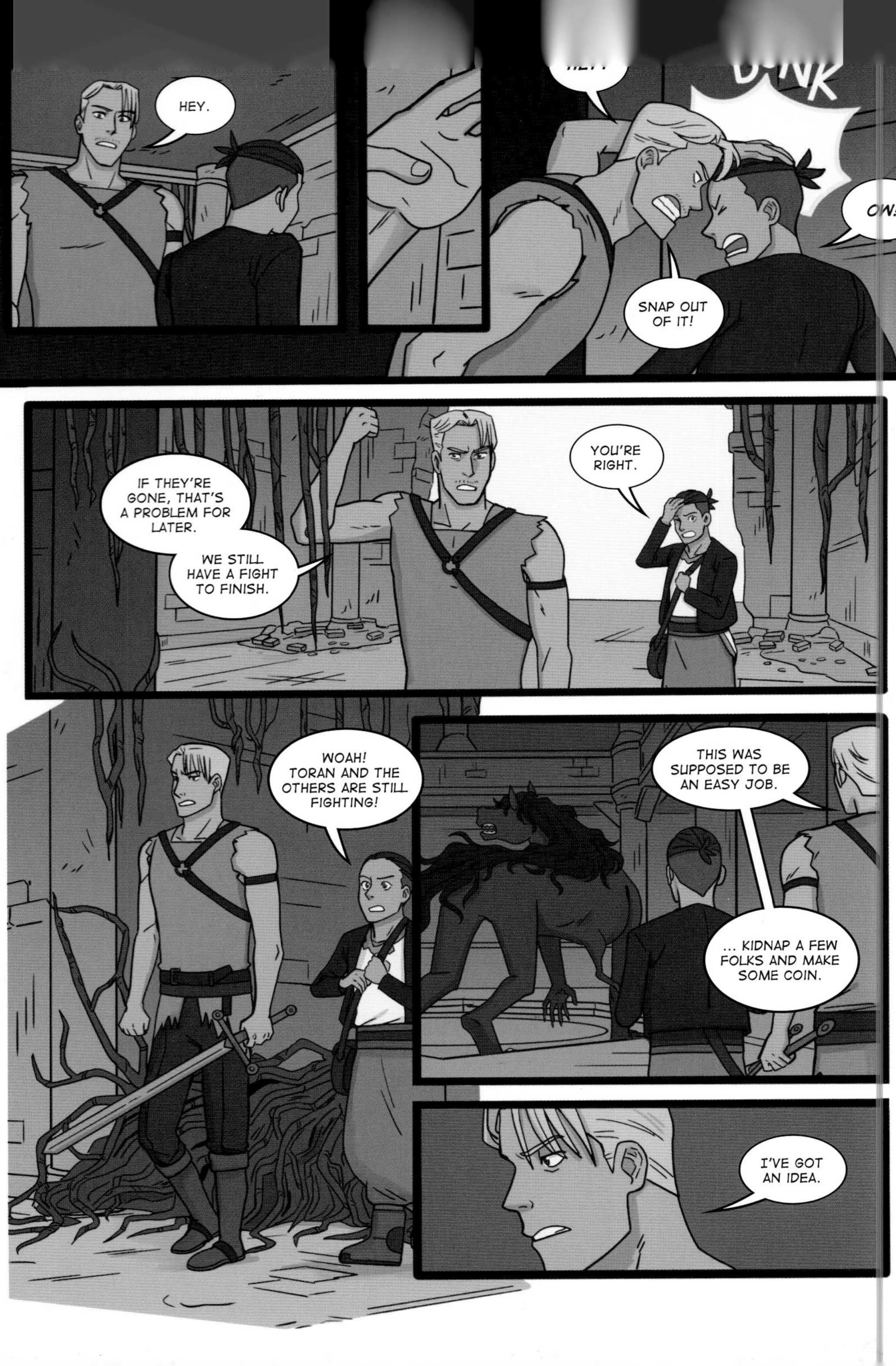
HEY.
OW!
SNAP OUT OF IT!
IF THEY'RE GONE, THAT'S A PROBLEM FOR LATER.
WE STILL HAVE A FIGHT TO FINISH.
YOU'RE RIGHT.
WOAH! TORAN AND THE OTHERS ARE STILL FIGHTING!
THIS WAS SUPPOSED TO BE AN EASY JOB.
... KIDNAP A FEW FOLKS AND MAKE SOME COIN.
I'VE GOT AN IDEA.

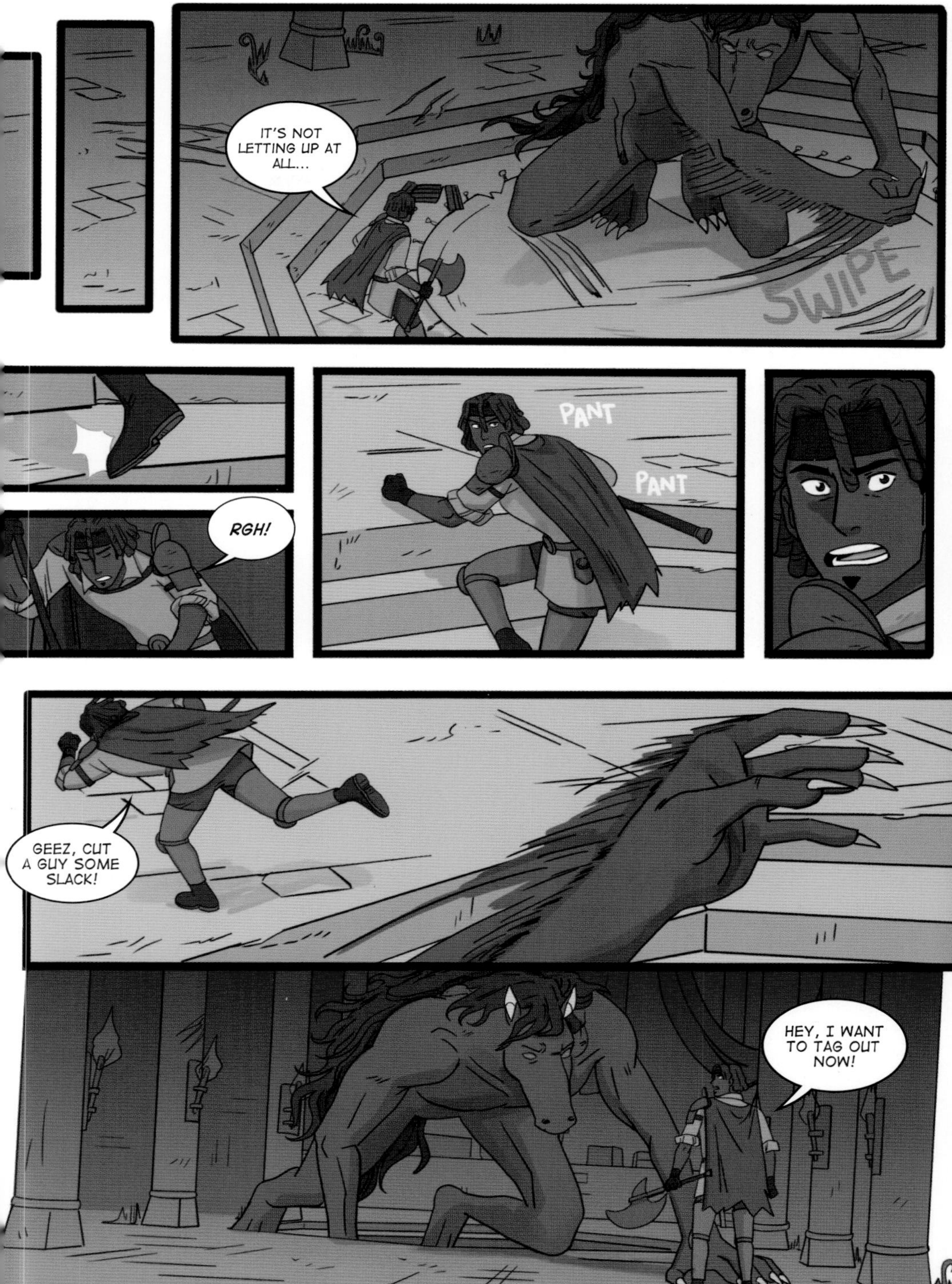
IT'S NOT LETTING UP AT ALL...
SWIPE
RGH!
PANT
PANT
GEEZ, CUT A GUY SOME SLACK!
HEY, I WANT TO TAG OUT NOW!

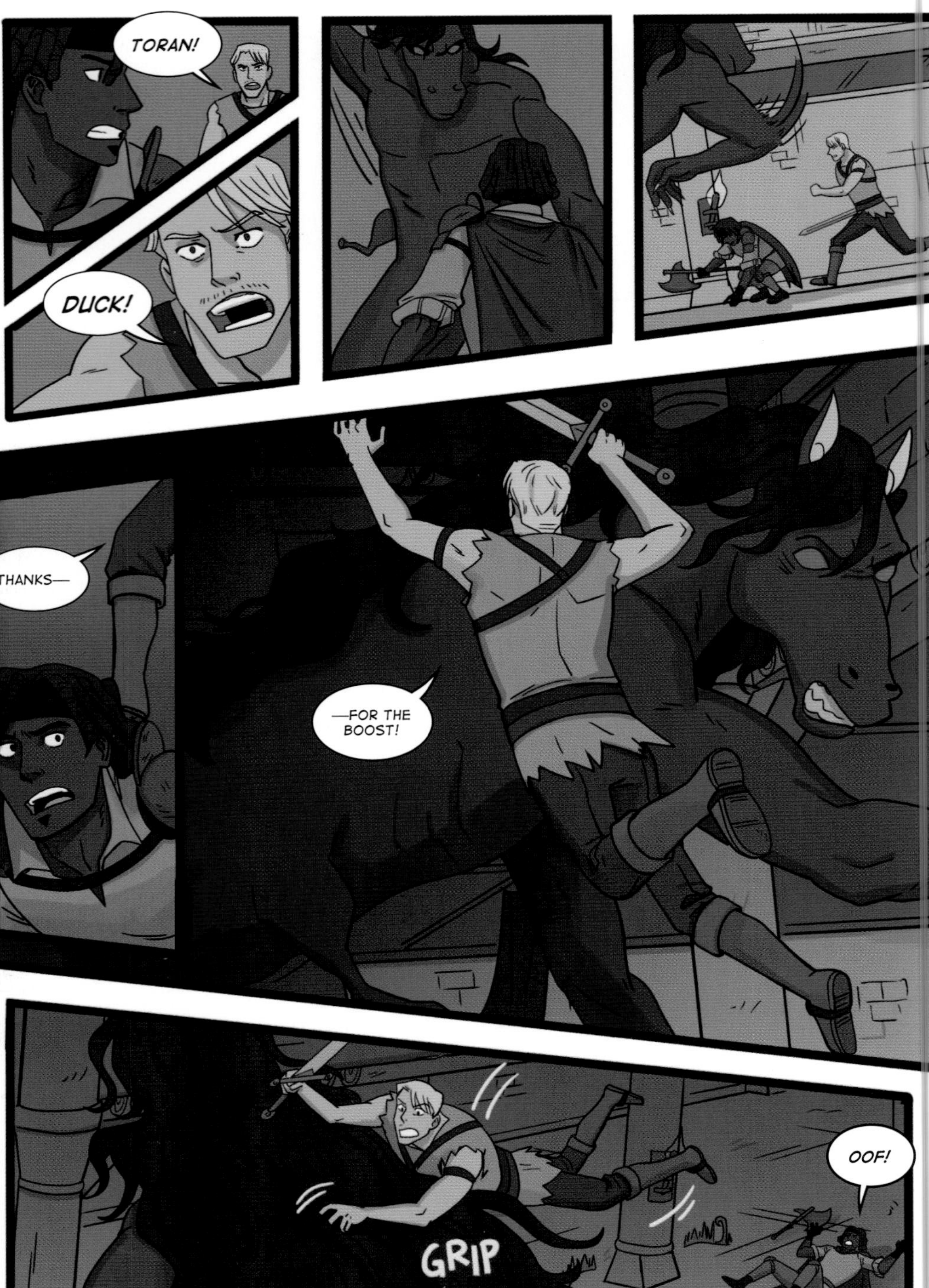
TORAN!
DUCK!
THANKS—
—FOR THE BOOST!
GRIP
OOF!

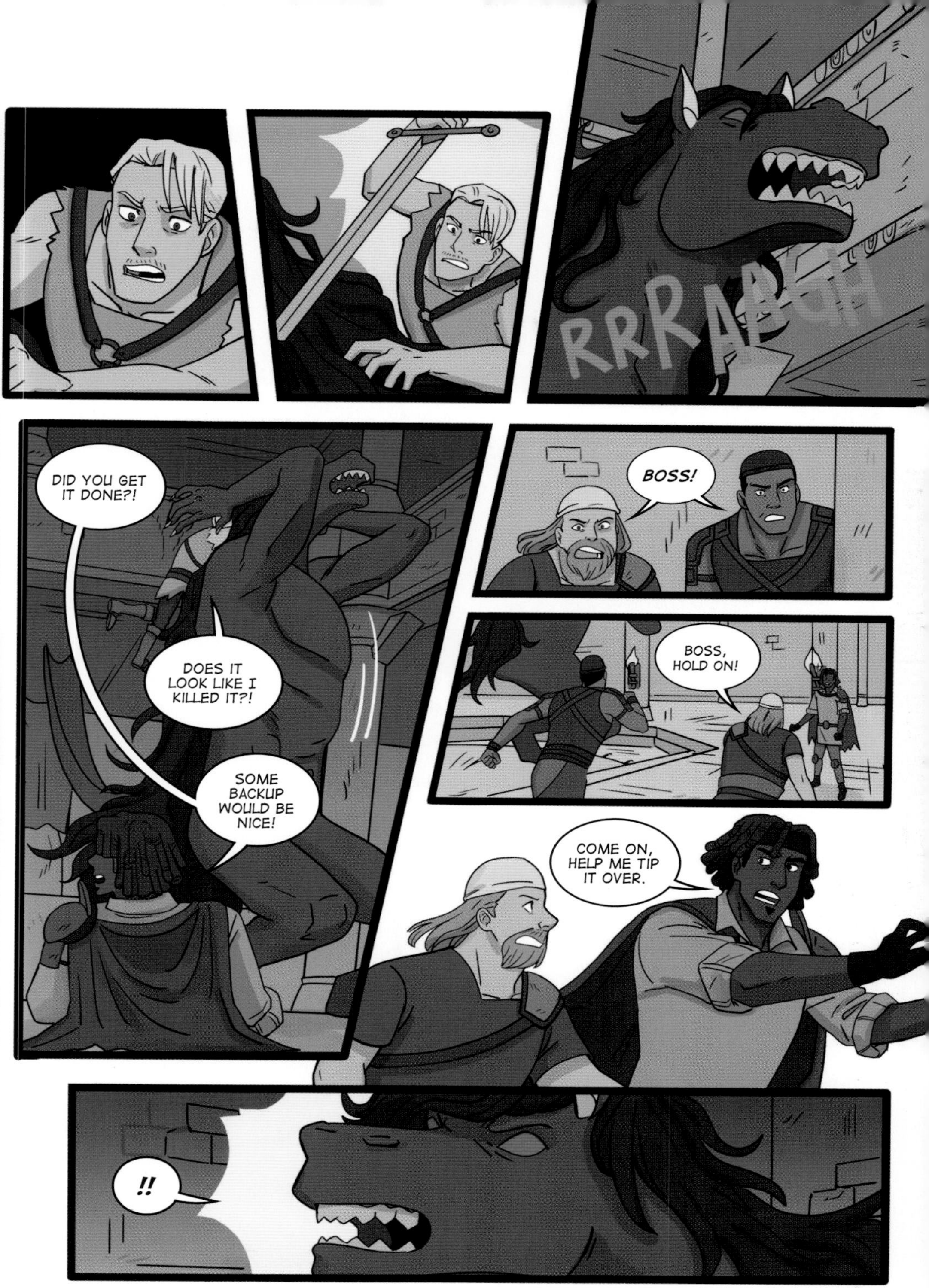
RRRAAGH
DID YOU GET IT DONE?!
DOES IT LOOK LIKE I KILLED IT?!
SOME BACKUP WOULD BE NICE!
BOSS!
BOSS, HOLD ON!
COME ON, HELP ME TIP IT OVER.
!!

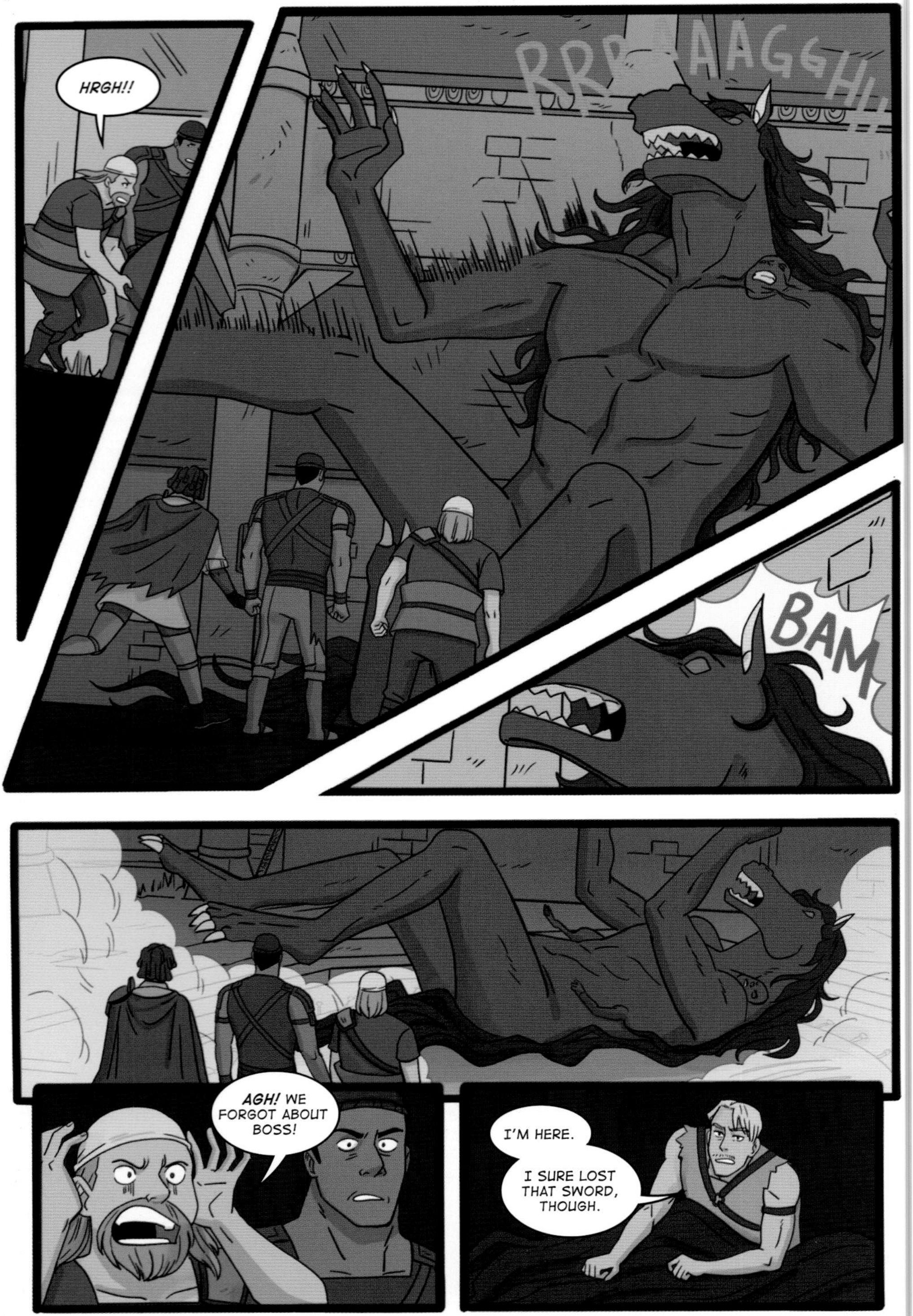
HRGH!!
RRRAAAGGH!!
BAM
AGH! WE FORGOT ABOUT BOSS!
I'M HERE.
I SURE LOST THAT SWORD, THOUGH.

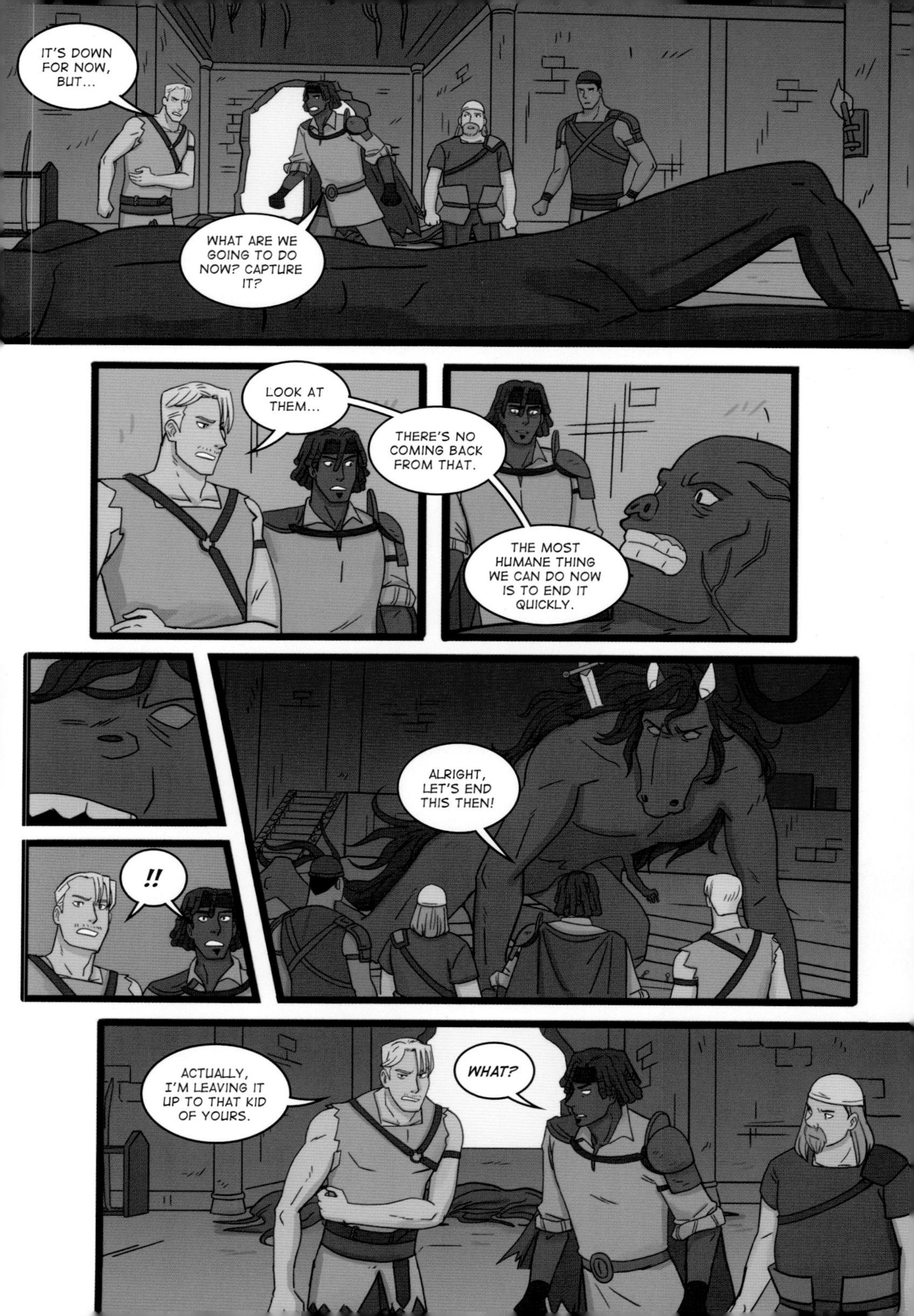
IT'S DOWN FOR NOW, BUT...
WHAT ARE WE GOING TO DO NOW? CAPTURE IT?
LOOK AT THEM...
THERE'S NO COMING BACK FROM THAT.
THE MOST HUMANE THING WE CAN DO NOW IS TO END IT QUICKLY.
!!
ALRIGHT, LET'S END THIS THEN!
ACTUALLY, I'M LEAVING IT UP TO THAT KID OF YOURS.
WHAT?

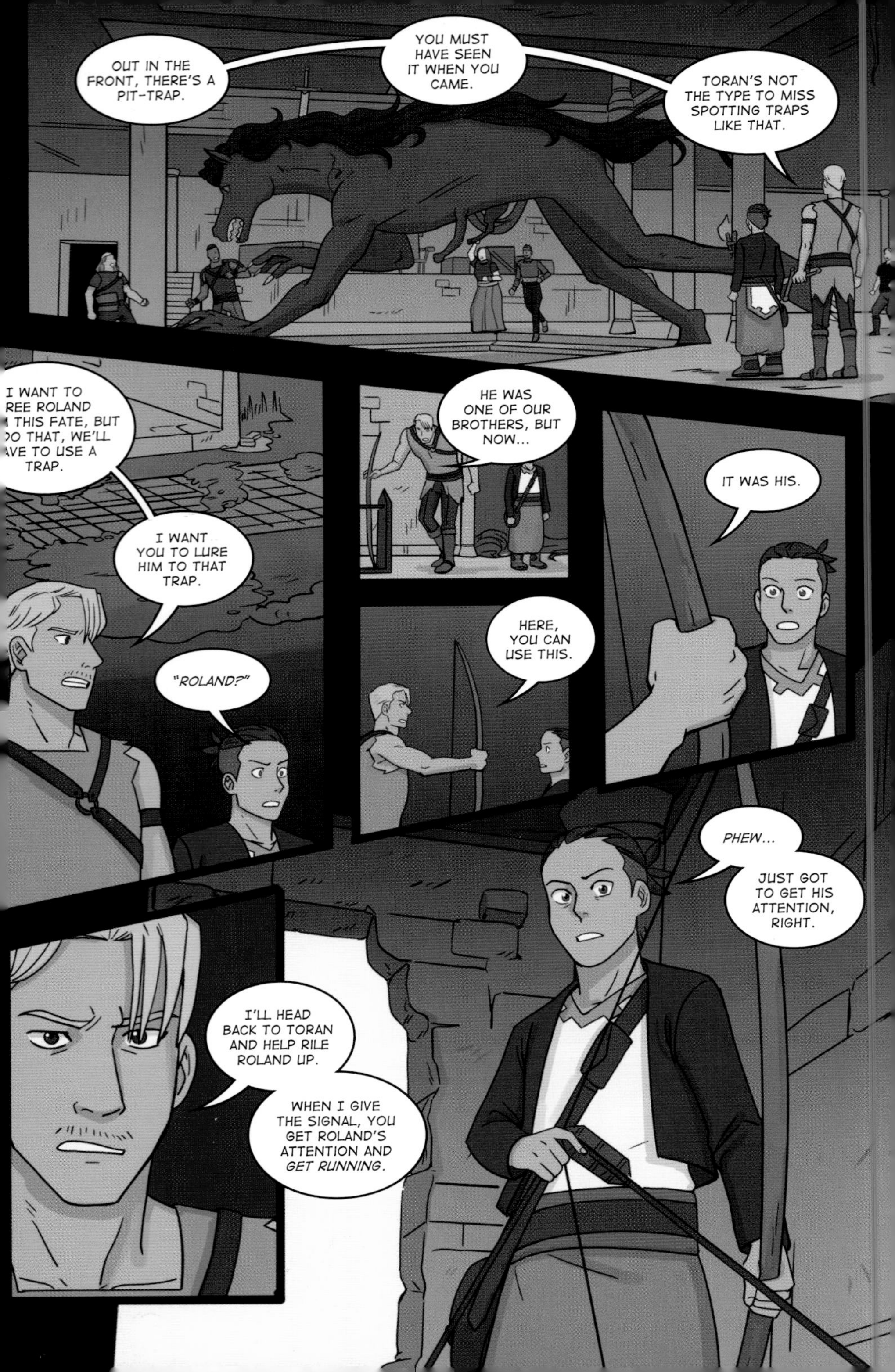
OUT IN THE FRONT, THERE'S A PIT-TRAP.
YOU MUST HAVE SEEN IT WHEN YOU CAME.
TORAN'S NOT THE TYPE TO MISS SPOTTING TRAPS LIKE THAT.
I WANT TO REE ROLAND M THIS FATE, BUT DO THAT, WE'LL AVE TO USE A TRAP.
I WANT YOU TO LURE HIM TO THAT TRAP.
"ROLAND?"
HE WAS ONE OF OUR BROTHERS, BUT NOW...
HERE, YOU CAN USE THIS.
IT WAS HIS.
I'LL HEAD BACK TO TORAN AND HELP RILE ROLAND UP.
WHEN I GIVE THE SIGNAL, YOU GET ROLAND'S ATTENTION AND GET RUNNING.
PHEW...
JUST GOT TO GET HIS ATTENTION, RIGHT.

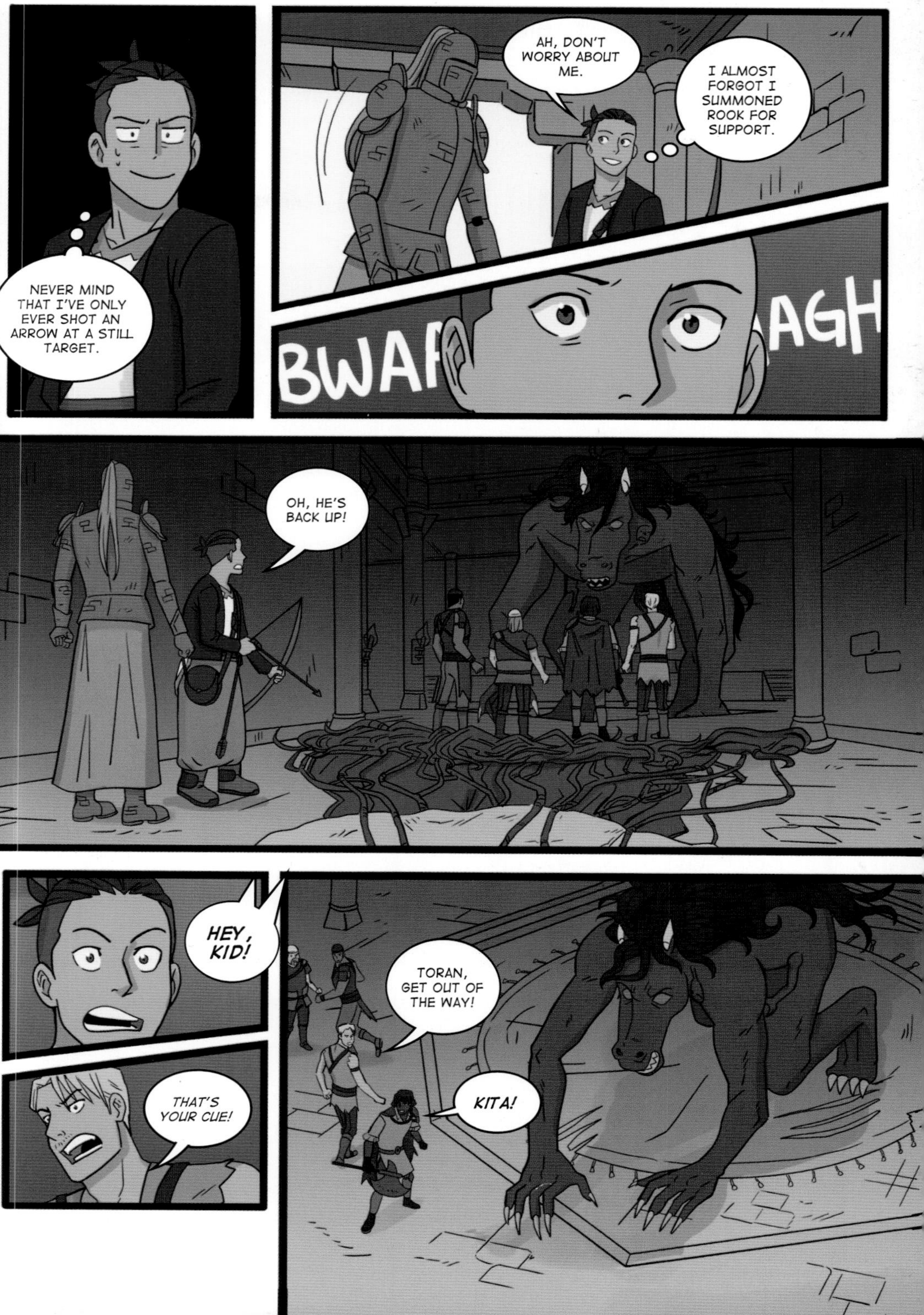

NEVER MIND THAT I'VE ONLY EVER SHOT AN ARROW AT A STILL TARGET.
AH, DON'T WORRY ABOUT ME.
I ALMOST FORGOT I SUMMONED ROOK FOR SUPPORT.
BWAAAGH
OH, HE'S BACK UP!
HEY, KID!
THAT'S YOUR CUE!
TORAN, GET OUT OF THE WAY!
KITA!

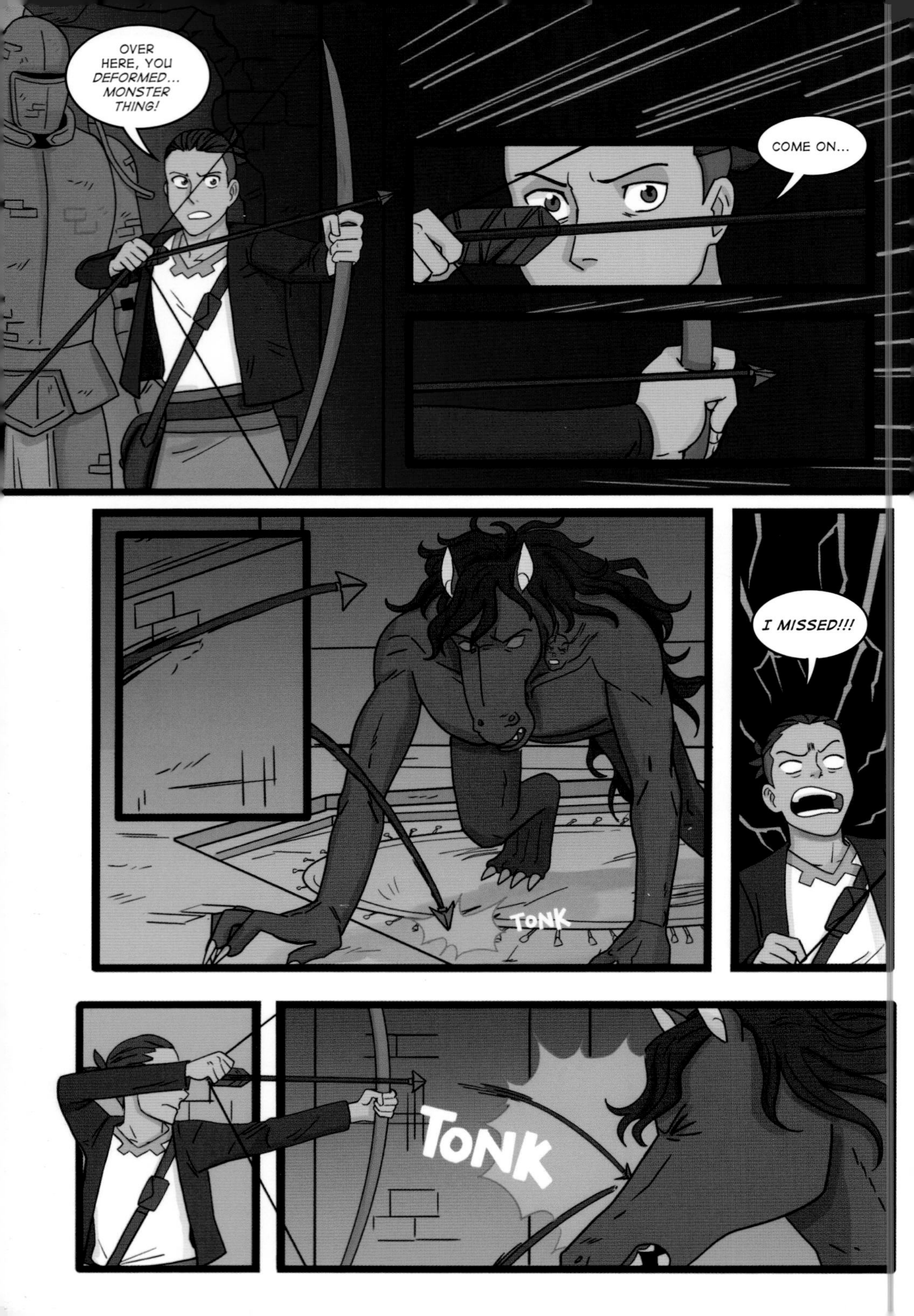
OVER HERE, YOU *DEFORMED*... *MONSTER THING!*
COME ON...
I MISSED!!!
TONK
TONK

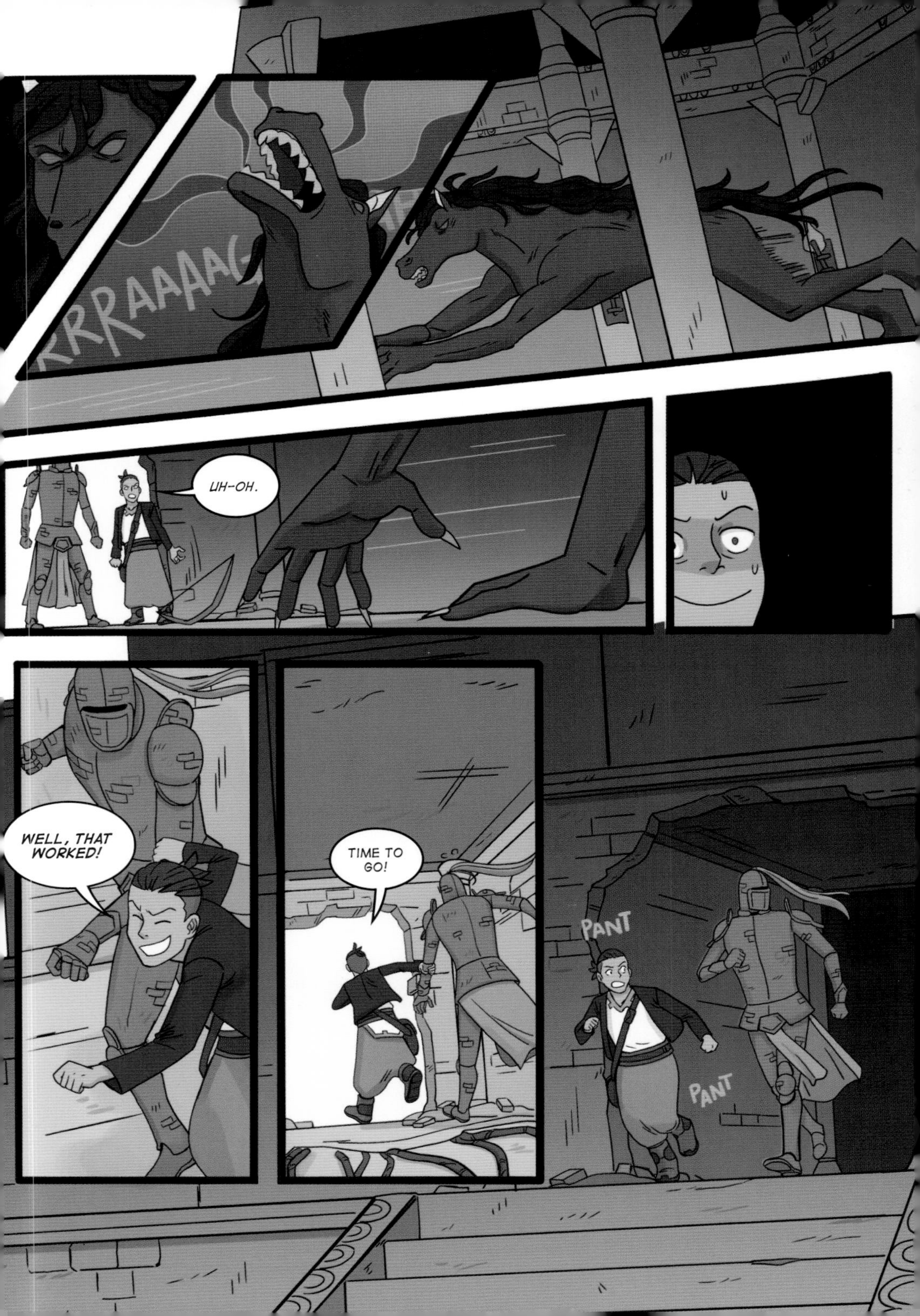
RRRAAAAG
UH-OH.
WELL, THAT WORKED!
TIME TO GO!
PANT
PANT

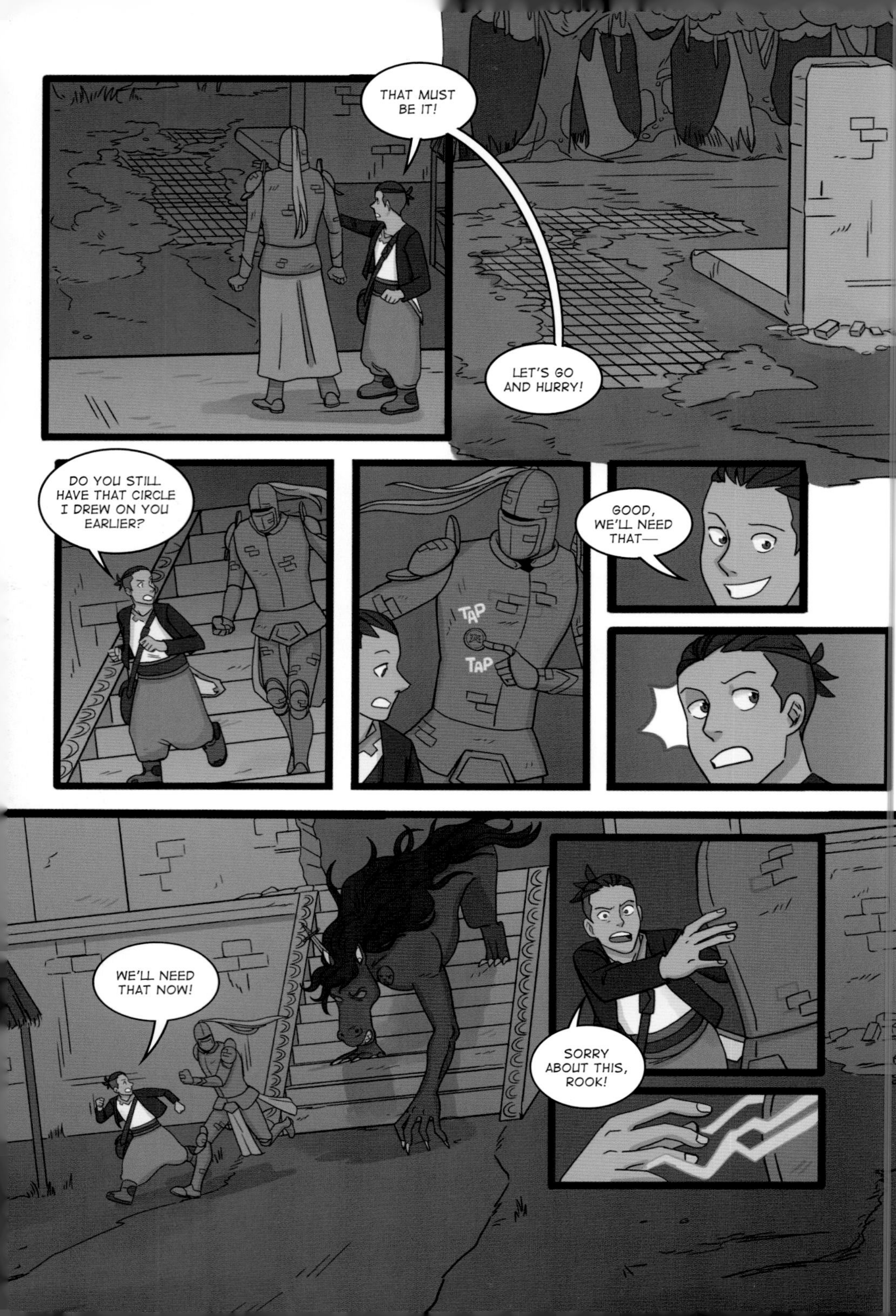
THAT MUST BE IT!
LET'S GO AND HURRY!
DO YOU STILL HAVE THAT CIRCLE I DREW ON YOU EARLIER?
TAP
TAP
GOOD, WE'LL NEED THAT—
WE'LL NEED THAT NOW!
SORRY ABOUT THIS, ROOK!

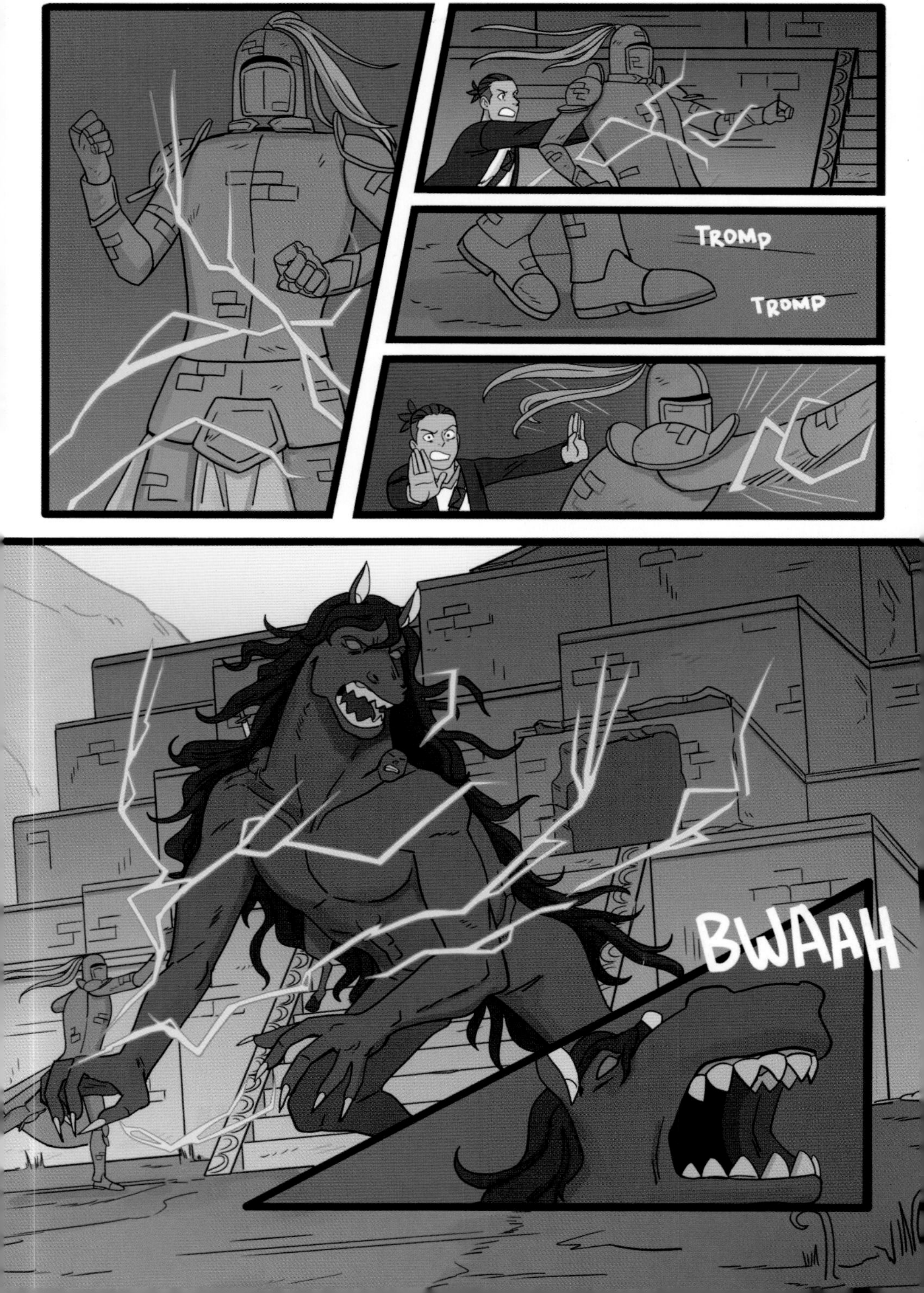
TROMP
TROMP
BWAAH

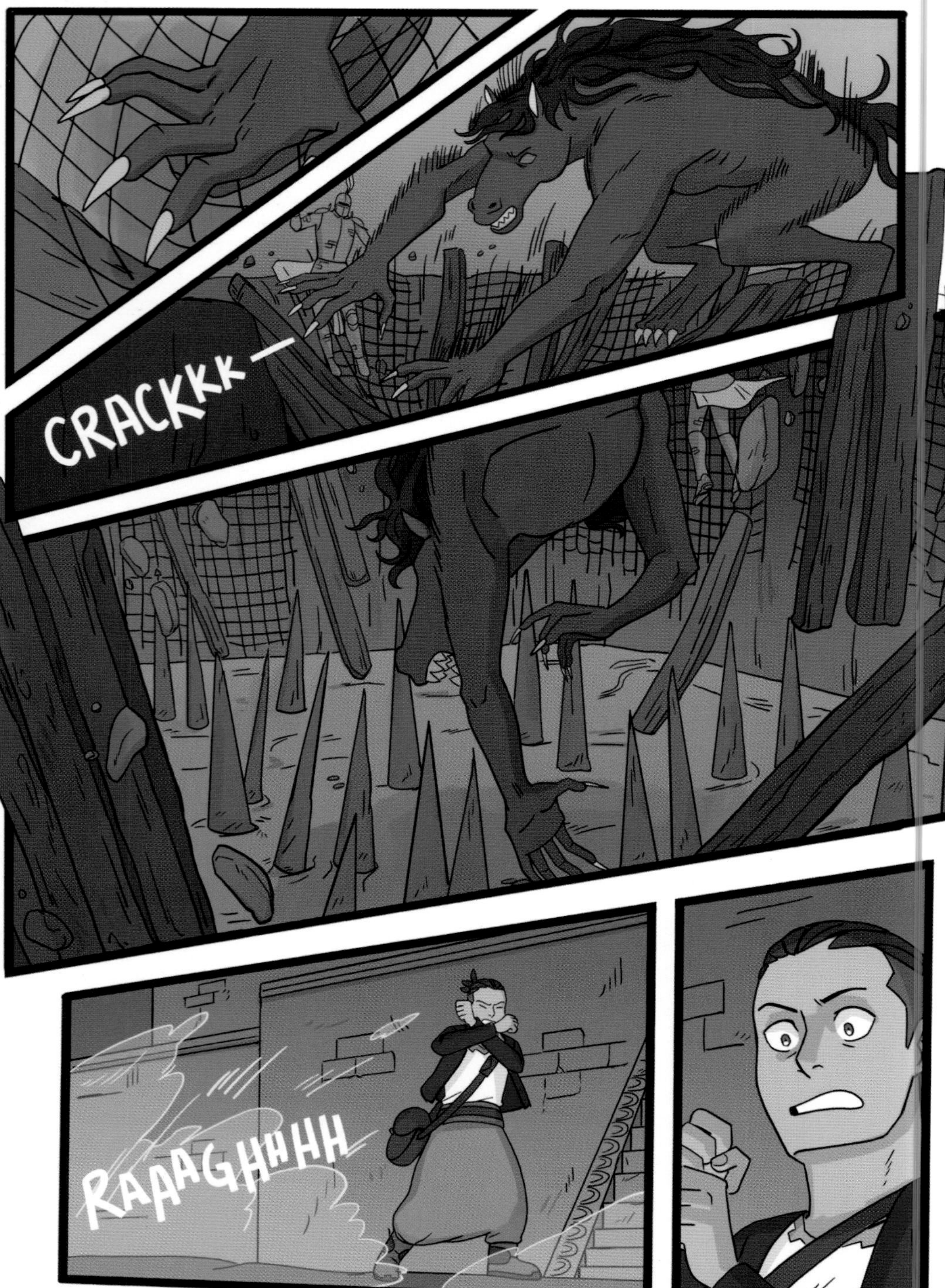
CRACKKK—
RAAAGHHHH

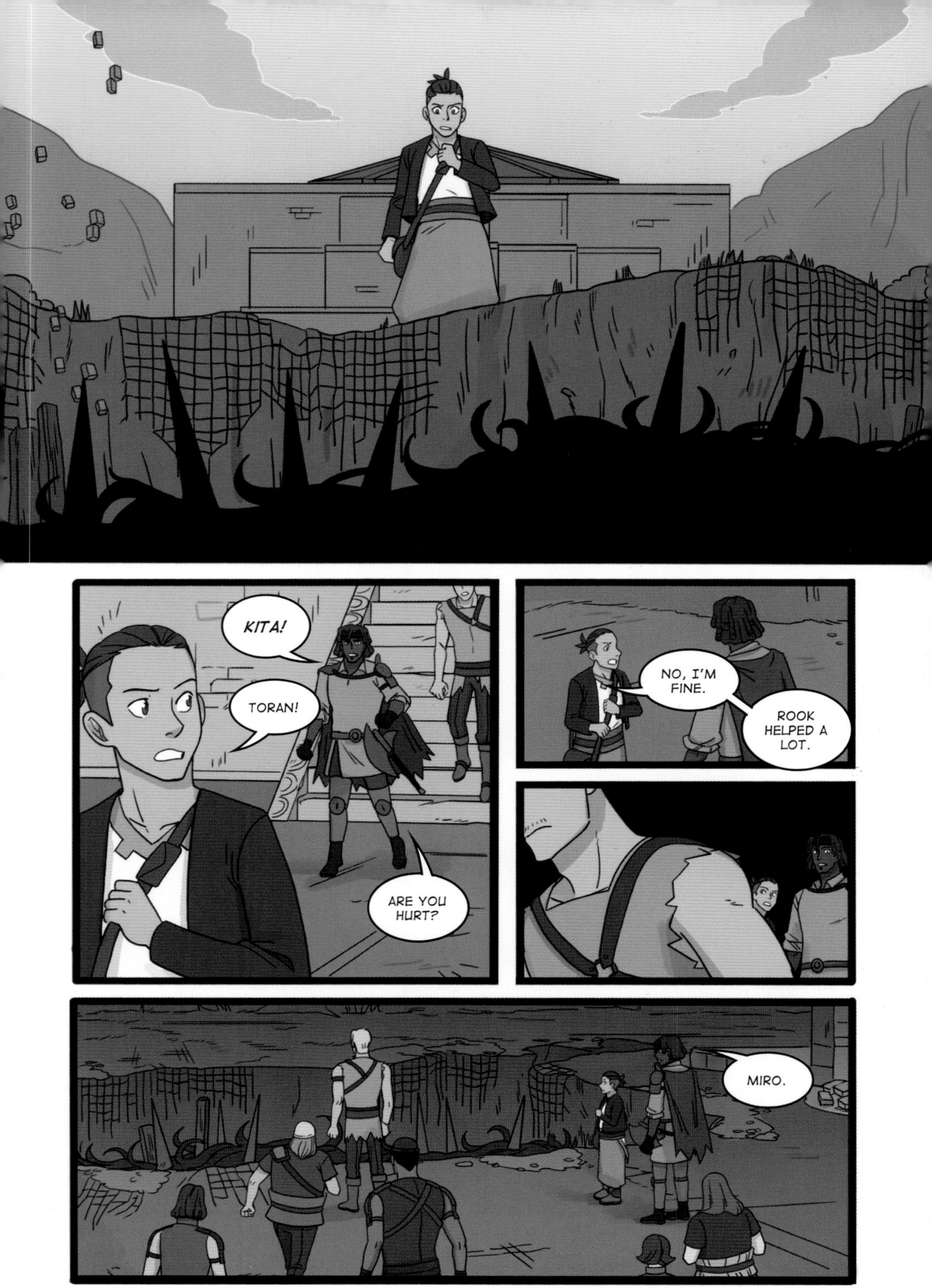
KITA!
TORAN!
ARE YOU HURT?
NO, I'M FINE.
ROOK HELPED A LOT.
MIRO.

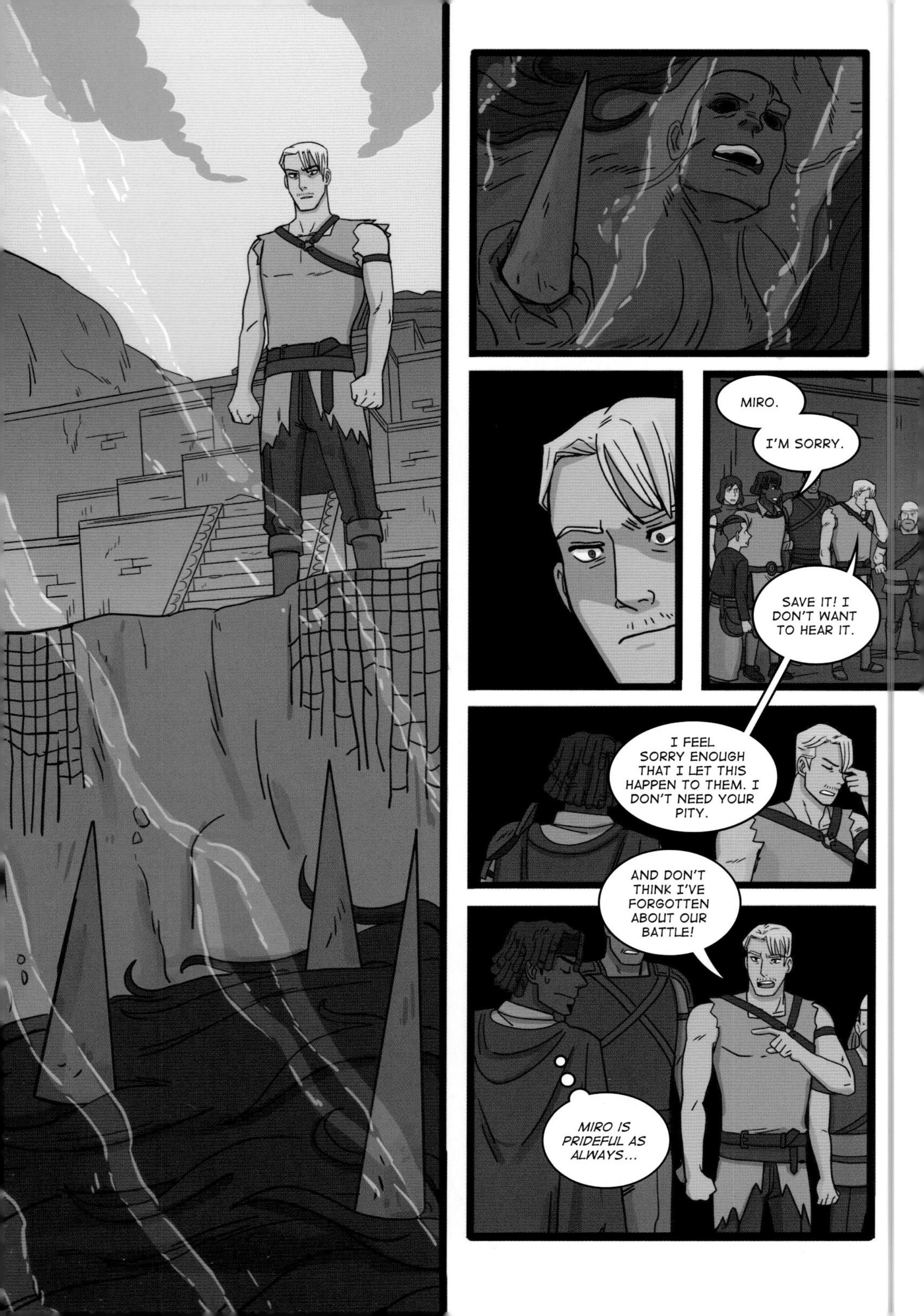
MIRO.
I'M SORRY.
SAVE IT! I DON'T WANT TO HEAR IT.
I FEEL SORRY ENOUGH THAT I LET THIS HAPPEN TO THEM. I DON'T NEED YOUR PITY.
AND DON'T THINK I'VE FORGOTTEN ABOUT OUR BATTLE!
MIRO IS PRIDEFUL AS ALWAYS...

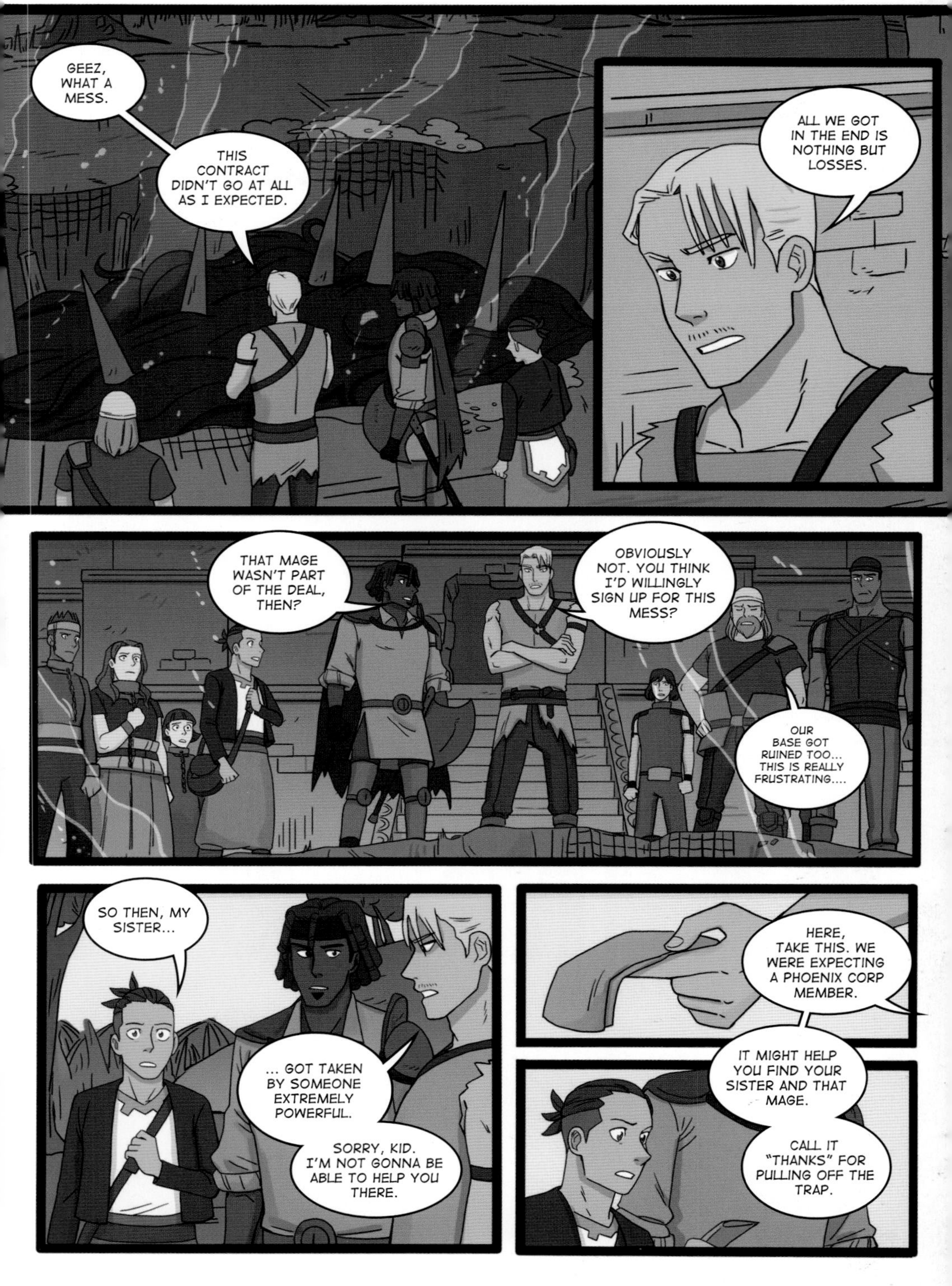
GEEZ, WHAT A MESS.
THIS CONTRACT DIDN'T GO AT ALL AS I EXPECTED.
ALL WE GOT IN THE END IS NOTHING BUT LOSSES.
THAT MAGE WASN'T PART OF THE DEAL, THEN?
OBVIOUSLY NOT. YOU THINK I'D WILLINGLY SIGN UP FOR THIS MESS?
OUR BASE GOT RUINED TOO... THIS IS REALLY FRUSTRATING....
SO THEN, MY SISTER...
... GOT TAKEN BY SOMEONE EXTREMELY POWERFUL.
SORRY, KID. I'M NOT GONNA BE ABLE TO HELP YOU THERE.
HERE, TAKE THIS. WE WERE EXPECTING A PHOENIX CORP MEMBER.
IT MIGHT HELP YOU FIND YOUR SISTER AND THAT MAGE.
CALL IT "THANKS" FOR PULLING OFF THE TRAP.

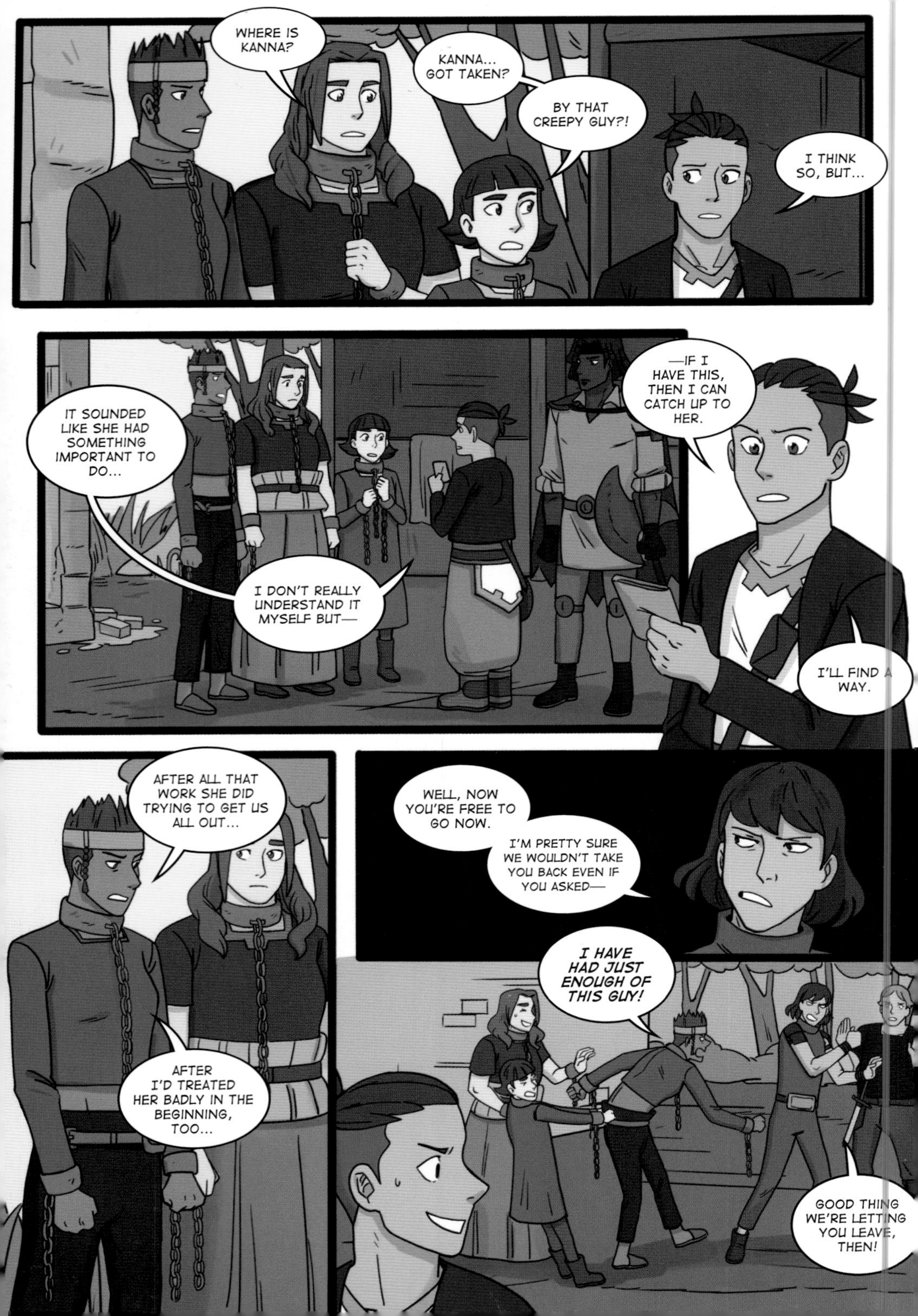
WHERE IS KANNA?
KANNA... GOT TAKEN?
BY THAT CREEPY GUY?!
I THINK SO, BUT...
IT SOUNDED LIKE SHE HAD SOMETHING IMPORTANT TO DO...
I DON'T REALLY UNDERSTAND IT MYSELF BUT—
—IF I HAVE THIS, THEN I CAN CATCH UP TO HER.
I'LL FIND A WAY.
AFTER ALL THAT WORK SHE DID TRYING TO GET US ALL OUT...
AFTER I'D TREATED HER BADLY IN THE BEGINNING, TOO...
WELL, NOW YOU'RE FREE TO GO NOW.
I'M PRETTY SURE WE WOULDN'T TAKE YOU BACK EVEN IF YOU ASKED—
I HAVE HAD JUST ENOUGH OF THIS GUY!
GOOD THING WE'RE LETTING YOU LEAVE, THEN!

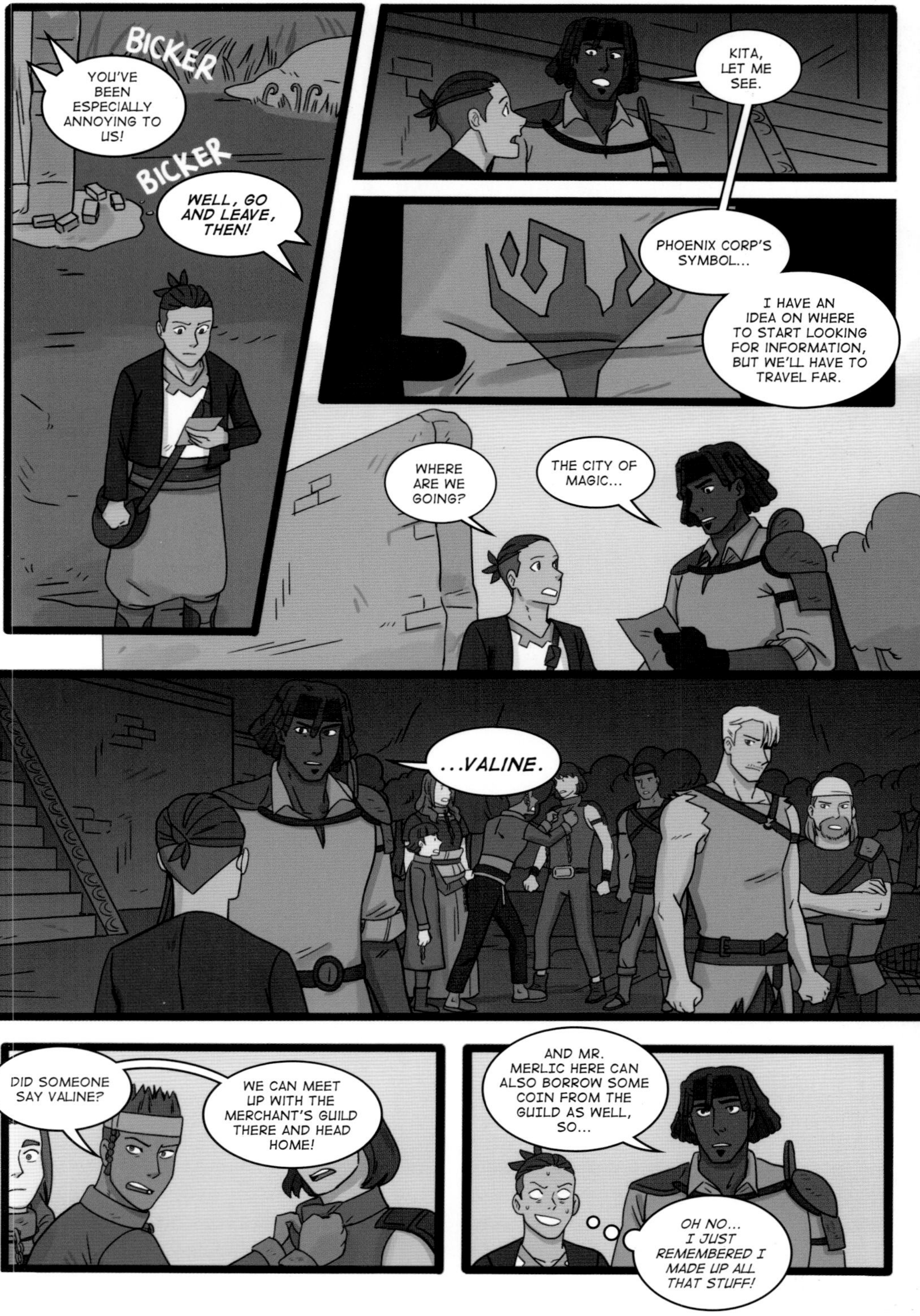
BICKER
YOU'VE BEEN ESPECIALLY ANNOYING TO US!
BICKER
WELL, GO AND LEAVE, THEN!
KITA, LET ME SEE.
PHOENIX CORP'S SYMBOL...
I HAVE AN IDEA ON WHERE TO START LOOKING FOR INFORMATION, BUT WE'LL HAVE TO TRAVEL FAR.
WHERE ARE WE GOING?
THE CITY OF MAGIC...
...VALINE.
DID SOMEONE SAY VALINE?
WE CAN MEET UP WITH THE MERCHANT'S GUILD THERE AND HEAD HOME!
AND MR. MERLIC HERE CAN ALSO BORROW SOME COIN FROM THE GUILD AS WELL, SO...
OH NO... I JUST REMEMBERED I MADE UP ALL THAT STUFF!

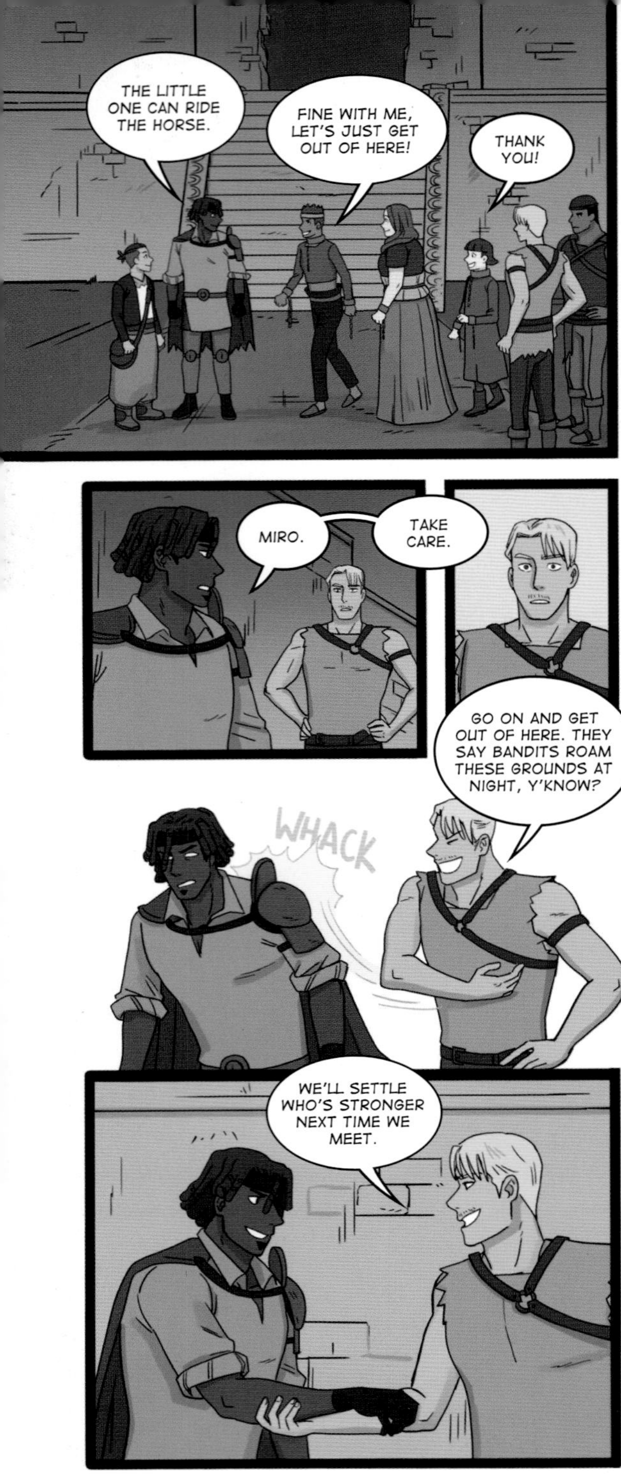
THE LITTLE ONE CAN RIDE THE HORSE.
FINE WITH ME, LET'S JUST GET OUT OF HERE!
THANK YOU!
MIRO.
TAKE CARE.
GO ON AND GET OUT OF HERE. THEY SAY BANDITS ROAM THESE GROUNDS AT NIGHT, Y'KNOW?
WHACK
WE'LL SETTLE WHO'S STRONGER NEXT TIME WE MEET.

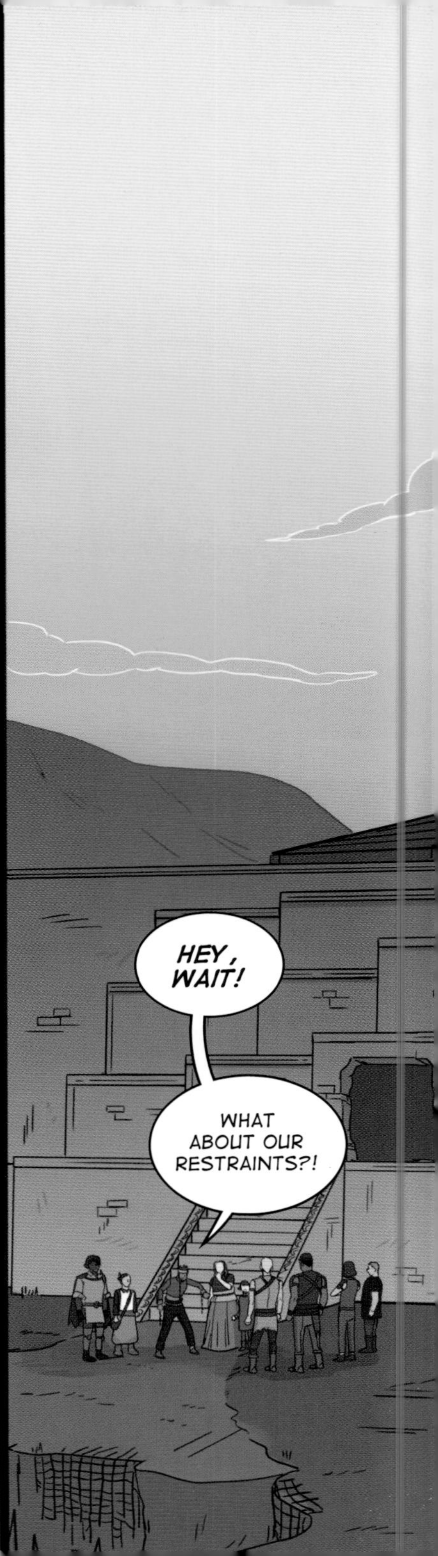
HEY, WAIT!
WHAT ABOUT OUR RESTRAINTS?!

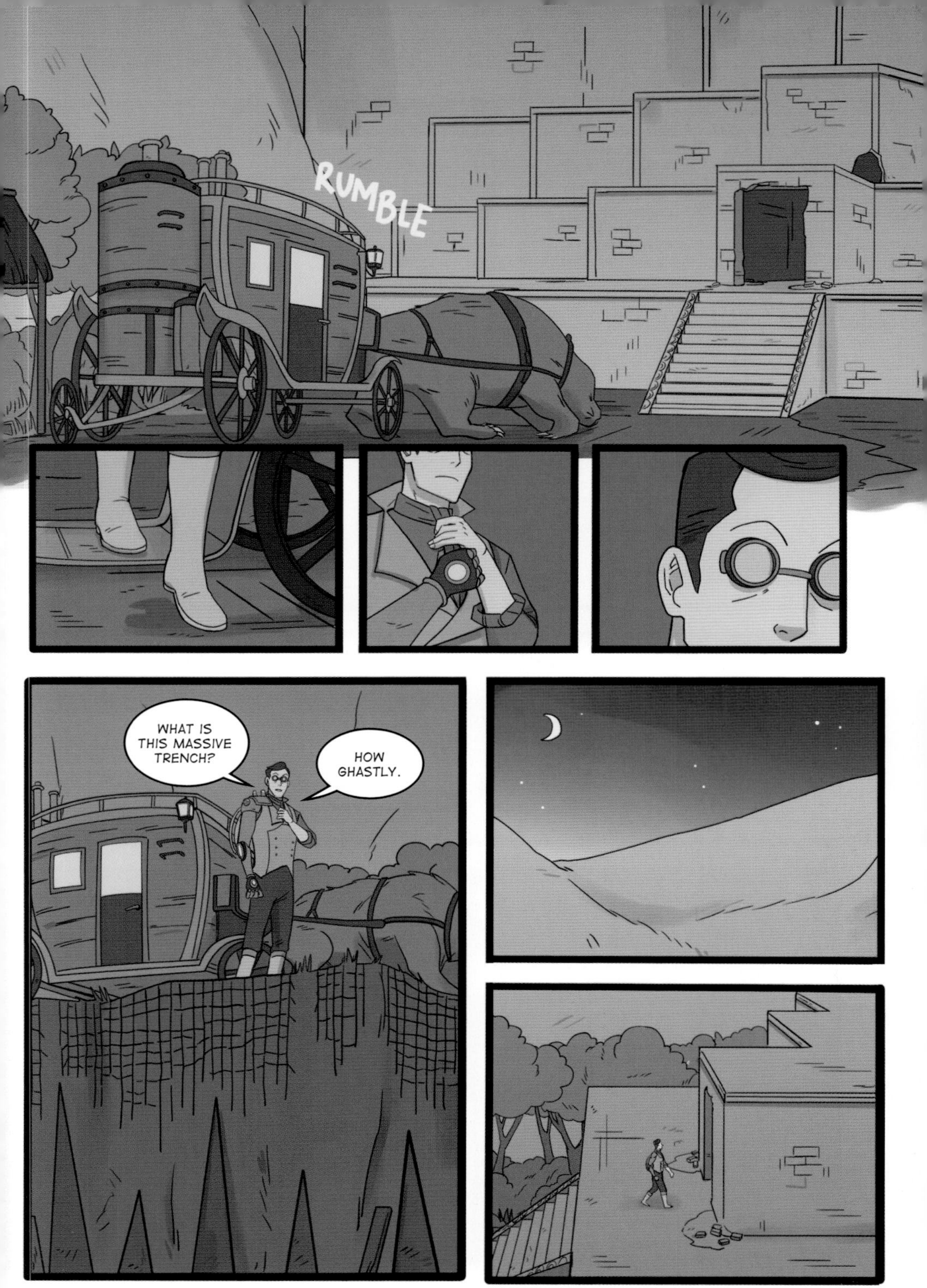
RUMBLE
WHAT IS THIS MASSIVE TRENCH?
HOW GHASTLY.

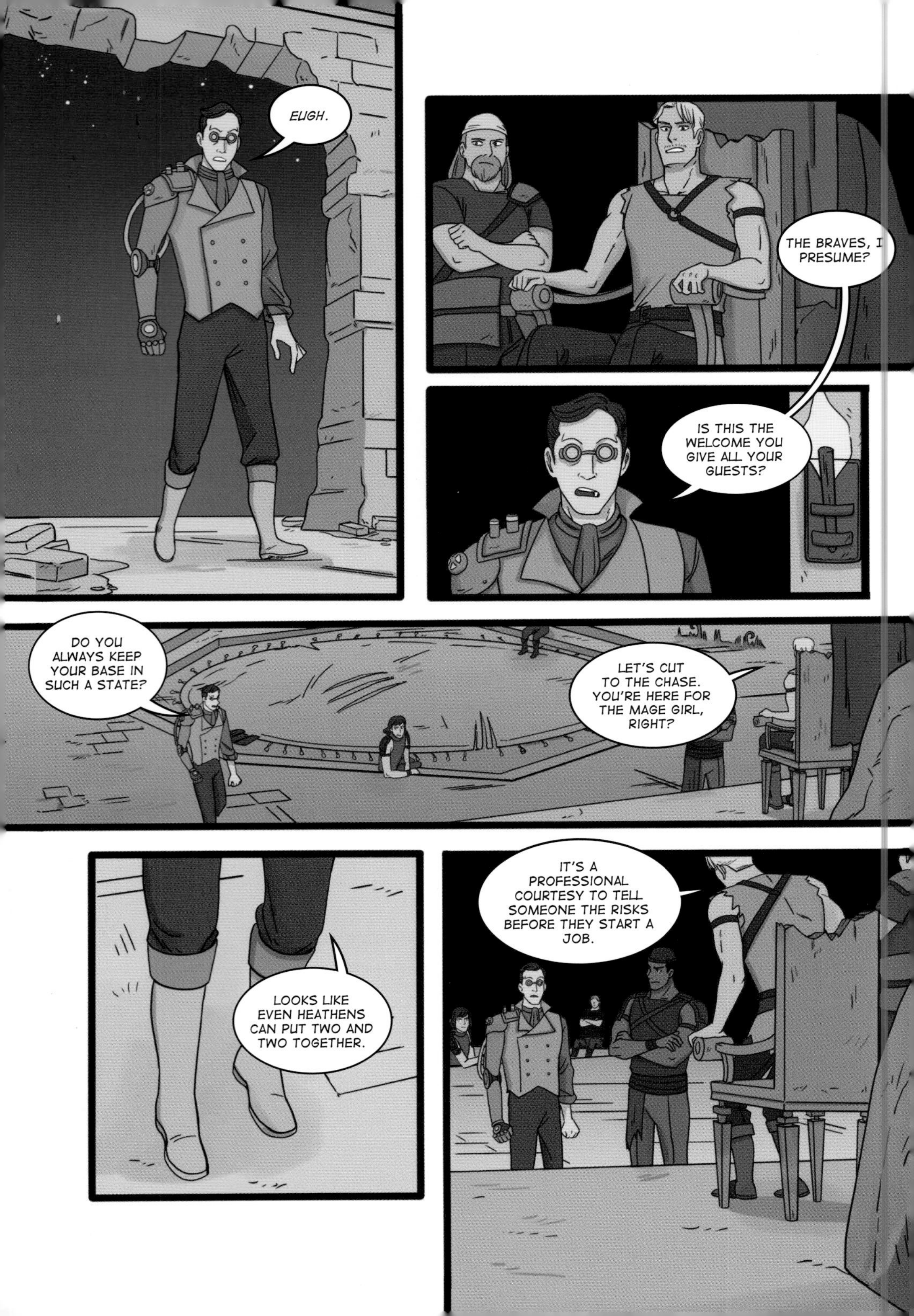
EUGH.
THE BRAVES, I PRESUME?
IS THIS THE WELCOME YOU GIVE ALL YOUR GUESTS?
DO YOU ALWAYS KEEP YOUR BASE IN SUCH A STATE?
LET'S CUT TO THE CHASE. YOU'RE HERE FOR THE MAGE GIRL, RIGHT?
LOOKS LIKE EVEN HEATHENS CAN PUT TWO AND TWO TOGETHER.
IT'S A PROFESSIONAL COURTESY TO TELL SOMEONE THE RISKS BEFORE THEY START A JOB.

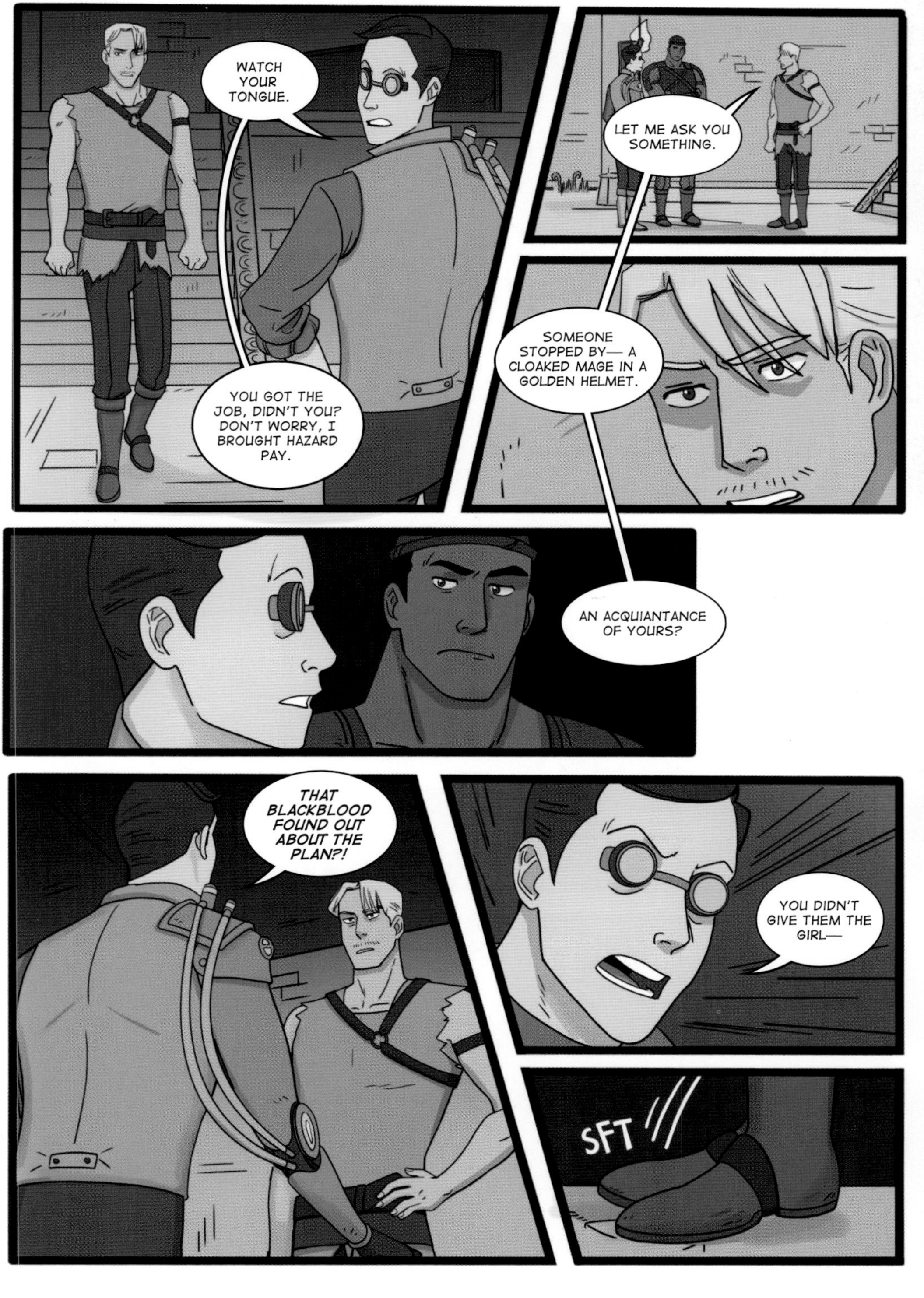
WATCH YOUR TONGUE.
YOU GOT THE JOB, DIDN'T YOU? DON'T WORRY, I BROUGHT HAZARD PAY.
LET ME ASK YOU SOMETHING.
SOMEONE STOPPED BY— A CLOAKED MAGE IN A GOLDEN HELMET.
AN ACQUIANTANCE OF YOURS?
THAT BLACKBLOOD FOUND OUT ABOUT THE PLAN?!
YOU DIDN'T GIVE THEM THE GIRL—
SFT

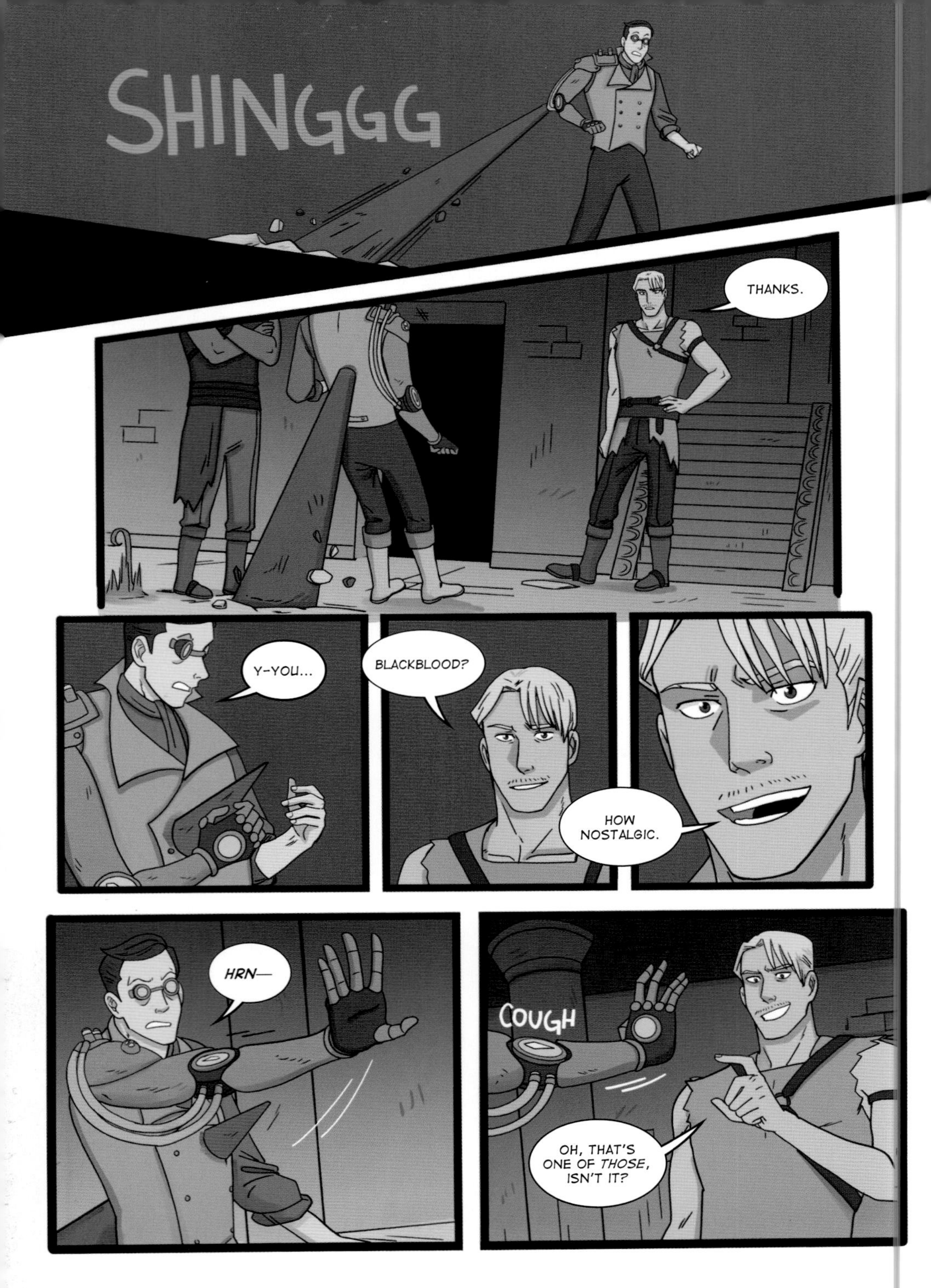
SHINGGG
THANKS.
Y-YOU...
BLACKBLOOD?
HOW NOSTALGIC.
HRN—
COUGH
OH, THAT'S ONE OF *THOSE*, ISN'T IT?

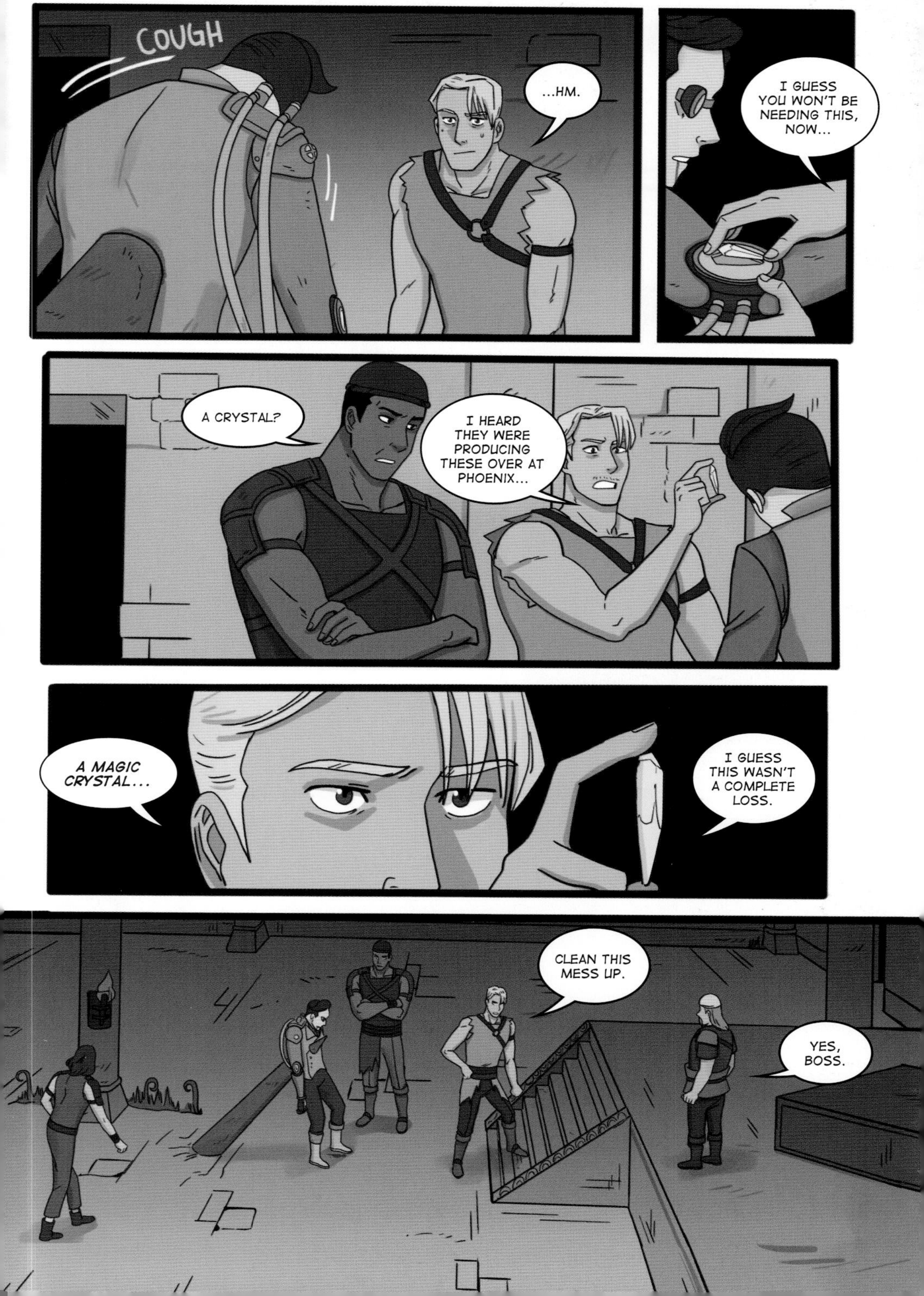
COUGH
...HM.
I GUESS YOU WON'T BE NEEDING THIS, NOW...
A CRYSTAL?
I HEARD THEY WERE PRODUCING THESE OVER AT PHOENIX...
A MAGIC CRYSTAL...
I GUESS THIS WASN'T A COMPLETE LOSS.
CLEAN THIS MESS UP.
YES, BOSS.

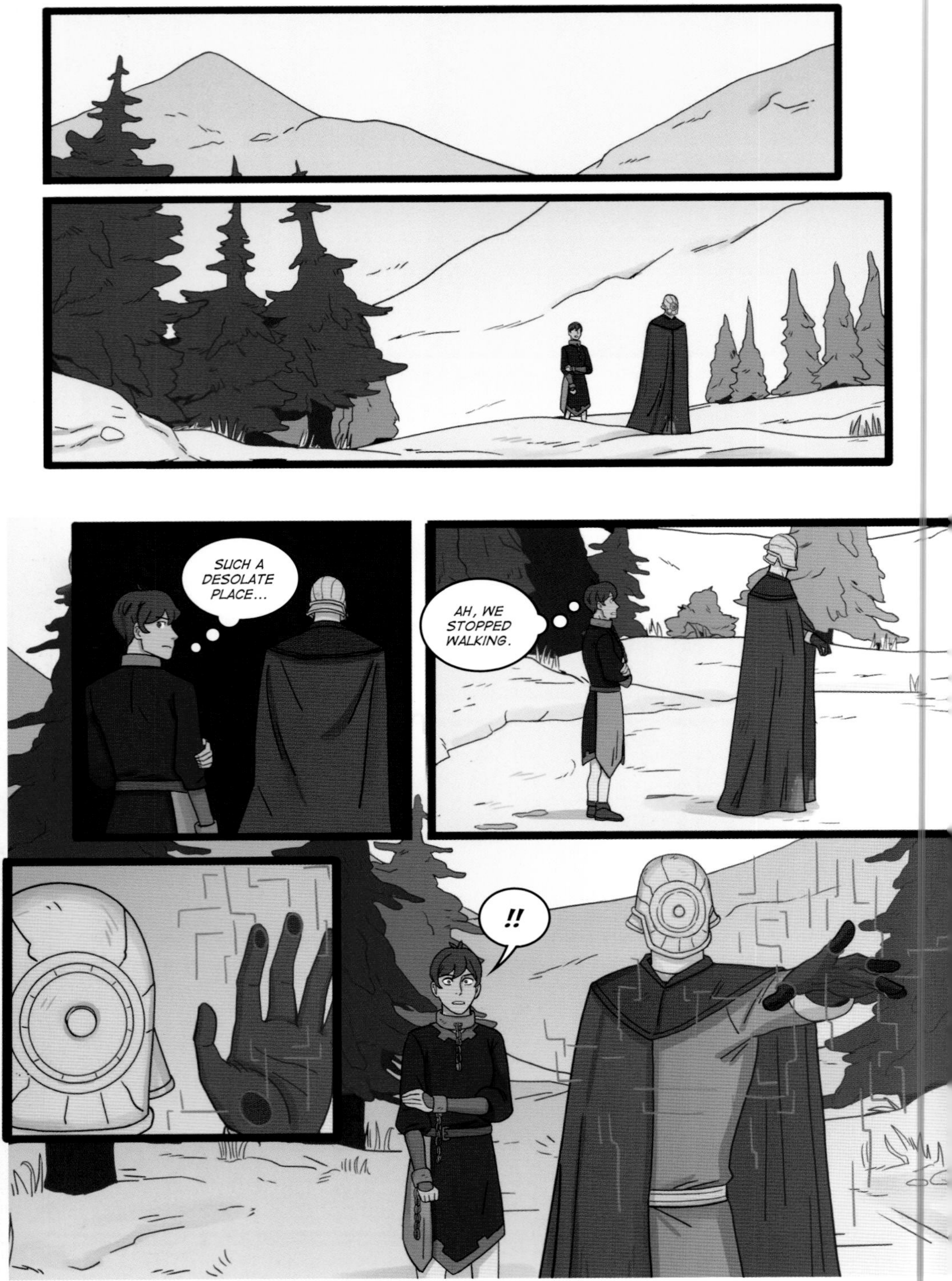
SUCH A DESOLATE PLACE...
AH, WE STOPPED WALKING.
!!

ZZZVOOM

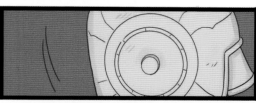

A BARRIER?

HOW DID HE PASS THROUGH SO EFFORTLESSLY?

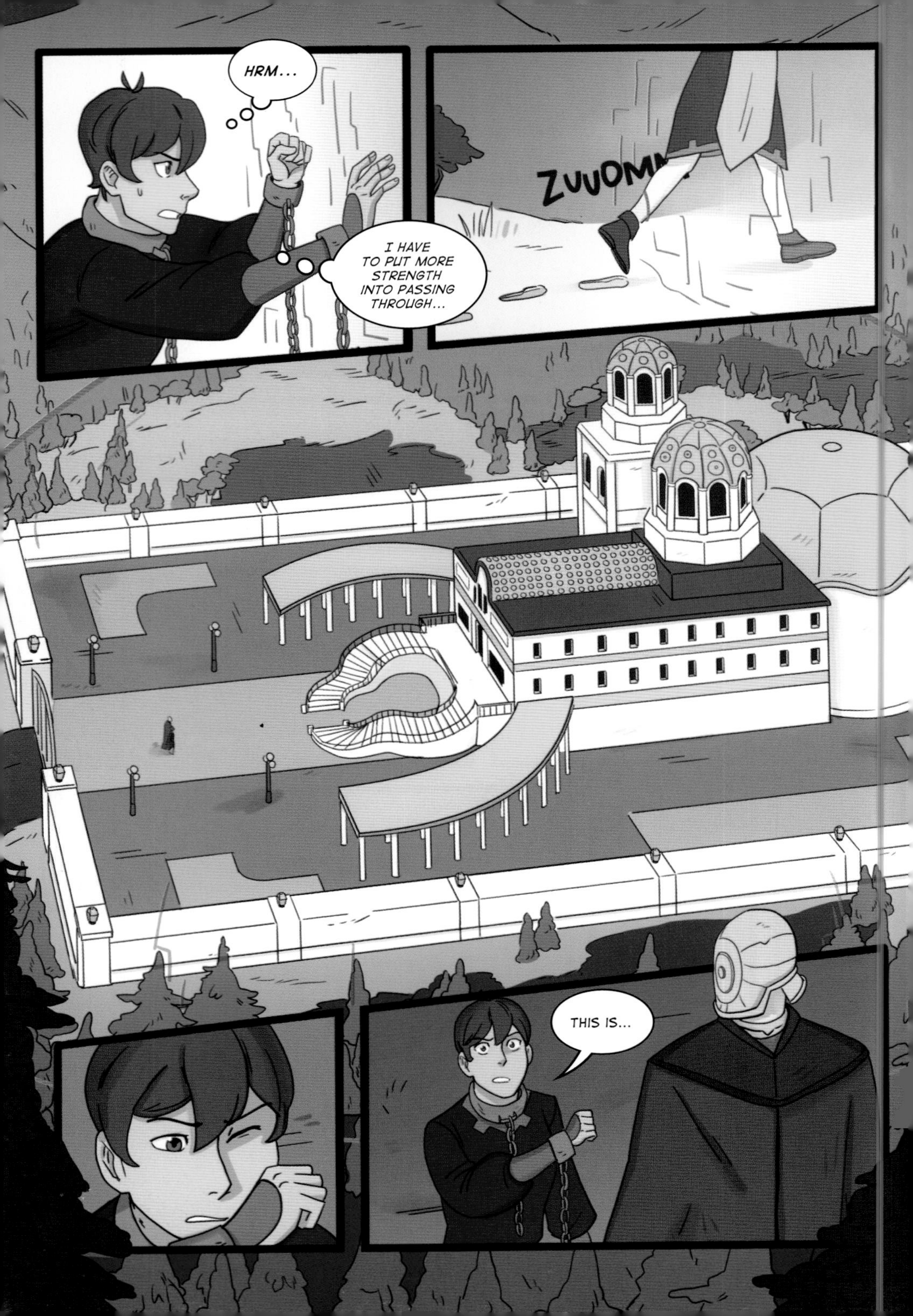
HRM...
I HAVE TO PUT MORE STRENGTH INTO PASSING THROUGH...
ZUUOMM
THIS IS...

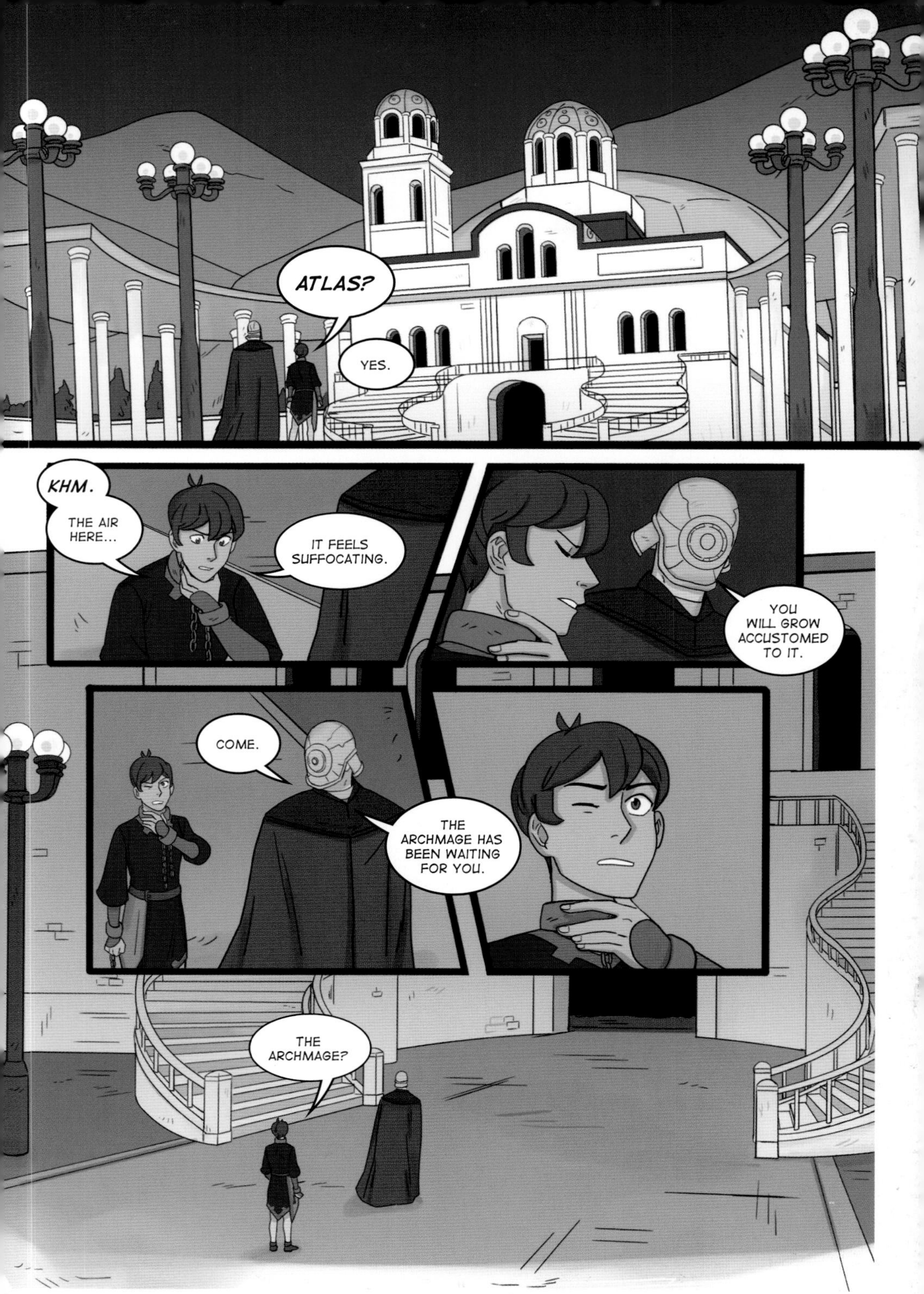
ATLAS?
YES.
KHM.
THE AIR HERE...
IT FEELS SUFFOCATING.
YOU WILL GROW ACCUSTOMED TO IT.
COME.
THE ARCHMAGE HAS BEEN WAITING FOR YOU.
THE ARCHMAGE?

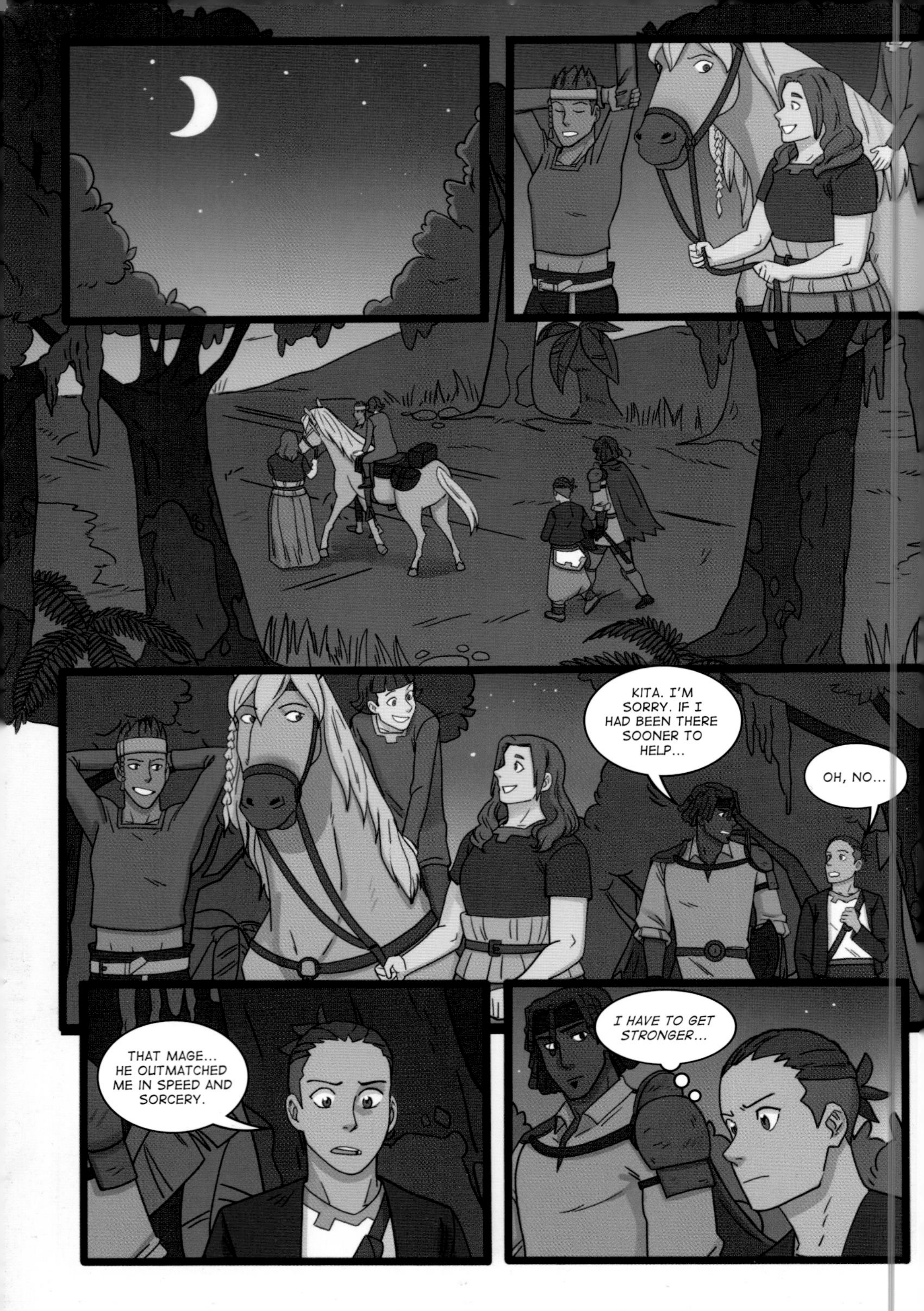
KITA. I'M SORRY. IF I HAD BEEN THERE SOONER TO HELP...
OH, NO...
THAT MAGE... HE OUTMATCHED ME IN SPEED AND SORCERY.
I HAVE TO GET STRONGER...

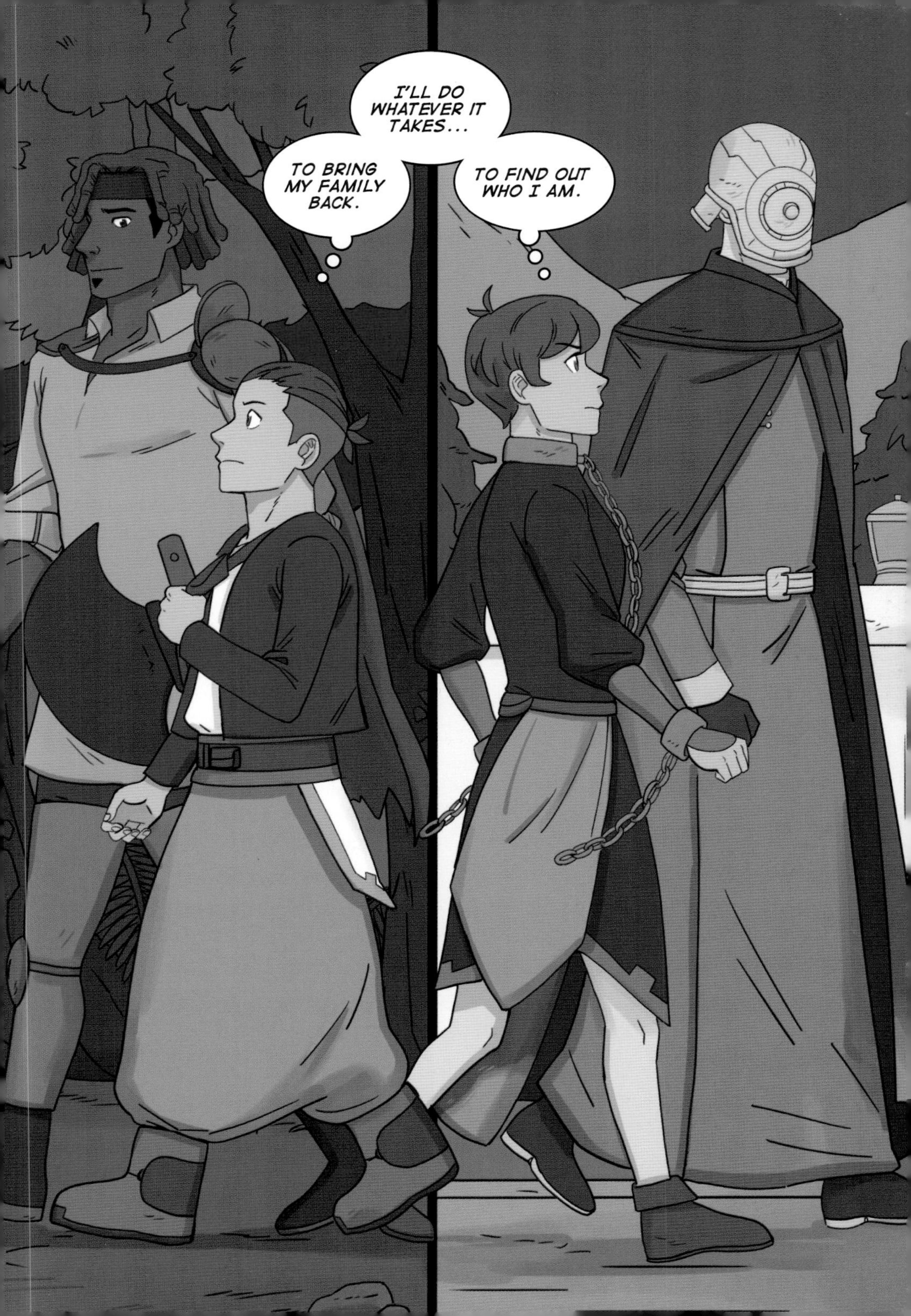
I'LL DO WHATEVER IT TAKES...
TO BRING MY FAMILY BACK.
TO FIND OUT WHO I AM.

Acknowledgments

Thank you first of all to Phu, who trusted me enough to share his ideas with me and incorporate many of my own, all while cheering me on while I finished the pages of each chapter and got started on a new one. None of this would have been possible were it not for you, and there are really no words to describe how thankful I am for how supportive you are and how great you are as a collaborator!

Thanks to Bianca Lesaca and Jes and Cin Wibowo, my schoolmates and friends who field my insecurities and feelings while inspiring me with their own paths as I grow as a comic artist. Thank you to my parents—you don't read comics or manga, but I wouldn't be anywhere now if you had not given me so much bootleg anime in my youth. "I saw this in Greenhills," my mom said to me as a twelve-year-old, passing a bootleg copy of *Perfect Blue* into my hands unknowingly. "You like this style, right?"

Thank you to all the readers of *Blackblood*, especially those from Webtoon/Tapastic. Your comments really motivated me to keep going and to push myself more as a new artist and keep consistent. Lastly, thanks to Charlie and Rob from Little Bee Books who gave this book so much helpful feedback and polish. Phu and I are so new, but you guys really gave us a chance!

—Isa

Thank you to my amazing girlfriend, Jessica, for encouraging me to chase my dreams! Thanks to my sibs, Trang, Tram, and Trung, who have been supporting *Blackblood* since it dropped as a webcomic! Thanks to my parents who let me watch a bunch of anime and play a ton of video games, this book wouldn't be here without y'all! Thank you to my Uncle David who was the person who originally brought me into the world of manga and anime!

Thank you to Alison, Junii, ELIUSHI, ttt., and Kat for the amazing feedback you guys gave while we were making the comic and hyping us up since the beginning! The extra sets of eyes were incredibly helpful!

Thanks to my classmates, Ryan, Brad, Brandon, Audrey, Otto, Matt, and Ian, for being my in-person squad to geek out about the graphic novel stuff with!

Thanks to Isa for believing in the idea of *Blackblood* enough to take a chance on it and being so essential to developing the world and characters! This project has become more amazing than I could ever have imagined thanks to you!

—Phu

Thank you to the Webtoons and Tapastic community for checking out and cheering *Blackblood* on during its fledgling webcomic days! We would not be here without all the support and excitement y'all brought us.

Thanks to Whitefox Designs for creating our wicked logo, Jessica and Jacinta Wibowo for the webcomic edits, Sarah Macklin for designing our map, Dot Valledor for helping out with flatting, Kat for illustrating a beautiful back cover, and Trung Tran for making our fire promo vid for the *Blackblood* webcomic! Shout out to Koi and RDC for the dope promo commish arts, too!

Thanks to everyone in the Little Bee staff, Rob, Charlie, and Mark for seeing something in our little fantasy adventure project and believing in it enough to bring it into the world as a book!

Final thanks to you for reading *Blackblood* and joining us on the adventure!

—Phu & Isa

We hope you enjoyed it!
Stay tuned for Volume 2!

WE HAD MADE THE FIRST CHAPTER AFTER MAKING THE SECOND CHAPTER, SO IT WAS FUN THINKING OF THE DESIGNS AFTER HAVING DRAWN KITA AND KANNA AND NEYLIN FOR A SHORT WHILE AND GETTING USED TO THEIR PERSONALITIES.

EARLY KITA HAD BLUE EYES.

I WANTED TORAN TO WEAR YELLOW SO BADLY. I WANT YELLOW TO BE A "COOL CHARACTER" COLOR.

DESIGNING THE FOUR BRUNETTES WAS A BIT OF A CHALLENGE...BUT I WAS EXCITED TO DRAW A LOT OF GIRLS.

I WAS LOOKING AT THE KELPIE DESIGN OF PERSONA 5 AND THE BLOODBORNE BOSS CALLED "BLOOD-STARVED BEAST" AS INSPIRATION. PHU AND I ALSO ENJOY FULLMETAL ALCHEMIST AND THINK THE MORE INTENSE CHARACTER TRANSFORMATIONS ARE REALLY COOL.